Robin Pilcher has work............................man
and PR consultant be............................n of
bestselling novelist Ros............................ four
children and lives near Dundee, his birthplace. He is the author of
four bestselling books, two of which, *A Risk Worth Taking* and
Starting Over, are currently being made into films.

For more information about the author, visit his website at
www.robinpilcher.co.uk

Praise for *An Ocean Apart*

'Sensitive and compulsive'
Mail on Sunday

'[A] perfectly constructed fairytale of loss and recovery'
The Times

'A total tear-jerker'
Woman's Journal

'An ideal read for a lazy winter weekend'
Woman and Home

For *Starting Over*

'Compulsive, sensitive and at times quite funny; one
wonders why Pilcher didn't take up writing years ago'
Ireland on Sunday

For *A Risk Worth Taking*

'A beautiful and heart warming tale . . . written with both
style and sensitivity'
Scottish Daily Record

'An absorbing story'
Woman's Day

ROBIN PILCHER OMNIBUS

A Risk Worth Taking

Starburst

sphere

SPHERE

This omnibus edition first published in Great Britain by Sphere in 2009
Robin Pilcher Omnibus copyright © Robin Pilcher 2009

Previously published separately:
A Risk Worth Taking first published in Great Britain in 2004
by Time Warner Books
Published by Time Warner Paperbacks in 2005
Reprinted 2005, 2006
Published by Sphere in 2007
Copyright © 2004 by Robin Pilcher

Starburst first published in the United States of America by
Thomas Dunne Books, an imprint of St. Martin's Press
First published in Great Britain in 2007 by Sphere
Copyright © 2007 by Robin Pilcher

A CIP catalogue record for this book
is available from the British Library.

ISBN 978-0-7515-4161-8

Typeset in Goudy by Palimpsest Book Production Limited,
Grangemouth, Stirlingshire
Printed and bound in Great Britain by Clays Ltd, St Ives plc

Sphere
An imprint of
Little, Brown Book Group
100 Victoria Embankment
London EC4Y 0DY

An Hachette UK Company
www.hachette.co.uk

www.littlebrown.co.uk

A Risk Worth Taking

For Oliver, Alice, Hugo, and Florence.
And for Tia Buffy,
who has always been my brilliant first-time reader.

Acknowledgments

My greatest appreciation goes to Nick Tudor, whose stories inspired the writing of this book.

Thanks also to Pippa and Kirsty, who gave the world the comfort of Tinkers, Pedlars and Pippers clothing; to Graham and Sandra, who acted as the Railway Children, waving me on along the track to completion; to Flora and Rosannagh, who so tunefully sang to me one of Mr Boom's greatest hits; to the staff at Fastnet, Fort William; and to Lisa Keany, Caroline Charles, Christo Sharpe, Jim Best, Charlie Cox, and Chris Clyne for keeping me straight on all things technical.

1

The alarm clock went off, as it had for the past fourteen months, at seven o'clock. Not at six, as had been the case when he had to get up to go to work. Nevertheless, it was still a shock to the system. Dan Porter groped out an arm from under the duvet and felt for the lever that would stop those infernal bells, but they rang with such vehemence that the clock juddered away from his searching hand and toppled from the bedside table onto the carpeted floor. There it continued its muffled clanging whilst the hand still blindly explored the surface of the table.

'Where the *hell is it?*' Both verbal and physical explosions came simultaneously. The duvet was thrown aside and Dan swung his legs over the bed and sat up. Not a wise act, he thought, as he screwed up his eyes to stop himself from being so completely aware of the oxygen pumping into his brain. As the sensation subsided and his hearing became oriented, he looked down at the clock on the floor, where its fading momentum spun it slower and slower, like a fly in its death throes.

He groaned and keeled forward to pick it up. It was still out of reach. He slid off the bed onto his knees and stretched out for the clock, but he never made it. He watched blearily as it was picked up by a beautiful, slim hand, its fourth finger bearing a band of gold that was held in place by a raised cluster of rubies set around a glinting diamond. A red-painted thumbnail flicked the lever on the clock and put it out of its misery. Dan turned his head to follow up a pinstriped arm, stopping when his eyes came to rest on the gold pendant that hung in the cleavage of her breasts, these being wholesomely accentuated by the way in which she had left open the top three buttons of her white cotton shirt. He turned his head only degrees more and looked up at his wife's face. He had often thought that if ever he had been called upon to write down a full description of her features, he would have sat forever in front of a blank piece of paper because he could never have written all that crap about her eyes being too wide set, or her nose too flat, or her ears too big. Maybe one word was sufficient. PERFECT in big black letters. Jackie always had been, and still was, a complete turn-on. Halfway through their twentieth year of marriage, and she still had that effect on him.

Today, however, it was obvious that the feeling was not reciprocated. Her mouth bore a trace of a smile, but it was one that he could read as meaning 'Dan, you really are a sorry sight' rather than 'Hello, my darling, how are you this morning?'

Dan pushed himself to his feet and flopped back on the bed. He lay there with his hand supporting the side of his face and watched as Jackie placed the alarm clock on the dressing table before slipping all her makeup necessities for the day into her handbag.

'Hey,' he said, creasing up the corner of his mouth into what he hoped might be taken as an evocative and sexy smile.

'What?' Jackie asked in a clipped voice, without looking in his direction. She walked over to the wardrobe and took a raincoat off one of the hangers.

Dan decided to persevere. 'Any chance of you lying back on this bed while I ravish you?'

Flipping the raincoat over her arm, Jackie now turned to look at him. She gave him concentrated appraisal, taking in his regular night-time attire of grey baggy sports shorts and faded blue T-shirt with the moth hole just above the left nipple.

'I wonder if I'm in the least bit tempted,' she said, slowly shaking her head.

Dan's hand fell away from his face and he slumped over in feigned dejection. 'Well, at least someone makes the suggestion every now and again,' he mumbled into the duvet.

'What was that?'

Dan pushed himself to his feet. 'Nothing.'

'I heard you.'

'Yes, well, it was just meant to be a joke.'

'And I don't think it was very funny.'

Dan let out a deep sigh. 'All right, then. Sorry.' He pushed his hands into the pockets of his shorts. 'Do you want me to make you a cup of coffee?'

Jackie shook her head. 'No, I've got to be in the office by eight. There's a finance meeting at nine, but before that I've got to give our set designer a kick up his backside. He was asked at least three months ago to do some modifications on our set for the show in Paris, and so far he hasn't come up with the goods.' She scanned the room briefly to make sure she hadn't forgotten anything, then turned and walked towards the door, reaching up and brushing a meaningless kiss onto Dan's cheek as she passed him. He followed on close behind her as she made her way along the narrow landing and down the staircase.

'What are you doing today?' she asked, throwing the question over her shoulder.

'I don't know. I might entertain myself once again with a spot of light housework.'

Reaching the bottom of the stairs, Jackie turned to look at him, and once more he realized that his witticism had fallen on a stony face.

'Did you call Ben Appleton?' she asked.

'Yes.'

'And?'

'Right now he's firing, not hiring.'

Jackie's eyes narrowed, as if trying to detect some evidence of an untruth being told. 'Did you really call him?'

'Of course I did.' Even though innocent of the apparent crime, he felt his face flush under Jackie's continued stare. 'Listen, contrary to what you think, I am still looking for a job.'

'Really? Excuse me if I find that rather hard to believe, Dan. There's certainly not much evidence of it up in your office.'

Dan's eyes momentarily flickered up the stairwell. 'When were you up there?'

'This morning.'

'Why?'

Jackie let out a long sigh. 'I wasn't actually going to your office, Dan. I went up to fetch the hairdryer from Millie's room. But the door of your office *was* open, and I did happen to notice that your computer didn't have its screensaver on.'

'So?'

'It still had an unfinished game of solitaire on it.'

Dan laughed. 'Oh-oh.'

'Don't think it's funny, Dan,' Jackie replied sharply. 'You cannot go on hiding up there, day after day, doing nothing.'

'For heaven's sake, I'm not doing nothing!'

'But you're not bringing any money into the household, Dan. That's what we need.'

'I know we do, but hey, listen, we're not on skid row yet.'

'We're not? In that case, I seem to have misunderstood our present circumstances. You've lost your job *and* most of your money on the dot.com fiasco, and because of that, the children have had to change schools, we cannot afford to go on a summer holiday for the first time since Josh was a baby, and you've also been forced to trade in your rather comfortable Mercedes for a fifteen-year-old Saab. Well, forgive me, Dan, if my opinion differs from yours. I would say that we're pretty damned close to being on "skid row". You need to get a job, Dan Porter, because my

4

income won't support us for ever. I may be the managing director of Rebecca Talworth Design Limited, but the position doesn't carry huge bucks with it, because we're still ploughing profit back into growth.'

'I understand all these things, but as I've said countless times before, it'll take a bit of time to find another job.'

'We don't have time, Dan!' Jackie cut herself short by glancing at her wristwatch. 'And I certainly don't have time to discuss all this now.' She walked along the short hallway, avoiding the schoolbags that lay ready for the day, and opened the front door, allowing the warm September sun to flood in across the stripped pine floorboards. Dan followed on behind her into the small front garden. He stood barefoot, his hands still thrust into the pockets of his shorts, as he watched his wife open the gate that led out onto the tree-shadowed pavement of Haleridge Road.

'Could you tell Nina that I will try to make her concert tonight?' she said, closing the gate behind her.

Dan nodded. 'See if you can be there this time.'

Once again, her expression demonstrated only too well her reaction to the remark. 'Not only is my job extremely important to the whole family, Dan, but it also happens to be quite full-on right now.'

Dan held up a hand in silent apology. He didn't want her to say any more, having just heard the front door of the adjoining house slam shut. There was no love lost between himself and Mrs Watt. She was their busybody of a neighbour, and Dan, on more than one occasion, had expressed those exact sentiments to her face. Nothing would give Mrs Watt more pleasure than to listen in on one of their marital disagreements, even though, over the past few months, she would have every reason to have become bored with their regularity. Her front gate clicked open and Dan watched as Jackie turned to smile a good morning to her. Mrs Watt appeared from behind the overgrown yew hedge that surrounded their property, and as she passed by Jackie, she slowed down long enough to shoot Dan a tight-mouthed glare of disapproval. He returned the disparaging greeting by thrusting forward his hands in the pockets of his shorts, giving the impression that he was more than a little excited to see her.

'Good morning, Mrs Watt,' he called out in an airy voice.

The woman quickly averted her eyes and, with a loud sucking of teeth, walked quickly on.

Jackie shook her head. 'For goodness' sake, Dan. When will you ever start to take things seriously?' She turned on her heel and disappeared from view behind the yew hedge.

Dan stood for a moment peering up into the cloudless sky as a Boeing 747 roared low overhead on its final approach to Heathrow Airport. He watched it disappear over the roofline of the houses opposite, then walked to the gate and peered over. He was in time to see Jackie's neat figure cross the street and head off down the low-stone-walled alleyway that led to South Clapham tube station. He thought about calling out something like 'Have a good day, my sweet!' but knew that she was in no mood for any of his lighthearted banter that morning, so he turned and went back into the house.

As soon as he opened the door into the kitchen, he could tell that one of their recent fosterlings from the Battersea Dogs' Home had done it again. What's more, it took no great powers of detection to work out who the culprit might be. Biggles, the cross collie/spaniel, lay cowering in his basket, whilst his smaller companion, Cruise, made a solid show of proclaiming his innocence by dancing energetically around Dan's feet.

'Bloody hell, Biggles!' Dan exclaimed, pinching his nostrils. 'Not again!'

He found the unwelcome evidence of the dog's misdemeanour centre stage in the conservatory extension to the kitchen. He picked up the coal shovel that now resided permanently beside the sliding glass door that led out into the small back garden.

'I don't know how good your geography is, my boy, but I should remind you that the dogs' home is only a half-hour's brisk walk from here.' He gave Biggles a hardened glare just to demonstrate how displeased he was, and the dog reacted by closing his eyes in shame, displaying the dark-ringed 'flying goggles' that had given rise to his name.

Having cleaned up the floor and clandestinely discarded the contents of the shovel over the fence into Mrs Watt's garden (he reckoned that, on that particular morning, she more than deserved it), Dan returned to the kitchen and picked up his mobile phone from the sideboard. As he filled up the kettle, he punched out a joint text message to Millie and Nina, informing them that it was time to get up. It was a ruse that seemed to work much more effectively than a yell up the stairs, his subtlety of thinking being that, even though his daughters were almost one hundred per cent sure that the text was from him at that time in the morning, there was always the slimmest chance that it could have been from someone considerably more exciting than their father.

It never failed to work. Just as the kettle came to the boil, he heard a thump on the floor above. Nina was on the move. He poured himself a cup of instant coffee, waiting for her usual riposte. When it came ringing down the stairs, he mouthed out her words in perfect synchronization. 'Dad, stop doing that! It's so unfa-*yer*!'

'Morning, Ni,' he called back. 'Make sure Millie's up, will you? You've got twenty-five minutes to get out of the house.'

'I'm not waking her up. She's a cow.' She said it in a crescendo, obviously wanting her sister to hear.

Dan shook his head and walked through to the hall. Nina, still in her pyjamas, sat slumped at the top of the stairs, her feet resting halfway up the banister post.

'She is not a cow, Ni. She is your loving, if not slightly tetchy sixteen-year-old sister who happens to be two years your senior, so I would be grateful if you didn't give her any more excuse than that to splatter your brains against the wall.' He took a gulp of coffee. 'Okay, tell me. Why is she a cow?'

'She's got my Atomic Kitten CD,' Nina replied moodily.

7

'Ah.' Dan paused. 'Well, she hasn't actually.'

'Yes, she has, Dad. Why do you always have to protect her?'

'I am not always protecting her. I know she hasn't got it because *I've* got it. You'll find it in the CD machine in my office.'

Nina's face sneered disapproval. 'That's so *sad*,' she said, getting up from the step and stomping off to her bedroom.

'Wake up Mill—' The door slammed shut before Dan could finish. Letting out a long sigh, he returned to the kitchen and pulled out a chair from the table. He sat down, resting his elbows on the table, and began to work his fingers at the throb of anxiety in his head. Biggles, noticing that this might be an opportune moment for reconciliation, crept from his basket and gently laid his muzzle on his master's knee. Dan looked down at the dog and smiled. 'Well, thank you, Biggles. At least someone in the world gives me a vague inkling that I'm still loved and appreciated.'

retirement age, having made his fortune in the City, which he is bound to do), they will be moving to a small cottage in the country (South Devon coast preferably) where Dan will sit with a smug smile on his face, knowing that he has not only done his bit to perpetuate the human race, but has achieved it with distinction.

At that time, it all seemed a bit pie-in-the-sky, really. Just the dreams of a young couple, both only two years out of their teens, who were fortified with too much Chardonnay and fizzing with excitement at the prospect of loving, honouring, and cherishing each other until death us do part. Yet for Dan, it could so easily have read something like:

Dan Porter and Sharon Pettigrew or Janice Longshaw or Kathleen Malloney (there were other girls with whom he had clothes-wrestled during midmorning break in the darkened store cupboard of the chemical lab at St Joseph's Secondary School, Tottenham Hale, North London – but they were the more likely ones to have ended up in the same full-stomached condition that Jackie now found herself to be in) are pleased to announce their plan for life. Following their wedding in St Mary's Episcopal Church, Tottenham Hale (his mother's local), Dan will take up employment in Baldwin Metals where he will work, on split shifts for £1.50 an hour, alongside his father in the dust-choking, earsplitting environs of the fabrication shed. They will be having only one child (the very same one that's got them into this bloody mess in the first place) because, until a council flat comes up, they will have to live with Dan's parents. Thereafter Sharon/Janice/Kathleen will be getting a job because otherwise they won't be able to afford to go out to the pub together on a Saturday night. Dan would like to take this opportunity to apologize to Tottenham Hotspur Football Club and to all his mates with whom he goes to matches, because one of the sacrifices that he'll have to make is giving up his season ticket. From now on, *he will only be able to watch those matches that are being tele-vised – that is, if Dixon's allows him to buy a television on hire purchase. And finally, once they have reached retirement age, the happy couple plan to . . . live off a state pension for a bit, then die.*

To be quite honest, that scenario had been in Dan's mind for a hell of a lot longer than the one that he and Jackie had formu-lated whilst polishing off the bottle of Chardonnay in the Central Park Diner. It was, in every way, his worst nightmare, and from his early teens had hung over his head like the sword of Damocles, heralding the inevitable progression of his life. He had been born in the wrong place at the wrong time, with neither prospect nor privilege.

So he decided to do his damnedest to avoid ending up like that. He kept his head down at school, both physically and academically, and watched as all his friends opted out as soon as they could with qualifications that suited them better for lives as mobsters rather than businessmen. When he eventually walked out of the gates of St Joseph's for the last time, he knew that the school's enduring and hard-earned legacy to him was that he was coming away with both these attributes.

University was out – his parents couldn't afford to support him during three years of further education, neither was he willing to burden himself with student loans. So, dressed in his cousin's ill-fitting wedding suit, he headed for the City with his exam certificate, showing his three top-grade A-level passes, carefully folded in his inside pocket. He had no idea what he was doing or where he was going, but he was determined not to catch the tube back to Tottenham Hale without securing some sort of employment for himself.

He would have no doubt been forced to change his mind about that had it not been for the intervention of a kindly commissionaire who had been standing on the steps of a large, gargoyle-fronted building in Cheapside. He had witnessed Dan walk up and down the street four or five times, stopping outside offices, bracing himself to enter, then turning away with a shake of his head.

'You're looking for a job, aren't you, son?' he had said in a voice that would have sounded more fitting on an army parade ground. Dan had nodded meekly, and the commissionaire had given him a wink and flicked his head to motion him into the building. Twenty minutes later, he came out into the late morning sunshine with a photocopied list of stockbroker firms clutched in his hand.

It took exactly four and a half hours and the heavy scoring out of eight names on his list before Dan found himself a job. Walking triumphantly from the lift of the office block in Leadenhall Street, he crossed the reception area, tightly balling up the piece of paper in his fist. As he pushed open the heavy glass doors, he lobbed it into a tall chrome litter bin, then stood outside on the pavement, feeling as if he had reached up to discover that the sword of Damocles was so blunt that it couldn't even cut through butter. Dan Porter, the office trainee from Tottenham Hale, had arrived in the City. From now on, he was going to do nothing but make money for himself.

And he had done just that for three years. No steady girl-friends, not too much excessive boozing. His two greatest expenditures were paying for his share of the rent on the flat that he had moved into with three other work colleagues just off Fulham Broadway, and the occasional sortie down King's Road to buy clothes. And then, one Saturday afternoon, he met Jackie Entwhistle.

Dan had been walking back to his flat when he passed the shop, situated at the unfashionable end of King's Road. It was the name on the sign above the small display window that had at first caught his eye. Rebecca Talworth. He had read about her in some newspaper or magazine. A young dress designer, fresh out of St Martin's, who they said was destined to make the grade. Dan peered through the window into the shop's crowded interior and almost immediately caught sight of a blonde girl, her face lit with animated humour as she served a customer. Maybe it was the intensity of his stare that had caused a slight tingling on the flawless skin of her cheek, because, for no apparent reason, she turned her head through ninety degrees and looked directly at him, and he was sure, if it was at all possible, that her smile broadened even more. It was on sheer impulse, but he decided not to go any further until he had asked her for a date. He entered the shop and reappeared on the street half an hour later with a grin on his face and a pain in his wallet. The price of the date had been the purchase of a £200 original Rebecca Talworth dress. Of course, Jackie had no idea that it was destined for her. He had said that it was for a friend, but he knew the moment that she held it up against herself to show off the style, that it would be sacrilege for anyone else to own it.

He had given it to her for her twenty-first birthday. Actually, it was four days after her birthday, because she had had to go up north for a big black-tie 'do' that her parents were holding in her honour at their golf club near Chester. But Dan had also organized a little celebration of his own. Back to his place, give Jackie the dress, get her to change into it, and then out to dinner at Quaglino's. Trouble was that Jackie never wore the dress and they never made dinner. The truth was that neither of them had worn very much that night.

And that was why they had come to be sitting making plans about their future over a bottle of Chardonnay in the Central Park Diner in Kensington High Street.

3

Stephen Turnbull strode across the office reception area, a neat cluster of files tucked under his arm, and shot a wink at the young temporary receptionist as he passed by. He kept his eye on her as he walked into his office and smiled to himself when he witnessed through the glass partitioning a slight colour rising to the girl's cheeks. It satisfied him that, at the age of twenty-nine, rising thirty, he still had the charisma and the looks to get that kind of reaction from a girl ten years his junior. He sat down at his desk and clicked the mouse of his computer, and stretching out his long, linen-clad legs, he leaned back in his chair and watched as the screensaver cleared to be replaced by the spreadsheet on which he had been working prior to the meeting.

Stephen had every reason to feel pleased with himself that morning. During the meeting that had finished half an hour ago, he had given a presentation to the company's financial backers demonstrating that everything was going pretty damned well with Rebecca Talworth Design Ltd. After only eighteen months since its inception, the company was performing way ahead of its fore-cast schedule, and if the spring/summer collection to be shown at Prêt-à-Porter in Paris in three weeks' time proved to be as successful as the previous one, then profit margins might just surpass all expectations.

And Stephen knew that it was he who had been entirely responsible for the whole thing happening. Two years before, whilst working for a small chartered accountancy practice in West Hampstead, he had been assigned a number of 'headache' clients, those whose accounting techniques consisted of submitting little or no ledger work and a pile of disordered receipts for reconciliation. Wading through them like an automaton, he had come across Rebecca Talworth's file, and was both surprised and bemused as to why one of the most successful and well-known fashion designers in the country should use such an unprestigious, out-of-the-way company to audit her books. However, having spent an hour scrutinizing her accounts, he had come to realize that the recognition that she had achieved for herself through her creative skills could in no way be complemented by an astute business sense. Rebecca Talworth was, to all intents and purposes, bust. He also surmised that she herself was probably fully aware of the fact and hoped that, by placing her books with a small, unknown firm of chartered accountants, she would be able to cajole them into throwing up a smokescreen to hide her dire financial situation.

It had never been Stephen's plan to become an accountant. When he had left school, he had every intention of going on to art college, having a greater aptitude towards all things creative than to any one thing in the academic field. But his overpowering father had bullied him into altering course, telling him that he expected his only son to take on the eventual running of his own business, and that accountancy was the best grounding with which to accomplish this successfully.

With not one iota of enthusiasm for the work, Stephen had scraped a lowly pass in his final accountancy exams, and consequently had only managed to find employment with the small West Hampstead practice. Every morning, he struggled to get himself out of bed, knowing that the day had little to offer him other than indescribable boredom. But now, as he scrutinized the Talworth file, he began to see a means of escape. He just had to manipulate it correctly.

He laid aside the file that day and went on to sort out the affairs of a self-employed jobbing plumber from Hackney. Then, that night, he took it home and began to put together a proposal for the designer. After a week of working well into the small hours of the morning, he devised a business plan that broadened the parameters of Rebecca Talworth's work into lucrative side-lines, whilst still granting her complete autonomy over designs and products. The control of expenditure and cash flow, however, was to be placed firmly in the hands of a financial director.

It took him five times of asking to arrange a meeting with Rebecca, something which confirmed in his mind that she was fully aware of the fact that her glitzy, jet-setting world was about to crumble around her feet. He was never put off by her complete refusal to speak to him on the telephone, because every time the line went dead, he became more assured that she had little option other than to accept his plan.

They met in her small mews house off Exhibition Road exactly three weeks after he had made his initial attempt to contact her. He handled the meeting with care, always putting across the harder points for her to accept with a generous massaging of her obviously extensive ego. Within an hour, he had struck the deal and was shown to the front door by a smiling, almost ebullient Rebecca Talworth. He left her waving on the doorstep and walked away down the narrow cobbled lane as the newly appointed financial director of Rebecca Talworth Design Ltd., a position that carried a healthy salary increment on the fulfilment of each of his proposed targets. By the time that he had emerged onto Exhibition Road, he had called the chartered accountancy practice in West Hampstead and told them that he was leaving without notice.

As he had imagined, raising the finance on the terms that he had set out in the business plan was plain sailing. In fact, he had managed to better them by narrowing down the offers that he had received from a plethora of financial institutions. They had fallen over themselves to get a foothold in the action, impressed by his proposals to tap into the huge marketing potential behind the goodwill of Rebecca Talworth's name.

Two weeks after the financial package had been finalized, he had negotiated a five-year lease, with an option to buy after that period, on 10,000 square feet of office space in a converted flour-mill on the north side of the River Thames, just west of the Wandsworth Bridge. Being on the top floor, it had an abundance of natural light flooding in through the large Velux windows that ran the full length of the roof, and there was ample room for the offices and large studio where the cutting and machining of design samples were to be carried out.

Within three months, Rebecca had closed down her two shops in King's Road, laying off all but two of her sales assistants, and had moved into the new premises. The shops were not part of the business plan. To begin with, retail was to be handled from rented floor space within one of the more prestigious department stores in the West End, depending on which was able to offer the better deal. Once manufacturing was in full swing, then units in similar department stores were to be sought in major cities throughout the world.

And it had worked. The base of the letterheading of Rebecca Talworth Design Ltd. now listed London, New York, Paris, Stockholm, Frankfurt and Madrid, and if his negotiations proved fruitful, then Tokyo would be added within the next month.

However, from the moment that the new company had started trading, there was one problem that Stephen had found hard to overcome, and that was his working relationship with Rebecca herself. She was still the creative genius, but still hopeless with money, and she displayed a wild extravagance with this new injection of finance. Having been on the receiving end, on a number of occasions, of her quick temper and irrationality of thought, Stephen knew that he had to handle Rebecca with the softest pair of kid gloves in order to maintain a measure of civility between them.

The solution to his problem presented itself in the form of Jackie Porter, a woman who had been working with Rebecca since she had first started and whom Rebecca had managed to persuade back from her role as mother to a young family to take on public relations for the company. Intelligent, strong-willed and beautiful, as well as being a good and trusted friend to Rebecca, Jackie had the ideal credentials to run the company and intermediate between Stephen and Rebecca. In a carefully worded address at one of the weekly management meetings, Stephen had proposed that the company should broaden its management base to allow Rebecca more time to expand the design division of the company. He felt that this could best be achieved by the appointment of a managing director.

Stephen did not put forward Jackie's name until the last moment. His timing was perfect. Rebecca agreed without a qualm, and it confirmed in Stephen's mind that she had already been harbouring concerns about how best to curb his own powers within the company.

As it turned out, the working relationship between Jackie and himself could not have been more successful. Rebecca allowed them full sanction to get on with the running of her company and, from the day of Jackie's appointment, never bothered to attend another management meeting. Jackie and he travelled to the States and across Europe together, setting up the retail outlets, and because they had to spend many days in each other's company, sometimes under quite tedious and frustrating circumstances, their friendship developed into one of mutual support and respect. At least, that is how Stephen felt that Jackie would read the situation. For him, it was different. He had found himself becoming increasingly attracted to her, even though he knew that she was unattainable. Not only ten years his senior, she was also the mother of three children and the wife of an extremely successful City man. However, there had been considerable

18

changes in Jackie's home life over the past year. Her husband had lost his job and there had been furtive whispers in the office that relationships within her family were becoming increasingly strained. Although it did not seem to affect the way in which she ran the business, Stephen now detected the slightest chink of vulnerability in Jackie's demeanour, one that had never before been apparent.

Stephen broke off his train of thought and glanced over the top of his computer screen. In the office opposite his own, Jackie sat at her desk, raking her fingers repeatedly through her long blonde hair as she wrote quickly on a jotting pad. She looked up to catch her thoughts and their eyes came into contact. He smiled at her and she smiled back, but there was little joy or frivolity in its delivery. She dipped her head and continued to write.

Stephen knocked out a quick rhythm with his hands on the desktop, then pushed himself out of his chair and walked out into the narrow glassed corridor that separated their offices. He gave a token knock on her door and entered.

'All right if I come in?'

Jackie looked up, nodded, then continued to write.

Stephen sat himself down in a chair opposite her. He folded his arms and crossed one foot over the other, but remained silent.

Jackie looked up again. She tilted her head questioningly to the side. 'Is anything wrong?'

Stephen shrugged his shoulders. 'I was about to ask you the same thing.'

Jackie held her pen six inches above the desk and let it go. It clattered down on the dark veneered surface. 'Listen, I'm sorry if I didn't seem very communicative at the meeting this morning.'

'There's no need to apologize. It couldn't have gone any better. They seemed more than happy with the way things are going.'

'As long as things keep going the way we've planned them.'

'Meaning?'

'Meaning that if Tom Headwick doesn't come up with the

modifications for the set design, then we've got a real problem on our hands.'

'But you spoke to him this morning. I was under the impression that he told you they were all but finished.'

Jackie scoffed dismissively. 'Well, that's what *he* says.'

'Have you spoken to Rebecca about it?'

'I haven't been able to get hold of her. She's been with a fabric supplier all morning and has her mobile switched off.'

Stephen raised his eyebrows. 'What's new?'

'And take a look at this, as well,' Jackie said, spinning a sheet of paper across the desk towards him. Stephen bent forward and picked it up.

'It's the schedule.'

'Yes. I've just taken it off the Internet.'

Stephen studied it for a moment. 'What's wrong with it?'

'Quite a lot, actually. We have a slot at one o'clock on Wednesday in the Bourdelle Museum.'

Stephen shrugged. 'That seems a good time. Means we don't have to get up at sparrowfart.'

'Yes, but look who's showing in the Louvre at exactly the same time.'

Stephen studied the schedule once more. 'Ah. Gaultier.'

'Exactly. So where's the press going to be?'

'Oh, hell!' Stephen muttered as he floated the schedule back onto Jackie's desk. 'And there's nothing that we can do about it?'

'Not a thing. The Chambre Syndicale set that schedule in stone. Do you want to hear more?'

Stephen groaned and scrunched up his eyes, as if preparing himself for a stinging blow to the face. 'If you insist.'

'Three of our star models have backed out. I would hazard a guess that they're probably going with him.'

'Can they *do* that?'

'I'm afraid so.' Jackie smiled. 'It's not really a big deal, though. I was half expecting something like this to happen, so I put a provisional booking on six other models from the agency.'

20

Stephen breathed out a sigh of relief. 'Thank goodness for that. Well done, you.' He pulled his chair forward and leaned his elbows on Jackie's desk. As he did so, one of his gold cufflinks momentarily caught the sunlight through the full-length window and flashed a brilliant pinpoint of light across Jackie's cleavage. 'Listen,' he said, moving his hand imperceptibly so that the oval reflection played upon the deep split between her breasts, 'are you going over to Paris before the show?'

'I had planned to. I don't think that one can tell the organizers too many times how *grateful* we are to be given a slot.'

'Right. I'll come with you.'

Jackie shook her head. 'There's no reason for you to come.'

'Oh, but I think I should. Two heads are always better than one, especially if there's a problem to negotiate. Anyway, my workload's pretty clear right up until the Tokyo trip.'

Jackie contemplated his offer for a moment, then reached across the desk for her diary. Stephen immediately dropped his hands to his lap in case she caught the positioning of the reflected light from his cufflink. She opened the diary and flipped through the pages. 'All right then. What about Saturday?'

'*This* Saturday?'

'I can't do next week. I have meetings every day.'

'I don't think that'll be much use then.'

'What do you mean?'

'Well, if we hit a problem, we're not going to get it sorted out on a Sunday. What meetings do you have on Monday?'

Jackie glanced back at her diary. 'One in the morning, one in the afternoon.'

'Are they important or could you put them off to another day?'

Jackie picked up her pen and began to turn it over in her fingers. 'You really think it's necessary?'

'As an insurance, yes, I do.'

She nodded. 'Okay then. I'll get Laurie to change them.'

Stephen pushed himself to his feet. 'Right. I'll get straight onto Eurostar and book the tickets.'

Jackie made no further comment about their arrangement, but swivelled around in her chair and stared out at the panoramic view of the River Thames and the uneven skyline of Wandsworth beyond. Sensing her deep distraction, Stephen stopped halfway to the door and then turned and walked over to the window, arriving in time to see a coxless four glide their boat upriver towards Putney.

'You're really *not* your usual dynamic self this morning, are you?'

'No, not really,' she replied quietly.

He turned and sat on the windowsill. 'Do you want to talk about it?'

She breathed out a laugh. 'No, not really.' She turned to look at him. 'Anyway, besides being unmarried and without the burden of children, I think you're probably the wrong age and the wrong sex to understand my problem.'

Stephen laughed. 'I don't know. I've always felt that I've been quite in touch with my feminine side.' His remark did not even register a spark of humour on Jackie's face. 'Things are a bit difficult at home, are they?'

'Just a little,' Jackie murmured. She rested an elbow on the arm of the chair, and closing her eyes, she began to rub a thumb and forefinger up and down the bridge of her nose. 'For some reason, it was so much easier to cope with Dan losing his job when it first happened. He was so . . . vulnerable and lost. But now he seems to be so complacent about it all, even happy, and it infuriates me. I don't think that he's making any effort at all to find another job.'

'What's he doing at the minute?'

'Not a lot. He does a bit of housework, he takes the dogs for a walk, and most days, he has lunch with one of his friends in the pub. He's also got heavily into cooking, which entails a great deal of watching Jamie Oliver on the television and serving up weird concoctions to me and the kids.'

'Well, at least he's doing that. Surely if you were both working, you'd be having to pay someone to look after the house.'

'Yes, but you can't count that as a job. Dan was earning close on two hundred thousand pounds a year in the City. That's a pretty expensive housekeeper, wouldn't you say?'

Stephen spread out his hands along the windowsill. 'So you are now the family's sole breadwinner.'

'Yes, in rather a large nutshell.'

'Well, in that case,' Stephen said, 'I would have thought that the way you're feeling is pretty natural. All your married life, he's been the security for your family – the provider. And now you've had to take over that role. Maybe . . .' – he paused momentarily, being caught in two minds as to whether he should continue – 'maybe you've just lost some of your respect for him.'

Jackie shot him a steely glance that told him he had over-stepped the mark. He immediately tried to backtrack. 'Not that you can't rebuild that.'

'Damn you.'

'I'm sorry. I shouldn't have said that.'

'No, I mean damn you for being so intuitive. I was wrong. Maybe age and sex have got nothing to do with it. But what you certainly won't understand is that, in marriage, losing respect for your partner is as bad as infidelity. There is no way that you can ever retrieve that complete, unassailable level of confidence that before existed between you as naturally as . . . . the creation of life itself.' She turned to look out the window once more. 'My word, you've stuck a spear deep into a wound that I was trying my best to ignore.'

'I'm sorry.'

'Don't be. You've stopped me from fooling myself.'

Stephen pushed himself away from the windowsill and moved quickly towards the door. 'Come on. You're coming with me.'

Jackie's expression was one of puzzlement as she spun around in her chair to track his exit. 'Where?'

'Out for lunch.'

Jackie shook her head. 'No way. I can't. I've got a pile of work to do.' She glanced at her wristwatch and laughed. 'Anyway, it's only half past eleven.'

'I couldn't give a toss. As financial director of Rebecca Talworth Design Limited, I consider it a necessary expense to take the company's managing director out for lunch in order to talk about the extremely successful meeting that we had this morning and . . . to lift her spirits so that she can continue to perform as brilliantly as she has done since taking over at the top.' He shot her a wink similar to the one that, half an hour beforehand, had succeeded in turning the young receptionist's knees to jelly. 'We'll only be an hour. What's more, you're not the only one who has work to do.'

Jackie smiled at him. 'All right. We'll have lunch, but let's leave it until midday. That should give you enough time to book those train tickets.'

4

Back then, the truth of the matter was that young Mr and Mrs Porter had struggled for a bit after they were married. But with the arrival of Josh, a beautiful, healthy nine-pound baby who had threatened to do permanent damage to Jackie's elegantly light frame, they were quite content to live in a state of impecunious bliss in the minute flat that they rented off Baron's Court Road.

Then, in 1986, when Josh was an eighteen-month-old bundle of trouble, all things changed and Dan had to alter his thinking about being born in the wrong place at the wrong time. It was the year of the Big Bang, the deregulation of the stock market, and the staid, formal image of the City took on a new and welcome vibrancy. Dan's firm benefited immediately, being one of the first to be taken over by a large American financial conglomerate, and within three months, he had been plucked from relative obscurity by the company's new senior vice president to be one of their market makers. And from the moment that he started, he thrived on it. His battling days at school had fitted him well for the job. He loved the quick decision, the adrenaline rush of making a deal, the subterfuge in offloading a nonperformer. But above all, he loved making money.

It was probably a much-needed energy release on Dan's part that resulted in Jackie's giving birth to Millie and Nina within the space of the next two years. The flat in Baron's Court had begun to groan with overcrowding, so Dan decided to make the largest personal investment of his lifetime and took out a mortgage on the three-storey, four-bedroom house in Clapham. It was not until they had spent their first few months there, happily throwing themselves about this newly acquired space, that Jackie reminded Dan of their conversation in the Central Park Diner. Three children and a house in a suburb south of the river. They had achieved it all, minus the dogs. Jackie said that the dogs could wait.

Dan had never paid much attention to the letters from headhunting firms that kept turning up in his in-tray. He was quite content to work in a familiar environment with colleagues that he knew and trusted. But there came the time when, at the age of five, Nina joined Millie at Alleyn's School, and with Josh already attending Dulwich College for Boys, Dan suddenly found himself faced with paying three hefty school fees. Having tied up the greater proportion of his extensive savings in long-term investments, the effect on the family's bank balance was immediate, even though Jackie had by now resumed work for three days a week with Rebecca Talworth. Either Dan had to find a better-paid job for himself or else such luxuries as their twice-yearly holidays abroad would have to be forfeited.

Within a month, Dan had been headhunted by a Hong Kong-based investment bank, and thereafter he played the field, never staying with any company for longer than a year. But he found that, no matter for whom he was working, he loved what he did, and he could never quite believe his good fortune in ending up doing a job that made him money and made him smile. It had always been a bit of a laugh, a game, like playing one schoolboy prank after another.

And then he had been badly caught out. Having decided to switch a substantial amount of his investments over to dot.com technology, he moved to another job that paid so well that the cash-in penalties incurred by the change were going to be written off in a year. But five months later, the dot.com bubble burst. Dan had seen it coming and had tried to offload his shares as fast as he could, but traders by now were wary of his techniques and treated them like leprosy. All he could do thereafter was to watch their value drop day by day. And then he had found the internal e-mail on his computer. At first he thought it a mistake that he had received it, obviously just sent out on blanket coverage. Nevertheless, he had read the e-mail through, two pages of corporate jargon, explaining that the company was being forced to shed jobs due to the collapse of the dot.com market. It wasn't until he reached the last paragraph that the true meaning of the e-mail hit him.

'This company has always adopted a policy of last-in, first-out, and for this reason, we find ourselves with no alternative other than to terminate your contract of employment.'

There were further remarks and apologies, but Dan hadn't bothered to read them. He picked up the telephone and immediately called the firm of headhunters that had secured his last position. Over the next hour, he tried time and time again to make contact with someone who could give him advice, but he never managed to get past the sweet-talking receptionist. Eventually, he replaced the receiver, and it slowly began to dawn on him that, for the first time in his working life, he was going to be without financial security and without a job.

At first, he had felt furious with himself for investing so recklessly and bitterly resentful at losing his job, but when, over the next few weeks, he received no offers from the headhunting firms that in the past had been falling over themselves to entice him away from one company to another, those feelings compounded to one of pure terror. At night, sleep deserted him and he would more often than not end up in the kitchen in the early hours of the morning drinking endless cups of tea and trying to blank out his thoughts by watching *Open University* or second-rate films on the television.

But those thoughts were all too pervasive, and during his lonely nighttime vigils, he constantly mulled over the effects that his new circumstances would have on the comfortable lifestyle that he and his family had enjoyed up until then. Due to his catastrophic investment in the dot.com market, he no longer had the financial resources to keep the family protected from the consequences of his unemployment; he had only been with the company for two months, so there was to be no substantial redundancy payment; he would have to freeze his pension contributions; the girls were just about to go back to Alleyn's for the start of the autumn term, and he knew that if his unemployment was to be long term, there was no way that he could keep them at the school; it was the start of Millie's sixth form year, so what would be least disruptive to her? Maybe it would be better to move them both to Clapham High School now, rather than halfway through Millie's A-level course.

He couldn't afford to lose the house, either. That was the bedrock of security for his family. At least he had made it a priority to pay off the mortgage, but he couldn't allow the bank to treat it as part of his estate if he were to go completely broke. It would be better to put it immediately into Jackie's name.

And what about Jackie? She was being supportive, but she had other things to think about now, especially with this new high-powered job with Rebecca Talworth. He knew that he disturbed her every time he got out of bed. She would make that aggravated clicking noise with her tongue and turn over to face away from him. They never used to bicker, but it had now become almost a daily occurrence. But he couldn't blame her for that. After all, it was he who had blown away the family's security on a bad investment, and it was he who had been like a bear with a sore head ever since he had lost his job, and everyone in the household had been affected by it.

All, that is, except Josh. He kept his own counsel. He had returned home, having dropped out of Manchester University during his first year, and had immediately set about making himself a stranger to his own family. He found himself a job stacking shelves in Tesco's and then spent every bit of money that he made in the ear-shattering depths of Horace's Inferno, one of Brixton's more notorious clubs. Dan was inwardly enraged that his son should have given up on an opportunity in life that he himself had never been afforded. Yet he'd never sought confrontation over the issue, thinking that it might quite easily result in his son's leaving home and setting himself up in some dive of a flat where he would be completely without parental control.

Always, when morning came and Dan had been woken from his fitful slumber on the kitchen sofa by the sounds of Jackie moving around upstairs, neither one scene from the film nor one equation from the *Open University* course had ever registered in his brain. There had always been too many other things flying around in his head.

5

Dan attempted to open the door of Josh's bedroom once more, this time with a dunt of his shoulder, but there appeared to be some object on the other side that only allowed it to open a mere six inches. He got down on his knees and put a hand through the gap, and at a full arm's length, managed to extract a battered Nike trainer, its toe caved in where it had been acting successfully as a wedge against his entry. He stood up and opened the door fully, and the strong, fusty odour of a youth's unventilated lair made him physically reel back. He took a deep inhalation of untainted air before entering, then stepped as gingerly as he would in a minefield over the disordered piles of clothing that were strewn across every spare inch of the darkened interior of the room. Having made it across the floor space without coming into contact with the prostrate body of any one of Josh's friends, who dossed down with him on an all too regular basis, Dan drew back the curtains and pushed up the window as wide as it would go. He then turned to survey the living quarters of his firstborn.

It was almost macabre, like a scene from a film showing the aftereffects of a raid by secret police. Every drawer was open and emptied, the doors to the fitted cupboard hung wide, the shelves empty except for one sock which drooped forlornly over the edge, as if caught making a valiant effort to join its companion somewhere on the ground. The walls were covered with posters, overlapping, askew, the majority showing the scowling, glary-eyed features of his son's favourite rapper, Eminem. And there, on the bed, completing this scene of violent mayhem, was Josh, lying facedown on the crumpled undersheet, his head hidden beneath a flaccid pillow that happened to be the only form of cover on his otherwise naked body.

Dan cast an eye over the prostrate figure from hidden head to outsized foot – the muscled arms, the wide shoulders, the lean back, the tight buttocks, the cluster of manhood between the dark-haired legs – and he laughed quietly to himself. How was it that such a beautiful, soft-skinned cherub of a little boy could have metamorphosed into this . . . lackadaisical monster?

He took in a breath of nostalgia, realizing immediately that it was the wrong thing to do. He discarded the Nike trainer, the key root to the problem, onto an unused chair, and took hold of Josh's heel and gave it a solid shake.

'Josh?'

He spoke loudly, but his voice sounded deadened in the clothes-padded confines of the room. There was not one twitch of movement from his son's body.

'Come on, Josh. It's time to get up.'

He grabbed hold of Josh's ankles and dragged him forcefully down the bed, away from the protection of the pillow. With his body now bent over the edge of the bed, Dan found the target too tempting to ignore and finished off the awakening process by delivering a short, sharp slap to his son's bare buttocks.

Josh turned his head slowly, his long dark curls falling across bleary eyes. 'Bugger off, Dad. That was sore.'

Dan picked up the sheet that lay at the foot of the bed and threw it over his son. 'Drastic action is sometimes called for, I'm afraid.'

Josh flumped his head down on the bed again. 'I heard you the first time.'

'Then you should have made a move earlier, shouldn't you?'

'What time is it?'

'Ten past twelve.'

Josh groaned. 'But my shift doesn't start until seven o'clock tonight. I don't have to get up yet.'

'Oh yes you do, mate. There's more to life than sticking cans of baked beans on a shelf and head banging in a bloody club all night.'

'Like what?'

'Like getting this room tidied up for a start.'

Josh swung his legs over the side of the bed and sat up, pulling the sheet across his lap. He surveyed the room through a curtain of hair, and his nose wrinkled in an expression of bewilderment. 'Jeez, I only did it two days ago.'

'Somehow, I don't think so.'

'I did.'

'Well, then, you must have worn every article of clothing that you possess over the last two days.'

A reluctant smile of acknowledgement creased Josh's mouth. 'Yeah, you're right. I must have done.'

Dan bent down and picked up a random pair of trousers from the floor. They seemed far too large for his son's lean figure, but that's how he liked them – worn so low on his hips that a vast expanse of knicker elastic was shown above the waistline. A pair of red, cupid-patterned pants were still inside the trousers. He extracted them and dropped both articles onto the chair occupied by the Nike trainer, then sat down on the bed next to Josh. 'So, how was it last night?'

Josh swept a hand through his hair, pulling it away from his face. It was the first time that Dan had seen it uncovered that morning. He studied his son's features, seeing so many similarities to his own. The full eyebrows, the dark brown eyes, the high-bridged nose. The small gold hoop, however, that adorned the upper part of his left earlobe was unique to Josh.

'It was all right. Good DJ anyway.'

Feeling little inclination to extract further information about his son's nighttime escapades, Dan turned and picked up a book from the bedside table. It was a copy of Steinbeck's *Grapes of Wrath*. He flicked through the pages. 'Are you reading this?' he asked with an element of surprise.

'Yeah. I think he's a great writer. He's brilliantly economic with his words.'

Dan replaced the book on the table and let out a deep sigh. 'Joshy, my boy, what *are* you going to do with your life? You're too damned intelligent to waste away your time like this.'

Josh turned and stared challengingly at his father. 'I don't know. What are *you* going to do?'

Dan snorted out a laugh and gave his son's unruly mop of hair a hard ruffle. 'Touché! A very good question.' He pushed himself to his feet. 'The truthful answer is that I don't know, but I'm sure something will turn up.'

Josh nodded. 'Yeah, that's sort of what I was thinking.'

Dan kicked aside the clothing to make a path to the door. 'If you take all these down to the kitchen, you can put a load in the washing machine. We'll get them hung out to dry when I get back.'

'Where are you off to?'

'I'm meeting Nick Jessop for lunch in the King's Head.' Dan turned when he reached the door. 'And incidentally, while I'm there, you can take the dogs for a walk around the block for me. And make sure you take a plastic bag with you in case Biggles decides to explode again.'

Josh's face expressed acute revulsion. 'Thanks a bunch,' he murmured, out of earshot of his father. 'Dad?'

Dan had left the room by the time Josh called out his name. He returned, leaning a hand against the doorframe. 'Yes?'

Josh's mouth was set tight, as if reluctant to speak.

'What is it?' Dan asked again.

'It's just . . . well' – Josh leaned forward on his knees and began flicking at one thumbnail with the other – 'things aren't going too well between you and Mum, are they?'

Dan paused briefly before replying. 'What makes you think that?'

'I heard you this morning.'

'When?'

'This morning. Just before she left for work. You were talking at the bottom of the stairs.'

Dan raised his eyebrows. 'Hell, I didn't think that we were talking loud enough to wake *you* up.'

'I was in the bathroom getting a glass of water.'

'Ah, right. Well, I didn't realize.'

'They're not, though, are they?'

'What?'

'Things between you and Mum. You seem to be arguing all the time.'

'Not all the time.'

Josh flicked back his head dismissively, but never raised his eyes. 'Who are you trying to kid?'

Obviously only myself, Dan thought to himself. 'Everything's all right, Josh. It's just . . . a bit difficult at the minute, what with Mum working every hour of the day and me being out of a job. That kind of pressure is enough to put a strain on even the strongest relationship.'

Josh nodded, but Dan could tell that his son was far from convinced. 'The girls are being a pain in the arse too,' Josh continued. 'They haven't been giving you much of a break recently, have they?'

Dan smiled at Josh's unexpected concern. 'No, not really. But again, I think it's quite understandable. They're both of an age when life can be, well, fairly traumatic, and I haven't exactly improved their lot by having them move to a new school. They're not particularly happy there . . . and, of course, they blame me for that.'

Josh blew out a derisive laugh. 'That's such a load of rubbish!

34

You're just too good to them because they're girls. I was never happy at *my* school, but you just kept telling me to knuckle down and get on with it.' He reached down and began to collect up some of his clothes. 'Or maybe the difference is that now you have *time* to realize that Millie and Nina aren't happy.'

Dan scratched a finger repeatedly against the side of his face as his mind fought for an appropriate dismissal to Josh's observation. He couldn't think of one. 'You could well be right.' He leaned his shoulder against the doorframe. 'So, are you saying that it's my fault that you dropped out of university?'

Josh laughed. 'No, actually, I'm not. And, to be quite honest, it wouldn't have made a blind bit of difference if you *had* sent me to another school. I've always had a natural aversion to all forms of education.'

Dan smiled at his son and walked back into the room and scooped up a pile of clothes from the floor. 'I'll put this lot in the washing machine. You bring down the rest.'

6

It had happened exactly one month and two days after he lost his job. At the precise moment when the first news report broke on the radio, he had been standing in the kitchen, making himself a mug of instant coffee to accompany his lunchtime sandwich. He remembered that he held the spoon brimming with coffee granules hovering above the mug, frozen in his actions, as he listened to the broadcast. By the time the reporter had signed off, promising to keep listeners up to date with news as it broke, and the incongruously lighthearted music had started once again, only two minute coffee granules had fallen to the base of the mug. In the plethora of reports that filled the newspapers for the next two weeks, it became clear that others throughout the world had also remembered exactly what they were doing, down to the last detail.

He had immediately turned on the television and watched, transfixed, at the scenes that were being beamed live from New York. He knew the building so well. He had been in it so many times before, but still he found it impossible to orientate himself, to tell from the shaking, street-level camera shots which tower had actually been hit. When he eventually realized that the one that housed the headquarters of the company for which he had worked for fifteen years still stood, apparently unscathed, he felt a moment's selfish relief that his colleagues would be all right and that they would be able to escape. It could only have been a moment, because as he stood there, no more than three feet away from the television screen, he watched in horror as the second aircraft hit the surviving tower.

Once he had managed to break himself away from the mesmeric images of utter catastrophe, he tried to call his old office in the City. The lines were jammed. He then tried Nick Jessop, an ex-colleague who had coincidentally lost his job at the same time as himself. The domestic help informed him that Mr Jessop had taken his baby son for a walk. At first, Dan couldn't believe that Nick was able to carry on with such a normal, everyday routine when, twenty minutes before, an occurrence had taken place that was destined to change the world for ever. And then he realized that it *had* only happened twenty minutes ago and that Nick wouldn't even know about it. He told the woman to get Nick to turn on the television as soon as he arrived back in the house.

He was now desperate to speak to someone that he knew, someone that he cared about. So he rang Jackie. The receptionist told him that his wife was in a finance meeting and didn't want to be disturbed. Dan had sworn at the girl, really sworn, and within ten seconds he was speaking with Jackie. 'Is this really important,' she had said, 'because I'm in the middle of an extremely tense meeting, and, by the way, don't you dare start calling the office and using the f-word with my receptionist.' Dan had said nothing more, other than to tell her to get her ear to a radio or her eyes to a television as soon as her meeting was over.

And then he had remembered that Josh was upstairs in bed. He rushed up the staircase and entered his bedroom with such force that Josh had awoken immediately. Even in his soporific state, Josh could tell that something had happened.

'What's the matter, Dad?' he had asked in a voice that registered real concern. 'Why are you crying?'

Until that moment, Dan hadn't realized that he was. 'Could you come downstairs, Josh, and watch television with me?' He heard his voice choke as he spoke the words.

'Why?' Josh asked, jumping out of bed and hurriedly pulling on a pair of boxer shorts. 'What's happened?'

'I'm not sure, but I think that I might have just witnessed a whole load of my friends being killed.'

They had sat on the sofa together for the rest of the afternoon watching the television. They never spoke, except to murmur an occasional expletive at the sheer magnitude of the devastation. Dan tried, on a number of occasions, to contact his old office in the City, but still the lines remained busy. He had never felt so helplessly out of touch in all his life.

When the newspapers eventually managed to compile lists of those who were missing, believed killed, he had counted eight close colleagues and three others whom he had met on a couple of occasions. John Fricker had probably been one of his closest friends, and in the instant that he read his name, he could recall every moment of the beautiful autumn weekend that he had spent with John and one of their work colleagues, Debbie Leishman, in upstate New York. It was after that weekend that John and Debbie started to become pretty serious about each other. Dan found their telephone number in his address book, but it took him a full week after reading the name in the newspaper to pluck up the courage to try to make contact with Debbie. When he eventually spoke to her, he found that he couldn't even begin to find adequate words to express the way that he felt, so for a quarter of an hour, he had just listened to the voice of complete incomprehension and desolation at the other end of the line.

It was after he had finished that telephone call, when he was alone in his office at the top of the house in Clapham, that Dan had started to reevaluate his whole life. His own troubles now seemed insignificant. He thought how lucky he was to have a family, how proud he was to have a seventeen-year-old son who had the sensitivity and strength to sit with a protective arm encircling his father's shoulder as they had watched those scenes from New York. He thought of the girls, miserable at their new school, and he vowed that he would be there for them, to help them through it. It was, after all, only a pinpoint of time in their lives. And he thought how unimportant it was to be without his high-flying job in the City. There were so many other things to cherish, to nurture. From that moment on, he was going to be happy, he was going to be fun, and he was going to be around for a family that needed him.

There was, however, one aspect of that day that Dan had never been able to comprehend. It left a chill where before there had been nothing but the warmth of mutual love and friendship. During those interminably long, dismal hours of September the eleventh, when families throughout the world, totally unconnected with those who had lost their lives, had telephoned each other just to touch base, just to express feelings of togetherness, Jackie had never bothered to call him.

7

There was only standing room available when Dan entered the King's Head, many of those who were having lunch being forced to balance plates upon beer glasses in order to free a hand with which to feed themselves. It therefore took Dan a certain amount of time and contortion to push his way to the bar. He tried to catch the attention of Martin, the landlord, but he was busy serving customers at the farthest end of the bar, so he turned his attention to Minty, the New Zealand girl who had been working in the pub for the past few months. She was serving a vociferous young businessman who had divested himself of his suit jacket to reveal a striking pair of red braces worn over a dark blue shirt with white starched cutaway collar. Dan thought how lucky he was that he no longer needed to wear the uniform of the City. He was much happier wearing his jeans and his leather jacket and his loafers. He had come to quite relish the fact that nobody could pigeon-hole him into any one particular job.

He watched as the man leaned across the bar and talked to Minty in a drawling tone of self-assuredness that obviously implied that the barmaid could not help but find him outrageously attractive. As she handed the man his change, Minty beamed him a sweet smile, and then spied Dan.

'Hi, Dan,' she said, giving her hands a quick rinse in the basin under the counter and air-flicking them dry. 'What can I get you?'

'Pint of Young's, please, Minty.'

'Coming right up.'

Dan cast an eye around the thronging mass of people. 'You haven't seen Nick around, have you?'

Minty was about to answer when they both heard a sound that was quite alien to a busy London pub. Above the roaring cacophony of conversation came a short, gleeful scream that could only be produced by a seriously underaged drinker. It brought an instant hush as heads were turned to source the perpetrator's whereabouts, but the interest was short-lived and the volume in the pub soon crescendoed once more. Dan, however, had no need to work out the origin of the sound. Only one person would be daft enough to bring a five-month-old baby into a smoke-filled pub, and he was sitting somewhere over by the cigarette machine.

Both he and Minty smiled knowingly at each other. 'Okay,' Dan laughed. 'I think I've got him.'

Nick Jessop was standing behind his table looking like a distraught kangaroo that had lost its joey. A baby sling hung forlornly empty against his tall frame as he watched with an uneasy smile on his face while young Tarquin's considerable bulk, resplendently dressed in a minute Chelsea Football Club team shirt, was being repeatedly thrown into the air and caught again in the arms of a thin, elderly woman with a squiggly lipsticked mouth and mirrored splodges of rouge on each of her sunken cheeks. Every now and again, she would cease her physical efforts to be fortified by a good slurp of gin and tonic and a deep drag on her cigarette. Then, encouraged by the child's gurning for more, she would again launch him into the air, her knees visibly buckling and a coughing wheeze being forced from her chest every time she clamped her arms around Tarquin's hurtling form.

Dan thought it not unlike watching a spider trying to catch a cannonball.

His arrival at the table was enough to break the attention being granted to the circus act, and Nick, with obvious relief, managed to retrieve his only child from the clutches of the woman.

'Thank God you arrived,' he breathed out, as he wedged Tarquin into the corner of the velour-covered bench, stopping his protestations by sticking a dummy in his mouth. 'I was just waiting for the moment when she got her timing wrong and took a swig and a drag when Tarquin was still midair.'

'Well, I'm afraid that you do slightly ask for it,' Dan replied, placing his pint on the table and pulling out the chair that Nick had been saving for him. 'You shouldn't keep bringing him in here.'

'Not an option, I'm afraid. Laura is working full-time now, and we haven't got any help in the house. Anyway, he likes being gregarious, don't you, my' – he leaned down over his son and blew a raspberry on his nylon-shirted tummy – 'cheeky, cheeky chappie!'

'So, how's life treating you?' Dan asked in an attempt to get the conversation back to adult level.

Nick made minor adjustments to Tarquin's position before turning his attention to Dan. 'Not bad, actually. In fact, I've got something here that I think might interest you.' He reached down under the table and pulled out a battered leather briefcase. He gave Dan a wink as he opened it and extracted a sheet of A4 paper. 'Are you ready for this?'

'I can't wait,' Dan replied with only a fraction of the enthusiasm being displayed by his friend.

Nick spun the sheet around on the table and sat back against the bench, a broad grin on his face as he watched for Dan's reaction. It was a drawing of something that loosely resembled an oversized banana with what looked like a dead stick insect laid across its top edge. Dan looked up at Nick, cleared his throat, and continued to study the drawing. Maybe it was meant to be the crescent moon, complete with anorexic elf reclining.

Dan shook his head. 'No, sorry. You've got me.'

Nick frowned. 'What do you mean, I've got you?' He spun the drawing around to face him. 'It's obvious what it is.'

It suddenly dawned on Dan that what was important about the drawing was not so much the content as the artistic prowess. He took back the drawing and studied it with renewed understanding. 'It's very good. He's got a very bright future.'

'Who has?'

'Tarquin.'

Nick snatched the drawing away from Dan. 'Okay, that's very funny. Listen, I might not be Van Gogh, but the idea behind it is a real winner.'

'Well then, you'd better explain what it is because I don't think that it's obvious at all.'

Nick laid the drawing once more in front of Dan and gave it a meaningful thump with his forefinger. 'I have designed a child's car seat.'

Dan looked back down at the banana and let out a silent sigh. Why the hell is it, he pondered to himself, that whenever men or women have their first offspring at a fairly advanced age, they either act as if theirs was the first household ever to be blessed with infant birth, or that all prior knowledge of rudimentary child care had been compiled by a moron?

'What's wrong with the ones you can get in Mothercare or Halford's?' Dan asked.

'Outdated. This is state-of-the-art technology.'

Dan chuckled. 'Nick, you're a banker. What the hell do you know about design and technology?'

Nick looked indignant. 'I'll have you know I was very good at making Airfix models at my prep school.'

Dan stifled a laugh. 'Jeez, I don't think those credentials will impress too many would-be users. I mean, you're not planning to *glue* the baby into the seat, are you?'

Nick leaned forward on the table and fixed Dan with a beady eye. 'Funny you should mention that.'

The smile slid from Dan's face. He slowly shook his head. 'Tell me you're not – please.'

Nick grinned excitedly. 'No. But it is revolutionary.'

'All right,' Dan said, leaning back in his chair and folding his arms. 'Go on then. Hit me with it.'

'Okay! What I've come up with is the idea of a seat without any form of retaining straps.'

Dan looked a little nonplussed. 'Oh?'

'Just wait.' Nick began to twist his hands around in the air as if caressing an invisible ball. 'Once you've put the child in the seat, you tilt it upwards so that the child's bottom is resting at the lowest point of the structure, and its feet and head at the top, so the only movement it could possibly make is upwards, and that, as you well know, is an impossibility in a car.'

'Unless you drive off the side of a motorway and roll ten times down the embankment.'

Nick looked peeved at Dan's negativity towards his idea. 'No one should be driving that stupidly if they have a child in the car.'

Dan let out a resigned laugh. He wasn't even going to bother trying to reason. 'All right, you win. I just don't see why you can't put straps on the seat.'

'Because they're damned uncomfortable for young babies.'

'Well, in that case, you'd be as well sticking their arse in a bucket and wedging them in behind the driver's seat.'

Nick shook his head. 'Come on, Dan, you've really got to understand what I'm trying to achieve here, because' – he aimed his forefinger at the centre of Dan's chest – 'I want *you* to handle the product marketing.'

Dan looked aghast. 'You've got to be joking! I'd be better trying to sell Kalashnikov rifles to Toys 'R' Us!'

'You'd be getting paid for it.'

'Oh yeah?'

'On commission. And don't tell me that a bit of income wouldn't come in useful.'

Dan's grin showed affection for his friend. Maybe he had been a bit cynical. Nick was only trying to help. 'Well, that is very kind and thoughtful of you, Nick. I'll tell you what, let's talk about it again once you've found a manufacturer.'

Nick balled his fist enthusiastically. 'Good idea.' He swept the drawing off the table and replaced it in his briefcase. He shot a glance of self-reassurance at Tarquin's now-slumbering form before leaning back on the table. 'Listen, I've got a plan for you and me tomorrow.'

'Really? And what might that be?'

'Well, how about heading up to Curzon Street and having a relaxed haircut and shave in Trumpers? It would be just like old times!'

Dan laughed. 'A good thought, Nick, but firstly, I don't need a haircut; secondly, I couldn't afford it anyway; and thirdly, just in case you've forgotten, tomorrow is our "brew" day. We can't go without our unemployment benefit now, can we?'

'Ah,' Nick replied quietly through clenched teeth. 'That was the other thing I wanted to talk to you about. The trip to Trumpers was meant to be, well, a sort of celebration.'

'Was it? Celebrating what?'

'The fact that I signed off the brew yesterday. I've got a new job.'

'Where?'

'In the City. With Broughton's.'

Dan raised his eyebrows. 'Well done, you. Congratulations. When do you start?'

'Two weeks on Monday. I hope to hell that I can find someone to look after Tarquin by then. I don't think that I'd be too popular if I turned up at work with him strapped to my front.' He paused. 'I don't suppose you'd consider . . .'

'No, Nick, I would not.'

'Right. Of course not. Well, it was just a thought.'

'So you're obviously not going to be relying on the child seat to make your fortune.'

'No. I was just planning for it to be a sideline.'

Dan laughed. 'Probably just as well.'

For the first time, Nick saw the funny side of Dan's ribbing. 'Yes, maybe you're right.' He drained the remainder of his pint, put the glass on the table, and began to spin it round with his fingers. 'Listen, Dan, once I've been with Broughton's for a bit, I'll put in a good word for you.'

Dan shook his head. 'Don't bother. I'm not going back to the City.'

'Come on, Dan!' Nick exclaimed. 'You're too damned good not to go back. I just don't understand why you haven't had any job offers since September eleventh.'

Dan shot him a wink. 'Ah, but I have, Nick. I just haven't told you about them. Six, maybe seven, actually, but I declined every one of them.'

'But why, for God's sake? You have to work, Dan.' There was almost a hint of desperation in Nick's voice.

'I will, but not in the City. I think I've probably mellowed too much to get involved in the cut and thrust of high finance again. Anyway, I had my fair share of the pot of gold over the years. Maybe it's time to put something back.'

Nick's mouth dropped open. 'That sounds a bit dangerous. You're not contemplating going into the church, are you?'

'Bloody hell, no! Could you see me in a dog collar?'

Nick visibly shuddered. 'No, you're quite right. Stupid suggestion. So, what *are* you thinking of doing?'

'I don't know, but I'm sure something will turn up.' His words struck a familiar chord, and he smiled to himself as he remembered Josh's clever riposte a couple of hours before.

On the bench, Tarquin made a gurgling noise and fluttered his eyelashes, threatening to wake up, but then he just turned his head and settled back into a deep sleep. Nick took his jacket off the back of the chair next to Dan and laid it gently over his son.

'When was the last time you heard from Debbie Leishman?' he asked.

'I got an e-mail from her two days ago,' Dan replied.

'How is she?'

'She's coping. Did you know that she'd had a baby?'

'Never. When was that?'

'In June.'

'How amazing!' Nick furrowed his brow. 'Could it have been John's child?'

'Of course it was John's child. She didn't even know that she was pregnant when he was killed on nine-eleven.'

Nick clicked his tongue. 'What a bugger, eh? On the other hand, it's pretty marvellous that she has something of his for always, if you get my meaning.'

'It would have been better still if they had been married. Then she would have got some compensation.'

'Are you still sending her money?'

'As much as I can, yes. I don't think Jackie would be too pleased if she found out that I was keeping another woman.'

Nick swept away a long string of blonde hair from his face. 'Are things going any better with you and Jackie, or is she still being a bit frosty?'

Dan snorted out a laugh. 'No, the girls are now the frosty ones. Jackie has turned into the ice maiden.' He let out a long sigh. 'But I keep smiling through it all and cooking them semi-delicious meals and coming out with jovial remarks that no one finds particularly funny, in the hope that my infectious happiness will lead us all to a better life.'

'And is there any sign of that happening?' Nick asked.

Dan chuckled. 'No. I just irritate the hell out of them all.'

Nick became thoughtful and began tapping his fingers on the table. 'Listen, Dan, why don't you try getting out of London for a bit? I mean, there's nothing to stop you from taking the whole family away somewhere for a week.'

Dan shook his head. 'The school term's just started, Nick. You can't just whip the kids away when you feel like it.' He glanced at Tarquin on the bench. 'Maybe you don't know about that kind of thing yet. Anyway, Jackie has Paris Fashion Week coming up soon, so there's no way that she would want to go.'

'Well, go over to Paris with her. Get Battersea Gran to look after the kids.'

The remark made Dan smile. When his father had died two years before, he had moved his mother from her council house in Tottenham Hale to a small flat in a high-rise block overlooking the River Thames in Battersea. It had never ceased to amuse him that she was now universally known as Battersea Gran. 'Yeah, I could, I suppose. I'll have a word with Jackie tonight when she gets home.'

Nick gave a quick nod of his head as if to finalize the point. 'Good.' He leaned over his son and carefully extracted a newspaper from the pocket of his jacket. 'Now, let's move on to more important matters. How about coming to Stamford Bridge on Saturday?'

'Who's playing?'

'Chelsea versus Spurs – their first clash of the season,' Nick replied, folding the paper across the back page and handing it over to Dan. 'Thought you'd like to come to support your old team.'

Dan glanced quickly at the prematch report before pushing the paper back across the table. 'I don't know. I can't really make any plans until I know what Jackie is doing.'

'Come on!' Nick cajoled. 'It would be just like old times.'

'Old times!' Dan laughed. 'Nick, whenever we've been to a match together, we've ended up sitting at opposite ends of the pitch, yelling tribal abuse at one another.'

'Okay, then, bring an extra Tottenham scarf with you. I don't mind being a Spurs fan for a day.'

Dan raised his eyebrows in surprise. 'My word, I think you mean it.'

'Of course I do. Anything for an old mate.'

'Well, that certainly would be the supreme sacrifice.' He paused. 'How many tickets could you lay your hands on?'

'How many extra are you looking for?'

'Just the one. For Josh.'

Nick gave him a thumbs-up. 'I'll see what I can do.' He picked up his empty beer glass and got to his feet. 'Right, keep an eye on Tarquin and I'll get another couple of pints in. Do you want anything to eat?'

'Not really. I'll share a ham sandwich with you, if you want.'

'Right, coming up!' He slapped Dan's shoulder as he passed him. 'And while I'm away, think about how we can improve on the design of the car seat.'

8

As he sat in his office at the top of the house that evening, desperately seeking an e-mail that had vanished from the screen of his laptop, strong evidence came to Dan's nostrils that his carefully prepared gourmet meal was fast becoming a burnt offering. He jumped up from his desk, squirting the screen arrow off to oblivion, and bolted down the stairs, two at a time. He raced into the kitchen and threw open the oven door, reeling back as the scorching fumes hit his face. He picked up an oven glove from the work surface and waved it about to clear the air, then gingerly extracted the smouldering roasting pan from the oven and hurried out through the French doors into the garden. As the heat from the pan began to penetrate through the flimsy glove, he looked around in desperation to try to find a suitable surface on which to put it. He opted, more out of necessity than choice, for the bird table.

Pulling off the glove, he blew hard on his seared fingers to relieve them, and despondently viewed the blackened lump that was to have been Nigella Lawson's Loin of Pork with Bay Leaves.

'Bugger it!' he said quietly to himself, and turned and walked back into the kitchen.

The fumes had now risen to the ceiling and hung above his

head like a swirling sea mist, and for the first time he became aware that he had not been alone in the kitchen when he had attempted his rescue. Millie sat with her chin resting on her hands at one end of the long pine table, her homework spread out in front of her. There was not much indication, however, of any great learning taking place, unless she had found a way of indoctrinating her brain with an enormous pair of Sony earphones clamped about her head, whilst her eyes feasted on a video recording of that day's episode of *EastEnders*.

Dan kicked the oven door closed and lobbed the oven glove onto the work surface. 'Millie, you twit, you might have called me. The whole house could have caught fire.'

Millie made no move, except to pull a long string of chewing gum from her mouth and then reel it back in again with her tongue. Dan moved up behind her and lifted the earphones off her head. 'Millie!'

His daughter jumped round in her chair. 'What?'

'Your dinner is cremated. It is burned to a frazzle.'

'So? You can't blame me for that.'

'I'm not blaming you for anything, but didn't you happen to notice that it was nigh on impossible to see the television for smoke?'

Millie once again resumed her chin-in-hands position and fixed her eyes on the television. 'How was I to know that it wasn't *meant* to be like that?'

'Well, I would have thought that the smell might have given you just the smallest indication that something was burning.'

'I didn't notice the smell.'

'Millie! Come on, pull the other one!'

She twisted round again, her hands outstretched to accentuate her blamelessness. 'I didn't! How could I? I was listening to music.'

Dan was left speechless by the reply. He shifted his baffled gaze from the earphones in his hand, which were still linked to the portable CD on the table and still blaring out music, to Millie's ears, wondering if there was some appalling defect in his daughter's sensory organs about which he had not previously known. He eventually accepted it for what it was, a complete non sequitur to stop him from pestering her during her nightly vigil with *EastEnders*.

Dan let out a sigh. 'Right then, where's Nina?'

'Upstairs, practising her flute,' Millie replied, without dragging her eyes away from the sight of pint-sized Barbara Windsor pulling yet another man-sized pint in the Queen Vic.

'For heaven's sake, she's just had a concert! Hasn't she played enough for one day?'

'She thinks she played rubbish.'

'Oh? I thought it all sounded pretty good. Who put that idea into her head?'

Millie looked at Dan out of the side of her eyes. 'Probably everybody in the orchestra, if not the school.'

Dan shook his head. 'Come on, Millie, surely things aren't that bad, are they?'

'Don't you believe it!' she mumbled in reply.

Dan put down the earphones on the table. 'Right, well, let's cheer everybody up. Seeing that the dinner's burned, I'll have to get a takeaway. What do you want? Indian or Chinese?'

Millie's eyes suddenly brightened. 'Can we have sushi?'

'No, Millie, we can't.'

'Why not?'

Dan leaned one hand on the worktop, the other on his hip, as he gave overplayed thought to Millie's question. 'Two reasons, mainly. One, because the nearest sushi bar is in Victoria, and two, because the car is being extremely fickle and has decided not to start. Therefore, we have no way of getting sushi.'

Millie despondently slumped her face back into her hands. 'Couldn't you get Mum to pick some up on the way home?'

'Indian or Chinese, Millie?'

Millie fixed her eyes on the television once more. 'Don't mind. Whatever.'

Dan flipped open the rubbish bin and dropped in the three card-board lids. 'Right, on the menu this evening we have chicken rogan mush, chicken pathia, and pilau rice.' He took a serving spoon from the drawer and stood with it hovering above the tinfoil containers. 'What's it going to be? Ni, you can have first choice.'

Both Millie and Nina remained transfixed in front of the television, as they had done since he had walked back into the kitchen bearing the two pale blue plastic bags.

'Listen, can we have the television off for a bit?'

It was like talking to a brick wall. Dan walked over to the table and stretched across Millie's shoulder and took the remote from her grasp. The television clicked and died. To his surprise, there were no vociferous complaints, both girls seeming to accept it with bland indifference.

'I've got to go to the loo,' Millie said, sliding off her chair.

'Come on! You could have done that while I was out.'

'Didn't need to go then,' Millie retorted as she left the room.

Dan let out a resigned sigh. 'Right then, Ni, what do you want?'

Nina walked over to the sideboard and eyed the contents of the containers with an expression that registered supreme distaste. 'What is that?'

'Well, for the second time, it's chicken rogan josh, chicken pathia, and pilau rice.'

'Haven't you got any poppadoms?'

'Yes, I have. They're in the oven keeping warm.'

'Which is the mildest?'

'I think the rogan josh.'

'Could I just have rice and poppadoms?'

Dan stood with the spoon still poised. 'No, you have to have a bit of one or the other.'

'Why?'

'Because . . . I bought it for you, that's why.'

'You could always put my share in the fridge for Josh. He doesn't mind what he eats.'

Dan decided that he had reasoned enough. He spooned out some rice and a small amount of rogan josh onto a plate and handed it to Nina. 'If you get the poppadoms out of the oven, you can have mine if you like.'

As Nina carried her plate over to the table, Millie came back into the kitchen. Dan gave her a plate already filled with food. He wasn't going to go through the same rigmarole with her.

'Can we put the television back on?' Millie asked.

'No, we can't,' Dan replied, putting the containers into the oven before taking his own plate over to the table.

Millie groaned at the same time that Nina asked, 'Why not?'

Dan handed a fork to each of his daughters. 'Because I thought that we might talk instead.'

'What about?' Nina asked halfheartedly, sticking the fork into her rice and letting it dribble back onto her plate.

'I don't know. What would you like to talk about?'

His question was met by silence. Dan took a mouthful of food, hoping that one of the girls might have said something by the time he had finished it. It didn't work. 'All right, then. Ni, I thought your concert went very well tonight.'

'Dad, you fool!' Millie hissed through clenched teeth. 'I *told* you about that.'

Dan ignored his elder daughter. 'I thought you played really well.'

'I did not,' Nina mumbled.

'Well, I disagree with you and I know for a fact that Mrs Partridge does as well.'

Millie and Nina turned to look at Dan simultaneously, both with questioning frowns creasing their foreheads. 'Who is Mrs Partridge?' Millie asked.

'Come on, Millie,' Dan exclaimed. 'You know as well as I do who Mrs Partridge is. Nina's music teacher.'

For a moment, both girls stared open-mouthed at him before bursting out laughing, Nina managing to spray her mouthful of food across the table in the process.

'Nina!' Dan exclaimed, reaching over to wipe the splattering of pilau rice off the television screen. 'Okay then, what have I said that's so funny?'

Millie swung around in her chair to face Dan, her eyes sparkling with intrigue – or maybe it was humour – Dan couldn't work out which, but it was certainly the most animated that he had seen his elder daughter all evening.

'So what did you say to Mrs *Partridge*, then, Dad?' she asked. 'Was it something like "My word, Mrs *Partridge*, didn't the orchestra play well tonight? Do you think Nina has any chance of getting an A in her GCSE's, Mrs *Partridge*?"'

Dan was bemused by all the hilarity, but nevertheless pleased that he had at least succeeded in making his daughters laugh. It didn't happen very often. 'Maybe not those exact words, but something like that, yes.'

Nina was laughing so much now that she fell forward and thumped her forehead on the table. The blow obviously caused her pain because she immediately straightened up, her only reaction to the blow being a silent, round-mouthed 'Ow'.

Millie took in a deep breath to control herself. 'Her name, Dad, is Miss Peacock, not Mrs Partridge.'

Dan smacked his hand against his mouth. 'It's not.'

Millie nodded, then burst out laughing again.

'Oh, hell,' Dan said quietly.

'Have you always called her Mrs Partridge, Dad?' Nina eventually managed to ask.

'Yes, I'm pretty sure I have,' Dan replied, looking as if he had just sucked on a sour lemon.

As the kitchen filled with laughter once more, the door opened and Jackie walked in. She surveyed the scene of conviviality as she shrugged off her raincoat. 'My word,' she said flatly. 'You all seem very happy this evening.'

'You'll never guess what, Mum,' Nina said, using her mother's entrance as a diversionary tactic to jettison the remainder of her rogan josh into the rubbish bin.

'No, I probably won't,' Jackie replied distractedly as she walked across to the telephone to check the notepad for messages.

'Dad has been calling Miss Peacock, my music teacher, Mrs Partridge.'

Jackie gave Nina a half-smile and ran a hand over her daughter's long dark hair. 'Sorry I didn't make the concert, darling. I just couldn't get away from work.'

The humorous twinkle vanished from Nina's eyes. 'That's all right,' she replied quietly.

Millie pushed back her chair and got to her feet. 'Can we go upstairs to watch television, Mum?'

'Sure you can.'

'Thanks. Come on, Ni.'

As the two girls left the kitchen, Jackie slumped down onto the chair that Millie had just vacated. Dan cleared the dirty plates off the table and carried them across to the sink.

'How's your day been?' he asked, rinsing them off under the tap.

'Exhausting,' Jackie replied.

Dan took the containers from the oven and put them on the worktop. 'I'm afraid we're on takeaway tonight. I had a bit of a disaster with the loin of pork.'

Jackie held up a hand. 'Thanks, but I really couldn't eat a thing. I had a huge lunch.'

'Right.' He scrutinized the contents of the three containers. 'Well, I don't think I'll risk giving it to the dogs,' he said, mainly for the benefit of himself. 'That might just be tempting providence.' He discarded everything into the rubbish bin and rubbed his hands clean on a dishtowel. 'Can I get you a glass of wine, then?'

Jackie shook her head. 'No, don't bother. I thought that I might just have a bath and go straight to bed.'

Dan sat down on the chair next to her. 'So, how did you get on with the set designer?'

'Oh,' Jackie replied. 'So you remembered.'

'Of course I remembered. What makes you think I wouldn't remember?'

'Well, I just thought . . . Look, don't let's get started into another argument. I'm too tired.'

56

'We're not having an argument! I was just asking!'

'All right! I'm sorry.' Jackie leaned her elbows on the table and covered her face with her hands. 'I really do feel exhausted.'

Dan reached across and gave her arm a gentle pat. 'It's not surprising. You're working bloody hard.' He got to his feet and walked over to the fridge. 'Are you sure you don't want to have a glass of wine? I'm going to have one.'

'All right then, but just half a glass.'

Dan poured out the wine and handed her the glass. He sat down again. 'Listen, when is Prêt-à-Porter?'

'In three weeks' time.'

'Do you have to go over beforehand?'

Jackie turned to look at him. She paused before replying. 'Yes, actually. I do.'

'Good. In that case, I thought that I'd come with you.'

Jackie's eyes opened wide. 'What?'

'Well, I just thought that we needed a bit of time together. It would be the perfect opportunity.'

Jackie bit at her lip. 'Dan, I've got to go over this weekend. I was going to tell you tonight.'

'Oh. Right. Well, I could try to get Battersea Gran to come over, but it's a bit short notice.'

'Dan, I'm going with Stephen.'

Dan's eyes shifted around the room as he tried to work out who the hell Stephen was. 'Stephen? Who might that be?'

'Our financial director.'

'Ah.'

'It's business, Dan. I've got some serious negotiations to do with the organizers. Stephen said that he would come over and give me a hand.'

Dan pulled a long face. 'Well, I hope you're only speaking metaphorically.'

'Don't be so bloody stupid. You know as well as I do what I mean.'

'Right. So when will you be back?'

'Probably Monday or Tuesday. Stephen thought it better to spill the visit over into a weekday, just in case we hit problems at the weekend.'

Dan scratched a finger across his forehead. 'Why is it that I haven't heard of this Stephen before?'

Jackie let out a long sigh. 'Maybe because you've never been interested in what I do before.'

'Jackie, that's nonsense and you know it.'

'Well, if you were so well up to speed, you would know that it was Stephen who is wholly responsible for setting up Rebecca Talworth Design Limited, and I think probably wholly responsible for getting me the job as managing director.'

Dan cocked his head to the side and winked. 'Sounds like some guy, this Stephen.'

Jackie drained her wine glass in one gulp. 'Right, I'm going upstairs.' She pushed back her chair and stood up.

'I was only joking, you know.'

'That's your problem, Dan. You're always joking. Maybe you should think about trying to take life a little more seriously and get yourself a bloody job!'

She grabbed her raincoat from the back of the chair and stormed out of the kitchen, slamming the door behind her. In the silence that ensued, Biggles crept out of hiding from his basket in the conservatory and came over and laid his head on Dan's knee.

Dan gave the dog a solid pat on his large black-and-white head. 'Biggles, my boy, your timing seems to be a hell of a lot better than mine.'

9

Dan sat in the ageing Saab outside St Bartholomew's Church in Battersea, killing time until his mother appeared by attempting to fit the convertible hood flush with the top of the windscreen so that they wouldn't have to make the journey back to Clapham with frozen scalps. He had never really been aware of the draught himself until the day before when he had whisked Jackie up to Waterloo Station and had dropped her outside the Eurostar terminal with her woollen scarf tied Russian-peasant-style around her head. He had secretly hoped that wonderboy Stephen could have seen her like that, but as he watched her walk into the building, she had pulled off the scarf, given her head a quick shake, and once more looked immaculate. Well, from the rear view at any rate. She hadn't actually bothered to turn round, not even for a final goodbye.

Two young children, clutching crayoned drawings in their hands, came running out through the doors of the church, heralding the end of the service. Dan watched as they hid behind one of the stone pillars, whispering excitedly to one another, and then jumped out when their parents appeared. Neither mother nor father showed any reaction to their children's sudden appearance.

Go on, Dan thought, do something! At least clutch a hand to the heart or stagger back in feigned shock. But no, they just pushed their children on in front of them and headed up the street in animated and godly conversation with each other.

Dan watched the procession of worshippers stream out of the church and shake hands with the storklike vicar at the door; there were a couple of ex-military types who stood ramrod straight and threw back their heads in laughter at the punchline of the story their wives simpered out to the vicar; there was a bevy of Born Agains, with their nonexistent dress code and their smiles of sheer goodness and radiant sincerity; there was an old woman with a woolly hat pulled down over her tangle of matted hair who shuffled past the vicar without a word and went off down the street, muttering to herself as she carried her worldly belongings in several plastic bags, their handles entwined in her grubby, mitted fingers; and then there were the stalwarts – the ladies who cleaned the floors, polished the brasses, arranged the flowers, and organized midweek fund-raising coffee mornings to which only they turned up. They were dressed in drab Sunday best coats done up to the neck, carrying handbags on their forearms and gloves in hand, and they wore hats that appeared to have been beaten into submission with cudgels before adorning their tightly permed white hair.

Dan could never quite fathom why it was that, as long as he could remember, old ladies always seemed to have dressed in exactly the same way. Was there never a time in their lives when they favoured bright figure-hugging clothes and glossed their mouths with devil-red lipstick? Had those pink-spectacled eyes never flashed a 'Come on, try your luck with me' to some cool young dude on the other side of the dance floor? It was hard to imagine. Maybe they all went through some bizarre metamorphic process as they approached their golden years, entering into some weird extrusion plant dressed as butterflies and coming out the other end as mothy pensioners.

Thank God for Mum, Dan thought to himself. There she was,

rounded and wholesome, dressed in a fuchsia pink raincoat, her grey, loose-curled hair blowing free in the breeze, standing amongst them like a rose in a cabbage patch. It didn't take much to imagine her still as that young, vibrant teenage girl, dressed in flared skirt and bobby socks, who had walked away with every jive competition held at the Metropole Dance Hall in Tottenham Hale.

Dan got out of the car and went around to the passenger door and held it open for his mother. She gave him a little wave but remained on the pavement talking with one of her fellow church slaves, no doubt fixing up the next scintillating meeting of the Scrape-Your-Knuckles-to-the-Bone-for-the-Welfare-of-the-Church Club. A nod and a gentle pat on the arm confirmed the arrangement and Battersea Gran crossed over the road to the car.

'Hello, dear,' she trilled, offering up her cheek for a kiss. Dan obliged. 'My word, hasn't it got cold all of a sudden? What's happened to the Indian summer that nice Mr Fish promised us on the telly?' She reached up and gave the lapel of his leather jacket a shake. 'And look at you without a jersey. You may think you look sexy in that thing, but it's not going to keep out the chill.'

'I'm fine, Mum,' Dan replied, wrestling his jacket from her grip. 'In fact, I'm feeling quite hot.' For heaven's sake, Dan thought to himself, nearly forty-one years old and you're still rising to her overprotective quips.

'Oh well, if you say so,' his mother sighed as she reversed her bottom onto the car seat and pulled her raincoat around her. Shutting the door more carefully than usual, Dan walked around to the other side of the car and got in.

'My word, this is very nice,' his mother cooed as she rubbed a hand along the wood veneer finish of the dashboard. 'Very plush indeed. Is it new?'

'Is what new?' Dan asked, clipping in his seat belt.

'The car.'

'Mum, it's fifteen years old,' Dan replied, wondering how his mother could have possibly missed the fact that the interior of the car looked as if it had been used for carting livestock at some time in its past.

'Well, you wouldn't think it, would you?' She nosed the fetid air in the car and her mouth pursed with disgust. 'Have you been smoking?' she asked tartly.

'No, I haven't. It must have been the last owner.'

Battersea Gran sucked her teeth. 'Probably died of lung cancer. Why else would anyone want to get rid of a nice car like this?'

'Right, Mum. Pull over your seat belt and I'll do it up for you.'

Dan clipped in the belt and started the car on the third time of asking. He executed a five-point turn in the middle of the narrow street, much to the annoyance of a taxi driver and a motorcyclist who were forced to wait while he carried out the manoeuvre. 'Okay, then,' he said, holding up a hand in apology and accelerating the car towards Battersea Park Road, 'Clapham next stop.'

'I think that I should go back to the flat first, dear.'

'Do you really need to? It's just that I've left the roast in the oven and the girls won't have the sense to take a look at it.'

'Nature calls, I'm afraid. I don't think that I'd make it to Haleridge Road.'

'Wasn't there a loo in the church?'

'Oh, yes, but I wouldn't dream of using that one.'

'Why not?'

'Because . . . well, you know . . . going to the toilet in church. Just doesn't seem right.'

'Mum, even Jesus had to have a pee sometimes.'

'Of course he did, dear, but I'm sure that he would have taken himself off somewhere very discreet to do it.'

Dan suppressed a laugh. 'What? Like the desert?'

'Probably.'

'A bit of overkill, though, wasn't it?'

'What do you mean?'

'Forty days and forty nights.'

Battersea Gran narrowed her eyes at her son, but it was insufficient to mask a sparkle of humour. 'No need to be irreverent now, Daniel Porter.'

The block of flats, situated overlooking Battersea Reach Wharf, was typical of uninspired sixties architecture. Originally council flats, it had been bought for a song in the early nineties by some property developer who saw the potential in its riverside location. Having refurbished the building from leaky top to graffitied bottom, he stuck a uniformed concierge in the hallway, gave the block a smart new name, and flogged the flats off as 'exclusive residences'. The building had been inhabited in the main by retired gentlefolk, and when Dan had moved his mother there after the death of his father, he had had grave misgivings about whether it would be for the best, taking her away from her simple lifestyle in Tottenham Hale and placing her in this somewhat up-market environment.

But his doubts proved to be unfounded. His mother treated the place as if it were an outpost of her own little street in North London, and single-handedly went about developing a community spirit in the building that had never existed before her arrival. She forced greetings from her reticent fellow residents in the lift and went around knocking on doors and inviting her somewhat surprised and lonely neighbours around to her little flat for cups of tea and mountains of her own homemade scones. Even the grumpy old concierge was soon won over by her open friendliness and hospitality. Flat 10F2 in Cavendish Rise soon became the focal point for residents' meetings and fund-raising campaigns to pay for pot-plants in the foyer and Christmas parties for the few children who lived in the block. Not that Battersea Gran was much good at constitutional matters, or discussing things like plumbing problems and rent reviews, but she put herself in charge of refreshments, and that proved an excellent rallying call to all those with empty stomachs and infinitely greater discussion skills than her own.

'I'll only be a moment, dear,' she said as she let herself into the flat and hurried off down the narrow passage to the lavatory. 'Just go into the lounge and I'll be with you in a minute.'

The furniture in the small room was set out exactly as it had been in the front room of the Porters' little terraced council house in Tottenham Hale. Dan had offered to buy her new furniture from Habitat, but she didn't want 'that rubbish' and insisted on moving everything from the old house. The ducks still flew up the wall, the picture of the Siamese girl with tear in eye still hung opposite the black-and-white photograph of his mother as an excited young teenager, standing onstage at the Metropole with Bill Haley and the Comets, and the brown velour suite was still set around the fireplace (albeit now a false one) and angled towards the television. The only real difference was that, where the netted window in the front room of the old house looked out onto a line of parked cars and the dirt-engrained façade of the houses opposite, the view from the full-width window on the tenth floor of the block was unimpeded, taking in the curve of the River Thames from Wandsworth Bridge to Battersea Bridge and a broad panorama across Fulham and Chelsea, stretching on out to the White City Stadium and beyond.

Dan glanced at his watch and began worrying about yet another roast ending up on the bird table. He walked across to the door. 'How are you doing, Mum?' he called down the passage.

'Just a minute, dear.' Her voice came from the bedroom. 'I'm just slipping into a thermal. I'm feeling the cold a bit.'

'Be as quick as you can, then.'

She appeared at the door of the bedroom with only one arm slipped into a sleeve of her vest, revealing an ample frontage encased in a flesh-coloured brassiere. 'I am, Dan. Just be patient.'

'Okay. It's just the—'

'The roast. I know, dear. And while your mind is on cooking, you should have a look at that recipe I found for you in *Woman's Weekly*. I left it open on the coffee table.' She eventually managed to struggle into her vest. 'I thought it looked rather good.'

I'm sure it will be, Dan thought, as he went back into the lounge and walked over to the table. Her idea of a good recipe was cheesy chicken or spiced meatballs in gravy. He picked up the magazine. Yes, that would be about the norm. An exciting lamb stew with kidney beans. He dropped the magazine back on the table.

His mother appeared, doing up the buttons of her overcoat. 'Right, that's me ready.'

'Good. Let's go then.'

'Don't forget the magazine.'

Dan blew out a resigned sigh and scooped up the *Woman's Weekly*.

As it turned out, lunch happened to be a great success. Apart from the roast beef appearing from the oven in a state of readiness that Dan had always strived to achieve – a crispy coating of fat on the outside and succulently red in the middle – the meal was, as far as Dan could remember, the first for many a moon that had been conducted without one cross or needling word being fired across the table. That was, of course, the doing of Battersea Gran. When she had been married to Dan's father, she had considered it her role in life to lavish him with praise and undying devotion (or 'devoshun', as she would pronounce it when warbling out one of her favourite songs, Johnny Tillotson's 'Poetry in Moshun'). However, since his death, that instinct had now been shifted onto her grandchildren, and in her simple, down-to-earth way, she always seemed able to extract from them the best of their characters. No matter what they did, it was always right by Battersea Gran – and they loved her for it. She was delighted by Josh's ability to stack shelves in Tesco's and intrigued by his visits to Horace's Inferno; she became tearful with pride when, after lunch, she sat listening to Nina as she stuttered through the *Braveheart* theme on her flute; and, even though Dan had tried to admonish her for it, she roared with laughter at Millie's stories of how she had been caught standing on top of the lavatory cistern in the school cloakrooms, blowing cigarette smoke up towards the Xpelair fan, or how she had given a one-fingered reply to the class geek when he asked her to go out with him.

As well as being a listener, Battersea Gran also had infinite knowledge of all things that interested the children, gleaned from the television in her flat. She knew more than either Dan or Josh about how Tottenham Hotspur were doing in the league table, who scored the goals during their last match, and who the manager was lining up for his next multimillion-pound signing; she watched *Top of the Pops* every week so that she could baffle the girls with her knowledge of rappers and heavy metal bands and the endless stream of manufactured boy groups, girl groups, and mixed groups; and when Josh went to Manchester University (the first Porter ever to achieve this distinction), she would wake herself at five o'clock every morning to watch *Open University*. She even began to achieve a vague understanding of some of the complex mathematical problems that the ginger-moustached lecturer was writing down on his flipchart. But then she discovered that Josh was studying English, so thereafter she decided to give up her early morning vigils and just stick to the less erudite information that daytime television afforded her.

Every birthday and every Christmas, the children received expensive, jaw-dropping presents from their grandparents in Chester, but during their visits to London (which thankfully for Dan were both brief and scarce), neither of Jackie's parents showed themselves capable of any degree of spontaneity or fun with the children. But then, Josh, Millie and Nina had Battersea Gran to provide that, and they had an instinctive understanding that having her constantly in their lives was worth much more than the material goods bestowed upon them by *the others*. If there was ever to be a battle of loyalties, then Battersea Gran was always going to win hands down. Josh spoke for them all when he once described her as being the *ultimate* Gran.

That evening, the weather had displayed typically fickle British tendencies and changed from winter back to the Indian summer that Mr Fish, the television weatherman, had promised. As Dan drove home after taking Battersea Gran back to her flat, he had to make use of the visor to shield his eyes from the watery rays of the setting sun, and the freezing draught that had earlier blown in through the gap at the top of the windscreen had now become a warm and comforting blast. Even though it was just before seven o'clock in the evening, Clapham Common was now awash with people who had been lured from their homes by the rise in temperature. As he sat in the queue for the traffic lights, Dan watched the walkers, the joggers, the footballers, the Frisbee throwers, and the kite flyers, as well as the bedlam of unruly dogs that joined in with any game that would accommodate them.

All was quiet when he entered the house. There was a note on the third step of the stairs that explained the silence. Jessica Napier, one of Millie's closest friends from her previous school, had rung to ask Millie and Nina around to her house for the evening. Dan scrumpled up the paper in his fist and walked through to the kitchen. He was pleased about that. Millie had had little contact with Jessica since she left Alleyn's. Maybe this heralded a new beginning to their relationship.

He briefly considered taking Biggles and Cruise out to join the hordes on Clapham Common, but then decided that, for once, they could make do with their nightly traipse around the block. It was a better idea to enjoy the tranquility while it lasted. He took a beer from the fridge, picked up a Sunday magazine from the table, and made his way out into the back garden.

He flicked the ring pull on the can and sucked away the froth, then pulled a lichen-covered garden seat from under an untamed honeysuckle at the bottom of the garden and positioned it in the sun, giving the seat a perfunctory sweep with his hand before sitting down. He opened the magazine at a page that showed the unappetizing image of a lamb stew with kidney beans floating like drowned beetles on its grease-bubbled surface. He turned back to the front cover and swore quietly to himself, realizing that he had picked up his mother's *Woman's Weekly* by mistake. He took a long pull from his beer can and spun the magazine onto the seat beside him. It fell to the ground and lay with its pages flapping over in the breeze.

Dan sat with eyes closed and head tilted back until he sensed the sun's warming rays leave his face. He watched as its fiery tip sank behind the rooftops of the houses at the end of the street, taking with it what little heat had been afforded the day. Feeling a shiver run through his body, he decided that it was time to head indoors.

As he leaned forward to pick up the magazine, he noticed a spider crawling its way across the page, perfectly dissecting the face of a woman with high cheekbones and bright blue eyes that caught the blinding glint of a camera flash. As it continued on its way, the spider was momentarily lost against a background of spiky brown hair before appearing once more on the cold grey of the rain-clouded sky. And then, with a few tentative steps, it descended from the magazine and scuttled away across the bricked patio to the sanctuary of the weed-infested flower border.

Dan picked up the magazine and studied the photograph. The woman was standing with her arms around the shoulders of two small children whose impish grins would seem to indicate that her loving envelopment was probably more a necessary entrapment for the benefit of the photographer. Behind the three figures, dark, colourless hills ran down into the dull, glassy waters of some kind of lake or reservoir. Against this background, the multicoloured plaid trousers that the woman and two children were wearing contrasted brightly.

Dan stood up from the bench, beer can in hand, and made his way across to the French doors that led into the house. As he walked, he read the headline that was written below the photograph. 'Too Good Boss Decides to Sell Business.'

He deposited the empty can in the rubbish bin as he passed, and then sat down at the table, laying the magazine open in front of him. The headline intrigued him. Surely this homely-looking woman, with not a trace of makeup on her face, wasn't the one being described as a 'too good boss'? Dammit, if she was, she was a far cry from any of the high-powered businesswomen that he had ever come across. He knew for a fact that Jackie would never set foot in *her* workplace with features that looked as if they had been scrubbed clean with a pumice stone. What the hell did she do to be described as a 'too good boss'? He leaned forward on the table and began to read the article.

Twelve years ago, Katie Trenchard (42) had everything set out for what she thought would be a peaceful and comfortable life. She and her husband Patrick (45) lived in a handsome detached house in the village of Cloveden, five miles from Plymouth, where Patrick worked as a lecturer in marine biology at the university. There were shops, cinemas and theatres within easy reach, they entertained on a regular basis, and they were able to make use of the many facilities that the university had to offer. And then, in one crazy month, they made a decision that would change their lives for ever. They sold their beloved house, said goodbye to their friends, and moved to Fort William in the northwest of Scotland where they ploughed every last penny into the purchase of Seascape, a small prawn-processing factory.

'It was Patrick's fault,' says Katie, narrowing her strikingly blue eyes. 'It had always been his lifetime ambition to run a business of his own. He had carried out a number of small research projects for Seascape and heard through the grapevine that it was for sale. He knew that it was an opportunity he couldn't let slip.'

Dan raised his eyebrows. Bloody fools, he thought to himself. What a madcap thing to do.

Within three months of taking over the business, the Trenchards had set up new agencies in France, Italy and Spain, and very soon found that demand for their product outstripped supply.

However, any profit that was being made had to be ploughed straight back into the business to upgrade its ageing equipment and meet the stringent regulations laid down by the Health and Safety Office of the Highland Regional Council. Consequently, there were no funds available for sumptuous accommodation, and for the first two years, they lived in only just bearable comfort in a three-room crofter's cottage on the shores of Loch Eil.

'Mind you, we very rarely seemed to be at home,' says Katie. 'The workers started at seven o'clock every morning and Patrick and I were always there half an hour before they arrived. During the high season, when the prawns were coming in thick and fast, the packers were producing over 10 tonnes a day, which meant that we all had to work on into the night just to keep up with our intake. Patrick and I would walk around like zombies for about four months of the year!'

Bloody fools, Dan repeated to himself. Fancy having to work hours like that and not make any money.

Katie's involvement in the company, however, ended on the eve that Max (now 10 and pictured left) was born. Her duties then changed from office administration to child care, a task that included trying to stop the little baby from freezing to death.

'Scotland was hit by one of the severest winters ever experienced for about twenty years,' says Katie. 'The only source of heat in the cottage was an ancient wood-burning range in the kitchen, which filled the room with smoke if there was even a hint of dampness on the logs. It was pure hell. I think Max spent the first six weeks of his life, day and night, cocooned in an old sleeping bag that, judging from the smell, had been at one time occupied by a family of mice. I think that was when I reached my lowest point. I just longed to be back in our old life in Plymouth.'

I bet you did, thought Dan.

*A year and a half later Sooty (8, pictured right) was born, making
her first appearance into the world with a mass of jet black curly
hair. Although christened Sacha, the nickname that Patrick gave
her on first seeing his new daughter in the hospital has stuck.
'Sooty's arrival spurred Patrick into action,' says Katie. 'He knew
that if I was to go through yet another freezing winter with two
children, let alone one, then he ran the risk of losing his whole
family. By this time, we were beginning to see the light at the
end of the tunnel with Seascape, so Patrick managed to persuade
the bank to let him take out a mortgage on a nearby farmhouse
that was being sold by the estate from which we rented the cottage.
The house was pretty run-down, but at least it had an oil-fired
Rayburn and central heating, so my days of shifting around
armfuls of wood thankfully came to an end!'*

Getting up from the table, Dan walked over to the fridge and
took out another can of beer. He flicked the ring pull and took
a drink. He was beginning to have a certain amount of admira-
tion for this family stuck away up in the north of Scotland. They
may have been mad, but by God, they were resilient. He sat back
down and found his place in the article.

*Living on the breadline, however, continued to be the name of
the game for the Trenchard family. One of the ways in which
Katie embraced this culture was by starting to make clothes for
her children, using off-cut fabrics that she bought from the local
drapery store in Fort William. Her design principle was based
on what her children seemed to be comfortable wearing. Baggy
trousers in brightly coloured brushed cotton with elasticated
waists, and big pockets in which useful things like toy tractors
and crumbling biscuits could be stored. The design for her skirts
followed a similar vein. Next came sweaters with wide, easily
rolled up sleeves, and made out of a polar fleece material that
Katie sourced from a factory in Inverness which specialized in
clothes for hillwalkers and mountaineers.*

'What I hadn't bargained for,' continues Katie, 'was the demand from mothers at Max's playschool for me to make similar clothes for their own children. At the time, we needed every bit of spare cash that we could lay our hands on, so the kitchen became like the Tailor of Gloucester's workroom!'

One of her greatest aficionados, however, just happened to be the nine-year-old son of the chief executive of the Local Enterprise Company, a burly red-bearded Highlander called Rhuraidh MacLeod. Rhuraidh was a good friend of Patrick's, having helped him on a feasibility study for an expansion plan for Seascape, so there seemed nothing unusual in his visiting their house one evening with a clump of papers stuck under his arm.

'He wasn't there to talk about Seascape, though,' says Katie. 'He wanted to talk to me about my clothes.'

Over a glass of whisky, Rhuraidh explained that there was a small clothes manufacturing unit on the same industrial estate where Patrick's plant was based that had just lost its main customer, a large retail chain in the south that had decided to cut costs by moving its manufacturing base to Eastern Europe.

Quite right too, Dan thought to himself. I'd have done the same. He turned the page. There was another photograph, this time of a brooding young male model with thick brown hair worn fashionably messy and a crucifix dangling from his left earlobe. He was wearing a black T-shirt that fell well below the waistline of his open bomber jacket and a pair of trousers cut like army fatigues, their cuffs caught up on the padded tops of his Nike trainers. The image took up the whole page with the typeset of the article wedging the young man in from all sides. It was large enough for Dan to be able to make out a label with the name Vagabonds sewn onto the right-hand side pocket of the trousers.

'Rhuraidh said that the twenty jobs that were to be lost at the factory might not seem that much, but it would be felt like a hammer blow in such a small community as Fort William. He

72

felt, however, that it could be saved, and before he took his leave of us that evening, he presented Patrick and me with a brief, three-page document which outlined his plans.'

Rhuraidh MacLeod had given the company a working title, *Vagabonds*, a word that Katie had heard him use quite often to describe his young, hyperactive son. He envisaged the new company to be mail order, so that manufacturing, ordering and packaging could all be handled from the same unit, and payment for articles would be up front. Rhuraidh's idea was that the work-force should be laid off for two months during which time he had set Katie the monumental task of sourcing fabrics, producing samples and photographing the catalogue while he would use the expertise in his office to set up the computer system and buy in mailing lists.

'It was pretty daunting,' admits Katie, 'but the carrot that Rhuraidh cleverly dangled in front of my nose was that, for the first six months, manufacturing costs would be borne jointly by the Local Enterprise Company and the District Council.

'So I decided to take on the challenge – not so much because I wanted to do it, but more out of a sense of loyalty to Rhuraidh. If he had taken this much trouble to save twenty jobs, then it had to mean a great deal to him. So Vagabonds became the name of the company, and exactly two months after Rhuraidh's visit, the first little pair of baggy trousers with elasticated waist and oversized pockets rolled off the production line and were sent off to our first mail order customer. It was a very exciting moment!'

Two years later, when demand for Vagabonds was spreading right across Europe, Katie was approached by the headmaster of Fort William High School to help their final-year Art and Design students with design technique and manufacture.

'I agreed to do it, although somewhat reluctantly,' says Katie. 'I really felt that I couldn't spare the time. But thank goodness I did. Those kids were so much more in tune with what everyone was wearing, and from that first year onwards, I incorporated many of their ideas into the Vagabonds range of clothes. I always

credited their names in the catalogue under the heading 'Designers',
which I think made them feel that they had hit the big time!'

Almost six years to the day since the company started, Katie
has decided that the time has come to sell up.

'The company is now in the position to be taken to a worldwide market,' says Katie, 'and it needs someone with a greater
business brain than I to be able to accomplish that! What's more,
I have been so occupied with Vagabonds over the years that I
feel that I have missed out on a great chunk of my children's
lives. I just want to spend more time with them.'

Dan looked up as the door of the kitchen opened and Josh
walked in.

'Hi there. Where have you sprung from?'

'Upstairs,' Josh replied, pulling the flex from the kettle and
filling it up from the tap.

'Really? I thought I was alone in the house. Aren't you working
tonight?'

'No. I couldn't be bothered. I rang in and said I was ill.'

'Oh,' Dan murmured before turning back to the magazine to
read the final paragraph of the article.

'Vagabonds is not only a niche market, but our products would
seem to be considered a classic, judging by our ever-escalating
order book. It will quite simply run and run.'

'Hey, Vaggas. Awesome wear.'

Dan turned to find Josh looking over his shoulder at the
magazine.

'What?'

'Those trousers. They're called Vaggas.'

Dan frowned quizzically at his son, then shot a glance back at
the photograph of the young male model. 'You mean you *know*
about them?'

'Of course I do. They're Vaggas.'

'Which I suppose has to be an abbreviation of Vagabonds, the name of the company that makes them.'

'Whatever,' Josh said, moving over to the sideboard to make himself a cup of coffee. 'I just know them as Vaggas.'

'But how on earth do *you* know about them?'

'I've seen them worn in the Inferno. They're great for clubbing, being loose-fitting and all that.'

'Are you telling me that these trousers are considered "cool wear"?'

Josh laughed. 'No, I'm not telling you that because I wouldn't use a phrase like that. Maybe . . . um . . . "ultimate" wear would be better.'

'For heaven's sake,' Dan murmured incredulously, knowing that Josh's use of that word was reserved for only the best things in life.

'They're pretty difficult to get hold of, though. All I've ever managed to lay my hands on is one of their baseball caps, and that's because I nicked it off a friend. You know the one. It's got a V on the front with sort of squiggly bits at the side.'

Dan nodded slowly. 'Yes, that does ring a bell.'

'I've tried to find the company on the Internet, but I don't think they've got a website. From what I gather, you can only buy them on mail order.'

Dan flipped over the page to study once more the unassuming, countrified woman who had obviously stumbled upon a style phenomenon. 'If these trousers are such a success, why has nobody ever tried to copy them?'

'I'm not sure – but if I was going to buy a pair, I'd only want them to be the genuine article. It's like you buying a pair of Levi's, isn't it? You wouldn't want to walk around in a pair of denims with the name of a supermarket stuck on your backside.'

Dan took Josh's point with a flick of his head. 'Probably not. So, in your opinion, the market for Vaggas, as you call them, could grow?'

'And how!' Josh replied, taking a swallow of his coffee and

pulling out a chair for himself next to Dan. 'I wouldn't think they're even scratching the surface yet. I'm not the only one who's been trying to get hold of a catalogue. Nobody even knows where the wretched company is based! I mean, whoever's running the business at present has no idea what a huge market he's missing out on.'

'Seemingly, it's all run from the north of Scotland.'

'Is it? Well, maybe the boss should lay down his bagpipes and get down here and do some marketing.'

Dan slid the magazine across the table to Josh. 'That's the "boss" there,' he said, stabbing his finger on the face of the woman. He could tell from Josh's expression that he was unimpressed, almost disappointed.

'Doesn't look particularly dynamic, does she?' Josh remarked.

Dan smiled. 'Not really. But give her her due, she did start the company as a hobby. She's obviously done bloody well to get it to where it is now.'

Josh drummed his fingers on the table. 'Maybe, but what they need to do is find someone who really *knows* how to run a business like that. Like Mum, for instance. If she took it over, she'd just make the whole thing explode.'

Dan bit thoughtfully at the side of his cheek. 'I wonder. I mean, I don't doubt your mother's capabilities, but this really is a completely different kettle of fish. Rebecca Talworth's name was pretty well established before Jackie started building up the company.'

'Dad,' Josh replied, shaking his head, 'go into any club that has a name for itself south of the river and ask if either the names Rebecca Talworth or Vaggas mean anything to them. I know what the answer would be.'

'You're going to tell me Vaggas, aren't you?'

'Probably ninety per cent?' Josh hazarded a guess.

'This is unreal!' Dan stated incredulously. 'I can't believe that something started from sewing scraps of cloth together in the north of Scotland should become sort of cult wear.'

'Well, it seems to have worked.' Josh drained his coffee. 'Hey, that article doesn't give a contact number, does it?'

Dan flipped over to the end of the article. 'No. Nothing. I suppose you could get it through directory enquiries.'

'Yeah, I suppose.' Josh rinsed out his mug under the tap. 'Don't think I'll bother, though. I'm a bit skint at the minute. I'd just get tempted.'

'They don't cost *that* much, do they?'

'About fifty quid, which is more than I can afford at the minute.'

'Fifty quid! Bloody hell!'

'Well, they don't seem to have any difficulty shifting them at that price.' Josh got up from the table, walked across the kitchen, and opened the door that led into the hall. 'Listen, I'm going to have a quick bath, and then go around to see Phil Neilson. We were supposed to meet over the weekend, but we never got our act together and he's heading back to university tonight.'

Dan pushed himself to his feet. 'Okay. Maybe see you later, then.'

Josh nodded. 'Are the girls not here?'

'No. They're spending the evening with one of Millie's friends.'

'Right. Are you okay by yourself, then?'

Dan smiled at his son's unnecessary but kindly concern. He shot him a wink. 'I'm fine. Thanks.'

As he heard Josh's footsteps ascend the staircase at speed, Dan picked up the Sunday magazine that he had initially sought out and took it over to the table. He pushed the *Woman's Weekly* to the far side of the table and sat down. He read one paragraph of an article about some high-flying interior designer in London, but his mind was elsewhere. His eyes went back to Battersea Gran's magazine. He reached over the table and drew it towards him, opening it once more at the photograph of Katie Trenchard and her two children.

If Josh was really right about this, then maybe it was worth finding out a little more about the company. If there was this huge untapped market, then maybe it could be a winner. He'd always gone on about something turning up. He'd never believed in omens, but nevertheless, the way that this had come to light was all pretty strange. A woman's magazine given to him by his mother for some ghastly recipe, the article, the company for sale, and then Josh telling him that their product was one of the hottest things around. Maybe he was right about Jackie's expertise. Of course, she had her job with Rebecca Talworth, but if he were to take on the management of the company, they could work on the marketing together. In fact, doing something in which they both had a common interest might be the stimulation their relationship needed at that precise moment.

Dan pushed back his chair and pulled out the drawer in the table. After a bit of rummaging, he found a blunt pencil and one of Nina's old exercise books. He creased it open at a blank page. Right, he thought to himself, let's give this a bit of thought.

i.   Source a manufacturer in Eastern Europe. Cheaper production costs.

ii.   Mail order *and* Internet sales. Spread the market worldwide.

iii. No need to live in Scotland. Could run everything from Haleridge Road.

iv. Not stock, though. Need to rent a small industrial unit nearby.

v.   Fabrics, designs, etc. No knowledge of that. Maybe have to keep Katie Trenchard on as design consultant for a year. On second thoughts, maybe not. Contention between her and Jackie?

vi   Funding. Mortgage house? Idea dismissed. Telephone Nick Jessop to see if he could wangle a short-term loan without collateral through Broughton's.

Nick. Of course. That was exactly to whom he should be talking. Dan got up from the table and walked over to the telephone. He dialled his number from memory.

'Nick?'

'Hi, Dan.'

Dan heard a loud splash of water in the background. 'Sorry, have I caught you at a bad time?'

'Sort of. I'm just giving Tarquin his bath. Hang on a minute while I get him out.'

Dan waited, hearing Nick's muffled voice talking away to his son.

'Right,' Nick said eventually. 'That's him sorted. I hope you're not ringing up to do more gloating about that result yesterday.'

Dan laughed. 'Now would I do a thing like that?'

'Yes, too bloody right you would!'

'Well, you have to admit, it *was* a pretty good match. Anyway, thanks, Nick, for getting me those tickets.'

'No problem.'

'Listen, that isn't actually the reason for the call. You're a wealth of information about all things to do with young children, and I just wondered if you had ever heard of a mail order company called Vagabonds?'

'Yes, sure I have.'

Dan was momentarily struck dumb by Nick's instantaneous reply. 'What? You *know* of them?'

'Of course I do. It's a pretty well-known company. I think Laura came across them about a year ago. She gave a pair of their trousers to one of her godchildren, and we've been getting their catalogues ever since. In fact, Laura was thinking of ordering up pairs for both herself and Tarquin.' Nick's voice went distant. 'Weren't we, my little man?' His mouth came back to the receiver. 'So, why this sudden interest in Vagabonds?'

'Oh, no particular reason,' Dan replied airily. 'It's just that I read an article about the woman who started it.' He paused for a moment. 'So, do you know others who buy from Vagabonds?'

'Sure. I couldn't tell you right now who they are, but yeah, I've seen adults and kids of all ages wear the trousers.'

'Right. And you think it's probably quite a well-run company.'

'I've no idea, Dan, but I reckon it would be more successful than many of the other mail order companies. For a start, their catalogue is brilliant.'

'Do you have one there?'

'Not right beside me. I'm actually in the bathroom, Dan.'

'You wouldn't be able to give me a telephone number, would you?'

Dan heard Nick let out a long sigh. 'Well, you'll have to hang on a minute. The catalogue is downstairs somewhere.'

'Okay. Sorry about this.'

The LCD readout on Dan's portable telephone registered a further three minutes before Nick came back on the line. 'Right. Are you ready for this?'

'Fire away,' Dan replied, hovering his pencil over Nina's exercise book.

'Telephone number is 01397 890000 and fax is 01397 890110. There doesn't appear to be an e-mail number.'

'No, that's fine. Many thanks, Nick.'

'Okay. Can I return to the peace of my Sunday evening routine now?'

'Of course you can, my son. With my blessing.'

Dan didn't even bother to hang up the receiver. He pressed the button to disconnect the line and then immediately dialled the number that Nick had given him. He just planned to leave a message on the Ansaphone and get them to send off a catalogue to him. He never imagined for one moment that, on a Sunday night, his call would be answered.

'Hello?' It was a woman's voice, shrill and questioning, and it gave Dan the immediate impression that his telephone call was not particularly welcome. In the background, there seemed to be a steady, rhythmic thrumming that was loud enough to make Dan hold the receiver an inch or two away from his ear.

'I'm sorry,' Dan said. 'I'm not sure if I've got the right number. I was trying to get hold of a company called Vagabonds.'

'What?' the voice shouted. It was then that Dan realized that her shrill tone was probably only a consequence of the background noise.

'Vagabonds. Is that Vagabonds?' Dan asked distinctly.

'Yes. Sorry. I should have said that, shouldn't I? It's just that we're a bit hectic here.'

'Well, I was expecting to talk to an Ansaphone. I didn't think that anyone would be working on a Sunday night.'

'Sorry, I didn't catch that. I'm afraid that I'm in the workshop and all the machines are going.'

Dan decided then that it wasn't going to be worth asking for a catalogue. Better all round if he called back in the morning. On the other hand, he couldn't just hang up.

'Am I talking to Katie Trenchard?' Dan asked, stepping up the volume of his voice.

'Yes. Who's that?'

'You don't know me, but my name is Dan Porter. I live in London.'

'Yes. Excuse me, can you hold the line for a moment, please?' Dan heard a muted question being asked and the woman replying, 'No, just finish off the XLs tonight. We can put out the Ls tomorrow evening.' She returned to the receiver. 'I'm sorry. How can I help you?'

'Right, well, I've just read this article about you in a magazine.'

'Magazine, yes.' Another machine seemed to have been added to the general cacophony of background noise, this one being situated not very far from Katie Trenchard's mouthpiece.

'And there were a couple of photographs too.'

'So you'll want to come up to see me.'

'What?' Dan asked, taken aback by the woman's directness.

'When do you want to come up, then?'

Dan felt strangely bemused. My word, he thought, it's not a wonder this woman has made a success of her company if she's able to catch people off guard like this. 'Hold on, I wasn't thinking exactly . . .'

81

'What?'

Dan took a deep breath to steady himself. 'I just wanted to ask a few questions.'

'That's fine. I'm quite happy to do that. How about sometime this week then?'

Dan now began to laugh to himself. Katie Trenchard was obviously a born seller. All he had been meaning to do was to ring up for a catalogue, and here he was, on a Sunday night, being invited up to the wilds of Scotland as a prospective buyer of her company. He, Dan Porter, who had never been north of Manchester in his life!

'Erm,' he muttered, trying to think of some way of stalling her for a moment. 'Right; just let me have a look in my diary.' He clamped his hand over the receiver. What the hell was he doing? Just say 'Thanks, but no thanks' and end the call. He stared down at the notes he had made in Nina's exercise book. Come on, you fool, he thought to himself, there *is* an opportunity here. You know that. If you just say you're not going to go, you'll regret it in the long run. And anyway, why the hell suddenly be so cautious? You were never that way in the City.

Dan made a quick surmise of his present domestic situation. Jackie was in Paris, back on Tuesday; the kids were at school for the week; Battersea Gran would probably be able to come round and look after them and the dogs. So why should he not just go? It would probably do him a load of good to get away from the house and from London for a couple of days. What's more, even if nothing came of it, it would at least give Jackie the impression that he was actively pursuing some form of gainful employment.

He took his hand away from the receiver and held it to his ear. The background noise seemed to have increased in volume. 'When could I come up?' he asked.

'What? Listen, I'm sorry. I'm going to go outside the building.' Dan heard a door slam and immediately the noise became a distant hum. 'That's better. Now, what did you ask me?'

'When would it be suitable for me to come up?'

'Well, the earlier part of the week would be best. I'm going to be away all day tomorrow, but Tuesday would be good.'

'Right. And what's the best way of getting to where you are?'

'Did you say you were based in London?'

'Yes.'

'Well, there's an overnight sleeper that goes direct from Euston to Fort William. That gets you here at about a quarter to ten in the morning. Or you could fly to Glasgow, and then take the train. Either way, if you call this number when you get to the station, I could get someone to meet you.'

'Okay.' Dan took a deep breath. 'So Tuesday's fine with you?'

'Absolutely. I look forward to meeting you . . . er . . . sorry, what was your name again?'

'Dan Porter.'

'Right . . . Dan. And, as a matter of interest, what was the magazine again?'

Dan walked over to the table and flipped it over to the front cover. '*Woman's Weekly.*'

'Oh, all right then.' Her reply seemed flat, almost registering a slight air of disappointment. 'I'll see you Tuesday, then.'

The telephone call to Battersea Gran was brief. She was quite happy to look after the children for a couple of days, but for once she kept the conversation brief, being engrossed in her regular Sunday night viewing of *Monarch of the Glen*. Dan put down the receiver with a wry smile on his face. If she had but known that he was heading off to a place that had to be similar in many ways to the untamed wilds of Glen Bogle, then she would have gleaned from him every last bit of information about his motives for going – as well as asking him to get Susan Hampshire's autograph while he was there.

Dan left the kitchen and ran up the two flights of stairs to his office. He pressed the START button on his computer before returning to the landing.

'Josh?' he called down the stairwell.

He heard a splash from the bathroom.

'What?'

'Come up to my office when you're finished, would you?'

He went back into his office and sat down at his desk, simultaneously clicking the mouse on the Internet icon. By the time Josh appeared, still dripping wet with a towel wrapped around his lower torso, Dan had the train schedule from Euston to Fort William up on the screen.

'Yeah?' Josh asked.

'Listen, I'm going up to Scotland for a couple of days,' Dan said, without taking his eyes away from the screen.

'You're what?'

Dan laughed. 'I'll be back on Wednesday or Thursday, depending on train times. I've called Battersea Gran and she's coming over to look after you all until Mum gets back.'

'Why on earth have you decided to go up to *Scotland?*'

Dan bit on his lip, then turned to Josh. 'I'll tell you only if you promise that it won't go any further.'

Josh raised his eyebrows. 'In-trigue.'

A new page had come up on the screen. Dan made a selection before continuing. 'I'm going to take a look at that company, Vagabonds.'

'*Vagabonds?*' Josh asked. 'For what reason?'

'Because it's up for sale.'

Josh let out a short, derisive laugh. 'Hang on, you've lost me. You're not saying that you're thinking of buying it – are you?'

'Well, let's just see, shall we? You said yourself that the market has hardly been scratched. I think it's worth finding out a bit more about them.'

'Wow!' Josh exclaimed in quiet incredulity. Dan felt a light punch on his left shoulder, and he turned to look at his son who was slowly nodding, a grin of 'ree-spect' on his face. 'Nice one, Dad. Go for it.'

'Keep it to yourself, though.'

Josh gave him a wink and tapped the side of his nose with a forefinger. 'Mum's the word.'

Dan smiled and shook his head. 'No, Josh, that is definitely *not* the word.'

10

As Jackie entered her hotel bedroom that evening, a soft wedge of reddened sunlight flooded across the thick patterned carpet, eventually trapping itself under the footwell of the small leather-inlaid desk that stood against the wall. Throwing her handbag onto the bed, she took a coat hanger from the wardrobe and hung up her suit jacket, then walked across to the full-length window and opened it. She leaned her hands on the wrought iron guardrail and breathed in the warm air, filled with the rich aromatic smells of the city, as she looked out over the glinting skyline of Paris from her vantage point on the heights of Montmartre. The incessant traffic hummed busily below her on the Boulevard de Clichy, broken now by the melodious bells of Sacré Coeur calling out the evening mass.

A smile of contentment brushed across her mouth. Everything had gone to plan over the weekend – the meeting with the Chambre Syndicale, the suitability of their venue in the Bourdelle Museum. And what's more, she had received e-mails both from the agency in London confirming the model bookings and from the set designer saying that all would be completed by the time that she returned to London.

Back to London. The mere thought of it immediately replaced her calm with a stomach-knot of agitation. She loved having her own space, being able to return to her hotel bedroom every evening and relish the successes of each day. She couldn't do that in London. Every evening was the same when she returned to the house in Clapham. No matter what her mood, the oppressive atmosphere of gloom and despondency that emanated throughout the place would envelop her and she would almost physically sense her own character being overpowered by ill-feeling and contempt. And she knew that it was Dan who was wholly to blame for bringing about that change in her.

Taking in a long, steadying breath, Jackie closed her eyes and concentrated on locking those bad thoughts away. She cast her mind back over the past few days and realized that since boarding the Eurostar at Waterloo Station, she had neither been stressed nor bad-tempered. She had had no reason to be, or what was maybe more accurate, nobody had given her reason to be.

Yet she hadn't been by herself, had she? When Stephen had first suggested that he come with her to Paris, her immediate reaction had been to put him off the idea. She had wanted to be free from male company, to do her own thing without having to make the effort of conversing with another man. But she had realized soon after their arrival in Paris that the disruption at home and the possible problems that she thought might arise during her visit had left her feeling quite vulnerable and unsure as to whether she would be able to cope. Over the course of the weekend, Stephen had proved himself to be a true friend and a wonderful support, and being in the company of someone so much younger than herself and without having the burden of her family weighing constantly on her mind had made her feel enlivened and youthful and carefree.

That day, having wrapped up their workload by noon, they had enjoyed a prolonged lunch together in one of the small restaurants below the steps of Sacré Coeur, where cars rattled at speed along the cobbled street. The waiter, dressed in a starched white ankle-length apron, served the six tables with an unquestioning attentiveness, and although Jackie had tried to banish the idea from her mind, she could not help but sense a notion of illicit romance about them being together, tucked away in the little backstreet restaurant, with the warming flow of red wine in her throat and the lingering tang of garlic on her tastebuds. As she and Stephen had laughed together across the table, she had had a momentary pang of guilt, thinking that if she *had* made the trip with Dan, maybe it would have been beneficial to their relationship. But even that one fleeting thought had pervaded her being with a shivering anxiety and she had dismissed it immediately, determined to free herself of reality for as long as their trip lasted.

A rhythmic knock on her bedroom door broke her away from her thoughts. She closed the window and walked across to the door and opened it. Stephen stood outside in the corridor, a grin on his face and a bottle of champagne and two glasses in his hands. He raised them up, a questioning slant on his mouth.

'How about a bit of a celebration?'

Jackie leaned a hand against the door, a barrier against his entry. 'I thought that's what we were doing at lunchtime.'

'This one's on me,' he said, sidling his way past her into the bedroom.

'I really think that I've had enough,' Jackie stated without moving away from the door. It could have been taken as a flat refusal, had she not followed it with a bubble of laughter as she watched Stephen disregard her opinion entirely, untwisting the wire and exploding the cork from the bottle. He poured a froth of champagne into each glass, waiting for it to settle before topping both up. He held out a glass at arm's length towards her, leaving Jackie no option other than to shut the door and walk over to take her glass.

'Here's to you, then,' Stephen said, clinking his glass against hers.

'And to you, too. I think we've both done a pretty good job

sewing up all the loose ends.' Jackie took a mouthful of champagne, feeling it pierce the sides of her mouth like icy needles before slipping in a cold cascade down her throat. 'Ooh, that is delicious.'

She would have put her hand over the top of her glass, but Stephen moved too fast for her. He filled it to the brim once more. 'I don't think that *we've* done a pretty good job. It was entirely you. I've never felt such a spare prick in all my life. I admit that, on this occasion, I was wrong. One head turned out to be infinitely better than two.'

'That's not true. I'm really glad you came.'

Stephen paused. 'Are you?'

'Yes. I know now that I did need the moral support.'

Stephen moved towards her. 'Listen, I hope you don't mind me doing this, but I find it rather disconcerting talking to you with that speck of dirt on your face.' He reached up and brushed the side of her cheek gently with his thumb. The particle disappeared, but Stephen kept his hand inches away from her face, trying to judge what her reaction had been to his touch. He felt butterflies rise in his stomach when Jackie made no attempt to move away from his outstretched hand.

'Must have got there when I was at the window,' she said. 'Has it gone?'

'Yes,' he replied. 'Your face returns once more to its usual perfect flawlessness.' He inched his hand back and rested it against the peach-smoothness of her skin. Then he felt the pressure as her head tilted to his touch. That was enough. He didn't need to know any more right now. She had showed willingness by that one almost imperceptible action. But he had to play this game so carefully. Everything depended on it – his job, the future. He dropped his hand to his side, noticing as he did so a momentary look of surprise on Jackie's face. He smiled at her, knowing that she would probably take it as one of affection. Only he knew that it was indeed one of satisfaction.

'I'm sorry,' he said, placing the offending hand in the small of his back. 'That was uncalled for. I shouldn't have done that.'

Jackie shook her head. 'There was no harm in it.' She smiled. 'At least we're both adult enough to know that it couldn't have been taken any further.'

'Of course not.' He filled up his champagne glass and took a swig. 'What would you have done, though?'

'What do you mean?'

'If I had tried to take it further.'

Jackie shifted her glance away from Stephen. He noticed a pinky glow rise to her cheeks, but he had an idea that it was embarrassment, or maybe a flush of excitement that had caused it, rather than anger at his suggestion. 'I'm a married woman, Stephen, with three teenage children. You shouldn't ask me that kind of question.'

Stephen shrugged his shoulders. 'Maybe you're right. I do know, however, that you have been in better form over these past few days than I have ever witnessed in all the time that I've known you. The trouble is that I *know* the reason for that, because you've told me – on more than one occasion. When we walked into that restaurant today, I saw men stop eating and turn to look at you, and I can tell you that to be able to draw a Frenchman's attention away from his food takes some doing. I bet that if you had stopped to tell *them* that you were the mother of three teenage children, you would have been met by a chorus of *"Mais ce n'est pas possible!"* I tell you, I was proud to be with you, even though it was under slightly, well, false pretences.'

Jackie smiled at him. 'That's a very kind thing to say.'

'For heaven's sake, I'm not being *kind*! Don't demean yourself! I'm being "kind" when I go to visit my granny in her sheltered accommodation in Welwyn Garden City. I'm being "kind" when I scratch the tummy of the smelly old spaniel that my parents dote on, even though I'd rather guide it out of the house with a boot. You've got a long way to go before I start being *kind* to you.'

Jackie said nothing and looked away.

Stephen drained his glass. 'I can take a hint.' He moved close to Jackie, and placing his hands on her shoulders, planted a loud, brotherly kiss on her forehead. She closed her eyes and Stephen could sense by the way her head tilted back that she would probably be a willing recipient for something a little more intimate. But he left it there. If anyone was to make the first move, it had to be her. He turned and walked across to the door and opened it. 'Use your days here well, Jackie. While you're happy and relaxed, which I know you are, just try to work out exactly what it is that you want to do. You're a beautiful, clever woman with a wonderful sense of humour, and I love being with you – as would any man. So please don't spend the rest of your life in discontent and bitterness. It would be such a waste.'

Jackie stood where he had left her, her arms crossed as she looked down at the floor and traced the point of her shoe around the pattern of the carpet.

'I'll give you a call, say about nine o'clock, and we can go out to get something to eat, all right?' Jackie seemed not to have heard him. 'All right?' he repeated.

She looked up at him and nodded.

Closing the door behind him, Stephen thrust his hands deep into his pockets. Dammit, maybe he had pushed it too far at the end. There was no way of knowing whether her silence was out of contempt for his forthrightness, or whether she was already considering what he had said. He felt a momentary frisson of guilt, knowing that he had been playing an uncompromising game with her own deep vulnerability. He let out a sigh and started off along the corridor towards the lift. He pressed the button and watched as the lift lumbered its way down towards him. As it pinged to a halt, he heard a door open at the end of the corridor.

'Stephen?'

Jackie stood in the open doorway, her arms still crossed, and he felt the butterflies rise once more in his stomach when he noticed that it enhanced the deep cleft of her breasts into which he had played the reflected light of his cufflink days before.

11

During the past twenty years, the life of a banker had taken Dan to many far corners of the world. He liked to think of himself as a seasoned traveller, flying in the relative comfort of business class to America and Europe, to Russia and Australia, to the Middle East and the Far East. Over the years, he had worked out how to combat jetlag so that he was able to get off a plane and go straight into a meeting without feeling that his brain was swimming in syrup. But never, in all the time that he had been circumnavigating the globe, had he experienced quite such an uncomfortable journey as the one that he was undertaking now, as the overnight sleeper from Euston rocked and juddered its way northwards towards Scotland.

By three o'clock in the morning, he had all but given up trying to get any sleep. The coarse linen sheet and meagre woollen blanket that were his allotted coverings for the night seemed to be drawn magnetically towards the floor, and he had had to get up at least five times (twice thumping his head on the extremely hard wooden edging of the upper bunk) to try to work out yet another way of getting the bloody things to stay on his bed. If the stifling heat in the compartment had been consistent, then he wouldn't have bothered, but every now and again the heating system would go into reverse thrust and the temperature would drop sharply to a level that would render a sealskin-clad Eskimo incapacitated with frostbite.

His travelling companion, a rotund tractor salesman from some market town just outside Glasgow, was having no such problems in sleeping. He had engaged Dan in lively conversation from the moment that he had entered their shoebox-sized compartment and Dan had understood absolutely nothing of the guttural solil-oquy that had been imparted to him. It had been even more disconcerting when the man had started to undress himself in an area that only allowed for one foot to come into contact with the floor at any one time. Dan had wedged himself into the corner of his bunk, watching in trepidation as the man's huge, boxer-shorted backside came ever closer to him. It reminded him too much of a film in which an unfortunate Mafia victim came to a grisly end inside a giant hydraulic scrap metal press. The man had then heaved himself up the ladder to his bunk (Dan had averted his eyes at that point as the boxer shorts left nothing to the imag-ination), turned off his light, thumped his pillow twice, broke wind loudly, and immediately fell into a deep and sonorous sleep.

Having eventually sorted out his cover problem by wrapping both sheet and blanket tightly around him, Dan had contorted himself back onto the bunk and eventually fallen into a fitful sleep. It seemed like only ten minutes before there was a sharp rap at the door. The tractor salesman slept peacefully on, so it was left to Dan to reach up and open the door to the attendant.

'Glasgow in half an hour,' the thin, waistcoated man said, his breath staled by cigarettes, as he thrust a small tea tray into Dan's hand.

'It's not for—'

But the attendant was obviously working to a tight schedule because he was already banging on the next door before Dan could finish his dozy remonstration.

There could be few more awkward situations in life than to

be starved of sleep, then handed a tray that contained boiling hot tea whilst lying prostrate on the bottom of two shelves and wrapped in swaddling clothes. Fixing his sandpapered eyes on the level of the tray, Dan first tried sitting up, but his upper body had only reached an angle of forty-five degrees before his head came into contact with the top bunk. He then tried lifting his legs but only managed to hold the position of a bent banana for a few seconds. After a moment's intensive thought, he decided to attempt a rolling action, but again was thwarted when the teapot slid precariously to the edge of the tray. It was only that near disaster that shot a bolt of adrenaline into his befuddled mind and enabled him to engage a small measure of lateral thought. He found beside him the small shelf that was specifically designed for the purpose of holding the tray, and having rid himself of the element of danger, he was able to unravel himself from his bedclothes and stand up.

Dan gave the man a friendly shove. 'Excuse me, but it's time for you to get up.'

The tractor salesman grunted and somehow managed to turn his overweight body around on the plank-sized bunk. Had Dan not ducked to retrieve the tray at that precise moment, he would probably have been knocked senseless because the man's arm flailed out across the open floor space.

'Whassamatter?'

That was when Dan lost his cool. He stood on the bottom rung of the ladder, unclipped the shelf above the man's head, and thrust the tray upon it. 'It's time for you to get your fat arse out of that bed, mate. The train will be stopping in Glasgow in five minutes.'

The man woke immediately and stared wide-eyed at Dan. 'All right, laddie. Keep your hair on,' he whined defensively.

Those were the last words that passed between them. Dan lay on his bunk, head turned towards the wall, as he listened to the man hurriedly wheeze his way through his dressing routine. He then thumped his suitcase off the luggage shelf, opened the door, and was gone. Dan reckoned that it was a good twenty minutes before the train eventually stopped in Glasgow, and with a satisfied grin on his face, he fell into a deep sleep.

'Fort William in half an hour.'

Dan had been ready for the attendant this time. He had swung his legs off the bed and stood up as the door was opened so that when he received the tray, he was able to place it straightaway onto the tractor salesman's bunk. He closed the door and stretched out his cramped limbs, then turning around, flipped up the blind on the window. He blinked twice. 'Bloody hell!'

The sky was the colour of dirty washing-up water and the dark hills were only just visible through a curtain of sleety rain. There didn't appear to be any sign of life forms. No roads, no houses, no animals. Nothing. It was a complete wilderness. This train was taking him to the ends of the world. For at least five minutes, he kept looking out the window, hoping, almost praying that he could find solace in seeing one twinkling light, one smoking fire, one moving car. But all that he witnessed were the hills getting higher and the day getting darker. Just before he turned away, he did manage to spot a huddle of sheep, crammed up tight together in the shelter of a stone wall, and he thought that their expressions of abject misery must have matched his own.

'You girls should all move to London,' he muttered to himself as he turned away from the window. He let out a short, manic laugh. God, he thought, is this what happens when you come up to Scotland? You start talking to *sheep*?

Dan was quite heartened, yet somewhat amazed when at least thirty other fellow passengers disembarked from the train at Fort William. He also noticed that every one of them was much better equipped than he for the current weather. A jolly group of climbers, dressed in hooded anoraks and breeches and gaudy coloured socks, strode towards him along the platform, making light of their weighty rucksacks, and even less of the freezing sleet that blew about the unsheltered station. As they passed by, they shot amused smiles at each other as they saw Dan struggle with already numbed fingers to do up the zip of his trendy but totally inadequate leather bomber jacket. He was glad that they weren't around to witness his next move. He started out towards the station exit, with head bowed against the icy blast, and immediately stepped into a puddle that was deep enough to fill one of his Gucci loafers with freezing water. It was at that point that he almost felt like crying with frustration and misery. He stood on the platform, holdall in hand and leather shoulders sagging, wondering to himself what the hell he was doing there and wishing that he was back in the warm, familiar surroundings of good old Clapham.

He found a moderately sheltered bench in the lee of the ticket office and there took off his shoe and poured a rivulet of slush from its soft tan interior. He dried it out as best he could and then changed into his only spare pair of socks. By the time that he had finished, he was the only person on the platform, save for one extraordinary figure that stood by the exit, looking in his direction. He or she was dressed in a pair of black Wellington boots and a long red anorak with an attached hood, the drawstrings of which were pulled so tight about the face that it looked as if all necessary sensory functions were carried out by means of one rather large, red nose. Dan picked up his holdall and walked along the deserted platform towards the figure, and it was then that he was suddenly struck by its uncanny resemblance to the murderous Venetian dwarf in the film *Don't Look Now*.

'Are you Dan Porter?' a voice mumbled deep within the hood.

'Yes.'

'Come on quickly, then. The van's outside.'

There were no introductions, no pleasantries passed on how he had fared on the journey, no lighthearted apology for the state of the weather. At that precise moment, he almost felt like walking in completely the opposite direction to the obtuse, red-coated figure, seeking out a good hostelry, and staying there until such time as he could crawl, pissed out of his tiny mind, back onto the train for London.

He found consolation in the fact that the van was a brand-new Ford Transit with the word *Vagabonds* written in a wavy, multicoloured line along its side. At least that reassured him that he wasn't going to be taken off to some dank hovel on a remote hillside and tortuously cut into little pieces with a blunt bread knife. He waited at the side of the passenger door while the figure got into the driver's side and reached over to unlock it for him. He climbed in and felt immediately the comforting warmth of its interior. The engine was started and then the figure undid the drawstrings of the hood and pushed it back. For the first time, Dan was assured that his driver was a woman, and as she ruffled her spiky brown hair, he recognized her features from the photograph in Battersea Gran's magazine.

She turned to him, a smile on her bright, scrubbed face. 'Hello, Dan. I'm Katie Trenchard,' she said, holding out a hand. 'The weather's so bad that I thought I'd come to meet you rather than wait for your telephone call.'

'Pleased to meet you,' he replied. Shaking her hand was like gripping an icicle.

'I'm sorry that I didn't introduce myself earlier. You just looked so cold and miserable standing on the platform that I thought it would be best to get you into the heat before we started having any conversation. Anyway, how was your journey?'

'Interesting.'

'Let me guess. You got no sleep, the heating blew hot and cold, and you shared your compartment with someone who snored.'

Dan was amazed. 'That's a bit *too* accurate. You didn't arrange it, by any chance, did you?'

Katie laughed. 'No. It's just par for the course. The secret is to slip a tenner into the attendant's hand before you set off. They're usually very good at juggling around with the berths.'

'Thanks for the tip. I'll make sure I do that on the way home.'

Katie revved up the engine, engaged gear, and moved off towards the exit of the station car park. 'Are you returning to London tonight?'

'Probably. I left the return open in case I needed more time up here.' As they turned onto the street, he looked out of the window at the people scurrying from shop to shop with their umbrellas angled in protection against the driving sleet. He let out a rueful laugh. 'But I think that I'll try to get back there as soon as I can.'

'So you don't think much of our wonderful weather, then?' Katie asked, her voice lilting with amusement.

'I can't believe that there could be such a change over five hundred miles. It was like summer when I left London last night. Is September always like this up here?'

'No, not at all. This is just a bit of a freak. The forecast is quite good for tomorrow.' She glanced across at him. 'So if you do stick around for another day, you won't be needing to invest in an unglamorous article like my anorak.'

Dan looked down at his attire. The sodden leather jacket was now beginning to steam in the heat of the van and his damp jeans felt warm against his skin. Only his foot inside its greasy loafer refused to give any indication that it was thawing out. 'I had no idea what to expect,' he said quietly.

'Obviously not,' Katie laughed.

Dan bit at his lip. 'Okay, point taken.'

'Sorry. I shouldn't laugh. It was just that you did look quite out of place on the platform back there.'

'Just as you would have done if you had arrived at Euston with nothing but your nose revealed to the world.'

'Maybe. I could have been taken for some eccentric Muslim woman, though.'

Katie accelerated the van towards a set of traffic lights that had just changed from green to amber. She thought about crossing them, but at the last moment slammed her foot on the brakes, skidding the van to a halt. Dan felt a crashing blow on the back of his head and a millisecond later found himself hemmed in by long rolls of brightly coloured fabric.

'Heavens, are you all right?' Katie asked with concern as she pushed back the rolls into the rear of the van. 'I hadn't realized that they were still there. They should have been taken into the factory last night.'

Dan decided against passing comment about how his head felt. The dull thumping simply blended itself into his overall feeling of sheer discomfort. 'Are we going there now?'

'Yes. It's on a small industrial estate just outside town. It's not very far away.'

Ten minutes later, they crossed over an unmanned level crossing and drove through a set of gates beside which stood a large white sign announcing that they were entering the Cruach Industrial Estate. The road weaved through a line of long, low prefabricated units, the majority of which had untidy stacks of fish boxes and pallets outside their large blue doors. These were slid closed against the bite of the wind blowing in across the choppy waters of the sea loch, on the exposed shores of which the industrial estate was situated.

Katie pulled the van to a halt outside an unmarked building and switched off the engine. 'This is it then. Home to my empire.'

'Looks good,' Dan replied, trying to sound enthusiastic as he surveyed the rusting pillars that supported the ineffectual porch above the glass-panelled entrance door, its paintwork weathered and peeling.

'Come on, then. We'll go inside and I'll make you a warming cup of coffee.' She picked up a large canvas bag from the floor of the van and opened the door. She stopped halfway out and turned to him. 'Heavens, it's just occurred to me that you've probably not had anything to eat. Would you like me to get you a bacon sandwich?'

'That would be great – if it's not too much bother.'

'Not at all. I'll get Hilary to go round to the café for one.'

As soon as Dan opened the door of the van, his nostrils were invaded by the overpowering smell of fish. Even though the wind was blowing in fresh across the loch, the odour had an irrepressible permanence about it as if it were deep-set into the fabric of the buildings and exuded through every warped crevice. Katie led Dan through the entrance door and into an open-plan work area, and immediately he could hear the hum of sewing machines from beyond the room. He spied, through the glass panel of an adjoining door, a line of women sitting intently at work.

The room in which he was standing was cluttered but businesslike with multipinned progress charts and Vagabond photographs lining every wall. The reception desk was manned by a young girl who had smiled broadly at him as he entered. Behind her, two women clicked away on the keyboards of their computers, talking as they did into hands-free mouthpieces. He heard one say in a lilting, friendly voice, 'Good morrrning! Vagabonds. This is Maggie speaking. How can I help you?'

'Hilary,' Katie said to the girl behind the reception desk, 'this is Mr Porter from London.' The girl stood up and forthrightly shook Dan's hand. 'Could you do me a great favour and pop round to the Greasy Spoon and get him a bacon sandwich?'

'Of course,' she replied keenly, immediately retrieving her raincoat from the stand beside her desk.

Dan thrust his hand into his pocket for change. 'Listen, I must—'

'No, don't be silly,' Katie interjected. 'I think the least we can do after your desperate trip to the frozen north is stand you to a bacon sandwich.' She took off her anorak and hung it up on the coat stand, then pulled off her Wellington boots and kicked her feet into a pair of old brown sailing shoes with broken backs, an indication that changing her footwear was a pretty regular occurrence. It was the first time that Dan had seen her free from her somewhat unflattering rainwear and he was impressed with what he saw. He watched her as she walked over to where the electric kettle teetered rather precariously on one of the windowsills. She gave it a shake to check that there was sufficient water in it and switched it on. Although no taller than five and a half feet, she had a figure that was totally in proportion to her height. Her hips were slim, her bust was full but firm inside her blue cashmere polo-necked jersey, and although she was wearing a brightly coloured pair of Vagabonds, the generous cut of which would no doubt have delayed many a 'heavier set' woman from going on a crash diet, he could tell that, in Katie's case, they were hiding from view a pert bottom and a shapely pair of legs.

'Right,' she said, returning to where he stood at the reception desk. 'While we're waiting for that to boil, would you like me to explain what's happening in here?'

Dan took off his leather jacket, which had begun to steam in the heat of the office and give off a smell like a bullock with a personal hygiene problem. 'Could I hang this somewhere to dry? It's soaked right through.'

'Of course,' Katie said, taking the jacket from him. 'I'm sorry. I should have thought.'

She walked to the far end of the room and spread the garment over a radiator at the back of an unoccupied desk that Dan reckoned to be her own. 'That should do it.'

'Are you sure it'll be all right like that?' Dan asked, eyeing his precious jacket with concern.

'I would think so. It won't harm the leather, if that's what you mean.'

Dan decided to trust her judgment. She, of all people, must know about that kind of thing.

'Okay, then,' she said, stopping behind the two women who sat at the computer screens, talking incessantly into their mouthpieces. She put a hand on a shoulder of each. They turned to give her a brief smile without faltering in their conversations. 'These two lovely ladies are Heather and Maggie. Come over here and I'll explain what they're doing.'

Dan moved around the side of the reception desk and walked over to stand beside her.

'Best to look at Maggie's screen. She's just started to take an order.' She paused as Maggie typed in the name of a Mrs Catherine Swift. Dan watched as the screen immediately filled with Mrs Swift's address, telephone number, and banking details.

'That's what I like to see,' Katie whispered to him. 'A satisfied customer returning for more.' She reached over Maggie's shoulder and pointed to one of the field boxes near to the bottom of the screen. 'That shows that Mrs Swift has already spent five hundred and eighty pounds with us this year.'

Dan was impressed. 'Are there many customers like her?'

'Oh yes,' she replied quite assuredly. 'Once Maggie has finished this order, I'll ask her to bring up our Top Ten list. I'm pretty certain that you won't find Mrs Swift's name on it.'

Maggie pressed a key, and the address and banking details were replaced by another screen format. She started to type in the order that was being given to her over the telephone.

'This is the stock handling format now,' Katie explained. 'Maggie types in what's required and then checks it against stock. If we have what the customer wants; then she reserves it and that's knocked off the stock list. If we don't have it, then it goes into a pending file. After each order is taken, it gets transferred to the monitor in the stockroom and, if all goes well, it should be in the post by the end of the day. If there is some part of the order that is pending, it gets printed out onto a manufacturing list, and along with stock update sheets, goes through to the girls in the workshop who then know what they have to produce.'

'Why do you bother printing out hard copy for them?' Dan asked. 'Why don't you have a monitor in the workshop like you do in the stockroom?'

Katie smiled. 'Because the girls in there don't like computers. We tried it once but it nearly ended in a walkout.' She walked over to the kettle, which Dan had heard click off a minute before. 'They much prefer good old-fashioned pieces of paper.' She spooned instant coffee into a mug and poured in the water. 'How do you like it?'

'Black's just fine.'

As Katie handed him the mug, Hilary walked in through the front door of the office, the shoulders of her raincoat damp with rain and her long dark hair plastered against the sides of her face.

She placed a silver foil package on the top of the reception desk, took off her coat, and then shook her head from side to side, spraying out water like a shaking dog. 'My word, that's *horrible* out there,' she exclaimed, tousling her hair with her fingers. She walked over to Dan and handed him the warm package before replacing her raincoat on its peg.

'I'm sorry about that, Hilary,' Katie said. 'I should have stopped by on the way here. I'm afraid my mind is a bit full of other things at the minute.'

'Not to worry,' the girl said brightly.

Dan smiled his appreciation at the young receptionist before she resumed her seat.

'What would you like to do?' Katie asked. 'We could either sit down and have a chat now, or we could continue with the tour?'

'If it's all the same to you,' Dan replied, 'I think it might be best to leave questions to the end.' Holding his coffee mug between arm and chest, he took the silver wrapper off the bacon sandwich and threw it in a wastepaper bin. 'As long as you don't mind me having breakfast as we go.'

'Not at all. Come on then, we'll start in the workshop.'

Katie led Dan through the windowed door at the back of the office and immediately he was hit by the whirring discord of the sewing machines and the blare of pop music from the speakers that were suspended from the metal rafters above the shop floor. Dan counted twelve machinists, all bent in concentration over their work, running the brightly coloured fabric through their machines, working foot pedal and hands in complete synchronization. Beside each workstation was positioned a stack of plastic boxes on the sides of which were written a series of numbers, preceded by two letters. Dan noticed that no two boxes were the same.

Katie saw him studying them. 'Those are the manufacturing codes,' she shouted into his ear. 'Different fabrics, different size garments, and different panels. Everything gets started at the back beside the cutting table and then moves forward, so that the finished article comes off over there by the door. Elsie here' – Elsie glanced up when she heard her name being mentioned, took one look at Dan, and went puce with embarrassment – 'is doing pockets, and once she's finished this batch, she'll push her boxes on to Karen in front there who'll put in the elastic.'

Katie led the way through the row of machinists to the back of the shop floor. As they walked, a shrill wolf whistle pierced the air and Dan turned to see the girl next to Elsie lean over and give her a teasing punch on the arm. Elsie's embarrassment was so intensified that her head almost disappeared into her lap.

Katie laughed. 'Don't worry. They give that treatment to any man who walks in here. You actually got off quite lightly.' She rested her hands on the edge of the large cutting table, and both she and Dan watched as a well-built girl wearing a baseball cap back to front deftly steered an electric cutting knife around a pattern that was laid upon a layer of fabric almost a foot deep.

'This is a pretty skilled job,' Katie boomed out. 'One slip of the knife and that whole lay of material may well have to be junked.'

'Has that happened before?' Dan asked.

Katie smiled at him and moved close to the baseball cap. 'Morag, he's asking if we've ever had to scrap a lay before?'

The girl's head jerked up to look at him, and Dan was quite taken aback by the obvious affront that flashed in her eyes. She shook her head once before resuming her work.

Dan could tell that Katie was suppressing a laugh. 'There's your answer.' She turned and made her way back towards the door. 'It is without doubt these girls who have made this company, not me. They think nothing of working over the weekend or well into the night if we fall behind on manufacturing. I seem to remember that when you called on Sunday night, it was pretty late, wasn't it?'

Dan nodded.

'Well, there you are then. In a way, you've already been witness to it. They all take pride in what they do, and what makes it even better is that they're all my friends. We're just one big happy family.'

Dan couldn't help but notice that there was almost a heaviness of heart in the way that Katie adulated her workers. As they returned to the office area, it came to him that of course she would feel that way. She was selling the business, after all, and the uncertainties regarding the future employment of her 'family' had to be weighing heavily on her mind.

By the time Dan had finished off his bacon sandwich and drunk his cup of coffee, they had completed the tour, having passed quickly through the high-shelved stockroom, with its neatly folded rows of trousers and jerseys, and the dispatch room, stacked with packets of tissue paper and smart blue boxes with *Vagabonds* written in gold italics across their lids. Returning to the reception area, Dan collected his holdall and followed Katie to the rear of the office. She pulled a chair away from the wall for him before sitting down at her desk.

'Right, then,' she said. 'Let's get to the questions. What would you like to ask me?'

Unzipping his holdall, Dan dug around to retrieve Nina's battered exercise book. 'May I?' he asked, reaching across and taking a biro from the wicker pen tray on Katie's desk. He sat down on the chair and crossed his legs. 'Well, let's start with the most important question. Can I ask you what your turnover is?'

Katie raised her eyebrows, seemingly startled by the forthrightness of the question. 'Right.' She hesitated briefly. 'Well, I think that last year we were at about the half-million mark, but I reckon that the company will surpass it this year.'

For a moment, Dan hovered pen above pad. He hadn't been expecting anything close to that. His mind raced back to what he and Josh had discussed in the kitchen in Clapham. If Vagabonds wasn't yet 'scratching the market', then, by hell, it wasn't doing badly as it was. Still, he found it hard to believe that a business such as this was housed in what looked like a

Nissan hut in one of the farthest outposts of the United Kingdom could ever be capable of achieving such a turnover.

'And your profit margin?'

Again Katie seemed perplexed by the question. She let out a sigh. 'I couldn't give you an exact answer to that. You would have to speak to our accountant. Our manufacturing costs are pretty high, but I would never think of changing the way we work. Last year, I think we cleared about twenty-five thousand after wages, but most of that went into paying off a medium-term bank loan.' She leaned forward on her desk. 'Can I ask *you* a question?'

'Sure,' Dan replied.

'Why would anyone reading *Woman's Weekly* be at all interested in profit margins?'

'I'm sorry?'

Katie sat back in her chair. 'Well, surely they'd be more interested in, well, less mundane matters. In fact, I was rather surprised that you wanted to do an article about me so soon after the last one.'

Dan frowned. 'I'm afraid you've lost me.'

Katie stared at him for a moment. 'You're wanting to write an article on me, aren't you? For *Woman's Weekly?*'

Dan laughed. 'No. What on earth gave you that idea?'

'But that's what you said on the telephone.'

'I never said anything of the sort.'

'But you are a journalist?'

'No, I certainly am not.'

Katie's fresh-faced complexion seemed to drain of colour. 'You're not from the Inland Revenue, are you? Because if you are, you'll have to—'

'Listen,' Dan interrupted her, beginning to feel an itch of irritation niggle at his sleep-starved mind. 'I saw an article about you in a copy of *Woman's Weekly* that my mother had given me' – that was a good start, he thought – 'for some recipe or other, and I read it. I then rang you up and said that I wanted to speak to you about your company, and you told me to come up. So I have done exactly that.'

'But why?'

'Because,' Dan replied, his voice rising in frustration, 'you said that you were selling your business and I thought that I might be interested in buying it.'

Katie thumped a hand to her mouth. 'Oh, no,' she mumbled.

'What do you mean, "oh no"?'

'I didn't hear you say that.' She paused for a moment, biting at her bottom lip. 'Oh my goodness, I think that I must have picked up the wrong end of the stick altogether.'

Dan shook his head dismissively. 'Oh well, there's no harm done.'

'But there is,' Katie replied quietly. 'I've brought you all the way up here to Scotland for no reason.'

'Well, let *me* be the judge of that.'

'There's nothing to judge!' Katie exclaimed. 'I sold the business two weeks ago!'

For a moment, Dan was rendered speechless. He sat staring at her as her words sank into his brain. 'What do you mean? It can't be . . . I mean, so soon?' he stuttered. 'I'd only just read about it in the magazine.'

'Didn't you look at the date?'

'What?'

'The date on the *Woman's Weekly*. That article was published about four months ago.'

Dan screwed up his eyes in disbelief. 'You've got to be joking!' He leaned back in his chair and smacked his hands on his forehead. 'For heaven's sake, I never even thought to look.'

'I really am so sorry. If I'd known that—'

'No, no, it's entirely my own fault. I should have checked. It just never occurred to me.'

Katie made a brave attempt at a smile. 'Would you like another cup of coffee?'

'No . . . thank you.' Jeez, he thought to himself, being out of work must have stagnated his brain. If someone in the bank had carried out such an appalling research job, he would have been out on his bloody ear! Moreover, what a waste of time! What a damned waste of *money*! 'Can I ask who bought the business?'

'A young couple who wanted to downshift from London. I had three offers, one of them being higher than theirs, but they were the only ones prepared to keep the factory running up here.'

Dan let out a deep sigh, and leaning forward, replaced the biro in the pen tray. 'Well, that's that, then,' he said, dropping Nina's exercise book back into the holdall.

'I feel awful about this,' Katie declared, her teeth clenched in embarrassment.

'There's no need to. It can all be blamed on my own stupidity.' Zipping up the holdall, he got to his feet and took his jacket off the radiator behind Katie's desk. He was pleased at least that it had dried out. 'Well, I won't take up any more of your time,' he said, putting on the jacket.

'I really am sorry that your trip was so abortive.'

'As I said, it was my own fault entirely.' He picked up his holdall. 'Listen, you should maybe tell the new owners of the company that there is a huge untapped market for Vagabonds in London. My son told me that all his friends are after them. They are apparently the ideal wear for clubbing.'

'Really?'

'That's what he says. They're supposedly deemed to be "*ultimate*" wear, and believe me, that's some praise coming from my son.'

Katie rose to her feet. 'In that case, I certainly will tell them.' She pushed her hands into the pockets of her trousers. 'What are you going to do now?'

Dan remembered his thoughts of earlier that morning about going into a local pub and anaesthetizing his chilly discomfort with drink. The idea of it had suddenly increased its appeal by at least the power of ten. 'I'll just head back to town and kill time until this evening.'

Katie started towards the entrance door. 'I'll give you a lift, then.'

'No, don't bother. I feel that I've wasted enough of your time already. I'd be grateful, though, if you could ask Hilary to call me a taxi.'

Katie sucked her teeth loudly. 'This is ridiculous,' she said, marching across to the coat stand and taking down her anorak.

'What's ridiculous?' Dan asked as he followed on.

'I can't have you waiting in Fort William all day for your train.'

'Look, please don't bother about—'

'Well, I'm sorry, but I do bother.' She turned to Hilary. 'I'm going to take Mr Porter back to Auchnacerie, so if anything urgent crops up, you can get hold of me there.' She dug her hand in the pocket of her anorak and took out a bunch of keys. 'Right, come on then. Let's go.'

'Where exactly are we going?'

'Back to my house.'

Dan sighed quietly. Under the circumstances, he would much rather be alone in his own company with a large drink in hand. 'I don't suppose it would do any good to raise an objection?'

'None at all. No matter what you say, I feel responsible for bringing you all the way up here under false pretences. It's the least I can do.'

Dan shrugged his shoulders. 'Okay. I'm in your hands, then.'

Two minutes later, they were out of the industrial estate and heading westward at speed in Katie's bright red Volkswagen Golf GTI, having thankfully (for Dan's head) by-passed the Vagabonds van in the car park. The day had got no brighter, but at least the dark clouds that shrouded the surrounding hills were valiantly holding back the sleet.

'Nice car,' Dan commented, not really wishing to make conversation, but thinking it would be rude if he just sat ruminating over his own incompetence.

'My little perk,' Katie replied. 'Vagabonds has literally taken over my life the past few years, so I felt I deserved some sort of reward for all the effort.'

'I would have thought that you'd all have four-wheel drives up here.'

'They're not necessary. If there's a bit of snow, a normal car will cope just as well, as long as you drive carefully.' Katie smiled at him. 'Is it not true that there are more four-wheel drives in London than there are in any other part of the country?'

Dan laughed. 'I wouldn't know the statistics, but yes, there do seem to be quite a number of them around.'

'Probably quite useful for getting over zebra crossings without getting stuck on pedestrians.'

Dan sucked in a breath through his teeth. 'Do I detect a hint of sarcasm in your tone?'

Katie chuckled. 'Maybe just a little.' She swung the car to the right and drove up a steep tarmacked gradient and pulled to a halt in front of a drystone wall, behind which Dan could spot every now and again the bobbing head of a child.

'Thank goodness! It's break time,' Katie said as she turned off the engine. 'Listen, I won't be a moment. I'm just going to pick up my daughter, Sooty. She wasn't feeling very well this morning, so I think a half-day off school might do her some good.'

'As long as Max doesn't catch sight of you taking her away.'

Katie frowned. 'What?'

'Or maybe he's not at the same school.'

Her eyes suddenly lit with understanding. She pointed a finger at him. 'Of course. The magazine. You know it all.' She pushed open the door. 'You're right. Max is here, but he can get the bus back later. I will endeavour to spirit Sooty away without causing a scene.'

Dan watched as she jogged across to the gates of the school and entered the playground. Finding himself alone for the first time since being given the news about the company, Dan now felt able to vent the pent-up rage at his own stupidity. He screwed up his eyes and knocked hard on his forehead with a clenched fist. 'Shit. Shit. *SHIT!*' He thwacked a hand down on the plastic fascia, his voice resounding around the confines of the car. As he continued to rebuke himself under his breath, he witnessed

111

a small pair of hands grasp the top of the playground wall and a carrot-topped head came into view, peering quizzically around. The boy caught sight of Dan, and then dropped behind the wall. Five seconds later, he appeared again, this time as if catapulted upwards. He swung his legs over the wall and sat staring at Dan, nonchalantly twiddling his thumbs.

At first Dan thought it best to ignore the boy. He pretended to play around with the catch of the glove compartment for a few seconds, but when he looked up, he still found himself fixed in the boy's beady gaze. Maybe he should say something to him. He tried the electric windows, but they didn't work without the ignition being switched on, so he opened the door a fraction, eager to keep the heat in the car.

'Hello,' he said, trying to sound bright and friendly.

The boy nodded once.

'What's your name, then?'

'Murdoch,' the boy answered in a drawn-out monotone.

'So how old are you, Murdoch?'

'Eleven,' the boy replied without altering the pitch of his voice.

'Right.' Dan heaved out a sigh at the effort of trying to continue this stilted conversation. 'And do you enjoy school?'

The boy shrugged his shoulders. 'S'all right.' He tilted his head slightly to the side. 'Was that you?'

'What do you mean?'

'Was that you who called out "shit"?'

Dan bit at his lip in embarrassment. 'Ah, well, yes, I'm afraid it was. Sorry about that.'

Murdoch thumped a fist down on the fingers of some unfortunate schoolmate who was grappling at the wall in an attempt to join him in his lofty position. 'My dad never says "shit".'

'Quite right too. It's not a good thing to say.'

'He says "shite".'

Dan cleared his throat. 'Well, neither are very good words,' he said, his voice sounding oddly schoolmasterly. 'Better not to say them at all.'

'No, probably not,' Murdoch replied quietly, slipping back into his monotone.

Dan gave the boy a wink, feeling quite pleased with himself that his short lesson in the avoidance of bad language had obviously penetrated the carrot-topped head.

Murdoch, however, looked menacingly questioning again. 'What about "bugger"? Do you think that's a good word?'

Dan was mercifully spared from answering the question by a male voice that boomed out from the other side of the wall. 'Murdoch! Get yourself down from there and into your classroom.' The boy disappeared like a coconut that had been knocked off its perch in a fairground stall.

Dan was still staring at the vacant space when Katie, clutching the hand of a skipping girl with tousled dark hair, walked towards the car. She opened the door and pushed forward the seat, and the little girl clambered into the back.

'Sorry about that,' Katie said, as she got into the car. 'You were right. There was a bit of a showdown with Max.'

'Not to worry. I was pleasantly entertained by a young man called Murdoch.'

The little girl in the back of the car made a noise that sounded as if she was being violently sick. 'Murdoch is *revolting!*' she cried out. 'He picks his nose and *flicks* it at people.'

'All right, Sooty,' Katie protested as she reversed the car. 'I don't think that we need to know that. Anyway, you haven't said hello to Mr Porter yet.'

'Dan, please.' Dan turned around and smiled at the young girl who was struggling with the buckle of her seat belt. 'Hello, Sooty. Nice to meet you.'

'Where are you from?' Sooty asked without making eye contact with him.

'London.'

'I fought so.'

'Really? Now, how would you know that?'

''Cos you sound as if you are off *EastEnders*.'

'Sooty!' Katie exclaimed reproachfully. 'You mustn't be so forward.'

'But he does.'

Dan laughed. 'You're right too. Mind you, my accent used to be a lot stronger than it is now.'

'Why has it changed?' Sooty asked.

'Probably working in the City all my life.'

'Why does that change your accent?'

'Well, in the City, you work with different people from all over the world, and sometimes they don't speak very good English, so you have to make yourself understood as best you can. That means knocking out the accent a bit.'

'Do I have an accent, Mummy?'

'I'm not sure,' Katie replied. 'Maybe you should ask Dan if you do.'

'Do I, Dan?'

'Well, yes, I can tell that you're from Scotland. Your accent's not nearly as strong as Murdoch's, though.'

'*Pleeease* don't talk about Murdoch,' Sooty moaned. 'He makes me feel ill!'

Dan shot a grimace at Katie who returned a similar expression. 'Murdoch's father is a gamekeeper on one of the estates here,' Katie said. 'The whole family's a bit . . . well, how can I put it? A bit undisciplined.'

Dan nodded. 'That would seem to figure.'

Katie stuck the car into third gear and edged out into the centre of the road to see if it was safe to overtake a large articulated lorry with foreign number plates and a logo of a fish on its tailgate. 'So you work in the City, then?' she asked, accelerating past the lorry.

'I did, yes, for twenty years.'

'Doing what?'

'For most of the time, investment banking.'

'And now?'

'Nothing . . . at present. Just waiting for the right opportunity to come along.'

Katie let out a sigh. 'And you thought that Vagabonds might have fit the bill.'

'It might have done.'

'God, I feel so awful about that.'

'Well, you don't have to. It was just a misunderstanding on both our parts.'

'Mummy,' Sooty piped up from the back of the car, 'can you put on the tape?'

'No, angel, Dan and I are talking.'

'But it's so *boring*! You can talk when you get home.'

'Sooty!'

'I don't mind,' Dan cut in, feeling that he too would like an excuse not to hear any more of Katie's heartfelt apologies.

'You haven't heard the tape yet,' Katie murmured out of the side of her mouth.

She pressed the button on the stereo, and immediately the car was filled with the nasal tones of a man who sang in a Scottish accent far exceeding the bounds of wee Murdoch's humble offering.

*There was a little girl who had one little goldfish, one little gold-
    fish, one little goldfish,
There was a little girl who had one little goldfish, and the gold-
    fish's name was Doris.*

*There was a little boy who had two little goldfish, two little gold-
    fish, two little goldfish,
There was a little boy who had two little goldfish, and the gold-
    fishes' names were Doris . . . and Horace.*

The road meandered gently as it ran eastwards alongside a single-track railway line that followed the rocky shoreline of a dark-watered loch. As the little girl in the song acquired another goldfish called Clovis, Katie pointed a finger in front of Dan's chest.

115

'Our house is somewhere over there in the mist on the other side of the loch. I'm afraid that we have to go right up to the end and then back again to get to it.'

'How far are you from Fort William?' Dan asked.

'About twenty miles.'

'And you do the journey every day?'

'Not just once. I come home every day for lunch.'

'That's eighty miles a day!'

'And more. I have to pick up the children from the school bus as well. It's probably nearer ninety.' Katie glanced across at him. 'Different from living in London, isn't it?'

'Just a little. On the other hand, one leg of your journey would most likely take less time than it would take me to travel from Clapham up to the City.'

Katie changed up a gear once more and zipped past a slow-moving car. 'Most likely.'

Dan gave the fascia of the dashboard an appreciating pat. 'And much more fun too.'

By the time they pulled off the road and drove through a pair of rough stone pillars, they had listened to Sooty's song three times. The tune now hung in Dan's brain like a constant taunt, and he had begun to make up names for the bloody goldfish that could never be mentioned, other than maybe at a rugby club dinner. The short drive led up past an unkempt garden with over-grown flowerbeds bordering a lawn that was in desperate need of mowing. In the centre of this hayfield, a large round trampoline with a gaping hole in the centre of its bouncing mat dripped inconsolably. The stone-built farmhouse, on the other hand, which was situated at the top of the garden, looked comforting and happy, its white-astragalled windows smiling out across the loch, despite the fact that its view was significantly curtailed by the low-lying mist.

Katie drove around to the back of the house and parked the car in one of a series of arched openings in a long, barnlike building, next to an ageing Mercedes estate car. She retrieved her canvas bag from the well at Dan's feet and got out of the car, pulling the seat forward for Sooty.

Dan squeezed himself out of the passenger door, trying to avoid bumping the lurid purple mountain bike that leaned against one of the heavy wooden beams supporting the floor of the loft above.

'Take care you don't slip on these flagstones,' Katie said as she stepped deliberately across the courtyard to the back door. 'They're an absolute deathtrap.'

Dan brought up the rear as they entered the house and walked through a small glory hole, filled with gumboots and fishing rods and shelves stacked with DIY paraphernalia. Another door led into a large kitchen, which, despite its size, seemed equally as cluttered. A drying pulley, lined with clothes, hung above the Rayburn cooker, and the round leafed table that was pushed in against the curved window seat was piled with books and files and fabric samples. A large ginger cat, with its front feet tucked under its chest, sat upon the closed lid of a laptop computer and ignored their arrival entirely. Dan wondered why it had chosen that resting place in preference to the obvious comfort of the old sofa, with its plaid rug covering and piles of colourful cushions, situated against the wall next to the television.

'Would you excuse me for a moment?' Katie said, dumping her canvas bag on the table. 'I just have to go upstairs.' She walked across to a door wedged into the corner of the room by a large pine Welsh dresser. 'Sooty will keep you company until I get back, won't you, Sooty?'

As soon as she had left the room, Sooty jumped onto the sofa, reached for the television remote, and switched it on. Hands on chin, elbows resting on the arm of the sofa, she became immediately absorbed in the antics of a cartoon dog that was frantically trying to bury a smouldering stick of dynamite. Dan glanced around at the countless examples of children's artwork that adorned most parts of the yellow walls, then as the television boomed out the demise of the unfortunate dog, he walked across to the window and stared out into the cold, grey shroud of mist that seemed to be baulking any chance of brightness from the day.

He couldn't even begin to live with this kind of weather. Not day after day. Especially being stuck out in the middle of nowhere, with neither sight nor sound of another person for miles around. It began to dawn on him that the most thankful thing that had happened to him all day was that Vagabonds *had* been sold, and the best of British luck to the young couple from London who had bought it. If they weren't both clawing at the doors of the sleeper train within the next few months, then, more than likely, they were already flying pretty high over the cuckoo's nest.

Dan heard the sound of Katie's footsteps come down the stairs. She opened the door and walked in. 'Right. What time is it?' She glanced up at the kitchen clock above the Rayburn. 'A quarter to twelve. I suppose it's a bit early, but let's have some lunch anyway.' She pulled open the door of the fridge. 'Would you like a beer?'

'If you have one, that would be great,' Dan replied.

Katie took out a can and lobbed it over to Dan.

'Now, what have we got?' she said, peering into the fridge. 'Not a lot, I'm afraid. Tomorrow's usually the big shopping day, so we're pretty low on supplies. How about . . . cheese on toast and tomato soup?'

Dan pulled the ring off the can. 'Sounds good to me.'

Sooty had her lunch in front of the television while Dan and Katie sat on the window seat eating theirs. Katie resumed her questioning of Dan, and by the time that she had stacked the dishwasher with their bowls and plates and they had finished off their mugs of coffee, he had told her about the house in Clapham, about Jackie and her high-flying and demanding job, about Josh and his low-flying and undemanding job, and about Millie and Nina and their supreme wish that Dad would get another job so that they could return to their old school and be with their friends. Battersea Gran's name was explained in full, both Biggles and Cruise were discussed, and even his old mate Nick and doted-upon son Tarquin got a mention.

'Heavens above!' exclaimed Katie, glancing at the clock and jumping to her feet. 'It's half past two! I was meant to get Patrick at two o'clock.'

Dan slid off the bench. 'Can I be of any help?'

Katie cleared the two mugs from the table and put them in the dishwasher. 'No, it's all right. I can manage.'

'Are you sure? I know that his factory is quite close to your workshop. I could easily find my way back there. My own insurance probably covers me for driving your car.'

Katie slowly straightened up from the dishwasher and stood staring at him, biting her lip. 'Ah,' she said quietly.

'Daddy's not at work, Dan,' Sooty said, breaking herself away from the television. Still leaning on the arm of the sofa, she bounced up and down on her knees. 'He's upstairs, isn't he, Mummy?'

Katie smiled forlornly at her daughter. 'Yes, angel, he is.'

Dan pushed his hands into the pockets of his unzipped bomber jacket. 'Sorry. I didn't realize that. I thought that when you said you had to get him, you meant from—'

'I think that I should maybe explain something,' Katie cut in. She glanced over to where Sooty was once more engrossed in yet another television programme. She crossed her arms and leaned against the towel rail of the Rayburn. 'There *was* a slight untruth told in that magazine article about me. I said that the reason I had decided to sell Vagabonds was that I wanted to spend more time with the children.'

'And that you felt it could expand to a worldwide market,' Dan added.

'Exactly.' Katie paused, twisting up the side of her mouth, as if steeling herself to continue. 'The real reason, however, is that I don't want to be away from the house much anymore.' Dan watched her intently as she once again gathered her thoughts. 'You obviously know that Patrick runs his own prawn-processing business.'

'Yes. Seascape.'

119

'Right. Well, five years ago, in June I think it was, Patrick had been up in Mallaig picking up a load of prawns from the boats, and he was driving back to Fort William in the lorry when he had an accident. It wasn't too serious. He just drove rather slowly into a ditch. However, when I eventually managed to drag out of him the reason for it happening, he said that he had suddenly got a really bad attack of pins and needles all the way down his right side, and that he had lost control of the lorry. I told him to go straight to the doctor, but he wouldn't. At that time of year, the factory is at its busiest, and he said that he couldn't afford to start getting all namby-pamby about his health. Anyway, about two weeks later, it happened again, but this time he lost all feeling in his right leg. Thankfully, he was in the office at the time, because he fell over quite heavily and thumped his head against the side of a desk. The whole episode gave him quite a shock, so he was more than willing to go to see the doctor after that. The consultation lasted five minutes and Patrick was immediately hustled off to Inverness for tests. And the long and the short of it is that he was confirmed as having multiple sclerosis.'

'For heaven's sake,' Dan muttered.

'The specialist said that it was early days and there was no way of knowing how fast the disease would develop. However, taking Patrick's age into account, he said that it was more likely to be the progressive form of the disease rather than the relapsing remitting form, especially as he had already experienced some numbness in his limbs. Having said that, he felt that Patrick would have periods of remission at this stage and saw no reason why he shouldn't just keep on working as normal. That, of course, came as music to Patrick's ears. After that, he kept going harder than ever. I never tried to stop him, because I knew it was his release.'

'How did it affect him?'

'Once he was in remission, it didn't at all, except that he would be exhausted at the end of a working day, but I was never sure whether that was a symptom of the disease or just because he was going at it all hours.'

'Has he had a relapse?'

'Yes, one about three months after the initial bout. That lasted for about three weeks, but again it didn't seem to leave any permanent damage, so he just kept going on as normal. Then there was this brilliantly long period of remission when we almost forgot that he had the wretched disease.'

'And that came to an end?'

Katie nodded. 'About five months ago, and this time, I'm afraid, he was left with acute weakness in both legs.'

'Is there any chance that that'll improve?'

'The specialist didn't say anything to Patrick, but he told me that I should expect that to be the norm from now on.'

'Is he still working?'

'Oh, yes. There's nothing wrong with his brain. It's just his body that doesn't work too well. He *has* had to delegate a lot more work now, but I still take him into the office about three times a week, depending on how he's feeling. But at other times' – she pointed over to the table in the window – 'that's where he works.'

'Is there no treatment he can get?'

Katie smiled. 'Yes, but it's all fairly unorthodox. He is in constant contact with this strange little lady who lives up near Spean Bridge. She's a faith healer. The funny thing is that Patrick was such a sceptic before all this happened, but now he hangs on her every word.' Her smile faded. 'Also, one of the boys from the factory drives him up to Inverness every fortnight where he goes into a hyperbaric chamber for about an hour.'

'What's that?'

'It's like a diving bell. I'm not entirely sure how it all works, but I know that it's pressurized to a certain depth and then pure oxygen is pumped into it, and Patrick sits there like a goldfish, getting extremely bored.' She pushed herself away from the towel rail. 'In fact, that's where he's been this morning. He feels absolutely knackered when it's all over, so, more often than not, he goes to bed when he gets home. That's why I went upstairs when we arrived. He gave me strict instructions to wake him at two o'clock.'

Dan blew out a long breath. 'What a hell of a pressure *you* must have on you at the moment.'

'Well, life is certainly not as easy as it was. I've had to juggle my time as best I can, keeping Vagabonds going and trying to look after Patrick and getting the children to and from school. But it really wasn't working, and that's why I decided to sell my business. And then, of course, Patrick is a completely different person.'

'In what way?'

'Oh, he can be morose, insufferably bad-tempered, and he gets extremely frustrated at his inability to carry out even the simplest tasks. I'm sure you can understand that.'

'Of course,' Dan replied, wishing that he hadn't asked such a blatantly stupid question. He glanced across at Sooty on her sofa. 'What about the children? How have they reacted to it all?'

'Max, I think, understands that Patrick is quite ill. He hasn't really changed in any way towards his father, which is a good thing, but he has become very tactile and loving towards me. I think he's just trying to lend his support in the best way that he can.'

'And Sooty?'

'I don't think that she's really taken it in. The innocence of youth, no doubt. She just calls her father Mr Wibbly Wobbly.'

'It's that bad, is it?'

Katie walked towards the door that led to the stairs. 'You'll soon see for yourself.'

'Can I do anything to help?'

Katie smiled back at him as she opened the door. 'No thanks. We've got a good routine going.'

12

Jackie stood, suitcase in hand, on the pavement outside the house in Haleridge Road and watched until the taxi had reached the bottom of the avenue, turned the corner, and disappeared from sight. She turned her gaze to the house and let out a deep sigh. She couldn't remember feeling this way since the days when she had had to go back to boarding school after a long, carefree holiday. The journey back from Paris had been wonderful, but the stone of foreboding had been sitting heavily in her stomach from the moment that she had got out of bed that morning. And now she was here. Back to reality.

She took in a nervous breath and opened the gate, and taking the house key from her pocket as she walked up the short path, she pushed it into the lock and opened the door. She was relieved that the house seemed quiet. She didn't bother to call out, but dropped her suitcase in the hall and walked along the passage to the kitchen.

Battersea Gran was standing at the sink when she entered, scrubbing away at a pot with a Brillo pad, unaware of Jackie's presence. The dogs, however, caught sight of her and Biggles let out a deep throaty bark before sidling over to greet her. The pot clattered into the sink and Battersea Gran turned quickly, a look of fright on her face. She clasped a pink rubber-gloved hand to her bosom. 'Oh, Jackie, it's you! What a terrible shock that dog gave me!'

Jackie shot her the thinnest of smiles. 'Are you all right?'

Battersea Gran leaned a hand against the sink. 'Yes, I'll be fine. Just set the old ticker thumping a bit.'

'Why not have a seat for a moment?'

'No, no, that's not necessary,' she replied, returning to her cleaning duties on the pot. 'I'll just get this all cleared away for you.'

Jackie took off her coat and dropped it over the back of one of the kitchen chairs.

'So, how was Paris?' Battersea Gran asked.

Jackie immediately felt the guilt well up from some hidden place in her subconscious and prickle at her cheeks. She turned and pretended to sift through some unopened letters on the table. 'Fine.'

'That's nice, then,' her mother-in-law replied, bending with a degree of effort to put the pot away in the cupboard below the sink.

Jackie brought herself under control. 'Is Dan not here?'

'No, dear, he's away at the minute.'

Jackie frowned. 'What do you mean, "away"?'

'He's in Scotland, dear,' Battersea Gran replied, pulling off her rubber gloves. 'He went up there last night.'

'*Scotland?* What on *earth* is he doing in Scotland?'

'I've no idea. He just rang me on Sunday night and asked if I could come over and look after the kids because he had to go to Scotland.'

'But he doesn't *know* anybody in Scotland.'

'I wouldn't know about that, dear, but he must have gone up there for some good reason.' She cast a quick glance around the kitchen before walking through to the hallway.

'When is he going to be back?' Jackie called after her.

'Tomorrow, or maybe the next day. He wasn't very sure.'

Letting out a sigh of incomprehension, Jackie leaned her bottom against the kitchen table and folded her arms. Battersea Gran came back into the kitchen, tucking in a scarf at the neck of her pink raincoat.

'Where are you going?' Jackie asked.

'Home, dear.' She took a pair of gloves from her pocket and pulled them on. 'I've made a nice steak pie for the girls, and—'

'But you can't go home yet,' Jackie cut in, her voice rising in agitation.

'I beg your pardon?'

'I mean, what about tomorrow?'

'Well, you're back from your travels now. You'll surely be able to look after the place now.'

'But I can't! I've got to go to work.'

Battersea Gran gave her a broad smile. 'Oh, I'm sure you can phone in to say you're going to be a little bit late.'

'Gran, I cannot afford to be late,' Jackie snapped at her. 'This is probably the busiest time of the year for me. You simply cannot go.'

'Well, I'm very sorry, dear, but I *am* going.'

'But . . . what about the dogs?'

Battersea Gran eyed the two dogs, both of whom had skulked away to their baskets the moment that Jackie had raised her voice. 'Ah, yes. I can see that they might be a bit of a problem. Well, never mind' – she reached up and gave Jackie a peck on the cheek – 'I'm sure that you'll be able to work something out.' She turned and made her way towards the door, only to have her exit blocked by Jackie.

'Please, Gran, you can't go.'

'But I must, dear. I have to make tea for a residents' meeting tonight.'

Jackie stood in the kitchen doorway and watched her mother-in-law bustle along the passage to the hall. 'Did Dan put you up to this?'

Battersea Gran turned, a questioning frown on her brow. 'Now, what could you mean by that?'

'It was Dan, wasn't it? He said to you that I would be home tonight and that I would be able to look after the kids.'

'No, that's not right, dear. I don't think you told him *when* you were going to be home.'

'I did tell him!'

'Well, in that case, he never told me.' There was more than a sense of finality in Battersea Gran's reply. She picked up her handbag from the hall table, opened the front door, and left the house.

Still standing with arms folded, Jackie leaned her head against the doorframe and closed her eyes. 'You bastard, Dan Porter. You damned *bastard*!'

She turned and walked back into the kitchen, and the dogs cringed when she glowered in their direction. She went over to the fridge, tugged open the door, and took out the cellophane-wrapped steak pie of Battersea Gran's making. As she thrust it into the oven and turned on the dial, the telephone rang. She sprang to it and picked it up.

'Hello?' she asked irately. She moderated her tone as soon as she heard the voice. 'Oh, hi, it's you . . . Yes, I know, I'm sorry. I've just been left up the creek without a paddle by my mother-in-law . . . Because Dan's gone off to Scotland for some reason and I've been left to deal with the kids and the dogs . . . No, I can't. Millie and Nina will be back at any minute . . . I know, I would like that too . . . It was great. I really enjoyed myself. Thank you for everything, Stephen.'

She put down the telephone, and for the first time since entering the house, a broad smile spread across her face.

13

He entered the kitchen slowly, his weight resting heavily on two walking sticks. He shuffled painstakingly past Katie, who stood holding the door open for him, and drew his arm sharply away from the touch of her outstretched hand. Dan could tell by the look on her face that it had always intended to be more a caring gesture than a supportive grip. He was a couple of inches shorter than Dan, but built as powerfully as a rugby prop forward, and the rolled-up sleeves of his checked shirt showed off muscles that bulged with the effort of keeping himself on his legs. His features were pallid, but bore signs of having been, at one time, healthily weather-beaten, and although his unbrushed mop of brown hair was thinning on the crown, Dan could not detect one hint of it going grey.

It was his eyes, however, that struck Dan as fascinating. There was an incredible brightness about them, and he could read in them a spirit of adventure, a sparkle of wicked humour, and a wildness at the injustice of being struck down in his prime by such a disabling disease.

Katie moved between them. 'Patrick, this is Dan Porter from London.'

'All right, just hang on a minute. Let me just get myself organized before I say hello.' It came out as an irascible retort, making Dan turn instinctively to watch for Katie's reaction. But she never broke her gaze away from her husband, and Dan could read only love and concern in her expression.

Patrick moved slowly over to the window seat and leaned heavily on the table while he hooked the sticks onto the back of a wooden chair. He edged himself round and sat down heavily. Blowing out with the effort, he ran his fingers through his hair and smiled up at Dan.

'Nice to meet you, Dan,' he said, offering a hand. 'Sorry about the delay in introductions.'

Dan stepped forward and shook his hand, and immediately noticed that the zip on his faded yellow corduroy trousers was undone.

'Good to meet you too, Patrick.' He shook the hand as gently as he could without it seeming that he was making allowances for the man's condition. 'Maybe I should tell you confidentially that your shop's open.'

Patrick glanced down into his lap and let out a disparaging guffaw. 'Oh, bugger, I'm always doing that.' He began to struggle with the zip. 'It's a damned good thing that I don't get out of the house much nowadays. No doubt living in this bloody politically correct country of ours, I'd have been arrested for public indecency about eight times by now.' He seemed to be making no headway with the zip. 'Oh, bloody hell, Kate, can you do it?'

Katie stepped forward and slid up the zip. 'Watch the language, Patrick,' she murmured quietly, her face inches away from his. 'Sooty's over there on the sofa.'

'Oops! Never saw her,' he said, smirking like a naughty schoolboy. 'Hi, Soots, how've you been? Feeling any better?'

Sooty ended her afternoon's television watching with a long stretch. 'Yes, fanks.' She climbed off the sofa and came over to her father and began to climb onto his knee.

'Can you cope?' Katie asked her husband.

'Of course we can, can't we, Soots? As long as you don't start bouncing.'

Sooty leaned her curly black head against her father's chest. 'Have you been diving today, Wibbly?'

'I certainly have. All the way down to forty feet, my girl. We're only a stone's throw from that wreck now, so it won't be long before I bring up all that treasure and we'll all be multimillionaires.'

Patrick tickled his daughter's tummy and she squealed with laughter. 'Can we make Dan a multimillionaire too?' she asked her father.

Patrick pushed Sooty gently off his knee. He looked up at Dan, a smiling glint in his eye. 'Of course not! We don't know him nearly well enough.'

'Oh, *please*, Wibbly!'

'Okay, well, let me interrogate him first and see if he's a trustworthy sort of a bloke.' He pointed to the other side of the curved window bench. 'Have a seat, Dan. I don't like people standing in front of me. It makes me feel inferior.'

'Come on, Sooty,' Katie said as Dan slid onto the bench. 'Let's put the kettle on.'

Patrick shifted awkwardly around on his bottom and rested his elbows on the table. 'So, I hear that your trip up here has been a bit abortive.'

'You could say that. It was my fault entirely, though.'

'Well, from what Kate says, it doesn't sound like it. I think it's high time that she had her ears syringed.' Katie turned from filling the kettle at the sink and stuck out her tongue at her husband, to which he reciprocated in similar fashion. 'So, you worked in the City, then?'

'Yes, for about twenty years.'

'So you were there through the Big Bang.'

'I certainly was. That's when everything took off.'

'And were you one of the infamous Dagenham boys that took the trading floor by storm?'

129

Dan grinned. He liked the directness of this man. 'No. I was from Tottenham Hale, but I suppose my background was pretty similar to theirs.'

Patrick seemed impressed. 'Good for you. Nothing like taking the bull by the horns.'

'We were lucky to be given the opportunity. I could quite easily have ended up working with my father in a north London metal works.'

'But you didn't, did you.'

'No.'

Patrick used both hands to shift a leg to a more comfortable position. 'I've always thought that it must have been a pretty hairy business, trading on the floor. I mean, you must have been fairly young at the time, weren't you?'

'Early twenties.' Dan paused. 'I suppose the best way I could describe it is like having one huge but permanent adrenaline rush. We worked hard and played hard. Well, most of the other guys did. I was more concerned with making as much money as I could and keeping hold of it so that I'd never have to return to Tottenham Hale again.'

'If you enjoyed it that much, why give it up, then?'

'Well, I never really gave it up. It gave *me* up. I was made redundant about fourteen months ago.'

'But surely, with *your* experience, you could have got another job?'

'Yes, you're right.'

Patrick cocked his head to the side, waiting for Dan to continue. 'So? Why not?'

Dan let out a deep breath. 'Because of nine-eleven. I lost one of my best mates in the building, as well as a good number of work colleagues. I just decided then that there were more important things in life than trying to make piles of money.'

Patrick nodded slowly. 'I can understand that.' He leaned forward on the table and fixed Dan with an intense stare. 'But you miss it, don't you?'

Dan smiled. 'Yes, I do. Every day. If you've had a pretty tough upbringing without any of the niceties of life, then you have to fight to survive. You have to be one step ahead of the gang on the street, otherwise you're going to end up lying facedown in the gutter nursing four broken ribs . . . or worse. The job was made for me, like it was made for every other boy and girl who started from nothing and ended up dealing in the City. We all sailed pretty close to the wind, but we knew instinctively how to handle a situation that was as volatile and as unpredictable as our backgrounds in life. It was just . . . the survival of the fittest. Cowboy country, really.'

'Hah!' Patrick exclaimed, slamming his hand down on the table. A fierce excitement suddenly burned in his eyes as he turned to his wife. 'Kate, did you hear that?'

Katie grinned broadly at him and nodded as she poured hot water into the teapot.

'You . . .' Patrick continued, pointing his finger at Dan, 'have just come out with my expression. I could almost have taken a bet that you would too.'

Dan laughed. 'Why?'

'Because' – Patrick clenched his fists and waved them about in the air, trying to find the right words – 'because that kind of business is so vibrant, so cut and thrust, so . . . basic that it puts a fire in your belly and you know that if you don't just go out there and grab every opportunity that arises, you're going to . . . shrivel up and die.'

'And you reckon that your business is like that too, do you?'

'Exactly.'

'In that case, it must have been a hell of a change from being a lecturer at a university.'

He seemed surprised. 'How did you know about that?'

'Dan knows everything about us,' Katie said, placing two mugs of tea in front of them on the table. 'He gleans all his information from *Woman's Weekly*, don't you, Dan?'

Dan twisted his mouth to the side at the teasing remark. 'Not always, but on this occasion, yes.' He turned his attention back to Patrick. 'So how did it come about?'

'Do you really want to hear it?' Patrick asked, casting a challenging look at Dan.

'If you can be bothered.'

Patrick took a drink from his mug. 'Okay then. Well, you're right, I was a lecturer – in marine biology at Plymouth University. The department there also used to carry out research projects for fish farming businesses and the like, and that was how I first came across Seascape. But anyway, that part of the story is quite a bit down the line. What really happened first was that an old mate of mine from London came down to stay with us for the weekend. He was running a successful wholesale business, supplying fresh fish and scallops and the like to restaurants throughout the West End, and he just happened to mention that he was on his way down to Penzance to find a new buyer.' He paused to take another gulp of tea. 'Anyway, all the students were away on holiday at the time and there was no ongoing research in the department, so I asked him what it entailed. He said that it was pretty simple. One just had to go into the buying shed and buy the right quality at the right price.' He looked over to Katie who was watching Sooty busily colour in a picture on a large piece of paper that she had spread out on the floor in front of the Rayburn. 'It was just twice a week, wasn't it, Kate?'

Katie looked over and nodded.

'So I asked him if there was any reason why I shouldn't be able to do it. He wasn't too sure to begin with, because he was concerned that once the university started up again, I wouldn't have the time. Anyway, I suggested that if he paid for my fuel, I'd work without commission for the duration of the holidays, and then if it didn't work out or I proved completely inept at the job, he hadn't lost out too much. So, at about four-thirty on the Monday morning, we both headed down to Penzance. We did a bit of buying and – well, if you'll excuse the horrible pun – I got hooked.'

'So you did continue doing it?'

'Yes. It all worked in very well. Just before the beginning of the next semester, I juggled around with the timetable and made sure that I wasn't giving lectures on the mornings that I went off buying.'

'How long did you do that for?'

'Oh, now,' Patrick drawled, scratching at the unshaven stubble on his chin, 'I took over Seascape in 'ninety-one, so . . . maybe, two years?'

'And then Seascape came on the market.'

'Yes. Well, to be quite honest, it never actually *came* on the market. I knew Archie Brannon, the owner of Seascape, quite well, and I'd been up to Fort William a number of times to see him. He had started a really good business, processing langoustines and prawns for the European markets, primarily Spain, Italy and France. He found out that when all the fishing boats came into harbour up here, they were just dumping the small catch over the side. So he decided to capitalize on it and he made a bloody good job of it too. The only trouble with Archie was that he had one appalling failing. He couldn't keep his pants on. Eventually, his wife ran out of patience and dragged him through the divorce courts, and she came out with a hefty settlement. Archie was already heavily borrowed at the bank, so he was left with no alternative other than to sell the business.'

'How did you find out about it?'

'We were working on some research for Seascape at the time, and I got a telephone call from Archie saying that we had to stop everything. He told me the whole story, and that night I went home and discussed it with Kate.'

'What do you mean? Buying the business?'

'Exactly. I wasn't going to hang around. At the time, we'd only been married a couple of years. We had no children, no animals, no commitment to anyone else but ourselves. Kate was working as a secretary in some law firm in Plymouth and was bored out of her skull, and I would much rather have been working full-time around the harbours in Falmouth and Penzance than teaching hungover and apathetic students in the classroom. So we grasped the opportunity. I negotiated a price with Archie, we sold the house in Plymouth for a packet, and then moved up here, the proud owners of Seascape.'

'And how did you cope with the change?'

Patrick smiled at Katie. 'Oh, we managed, didn't we? It *was* completely different, though. I had never come across xenophobia before, but by God, it hit us in the face when we got here. I was known universally as "the Englishman" at every harbour in Scotland. Seascape had been in business for five years, but when I started buying, it was always "sold to the Englishman"!' He smiled and shook his head. 'But, my word, it was fun. I remember going up to Ullapool for the first time, and driving down the hill into the town. There were all these boats in the harbour, nearly every one of them was flying a different national flag, and sitting out in the bay were these bloody great Russian trawlers. When I got down to the harbour, I couldn't believe my eyes. It wasn't just fish that was being traded. It was everything! The Russians were bartering with their vodka and caviar, and the Scottish fishermen were dealing in Levi jeans and whisky, and the Spanish were in there too. It was just one big international, free-for-all market.' Patrick let out a scoffing laugh. 'In Ullapool of all places! Stuck right up there in the northwest of Scotland!'

Dan smiled. He was beginning to warm to this man more with every moment that he was in his company.

'But it was hard to start off with, I have to admit,' Patrick continued, 'especially for Kate. We'd sunk every last penny into the purchase of Seascape, so we were forced to live pretty much hand-to-mouth for a couple of years before we really got it going. And to do that, we had to expand the business, and that meant buying from other harbours. It was then that we came up against some pretty shady characters who didn't like us butting in on their market.' He settled his elbows on the table. 'I remember one time returning from the East Neuk of Fife with the refrigerated lorry stuffed full of prawns, and about twenty miles into the journey, the bloody thing just stopped dead. Now, what you've got to realize is that if the lorry stops, then the refrigeration unit packs up as well. So I was desperately looking around under the bonnet, but I just couldn't work out what the hell the matter was with the damned thing. Anyway, having checked absolutely everything else, I eventually took the cap off the fuel tank and it sort of grated as I turned it. There was still sand stuck in the neck of the tank.'

'Someone had put *sand* in it?' Dan asked incredulously.

Patrick shrugged. 'It was a warning. "Don't come back here, Englishman." That sort of thing.'

'What about the load of prawns?'

'Oh, we unloaded this oozing, smelly load of pulp when I got back to Fort William.'

'You lost the lot?'

'Yes. About three thousand pounds' worth.'

'Did you ever go back to buy in Fife?'

Patrick held up his hands defensively. 'No way. Those guys meant it. I didn't want to end up floating in the harbour.'

Katie came across with a mug of tea and slid herself onto the bench beside Dan. 'There *was* one time when you nearly got killed in the line of duty.'

Patrick shot her a quizzical look. 'When was that, Kate?'

'In Italy.'

'Jeez, yes. Now that wasn't funny.'

'What happened?' Dan asked.

Patrick contorted his face. 'I had a new customer in Pisa. I didn't know much about him, but he'd put in a big order and he insisted that I go over there with the shipment. Anyway, I'm pretty convinced now that he was Mafia. I arrived at his place in the evening, and he took one look at the prawns and said that I was trying to swindle him. "They are all *deefferent* sizes," he said. So he and two of his henchmen pushed me into the cold store, threw in a lightweight anorak, and locked me in with two pallet loads of prawns. 'I want them *sorrted* out by the *morrning!*'

'Don't tell me you were left in there overnight?'

'Too bloody right I was.'

'How on earth did you survive that ordeal?'

'Not very well. I returned back here with double pneumonia and my bank balance about five thousand pounds short.'

Dan laughed. 'This is unreal! I wouldn't have thought that running a prawn business could prove to be such a dangerous occupation.'

Patrick shot him a wink. 'Ah, but that's what makes it so much fun. You're dealing in' – he clicked his fingers and pointed at Dan – 'well, you said it. Cowboy country.'

'Yes, but my line of business was pretty tame compared with that,' said Dan, leaning back against the window and pushing his hands into the pockets of his jacket. 'You don't get into those kinds of situations in the City.'

'I bet *you* did. I bet you laid your life on the line every time you made a deal.'

'Not literally.'

'All right then, your livelihood. Weren't there times when you thought, If this deal doesn't go through, then that's me finished?'

Dan smiled. 'Yes, constantly.'

'Well, there you go then.' Patrick thumped his fists on the table. 'I think there are great similarities between us, Dan. Neither you nor I have ever had anything handed to us on a plate. We've both had to fight hard to succeed in businesses that were never our absolute destiny. And that's what makes success all the sweeter.' He glanced round at the kitchen clock. 'Listen, Kate said that you were catching a train this evening. What time does it leave Fort William?'

'Just before eight o'clock.'

'Great! That gives us just under four hours,' Patrick replied excitedly, as he grabbed the two sticks off the chair and began preparing himself for a move to his feet. 'How would you like to see around the factory?'

Katie broke her silence. 'Wait a minute, Patrick.'

'What's wrong?' Patrick asked, a questioning scowl on his face.

'Do you really think you should?'

'Of course I should!' he retorted, pushing himself with a great deal of effort to his feet. 'There's nothing wrong with me!'

'How will you get to Fort William? I can't take you. I've got to pick up Max.'

'That's no problem. Dan can drive the Merc and I'll get Pete Jackson to bring me back.'

Katie shrugged her shoulders. 'Well, if you're sure. Just don't overdo it.'

Patrick gave her a sweet, innocent smile. 'I shall be a model of tranquillity and calm.'

'Oh yeah? That'll be the day!' Katie laughed.

Even though Dan had reversed the car out of the barn and parked close to the back door, it was still a full ten minutes before Patrick managed to heave himself into the passenger seat. Despite having to negotiate the lethal flagstones in the courtyard, he dismissed any offer of help, and there was nothing that Katie or Dan could do other than to stand watching in fearful trepidation as he laboriously wobbled his way around the car, the rubber tips on his walking sticks losing their grip on more than one occasion. Once he was settled in the car with his sticks tucked in around his feet, Katie leaned in and gave him a kiss on his cheek before closing the door.

Dan walked round and met her at the rear of the car. 'Thanks for the hospitality, Katie,' he said, 'and probably the best idea would be to draw a thick black line through our meeting this morning.'

'Agreed,' replied Katie, 'but nevertheless, it's been a pleasure to meet you, and I have to say, selfishly speaking, that I am delighted that you made the trip. You've been a real tonic for Patrick. He doesn't get to meet many kindred spirits up here, and I haven't seen him so stimulated for ages.'

'He's a great man – and a survivor, too.'

'I sincerely hope so.' She surprised Dan by reaching up and giving him a kiss on his cheek. 'You must give Patrick your telephone number in London. He'd love to speak to you every now and again.'

'Of course. I'd like that too.'

'What are you lot doing?' Patrick's muffled voice boomed in the car.

Katie smiled. 'You'd better go. Have a good trip back to London.'

'I will,' Dan replied, walking to the driver's door and opening it, 'and I'll remember your tip about giving the backhander to the steward.'

'You do that.'

'And please say goodbye to Sooty for me.'

'Of course.' She shooed him away with her hands. 'Now go, before he starts getting hopelessly agitated.'

Katie had been right about the weather, only she had been a good twelve hours out with her prediction. As they pulled out onto the main road at the head of the loch, Dan suddenly realized that the mist had dispersed, and the sun beamed through the broken clouds as they scudded westwards towards the dark, towering presence of Ben Nevis. The waters of Loch Eil had turned from murky brown to muted blue and the hills on the far side were transformed to purple and green in their newly acquired light. Even though the ground rose steeply to one side of the road, Dan was now made aware of the vastness of the countryside that surrounded him. There was a mysticism about it, a power in its complete emptiness that seemed to diminish even the need for human existence. Yet, for some reason, he didn't feel uncomfortable with it. It was as if every stone, every tree, every shadow-filled crevice on the hills was saying, 'Don't be frightened. Don't run away. You are quite welcome to be part of our world.'

'You haven't been listening to anything I've been saying, have you?'

Dan turned to look at Patrick. 'Sorry?'

'I was just attempting to point out to you that that's our house over there on the other side of the loch.' Patrick smiled. 'Ah! I see you've got that look in your eye.'

'And what look might that be?'

'The same one that I had when I first came up here. This countryside has a hell of a draw, doesn't it?'

Dan laughed. 'I'm a Londoner, Patrick, right to the core.'

'So was I.'

'Really?'

'Well, southwest London. Wimbledon, actually.'

'Ah,' Dan said with a smirk on his face. 'Home of the well-heeled. Educated at public school, were you?'

Patrick cleared his throat. 'As a matter of fact, yes. You wouldn't hold that against me, would you?'

Dan shook his head. 'No. As a matter of fact, I don't think that I hold many things against anybody. I feel that if you end up being content with your own existence, then you take everyone at face value.'

'And my face fits?'

Dan shot him a wry smile. 'It'll do.'

Patrick laughed and slapped a hand on Dan's arm. 'I like you, Dan. You're a man after my own heart.'

The factory was situated on the north side of the small industrial estate through which Dan and Katie had driven earlier in the day. It was longer than most of the other buildings but still constructed in similar prefabricated fashion. At one end of the shed, next to the main road, a paling fence did rather an ineffectual job of hiding from view a motley line of rusty containers that were jacked up on metal supports, and most of the car parking space was taken up with stacks of empty pallets and blue plastic boxes. Dan waited for a small forklift truck to buzz backwards at speed across the forecourt before pulling into a parking space in front of an insignificant door marked Office. He switched off the engine and got out of the car, and immediately could tell that Patrick's factory was partly responsible for the all-pervading smell of fish that emanated throughout the area.

Dan walked around to the passenger side and held the door open for Patrick. 'Can you manage?'

Patrick replied as Dan thought he might. 'No problem.' He shifted his legs manually out of the car. 'Listen, I'll tell you what you can do. See that shed over there?' He pointed to a wooden building wedged in between the paling fence and the nearest container. 'You'll find a wheelchair in there. I hate using the bloody thing, but the floor in the factory is always soaking wet, and that's lethal for me.'

Dan made his way over to the building, located the wheelchair, and brought it back. Once more Patrick refused his help as he shifted around on his sticks and thumped himself down into the chair.

'Right!' he said. 'I'll start the explanation here. The lorries pull in right where we are now and the prawns are offloaded in twenty-kilogram boxes, and usually they go straight into the factory.' He pointed to the row of containers. 'If, however, we get a backlog to process, we use those for chilling. That's more likely to happen in the high season, which is about May to September, but it mostly depends on how much is coming in from the boats. There's a monitor in the office that gives a readout of the temperature in each container. You'll understand from the story I told you about the sand in the fuel tank that it's vital that they're kept at exactly the right temperature.' He glanced up at Dan. 'Any questions yet?'

'No. Brilliantly explained so far.'

Patrick pointed to the open bay at the end of the shed. 'Okay, then. Wagons roll!'

Dan pushed the wheelchair across the car park and entered the building.

'Stop!' Patrick ordered, holding up his hand. 'Get yourself a white coat and a hat from the hook over there, and stick a pair of wellies on your feet. You'd better get the same for me.' As Dan walked over to the line of hooks, Patrick added, 'Minus the wellies, of course.'

Over the next hour, Dan was once more fully indoctrinated into yet another thriving Trenchard business. He walked beside Patrick as he guided his wheelchair slowly through the prawn washing area, the packing room, and on into the bay where the prawns, packed neatly into polystyrene boxes, were cryogenically frozen in a vast, stainless steel chamber. They stood for barely a minute in the dispatch freezer, where the temperature was kept controlled at −25 degrees Centigrade, as they watched the well-muffled storeman scoot back and forth on his forklift, shifting around shrink-wrapped pallets loaded with the polystyrene boxes. As they went, Patrick talked with incessant enthusiasm about the business, while Dan broke in with questions that he hoped would not show himself up as a complete ignoramus.

'How many people do you have working here?'

'Fifty-five maximum, but that goes down to about forty in the low season.'

'And what's the output of the place?'

'Again, it depends on the time of year, and what the weather's like. After a storm, for instance, it can take three days for the seabed to settle, so it can be feast or famine quite often. But generally speaking, in the winter months we can process about six tonnes per day, but that can go up to ten tonnes a day, no problem, in the high season.'

'So summer is when you put in the hours, then?'

'Do we not! We start at seven o'clock every morning regardless, and sometimes we don't get away until about two o'clock the following morning. That's why most of our workforce comes from abroad – Spain, Russia, those kinds of places. For most of the year, we work pretty antisocial hours, and the locals aren't too keen on that.'

'And your principal markets are France, Spain and Italy?'

'That's right. We pack the prawns according to the requirement of each country. For France, it's one-kilo boxes for the frozen market and three-kilo boxes for fresh. The latter get sent down to Glasgow and are being sold in the market next morning in Paris. For Italy, it's eight hundred grammes frozen, and Spain, one and a half kilograms frozen. The quality specifications differ as well. The French and the Italians, for instance, love greensacks, but the Spanish won't touch them.'

'What's a greensack?'

'A prawn that is carrying its eggs. They show up on the neck and give a sort of greeny tinge to the overall colouring of the prawn. Greensacks are only caught in June and July, though.'

'So, which harbours are you buying from now?'

'Campbeltown, Oban, Mull, Mallaig, Peterhead, Buckie, Fraserburgh. All over the north and west of Scotland, really. However, it's only from Campbeltown and Mull that we buy for the fresh market. Campbeltown is renowned for landing the best prawns. Clonkers, we call them.'

'Surely you can't get around to all these places yourself?'

'No way. I use agents now. They call the office in the morning and tell us what the catches are. There are a couple of small boats that come into Mallaig with whom we deal direct, but that's only because I've built up a good relationship with them over the years. We still buy on the stone weight for everything, even though everything goes out of here on metric weight. Fishermen aren't too keen on change, if you know what I mean.'

The questions and answers went on into the evening as they sat together in a pub in Fort William, drinking beer and eating wholesome plates of homemade steak pie and chips. At seven-fifteen, Pete Jackson, Patrick's production manager, was dropped off to drive him home.

'We'll give you a lift to the station,' Patrick said.

'No need to bother,' replied Dan, getting up from the table

and picking up his holdall. 'I'll just walk along there. It's not far, and I need a bit of fresh air.'

Patrick held out a hand. 'It's been good meeting you, Dan.'

'I've enjoyed it too, Patrick.' He shook his hand. 'Thanks for showing me around the plant. You really have built up a pretty good business here.'

'Yes, I know it.' He gripped his two sticks in one hand and brandished them at Dan. 'Let's just hope I can keep it going.'

Dan smiled at him. 'I have no doubt in my mind that you will. Give my regards to Katie, won't you? Oh, hang on!' He put the holdall on the table, unzipped it, and took out Nina's exercise book. 'I told her that I'd give you my telephone number in London.' He wrote down the number, ripped the page out of the book, and gave it to Patrick.

'Anytime you feel like a chat, give me a call.'

Patrick folded up the piece of paper and put it in the top pocket of his shirt. 'I will do. I'd like that very much.'

Dan zipped up the holdall once more and slid it off the table. 'Best of luck, Patrick, with everything.'

Patrick nodded slowly. 'Thanks. I'll be needing plenty of that.'

14

As Jackie opened the door of the house, the dogs burst past her, nearly taking her legs from underneath her, and disappeared at speed along the passage into the kitchen. She threw the leads onto the hall table and glanced at her watch. It was nearly ten past nine. She felt a tremor of panic run through her as she hurried after the dogs.

'Millie! Nina!' she yelled as she walked past the bottom of the stairs. 'For goodness' sake, get your act together! You're ten minutes late for school already.'

Millie appeared at the kitchen door with a half-eaten piece of toast in her hand. 'We're just having our breakfast.'

'Well, eat it on the way to school,' Jackie snapped as she pushed past her into the kitchen. Her eyes fixed on Nina who was hunched over a bowl of cereal, her eyes glued to the television. 'Nina! What the hell are you doing?' She picked up the remote from the table and zapped the television. 'Would you two stop moving like dead turtles and get out of this house?'

Millie pulled a face at her sister. 'Chill out, Mum,' she murmured.

Jackie turned and glared at her. 'What do you mean, "chill

out"? I was meant to be in the office at eight o'clock this morning, and I'm still here at ten past nine because I've had to walk the damned dogs and try to get you two off to school.'

'Wasn't our fault,' Nina grumbled. 'You didn't wake us up in time.'

'That is not true, Nina. I woke you both at seven-thirty. If you'd got up then, *you* could have taken the dogs for a walk and we wouldn't be running round in circles now.'

'Dad always wakes us twice,' Millie said.

'Yes,' Nina agreed. 'First with a knock and then, half an hour later, with a text.'

Jackie unplugged her mobile phone from the charger and put it in her handbag. 'I really do not feel like speaking about your father right now. I don't know where the hell he is, but he should be here. He *knows* that this is probably my busiest time of the year.' She picked up her coat from the back of a chair and put it over her arm. She took in a deep, settling breath. 'Right. I'm off. Make sure you double-lock the door, okay?'

She looked curiously at Nina who had turned slowly in her chair, her nose wrinkled and a sneer of disgust on her face.

'What's that smell?' Nina said, getting to her feet and walking around the work island. 'Eeeugh! Biggles has done a poo.'

'You cannot be seri . . .' Jackie came over and witnessed the mess on the floor. 'Oh, you bloody dogs,' she whimpered. 'What's the point in my taking you for a walk? That's what you're supposed to do *then*!' She skirted gingerly around the affected area and threw open the French door. 'Get out! Get out, you revolting animals!' she screamed at the dogs. Biggles, who had pressed himself into the farthest corner of the room, moved like lightning out into the garden as if expecting a boot to help him on his way, while Cruise trotted nonchalantly after him.

Both Millie and Nina hurriedly picked up their schoolbags and made a break for the door. 'We'd better get off to school, Mum,' Millie said, a sudden urgency in her manner.

'You can't go yet!' Jackie howled. 'What am I going to do with *this*?'

'You could always leave it for Josh,' Nina suggested as she pushed her sister out of the door in front of her. 'He doesn't mind smelly things.' She giggled. 'He is one himself.'

As Jackie stared with abhorrence at the task that faced her, she heard the girls laugh their way along the passageway and slam the front door on their departure from the house. Letting out a choking sob, she dumped her handbag on the work island, threw her coat back over the chair, and went to retrieve the pink rubber gloves, last used by Battersea Gran for a much more pleasant task than the one that faced her.

She was standing with a dumbstruck expression on her face, a cloth held between thumb and forefinger over a bucket filled with dirty brown water, when Dan walked into the kitchen.

'Hi,' he said airily, as he dropped his holdall to the ground. 'I didn't expect to find *you* here.'

He walked towards her with the intention of giving her a kiss, but Jackie backed away from him.

'Don't you come near me,' she croaked in anger.

Dan stopped in his tracks. 'Why? Have you got the flu or something? Come to think of it, you don't look too good. You're as white as a sheet.'

Jackie was speechless with rage.

'Look, why not have a seat while I make you a cup of coffee? You shouldn't be doing housework if you're not feeling well.'

'Where have you been?' Jackie asked quietly, her teeth clenched.

'Me?' Dan said brightly, filling the kettle with water. 'I've been up to Scotland for a couple of days.'

'I know,' Jackie replied in the same tone of voice.

'Oh?' Dan turned, a perplexed expression on his face. 'Why ask, then?'

'Because I want to know what the *hell you've been doing up there*?' Her voice crescendoed to a scream.

'All right, all right. What's all the aggro about?'

Jackie dropped the cloth into the bucket with a splosh and started tugging the rubber gloves off her hand. 'Aggro? I'll tell you what the aggro's about. I come back here yesterday from Paris, having had an appallingly hard weekend's worth of business to deal with, only to find your mother looking after the place because you've decided on a whim to swan off to Scotland.'

'It wasn't on a wh—'

Jackie held up a hand. 'Let me finish, please. Despite an inordinate amount of pleading on my part, your mother then puts on her wretched pink raincoat and leaves, saying that I can look after the place, the children and the dogs.' She moved slowly towards Dan, swinging the plastic gloves from side to side. 'But the one itsy-bitsy problem with that, Dan, is that I can't. Why, you might ask yourself? Because I have a job, an extremely important job both to me and to this family, and right at this wonderful moment in time, it just happens to be the busiest time of the year for the company for which I work. You, on the other hand, do *not* work, therefore your input to this family at the best of times is fairly useless. So I think it not wholly unreasonable for me to ask what the *hell you were doing in Scotland*!'

Dan handed her a mug of coffee, but she never took her anger-filled eyes away from him. He placed it on the work island beside her and walked over to the table and sat down on a chair. 'I went up there to have a look at a company.'

Jackie was silent for a moment. She began drumming her red-painted fingernails on the top of the island. 'What kind of company?' she asked, her voice now sounding more controlled.

'A clothing mail order company.'

'Why?'

'Because it was for sale.'

Jackie frowned. 'And you were looking to *buy* it?'

'Well, I certainly wanted to have a look at it before making up my mind one way or the other.'

'And?'

147

'It had been sold two weeks ago.'

'Hah!' Jackie scoffed loudly, placing clenched fists on hips. 'You went all the way up to Scotland to look at a business that had been sold two weeks ago?'

'It happened to be quite an understandable mistake.'

'Oh, I'm sure. Pray tell me, Dan, how were you supposing to fund this purchase?'

'Well, my thoughts were that if I felt that the company was a goer, then we could maybe have remortgaged the house—'

'Wait a minute,' Jackie cut in. 'What do you mean "we"?'

Dan let out a sigh. 'I wanted to talk to you properly about all this.'

'We are talking properly about it. What do you mean "we"?'

Dan slid his coffee cup across the table. 'Okay. I thought that if this company looked good, then, with your skills in the fashion business and mine on the financial side, we could grow it into a worldwide business on the Internet.' He paused. 'I just thought that it would be good for our . . . relationship if we did something together, you know, jointly, and made a bit of money at the same time.'

Jackie rolled her eyes. 'And you took it upon yourself to presume that I would give up my job as managing director of Rebecca Talworth to come and help you run some poxy little mail order company that you'd just happened to unearth somewhere up in Scotland?'

'Actually, it happens *not* to be a poxy little company, and anyway, I didn't presume anything of the kind. I just thought that you could have helped sort of part-time.'

'Part-time! Dan, I don't have time for part-time! I work all hours of the day as it is. You could not find a job that is more demanding than mine right now.' She shook her head. 'I can't believe this. I really can't believe what you're telling me.' She looked around and, for lack of something better to do, took a large gulp of coffee that was still far too hot to consume in that fashion. She rushed over to the sink, threw away the remainder of the coffee, filled up the mug with cold water from the tap, and drank copiously.

'For God's sake, Jackie, it was only an idea.'

Jackie took in a few deep breaths before replying. 'Really? And I suppose that if it *had* been for sale and you liked what you saw, you would have asked me to give up my work, sell up my house – remember that, Dan – *my* house, and move lock, stock and barrel up to some heathen part of Scotland.'

'That was not what I thought. The business could quite easily have been run from here.'

'Oh, Dan, get a grip on your bloody senses!'

'Oh, piss off! Just because you think you're so bloody wonderful.'

The door was pushed open and slammed against the wall. Josh stood in the doorway like a gunslinger entering a saloon bar. He was wearing nothing except a pair of boxer shorts. 'What – the – hell – is – going – on – here?' he drawled out.

'Keep out of this, Josh,' Jackie snapped at him.

'I'm sorry?' he said, entering the room slowly. 'I thought by the volume of your voices that you were intending for the whole street to be involved in your little discussion. What the hell has got into you two? You seem to have become incapable of saying one civil word to each other.'

'Your father—' 'Your mother—' Dan and Jackie started in unison, then both stopped abruptly and stared at one another with foolish embarrassment.

Jackie spoke first, her voice deliberate. 'We were just discussing your father's trip up to Scotland. It seems that he went up there to look at a small mail order company with the intention of buying it.'

Josh's face brightened. He turned to Dan. 'Oh, yeah! How did you get on?'

Dan looked daggers at him.

'Wait a minute,' Jackie said, looking from one to the other. 'You knew about this?'

'Yes. I thought it was a great idea. Vagabonds is a terrific company. They make brilliant clothes.' He smiled excitedly at his father. 'What's the story, then?'

'The company has already been sold,' Dan replied quietly.

Josh sighed. 'Oh, what a bummer.'

Jackie spluttered in disbelief. 'You two are as bad as each other. You're just two bloody wasters, ruining your lives and ruining everybody else's at the same time.'

Josh held up his hands defensively. 'Wait on, now! That's a bit heavy. I don't like being called a waster, and I certainly am not involved with anybody else's life other than my own.'

The tension in the room was broken by the sound of the telephone ringing. Jackie walked over and picked it up. She turned and held the receiver out to Dan. 'It's for you,' she said curtly.

'Hello . . . Who? . . . Oh, hello, Patrick, how are you?' Dan held up his hand to stop either Jackie or Josh from leaving the room. 'Yes, thanks, it was a good journey. I managed to get a compartment to myself, thanks to Katie's advice . . . Sure, go ahead.' He held up his hand once more to reaffirm his request for them to stay put, and then turned and stared out into the garden as he listened.

'Dan, I can't wait any longer,' Jackie said as Dan put down the receiver five minutes later. 'I *have* to get to work.'

'Please – if you could just wait a minute.' He walked back to the table and pulled out two chairs for Jackie and Josh. 'Sit down, would you?'

'Dan, I can't—'

'Please.'

Jackie let out a loud sigh as both she and Josh sat down at the table. 'So? What is it?'

'I've been offered a job . . . for four months.'

Jackie raised her eyebrows. 'Well, I suppose that's better than nothing. After all, it's a foot in the door and if it all goes well, you might be kept on for longer.'

'No. It's only for four months.'

'Right. Where is it? In the City?'

Dan shook his head and looked directly at Jackie, anticipating already her reaction to his answer. 'Scotland.'

Jackie placed her elbows on the table and slowly keeled her head forward into her hands. 'Who has offered you a job in Scotland? Not this . . . mail order company?'

'No. It's another one, but it does belong to the husband of the woman who has just sold that company.' He paused. 'Listen, please don't say anything until I've explained it all to you.'

Over the next ten minutes, Dan told them everything that he knew about the Trenchards. Josh sat staring at Dan throughout, enthralled and captivated by the story, whilst Jackie never lifted her head from her hands.

'What an amazing guy,' Josh said when Dan had eventually finished.

'Yes, he is.'

'So,' Jackie sighed, sitting back in her chair. 'I suppose that means that you're going to take the job.'

'I don't know,' Dan replied. 'I thought we might discuss it.'

'Why did he not ask you yesterday? Why wait for you to come all the way down to London before asking you?'

'Because yesterday he had someone lined up to help him run the business. The chap telephoned him this morning to say that the company that currently employed him had changed their tune and were now insisting that he serve out his contract.'

'And that just happens to be four months,' Jackie stated slowly.

'Exactly. Patrick is now desperate. He can't really cope by himself, not after his last relapse. It was his wife who made him call me.'

'I think you should do it,' Josh said forthrightly.

'Wait a minute,' Jackie exclaimed, holding up her hands. 'Don't let's be too hasty here. Maybe this guy can't cope up in Scotland, but how on earth am I going to be able to cope down here? I haven't got the time to look after the place and the girls and you, Josh. I'm having to go back over to Paris in a couple of weeks.'

'Maybe Battersea Gran wouldn't mind coming round to stay,' Josh suggested.

Jackie shook her head. 'This is all going too fast,' she sang out in a desperate voice. 'Listen, there's no way that Battersea Gran can manage for that length of time. Damn it, she proved that over the weekend. She was out of here like a bullet.'

'That's because you were back here,' Dan said. He looked around the kitchen. 'And you have to admit that there's not much sign of the fact that she wasn't able to manage.'

'Well . . . what about the dogs? They can't be left all day in the house. Battersea Gran won't be here *all* the time.'

'Could you do without the car?' Dan asked.

'I don't drive it anyway, Dan,' Jackie answered tersely.

'Well, in that case, I could take the dogs with me.'

Jackie bit at her lip as she watched him silently. 'You're going to take the job, aren't you?'

Dan nodded slowly. 'If Battersea Gran can help out, then, yes, I think I will take it. I'm not doing anything else, and the man is desperate for help.'

Jackie took in a deep breath and got to her feet. 'Well, that's that, then. End of discussion.'

'It's only for four months, Jackie,' Dan said.

She picked up her handbag and her coat. 'Yes. Of course. Only four months.' She walked towards the door. 'By the way, your dog shat on the other side of the island this morning. Maybe you could finish clearing it up before you go.'

Dan pushed himself to his feet. 'Jackie, don't be unreasonable. I wasn't thinking of going *today*.'

Jackie walked towards the door and opened it. 'Well, I would if I were you, Dan. For all our sakes, I think you should.' She walked out of the kitchen, and a moment later the front door slammed behind her.

'Oh, for God's sake,' Dan murmured under his breath.

'Don't worry about it,' Josh said quietly. 'She's just a bit cranky at the minute.' He got up from the table, picked up Nina's cereal bowl and Dan's mug, and walked over to the sink. 'So, what are you going to do?'

'I don't know.'

Josh picked up the telephone and pushed in a quick-dial code. He held the receiver out to his father. 'Have a word with Battersea Gran and explain the situation. Knowing her, she'll be more than happy to help out, especially if she knows about your friend's circumstances.'

'What about the girls?' Dan asked, taking the receiver from Josh.

'They'll be fine, Dad. They're a unit on their own. Just leave a note for them. They'll understand.'

An hour later, Dan had a large suitcase in the boot of the car and the dogs sitting looking rather puzzled on the backseat. He was pretty sure Biggles was thinking that his misdemeanor that morning had been the final straw, and that now he was being returned to the dogs' home. Dan walked back into the house, licking the envelope in which he had put the note for the girls. He placed it on the hall table, next to the one that bore Jackie's name, and then went to the bottom of the stairs.

'Josh?'

'Hang on, I'll be down in a minute,' Josh's voice rang out from his bedroom.

'I'm heading off, Josh.'

'I heard you. Just give me a minute.'

Dan leaned against the banister rail. He heard Josh's footsteps coming along the passageway. He appeared at the top of the stairs, fully dressed in a pair of his bum-showing jeans and a blue parka, a beanie pulled hard onto his black, curly head. On his back was an overstuffed rucksack with a white T-shirt streaming out its side.

Dan looked questioningly at him. 'Where are *you* off to?' he asked as Josh came down the stairs.

'Scotland,' Josh replied with a broad grin on his face.

Dan couldn't help but laugh. 'Josh, you can't come.'

'Why not?'

'Because . . . it's totally different up there. You wouldn't enjoy it. There aren't any nightclubs or venues or things like that. I don't even know if there's a Tesco's.'

Josh blew out derisively. 'Oh, what the hell! Listen, Dad, I'm in a rut here. You said it in so many words the other day in my bedroom. I'm going noplace. I'm sick of my dead-end job and I'm sick of life in London. Even Horace's Inferno has been taken over by West End posers.' He shrugged the haversack higher onto his back and adjusted the shoulder straps. 'I've been trying to think of something else to do for the past few months, but I just came up blank every time. I know this is impulsive, but what the hell, you're doing something pretty impulsive as well. So come on, man, I'm quite willing to do something adventurous if you are.'

Dan felt the unaccustomed prickle of emotion in his eyes. 'All right, Josh. Come on, we'll do something impulsive together.' He put an arm around his son's shoulder and held him tight. 'Nothing ventured, nothing gained, eh?'

Josh grinned at his father. 'Let's hit the road, then.'

15

It was only a short distance, barely a mile, between the Trenchards' house and the cottage. Dan drove hard on the heels of the red Golf as it sped along the narrow road that followed the south shore of Loch Eil. He was almost taken unawares when Katie's brake lights suddenly shone red. She swung the car to the right through a rusting gate that hung askew from one hinge, and drove up a short, rutted track, the grass in its centre brushing heavily on the underside of her car.

'Oh, gawd,' Josh muttered as they followed the Golf up the track. 'I saw this place from back there, and I was going to make some stupid joke about it being our new home in the Highlands.'

The low, corrugated iron-roofed cottage was situated thirty yards back from the road on a small hillock, its three front windows giving out to a view across the loch. That was its only plus point. Sections of the wooden fence that surrounded its small, overgrown garden had fallen victim to the wind and those that still stood were covered with greeny-black lichen. A nondescript climbing plant, devoid of much of its foliage despite it being only September, grew in a tangled heap up the rough stone wall and hung like an unkempt fringe over the drab brown front door. At the back of the cottage, there was a flat-roofed harled extension with a small metal window that was, in architectural terms, utterly discordant with the rest of the building.

'Still pleased you came?' Dan laughed, as he creaked open the Saab door.

Josh leaped enthusiastically from the car. 'Wouldn't miss it for the world.'

They had arrived late the previous night after a drive that had included numerous stops for the dogs and at least three completely unnecessary excursions, thanks to Josh's appalling map-reading skills. Due to his fraught exchange of words with Jackie and the subsequent speedy departure from London, it had completely slipped Dan's mind to telephone Patrick and Katie to say that he was on the way north, so they were amazed at his quick response to their cry for assistance, and even more so when they saw his extraordinary entourage. It was decided over a beef sandwich and a couple of restoring glasses of Glendurnich malt whisky that Dan and Josh should stay the night in the small downstairs spare bedroom, but Katie had told Dan out of earshot of Patrick that the room had to be kept free for him, as there were times when he couldn't make it up the stairs to their own bedroom. It was at that point that the Trenchards' former home, about which Dan had already read Katie's gruelling account of damp discomfort, was mentioned.

'We had a holiday let in July,' Katie said, as she ducked under the sparsely leaved vine and put an enormous key in the door lock, 'but that was the last time it was used, so please don't expect too much.' She shouldered open the door and Dan and Josh followed her in.

There was a distinctly musty smell about the place, and dust, highlighted by the sun that glanced through smeared windows, showed up on every surface. The front door led straight into a kitchen-cum-sitting room, this being made apparent by the presence of a cream-coloured stove, with scoured chrome tops and hardened dribbles of brown grease below its oven door, at one end of the room, and a moth-eaten three-piece suite in a nice

156

shade of dung at the other end. Other than that, the room was sparsely furnished, save for a small fridge next to the stove, an old sideboard with a glass-fronted cabinet above it, both painted in gaudy green to make them look as if they were one unit, and four plastic-seated chairs pushed in around a small table that was covered by a faded oilcloth, and upon which sat two bottles that flowed with candlewax.

'For heaven's sake!' Katie exclaimed, holding a hand to her mouth. 'You know, I think I must have forgotten to come in to clear up the place after they'd gone.' She let out a sigh and shook her head. 'That's what happens when you have other things on your mind.'

Dan shrugged. 'It doesn't seem too bad.' He turned to Josh. 'What do you think?'

'Does the telly work?' Josh asked, pointing to an enormous television set that dwarfed the three-legged table on which it rested in the corner of the sitting area. Judging from its antiquity, Dan thought it highly unlikely that it had been switched on since Muffin the Mule graced the screen.

'I think so,' Katie replied. 'I seem to remember that it's quite like viewing through a snowstorm, though.' She walked across to a door at the back of the room. 'I hardly dare look in here,' she said, pushing it open. She shuddered as she entered the bathroom, built into the flat-roofed block at the back of the house. 'Well, it's freezing, but it's clean enough.'

Dan and Josh peered through the doorway. There was an old cast-iron bath with sticky-out feet and peculiarly bulbous taps, a basin with a mirrored cupboard above it, and a lavatory with a wooden seat.

'How is the water heated?' Dan asked.

Katie smiled as she walked past them into the main room. 'Ah, well, now that's another thing. The stove does it all. The water, the radiators in the bathroom and the bedrooms, and, of course, the cooking too.'

Dan was pleasantly impressed. 'That sounds quite efficient.'

'Quite,' said Katie, biting at her bottom lip. 'The trouble is that the stove burns solid fuel.'

'Oh yes,' Dan chuckled. 'I remember now. It takes whole forests to feed it.'

'Actually, it's not that bad. It's a bit of a pig to get started, but once it's going well, you can close it right down and it just burns slowly.'

'What about getting the wood?'

'I'm sure there'll be some logs in the lean-to at the back of the cottage, but if not, I can get Patrick to order you up a load.'

She threaded her way through the three-piece suite and opened up a door at the east end of the cottage. 'That's one of the bedrooms. It's got a double bed.' She opened the door next to it. 'And there's a single bed in there.' She turned to Dan and Josh. 'That's it, I'm afraid. Not quite the Ritz, but it's all we have. What do you think?'

Dan blew out a breath that was visible in the cold of the room. 'Well, it's the right size for us both.'

Katie took that as a noncommitment. 'I'm sorry. It's not brilliant, is it? I suppose we could try and find some lodgings for you, but it's just the dogs that—'

'I think it's great!' cut in Josh. He turned to his father. 'Come on, Dad, it'll do us all right.'

'No, I wasn't meaning . . .' He paused to get his words right. 'Yes, it's absolutely fine for us. We'll get it cleaned up and heated in no time. It's . . . perfect.'

Katie's eyes expressed relief. 'That's great, then!' She walked across to the kitchen sink, which was situated in front of the window nearest the stove, and opened up the cupboard beneath it. 'There's some cleaning stuff in there, and' – she got down on her hands and knees and put her head into the cupboard, and there was an immediate sound of trickling water above in the roof space – 'that's your water turned on.' She got to her feet and pulled open a door next to the stove. 'And there's a mop and bucket and a vacuum cleaner in there.'

'Okay,' said Dan. 'Just leave us to it, then.'

'Would you mind if I did?' Katie asked. 'I really have to make sure that Patrick's all right before I go to work.'

'Of course. We can easily cope here.'

'Good. And then you must both come over to the house for lunch, say about half-past one? I think Patrick is pretty eager to take you into Seascape this afternoon, so maybe after that you could go to the supermarket in Fort William and buy some provisions for yourselves.' She turned to Josh. 'I don't know what plans you have, Josh, but Patrick said that, if you wanted, he could give you a job in the factory.'

'Nice one!' replied Josh enthusiastically. 'That would be sound.'

'Right then. Well, best of luck and we'll see you at lunch.'

Having pulled the Saab up onto the side of the track to allow Katie to reverse down to the road, both Dan and Josh watched as she accelerated away, giving a short blast on the horn before disappearing around a bend in the road. Dan shot a sideways glance at Josh and snorted out a laugh. 'Bit of a change of lifestyle, eh?'

Josh turned and surveyed their new abode. 'They should film us for the next episode of *Survivor*.' He let out a resigned sigh. 'Could be character-building, I suppose.'

Dan reached over and pulled his son's beanie down over his eyes. 'I'm glad you came, Josh. I think I'd be near suicide by now if you hadn't.' He gave him a macho slap on the shoulder. 'Come on. Let's get started.'

As they walked up the track, Dan opened the back door of the Saab to let out the dogs. Cruise came out like a bullet and stood looking around, ears cocked and nosing the air, as if already getting himself in tune with the whereabouts of interesting females. No scent was carried on the chilly wind, so he lost interest and headed off to cock his leg against a large stone at the side of the track. Biggles, on the other hand, was reluctant to get out. After the long journey, and still not totally convinced that he wasn't being taken back to the dogs' home, he regarded the car as his refuge. He lay on the backseat, feet skywards, with his upper lip curled back to give the best view of his curved white teeth.

'All right, I'm not going to force you to get out,' Dan said, leaving the door open for him. 'You just don't know what you're missing, though.'

If there had been a passing stranger that morning inquisitive enough to find out who now lived in this remote cottage, it would have become immediately apparent to him that the new occupants had survived their years without once putting a match to an open fire. For an hour, Dan and Josh knelt in front of the stove, trying to coax some form of incendiary reaction from a six-month-old edition of the *Press & Journal* that they had found lining a cupboard, a roll of lavatory paper, five unpaid parking tickets issued by the London Borough of Chelsea (courtesy of the glove compartment of the Saab), a flier announcing the impending visit of a celebrated DJ called JamHamFister to Horace's Inferno (plucked in desperation from the pocket of Josh's parka), and a pile of damp twigs. It was the plastic sheaths on the parking tickets that eventually got it going, but the whoops of delight that met this monumental achievement immediately turned to choking coughs of asphyxiation as the damp chimney refused to draw away the dense blue smoke. Instead, it regurgitated it out, along with a good dollop of soot, into the joyous faces of Dan and Josh.

'Bloody hell!' exclaimed Dan, jumping back from the stove and wiping his blackened hands down the front of his leather jacket before he knew what he was doing. 'Shit!'

'Don't worry! It's going to go. Look!'

The smoke was now curling back into the stove, like someone exhaling cigarette smoke from his mouth and sucking it up through his nose.

'Put more wood on it, then!' Dan cried out urgently.

Josh stuffed the remainder of the pile of twigs into the fire. 'Should I close the door?'

'No, just leave it for a moment.'

They stood back and watched mesmerically as the flames slowly crept up through the twigs and then began to curl up the chimney. Thirty seconds later, there was a healthy roar from the stove.

'Right,' said Dan. 'I think that's cracked it. We'll stick a couple of logs in there too, and pray that it doesn't go out.' He glanced at the watch on his sooty wrist. 'God, it's eleven o'clock and we haven't even started yet.'

'How are we going to wash?' Josh asked, staring at his filthy hands. 'The water will still be freezing.'

'Hell's teeth, Josh! What's the point of cleaning ourselves up now?' He swept a hand around the dust-covered room. 'We've got this to do yet.' Josh looked suitably despondent. 'Never mind, by the time we've finished, the water should be hot.' He walked over to the cupboard and took out the mop and bucket and handed them to Josh. 'Right, now for the real work.'

An hour and a half later, they had the place cleaned from Ajaxed bath to Flash-sparkled floor. By that time, the stove had managed to heat the water to a bearable tepidity, and they were able to wash off the worst of their ingrained dirt before taking their belongings in from the car and starting to unpack them.

Dan was shoving a pile of shirts into his small chest of drawers when Josh entered the bedroom, frowning quizzically at his mobile phone.

'This thing's broken,' he said, giving it a shake. 'The battery's full, but all it does is bleep at me.'

'Probably because there's no reception here.'

'What do you mean, no reception? Mobile phones work everywhere, don't they?'

'Not in a tube train, they don't.'

'We're not *in* a tube train, Dad.'

'I know, but the principle's the same. If you're out of range of a signal, then you don't get reception.'

'Do you mean to say that we're out of range up *here*?'

'Probably.'

'But this is mainland Britain. I thought the whole place was covered.'

'Obviously not.'

'Well, how am I meant to text my mates?'

Dan laughed as he threw a handful of socks into a drawer. 'I don't know. Try walking up the hill at the back of the cottage. You might get lucky up there.'

With a discontented groan, Josh slipped the mobile into the pocket of his trousers. His eye caught the contents of Dan's suitcase on the bed. 'What on earth is *that*?'

'What on earth is what?' Dan asked, following Josh's baffled gaze.

'That beige thing.'

'It's my skiing outfit.'

'Why have you brought that?'

'Because, Josh, it can get like the Arctic up here, and I don't possess any other clothes that suit extreme weather conditions.'

Josh laughed. 'Maybe, but you *can't* walk around in a pair of sludge-coloured salopettes. It's just . . . geeksville.' He pulled the bulky outfit out of the suitcase and threw it onto the bed. 'What else have you got in here?' He flicked through Dan's clothes. 'Dad, you've brought at least three of your Armani suits! When are you thinking of wearing them?'

Dan gave his son's hand a slap to get him away from his suitcase. 'All right, mastermind. Just because your daily attire makes you look as if you're about to muck out a pigsty.'

'Oooh!' Josh sang out. 'That's a bit acid.'

Dan smiled. 'Okay, point taken. We'll find a shop in Fort William this afternoon and I'll get myself kitted out in some appallingly countrified attire. How would that suit you?'

'I'm sure whatever you wear, Dad, you won't forego your usual sartorial elegance.'

Dan blew a raspberry. 'My word, you are an eloquent little devil today, aren't you?'

162

At twenty past one, having shared the peaty-brown water of a deep and luxuriously hot bath, they left a warming cottage and drove to the Trenchards' house for lunch. It turned out to be a hurried affair, mostly because Patrick was champing at the bit to get to the factory and start showing Dan and Josh the ropes. By a quarter to three, he had both father and son standing in the packing room, wearing identical garb of a blue boiler suit with matching peaked cap, a pair of Wellington boots, a long plastic apron, and a pair of bright yellow rubber gloves. Both looked awesomely surprised at the speed of their incumbency and at the task that Patrick had set for them.

'Best way to learn about this business is from the grass roots upwards,' he said, pushing himself in his wheelchair over to one of the long, stainless steel packing tables. 'Maria José! Could you come over here for a minute?'

A young Spanish girl with flawless sallow skin and dark brown eyes walked across from the far side of the packing room. Her black hair was gathered in a ponytail and pulled through the adjusting band at the back of her cap, and even though she was dressed in the similarly unsexy style of both Dan and Josh, it did nothing to diminish her obvious Latin good looks.

'Right,' Patrick continued. 'Maria José, this is Dan and Josh.' Sticky rubber-gloved handshakes ensued between them. 'Maria José is in charge of both our packer training and quality control. She's going to show you everything you need to know about prawns; how to grade them, how to pack them, how to tell a bad one from a good one. By the end of a week, you should both know instinctively the source of a consignment by its quality, as well as the destination of each of the boxes you have packed.' He laughed out loud at the expression of horror on Dan's face. 'Don't look so worried, Dan. You'll manage fine.'

'Talk about being thrown in at the deep end,' Dan groaned. 'I'm not the most practical of people, you know.'

'Neither was I when I started in here. In fact, it took me about two months to get to grips with it all.' He reached out and gave

Dan's arm a shove. 'It's important that you do this, Dan, not only to help you understand the business, but also it shows the others that you can work alongside them. It's only for a week, and Maria José will be looking after you the whole time. She won't let you make a mistake. Anyway, look at Josh.' Dan turned to see that Josh had already started to sift through a large yellow box of prawns that stood beside the packing table, listening attentively to what the Spanish girl had to say about them in her husky, broken English accent. 'He seems to be enthusiastic enough.'

'I'm not sure if the enthusiasm stems from the sorting of the prawns,' Dan said out of the corner of his mouth.

Patrick laughed. 'In that case, he'll learn fast.' He backed his wheelchair away from the table. 'Kate said that you'll be wanting to buy some provisions?'

'Yes, and I've also got to find myself something a little more suitable to wear for your unpredictable Scottish weather.'

'Probably not a bad idea. Well, we're only going to be working until four o'clock this afternoon, so we'll head into Fort William after we've finished up here. Then tomorrow morning, it would be best if you both started with the rest of the gang at seven o'clock. Reckon you're up to that?'

'It'll be just like old times.'

'Good.' He turned his wheelchair towards the door that led through to the office, and then glanced back over his shoulder. 'Oh, and another thing. Does Josh drive?'

Dan sucked in a breath. 'He's passed his test, but he's hardly been behind the wheel since then. He always used public transport in London.'

'Well, this is probably the best place for him to get back into it again. The reason why I mentioned it is that, eventually, you and I will be away from the factory quite a bit, and he'll need to have a way of getting to and from work.'

'In that case, we can both take our lives in our hands and let him start this afternoon.'

'Okay. And then maybe in a couple of days when he's got back into the way of it, you can stop by our house on your way into work and drive me here in the Merc.'

Dan looked uncertain. 'Well, let's just see how Josh gets on, shall we?'

'What's the matter? Don't think I can manage it?'

'I'm sure you can, Patrick, but maybe Katie might think differently.'

'Don't worry. I know my limitations – and that's all that matters, right?'

The remark was not made as a lighthearted quip, but more as a firm directive. It took Dan by surprise.

'If you say so,' he replied, determined not to show outright acceptance of the idea. He watched as Patrick negotiated the shallow ramp that had been built for him at the door, then turned to find that Josh had two boxes of neatly packed prawns already sitting on the table in front of him. Dan guessed that the expression of delight on his face was not so much due to the successful completion of the task as with the fact that Maria José was standing close to him and bathing him in brown-eyed congratulations.

16

'That's your full fry-up, Ronnie,' said Eck, the proprietor of the Cormorant Café, as he slid a plate brimming with eggs, bacon, sausage, black pudding and tomatoes across the table.

Ronnie Macaskill held a hand to the edge of the Formica top to stop the plate from overshooting and ending up in his lap. He rolled his copy of the *Daily Record* into a tube and placed it at the side of the table next to the battered black notebook and mobile phone. 'Thanks, Eck,' he said, glancing up at the man as he sidled back to his place behind the counter, wiping his hands on his stained white apron.

He took a large mouthful of his breakfast just as his mobile rang. He pulled a small paper napkin from the dispenser on the table and wiped his hands, and then picked up the phone, checking the source of the call on the screen before hitting the SPEAK button. 'Good morning, Betty,' he said, gulping down his food. 'How are things with you in Fort William?'

'Oh, it's a fine day here now, Ronnie,' the office manager at Seascape replied in her euphonious voice. 'That wretched cold weather seems to have moved on, so maybe we'll be getting that Indian summer after all.'

'Aye, that would be suiting us now, would it not?' Ronnie replied, before taking a swig of hot, sweet tea from his mug.

'And what like is it in Oban?' Betty asked.

'Much the same.' He looked out of the window, catching sight of a seagull settling itself awkwardly on the top of the winch drum of one of the trawlers. 'There's quite a stiff breeze down here at the harbour, but the sky seems settled enough.'

'So have you been buying for us today?'

'Aye, I have.' He reached over for his notebook, opened it, and flicked through the pages. 'I gave you a call earlier, but your phone was engaged.'

'Och, I can well believe that. It's been havoc here this morning. Jimmy called in from Buckie, and then Patrick from Mallaig, so the line has been red hot.'

'Patrick's up in Mallaig, is he? Now, how would he be managing that?'

'He went up with this new chappie from London. Did you not know about him working for us?'

'No. Never heard a word. How long has he been with Seascape?'

'Just over a week now. Dan Porter's his name. He came up with his son Josh, and they've both been working in the packing house to get the feel of the place. This is the first morning that Patrick and he have been off buying together.'

'And what's this Dan Porter from London like?'

'He seems to be a pleasant enough man. He's managed to put Patrick in a better mood, at any rate.'

'And does he know anything about the prawn?'

'He knows more now than he did a week ago. He's been a banker in his life – not a fisherman or the like.'

'A banker, eh? So what happened to the lad that we were to be getting from Ocean Produce in Aberdeen?' Ronnie broke the yolk of his second fried egg with a piece of bread and put it in his mouth.

'The company's not letting him away for the next four months.

Dan Porter is only here temporary-like, just to give Patrick a hand.'

'And how does Patrick seem to be keeping?'

Betty's voice seemed to hush. 'I wouldn't say he's that good, Ronnie. When did you last see him?'

'Not for a couple of months or so.'

'Well, you'd see a big change. He's still walking around on sticks, but to my mind, it's awful dangerous for him. He's fallen over in the office a number of times now.'

'Aye, it's truly a bad thing, especially for a man so active as himself.'

'If he wasn't so active, it might be a great saving to him. Since Dan Porter has started in the job, Patrick has been coming into the factory at seven o'clock every morning.'

'That's Patrick for you, though. He'll keep going to the end.'

'Which could well be hastened, Ronnie, if he goes on like this.' Betty rustled some papers. 'Look here, I've been speaking too long again. You'd better be letting me know what you have for us.'

Ronnie ran a stubby finger down the page as he gave Betty the names of the boats, the number of boxes that were coming off each, and the price paid. He read slowly, knowing that Betty would be entering them in the database as he spoke. *Bonnie Maud*, 4 boxes, £14 per stone; *Misty Blue*, 5 boxes, £16 per stone; *Minch Hunter*, 6 boxes, £18 per stone. They weren't the best, having been caught by deep-sea trawlers working the inky depths of the Minch. He much preferred to buy off the small fishing boats that set their creels close into the rocky shoreline of the Mull of Kintyre. That was where the clonkers were caught.

'And that's it for the day,' Ronnie said, holding the mobile between his cheek and shoulder and slipping the elastic band over the notebook.

'Thanks, Ronnie. Will you be buying from Oban tomorrow as well?'

'I'll have to find out if there are any boats due in. If not, I might just take a ride down to Campbeltown and see if I can pick up some clonkers for you.'

'Well, we certainly could do with some. Mercamadrid were on the phone this morning from Spain looking for some big ones.'

'I'll do my best, Betty. Speak to you tomorrow.'

He pressed the button on his mobile and put it down on the notebook, and went back to enjoying his breakfast.

'Mind if I join you?'

Ronnie looked up to see Billy Inglis, the buyer for one of Seascape's rival companies, standing in front of him. He glanced over to the table that Billy had been occupying up until a moment ago, and wondered why he wanted to come over to his table. Besides being rivals at the bid, Ronnie never felt that he had much in common with the lanky East Coast man.

'Aye, if you wish,' Ronnie said, pointing to a chair with a fork laden with bacon and black pudding.

Billy pulled out the chair and sat down, and immediately leaned forward on his elbows and blinkered his eyes with his hands.

'Is something wrong, Billy?' Ronnie asked, his brow creased questioningly.

'Have ye no' seen the car that's just pulled up ootside?'

'No.'

'Well, hae a look.'

Letting out a sigh, Ronnie laid down his knife and fork, got to his feet, and went over to the window. He angled his vision so that he could see farther up the pier, and caught sight of the ageing BMW, lovingly polished as always so that its bright red paintwork gleamed in the morning sun.

'Och, for heaven's sake,' he mumbled to himself. 'It's the bloody politician.' He returned to the table, where Billy continued to shield his face. 'Aye, I see what you mean. What the hell's he doing down here?'

'Probably bored a'body else on the West Coast.'

'Did he see you?'

'I canna be sure aboot that. I'm takin' no risks, though.'

The door of the café opened and a large man in his early thirties with a bull neck and a supercilious smile on his florid face heaved himself up the steep step. His football-sized head was prematurely balding and those few strands of hair that still survived were splayed out across his scalp like parched rhizome roots in a desert. He pulled off a pair of string-backed driving gloves, finger by finger, before unbuttoning his blue serge overcoat to reveal an enormous belly that overhung the trousers of his charcoal grey suit.

'God's sake,' Ronnie murmured, sliding lower in his chair so that he could use Billy as a screen. 'Imagine getting that stuck in your fishing net.'

'Is it him?' Billy asked, darting his eyes from side to side, trying to use his peripheral vision to catch a glimpse at what lay behind him.

'Who else? He's not seen us yet, though.'

Ronnie noticed that Eck, the owner of the Cormorant Café, had done his utmost to avoid catching the eye of the man, but eventually had to turn from the grease-splattered cooker to thump yet another full fry-up on the counter. The man greeted him loudly, and did a jumpy little dance as he tucked his thumbs into the waistband of his trousers and pulled them up. He had called Eck by name and followed it by casting his piggy eyes around those tables closest to the counter to see if anyone had noticed that he had done so. But no one took a blind bit of notice of him. It was clear that others felt the same as Ronnie and Billy – that being acquainted with the man would do nothing to enrich one's life.

Unfortunately, Ronnie was acquainted with him. It wasn't that Maxwell Borthwick had ever done him any harm or injustice. It was just that he was one of those self-opinionated, thick-skinned, conniving individuals that Ronnie had done his best to avoid most of his life. He came from Inverness and spoke in a thin, whining accent, and Ronnie had always imagined him as the

170

kind of young boy who either would have been dragged off into some teacher-free corner of the school playground to get beaten up quite regularly or, if he was ever lucky enough to be involved in a game with the other boys, would have been made to play the role of 'the enemy'. That was probably the reason why he had gone into politics – to give back a little of what he had received, and to give himself the power that he knew he had so blatantly lacked in his earlier days.

Not that his chosen career had been as successful as he would have liked. When the new Scottish Parliament had been formed, he had put himself forward as a Scottish Socialist Party candidate for the Highlands and Islands. He wanted to see a Democratic Scotland – power to the people and not allegiance to the Crown. He wanted Scotland for the Scots and he wanted to rid the country of the parasitic presence of its landowners, no matter if they were English, Dutch, Danish, Swedish, or whatever, those who lived privileged existences, in many cases in absenteeism, off the struggling labours of those unfortunate enough to work for them or live as tenants on their vast estates. Absolute partition was the only way forward.

It was a simplistic manifesto, yet an emotive one, and during the run-up to the election, Maxwell's words were seldom out of the local press, his high-pitched voice constantly heard on Moray Firth Radio, expounding his views with such nationalistic vehemence that it appeared that he was not going to be satisfied until he had seen every haw-haw-speaking toff living in Scotland lose his head on the guillotine. He wanted a new pecking order in *his* country, and he wanted to be at the top of it.

Maxwell felt that nothing could stop him from taking his seat in the Assembly Rooms in Edinburgh, and he therefore adopted for himself an image that he thought reflected the importance of his new status. He bought his clothes from Austin Reed, joined a new golf club on the outskirts of Glasgow that was frequented by some of the hierarchy of Scottish politics (even though it was a good four-hour drive from his home in Inverness and he barely knew the difference between a driver and a putter). He made sure he was seen at all the events that would be featured in *Caledonia* magazine, and to transport himself from Inverness to his place of work in Edinburgh, he had purchased the second-hand BMW 525i.

However, it was all to no avail. Five weeks before the election, he had had to undergo an operation on a delicate part of his anatomy, and even though he craved notoriety and publicity for himself, he was mortified when some Conservative-voting doctor or money-grabbing porter in the hospital had leaked it to the newspapers. Most of the tabloids had picked it up, but the most humiliating for Maxwell was the *Daily Star*, which printed a short, four-line paragraph directly opposite the right nipple of the Page 3 girl under the headline 'Borthwick Drops a Ball'. It was assured that everyone was going to read it.

Maxwell had thereafter gone to ground, or to be more precise, had hidden himself for a week beneath the stiff white sheets of his hospital bed before leaving the scene of his betrayal in sunglasses and a broad-rimmed hat to return, tail between legs, to the neat little council house of his doting mother in Inverness. There, he had been able to unleash the full power of his political authority by banning her from reading a newspaper or watching any programme on the television. Not that anyone in the media was remotely interested in Maxwell Borthwick anymore.

But then he had bounced back, still fired by his convictions, and found himself a job as a junior councillor with the Highland Regional Council. It was only a stepping-stone, in Maxwell's view, until the realms of Holyrood opened up their arms and welcomed him as a key figure in the development of the New Scotland. Until then, he made sure that he was going to be seen in all the places where he felt there were ardent, 'grass-roots' feelings for his policies. Places like the Cormorant Café in Oban.

He took the cup of coffee that Eck had banged down on the counter, and having poured the contents of the saucer back into the cup, he gently stirred it with the bent teaspoon as he glanced around the place.

'My wordie, he's seen us,' Ronnie said, rubbing his fingers across his forehead.

'Good morning, gentlemen,' Maxwell said brightly, his voice sounding like an over-revving chainsaw. 'Would you mind if I have a seat at your table?'

'Ye can have mine, if ye like,' Billy said, getting up from his chair.

'I'm sure that Mr Borthwick can quite easily pull one over from another table,' Ronnie responded, giving Billy a look that dared him to leave at his peril.

'Of course I can. No need to move, Billy.' He put his cup down on the table, and as he turned his back on them to retrieve a chair, Billy shot Ronnie a sneering thanks and sat down again.

'So,' said Maxwell, spilling his bulk over the edges of the red plastic chair, 'what's the trade been like?'

'Above average,' Ronnie replied, knowing that the man's understanding of the fish trade was below minimal and that he could have said anything. Billy, however, had decided not to be so forgiving.

'Prawns the size of elephants this morning. It's aye good when the boats are fishin' aff the Azores.'

Maxwell nodded understandingly. 'Yes, so I have been told.'

The two buyers caught each other's eye across the table. Ronnie took a drink of tea to stop himself from laughing and Billy dug frantically in his pocket for a handkerchief and gave his nose a prolonged blow.

'So who have you been buying for today, Ronnie?'

'Seascape.'

'Ah, right. I hear that the Englishman is not keeping so well.'

Ronnie glowered at the man. 'Now, would that be Patrick you're talking about, MacSwell?' He always liked to get the accent wrong on his name. He felt that it was more fitting for the bumptious blimp of a man.

'Of course. There's no other Englishman that works for Seascape.'

Ronnie cocked his head to the side. 'Well, that's where you're wrong, MacSwell. Seemingly, Patrick has just hired another man to help him. From London, I believe. A banker, no less.'

Maxwell stared at Ronnie, unaware of the dribble of coffee that ran down the deep, podgy cleft at the side of his mouth. He placed his cup with a clatter onto its saucer. 'Now, that's just typical, isn't it?'

Billy drummed his fingers on the table. 'Whit dae ye mean by that?'

Maxwell clasped his sausage fingers together and rested them on his stomach. 'Well, it just seems to me that there are plenty of good men up here looking for jobs. Why give priority to someone coming up from the south?'

Ronnie let out a quiet sigh. He was a Scotsman through and through, yet he didn't like these 'us and them' ideas that Maxwell had spouted so readily to the media. His own father had been a forester all his days, working on an estate up near Lochcarron in Wester Ross. Ten years ago, it had been bought by a Danish industrialist who had ploughed money into the place to improve its infrastructure. He employed thirty staff where before there had only been ten, and had funded the building of the new community hall, which thereafter became the main focal point of the area, being the venue for the various local council meetings and for the Saturday night *ceilidhs*. His father had always maintained that the Dane would have got a poor return on the capital that he had invested in the property.

'So what brings you down to these parts, MacSwell? You're a long way from your jurisdiction, are you not?'

'Always good to get out and meet the people,' Maxwell replied with a smug smile.

'Does yer boss ken that ye're doon here?' Billy asked, narrowing his eyes at the man.

Maxwell drew himself up in his chair. 'I am my own boss, Billy.

I have been for some time now. I am one of two coordinators of business development for the Highland Regional Council.'

Billy scratched his head quite theatrically, giving the impression that he was totally perplexed. 'Aye, that may be so, but are we not in Argyll at the minute?'

'Well, yes, but . . .' Maxwell spluttered.

'Maybe he was just wanting to give the car a wee bit of a run,' Ronnie said to Billy, a wry smile on his face. 'It's still going well, I suppose?'

'Like a dream,' Maxwell replied, glad that the direction of the conversation had changed. 'I had it tuned the other day by Frangalini Motors in Inverness.'

'Tuned, eh?' Ronnie sang out as he drained the last of the tea from his mug. 'Well, there's a thing.'

Maxwell glanced over both shoulders, and then leaned forward in his chair. 'I got it up to a hundred and fifteen miles an hour on the A9 this morning.'

Billy had taken a tin of tobacco from his pocket and was busy rolling an anorexic cigarette. 'In that case, ye'd better watch oot for yersel', boy.' He licked the paper, squeezed the cigarette, and put it in his mouth. 'Itherwise ye'll soon be withoot yer precious car.'

Maxwell flumped back in his chair. 'Oh, I don't worry about that kind of thing. I've got a radar detector fitted.'

'Aye, I reckon you would have,' said Ronnie, picking up his notebook and mobile phone. 'Well, gentlemen, it'll do me no good sitting around gossiping all day.' He pushed back his chair and got to his feet. 'So if you will both excuse me.'

'Aye,' said Billy, hurriedly getting to his feet. 'And I've got tae see a man aboot a dog.'

Maxwell watched the two men as they hurriedly paid Eck at the counter and then jostled with each other to get to the door. He turned back to the table and finished off his cup of coffee with a smack of his lips. So the trip had been worth it. He had found out about this new Englishman working for Seascape. That was not good news. That bloody man Trenchard had always got up his nose. Maybe the time would be right to have a quick word in the ear of Allan Duguid in Buckie. His prawn business had been suffering from the day that Trenchard took over Seascape. A little leverage on his part in Allan's favour might well be rewarded quite handsomely.

As Maxwell pushed himself to his feet, pulling the folds of his overcoat around his stomach, a mobile sounded in his pocket. He extracted it from the depths and pressed the button.

'Hello? . . . Oh, yes, good morning, Cyril . . . Where am I? Oh, well, at the minute, I'm in, er, Dingwall . . . Yes, Cyril, as soon as I can . . . Well, I can't be there that soon because my, er, car is in the garage . . . No, I can't take the bus, because the garage is here in Dingwall, and I couldn't then . . . all right, Cyril, I'll get there as soon as possible. Thank you, Cyril . . . Goodbye.'

Maxwell's face had changed from ruddy red to deep purple. He waddled quickly over to the counter and paid his bill, then left the café at speed. It would be that creep Cyril Bentwood, he thought to himself, as he pressed the key fob to open the doors of the BMW. He had always seen it as the final insult, having an Englishman as a boss.

17

As Betty, the office manager at Seascape, had hoped, the weather settled into the warmth of a prolonged Indian summer that spilled over from September into the first few weeks of October. The garden at the cottage, which had been a colourless wilderness when Dan and Josh had arrived, took on a new lease of life, bursting forth in resurgence with hollyhocks, larkspur and foxgloves that splashed pink and blue and purple along the narrow border of the property. Even the dormant honeysuckle that had clung so miserably to the front wall of the cottage responded by producing a thin covering of dark green leaves and even the occasional small but heavily scented flower.

Although Josh was working most days in the factory, he found time to plunder Patrick's tool shed for the necessary hardware to restore order to the garden. He pulled free the wind-blown sections of the fence from the tangled mat of overgrown grass and hammer-and-nailed them back into place with a volley of missed blows and wind-absorbed expletives. He then put to use his teenage ingenuity by enticing an itinerant Blackface ewe into this now secure palisade to eat down the grass, but her gourmet tastes turned out to be more for the sweet stalks of the flowers than the rank, tasteless roughage. Consequently, Josh had to hurriedly dispense with her services by wrestling her reluctant form from the garden, during which exercise he was given little creditable assistance from the dogs. Biggles sat cowering by the front door of the cottage, having never before encountered on his jaunts around Clapham Common anything quite so weird as this long-haired, violent creature, while Cruise, who had not scented one decent bitch in all the time that he had been in Scotland, sniffed hopefully at the ewe's backside. The unfortunate result of this failed experiment was three hours' hard labour on Josh's part, kneeling on damp ground with a pair of rusty garden shears, to get the grass to a height that could be managed by Patrick's mower. Having discarded the raked-up piles over the fence to the expectant Blackface ewe, who was now content with any slim pickings, Josh had steered the groaning mower up and down, and at the end of a further hour, stood back with pride as he surveyed his new, perfectly striped and perfectly yellow front lawn.

The interior of the cottage had also been restored to full working order. Dan had managed to conquer the temperamental idiosyncrasies of the cooking stove, his success being such that even with the vents shut right down and with the wood barely glowing, he was forced to throw open the front windows to allow out the heat generated both by the stove and by the hot water tank that gurgled as dangerously as a capped geyser. The walls throughout the cottage had been given a fresh coat of white paint, courtesy of Patrick and the odd-job man at Seascape, the kitchen table adorned with a new oilcloth, while the three-piece suite, now swathed in a mass of brightly coloured bothy rugs, had been rearranged so that each seat commanded an excellent view of the new television-cum-video that Dan had rented from a small electrical store in Fort William.

Not that their new daily routine allowed much time for watching it. They would set out each morning at six-fifteen, leaving the front door wedged open to allow the dogs the run of both the house and the garden, and then drive along the narrow road to Auchnacerie, the headlights of the car beaming forth bravely into the soulless black void of the surrounding countryside. At first, Dan had felt his skin creep with uneasiness at the eerie desolation that enfolded him, having never before driven without a set of headlights blasting into his rearview mirror and the red taillights of the preceding car only yards in front of him. But now, he had come to find it exhilarating, as if every day he and Josh were setting out on a new voyage of discovery, 'going where no man had gone before'. Josh would then drop him off at the end of the road leading up to the Trenchards' house, where Dan would stand watching as the lights of the car twisted through the bends in the road, like the sweeping beams of a lighthouse, until they disappeared around the edge of the hill that dropped sharply down into the depths of Loch Eil.

After the first few weeks of this routine, Dan had tried his best to change it. At the outset, he had always found Patrick in the kitchen, sitting expectantly at the table and beginning his slow ascent to his feet as soon as Dan walked into the room. But soon, it was Dan who had to wait while he listened to the frustrated oaths that rang down the stairwell from the Trenchards' bedroom above. Later still, both he and Katie would sit in the kitchen discussing how best they could persuade Patrick to take things easier while he slept on, undisturbed by the blast of his alarm radio. On such mornings, it was always Katie who bore the brunt of Patrick's fury as he castigated her for not making sure that he was awakened when the alarm went off.

Yet Patrick was not for persuasion. Dan suggested that he could quite easily handle the buying at Mallaig by himself, but this was met with that steely glint of determination in Patrick's eyes. 'Nothing wrong with me, Dan,' he had said. 'Body may be a bit tired, but the brain's still active. Anyway, you've still got a lot to learn.'

And so they had continued to head off on their buying trips together, Patrick more often than not falling fast asleep in the passenger seat as soon as Dan had the old Mercedes in motion.

As he drove, Dan would study the slumbering form of the man, every day seeing visible changes in his features. His face had lost its weather-beaten glow and the skin on his sunken cheeks had now taken on the colour and texture of putty, whilst the sheer effort of concentrating on the movement of his limbs had produced lines on his forehead that were as deep as plough furrows. Witnessing this decline in Patrick's health, Dan now had mixed feelings as to whether his decision to come up to Scotland had been the correct one. Patrick would have continued to use a buyer at Mallaig and would not have been capable of getting into the office so much. He would have had to stay at home, using the kitchen table as his workplace, taking it easy, pacing himself, and no doubt every day getting more and more frustrated and angry with the world. So it was a no-win situation. Yet what really upset Dan was to have met this man with whom he had such an immediate and powerful rapport and to be able to do absolutely nothing but watch as this deterioration took place. And if he felt that way after such a short space of time, he could not begin to quantify the emotional turmoil that Katie had to be suffering.

There was, however, an up side to it all. Dan hadn't felt as exhilarated in a job since the days when he had worked as a money broker on the Stock Exchange floor. He loved the atmosphere of the auction, the wry smiles and cutting banter that were exchanged when he and Patrick had caught out a rival bidder. He loved the postmortems in the harbour café afterwards when they would sit with the other buyers, discussing over a gargantuan and totally unhealthy breakfast the quality of the day's catch. He loved dealing directly with the fishermen in the smaller boats, watching with incomprehension as the spokesmen for their buying cartel gathered lobster creels into a circle on the quayside and sat in a waft of cigarette smoke while they discussed in Gaelic the various offers for their prawns. A man would eventually turn from the group, there would be a click of fingers, and simultaneously he would point to the purchaser and call out his name in an accent that was as foreign to Dan's ears as any that he had heard before. *'Meester Trrenchard, ye can tek eet feer Seascape the day.'*

And then, of course, bringing Josh had been the best thing that he could have done. With every day that passed, Dan realized how little he had known about his son before. Josh was certainly not the useless layabout that Jackie had accused him of being. Over the weeks that he had been in the factory, he had proved himself to be a hard worker, determined to do the job well, if not better than anyone else in the packing room. And that was not Dan's own judgement of the boy's capabilities. That was Patrick's.

Dan also loved having his company in the cottage. Josh turned out to be surprisingly house-proud, something that Dan found most odd, remembering only too well the orderless upheaval of his son's bedroom in London, and his enthusiasm for their home diminished any small feeling of sparseness and discomfort that Dan might have secretly harboured about the place. On those evenings when Dan arrived back at the cottage earlier than usual and Josh was working overtime in the factory, he missed having him around. He loved their new man-to-man relationship, feet up in front of the television, beer in hand, watching a football match or a film that Dan had picked up at the local video store on the way home. He therefore felt a momentary pang of resentment, before giving instant and laddish congratulations, when Josh broke the news to him that, on some occasions, the reason for his delayed return had been due to Maria José, the young Spanish girl in the factory, with whom he had either been going for a drink in the Nevisview Inn or seeing a film at the local cinema.

Besides this unexpected but pleasing revelation, there were other hidden depths to Josh's character that took Dan completely by surprise. After his success with the cottage lawn, which he had managed to transform to a deep and healthy shade of green following nightly floodings with buckets of water, Josh had become quite passionate about gardening, so much so that when all was in order, and when work and Maria José allowed, he turned his attentions to the much greater challenge of restoring the Trenchards' garden to some degree of horticultural sanity. It

181

existent, even though Josh had found a place next to a lone, windswept silver birch a hundred yards straight up the hill from the back of the cottage where three blips of reception could be achieved on a mobile phone. Every night, Dan would walk the dogs up to the tree and call the house in Clapham. Sometimes he spoke to Battersea Gran, with whom he had long and informative conversations; sometimes it was Millie or Nina, both of whom displayed little interest at hearing their father's voice at the other end of the line. But he never got to speak to Jackie. He had tried to call her at work, but she was never there, the first week being out at business meetings and the second week in Paris. He left voicemail messages on her mobile that she never answered, although she did eventually reply to a text. It read only *Taking Josh with you was a clever move.*

The message upset him greatly. He hadn't realized until then that there was this measure of vindictiveness about their relationship. Okay, they had had their disagreements and arguments, but that kind of statement was more in tune with a couple getting a divorce and wrangling over the custody of their children. He sent her another text saying that it had been Josh's decision to come with him, that Josh was now working in a good job and making good money, and that she would be extremely proud of him, because *he* certainly was. Dan decided to leave it at that, hoping that she would now be satisfied that there had been no scheming rationale behind the move to take Josh.

Thereafter, he did continue to call her every second night, but it was always Battersea Gran, Millie or Nina who answered the telephone. Then, one evening, as he picked his way down the hill in the dark, following the winding sheep track through the heather, it dawned on him that, in all their years of marriage, he had never gone so long without speaking to his wife.

18

Dan had no idea that the Seascape refrigerated van was parked at the back of the Trenchards' house. He had become used to measuring his steps in the darkness of the early morning – up the road, into the courtyard, and across to the back door – but on this occasion, it was only a sixth sense that stopped him from slamming his face into the rear door of the vehicle. He skirted around it and entered the house. Katie was standing by the Rayburn, her mouth stretched open in a long, shuddering yawn.

'Everything all right?' Dan asked, sensing that there was something amiss.

Katie pushed the heels of her hands deep into the sockets of her eyes. 'Not really, no. Patrick had an appalling night. He was sleeping downstairs and got up to go to the loo, and then fell over. I couldn't move him and he couldn't move himself, so I had to put a mattress on the bathroom floor and roll him onto it.'

'Is he still there?'

'No, Pete arrived about half an hour ago with the van and he carried him back to his bed before heading to the factory in Patrick's car.'

Dan had no doubts that Pete Jackson would be able to manage

such a Herculean task. The factory manager at Seascape was built like an ox and had an awesome reputation in the heavy events at Highland Games throughout Scotland.

'What time did this happen?'

'About three o'clock.'

'You should have got hold of me. I would have come straight over.'

Katie lifted the lid of the Rayburn and put on the kettle. 'I did try. I left a message on your mobile.'

'Hell, I'm sorry about that. The wretched thing doesn't work in the cottage. We have to yomp up the hill to get a line.'

'That's what I thought.'

'And I don't suppose you could have left him for a minute and come over in the car.'

Katie shook her head. 'No. For all Patrick's bluster and bravado, he is absolutely terrified of what's happening to him. As I was putting the duvet over him, he grabbed hold of my hand, and he wouldn't let go.'

'Do you mean you spent the whole night with him in the bathroom?'

'I hadn't much option. It was bloody cold and extremely uncomfortable as well. I must remember to put a rug down on those tiles in case it happens again.'

'You must be feeling exhausted.'

Katie poured boiling water into two cups of instant coffee and gave one to Dan. 'You get used to it. Most nights, there's something going on. Not usually as bad as that, though.'

'What happens now, then?'

'Well, much against Patrick's wishes, I've told him to stay in bed and I've called the doctor. He's on his way out from Fort William.'

Dan took his coffee over to the table and sat down on the window seat. 'In that case, why don't you let me deal with the children today? I can easily drop them off at school and pick them up later. That'll give you time to catch up on some sleep.'

Katie shook her head, using the opportunity to dispel some of the fatigue from her brain. 'No, I'll be fine. Anyway, I'm afraid that you've got *your* work cut out for the day.'

'Oh?'

Katie came over and sat down opposite him. 'Patrick wants you to take the refrigerated van down to Oban. There was a lorry scheduled to pick up this morning's catch, but it's been redirected over to the East Coast.' She dug into the pockets of her Vagabonds and brought out a piece of paper. 'That's the mobile number of Ronnie Macaskill, our buyer in Oban. Give him a call when you arrive there and he'll arrange a meeting place with you down at the harbour.'

Dan scratched the side of his face and laughed. 'Right. So which way is Oban?'

'Pete has written out directions for you and left them on the passenger seat in the van,' Katie replied. 'He says that it should take you no more than two hours at this time of the morning. It's only about sixty miles.'

'And then I head straight back to the factory?'

'Yes, as quickly as you can. There's a shipment meant to be going out tonight to Mercabarna and there's a shortfall in the order, so Pete wants you back as soon as possible.'

Dan drained his coffee. 'Well, I'd better be going then.' He rinsed out his cup under the tap and placed it on the draining board. 'Listen, if you want anything, give me a call on the mobile. I'll bring Patrick's car back from the factory, so I could easily pick up Max and Sooty on the way home.'

Katie nodded appreciatively. 'Thanks. I'll let you know. It really depends on what the doctor says.'

'Okay.' He waggled a finger at her. 'You just take it easy, do you hear? You've got backup now.'

Dan made Oban in exactly two hours. He reckoned that he would be able to do it in less time on the way back to Fort William because it had taken him a good half hour to get used to the van's hefty gearbox and more than an hour to judge the width of the vehicle on the tight-bending road that wound its way down the eastern side of Loch Linnhe. He telephoned Ronnie Macaskill when he was three miles from Oban, stopping off to make the call at the entrance to the Dunstaffnage Yacht Marina.

The harbour was not difficult to find. As he drove down the hill into Oban, he could see the boats clustered together beyond the buildings that lined the promenade, above them protruding the distinctive red and black funnel of a Caledonian MacBrayne ferry. He followed the mainstream of traffic and found himself quite unexpectedly driving out onto the pier.

The Cormorant Café was an insubstantial pale blue clapboard edifice resting on a pile of railway sleepers and tucked in protectively against the harbour wall. There was a gap of about two feet between the ground and the door, and therefore an upturned fish box had become a permanent fixture in front of the café to act as a step. Dan entered the establishment and looked around for his contact. He immediately saw a slightly built man wearing a pair of brown corduroy jeans, a dark blue donkey jacket and a wise look on his agreeable face who rose to his feet at the far end of the café. He picked up a notebook and mobile phone from the table and walked towards Dan with easy strides.

'Mr Porter, I believe,' he said in a slow, deliberate voice, holding out a hand.

'Dan,' he replied, shaking the hand.

'Good to meet you, Dan. I'm Ronnie Macaskill.' He flicked a thumb towards the counter. 'Are you wanting to get yourself a cup of coffee?'

'No, I won't bother. I've got to get this load back to the factory as quickly as I can.'

Ronnie nodded slowly. 'So Pete told me this morning. We do, however, have a slight complication.'

Dan frowned at the man. 'Being?'

'Being that I have four boxes of clonkers on their way up from Campbeltown and Pete Jackson wants you to take those back with you as well. The lorry is heading on to Glasgow, so I'm going to be meeting him in Lochgilphead in about three quarters of an hour.'

'That's going to make me pretty tight for time.'

'Aye, I realize that, so I'm thinking that it would be best if we met up again outside of the town so that you can get away up the road as quickly as possible. Now, would you be knowing any landmarks around here?'

Dan scratched at the back of his head. 'Not really. Oh, except that yacht marina about three miles north from here.'

'Dunstaffnage. That would do just grand. If you get yourself there in about an hour and a quarter, I'll see if I can drive like the wind and get to you as soon as I can.'

'Right. So where do I get loaded up here?'

Ronnie pushed open the door of the café. 'I'll show you.' He stepped down onto the fish box and Dan made to follow him, but the man turned around quickly and pushed Dan back into the café, closing the door behind him.

'Oh, damn the world!' he muttered, as he walked over to the window and peered out at the side. 'What the hell is he doing down here again?'

'What's the matter?' Dan asked.

Ronnie beckoned him over. 'Have a look here.' He moved out of the way to give Dan his space. 'You see that red BMW there?'

Dan saw the distinctive badge above the grille of the car, its nose just visible at the far side of the Seascape van. As he watched, a hugely overweight man with a head like a turnip and dressed in a billowing blue serge overcoat appeared from the back of the van and walked slowly along its side, casting a furtive glance into the cab as he passed by.

'Is that the owner of the car?' Dan asked.

Ronnie stepped forward and glanced out the window. 'Aye, that's Maxwell Borthwick, our self-styled Robin Hood of the Highlands.'

'What do you mean by that?'

'He's all for taking from the rich and giving to the poor,

188

excepting that he's got his wires a wee bit crossed over what he's trying to achieve.'

'Which is?'

Ronnie twisted his mouth into a wry smile. 'To put it in a nutshell, he would be a happy man if he were to be given credit for ridding this land of all those who spoke with anything other than a Scots accent.'

Dan grimaced. 'In other words, he wouldn't be very pleased to meet me.'

'Oh, he'd like to meet you all right. He knows all about you, but I'm thinking that we won't give him the pleasure. He's a dangerous man, that Maxwell Borthwick. Like all quasi politicians, he has friends in all the wrong places, and his number one enemy just happens to be Patrick Trenchard.'

'How did that come about?'

'Patrick had a head-to-head with him once during a political discussion on the local radio station and he succeeded in leaving the man spluttering for answers. Unfortunately for Maxwell, the programme was heard by a journalist who wrote a scathing report on the man's inability for debate. It was printed in most of the national newspapers the following day. Now, Maxwell is the type of man who doesn't take kindly to being made to look a fool. He'd certainly like to get his pound of flesh off Patrick.' Ronnie pulled back from the window. 'Right, that's him away now. I don't know where he's headed off to, but hopefully, it will give you time to get loaded up and away out of here before he finds out that it was you who was driving the van.' He opened the door of the café and jumped down to the ground without using the step. 'I'd better be getting myself off to Lochgilphead.' He pointed to a large shed two hundred yards away at the town end of the quay. 'If you take the van round the back of that shed there and ask for Tommy, he'll get you loaded up. He's expecting you. And take care going in through the gate. It's awful narrow.'

'Right, and I'll see you at Dun' – his mind went blank – 'at the yacht marina in about an hour and a quarter.'

'Aye, that'll be fine.' He walked over to a small white Peugeot van parked at one end of the Cormorant Café and got in, and there hardly seemed time for him to start the engine before he sped off along the quay.

There were two other lorries waiting to be loaded when Dan arrived at the shed. He negotiated the tight entrance gate with care, pulled the van into the line, and then went off in search of Tommy. He was informed by one of the lorry drivers that it was Tommy himself who was negotiating the restricted loading space at speed on a forklift truck. When he caught sight of Dan and the Seascape logo on the side of the van, he held up his hands, fingers outspread, to indicate that he was going to be no longer than ten minutes.

In typical West Coast fashion, it was three quarters of an hour before the second lorry was finished being loaded. Dan pulled the van hard against the wall of the loading area to allow the lorry to reverse out past him, and then drove into the shed.

'Sorry about that,' Tommy said as he jumped off his forklift and started to manhandle the prawn boxes off the pallet and into the back of the van. 'You'll be Dan Porter then.'

'That's right,' Dan replied, pulling on a pair of leather gloves that he had found in the cab's cubbyhole. He went to pick up three boxes from the pallet, realized that he wasn't going to manage them, and settled for two.

'And how's Patrick keeping?' Tommy asked as he collected his next load.

'Not so good, I'm afraid. He had a bad night last night.'

Tommy rested his hands on top of the boxes. 'It's a real bastard, that kind of thing happening to a man like Patrick. He's such an active man.' He heaved up the boxes and walked around to the back of the van. 'He's awful well liked in these parts, you know,' he called out.

'I can well see why. He's a great man.'

Tommy came back to his forklift and rested once more on his

next load of prawn boxes. 'I'll agree with you entirely on that. Now, I mind the time when . . .'

The story took all of ten minutes to recount, and Dan began to cast surreptitious glances at his wristwatch. He was meant to be up at the yacht marina in fifteen minutes. He realized now why the lorries had taken so long to load. Tommy was a born storyteller. Dan wanted to grab the boxes on which the forklift driver rested his hands and get on with the loading, but he knew that it would be taken as an unfriendly action, so he resigned himself to listening to the whole drawn-out account.

'Aye, he's a fine man,' Tommy concluded eventually, picking up the boxes and thus allowing Dan to dive in for his next load. 'Right, just one more pallet after this one.'

Dan groaned quietly.

Exactly at the time of his rendezvous with Ronnie, Dan slammed shut the backdoor of the van and pulled down the heavy levers on the airtight doors. Pulling off his gloves, he glanced toward the narrow entrance gates, just to get a judgement on their width before he reversed out. 'Oh for God's sake!' he exclaimed, throwing his gloves to the ground in frustrated fury. 'What the hell is he doing parked there?'

The red BMW, which he had seen earlier down at the harbour, was drawn up perfectly into the gateway, leaving no more than six inches' gap between each of its bumpers and the gate pillars. Dan ran over to the entrance, squeezed his way past the car, and looked up and down the street. He saw the bulky figure of the man waddling his way jauntily up the street.

'Hey, mate!' Dan yelled out.

The man turned and looked back towards him. 'Are you, by any chance, addressing me?' he asked in an aggravatingly high-pitched voice.

'Too right I am. What the hell are you doing parking your car there? It's a bloody gateway.'

'Well, that may be so, but there's no sign of a yellow line. I'm quite within my legal rights to park there.'

'Come on, that's being bloody obtuse. There are no lines at all on this street. You could have parked anywhere.'

'And I choose to park exactly there.'

Dan realized that being rude to the man wasn't going to help matters. 'All right, then. Would you mind *please* moving your car? I happen to have a pretty valuable load of prawns on that van, and I have to get them back to Fort William as soon as possible.'

The man's flabby features spread wide into an ingratiating smile and he took a few steps back towards Dan. 'Do I have the pleasure of meeting Mr Dan Porter?'

Dan breathed a sigh of relief, thinking that his diplomacy was working. 'You do. And you must be Mr Maxwell Borthwick.'

The man stopped. 'That's right.' He pulled up the sleeve of his overcoat and studied his watch. 'Well, Mr Porter, I have an extremely important meeting to attend, and I'm afraid that I'm late as it is' – he turned and waved his hand in the air – 'but it should take no more than an hour.' With that, he hurried away with the grace of a seal making for water.

Dan thought about running after the man and laying into him, but realized that it would be a pointless exercise. As he squeezed past the car again, he felt like turning and sinking a foot into its highly polished side, but again knew that it would only lead to trouble.

He was walking back to the van to get his mobile to call Ronnie when he saw the pile of pallets at the side of the load yard. They were stacked three deep and to a height of at least eight feet. He studied them for a moment, then walked over and gave them a shake. They were as solid as a rock. He glanced back at the car, his head to the side as he studied the minuscule gaps at either end. Then he turned and went off to find Tommy, the forklift driver.

Tommy was a complete artist with his truck. Having coupled on fork extensions, he edged them carefully under the BMW and jammed some old sacks and a couple of blankets between the bodywork and the retaining frame so that there would be no possibility of damaging the car. Then he lifted the car effortlessly off the ground and slowly moved backwards, his eyes darting from one end of the car to the other as he negotiated it through the gateway. Once clear, he picked up a little more speed, reversing back and twisting the forklift round so that it sat directly opposite the pallets.

'Are you sure they'll take the load?' Dan asked, having second thoughts as to whether his idea had been such a good one after all.

'Without a doubt. They could hold a lorry up there.'

He drove the forklift forward until the car was inches from the pallets and then continued to lift it until the wheels were exactly level with the top of the stack. He once again edged forward, working his lift, tilt and sideshift levers as quickly and as accurately as a touch typist, until he had the car exactly where he wanted it. Then he settled it down, without so much as a scuff mark on its shiny red bodywork, high up in its new parking place.

As he reversed the forklift back, Tommy turned to Dan and shot him a wicked grin. 'Aye, and there are no yellow lines up there either. He can park on my pallets as long as he likes, which is just as well, because I'm going off for the day now.'

As he sped away into the shed, there was a squeal of tyres and Ronnie's little Peugeot came careering into the yard. He pulled to a halt and emerged slowly from the van, his eyes fixed on the BMW teetering up on its perch, his mouth bearing the expression of a surprised goldfish. 'Now what, may I ask, is going on here?' he asked in a voice that trilled with laughter.

'Sorry for not making the rendezvous, Ronnie. I had a bit of a run-in with our friend Mr Borthwick. He parked his car right in front of the gates so that I couldn't get the van out.'

Ronnie's shoulders had begun to shake with silent mirth. 'Oh boy,' he said, still staring at the car, 'wait until Patrick hears about this. He will surely laugh himself clean out of his bed.'

With a click of his fingers, Ronnie hurried round to the back of his van. 'I think we should get you away from here before the local constabulary hear about your wee escapade.'

Less than a minute later, the Campbeltown consignment was loaded into the refrigerated van. Dan slammed shut the back door, pulled hard on the levers, and turned with his hand outstretched to the still-chuckling buyer.

'Good to meet you, Ronnie.'

'Aye, and it's been a pleasure meeting you too, Dan Porter. You're a man after Patrick's heart, and I dare say that you'll be making a good few friends while you're up here in Scotland as well.'

Dan raised his eyebrows. 'And probably one or two enemies as well.'

Ronnie glanced up at the BMW. 'Aye, that is probably quite an understatement of fact.' He gave Dan a friendly slap on the arm. 'But no doubt you'll be able to cope with that.'

Dan walked around to the driver's door and pulled it open. 'I've coped with worse in my time.'

Ronnie shot an index finger at him and winked. 'I'm sure you have, Dan Porter. I'm sure you have.'

19

The new full-time receptionist at Rebecca Talworth Design Ltd. sorted through the morning's post with practised speed. Even though still at the tender age of nineteen, she had had the experience of working for a large litigation law practice in the Docklands where filing precision had been considered an essential and integral part of the firm's success. She checked each envelope first to make sure that it didn't bear a mark of confidentiality, and then, slitting it open with a letter knife, she discarded the envelope into the wastepaper bin and placed the letter in its relevant in-tray. Once she had finished, she gathered up the contents of each tray, slipped them into individual cardboard folders, twanged on the elastic retainer bands, and then, cradling the folders in her arms, she went off to deliver them to their respective recipients.

Her first port of call was to the office of Stephen Turnbull, the young and, to her mind, extremely good-looking financial director of the company. As she made to knock on the glass door of his office, he looked up and saw her, his face lighting up in a broad smile, and there was a glint in his eye that made her knees turn to jelly. She could sense immediately the involuntary flush that had been brought to her cheeks. He come-hithered her with his index finger and she entered the office.

'Good morning, Carrie,' he drawled, leaning back in his chair and folding his hands behind the slicked-back hair on his head. 'How are you this morning?'

'I'm well, thank you, Mr Turnbull,' Carrie replied, trying to avoid looking into his dark-brown eyes by casting a glance first at her armful of files and then out of the window behind him. A pigeon had settled down to preen itself on the rooftop of the building opposite and it was positioned in such a way that it appeared to be sitting on top of his head. She bit at her bottom lip to stop herself from laughing. 'And how are you?'

'Couldn't be better.' He pushed himself forward and leaned on the desk. 'Listen, let's drop this "Mr Turnbull" bit. This is not a stuffy old law firm. Stephen'll do fine.'

'All right' – Carrie felt her face colour even more – 'Stephen.'

'Good.' He held a hand out for his file. 'Anything interesting for me today?'

'Not a lot, I'm afraid,' she replied, handing him the file. 'Oh, there are the press cuttings from Paris. I didn't read them, though. I thought that you might like to see them first.'

Stephen flicked the elastic bands off the file, and then hurriedly sifted through his mail before extracting the stapled pages of the press reports. He glanced quickly through them, dropped them on his desk, and clenched his fist into a tight ball.

'Are they good?' Carrie asked tentatively.

'They are bloody wonderful, Carrie. They are truly bloody wonderful.'

Carrie lifted her shoulders in girlish glee. 'Oh, that's terrific. Jackie will be delighted.'

'You bet she will,' Stephen replied, casting a smiling glance past the receptionist and across to the office opposite where Jackie sat at her desk. The steely glare that met him made the smile quickly disappear from his face. 'Right,' he said, his voice suddenly becoming brusque. 'I think that will be all, thanks,

Carrie. I won't hold you back. I'm sure you've got lots to do.'

The young receptionist became flustered at his sudden change of tone. 'Right, yes, of course I have. I'm sorry I've kept you.' She hurriedly left the financial director's office and averted her eyes from his gaze as she walked along the corridor to make her next delivery.

Stephen pushed aside the file and picked up the press reports. He held them up, facing Jackie, and brushed their top edge against his mouth. She looked at him quizzically before her mouth dropped open in realization of what he was showing her. He shot three consecutive winks at her, and she immediately understood their meaning. She jumped up from her desk and ran through to his office.

'What are they like?' she asked breathlessly.

Stephen spun the press cuttings across the desk towards her. 'See for yourself.'

Jackie picked up the pages and flicked through them, her face becoming more animated with each one. 'They're brilliant, Stephen. Every one of them is absolutely brilliant!'

Stephen laughed. 'I know. And that's even with Gaultier showing at the same time.'

'Has Rebecca seen these?'

'I wouldn't have thought so. She's still at home. We'll fax them through and see what she has to say about them.'

'She couldn't be anything but pleased.'

'I would hope so. It depends on how the mood takes her.' Stephen pushed back his chair and got to his feet. 'However, I think that we should feel extremely pleased with ourselves,' he said, walking around behind her and putting his hands on her shoulders, 'because it was us who put the whole thing together.' He blew gently on her right ear.

Jackie, who had been engrossed in the press reports, suddenly realized what was happening. She pulled away from his hold and began casting furtive glances around the open-plan office. Nobody appeared to be looking in their direction. 'Stephen!' she exclaimed in a laughing whisper. 'For goodness' sake, don't do that! I've told you before, we don't mix business with pleasure.' She leaned back on his desk, keeping a safe distance between them, as she nonchalantly continued to read the reports.

'What a pity,' Stephen replied, pushing his hands into the pockets of his trousers, 'because I wouldn't mind taking you right here and now on my desk.'

'Oh, wouldn't you?' Jackie asked, without shifting her eyes from the paper. 'And I suppose that Carrie would be in line for the same kind of treatment.'

'She's not my type. I don't go for—'

'Younger women?' Jackie cut in, lifting her head sharply to watch for his reaction.

'That was not what I was going to say.' He moved towards her, made to put his arms around her, but then checked himself and instead folded them across his chest. It was he, this time, who cast a glance around at the other offices. 'You know how I feel about you, Jackie. I wouldn't muck around.'

Jackie let out a sigh. 'Aren't we both guilty of that already, Stephen?'

Stephen grabbed the press reports out of her hand and waved them in front of her face. 'Listen, we shouldn't be talking like this today. We've got great news. Rebecca Talworth is made, and all thanks to us. We should be celebrating.'

Jackie smiled at him. 'You're right. We should be.'

Stephen let out a sigh of relief. 'Jeez, I'm glad you said that. You had me worried there for a minute.'

'I worry myself quite often.'

'Well, don't.' He gave her arm a quick squeeze. 'Listen, I've got a great idea.'

'And what might that be?'

'I have to head off to Milan the week after next to see if I can strike a deal over the rental of the new premises. Why don't you come with me?'

Jackie shook her head. 'I can't.'

'Why?'

'Because I've got something on.'

'What have you got on?'

Jackie laughed. 'I don't know exactly *what*. I'd have to check my diary.'

'Come on, then.' He grabbed her forcefully by the arm and marched her out of his office, across the corridor, and into her own. 'Right, let's check it.'

Having been made to hurry, Jackie now took her time, deliberately flicking through the pages of her diary. She came to the appropriate date and ran her finger down the central spine to smooth them open. 'Can't do it, I'm afraid. It's Millie and Nina's half term.'

Stephen detected the hint of disappointment in her voice, and sensed that all was not lost. 'Surely the great and wonderful Battersea Gran could look after them?'

'God, don't talk about her. She's been a nightmare lately. I get a different lecture every time I go home.' Jackie drew down the sides of her mouth as she reeled off a host of Battersea Gran's requests in a whining Cockney accent. 'Why can't you make an effort to go to one of Nina's concerts? Can't you do some of the shopping for a change? It would be nice if you could *at least* be here at the weekends, so I could go back to my own place for a bit. And why don't you ever phone Dan?'

Stephen's eyes lit up. 'Why don't you?'

Jackie shot him an acid look. 'Don't you start as well.'

'I'm not meaning it in *that* way. Why don't you call and ask if the girls can go up to stay with him and your son for half term? It would be a great adventure for them. Have they ever been to Scotland?'

'No,' Jackie replied with a shrug.

'Well, there you are. There's your solution. And what's more, you'd be scoring a few Brownie points with Battersea Gran by letting her get back to her flat for a week.'

Jackie pulled the arms of her chair forward and sat down, and began kneading her forehead with her fingertips.

'What's the matter?' Stephen asked.

She dropped her hands to the desk. 'I don't think you quite realize how difficult all this is for me.'

Stephen moved behind Jackie, leaning one hand on the back of her chair, the other on her desk. To anyone who might have witnessed this action from the corridor, it would appear as if he had just made the move to read something over her shoulder. But Stephen was close enough to see the goosebumps rise when he blew softly on the back of her neck and he could smell the heady muskiness of her perfume.

'I do understand, Jackie, believe me, I do, but I want you to be with me all the time. I *need* you to be with me all the time. And I know that you feel the same way about me. I don't want anything ever to come between us, Jackie, because if that happened, I just couldn't cope with working here anymore. We're a great partnership, my girl, not only in business, so why should we do anything to break that up?' He reached for the telephone receiver, picked it up, and held it out for her. 'Go on, give Dan a call' – he leaned over and pressed his mouth to her ear – 'and think about Milan!' he whispered.

Jackie took the receiver from him but made no attempt to dial. 'Do you really mean that, about wanting me, Stephen?' she asked without turning her head to look at him.

'I think you know me well enough by now, don't you? When I want something badly enough, I'll go all out to get it. And once I've got it, I'll never let it out of my grasp again.'

Jackie closed her eyes as she felt his breath tickle the back of her ear. 'Would you mind leaving the office, then, while I make the phone call?'

Stephen glanced out at the corridor, then over to the other offices, and finally across to the reception desk. When he was sure that everyone was occupied at work, he planted a light kiss on the nape of Jackie's neck. 'Of course. Good luck.'

Jackie waited until he was back at his desk before punching in the quick-dial number of Dan's mobile. As it rang, she pulled in a long, settling breath, feeling herself shudder nervously as she let it out.

'He-llo?'

Hearing his voice again after so long sent an involuntary shock-wave of guilt through her body, but it was countered by the resentment that she felt at the cheeriness of his reply.

'Dan?'

'Jackie, is that you?'

'Yes.'

'Just hang on a minute, can you? I'm just going to pull over onto the side of the road.' In the background, she could hear the muffled sound of the engine dying as he brought the car to a halt. 'Sorry, I didn't look to see who was calling. How *are* you?'

'I'm fine.'

'It's so good to hear. I haven't spoken to you for ages.'

'I know. I've been really busy.'

'How did Paris go?'

Jackie wished that he wouldn't be so bloody interested in everything that she did. 'It went really well. The press reports were excellent.'

'That's terrific. Well done, you. That's a real feather in your cap.'

'Dan?'

'How's everything at home? Battersea Gran coping all right, is she?'

'Yes, she's being wonderful. Dan?'

Once again he cut across her question. 'And how are Millie and Nina?' She heard him laugh. 'Still watching the soaps instead of doing their homework, are they?'

Jackie grasped the opportunity. 'That's what I was calling you about, Dan.'

That seemed to quieten him. 'There's nothing wrong, is there?' She could hear the concern in his voice.

'No, nothing at all. It's just that . . .' She glanced across to Stephen's office. He was eyeing her intently. She spun her chair round to avoid his gaze. 'It's just that it's the girls' half term the week after next, and I have to go over to Milan so I won't be here.'

'Right. So, can't Battersea Gran look after them?'

Jackie suddenly saw her direction. 'Well, I think your mother could do with a rest. She's longing to go back to Battersea for a bit, and I'm afraid that I just haven't been able to give her the chance.'

'So what are you suggesting?'

'Well, maybe that they could come up and stay with you and Josh for the week.' She paused to hear Dan's reply, but none was forthcoming. 'It would be a bit of an adventure for them.'

Dan laughed. 'You must be joking, Jackie. They'd *hate* it up here. They'd get more enjoyment going to the moon! Anyway, there's hardly enough room for Josh and me to swing a cat in the cottage, let alone have the girls come to join us.'

Jackie narrowed her mouth petulantly. 'So you don't want them, then?'

'That's not what I said. I would love to have them come to stay more than anything, but I don't think it's, well, very practical. Josh and I leave the house every morning at six-fifteen and we don't get back until early evening. What would they do with themselves?'

'They could look after the dogs.' She regretted saying it the moment she opened her mouth. She knew as well as Dan that the last time the girls had shown any interest in the dogs was when the Porter family, en masse, had driven to Battersea Dogs' Home to collect them and Nina had given Cruise his name. 'And they both have a lot of work to do, especially Millie. It would be so much better for them to be up in Scotland where there are obviously no distractions. They could just get on with it.'

'I don't know, Jackie.'

She could sense his resolve falter. 'They really have missed both you and Josh, you know.' She thought that a little friendly

202

laugh wouldn't go amiss at that precise moment. 'Not your cooking, I have to say.'

'Jackie, you have to understand that we're *miles* away from the nearest McDonald's.'

'Scotland's famous for its fish-and-chip shops, isn't it?'

Jackie bit at the side of a fingernail when she heard him laugh. 'That's true. Maybe I could wean them slowly onto my cooking.'

'It really would be an ideal environment for them to catch up on their work, Dan.'

'Yeah, I can see that.'

'So could they come?'

'It would be a hell of a squash.'

'They wouldn't mind that.'

'They'd have to bring sleeping bags.'

'They're used to kipping on the floor. You know as well as I do how many sleep-overs they go to.'

Dan was silent, and Jackie sensed it as being the moment of decision.

'Oh, all right, then, but you'll have to clear it with Millie and Nina first. I don't want them coming up here and just moping around the place.'

'Of course I will!' Jackie replied, stifling the urge to jump to her feet and let out a whoop of triumph. 'I'll build Scotland up as *the* happening place.'

Dan chuckled. 'For goodness' sake, don't do that.'

'Leave it to me. I'll say all the right things. Now, how do they get up there?'

'Probably best putting them on the overnight train from Euston to Fort William. When are you thinking of sending them up?'

Jackie turned her chair around and glanced at her diary, realizing immediately that she had no idea when Stephen was planning to go to Milan. 'Just hang on a moment.' She caught Stephen's eye and beckoned to him frantically. He raced over to her office.

'How did you get on?' he asked as he entered, his voice reverberating around her room.

She mouthed at him to shut up and gesticulated towards the mouthpiece of her telephone before clamping her hand over it.

'Who was that?' Dan asked.

Jackie took her hand away. 'Just somebody coming into my office to find out how we got on in Paris.'

'Ah, right. So when are they coming up?'

'I'm still trying to find my diary.' She put her hand over the mouthpiece again and glared at Stephen. 'You nearly blew it then,' she whispered angrily at him. 'When are you wanting to go over to Milan?'

'I've booked two seats on the Tuesday morning flight out of Heathrow.'

'Oh, have you? Was that before or after our little conversation just then?'

'Jackie?' Dan's voice sounded down the telephone. 'Are you still there?'

Jackie took her hand away. 'Yes, sorry, I've found it now. How about if I put them on the Monday night train? They'd be with you then on Tuesday morning.'

'Okay. And when would they have to be back in London?'

Jackie turned the page on her diary. 'The following Monday morning would be fine. They are meant to be starting back at school that day, but I'm sure they could be a little late.'

'Would you meet them at the station?'

'Yes, or if not, they could always get the tube.'

'No, I want you to meet them. If I'm going to have them for the week, I think you could take a bit of time off work just to do that.'

'All right. Of course I'll do that. Listen, Dan, I have to go. I've got a meeting about to start. I'll text you their train times.'

'You could always ring me during the day.'

'I'll see. And everything's all right with you and Josh?'

'Yes, all's well. I'm just on my way back from Buckie at the minute. Hell, Jackie, you'd have laughed. I had this contretemps with a guy down in Oban—'

'I have to go, Dan,' Jackie cut in. 'They're calling me into the meeting. Tell me another time.'

'Oh, all right.' She could hear the tone of his voice dip with disappointment. 'It's been great talking to you, Jacks. You know, the other day, I was just thinking that in all the time that we've been married, I don't think that—'

'Your line's breaking up, Dan. I can't hear you very well.' She put her finger on the button to end the call, and slowly replaced the telephone on its cradle.

Stephen had not bothered to return to his office, but had remained standing by her door until she finished the call. 'Sorry about that,' he said quietly. 'I didn't know that you were still speaking to him.'

'I realized that.'

'So are we on for Milan?'

Jackie smiled at him and nodded.

Stephen gave her the thumbs-up. 'That's wonderful. You just wait. I'll give you the time of your life.'

The story about Dan's little escapade in the loading yard in Oban was recounted to Patrick, with all the exaggeration of a game of Chinese Whispers, long before Dan arrived back at Auchnacerie that evening. Patrick did indeed laugh, but contrary to Ronnie Macaskill's predictions, he never managed to shift himself from his bed that day, nor for a week after. Dan's reputation, however, was given a healthy boost by his actions, and the true animosity felt against Maxwell Borthwick in the area was confirmed to Dan every time he went into a shop or a pub or a filling station. Everyone had heard the story, and everyone had heard it differently.

Also, it had helped to create a real bond in his relationship with Ronnie Macaskill, a man renowned for keeping himself to himself and having a total inability to suffer fools. Thereafter, no matter where Dan was, Ronnie would call him on his mobile every morning at ten o'clock to find out what prices Dan had been paying and with which boats he had been dealing. Ronnie relinquished to Dan every shrewd bit of knowledge in his possession about buying prawns.

Dan's own opinion of the man, however, was slightly dented

the following weekend when Ronnie inveigled both him and Josh into representing Seascape in a game of *camanachd* against a rival company from Elgin.

'Played a bit of sport in your time, have you, Dan?' Ronnie had asked him during one of their morning telephone calls.

'I used to play a bit of football, yes.'

'That would set you up well, then.'

'Set me up for what?'

'I'm short of a few players to play *camanachd* for the company on Saturday, so I was hoping that maybe you and Josh would be good enough to take part.'

'*Cama*-what? Ronnie, I can't even pronounce it, let alone play the game.'

'You'll know it better as shinty, no doubt.'

'Oh, right. I've got you now. That's a hell of a rough game, isn't it?'

'No, no, not at all. It's a wee bit of a mixture between hockey and lacrosse, not unlike the kind of games that you see played at girls' schools. It should be nothing more than a doddle for you.'

The tinge of sardonic humour in Ronnie's voice as he imparted this information did nothing to convince Dan of its total truth.

'How long does the game go on for?'

'It would just be two halves of forty-five minutes each.'

'*Ninety minutes?* Ronnie, I'd have a heart attack! I haven't taken any exercise for about eighteen months.'

'That's not a worry. We're short of a goalkeeper anyway, so you won't be having to do too much running about.'

'I don't know about this, Ronnie. I have a feeling that I might just let everybody down.'

'Not at all. We're just a bunch of amateurs having a wee bit of a hit-around.'

Having eventually agreed to play, Dan found out later from a knowledgeable, though clearly inebriated, aficionado of the sport over an evening drink in the Nevisview public bar that even those who played for the teams that made up the Marine Harvest National Premier League were of amateur status. He was also informed that, five years previously, Ronnie Macaskill, that unassuming and mild-mannered individual who had sweet-talked him into playing, had been the centre forward for Kingussie, and that during the time that he had worn their colours, the team had walked away with the prestigious Glenmorangie Camanachd Cup no fewer than three times. What's more, he had represented Scotland twice in the annual Shinty Hurling International against Ireland.

It was therefore quite understandable that the following Saturday, Dan's nerves were jangling to such an extent that he was forced to have a number of unscheduled stops at the side of the road on the way from the cottage to the playing field in Fort William. As he nonchalantly viewed the beauty of the surrounding countryside while being stared at by the occupants of passing cars, he wished that he could have had a fraction of the youthful enthusiasm for the forthcoming battle displayed by his bandana-headed son who sat sucking his teeth in the car, desperate to get to the field of conflict and to get stuck in to the opposition.

Having given his team a pep talk that started with a secretive message on tactics and crescendoed into a motivational war cry, Ronnie broke free from the huddle of players and walked over to Dan, who was standing by the touchline, leaning on a *caman*, his designated weapon for the day, staring open-mouthed towards one end of the pitch.

'What the hell is *that*?' he asked, pointing his *caman* at the gigantic goal.

'That's the *tadhal* – the goal.'

'But it's bigger than the bloody gates of Buckingham Palace!'

'Not quite. It measures about twelve foot by ten foot.'

'Ronnie, that's one hundred and twenty square feet! How the hell am I meant to stop the ball from going in there?'

'Well, there would be three ways, actually. You can either

'cleek' it with your *caman*, slap it away, or stop it with your open hand.'

Dan shook his head in desperation at Ronnie's calculated misunderstanding of his complaint. 'Thanks, Ronnie.'

'Oh, and you can stop the ball with your foot, if you like, but you're not allowed to swing a boot at it' – he let out a chuckle of a laugh – 'nor at any of your opponents, for that matter.'

Dan let out a resigned sigh. 'Right, I suppose I'd better get ready, then.'

Ronnie gave him an encouraging pat on the back. 'Aye, a good idea, lad. Take a couple of turns around the pitch to get warmed up.'

Dan narrowed his eyes at the man. 'I wasn't meaning that. I meant that I should put on my protective gear.'

Ronnie clicked his fingers. 'Och, I was forgetting about that.' He ran off into the hut at the side of the pitch and returned far too quickly holding out Dan's armour to him.

Dan ran his tongue against the top row of his teeth, wondering if it would be the last time that he would ever be able to do such a thing. 'What is that?' he asked quietly, looking at the wafer-thin pair of shin pads and the soft leather gloves that Ronnie held in his hand.

Ronnie dropped the meagre collection on the ground in front of his goalkeeper. 'That, Dan, is your gear.'

'You have got to be joking.'

Ronnie gave him a wink. 'Don't worry. Those laddies will never get near your goal.'

The game ended after ninety minutes of play, plus a full ten minutes of injury time, in a resounding 5–1 victory for the Seascape Camanachd Club. For Dan, however, it ended after only twenty minutes of the first half. He had been standing quite happily minding his own business in the goalmouth a good seventy yards from where the action was taking place, when the ball suddenly came looping through the air in his direction. The centre forward of the opposing side, a deceptive little devil who looked as if he trained on four pints of lager before each game but who, in truth, had the same fleetness of foot as Pegasus, covered fifty yards of the pitch at such a speed that he arrived with at least two seconds in hand at the spot where the ball was destined to make contact once more with terra firma. This fractional moment in time gave him the opportunity to steady his feet and to swing his *caman* around his head like a hammer thrower, before hitting a first-time ball absolutely fair and square in the direction of Dan.

Dan stood transfixed, like an earthling who was caught in the path of a mighty meteor from space, his eyes rooted on the cork and leather missile that flew towards him. In the last few seconds before his eternal demise, and as he found out later, much to the disgust of his fellow players, Dan took cowardly avoidance action, ducking unceremoniously and covering his head with his arms. He felt a whistling wind rush past him as the ball screamed over his quaking shoulders, immediately followed by the zing as it concaved into the back of the net. Dan unfurled himself and stared at the ball on the ground, convinced that a few wisps of smoke still rose from its leather casing. The blood in his body, which had been hitherto pumping madly somewhere about his feet, began to boil up to his head and he turned, his eyes bulging in fury, as he glared at the perpetrator of this unsportsman-like deed.

'You stupid bastard!' he yelled as he charged up the pitch, with *caman* raised, like Rob Roy leading the final charge against the Redcoats at the Battle of Killiecrankie. 'You had at least a hundred square feet of fucking goal to shoot at, and you had to hit the fucking ball straight at me!'

It was now the turn of Pegasus to stand immobile, and if it had not been for the intervention of Josh who, just before the moment of contact, yelled out, 'Dad, for goodness' sake, what the *hell's* got into you?' Dan would have cleaved the man from head to foot with one blow.

Dan's reputation was therefore further enhanced by being the first Seascape Camanachd Club player ever to be red-carded from the field of play. Not that he minded much. Josh took over the goalkeeping duties thereafter and, no doubt in part due to the presence of Maria José on the touchline, performed for the rest of the game with the alacrity of a scalded cat.

21

Dan's heart sank the moment he woke up on the morning that the girls' train was due to pull into Fort William Station. He had become quite accustomed to lying in bed for those few precious seconds after his alarm had gone off, listening to the wind lightly blowing on the start of yet another sun-filled day. However, on this occasion, it whistled through the gap in his open window and splattered rain off the tin roof like the incessant roll of a snare drum, thus heralding the end of the long-running Indian summer.

He got out of bed and padded through to the main room, realizing as he went that the temperature in the house had dropped by about ten degrees. Having been lulled into a state of complacency by the continuance of the good weather, he had forgotten to bring in logs for the cooking stove the night before. He stuck his bare feet into a virgin pair of Wellington boots, chucked on a padded jacket, from which the price tag still hung, over his T-shirt and sports shorts, gave a short whistle to call the dogs from their bed, and ventured outside. He was back in the house no more than thirty seconds later. Having dumped the armful of logs into the wooden box by the stove, he began hopping from one foot to the other and beating his arms around his chest to get himself warm. The day was similar to the one when he had first arrived in Fort William five weeks ago, if not worse.

He was standing on the platform as the train slowly pulled into the station, the zip of his jacket done up beyond his chin, his hands thrust deep into its pockets, and a woollen hat, with *Ski Aonach Mor* emblazoned across its rim, pulled down over his ears. He looked down the length of the train at the unsynchronized motion of the doors being opened and slammed shut again, and watched as the drab-clothed mountain folk with their gaitered legs and crampon-festooned rucksacks disembarked from the carriages. And then into this fashionless scene stepped Millie and Nina, wearing such bewildered expressions and out-of-place clothes that it would seem they had just taken the wrong tube line from Notting Hill Gate.

By the time he reached them, the trailing hems of his eldest daughter's baggy jeans were already soaking up the dirty brown water that lay an inch deep on the platform, and she shivered as she pulled her minuscule army jacket around her in a vain attempt to give her bare midriff some protection against the elements. Nina, meanwhile, stood with a set of earphone wires hanging limply from her ears, moving her head from side to side like a short-circuited robot as she took in her new surroundings. Her bright yellow bell-bottomed trousers had started the same osmotic process as those of her sister, while the woolly white collar of her purple Afghan waistcoat had begun to take on the appearance, and no doubt the odour, of a miserably wet billy goat.

'Hi there, you two,' Dan exclaimed enthusiastically as he opened his arms to give Millie a hug. She jumped away as if being set upon by a deranged sex maniac, her sudden movement almost displacing the pair of rain-spattered Oakley sunglasses that held back her short blonde hair.

'Dad, is that *you*?' she asked, her nose wrinkling up in disgust as she visually ingested his attire from head to foot.

'Of course it is. I haven't been away from London *that* long, have I?'

'Why are you dressed like such a prat?'

Dan snorted out a laugh, realizing now why his initial meeting with Katie at this exact venue must have seemed like the first-time encounter of ET and its young earthling mate. 'Don't worry. You'll soon find out.' He leaned over and gave Millie an unreciprocated kiss on each of her freezing cheeks before turning his attentions to Nina. He needn't have bothered. She could have been set upon by that deranged sex maniac without even a look of surprise flashing across her sleet-stung features.

'Ni, aren't you going to say hello?' Dan asked, his head held to the side as he waited for some kind of reaction to their meeting.

The sideways movement of Nina's head eventually sped up to a definite shake of negativity. 'This has to be the arsehole of the world,' she said in a voice that would seem that she had just found herself eternally condemned to the depths of Satan's empire.

'Oh, it's not that bad,' Dan retorted cheerfully, 'although it is a real pity that it's raining today. We've just had a month of nothing but sun.'

Nina chucked back her head. 'Typical,' she tutted as she bent down and heaved up her canvas bag, its sides cascading off rivulets of icy rain.

Dan swept up Millie's suitcase and relieved Nina of her load. 'Come on, we'll get you back to the cottage. It's really cosy there. You'll be warm again in no time.' He had taken no more than a dozen steps towards the exit of the station before the cases were once more dropped to the ground, and he stood exercising his cramped and aching fingers.

'What the hell have you brought with you? Bags of cement?'

'I wish,' Millie replied morosely, tucking her hands under her armpits to keep them warm. 'Mum made us bring all our schoolbooks with us. Some half term this is going to turn out to be.'

They drove back to the cottage alongside the murky waters of Loch Eil, and once again Dan wished that the Indian summer could have held out for just a week longer. The air of despondency

214

inside the fuggy interior of Patrick's Mercedes was almost tangible, and Dan could tell that the false gaiety in his voice as he pointed out mist-shrouded landmarks was getting very close to manic level. The car, in fact, had been the only thing to date that had brought any kind of verbal comment from Nina.

'We had a car like this once, but it had leather seats and was much newer.'

It got worse. As Dan pulled into the lane that led up to the cottage, Nina, who had been sitting alone in the back of the car and had been trying to stave off the slavering attention of the dogs all the way from Fort William, suddenly burst into floods of tears. Dan glanced in the rearview mirror at the collapsed face of his younger daughter. 'Ni, what is it?' he asked concernedly.

'I want to go home,' she choked out in long, stuttering sobs. 'This is the worst place I've ever been to in my life.'

'Well, you can't go home,' Millie retorted with feeling. 'We've been banished, remember.'

'That's enough, Millie,' Dan said quietly out of the side of his mouth.

'But I had two parties to go to, and Barney was going to be at one of them.'

Dan stopped the car at the top of the lane, jumped out and opened up the rear passenger door, and got in beside his daughter. He put his arm around her and gave her a hug. 'It's only going to be for a week, Ni, and anyway, you'll enjoy yourself. Just wait and see.'

'But what's there to *do* up here?' Nina howled.

'Well,' Dan said slowly, trying desperately to think of something moderately exciting to lift his younger daughter's shattered spirits. 'Quite a lot, really.'

Millie, meanwhile, had decided to get into the promised warmth of the cottage as quickly as possible. Having got out of the car, she skipped from side to side up to the gate, doing her best not to get the track's now slimy mud on any part of her new silver-grey Reebok trainers. She was in the process of working

215

out Josh's complicated but totally dog-proof latch system, when she suddenly turned and raced back to the car at the speed of an Olympic sprinter, cares for her fancy footwear cast frivolously to the biting wind. She tore the car door open, jumped in, and slammed it shut.

'My God, that thing is *terrifying*!' she screamed out melodramatically, her eyes fixed on the far corner of the cottage. 'What *is* it, Dad?'

Her voice had expressed such fear and alarm that even Dan wondered momentarily whether he had been unconsciously living in the depths of Jurassic Park for the past five weeks. Then, around the edge of the wooden fence at the front of the garden, appeared the fiercely horned head of Dolly, the resident Blackface ewe, a piece of grass sticking out the side of her mouth and an expression on her face that would seem to suggest that she was deeply miffed that her welcome had been so mannerlessly rebuffed.

'Don't worry,' said Dan, taking his arm from around the heaving shoulders of his younger daughter and getting out of the car. 'That's just Dolly. She's as harmless as a . . .' He didn't bother to finish. He couldn't think of any happy, pleasing simile that would make any bloody difference to his daughters' miserable appraisal of their new surroundings. 'Come on, you two,' he sighed, 'out you get. It's time to survey the Taj Mahal.'

They declined the bacon and eggs that Josh had generously left for them on top of the cooking stove and breakfasted in silence on cereal and yoghurt, casting looks around the room and then at each other, lifting an eyebrow in foreboding of what they were to suffer during the course of their mid-term break. Dan whistled a merry tune as he went about his domestic chores, hoping that the false contentment that he displayed over his Spartan abode might in some way be infective enough to rub off on the girls. It was, indeed, a tall order.

'I have to go to work now,' he said as he returned the dustpan and brush to the cupboard next to the sink, 'so I would suggest

216

that you just get yourselves settled in. The telly works well enough and there are a few videos on the shelf over there. All I ask is that you keep the stove going, because that does everything here – the cooking, the heating and the hot water.' He proceeded to give a demonstration on the art of replenishing the boiler that would have worked well at playschool. 'You take the wood from here,' he said, picking up a log from the box and holding it out to show them what a log looked like, 'and then you take it to the stove and you open this door, like this, and then you put the log inside, and close the door again. Simple as that.'

'Ooh, do you think that we can manage that, Nina?' Millie squeaked in a little girl's voice. 'It looks *awfully* difficult.'

Dan laughed. 'All right. Just don't forget to do it, okay?'

'When will you be back?' Nina asked.

'No later than six o'clock.'

'*Six o'clock*? You're leaving us here all by ourselves until *six o'clock*?'

'I'm sorry, but I do have to work, Ni. You'll be all right. The dogs will be with you.'

Nina eyed disdainfully the two slumbering forms on the rug in front of the stove. 'Thanks a bunch.'

'I will have the weekend off,' Dan continued, feeling a sudden guilt about his departure. 'We'll all go off and do something together.'

'When does Josh get back, then?' Millie asked.

'That depends.'

'On what?'

'On whether he's finishing early or late at the factory and whether he's seeing Maria José. He usually gets back at—'

'Maria *what*?' Millie interjected, her eyes fixed questioningly on her father.

Dan bit at his tongue, wishing that he hadn't said anything. 'Maria José.'

He watched the girls' eyes sparkle as they looked at each other. 'Josh doesn't have a *girlfriend*, does he?'

217

'Well, yes, he does, as a matter of fact.'

'God, she must be blind or something,' Millie scoffed.

'Or so ugly that she can't find anyone else to go out with,' Nina added with a giggle.

'Or an illegal immigrant who needs to find someone to marry her so that she can stay in this country,' Millie continued.

'Well, you're both completely wrong about everything. Maria José is a very beautiful and intelligent girl, and she is obviously extremely fond of Josh, otherwise she wouldn't be going out with him.'

'What does she do?'

'She works in the prawn factory with Josh.'

Millie let out a derisive laugh. 'Come on, Dad, she couldn't be *that* intelligent if she works in a *prawn* factory!'

'And she must smell *horrible* as well,' Nina remarked as she feigned a vomit. 'Think of those *fingers* running through Josh's hair!'

Dan shook his head. 'All right, I've had enough of you two for now. I'm going. Have you brought your mobiles with you?'

'Of course we have,' said Millie. 'We want *some* kind of contact with the outside world.'

'Well, in that case, give me a call if you want anything. You'll have to walk up the hill at the back of the house if you want to get a signal, though. There's small tree up there where you'll find that it works.'

Nina stared fixedly at her father for a moment, then turned to her elder sister and slowly shook her head. 'You see,' she said miserably, 'this is the arsehole of the world.'

The weather during the next three days did nothing to disprove Nina's opinion of the place. They never ventured from the confines of their Highland prison and even suffered the self-imposed torture of being *ex-text-communicado* with their friends in London. On the first evening, while they had sat watching television, Millie had walked around the room, climbing up onto various bits of furniture, and while tottering precariously on her perch, had gazed fixedly at the screen of her mobile phone in the hope that even one blip of reception signal would appear. Eventually, the precious phone had been unlovingly discarded into her suitcase, its usefulness done, and she had flumped down onto the sofa between Nina and Josh to watch the film *Ten Things I Hate About You* for the fifth time.

There were, however, moments of diversion. On the Tuesday evening, Josh bravely took the girls with him into Fort William where they met up with Maria José for a drink in the Nevisview Inn. Neither Millie nor Nina contributed much to the flow of conversation, but instead sat picking their fingernails and staring at the dark-eyed Spanish girl, trying to find something about her that they could criticize. When Dan asked them on their return how they had got on, and whether they had liked Maria José, the girls, having been able to find a blemish neither in her character nor on her face, simply grunted and within five minutes had slipped themselves wordlessly into the comforting depths of their sleeping bags. All that Dan had done, thereafter, was to shoot a knowing wink at his son.

The following evening, they were asked over to Auchnacerie for supper. Dan had at first thought about suggesting that he should cook the meal, but then remembered that his daughters did not hold his culinary delights in such high esteem as did the Trenchard family. So he left it to Katie to produce exactly what was required – hamburgers, baked beans and chips – and for the first time since Millie and Nina had been in Scotland, Dan watched with relief how the simple comforts of fast food brought smiles back to their faces. With a good deal of help from Josh, Patrick made it to the supper table, his face drawn and dark rings under his eyes, but his indomitable spirit still burning as fiercely as a bush fire. He teased Millie rotten over her taste in clothes, and then suggested that Nina should hang on for Max, because even though he was five years her junior, he was going to be some looker. What delighted and surprised Dan was the way in which the girls took the ribbing, and Millie even gave back as good as she got when she told Patrick that his hairstyle was at the height of fashion – for scarecrows. Sitting next to Katie at the top end of the table, Dan caught her eye during the meal and the look that passed between read only that things were surely turning for the good. By the end of the evening, a slight flush of colour had returned to Patrick's pallid features, and there seemed at last to be the beginnings of a mild acceptance by Millie and Nina that their week's sojourn in the wild, unfashionable wastes of northern Scotland wasn't going to turn out as badly as they had at first predicted.

On the Friday morning, the wind dropped and the rain clouds once more moved off eastwards over the tall stack of Ben Nevis, leaving the adjacent waters of Loch Eil and Loch Linnhe bathed by a pale autumnal sun. Before slipping quietly from the house, Dan left a note on the kitchen table for the girls saying that he felt they had done enough homework for the week, and that they should take things easy for the day. He added that they should maybe take advantage of the good weather and walk up to the tree and telephone their mother to tell her how they were getting on. However, he had little doubt in his mind that they would treat the day in similar fashion to those that had gone before, and that when he returned from work, they would still be lying prostrate on the sofas, tucked into their sleeping bags with their eyes glued to the television.

That evening, therefore, it was with considerable surprise and a certain amount of consternation that he read the note that lay alongside his own on the kitchen table. It was written in Millie's flourishing scrawl.

Dad,
It's such a beautiful day that we have decided to go up to the tree to phone Mum and then take the dogs for a walk. We'll probably be back before you get the chance to read this, but thought I should just let you know.

Love Millie

Dan dropped the note on the table and glanced out of the window. Darkness was beginning to shroud the hills opposite, and already he could make out a pair of headlights darting through the trees on the road at the other side of the loch. He shrugged his jacket back on again and walked out into the garden, feeling the night drop its invisible veil of chilling dampness over him. He hurried round to the back of the cottage and ran up the hill to the tree. There, on the ground, he found a newly discarded Hollywood chewing gum wrapper. They had definitely been there.

'Oh, for heaven's sake! Where have you got to, you silly girls,' he murmured under his breath as he pressed on up the hill. He felt beads of sweat break out on his forehead at the effort of the climb and the constant lifting of his feet to clear the tall, springy heather, but they turned cold as they trickled between his eyebrows and down the side of his nose. Just as he reached the top of the hill, he fell flat on his face in the heather, his shoe having lost its grip on a lichen-covered stone. He pushed himself back to his feet and stood motionless, looking around him.

'Oh my God,' he said slowly.

He had never ventured that far up the hill before. In the near-darkness, he could see now that nothing lay beyond its summit except total emptiness. He could walk on and never stop, and he prayed to God that that was not what Millie and Nina and the dogs had chosen to do. He yelled out their names, but his voice was lost to the rising wind. He tried to whistle in a vain attempt to attract the dogs' attention, but his mouth had gone dry, and all that came out was a pathetic exhalation of air. He turned and began to make his way clumsily down the hill, fumbling in the jacket pocket for his mobile phone. He stopped long enough to get Josh's number up onto the screen, and then continued his descent, bouncing over the heather, with the phone clamped to his ear.

'Josh?'

'Hi, Dad. How are things?'

'Where are you?'

'Just leaving work. I'm going to come straight home this evening.'

'Josh, the girls have gone.'

'Have they? Where?'

'I don't bloody know. They left a note for me on the kitchen table, saying that they were going off for a walk. They're not back, Josh.'

'Oh, they'll be fine, Dad. Those girls have never walked farther than the length of Portobello market in their lives.'

'But I found a chewing gum wrapper up by the tree.'

'Ah, I see what you mean. So where are you at the minute?'

'I'm on my way back down to the cottage. Josh, if they're up on the hill, they'll never find their way back. They'll be lost, Josh.'

'What do you think we should do?'

'I've no idea.' Dan stopped to catch his breath. 'Yes, actually, I do. Go to the police station, Josh. Tell them that your two sisters left the cottage this afternoon at about three o'clock with two dogs and that they haven't returned. Give them descriptions and anything they want to know, and tell them that we'll need to get search parties out looking for them as soon as possible.'

'That's a bit serious, Dad. Do you really think it's that bad?'

'Too right, I do. I think they're in a heap of trouble.'

'What are you going to do?'

'I'll take the car along to Auchnacerie to find out if they've been there. If not, I'll call you back from the Trenchards' phone.'

'All right.' Josh paused on the line. 'Dad?'

'What is it?'

'I'm sure they'll be fine. I can usually sense if something's gone wrong.'

Dan silently blessed his son's ability to come out with the right words at the right time. It had been exactly that way when they had sat together watching the towers of the World Trade Center crumble to the ground. 'I hope you're right, Josh. I pray to God that you're right.'

He burst into the kitchen at Auchnacerie without so much

as a knock on the door, and found every member of the Trenchard family present, each occupied with a different project. Max lay on the sofa, fingers flicking the controls of a PlayStation as he stared intently at the darting figures and flashing laser beams that filled the television screen; Sooty was at one end of the kitchen table, absorbed in yet another pictorial masterpiece; while Patrick and Katie, seated at the other end, entered data onto the laptop computer from the untidy pile of bills and receipts that Patrick had in front of him. They were immediately united by their looks of surprise and concern when Dan entered.

'Everything all right, Dan?' Patrick asked, peering over a pair of half-moon reading glasses.

'You haven't by any chance seen Millie and Nina, have you?'

Patrick looked across at his wife. She shrugged her shoulders. 'No. Why? Are they not at the cottage?'

Dan let out a deep sigh of despair. 'They went off for a walk at about three o'clock with the dogs and they haven't returned.'

'Oh, for goodness' sake!' Katie exclaimed, getting up from her seat and pushing her way past Sooty. 'Have you any idea where they've gone?'

'No, but I've a horrible suspicion that they could have gone over the top of the hill at the back of the cottage.'

Patrick began to push himself to his feet. 'Kate, get on the phone to the police station in Fort William.'

'Don't bother to get up, Patrick,' Dan said. 'I've already done that. At least, I've called Josh and asked him to go round to tell them that they're missing.'

'I don't think they'll have gone very far,' Max said, sending a laser beam towards a grotesque creature that exploded in a splat of computer-generated gore. 'They're not the type.'

'That's enough, Max,' Patrick said sharply to him. 'This is really quite serious, you know.'

'That's all right,' Dan said. 'Josh said exactly the same thing. Would you mind if I called him to say that they're not here?'

Patrick gestured towards the telephone. 'Of course. Go ahead.'

Katie put a hand on Dan's arm as he went to pick up the receiver. 'I'm sure that they'll be all right, Dan. They can't have gone that far.'

'But this countryside is bloody treacherous, Katie!' Dan said vehemently, getting frustrated by their calmness. He began forcefully dialling Josh's number. 'I'm always reading in the papers about people being found dead up in the bloody Highlands. I mean, they're not even prepared for the weather up here. The kind of clothes they're wearing wouldn't keep an ant warm.'

Sooty sat with her pencil raised in the air, as if asking for permission to speak in a classroom. 'Dan the Man?'

'You said that they had the dogs with them,' Patrick stated.

'Yes.'

'Well, that's good, because they've been here long enough to get their bearings. What's more, if they do have to send out the search dogs for the girls, then' – Patrick caught Katie's eye and saw from her expression that she thought he should tone it down a bit – 'well, it'll help anyway.'

Sooty now supported her tiring arm with a hand under the elbow. Once more she tried to get a word in. 'Dan the Man?'

'Josh, it's Dad,' Dan said into the receiver.

Katie turned to her daughter. 'What *is* it, Sooty? Can't you see that Dan is on the phone?' She softened her voice. 'We're all a bit worried, angel, because Millie and Nina have gone missing somewhere.'

'I *know*.'

'So why don't you just get on with your drawing so that we can work out what best can be done to help find them?'

'But I don't think that they *need* to be found.' Sooty was all at once set upon by four sets of staring eyes. She wondered what she had said wrong *now*. 'Well, anyway, not up the hill,' she said quietly as she got on with her drawing.

The telephone was slammed down mid-sentence and Sooty suddenly found herself hemmed in on the bench by Katie and Dan.

'What do you mean, Sooty?' Katie asked her daughter.

'I *saw* Millie and Nina out of the window there.' She pointed out into the darkness. 'They were on the road and I waved to them, and they waved back.'

'Can you remember when this was?' Dan asked.

'When Mummy went to get Max from school. Daddy had gone to the loo, and I was sitting here by myself.'

Dan looked over the top of Sooty's curly black head at Katie. 'What time would that have been?'

'About quarter past four,' Katie replied.

Thumping his elbows onto the table, Dan slapped his hands to his forehead and let out a long sigh of relief. 'Thank goodness for that! At least they're not up on the hill.' He bent over and gave Sooty a kiss on the top of her head. 'Thanks, Sooty, you are a wonder girl.' He jumped to his feet and went back over to the telephone and dialled Josh's number.

'Josh?'

'Have you found them?'

'No, not yet.'

'Oh.' Josh's voice dropped in disappointment. 'I thought that when you hung up just then—'

'Sooty saw them earlier this afternoon, Josh, so they're not up the hill.'

Dan heard his son let out a long sigh. 'Well, that's something, anyway. Where were they heading?'

Dan looked over to where Sooty was continuing with her drawing. 'Can you remember which way they were going, Sooty?'

'That way,' Sooty replied, pointing the rubber on her pencil westwards. 'They were going towards the bridge at the top of the loch.'

'They were heading towards the main road, Josh.'

'Right, I'll tell the police.'

'Are you at the station?'

'Yes. They've got the Mountain Rescue Team on standby.'

'Well, tell them that I don't think that we'll be needing them, but could you ask the police to check the main road between

Kinlocheil and Fort William? I'll go out myself to see if I can find them. You'd better stay there just in case any word of their whereabouts comes through.'

'Okay.'

'Well done, Josh. And thanks.'

'No worries. I was right, you see, Dad. The girls are going to be fine.'

'I hope so, Josh. We've still got to find them, though.'

The telephone call came through just as Dan was moving off in the car from Auchnacerie. Katie came rushing out of the house and banged on the back window to stop him.

'They've been found, Dan.'

Dan jumped out of the car. 'Thank heavens! Where?' he said, walking quickly ahead of Katie into the house.

'Glenfinnan.'

'*Glenfinnan*? What on earth were they doing there?' He entered the kitchen and picked up the receiver from the sideboard. 'Hello?'

'Is that Mr Dan Porter?' The man spoke with a slow, easy accent that did little to accentuate the urgency of the situation.

'Yes, it is.'

'This is Constable Lamond here of the Northern Constabulary.'

Dan hurried him for information. 'You've found my daughters, Constable Lamond.'

'That I have, sir. That I have. The two girls and their dogs are in my van at this very moment in time.'

Dan blew out a relieved breath. 'Thank you, Constable Lamond. I very much appreciate your trouble. They're none the worse for wear, then?'

'Aye, well, it depends on what you mean by that, sir.'

'What do you mean?'

'Well, the control room at the station received a phone call from Jimmy Maclean, the landlord at the Jacobite Inn at Glenfinnan, saying that two girls had recently left his establishment in a state that would raise a wee bit of concern.'

'What do you mean? They were *drunk*?'

'Aye, well, sir, they would seem to be fairly inebriated. Jimmy Maclean feels awful ashamed and also a wee bit angry that he had been serving underage drinkers, but with all their fancy makeup, he thought that they were both of a legal age.'

Dan screwed up his eyes and ran a hand over the top of his head. 'Where did you pick them up?'

'On the main road, sir, about two miles out of Glenfinnan. They were heading back on the road to Fort William with a wee bit of difficulty. Certainly the dogs seemed to be making better weather of the walking than your daughters.'

'What had they been drinking?'

'Ah, well, the evidence was there for all to see.'

'Meaning?'

'Both were carrying packs of these Alco pop-thingies under their arms. Awful dangerous stuff, sir. Shouldn't really be allowed, passing off alcohol as lemonade.'

Dan pressed his fingers to his forehead. 'Oh, the *stupid* idiots!' he said quietly.

'Aye, I would agree, sir. I've already given them a good talking-to, but I don't think that a few words from yourself would go amiss.'

'They'll certainly get that, Constable. I'm really sorry that you've had to deal with this. We'd better arrange a meeting point and I'll come and pick them up.'

'Don't worry about that, sir. I'm on my way back to Fort William anyway, so I'll drop them off on my way past.'

'Do you know where I live?'

'It'd be the cottage where Patrick Trenchard stayed, would it not?'

'Exactly.'

'Well, I'll be there in about fifteen minutes.'

'I'll be waiting, Constable.'

The phone rang again before Dan had the time to turn round to witness the reactions of Patrick and Katie. He picked up the receiver without thinking.

'Hello?'

It was Josh. 'Dad? Have you heard the latest?'

'Have I not.'

'Bloody headcases. What the hell did they think they were doing?'

'That's what I'm going to find out in about fifteen minutes.'

'Well, don't go all soft on them, just because they've been missing. They won't have any idea how much trouble they've caused.'

'I wouldn't think so for a minute.'

'Just lay into them, Dad.'

'I'll deal with it, Josh.'

'Yeah, well. Listen, I don't feel like coming home right now. I'm going to give Maria José a call and meet her for a drink.'

'Good idea. Sorry, Josh, about all this. To be quite honest, I have no idea what I'm going to do with them after this escapade.'

'If I were you, I'd put them on the next train back to London. If they want to behave like that, they can damned well stay down there. This has done nothing for our family's reputation up here, you know.'

Dan found himself grimacing at the formality of the admonishment delivered by his ex-grunge son. 'I know, Josh. I do realize that, and I promise you that I'll make sure that they're fully aware of that.'

'Bloody *idiots*,' Josh said with a spit of animosity before ending the call.

Dan left the Trenchards' house immediately, only giving a brief account of what had taken place. Josh had been right. It was an embarrassment and he was glad to have the excuse to leave, saying that he had to get back to the cottage before the constable arrived with his wretched load.

There was no way that Dan could utter even one word of rebuke to his daughters that evening. He realized that the moment they entered the house, clinging to the arms of the constable as if being guided blindfolded along a precipitous mountain path.

228

Even the dogs skulked off to their bed in front of the stove without giving Dan their usual rapturous welcome.

'If I were you, sir,' said the tall, stern-faced policeman, 'I would just get them into their beds and then have a wee word with them in the morning.'

Nina's eyes tried to focus on her father, then her ashen features turned an impossible shade of green and she started to retch. Dan grabbed her and forcefully lifted her outside where she rid herself of at least some of the contents of her stomach.

As they came back into the cottage, Constable Lamond raised his eyebrows. 'Aye, we've had a number of forced stops on the way home for that kind of thing, I'm afraid.'

He stayed long enough to help Dan get the girls into their sleeping bags, and then, having seen him to the door with further thanks and apologies, Dan set about covering the floor around the comatose bodies of his daughters with newspapers and an assortment of receptacles that could be used in the event of further upheaval. He then sat on the sofa for the next three hours, staring at the girls, sometimes leaning forward to brush a hand against their foreheads just to make sure that they were still in the land of the living. And as he sat there, taking in the characteristics of their faces – the dimple on Millie's chin that was his, the fine blonde hair that was Jackie's, the arch of Nina's eyebrows that was his, the fullness of her mouth that was Jackie's – his heart began to ache at the thought that the evening's shenanigans could have turned out so much worse.

The girls did not wake until just before eleven o'clock the following morning. Josh had gone off to work at the normal time, which pleased Dan. He knew that his son would have had much harsher things to say to his sisters than those that Dan himself had planned. As soon as they raised their throbbing heads from their pillows, Dan handed each a glass of water and a couple of Nurofen capsules, and by the time they had ventured out of their sleeping bags and sat down at the kitchen table, the pained furrowing of their foreheads had lessened. Not a word passed between them as Dan placed the plateful of well-done toast and mugs of hot, sweet tea in front of them. The girls glanced across the table at each other and both simultaneously burst into tears.

Even though Dan's heart yearned to comfort them, he kept up his work in silence. He picked up their sleeping bags and folded them up and put them on the sofa. He cleared the buckets and saucepans from the floor and scrumpled up the newspapers and threw them in the dustbin. And all the while, the girls kept crying and picking at their toast and drinking their tea in mouse-like quantities.

It was Millie who eventually broke the silence. 'We are really sorry, Dad. We really are.'

'Right,' said Dan, and then began to wash up his own break-fast things.

'We didn't mean to do it,' said Nina, giving him full benefit of her doe-eyed meekness.

Dan turned to look at her, but his expression of displeasure never changed. 'Right.' He slung the dishcloth over his shoulder and began stacking away cups and plates in the cupboard next to the sink.

Millie began sobbing with renewed gusto. 'We are just so *miserable*, Dad. You don't understand. We just hate it *so* much.'

Dan threw the dishcloth onto the table between them with force. 'It was only for a week, you know. That's all. One week. And I think that the least you could have done, for my sake, was to just make the best of it. In fact, I really thought you were. Both of you were in sparkling form the other night at the Trenchards'. I was really proud of you. And then you have to go and do a stupid thing like that!'

Millie looked at him as if he had just slapped her across the face. 'But—'

'There is absolutely no excuse, Millie, so don't even bother trying to wriggle your way out of this one. What you did was inexcusable. You involved a hell of a lot of people last night, and every one of us was in fear for your safety. To be honest, I

230

couldn't give a shit about you getting drunk. I'm pretty sure that you'll be feeling the punishment for that right now. But what I can't excuse is the selfishness that you showed towards others.'

Millie dipped her head and stared into her lap. 'I know. I'm sorry.'

'We truly are, Dad,' Nina added quietly.

Dan shook his head. 'Do you know something? After that night at the Trenchards', I had an idea that I might ring up your mother and ask if you could all come up here for Christmas. I thought that it would be great fun because I thought you were beginning to enjoy yourselves. But that was a stupid idea, wasn't it?' He turned and stared out the window. 'You win, girls. You can get on that train on Sunday night and neither of you need ever come back to Scotland again.'

'But we love it up here,' Nina spluttered out, her face collapsing as only Nina's could.

'I don't think so, Nina.'

'But we do,' Millie carried on from her sister. 'We really love being like a family again. That other night with the Trenchards was good fun. I really liked Patrick and Katie and their children. It was just . . . fun.'

Dan turned and leaned against the kitchen sink, his arms folded. 'Excuse me, you two, but do you think I have a memory like a sieve? No more than a minute ago, you were telling me how much you *hated* it up here?'

Millie wiped the sleeve of her T-shirt across her dripping nose as she shook her head. 'Not here. School. We hate school so much, Dad. We just didn't want to go back, and that's why . . .' She didn't finish, but once more burst into tears, her action being copied to a T by her younger sister.

Dan was glad of the unscheduled break in their conversation. He suddenly realized they had been talking at cross-purposes. He pulled out a chair from the table and sat down. 'Why did you not tell me?' he asked, concerned.

Millie instantly stopped crying and turned to face him with

231

an expression of fury. 'What do you mean? We are *always* telling you, Dad, but you never, ever listen. You just go on about making the best of things and that it will only be for another few years of our lives. But what you don't understand, Dad, is that every day at the place is like another year.'

Dan covered his mouth with his hand. His misunderstanding of the situation went much deeper than just getting the wrong end of the stick during their recent talk. They were not the ones who were at fault here. It was he. He had been stupid, blind and pigheaded enough to think that he could just mess around with his daughters' lives. If he had gone out and found himself a job, as Jackie had always been telling him to do, then this would never have happened. But he had to have his principles, didn't he? He had to have his own way. All that business about 'being around for a family who needed him'. It was all a load of crap. They hadn't needed him around. They had needed him working.

He leaned forward in his chair and sat pressing the nails of his thumbs together, not wishing to look up at his daughters' faces. 'It really is that bad, is it?'

'Yes, Dad, it is,' Millie said quietly. 'My work is really suffering, and I know that Nina isn't being given a chance at all. And we just have no friends there, even though we've tried hard to make them.'

Dan let out a long sigh and scratched his fingers at the back of his head. 'This is just so stupid.'

Millie's shoulders slumped despondently. 'I knew that's all you would say.'

'No, I didn't mean it that way. I'm going to send you both back to Alleyn's.'

Millie looked up and glanced across at her sister. 'But you can't. It would mean . . .'

Dan shook his head. 'No. There's no alternative. You're going back to Alleyn's. I have no right to make your lives such a misery. If I wanted to give up work, that was my decision. If you wanted to stay on at Alleyn's, then that should have been yours. I should

232

never have taken that privilege away from you.' He laid his hands, palm-down, on the table. 'I'll speak to your mother when she gets back from Italy, or wherever she is, and tell her what we're going to do, all right?'

'But, Dad,' Nina said, her blue eyes taking on a brightness that he hadn't seen for ages, 'how can we afford it?'

'That is not, and never again will be, your problem, Ni. As soon as I finish up here with Seascape, I'll come back down to London and get a job. Maybe not in the City, but I'll make sure that it pays enough to keep you both at Alleyn's for as long as you need to be there. But one thing I ask is that you never go off and do something as stupid as that ever again.'

The two girls nodded solemnly, and then slid off their chairs and put their arms around his shoulders. 'Thanks, Dad,' Millie said, pressing her wet cheek against his neck. 'You're the best.'

Dan let out a self-deprecating scoff. 'No, Millie, I certainly wouldn't describe myself as that.'

'Dad?' Nina said from the other side.

'Yes, Ni?'

'I think I'm going to be sick again.'

22

Josh was fairly disgruntled with Dan when he heard the outcome of the stern lecture that he had given his sisters. He had always had the notion that Millie and Nina could twist their father around their little fingers, and here was the proof. If he had done exactly as they had and gone off and got drunk to prove that he hated his school, the reaction from his father would have been totally different. Dan had gone soft. He had totally capitulated to them.

However, despite Josh's opinion on the worth of the talk, it seemed to have had an immediate effect on Millie. That evening, of her own volition, she went into Josh's bedroom where she spent over an hour talking with him behind closed doors. Finally, they appeared, white-faced but united, a new understanding having been forged between them. And when the two girls left on the train to London the following evening, after a success-fully riotous family day-out to Mallaig, when hands had waved like octopus tentacles out of the open-topped Saab, the fondest farewell on the platform at Fort William Station was between the two eldest siblings.

After they had left, Dan tried to ring Jackie on her mobile to tell her about his plans to send the girls back to Alleyn's, but once more he found himself being patched through to her voice-mail service. He felt that what he wanted to say to his wife was too long for a text, so while Josh headed off to meet up with Maria José, he went straight to the Seascape office to send her an e-mail, asking Josh to pick him up in an hour's time.

It took him time to write the e-mail. He had always found it difficult to admit that he was wrong about anything, let alone his own family, and he had never been that eloquent with the written word. He wasn't entirely content with the final draft, but nevertheless sent it off to Jackie's home e-mail address, hoping that she would get to read it before she went to meet the girls the following morning.

He still had twenty minutes to kill before Josh was due to come to pick him up, so he went onto the Internet and opened up his own mail server to see if he had any unread e-mails. There were two. The first was from Nick Jessop, giving him the latest news on how he was surviving in his new job with Broughton's.

'Things are not the same, Dan,' he wrote. *'Everything has changed since 9/11. The fun seems to have gone out of the City. I sometimes wonder if I wouldn't have been better just trying to get that idea of the child's car seat off the ground. At least if I had done that, I'd have been able to spend more time with Tarquin.'*

The rest of the e-mail was a running commentary on the successes of Chelsea Football Club that season. Dan wrote only a few words in reply.

'Stick to what you're doing. Tarquin will be the winner in the long run. Anyway, you would only be spending time with him in hospital if you went ahead with that damned car seat! Turning into a wild Scotsman up here. You won't be able to understand a word I say when I get back! Dan.'

The other e-mail was from Debbie Leishman in New York.

'Dear Dan,' she wrote. *'I really don't know how I can thank you for continuing to be such a wonderful friend. Without your support, I could never have afforded to stay off work so long with the baby. He continues to do well, and very soon I shall send you a real long update on how he is progressing and a photograph so that you can see for yourself just how like his daddy he is turning out to be. I still have wonderful memories of that weekend we had up in Maine. Oh, that we could wind back the clock and make it all happen over again. With my love, as always, Debbie.'*

He wrote back, *'Dear Debbie, thanks for your e-mail. Don't give the money another thought. I'm so glad that the baby's doing well. I'll look forward to getting the progress report and the photograph. Remember to get in touch whenever you want. With love, Dan.'*

The next morning, when he arrived at the Trenchards' house to pick up the Mercedes, he found a note stuck in behind the driver's windscreen wiper. It was from Katie, asking him to come into the kitchen before he left.

She rose from her customary seat in the window as he entered and pushed her arms high above her head in a long stretch. 'Morning, Dan. You got my note, then.'

The strain of Patrick's 'bad patch' over the past few weeks had taken its toll on his wife. Her face no longer glowed with rustic health but had become pale with fatigue and worry. Yet, in a strange way, the change seemed to accentuate her attractiveness, and the vulnerability that was now displayed in one usually so capable brought out an ethereal beauty in her.

'Everything all right?' Dan asked.

'Fine. Did you get the girls onto the train all right?'

'Yes. They went off a great deal happier than when I first picked them up, at any rate.'

'Maybe things needed to reach an all-time low before they got better.'

'I think you're right. Talking of which, how's Patrick?'

Katie let out a laugh of frustration and shook her head. 'He wants to go with you this morning.'

'Really? Is he up to it?'

'*He* thinks he is, and try arguing against that.'

'Do you want me to have a word with him?'

The smile slipped from Katie's face. 'No, it would be no use.' She closed her eyes. 'If he wants to go on like that, I can't stop . . .' She faltered and Dan watched as she gulped to control her emotions. A large tear broke free from each of her tightly closed eyes.

'Hey, come on. It's all right.' He moved quickly over to her and put his arms around her. She responded immediately, pressing her face against his chest and holding hard to him. 'He'll be fine, Katie. I won't let him overdo it.'

'I just don't know what I would do if something happened to him.'

'I'll take care of him.'

Katie pushed herself away from his hold. 'What can you do that I haven't done already?' she snapped at him.

Dan grimaced. 'Look, what I meant was . . .'

Katie sat down on the edge of the window seat and covered her face with her hands. 'I know what you meant. I'm sorry, Dan. It's just that I can't control him. I've tried, but his will to keep going is just too strong.'

'In that case,' Dan said quietly, 'maybe you just have to let him keep going.'

Katie looked up at him and smiled bravely. 'I know. I'm only thinking of myself, aren't I?'

'No, you're not. You're being wonderful. I don't know how the hell you cope.'

'Kate!' Patrick's voice boomed along the passageway from the small downstairs bedroom. 'Is Dan here yet?'

'Yes, he is,' Katie called out. She walked across to the sideboard and took a wodge of kitchen towel from the roll and blew her nose. 'He's just coming.'

'Well, tell him to come and give me a hand, otherwise we'll be late.'

Katie shrugged her shoulders. 'Well, as you say, I'd better just let him keep going.'

Putting his hand on her arm, Dan gave it a quick, reassuring squeeze before leaving the kitchen and heading along the passageway to Patrick's bedroom.

'Did I ever tell you about the time I bought prawns from Newfoundland?' Patrick asked as they drove past the dark silhouette of Bonnie Prince Charlie's statue at Glenfinnan.

'No, I don't think so.'

'What a gas. The most expensive experiment I ever tried, but by God, it was worth doing just for the thrill of it all.'

'What happened?'

'I bought live prawns and chartered a plane to fly them overnight back to London. I wanted to see if I could get them into Billingsgate the next morning still crawling in their boxes.'

'And did you succeed?'

Patrick shot him a challenging look. 'Yes, of course I did.'

'But it wasn't cost-effective.'

'No, it certainly wasn't. I thought that I'd be allowed to travel with the prawns in the cargo plane, but they wouldn't let me.'

'So how did you get back?'

'Well, I wanted to arrive in the UK before the cargo, so I did the only thing I could do. I caught a flight to New York, then flew from there on Concorde.'

Dan glanced at him and laughed. 'And that's where the profit went.'

Patrick smiled. 'Sort of.'

Dan signalled to overtake a lorry. 'You are bloody mad, Patrick,' he said as he accelerated past it.

238

'I'd give any part of my useless body to do it all over again, though.'

'What? Fly live prawns from Newfoundland?'

'No, maybe not from there.' He gave Dan's arm a light nudge. 'But I'm thinking about it. If the opportunity arises, then I'm off.'

Dan turned to look at the man, his face seeming even more gaunt in the eerie green light that shone from the Mercedes dashboard. 'How are you feeling, Patrick?'

'Shit.'

'I thought so. You have to take it easy, mate. If not for your own sake, then for Katie's.'

Patrick grunted out a laugh. 'Have you two been conspiring against me?'

'No, we have not. I just know that she would be lost if anything happened to you.'

Patrick turned and shot him a wink. 'Nothing's going to happen to me, my friend. Not if I have anything to do with it.'

No further word passed between them until Dan dropped his speed to drive through the village of Arisaig.

'What are your plans, Dan?'

'When I go back to London, do you mean?'

'I suppose so.'

'Well, now that the girls are heading back to a fee-paying school, I don't think there's much alternative for me other than to get a proper full-time job.'

'Right.'

'Why do you ask?'

'No reason.'

'Oh yeah?'

Patrick laughed. 'I was going to ask if you would take on Seascape for me.'

Their lighthearted banter was brought to a sudden halt by Patrick's request. Dan was able to feign concentration as he picked up speed, guiding the Mercedes around the tight bends

239

in the road. In truth, he was thinking back to what Katie had said about her husband. All that bluster and bravado were just a cover. Patrick knew as well as any that there would come a time when he wouldn't be able to cope with anything much more than lifting his walking stick.

'What about the guy from Ocean Produce in Aberdeen?'

'I could put him off. Dammit, I've waited long enough for him.'

'But he's got the knowledge, Patrick. I don't.'

'Keep going the way you are at the minute and you'll have more knowledge than me in six months.' Patrick paused, flicking his thumbnail against a knot of wood on the handle of his walking stick. 'I couldn't pay you as much as you'd get in London, but it would be a decent enough salary. I'm sure it would be enough to keep the girls at that private school of theirs.'

Dan noted a tone in Patrick's voice that he had never heard before. It was almost as if the man was pleading with him to stay.

'Patrick, listen, I don't think that I could have enjoyed myself more over these past few months, and I feel really lucky to have had the opportunity of working with you and getting to know you and Katie and the kids. But I can't work up here for ever. I have a wife in London who would never, in a million years, consider moving to Scotland, and you've seen the girls for yourself! London is like a life-support system to them all. I can't split the family up, Patrick. I have to go back.'

Patrick glanced out of the side window at the pale dawn that glowed red upon the distant wedged slope of the Isle of Eigg. Dan heard him let out a quiet laugh. 'You'll be leaving the cowboy country, Dan. Can you do that?'

Dan let out a long breath. 'There always comes the right time for riding off into the sunset, Patrick.'

23

Although the Christmas lights in Fort William were like a pencil torch in comparison to the vast illuminations of Oxford Street, they had twinkled merrily on the snow-covered streets of the town for at least a month before Dan and Josh decided that it was time that the cottage should also be decked out in festive cheer. In his own typically enthusiastic way, Josh arrived home on the appointed evening of decoration with a Christmas tree sticking out at least four feet above the open-topped Saab. It was, of course, impossible to get it into the cottage without severe surgery. So the tree went back into the car and was chauffeured along to Auchnacerie where it was gratefully received. Consequently, the Porters were roped into helping with the decoration of the Trenchards' house under the slave-driving orchestration of Patrick, who sat at the kitchen table, pointing out misplaced baubles on the tree with his holly-bedecked walking stick. There was a moment of great consternation when the fairy for the top of the tree could not be found, so Patrick suggested that Katie had really nothing much to do for the next few weeks and could easily cope with being a stand-in. With screams of delight, Max and Sooty immediately set about winding tinsel around their mother, and it was left to Dan to hoist her onto his shoulder in a fireman's lift and climb precariously up the stepladder to put her in place. With a protesting creak of metal, the aluminium ladder gave way slowly under their combined weights, and they ended up helpless with laughter on the ground amidst the prickly branches of the fallen tree. And so the decoration process had to be started all over again.

As a result, Dan and Josh did not arrive home to their bare little cottage until two o'clock in the morning, and with a good number of Patrick's Glendurnich malts swirling around in their heads, both slept through the cacophony of their alarm calls three and a half hours later. It was only the crash of the front door opening that woke Dan from his alcoholic slumber.

He sat up in bed and rubbed at his gritty eyes, then squinted at the figure of Katie standing in the doorway of his bedroom. He glanced at his alarm clock.

'Oh, bugger!' he groaned as he threw back the bedclothes. 'Sorry, Katie. Is Patrick waiting?'

'I've had to call for an ambulance, Dan. I've got to get Patrick to Inverness.'

'Why?' Dan asked, looking up at her with concern as he stuck a finger down the back of his shoe to get it on. 'What's happened?'

'Patrick had another collapse last night on the bathroom floor, and I didn't hear him. I found him this morning and he was having real difficulty breathing. I just pray to God he hasn't got pneumonia.'

'For heaven's sake,' Dan exclaimed, standing up and banging his foot into the other shoe.

'He had a urinary infection about two years ago, and it really weakened him. The disease is so much more advanced now that this one could be a real problem.'

'Have you managed to move him?'

Katie shook her head. 'No. Max is sitting with him.' Her voice quivered. 'He can hardly speak, Dan.'

Pulling on a shirt and a pair of jeans over his T-shirt and sports shorts, Dan realized that it was time for him to take control. He walked through the main room, giving Katie a quick, reassuring hug as he passed her, and banged on Josh's door. 'Josh, get up! We've got a problem.'

Josh had appeared in the doorway of his bedroom by the time Dan had pulled on his jacket. True to the habit of a teenage male who had just woken from his slumbers, he scratched slowly at the crotch of his boxer shorts, but desisted the moment he realized that Katie was in the room.

'What's up?' he asked, a puzzled expression on his face.

'We've got to get Patrick up to Inverness. He's had another collapse.'

Josh was immediately galvanized into action by the news. He disappeared into his bedroom and started pulling on any article of clothing that came his way. 'What do you want me to do?'

'Look after Max and Sooty until we get back,' Dan replied as he did up the zip of his jacket. 'If they want to go to school, take them. If not, just stay with them at Auchnacerie. And call Pete at the factory and tell him what's happened and that we're all out of action for the day.'

They saw the ambulance turning into the drive as Katie hit the final straight to Auchnacerie at speed. By the time she had pulled the Golf into the courtyard behind the house, the paramedics already had the stretcher out of the vehicle and were standing at the back door of the house. Katie abandoned the car, leaving Dan to turn off the engine and shut her door.

He stood watching as Patrick was unceremoniously tilted from one side to the other as the paramedics negotiated the narrow doorway. Despite the oxygen mask covering his mouth and nose, his chest heaved at the effort of breathing, yet he turned his head fractionally and looked directly at Dan as he was being hoisted into the back of the ambulance. There was little movement in his facial muscles, but Dan noticed a slight wrinkling of the eyes as the stretcher was slid onto its tracks. It was the only way that Patrick could convey a smile.

'Could you follow on in my car, Dan?' Katie asked as she hurried out of the house, stuffing essentials into her canvas bag. 'I'm going to travel with Patrick.'

'Of course,' he replied, helping one of the paramedics to close the back door of the vehicle while the other started up the engine.

As the ambulance reversed back, the Saab shot into the courtyard, immediately pulling over to one side to allow it to pass. Josh got out of the car and walked across to his father, and they stood watching as the vehicle made its way slowly down the driveway.

'What did he look like?' Josh asked.

'Not too good. He's having a real problem breathing.'

'Shit,' Josh said quietly. He gave his father a pat on the back. 'Where are Max and Sooty?'

'I'm not sure. Probably in the kitchen.'

'Right, I'll go and see how they're getting on. I don't suppose you'll have any idea when you're going to get back from Inverness?'

'No. It'll depend on what the doctors say at the hospital.'

'Well, keep in touch. Have you got your mobile with you?'

'Yup, I have,' Dan replied distantly, continuing to watch after the ambulance had disappeared around the final bend in the road. 'So, what do you think this time, Josh? Is everything going to be all right?'

There was a pause before Josh answered. 'I don't know. All I can say is that I don't have that same feeling of total confidence about this one. But then again, this is Patrick we're talking about.'

Dan let out a quiet laugh. 'You're right. It is.'

The hospital was situated on the outskirts of Inverness, a tall, modern-looking building with every one of its windows protected from the sunlight by Venetian blinds. As the ambulance pulled into the emergency bay, Dan veered off and made his way to the car park.

He waited for an hour in the foyer of the hospital, then, having never been a great fan of the smell of medical establishments, he went out and sat in the car. With the sun on his face and still with the aftermath of a hangover, he dozed peacefully as he listened to the morning story on Radio 4.

He was awoken by the sound of the passenger door being opened. Katie got in and slumped back in the seat with a long, exhausted breath.

'How is he?' Dan asked.

'The doctor told me that he is "stable", whatever that means.'

He reached over and patted her knee. 'A lot better than "critical", I would think. How long do you reckon they'll keep him here?'

'No idea, but I have little doubt that as soon as Patrick kicks off the infection, he'll be yelling to get out of the place as quickly as he can.'

Dan laughed. 'No doubt.' He reached forward and turned off the radio. 'So what do you want to do?'

'I don't know. I don't think I should leave him.'

'No, I agree with that.'

Katie turned to Dan. 'What about you? You'll be wanting to get back to Fort William.'

'We only have the one car.'

'Yes, we do, don't we? So what should we do?'

'Right,' said Dan decisively. 'If you stay here with Patrick, I'll head into Inverness. I need to do some shopping and I've also got to go to the train station to book the girls' tickets for Christmas.'

'I never knew they were coming up.'

'One of their last requests before they left, believe it or not.'

'Is Jackie coming up too?'

Dan shook his head. 'Unfortunately not. She says that Rebecca Talworth has decided to hold a charity auction on Christmas Eve, of all the times to pick, so she's not going to be able to make it. She's not an easy person to persuade otherwise, either.'

'What a pity.'

245

'I know. Anyway, I'll give Josh a call and ask him to look after Max and Sooty for the night, and then I'll see if I can find us a couple of rooms in a hotel somewhere nearby.'

'I'm sorry, Dan. This is a complete nuisance for you. I should have driven up here myself, only—'

'Listen, it's no bother at all. Nothing matters except that Patrick gets better again. Seascape will survive without us all for a couple of days, and no doubt our offspring will as well.'

Katie reached over and gave him a long kiss on his cheek. 'You have been an absolute star over the past four months, Dan the Man, and I don't think I have ever thanked you for all you've done for my family.'

'It's been a pleasure, Katie. I really mean that. You helped me get out of a rut too, remember?'

Katie put a hand on his arm and sat back, staring at him quizzically. 'Tell me, what would you rather have done? Run Vagabonds or work with Patrick?'

Dan laughed. 'I don't think you need to ask that question, Mrs Trenchard.'

'You're right. I don't believe I do.' She opened up the car door. 'What time will you be back?'

'Say six o'clock this evening?'

'All right. I'll be waiting for you in the foyer.'

She closed the door and Dan watched in the rearview mirror as she ran across the car park, a small, brave figure in a pair of multipanelled tartan trousers.

24

The offices of the Business Development Department of the Highland Regional Council took up two small, fluorescent-lit rooms on the third floor of an ugly Victorian building on Bridge Street in Inverness. There were two desks in each room, and in order to get behind them, it was necessary to squeeze past the bank of filing cabinets that lined the high, cream-coloured walls. This posed an almost insurmountable problem for the well-built figure of Maxwell Borthwick every time he had to take a seat at his desk.

Hemmed in by these permanent reminders of just how boring his job was, Maxwell sat reading through a thick, acetate-covered business plan that had been placed on his desk that afternoon by the weasly faced director of business development, Cyril Bentwood.

'Could you have a quick glance at that for me, please, Maxwell?' he had asked, as he had taken his sheepskin car coat and ghastly porkpie hat from the chrome coat stand. 'And I would appreciate your thoughts on it first thing tomorrow morning.'

'Of course, Cyril,' Maxwell had replied, sticking up a middle finger at his boss as he turned and left the room, his work finished for the day at five o'clock precisely.

Maxwell detested Cyril Bentwood at the best of times, but his sentiments towards him had become even more acidic now that the little Englishman had been given the opportunity to tighten his control over Maxwell's geographical movements. And that had all come about due to the incident in Oban when that bastard from Seascape had hoisted his beloved BMW up onto those pallets.

It had taken a full six hours and a hefty £50 backhander before he had managed to persuade the obtuse forklift driver to bring the car down, and even though he had driven like the wind back up to Inverness, he had still missed out on a full day's worth of work. Cyril, of course, had revelled in it all. 'One has to be trustworthy as a civil servant, Maxwell,' he had said. 'We are funded by taxpayers' money, and, as such, it is our duty to honour our work commitment. I am disappointed that you do not feel ready to respect this. Of course, I shall overlook your unscheduled absence from the office on this occasion, but if there happens to be a reoccurrence, I'm afraid that I will be left with no alternative other than to recommend that you be moved to some lesser office in the Council.'

It had taken all Maxwell's self-control to stop himself from reaching over the desk, picking up the man, and hanging him up on the coat stand alongside his car coat and porkpie hat. What the hell did he mean, a 'lesser office in the Council'? What on earth did he think he was running? The bloody Bank of England?

But he had taken the telling-off. He had had no alternative, and now Cyril Bentwood was making sure that he curbed Maxwell's wandering instincts by getting out of him as many work-hours as he possibly could.

Maxwell leaned back in his chair and linked his podgy fingers behind his head. It was going to be a long evening. He had been reading the wretched document for nearly two hours now and he hadn't even reached the end of the background report. His mind was far too active for this kind of work. That was his problem. He was better suited to the realms of nationwide administration, applying his brainpower to the running of his beloved country. It was he who should be throwing documents onto the desks of insignificant little pricks like Cyril Bentwood to read.

He got up from his chair and picked up the electric kettle from on top of a filing cabinet and gave it a shake. He reckoned that there was enough water in it for one small cup of instant coffee. He certainly wasn't going to be bothered to go through the rigmarole of contorting his way out of the office just for a half-pint of water. He pressed the switch on the kettle, and then, pushing his chair hard into the footwell of the desk, he walked across to the tall, dirt-smeared window and looked down onto the crowded street.

With Christmas just two weeks away, the shops in Inverness were remaining open every night until eight. He loved the atmosphere of the bustling crowds, yet it was not so much that it put him in the joyous spirit of Christmas, but more that it resembled what he had always imagined that living in a big city, like Edinburgh or Glasgow, would be like. And that, above all, was what he yearned for.

He pulled a silk handkerchief from his trouser pocket and wiped away a bead of sweat from his enormous brow, a late reminder of the delicious tangy heat of the vindaloo curry that he had enjoyed at lunchtime. He stopped suddenly, his handkerchief pressed to his face, and stared down at the two figures that picked their way, side by side, through the crowds on the pavement. Well, speak of the devil, he thought to himself. Look who's turned up in Inverness. Seascape's own bloody Dan Porter. Maxwell cupped his hands against the glass to get a clearer view of his companion. He knew that he recognized her. Yes, of course, it was Trenchard's wife. He was sure of it. What on earth were they doing together so far from home at this time of the day?

He reached up and undid the catch on the window and

managed to slide it open on the third attempt. He leaned out onto the sill and managed to catch sight of them again just as they cut across the flow of pedestrians at the bottom of the street and entered the brightly lit foyer of the Caledonia Hotel.

Maxwell pulled his bulk back into the room and shut the window. He turned, a broad smile of satisfaction puckering up his flabby cheeks. 'Oh-ho-ho!' he said out loud. 'Now what do we have going on here?'

He took his jacket from the back of the chair and, as quickly as possible, squeezed his way to the door of the office, flicking off the switch of the kettle as he passed. He glanced momentarily at the document on his desk before killing the fluorescent lights and closing the door behind him.

'Can I help you, sir?' asked the bright-faced receptionist of the Caledonia Hotel.

'Yes, I do believe you can,' Maxwell replied cheerfully, as he glanced quickly over to the seating area in the foyer, just to make sure that the two persons in question were not present. 'You wouldn't, by any chance, have a Mr Dan Porter staying here at the minute, would you?'

'If you could wait a moment, sir, I'll just check for you.' The girl typed quickly on the keyboard of her computer and then ran her finger down the screen. 'Yes, we do, sir.' She put a hand on the receiver of her telephone. 'Would you like me to put you through to his room?'

Maxwell waved a hand dismissively. 'No, don't worry. I think I'll just surprise him. I'm an old friend of both Mr Porter and Mrs Trenchard. I take it that she's staying here as well?'

The girl consulted her computer once more. 'Yes, she is.'

'Oh, that's wonderful. I haven't seen either of them for so long.' He leaned forward on the top of the high reception desk and smiled conspiratorially at the girl. 'I know it's probably against company policy, but you wouldn't just give me their room number, so that I could go up and give them a bit of a surprise.'

250

The girl bit at her lip. 'I'm not supposed to, sir.'

Maxwell stood away from the desk. 'Of course. I quite understand.' He made sure the girl saw that he was pondering the dilemma. 'Would it be possible then to buy a bottle of champagne for them, so that I could send it up to their room?'

'Of course it is,' the girl replied with a smile before looking back down at her computer screen. It was she who leaned across the desk this time. 'Their room numbers are three twenty-one and three twenty-two,' she whispered to him.

Maxwell felt disappointed that they were in different rooms, but he managed not to make it apparent to the girl. 'Thank you. I very much appreciate it,' he replied in an equally secretive tone. He turned and made his way towards the lift.

'What about the champagne, sir?' the girl called after him.

Maxwell turned and shot her a wink. 'Let's leave that until later, shall we? One surprise at a time.'

For the rest of the evening, Maxwell became their shadow. He was desperate not to let this opportunity go a-begging because he knew that his chances to get even with Porter were going to be few and far between. Having found an open service room on their corridor, he kept watch through the barely open door until they eventually left their rooms together about half an hour later. He had never had to make his way down three flights of stairs so fast in all his life, but he managed to reach the ground floor just as they were walking out of the hotel. As luck would have it, they had parked in the car park down by the river, about three rows away from where his BMW sat.

He followed them at a safe distance as they made their way out of town, and for a heart-stopping moment, he thought they were heading for the A9, the main road that linked Inverness with the rest of the world. But just before the slip road, they signalled to the left and pulled into the car park of Raigmore Hospital.

He waited for them for an hour, killing time by listening to a

Runrig album on the minidisc system that he had had recently installed in the BMW. When they reappeared through the glass doors of the hospital, he stabbed at the OFF switch and slumped down into his seat. He watched them get into the Golf, reverse out of their parking slot, and move off towards the exit. He started his own car, but did not move. He wanted to see which way they turned at the bottom of the road. The indicator light flashed to the right, and he knew that they were heading back into Inverness.

Cutting the engine once more, he got out of the car and walked across to the hospital entrance. He had a pretty shrewd idea of what was going on, but he just had to make sure. He only had to ask a few words of the woman at the reception desk to have his thoughts confirmed, and he left the hospital with a smile on his face and a jaunty bounce to his step. He heaved himself into the BMW and let out a long, slow laugh. So Patrick Trenchard was in the High Dependency Unit, was he? He started up the car and reversed back at speed. Right, Maxwell, he thought to himself, let's see how we can turn this to our advantage.

25

It had been Dan's decision not to eat in the hotel dining room that evening. He had glanced into its dazzlingly bright interior and seen the young shirtsleeved businessmen seated at the tables, their mobile phones clustered around them as if they were an integral part of the dinner service, and he felt that he didn't want to be part of them. He also had a suspicion that the superior-looking headwaiter might take unkindly to the scruffy clothes that he had hastily thrown on that morning. So he and Katie left the hotel and walked across the street to a cheery-looking establishment called Buchan's Steak Bar. They sat opposite each other at a small table tucked away into the corner of the restaurant, next to the door that led to the gents' lavatory. They had been lucky enough to get a seat at all, as the place was seething with feasting late-night shoppers, and every square inch of the floor space was taken up with enormous shopping bags and parcels of every size and shape. Yet although the room was filled with the general clamour of pre-Christmas merriment, the mood at their table was solemn.

Dan placed his knife and fork down on his plate. 'Are you sure you don't feel like eating anything?'

Katie shook her head and took another drink from her wineglass. 'I had a ham roll at the hospital. That'll do me.'

'You've eaten nothing else all day, though.'

'For goodness' sake, please stop worrying about me, Dan. I'm fine.'

Dan flicked his head to the side. 'Okay.'

Katie let out a long sigh. 'I'm sorry. That was rude. I'm just so . . . keyed up about Patrick.'

Dan finished off a mouthful of steak, and then pushed the plate to one side. 'You don't have to apologize. I can imagine how you're feeling.'

'It just goes on and on, and I know that there'll be no respite for me, until . . .' – she bit at her bottom lip – 'until something pretty final happens to Patrick.' She paused to take another drink of wine. 'No, I don't think you can ever imagine how I'm feeling. Patrick has been my protection, my rock, ever since we were married. I was never cut out to take over that role from him. He knows it too and that's one of the reasons he feels that he has to keep going. But sometimes, it just makes me feel very vulnerable and very lonely, and I long for him to be whole again.' She gazed at her wineglass as she spun it around in her fingers. 'The worst are the nights. I lie in that huge double bed by myself and listen to him moving restlessly about in that poky little room downstairs. I long to just get up and go to him and lie down beside him and let him wrap me in those big powerful arms of his and hear him say, "Don't worry, Kate. I'll look after you." But, of course, I can't.' She let out a hopeless laugh. 'The bed's too narrow and his arms are too weak.' The unhappy smile slid from her face. 'And then, the following morning, I'm supposed to leap out of bed and be strong and resolute and supportive of my family.' She shook her head as she took another sip of wine. 'I can't really describe it, Dan, but I do know that you can never imagine how I'm feeling.'

'No, you're right. I don't think I probably can.'

Katie rocked back in her chair and threw her hands up in the air. 'But this is so unfair. I shouldn't be saying that kind of thing to you. All you've done is help us, Dan. Both you and Josh came out of the blue and you've been our . . . saviours. We could never have survived these last few months without you. So what gives me the right to come out and say something like that?'

Dan leaned forward on the table and rubbed at the two-days' worth of stubble on his chin. 'I hope it's because I'm a friend.'

Katie smiled and reached over and gripped his forearm. 'You are, Dan. A very dear friend, both to Patrick and to me.' She pushed back from the table and pressed her fingers against her eyes. 'I am just feeling so tired. I didn't sleep a wink last night, and all I really want to do is to crash out for about twelve hours without interruption.' She picked up her canvas bag from the floor. 'Would you mind if I went back to the hotel now?'

'Not at all. I'll come over with you,' Dan replied, catching the eye of a waitress and signalling for the bill. He then glanced at his watch. It was just before nine o'clock. He smiled across the table at Katie. 'If we're quick, you should just about make your twelve hours.'

Thank God hotels cater for unprepared travellers, Dan thought, as he made use of the disposable razor that he had found, neatly packaged, in the bathroom cabinet. He had already had a deep, luxurious bath and the empty sachets in the soap tray were testament to the fact that he had used every freebie that the hotel supplied. Throwing the razor into the waste bin, he towelled off what was left of the shaving soap on his face, and feeling clean and revitalized, he walked naked from the bathroom, flopped down on the bed, and rang the house in Clapham.

It was Jackie who answered. He had hoped that his decision to send the girls back to Alleyn's might have helped solve some of their differences, but he only managed a stilted conversation with her before she handed him over to Millie. Talking to his elder daughter was the complete antithesis. Over the telephone, Millie sounded loving and buoyant in spirit, and he had to hold the receiver away from his ear at her reaction to the news that he had bought their train tickets for Christmas. The call lasted a further ten minutes, during which time Dan hardly uttered a word.

He began to watch a film on the television but it wasn't long before the events of the day caught up with him as well. During a lengthy and deeply meaningful conversation between the two main actors, stuck in a wind-blown bivouac somewhere high up in the Himalayas, his head slumped on the pillow and he fell into a deep sleep.

It was the long, continuous beep of the empty screen that woke him. He fumbled for the remote, eventually finding it on the floor beside the bed, and turned off the television. He glanced at his watch before pulling the bedclothes over him, plumping up his pillow and settling himself for the rest of the night. He angled his wristwatch to catch the glare of the streetlights coming in through the window. It was two o'clock in the morning. He had at least another six hours' undisturbed sleep to enjoy.

As he became accustomed to the quiet, he heard what he thought was the sound of someone talking in hushed tones in one of the adjoining bedrooms. He switched on the bedside light and sat up, and turned his head one way and then the other, trying to work out from which side of the room the voice was coming. He threw back the bedclothes and got to his feet and walked across to the wall that separated his room from Katie's. The sound was coming from her room. He pressed his ear against the wall, and then immediately took a couple of paces back. He stood, scratching a finger thoughtfully down the side of his face as he fixed his eyes on the spot where his ear had been. Katie wasn't talking. She was crying.

He sat for a full quarter of an hour on the edge of his bed, listening to her intermittent sobs and wondering whether he should do anything about it. Maybe she was still asleep. Maybe she would wake up in the morning and she wouldn't know anything about it. Then he heard a definite change to the pattern.

He stood up and went back to the wall and listened. The volume was fluctuating, sometimes distant, sometimes close to the wall that separated them. He knew then that Katie was awake and was moving about in the room.

He went into the bathroom and took one of the white towelling dressing gowns from the back of the door. He put it on and walked out of his bedroom into the corridor, knotting the tie on the dressing gown as he went. He stood outside Katie's door, listening intently, his knuckle raised to knock. He thought for a moment that she had stopped, and he was about to turn and go back to his room when he heard her sobs of despair much clearer than he had done before. He gave two quiet taps on the door.

'Katie?' he whispered.

There was no reply.

'Kate, it's Dan.' He knew as soon as he had said it that he shouldn't have done so. He had only called her Kate because it sounded softer and less likely to disturb the other hotel guests. But it was Patrick who called her that. No one else.

The door flew open and Katie appeared and she threw her arms around him. The action opened up the top half of his dressing gown and she pushed her spiky brown hair against his bare chest.

'Oh, Dan! Oh, Dan!' she said in a voice that echoed down the corridor.

Dan glanced around him. 'Ssh, Katie. You'll wake everyone up.'

She reached a hand behind his neck and pulled his face down towards her and kissed him on the mouth and he felt her tongue trying to prise open his mouth. He flinched away.

'Stop it, Katie. Don't do that. It's not the answer.' He looked down at her tear-stained face, and his eyes settled unwillingly on the curve of her breasts, exposed by her half-open pyjama top.

'I'm Kate,' she sobbed, 'I'm Kate.' She turned her head and kissed his chest, and then pushing back the front of his dressing gown, her mouth sought out one of his nipples.

'For God's sake, Katie, don't do this,' Dan exclaimed, trying to push her away from him. 'We'll only regret it later.'

Katie stood back from him, her eyes flaming with defiance. 'No, I never will. I never will.'

She took hold of his hand and tried to pull him into her room. Dan used his strength to disengage himself from her grip. 'We're not going to do this, Katie.'

She stood watching him, a bewildered, hurt expression on her face, and then she slowly raised her fingers to the front of her pyjama top and undid the three remaining buttons before letting it slip to the ground. 'My name is Kate, and I want to be held and I want to be loved again.' She reached out and took his hand once more, and with a shake of his head, Dan allowed himself to be led into her room.

And while Katie began to take from him the long-lost sensation of physical comfort, a large figure appeared from the service room in the corridor and stretched out his aching limbs before setting off with heavy, tiptoe steps towards the lift.

26

'Why did you leave?' Katie asked as she walked quickly past Dan into his bedroom the following morning. 'There was no need to.'

Dan scratched at the back of his head and closed the door. 'Katie, we shouldn't have done that last night.'

'Oh, and why not? It was my decision. You have no reason to reproach yourself for what happened.'

Dan pushed his hands into the pockets of the dressing gown. 'We're both married, Katie. That's why.' He let out a long sigh. 'Patrick also happens to be one of the best friends I have ever had. And I have just slept with his wife.'

Katie raised her eyebrows. 'Well, bully for you,' she said quietly.

'Come on, Katie, can't you understand what—'

'No, Dan,' Katie interjected. 'It's *you* who has to understand. I'm not one of those women who can be comforted with a few kind words and a little friendly hug and a pat on the top of my head. I boil up inside every time that happens. I want to grab whoever's said it and tell them that I am bursting with anger and frustration and all I want to do is – shout at them, "Don't give me your . . . kindly condolences. Give me back my husband!"' She sat down heavily on the edge of his bed. 'You gave me, Dan, the one thing that could give me any small comfort at all, and that was physical love and physical protection. So don't start trying to envelop me in your own guilt.'

Walking over to the window, Dan swept his hands through his hair and linked them behind his head. 'Oh, Katie, I don't know what the hell I'm meant to say about all this.'

'You don't have to say anything.'

'But what *about* Patrick?'

'Patrick need never know it happened, and if it's any small comfort to you, it won't ever happen again.' She got up and went to stand beside him, and put a hand on his shoulder. 'But I needed it, Dan. I feel . . . different this morning. I feel able to cope with what's to come. And that's your doing, so I thank you from the bottom of my heart for helping me.'

Dan shook his head slowly. 'But it has changed everything, Katie.'

'Why?'

'Because I can't stay up here now.'

'Why not?'

'Because I couldn't face Patrick again.'

'Oh, come *on*, Dan!'

He spun round to look at her. 'No, Katie, *you* listen this time. I am not a liar. I am physically incapable of keeping something like this under wraps. Okay, I played games with the reality of situations in the City, but the truth behind them was plain for all to see, if they bothered to work it out. If a trader saw through a deal that I was trying to push onto him, I'd just give him a wink and say something like "Oh well, it was worth a go." Don't you see, Katie? I've always had to have people trusting me, otherwise I would never have been able to succeed in my job.'

Katie dropped her hand from his shoulder. 'I'm sorry,' she said quietly.

'Oh, Katie, don't feel sorry. Listen, it takes two to tango. Maybe I should pretend that I didn't enjoy it, but that would be way too far from the truth. Yet it has changed everything.'

Katie walked slowly over to the bed and sat down again. 'So what are you going to do?'

Dan turned and leaned against the window sill. 'I've found out that there's a bus leaving for Fort William at ten o'clock. Once I'm there, I'll have a word with Pete and tell him that I have to go. It's only another couple of weeks before the chap from Ocean Produce starts, so I'm sure he can cope until then. After that, I'll get Josh to take me back to the cottage to pick up my gear.'

'What will you tell them both?'

'The first of my lies. That I have been called back to London to start a new job.'

'Will Josh go with you?'

'That's up to him.' Dan let out a short laugh. 'I doubt it, though. Everything he loves is up here. His job, Marie José and, of course, the Trenchard family.'

Dan saw a tear trickle slowly down Katie's cheek. 'What do I say to Patrick?'

'I would suggest that you say exactly the same to him and to Max and to Sooty as I'm going to say to Pete and Josh. The trouble with subterfuge is that stories always have to match exactly.'

'He'll miss you so much, Dan.'

'As I will him.'

She looked up at him, a pleading look in her eyes. 'Could you not just see him for a moment before you go?'

Dan shook his head. 'No, Katie. We are pretty much alike, Patrick and I. He would be able to tell immediately that something had happened. We must never give him any reason not to get well again.'

She stood up and hurried towards him and encircled his waist with her arms. This time, Dan responded without reservation. He placed his arms around her neck, and leaning forward, he kissed the top of her spiky head. They stood holding each other for a minute before he turned her around to face the door. 'Now, go and see your husband, Katie. He needs you as much as you need him.'

Katie walked out of the doors of the hospital and stood beneath the canopy, looking up at the cold grey skies. She had noticed the first flurries of snow out of the window when she was sitting beside Patrick's bed. Yet, despite the bleakness of the weather, she felt contented, almost happy. Once more, Patrick was fighting back, and whilst in the presence of the doctor, he had slid the oxygen mask off his mouth and said in a laboured voice that he wanted to get the hell out of that bloody mausoleum as fast as he possibly could. The doctor, who had overheard every word, simply smiled at her and said that Patrick had progressed well enough to move him out of the High Depency Unit and that he would discharge him into Katie's care as soon as possible.

She pulled her coat around her and clutched the collar closed at the neck, then ran across the car park to the Golf. As she reversed out of her parking space, she took care not to clip the rear bumper of the red BMW that was parked beside her.

It had been pure devilment on Maxwell Borthwick's part to slot his car into the parking space next to the Golf. There were many other spaces available in the car park, but as soon as he saw her arriving, he moved his car adjacent to hers so that he could see her close up before he ruined her life for ever.

He watched as the Golf turned onto the main road, then he got out of the car, and wrapping his blue serge overcoat around him, he walked delicately across to the entrance door, taking care not to slip on the newly fallen snow. He approached the reception desk with a friendly smile on his face.

'Good morning,' he said in a bright, cheery voice. 'I wonder if you could direct me to the ward where I might find Patrick Trenchard.'

The woman clattered speedily on her keyboard, and then picked up the telephone and dialled an extension number. 'Hello, this is reception,' she said. 'Could I speak to Staff Nurse, please?'

She smiled at Maxwell as she waited for the staff nurse to come to the telephone. 'Hello, yes, this is reception here. Do you still have Patrick Trenchard with you? . . . Right, I see. And how long will that be? . . . Right.' She cupped her hand over the receiver. 'They are in the process of moving Mr Trenchard from the High Dependency Unit into a day ward. He won't be ready for visitors for about half an hour.'

Maxwell slapped his hands down on the desk. 'Not to worry.' He turned and pointed to an empty bench in the foyer. 'I'll just go and have a seat over there. Maybe you could let me know when he is ready.'

He walked over to the bench and sat down, and immediately let out a long, shuddering yawn. He hadn't had a moment's sleep all night. As soon as he had left the hotel in the early hours of the morning, he had gone back to the office to write the report for Cyril Bentwood. It had been a difficult task, because his mind had kept imagining with relish the conversation he was going to have with Patrick Trenchard later on in the day. But at seven o'clock on the dot, he had placed the report on Bentwood's desk, and at that point he had sworn to himself that, once he had disposed of Trenchard, he would then turn his attentions to the wretched little man with the sheepskin car coat and the porkpie hat.

It was a full hour before the receptionist walked over to him and woke him gently with a tap on his shoulder. 'That's Mr Trenchard ready for visitors now.'

Maxwell pushed himself to his feet. 'Thank you. Which way do I go?'

The receptionist gave him directions and he set off hurriedly along the corridor towards the ward. Not only was he desperate to see Trenchard's reaction to his revelations, but he was also keen to get back to the office before Bentwood saw fit to move him to a 'lesser' office.

The staff nurse waylaid him at the entrance to the ward. 'The doctor has requested that only family should be visiting Mr Trenchard for the time being,' she said.

'I quite understand that. It's just that I'm a very old friend and I was just passing through Inverness on my way up north. promise that I'll only stay for a couple of minutes.'

The staff nurse smiled and led him to Patrick's bed.

Maxwell was delighted to see just how ill Patrick Trenchard was. He lay prostrate on the bed, his mouth and nose covered by an oxygen mask, and his eyes flickered open and shut in synchronization with the effort of his breathing. He was a mere shadow of the loud-mouthed braggart with whom Maxwell had had dealings in the past. He leaned over Patrick and grinned into his face. He saw a stirring of recognition in the wrinkles on his forehead.

'I bet you're surprised to see me, aren't you, Trenchard?' he said in a quiet voice.

He detected a slight narrowing of Patrick's eyes.

'I am really sorry to see you like this, Trenchard. Never mind you'll soon be up and about, won't you?'

Patrick turned his head slowly as if trying to look for the bell

'No, no, we don't want to call the nurse, do we? Not ye anyway.' Maxwell looked around and saw a chair against the wall opposite. He went over and picked it up and brought it over to Patrick's bedside and sat down.

'So how is your friend Dan Porter? Been stacking any more cars recently, has he?'

He witnessed a slight stretching to Patrick's mouth.

'Oh you think it's funny, do you? Well, let's see if this wipe that pathetic smile off your face.' He moved his chair in close to Patrick's bed and leaned over so that his mouth was inche from Patrick's ear. 'You see, I just *happened* to be in the Caledonia Hotel last night, and lo and behold, who should be staying there but your wife and your good friend Dan Porter. Now, I though it was a bit odd that they seemed to be getting on rather to well, so I took it upon myself to do a bit of . . .' – he sucked loudly on his blubbery bottom lip – 'yes, a bit of "sleuthing", and I think that you'll be rather grateful that I did.' He cast a glance around the ward for dramatic effect. 'You see, at about two o'clock this morning, I was sitting, rather uncomfortably I might add, in a service room on the third floor of the hotel, watching their rooms. I could hardly believe my eyes when I saw what happened next. Do you want to know what I saw?'

Patrick stared fixedly at the man.

'I'll take that as a yes, then. Well, what happened was that your friend Porter came out of his bedroom and knocked on your wife's door, and in the blink of an eye, the door opened and your wife threw herself – no, maybe catapulted might be a more appropriate word – into Porter's arms. There was a moment when they just held each other, right there in the corridor, before your wife, very deliberately, undid the buttons on her sexy little pyjama top and let it fall to the ground. Well, I have to say, Trenchard, that I was sincerely impressed. She certainly has a good pair of paps, that wife of yours. And they were certainly good enough to get Porter jumping into that room.' Maxwell's face took on a serious expression. 'Well, now, I'm a man of integrity, and I did nothing untoward like listen at the door for the sound of heaving bedsprings, but I left in the knowledge that I could do you a great favour in letting you know what happened.' He sat back with a sigh and slapped his knees with his hands. 'Well, that's just about it. My story is told.' He leaned forward again. 'So what do you think of that, Trenchard?'

Watching carefully for Patrick's reaction, he was amazed, and somewhat perturbed when, beneath the clear plastic of the oxygen mask, he saw Patrick's mouth stretch into a grin. He saw Patrick's hand rise from the bed and a finger slowly beckon to him. Maxwell got to his feet and leaned over Patrick, watching him as he lifted the oxygen mask from his face. His voice was slow, but perfectly clear and perfectly precise.

'Why – don't – you – mind – your – own – fucking – business, you – fat – bastard.'

Maxwell jumped back from the bed as if Patrick had just poured boiling water into his ear. He watched with a shocked expression as Patrick let the mask plop back onto his face and then moved his hand slowly, but without faltering, towards the bell. He pressed the button and the buzzer sounded noisily around the ward. The staff nurse was at his bedside in a matter of moments. She could tell by the flick of Patrick's hand that visiting time was over. As she led Maxwell to the exit, he turned and glanced once more over to where Patrick lay. He was staring at the ceiling, and although most of his face was hidden beneath the oxygen mask, Maxwell could tell by the wrinkling of his eyes that he wore a smile of utter contentment. It was almost as if he had just been informed that his illness had been vanquished and that a full recovery was now a certainty.

27

As Dan had suspected, Josh had no wish to leave Fort William. They had talked about it as they drove back to the cottage, and Josh had made it plain that he never wanted to live in London again. His new life was in Scotland with friends the like of which he could never possibly meet in the seething mass of the metropolis. And so Dan had left him, with the dogs and with the Saab, and headed back to London on the overnight sleeper alone.

The taxi dropped him outside the house in Clapham at ten o'clock the next morning. Having paid the cabbie, Dan stood on the pavement, staring at the stained-glass front door and wondering if he was pleased to be back. And then he heard the sound of Mrs Watt coming out of her house and he made a bolt for the gate to avoid meeting her. He let himself into the house and slammed the door shut, dropping his suitcase to the floor. He leaned his back against the stained glass and shut his eyes, taking in the familiar smell of his own home. Yet, this time, it seemed alien. In the past it had given him comfort and a sense of security, but now it just seemed old and stale. It was as if he didn't really belong to the house anymore.

But it *was* his home, and it *was* his family, and he had made a commitment to the girls to let them finish their schooling at Alleyn's. He had to be thankful for everything he had achieved because, by God, it could have turned out so differently. He could have been stuck in Tottenham Hale with Sharon or Janice or Kathleen, and their one child, working in that bloody fabrication shed. But he had made it to here, to this fine house in Clapham, where he lived with his wife Jackie, their three wonderful children, and two deranged dogs. He was, indeed, a lucky man.

He walked through to the kitchen and realized as he entered the room that he had hardly ever done so without being greeted by the appalling smell of one of Biggles's misdeeds. He thought of the dogs, and then he thought of Josh, and then he thought of Patrick and Katie, and he yearned to be back with them all. He had only been away from them for a matter of hours, and already he missed the intuitive wisdom and boundless enthusiasm of Josh, the drive and the sense of humour and the fight in Patrick, and the quiet resilience and strength of character in Katie. And last night, on the train, as he tossed and turned on his narrow bunk, he missed having her body curled in next to his. He would never forget that night, as long as he lived, when he lay on top of her, absorbing her pain and sorrow into his very being.

He filled up the electric kettle and turned it on, and then saw the four piles of mail sitting on the shelf next to the telephone. He thumbed through the first one, sorting out the junk from the readable, and he was about to open a letter from Broughton's, the company for which Nick Jessop worked, when he heard the sound of footsteps coming down the stairs.

'Millie? Is that you?' It was Jackie's voice.

'No, it's me – Dan.'

He heard the footsteps stop, and then ascend the stairs at speed. He flicked his head back dismissively and continued with the opening of the letter. It was a brief five-liner.

Dear Dan,

I have been told by one of my colleagues, Nick Jessop, that you might be interested in seeking a job with Broughton's. I am, of course, familiar with your past achievements in the City and therefore was hoping that we might meet for lunch in the near future. I know that you are in Scotland at present, but on your return, do please e-mail me at j.burrows@ broughtons.com to let me know if you want to take this further.

Yours sincerely

Good old Nick, he thought to himself. He doesn't give up, does he? He fluttered the letter down onto the kitchen table and then heard the sound of Jackie's footsteps coming down the stairs once more. She entered the kitchen and stood in the doorway, wearing a pair of jeans and a T-shirt. She made no move to come towards him to greet him.

'Hi,' he said, smiling at her. 'This is a bit of a surprise. I didn't expect to find you here.' He walked over to her and made to give her a kiss on the mouth, but she turned her face so that it landed on her cheek. He put his arms around her and gave her a hug. It was like holding a lump of wood.

'I was going to say exactly the same thing myself,' Jackie said, pushing him away. 'What are you doing back? I thought you were going to be up in Scotland until mid-January.'

'I know,' Dan replied, walking over to the sideboard and unhooking two mugs. 'Do you want a cup of coffee?'

'No thanks.'

'How are the girls?'

'Fine. They both spent last night at Jessica Napier's house.' She bit at the side of her mouth. 'So why are you back?'

Dan spooned coffee into the mug. 'My contract finished early,' he said, realizing that he had just told Lie No. 2. 'So I thought that I would just come back and see if I could find myself a job.' He flicked his head over to where the letter lay on the table.

269

'Things look promising, as well. I've been asked to meet some guy from Broughton's.'

'But what about Christmas? The girls are meant to be joining you and Josh in Scotland.'

'I know. I've been thinking about that.' Dan poured water into the coffee cup, and then took a spoon from the drawer and gave it a stir. 'I made a bit of money with Seascape. Not a huge amount, but I never spent anything, so I thought that I might check out the Internet for a cheap skiing holiday somewhere.'

'What about Josh?'

'Josh didn't want to move out of Scotland. He's totally settled up there. I left him with the dogs and the car, and he's as happy as Larry.' He dropped the spoon into the sink. 'But you can come skiing if you want.'

Jackie shook her head. 'You know I can't. Rebecca's got this charity auction, and I have to be there.'

'Of course.' Dan took a sip of coffee. 'So, tell me, what's been the news with you? Are you taking a bit of a break at the minute?'

Jackie leaned her shoulder against the doorpost and fixed him with a steely glare. 'Dan, I want to ask you something.'

'Go ahead.'

'How long have you been having an affair?'

The mug jigged in Dan's hand and boiling coffee spilled over his wrist. 'What?' he exclaimed, transferring the mug to the other hand and flicking his wrist to cool down the scald.

'You heard me. How long have you been having an affair?'

'I don't know what the hell you're talking about.'

Jackie pushed herself away from the doorpost and pulled a chair out from the table and sat down. 'Dan, I know that you've been having an affair. You're not a very good liar, you know. You never were. Your face has gone beetroot, and so has your hand, thanks to that coffee.'

Dan bit at the inside of his cheek as he stared at his wife. I know I'm not a very good liar, he thought to himself. That's what I told Katie. 'I have not been having an affair, Jackie,' he said in a voice that was as controlled as he could make it.

Jackie slammed her hand hard down on the table. 'Come *on*, Dan. Let's at least be adult about this! Why don't you just admit it to my face? On the other hand, why do I need that kind of proof? Your actions speak well enough for you.'

Dan kept staring at her. How the hell could she have known? There was no way anyone could have told her, because nobody *knew* about it except Katie and himself.

'Did you not know, Dan, that the best way to express guilt is through silence?'

Dan heaved out a long sigh. He could not be bothered with telling Lie No. 3, because it would only lead on to Lie No. 4, and then Lie No. 5.

'It was only one night, Jackie.'

Jackie drummed her fingers hard on the table. 'One night. Well, at least that's a start.' She got up and walked towards him. 'But the trouble is that I don't believe you, you rotten bastard. I reckon that it was going on for a lot longer than one night.'

'It was not,' Dan replied, moving back from the threatening presence of his wife.

Jackie stopped inches away from him and glared into his eyes. 'And to think that you've made me feel so *guilty* about everything over the past few months. How *dare* you make me feel that way when you've been carrying on with another woman.'

Dan frowned at her, having absolutely no understanding of how she had found out about Katie and what she was talking about right now. 'What do you mean, I've made you feel guilty? Guilty about what?'

Jackie hit back. 'So what was it like screwing her, Dan? Was she *so* much better than me?'

'Oh, come on, Jackie. It was only one night, I promise you. That's all. Her husband was—'

'I know!' she interjected. 'I know everything! Her husband was killed on the eleventh of September 2001 in New York, and you, the kindhearted friend, stepped in with your solace and

271

your compassion, and you made love to her and you got her pregnant.'

'What *are* you talking about?'

Jackie marched over to the sideboard and opened a drawer, and pulled out a fistful of papers. She held them up in her hand and Dan could make out in the corner of the topmost sheet the black horse logo of Lloyd's Bank. 'Every month, from your bank account, there is a transfer of two hundred and fifty pounds into Debbie Leishman's account in New York.'

Dan put down the mug of coffee on the sideboard and covered his face with his hands. Oh my God, he thought to himself, it's all been a bloody misunderstanding. I've just admitted to sleeping with a woman, and Jackie had absolutely no idea about it.

'Oh, yes,' Jackie continued, 'you do that! You cover your face, Dan Porter, because I've found you out. And do you know how I did that?' She turned and pulled another piece of paper from the drawer. 'Do you know what this is?'

'No, Jackie, I have no idea,' Dan replied resignedly.

'It's an e-mail from your Debbie bloody Leishman. When I got back from Milan, I went to check my e-mails and of course you know as well as I do what pops up onto the screen when the computer is switched on. Your wretched in-box!' She held the piece of paper up in front of her as if she were about to sing an aria. *'Dear Dan, I really don't know how I can thank you for continuing to be such a wonderful friend.'* She read it in a whining American drawl. *'Without your support, I could never have afforded to stay off work so long with the baby. He continues to do well, and very soon I shall send you a real long update on how he is progressing and a photograph so that you can see for yourself just how like his daddy he is turning out to be. I still have wonderful memories of that weekend we had up in Maine. Oh, that we could wind back the clock and make it all happen over again. With my love, as always, Debbie.'*

She scrumpled up the piece of paper and lobbed it over her shoulder. 'So, Dan Porter, you are a father four times over. What a stud you are!'

Dan slowly shook his head. 'Are you quite finished?'

Jackie let out a short laugh. 'What do you mean, "quite finished"? I'm barely started, Dan.'

'The father of that baby, Jackie, was John Fricker, and for your information, he and Debbie were *not* married. They had, however, been living together for about three months before he was killed in the World Trade Center. And because they weren't married, Debbie was not eligible for compensation. She was a working girl and she wasn't dependent on John. She didn't even know she was pregnant when he died. Anyway, after the baby was born, I took it upon myself to help her in the only way I could.'

Jackie's mouth was set hard and her eyes narrowed with contempt. It was the first time ever that Dan had seen her look ugly. 'So what's all this about "the wonderful weekend that *we* spent together in Maine"?' Her voice changed once more to the sugary American accent.

'That was John, Debbie and myself. If I remember right, it was after that weekend that they became a couple.'

Jackie had had her direction planned from the start, but she knew now that it had been a false trail. She backtracked through their conversation to seek out her next point of attack, her head quivering with the effort. 'So, who *did* you have an affair with?' she eventually blurted out.

Dan flopped a hand dismissively at her. 'I've had enough of this witch-hunt, Jackie.' He poured the remainder of his coffee into the sink. 'I'm not telling you.' He turned to face her. 'Anyway, what's all this business of me making *you* feel guilty?'

Jackie bit hard on her bottom lip. 'I'm leaving you, Dan.'

'I beg your pardon?'

'I'm leaving you.'

'For heaven's sake, Jackie. Don't be so bloody ridiculous. You can't leave. We've got a marriage. We've got children. You can't just turn your back on twenty years of accumulation.' He leaned a hand against the sink. 'Jackie, it was only one night.'

Without speaking, Jackie turned and walked over to the door.

She opened it and cast a glance over her shoulder at him. 'Goodbye, Dan.'

'Jackie, you are being totally irrational.'

But she had closed the door behind her before he had finished the sentence.

Dan leaned his bottom against the kitchen sink and crossed his arms and looked out at the bare little garden at the back of the house. Better to leave her for a bit. It was just another of their rows. Admittedly, she had every reason to feel hurt and angry, but they would be able to sort it out. They had always been able to do so in the past. He heard her moving around upstairs, going from one room to the other, and then her footsteps began to descend the stairs once more. They sounded denser this time, and it occurred to Dan that she could well be carrying something of considerable weight.

He pushed himself away from the sink and walked quickly over to the door and opened it. He had been right. Jackie was standing in the hallway with a suitcase at her side. She glanced at him briefly and then up the stairwell, a worried expression creasing her brow. And then Dan heard a second set of footsteps descend the stairs.

He was a young man, maybe thirty years old, dressed in a pair of dark blue chinos, a black polo-necked sweater, and a blazer, and he was carrying another suitcase that Dan recognized as being Jackie's. By the time that he had reached the bottom of the stairs, Jackie had already opened the front door and placed her suitcase against it to keep it open. She took hold of the man's arm and ushered him quickly towards the door.

'Who is this, Jackie?' Dan asked, walking slowly up the two steps from the kitchen and along the passage towards them.

'Come on, Stephen, for God's sake, let's go,' Jackie murmured urgently at the man.

Dan heard every word. 'Stephen. Oh, for heaven's sake, it's the wonderboy Stephen.'

Stephen turned and gave Dan an uncertain smile.

Dan let out a long whistle as everything became clear in his mind. 'So, Jackie, this is your reason for feeling so guilty, is it? The wonderboy Stephen.' Dan looked hard at the man. 'Tell me, Stephen, how long have you been bonking my wife in my own house?' The smile slid from Stephen's face and he turned to look at Jackie for support.

'I'll be back for the rest of my things later, Dan.'

'Oh, will you? Well, you'd better get yourself a bloody great van, because you can take our bed with you as well. I would hate to deprive Stephen here of his *shagpit!*' He spat out the words only inches from the young man's face, and he noticed with pleasure that he flinched as spittle shot into his eye. Dan shook his head. 'Well, at least you had the decency to send the girls away so that they didn't have to listen to you rogering each other all night.'

Jackie took hold of Stephen's arm once more and guided him out of the house. 'Come on, Stephen, let's get out of here before he gets violent.'

But strangely enough, Dan had not one instinct towards physical violence. He just felt sad and tired and pretty much emotionally drained. He simply watched as Jackie and Stephen pushed and jostled each other awkwardly down the short path. They opened the gate and turned out onto the street, and Dan stood listening to the fast tap-tapping of Jackie's high-heeled shoes and the clattering wheels of her pull-along suitcase on the pavement as she hurried away to put the greatest possible distance between herself and her husband and her home.

Despite the emotional turmoil and heartbreak that had been caused by Jackie's departure, Dan did take Millie and Nina skiing at Christmas, having managed to pick up a cheap deal on a cancelled holiday in Andorra. It was the best thing he could have done. They were up on the slopes every morning at nine-thirty and they skied hard all day, thumping out their anger and frustration on the mogul fields until they heard the hooter sound out for the final cable car to take them down the mountain. And when they returned to the empty house in Clapham on New Year's Eve, the excitement of a party at Jessica Napier's house that evening and the prospect of returning to Alleyn's in just a few weeks' time helped to keep the spirits of Millie and Nina buoyant.

The hallway floor was scattered with Christmas cards when they entered the house, and Dan simply collected them together and placed them on the hall table. He didn't particularly feel like opening any of them. He knew that Jackie's name would be written on every one. So they remained there until that evening when he stood on the front step, waving the girls off to their party. He shut the door, picked up the pile, and took them through to the kitchen. He took a beer from the fridge, sat down at the table, and began to open them. After the fifth one, he pushed the pile aside and took a long drink from his can of beer.

His eye was caught by one envelope that was not the lurid pink or Caribbean blue of a Christmas card. He reached forward and slid it out of the disordered pile and immediately saw the Seascape logo in the top left-hand corner. It was addressed to him in type. He waved the envelope around in front of his eyes, wondering if he wanted to open this one any more than he did the Christmas cards. Blowing out a breath of trepidation, he broke the seal with his forefinger and took out the letter. He took another large swig of his beer before opening it up and reading it.

Dear Dan,

I'm dictating this letter to Betty in the office, because my handwriting now looks as if an inebriated spider has fallen into an inkwell and then crawled across the paper. For this reason, you will probably find not one of my usual expletives written down, because Betty is a very good editor. (Patrick wants me to write here that that is not what he said, but I am not going to type that kind of a word. By the way, I hope that you are well and keeping your spirits up.)

I was sorry not to have had the chance to say goodbye, but Kate told me about the job and I am delighted for you, although I am sure that it would have tasted a good deal sweeter if you had not been faced with such a devastating domestic crisis on your return. I do hope that you and the girls are being able to cope all right. Anyway, Kate and I keep sending huge amounts of love and strength to all three of you down the airwaves!

We had Josh for Christmas and he was obviously quite subdued after learning about it all, but the children loved having him with us. I think that he's heading off to Edinburgh for New Year with Maria José, so that should cheer him up a bit. I decided that he needed a bit of a boost just before Christmas so I sent him down to Oban for a couple of days to get a bit of work experience with Ronnie Macaskill. Ronnie kept him for a week! He said that the boy is a natural buyer and has 'a good eye for a prawn'! Definitely his father's son, Ronnie said. He also asked me to send on his best wishes to you, and said that if you're ever wanting another game of shinty, all you have to do is pick up the phone!

Your dogs seem to have taken up permanent residence at Auchnacerie. The kids think they're wonderful, although Biggles was definitely 'persona non grata' over Christmas, having grabbed the stuffing off the kitchen table before Kate had the chance to ram it into the turkey!

I managed to get out of hospital a week after you left. Can't stand those places. I'm not much good at the minute, though. That wretched chest infection rather took its toll, so the walking sticks have been retired and I'm on wheels all the time now. But I'm still alive and kicking, and Pete Jackson and Bob Murray, the guy who joined us from Ocean Produce, are managing to keep the business up and running.

But, Dan, what I really wanted to say in this letter was how much I have appreciated your help and your friendship over these past few months. I don't think I have ever enjoyed a time in my life more. I will remember with great fondness our trips together to Mallaig and all the laughs that you gave me. Talking of which, remember that dreadful man, Maxwell Borthwick? (BMW and forklift truck ring a bell!?) Well, I think that I managed to deflate his ego once and for all. I won't bore you with the details, but it was a wonderfully enjoyable experience!

Most of all, though, I want to thank you for the support that you gave Kate when I was in hospital in Inverness. This illness is a bugger (He made me put that – Betty) and sometimes it has been extremely hard for me to give the kind of support that Kate is in most need of. (Bad English – won't let *me change it!) You are a good, compassionate man, Dan Porter, and I feel blessed in knowing that it was you who was at Kate's side when she needed most the strength and understanding of a true friend. And that's exactly what you are — to all the Trenchard family.*

Keep well, Dan, and I hope that very soon you saddle up your horse and ride back into Cowboy Country. We'll have the steaks sizzling and the coffee pot on the stove when you do!

With very best wishes,

Patrick

Dan had to read it through three times before fully understanding the code that Patrick had adopted in his letter. He was now permanently in a wheelchair. He couldn't write himself. Pete Jackson and Bob Murray were coping with the running of the business, yet he went to all the trouble of going into the office so that Betty could type him out a letter. Why? Because he didn't want Katie to type it. He didn't want her to find out what he knew.

Dan tilted back the wooden chair and linked his hands behind his head. He knew now that he had made the right decision to return to London. Patrick had known instinctively what had taken place between him and Katie. He should have known that there was never the need to tell Lie No. 1 in the first place.

Although having been in constant contact with his mother since his return to London, Dan had never actually gone to see her. He knew that he had to tell her face-to-face about his marriage split-up, and he was just putting off the fateful day. However, he had always promised that he would bring in the New Year with her and her friends in Cavendish Rise, and it was therefore with a certain amount of foreboding that he let himself into her flat at nine o'clock that evening.

Looking up as he entered the stiflingly hot little sitting room, Battersea Gran levered herself out of the armchair from where she had been watching her television with the volume shut off.

'Hello, love,' she said as he bent down to give her a kiss on either cheek. 'Well, let's have a look at you.' She stood back and studied him with as much pleasure as she might have done having just won the star prize on the Wheel of Fortune. 'My word, that skiing holiday has done you the world of good. You've certainly got wonderful colour in your cheeks.'

'We were lucky. The sun shone every day,' Dan replied.

'Well, I'm sure that you'll really be feeling the cold now,' she said, stepping forward and rubbing the arm of his leather jacket between her fingers to gauge its thermal qualities. 'You know, Dan, you're of an age now when you shouldn't be bothering about dressing up in trendy gear. You should go and buy yourself a good cardy. That's what your father always wore, and he hardly had a day's illness in his life.'

Dan burst out laughing and grabbed his mother and gave her a long hug. 'It's great to see you, Mum. I really have missed you.'

'And I've missed you too, son.'

Dan took off his jacket and glanced at the television screen. 'So what are you watching?'

'I think it's the build-up to the big party in Edinburgh.' She smiled up at him. 'I kept the volume down so that I could hear you arriving.'

'Josh is going to be there.'

'Is he?' Battersea Gran exclaimed, walking across to the screen and peering at it. 'Do you think we'd be able to see him?'

'I doubt it. There are hundreds of thousands of people there. It's the largest New Year's party in the world, you know.'

'Really? I do hope he'll be all right,' she said, continuing to squint at the screen. 'It looks awfully cold up there. I hope he's wearing lots of clothes.'

Dan raised his eyebrows behind her back. 'Come on, Mum, let's get settled in to watch it, then. Did you buy some drink?'

'Oh, yes, of course,' she said, breaking away from the television and hurrying off towards the door.

'I'll get it. You sit down.'

'All right, then. I got some cans of lager for you, and because you've been in Scotland, I bought you a bottle of whisky. It was on offer at the local supermarket for nine pounds. It's all on the kitchen table.'

'What about you?'

'I'll just have a glass of sherry, please, dear.'

Dan went through to the kitchen and returned a moment later with a can of beer and the glass of sherry.

'Don't you want a tumbler for that?' she asked as he handed her the sherry.

'No, this is fine.'

'You'll get germs drinking it like that. You don't know who's been handling that can.'

'I think I'll survive.' Dan sat down on the sofa, and leaning back against the white lace antimacassar, pulled the ring off the can. 'Mum, I noticed that there were only two glasses laid out on the kitchen table. I thought you were having a few people round tonight.'

His mother stared at the silent television without answering.

'Mum? I said that I thought there were others coming in to spend New Year with us.'

His mother turned to look at him, and he could see from the way that her lipsticked mouth drooped at the corners that there was something wrong.

'What's happened?' he asked quietly.

'Nothing really, dear. Just a small misunderstanding.'

'About what?'

'About the residents' committee.'

'Tell me about it.'

'Well, dear . . .' – she placed her glass of sherry on the occasional table next to her and settled her elbows on the arm of the chair – 'when I got back from looking after Millie and Nina, I went around to the flat of the chairman of the residents' committee, and asked him when the next meeting was going to be, and he said that I didn't need to bother attending it. I said

281

to him that of course I had to be there because it was my job to make the tea and the scones and everything. And he said to me that because I had been away for so long, they had decided to appoint someone else to that position. And do you know who they have chosen instead of me?'

Dan shook his head. 'Who?'

'It's that dreadful woman Nancy Smith in flat 5F4. I mean, Dan, she can't even butter bread, let alone make a scone, and' – she waggled a finger at him to emphasize her point – 'and she has only been in her flat for six months.' She threw herself back in her armchair and shot a purse-mouthed expression at him. 'Now what do you think of that? It's a blooming scandal, that's what it is.' She pulled a handkerchief from the sleeve of her jersey and dabbed at her eyes. 'I have been usurped, Dan.'

'It sounds like it.'

'And now nobody will speak to me.'

'I'm sure they will, Mum. It'll all blow over in time.'

'It certainly will not, Dan, my boy. It's gone way beyond "blowing over", as you put it.'

'Why?'

His mother did not reply, but instead crossed her arms and pouted her mouth.

'What did you do, Mum?' Dan asked, trying to suppress a laugh.

'I took the one course that was left open to me.'

'Which was what?'

'I demonstrated.'

This time, Dan couldn't help but laugh. 'You demonstrated?'

Battersea Gran leaned forward on the arm of her chair again, a conspiratorial glint in her eye. 'Yes, and I have to say, Dan, that I made a very good demonstrator.'

'What did you do?'

'Well, I went down to the local shop and I bought one of those magic marker thingies, and then I made up this banner on a dish-towel that your Auntie Vi once gave me. I've never used it.'

'What did you write?'

'UNFAIR DISMISSAL. MAKING TEA WAS MY JOB in big black letters. Actually, I got the size of the letters wrong, so I had to write MY JOB on the other side and then keep turning it around.'

'So when did you demonstrate?'

'At the next residents' meeting. I arrived in the hall just at the right time, between Item Three on the agenda – the foyer flower rota, and Item Four – the sanitation of the dustbin area.'

'And what did you do?'

'I walked in, without so much as an invitation, sat down on the floor in front of the committee, and started turning my dish-cloth this way and that and chanting, "Unfair dismissal. Making tea was my job. Unfair dismissal. Making tea was my job."' She grinned excitedly at Dan. 'It's got a good ring to it, hasn't it?'

'And did they take any notice?'

'They certainly did. I disrupted the whole meeting.'

'Well done, you, Mum. I'm really proud of you.'

She dabbed at her eyes with the handkerchief once more. 'But then, I can hardly bring myself to tell you what happened next, Dan.'

'Well, if you can, I would very much appreciate it.'

She took in a deep breath. 'I was evicted.'

'Oh dear.'

'Thrown out I was, Dan. Like an intruder in my own block of flats.'

'And who was brave enough to carry out the eviction?'

'Stan Beardsley from the Fabric Committee. Dan, he used to be a commissionaire at the Hyde Park Hotel. I didn't stand a chance. I mean, it was like calling in the professionals. He lifted me bodily from the floor and put me down in the corridor.' Her face crumpled, and in that instant, Dan realized where Nina had inherited her aptitude for looking totally miserable. 'And I haven't spoken to anyone since. I have been sitting in my little flat over the past four weeks without so much as one knock on the door.'

Dan looked at her, a frown creasing his forehead. 'What do you mean, the past four weeks? Haven't you been staying at Clapham?'

'No, dear, I have not.'

'But who's been looking after Millie and Nina?'

'I suppose Jackie,' she replied tartly.

'But Jackie works, Mum.'

'I know she does, dear, but she said' – she faltered – 'she said that she could manage without me.'

'She never did.'

'She said that she never wanted me in the house again.' Battersea Gran wrung her handkerchief in her plump little hands. 'I'm sorry, Dan, I didn't mean to tell you that. I know that she's your wife, but we just had our differences, and try as I might, I could never seem to do or say the right thing.'

Dan put his head in his hands. 'Oh, Mum, I'm so sorry.'

'No, dear, it was probably my fault all along.'

'No, it certainly wasn't.' He dropped his hands onto the sofa and turned to look at her. 'Listen, Mum, this is not very easy to tell you, but . . . Jackie has left me.'

His mother's face expressed such immediate compassion that he felt like jumping to his feet and kneeling down in front of her and burying his head in her huge, pink-sweatered bosom. 'Oh, Dan. What an awful thing to happen. And you did love her so much.'

Dan shook his head. 'You're right. But I'm afraid "did" is probably the operative word.'

She leaned across and held onto his arm. 'Had she been playing around, dear?'

Dan nodded.

'I had my suspicions, I have to say.'

'Yes. I reckon you would have done.' Dan leaned forward on the sofa and looked at his mother. 'Are you happy here, Mum?'

'What, here in the flat, do you mean?'

'Yes.'

'No, I'm bloody miserable, if you will pardon my French.'

'Well, I wondered if you might like to come to live with me and the girls in Clapham.'

'Oh no, dear, I could never impose myself on you like that.'

'Mum, you would not be imposing yourself. Right now, I don't think there is anyone we would rather have in the house.'

'Do you really mean that, Dan?'

'Yes, I really mean it. As you know, the girls are going back to Alleyn's, so if we sell this place, it would certainly help me with the finances.' He took a drink of beer from his can. 'At least please think about it, Mum.'

His mother smiled at him. 'I don't need to think about it, dear. I can't think of anything I would rather do.'

'Good.' He raised his can towards her. 'Let's toast ourselves an early Happy New Year then, shall we?' He clinked his can against her glass. 'Cheers, Mum.'

'Chin-chin, love.'

Battersea Gran picked up the remote for her television and turned it up to almost full volume. The roar of the crowd in Edinburgh filled the room. 'Now let's see if we can spot Josh,' she yelled across the three-foot gap between herself and her son.

'What? no Tarquin today?' Dan asked as he placed his pint of beer down on the table in the King's Head pub.

'Not today,' Nick Jessop replied, folding up the business supplement of *The Sunday Times* and discarding it onto the pile of newspapers that lay beside him on the bench. 'Laura has taken him off to some fancy-dress party this afternoon. It was quite incongruous to see a pirate with a dummy in his mouth.' He took a gulp of beer. 'So what have you done with your family today?'

Dan took off his leather jacket and hung it on the back of the chair before sitting down. 'They're all out of the house. Battersea Gran headed off to church on the bus this morning, and then rang to say that she's going to have lunch with a friend. And the girls have gone round to see Jackie.'

'Ah. So contact has been reestablished.'

'Not really. It's mostly through the lawyers. One good thing, though, is that I had a phone call from her lawyer on Friday, saying that I could stay in the house for as long as the girls were in full-time education. That should give me time to build up enough capital to buy a flat somewhere.'

'That sounds a decent enough arrangement. How are the girls getting on at Alleyn's?'

'Loving it.' Dan took a drink of beer. 'I should never have taken them away in the first place.'

'C'est la vie,' Nick said, raising his glass. 'So it's back to the old times, then.'

'Almost.'

Nick leaned his elbows on the table. 'I've really enjoyed working with you again, Dan. It's been great having you in the office over the past few months. It's given the whole place a boost.'

'Well, I have you to thank for getting me the job.'

'Think nothing of it. By the way' – he picked up the business supplement and leafed quickly through it and then folded it twice – 'you've got your name in the papers again.' He handed it over to Dan.

Dan read quickly through the short article about the proposed merger between Broughton's and Carswell Asset Management and then lobbed the supplement back onto the bench. He noticed in the pile of newspapers the gaudy red front page of the *News of the World*. He scoffed and shook his head. 'Honestly, Nick, I don't know why you bother reading all that crap.'

Nick glanced down at his newspapers. 'To which publication are you referring in such disparaging terms?'

'The *News of the World*, Nick. It's a load of rubbish.'

'It is not!' Nick retorted, pulling the paper out from below the pile. 'I think it's great. The *News of the World* is the master of the pun.' He opened up the broadsheet and began scanning its pages. 'This, for instance. "Tellers a Story about Williams Bonk". Now *tellers* is spelt t-e-l-l-e-r-s. What do you think that's about?'

'I have no idea.'

'Two tellers were caught on the security camera of Williams Bank having it off in the safe.'

'That's very good. I wonder why I didn't guess.'

'Right. I'll try another one on you.' Nick turned the page and

287

sought out his next tacky headline. 'Okay, this one. "Strip Cartoon in Leicester Square Keeps Abreast with Technology." Any idea?'

Dan let out a sigh. 'Well, it's got to be something to do with breasts.'

'Yes?' Nick said, slanting his eyes at Dan, wanting him to go into a little more depth.

'I have no idea, Nick.'

Nick sucked his teeth. 'You're hopeless. "*Belinda Carter (24), a secretary from Bromley, Kent, gave everyone a thrill in Leicester Square on Friday night. Returning from a Cartoon Character party, held in the Planet Hollywood restaurant, she divested herself of every last stitch of her Minnie Mouse outfit and danced naked on a bench in the square. The crowd that gathered around to watch were not only captivated by her dance routine, but also by the enormity of her breasts. 'I'm very proud of them,' she told the policeman who had covered her indiscretions with his jacket before leading her away. 'It cost me six months' wages to get these silicone implants and I like to display them.'*" How about that, then?'

'Thank you, Nick. I am enlightened. Now, do you think that you could put that paper down so that we could have a normal conversation?'

'One more.'

'Oh, for heaven's sake.'

'Just a quick one.' He turned the page. 'Right, you should get this one.' He quickly read through the story. 'And you'll be pleased to hear that it's not even smutty. Are you ready?'

Dan didn't even bother to reply. He just nodded his head.

'"Prawn to Stay Alive."'

'No idea.'

'Not even going to hazard a guess?'

'No.'

Nick looked disappointed. 'All right then. "*When a rescue team reached the wreckage of a light aircraft that had crashed into a fog-bound hillside in remote Wester Ross, they were amazed to find that its cargo of prawns were still alive and crawling around on the ground.*

'It was amazing that anything survived that kind of an impact,' said Hughie McLeish of the Lochaber Mountain Rescue Team. 'They must be tough little creatures.' The pilot of the plane, Dick Freeman (52) of Inverness, was killed outright along with his passenger, Patrick Trenchard (45) of Fort Will—''

'Oh for God's sake!' exclaimed Dan, grabbing the paper from Nick.

'What's the matter? What are you objecting to now?'

Dan held up a hand as he continued to read the article.

Patrick Trenchard of Fort William. The plane, a Piper Aztec, had been chartered by Mr Trenchard, who owns Seascape, the Fort William-based prawn factory, to fly a shipment of prawns from the Outer Hebrides back to the mainland. 'I stuck a load of the prawns in a plastic bag and put them in my haversack,' continued Hughie. 'The wife and I had them for our tea and they were delicious!'

Dan tossed the paper back onto the table. 'I have to go, Nick.'

'Why?'

Dan got up and flipped his jacket off the back of the chair. 'I'll tell you later.' He hurried off towards the door of the pub, and then stopped and went back to the table. 'Listen, Nick, I might not be at work tomorrow. I don't know yet, but just be prepared if I don't show up.'

'Why? Come on, Dan, you've got to give me some idea of what's happened.'

Dan pointed at the News of the World on the table. 'Patrick Trenchard was the chap Josh and I worked for up in Scotland. He was a great friend of mine.'

'Oh, God. I'm really sorry, Dan, I had no idea.'

'No, you did me a favour. I'm not quite sure why Josh has never rung to tell me. So would you be able to cover for me if I do go AWOL?'

'Of course.'

'I'll keep in touch just in case there's any development on the Carswell merger.'

'How long do you reckon you'll be away?'

'Not long. I promise you that I won't leave you in the lurch, though.'

As Dan ran back to the house in Haleridge Road, he cursed himself for not having brought his mobile phone with him. He made it there in ten minutes flat. He opened the front door and went straight through to the kitchen and picked up the telephone receiver. He dialled Josh's mobile number.

'Come on, Josh,' he muttered under his breath. 'Answer it, for God's sake.'

The mobile was redirected to Josh's voicemail service, and Dan ended the call without leaving a message. Josh must have been out of range, no doubt at the cottage. He thought about ringing the factory, but being a Sunday, the switchboard would probably not be manned. Anyway, the place would more than likely be closed following Patrick's death.

That left him only one option. Auchnacerie.

For a moment, his hand hovered above the dialling keyboard before he punched in the number. As soon as the call was connected, it was answered by his son.

'Josh?'

'Dad, where the hell have you been? I've been trying to get in touch with you all morning. Dad, I've got some really bad news—'

'I know, Josh. I've just read about it in the Sunday papers. When did it happen?'

'Friday night.'

'Why didn't you contact me?'

'Because I only heard about it last night when I got back from Barcelona.'

'What were you doing there?'

'Patrick sent me and Maria José over on a sales trip.'

'Right.' Even though Dan was eager for information, he still experienced a swell of pride at Josh's obvious rise in status. 'So why are you at Auchnacerie?'

'Maria José and I are looking after Max and Sooty. Katie's had to go up to Inverness to have a meeting in the coroner's office. There has to be an enquiry.'

'How are the children?'

'They seem to be bearing up all right. Max is here with me, and Maria José and Sooty have taken the dogs for a walk.'

'Did you see Katie before she left?'

'Yes, I did.'

'How is she taking it?'

'She's obviously upset, but, on the other hand, she seems to be quite calm about it all. Maybe that's what comes from living with illness for so long. She's a pretty tough person.'

'I know she is.'

'Just before she left for Inverness, she told me that Patrick had been planning this trip for ages, and that he had been so excited about it. She said that he would have wanted to end his days doing something completely madcap like that, rather than fester away in a wheelchair.'

'I think that's very true.' Dan suddenly had a vision of Patrick, eyes glinting with excitement and intrigue, staring out of the plane windscreen into the all-enveloping fog. He shook his head to clear it from his mind. 'I don't suppose any arrangements have been made for the funeral?'

'Not yet. Katie reckons that there'll be a postmortem.'

'Of course.'

'Are you coming up, Dad?'

Dan ran a hand through his hair. 'I've got to work it out, Josh. I'll have to have a word with Battersea Gran and the girls before I make a decision.' He bit at his bottom lip. 'What's your gut feeling, Josh? You always seem to know.'

There was a brief silence on the line. 'I think you should come up immediately, Dad,' Josh said quietly. 'Katie needs your support. That's my gut feeling.'

Dan smiled. 'I'm glad you said that, Josh.'

'So will you come?'

'I'll try to get on the train tonight. Can I get hold of you at Auchnacerie?'

'Yes. Maria José and I are staying here until Katie gets back.'

'In that case, I'll make some plans and then give you a call. I'll just stay at the cottage.'

'All right, then,' Josh replied, 'and Dad, you'd better bring some warm clothes. It's bloody freezing up here.'

30

'There was no need for you all to come, you know,' Dan said to his mother as he walked with her and Millie and Nina along the platform at Euston Station.

'No bother at all, dear,' puffed Battersea Gran. 'Sunday night telly has never been quite the same since *Monarch of the Glen* finished. Anyway, I've always rather liked railway stations. There's such an air of excitement about them!'

Dan found his carriage and put his suitcase in through the door. He had taken notice of what Josh had said about the weather and now turned to face his farewell committee wearing his padded jacket and fawn-coloured corduroy trousers. 'I'll be back as soon as I can,' he said, bending down and giving his mother a kiss on the cheek. 'I'll let you know when.'

Battersea Gran put her hand on the sleeve of his jacket and her eyes brightened when she felt its soft, downy texture. 'Now that's what I call clothing. At last you've come to your senses.'

The girls began laughing behind her back. Dan shot them a wink before moving over to Nina and giving her a kiss and a long hug. Then he put his arms around Millie's neck. 'You be in charge,' he whispered into her ear. 'Give me a call if anything goes haywire.'

'All right, Dad,' Millie said, giving him a smacking kiss on the side of his neck. 'Even though you're dressed like a prat, I still love ya.'

Dan laughed. 'I'm glad to hear it.'

'Give my love to everyone up there.'

'I will do.' He broke away from Millie's embrace. 'Right, you lot, I think you should get away home. There's no point waiting until the train leaves.'

He stood watching them until they had reached the gate at the top of the platform. They turned and gave him an enthusiastic wave before disappearing into the crowded terminus. He shook his head slowly. What a difference, he thought to himself. Six months ago, those girls would hardly have acknowledged his existence, yet now they could not be more close to him. He tilted back his head and gazed up at the cavernous glass roof of the station. Six months ago, he had been precisely here, on his way up to Scotland on some whimsical jaunt, without one iota of realization that his selfish, insular existence had led his family into crisis. And what a price he had had to pay for it.

He turned and walked over to the carriage door, then glanced back to where he had last seen Battersea Gran and Millie and Nina. He could never afford to make that mistake again. Two families now depended on it. He knew that he owed that much to Patrick.

And as he boarded the train, he thought of Katie and he grinned as her shrewd advice came to mind. He took his wallet from the inside pocket of his jacket, and extracting a ten-pound note, he went off in search of the car attendant.

Starburst

This book is dedicated to the memories of
two incandescent fireflies,

JOANNA and HENRIETTA MACRAE

Who held the Big Umbrella
While Rowena played her fiddle
On the castle esplanade

Acknowledgements

There are many aspects of this book that had never been covered by my own experiences, so I had to rely on quite lengthy research to make it seem as authentic as possible. I am therefore indebted to the following people:

Wilf Scott, MVO, Master Pyrotechnic, of Pyrovision
Owen O'Leary of the Edinburgh Festival Fringe
Susie Burnet of the Edinburgh International Festival
Alistair Rae of Hartlepool Borough Council
Christine Beroff of Le Conservatoire National Supérieur de
    Musique et de Danse de Paris
Harry Bell of Tern Television
Sergeant Wilson Gove of Tayside Police, Traffic Division
Roddie Urquhart of A& WM Urquhart, WS
Amanda Bower of the Sheraton Grand Hotel, Edinburgh
Sarah Rymer, concert violinist
Graham Nicholson for his knowledge of Edinburgh
Anna Wemyss for her knowledge of the Underbelly
Jamie and Sarah Jauncey for brainstorming Dessuin with me

Also my daughter, Alice, who helped me work on the younger characters in the book, and my daughter-in-law, Abi, who gave me valuable assistance with the Edinburgh vernacular!

Walking around Edinburgh in late July, you'll likely feel the first vibrations of the earthquake that is festival time, which shakes the city throughout August and into September. You may hear reference to an 'Edinburgh Festival', but this is really an umbrella term for six separate festivals all taking place around the same time.

The best-known and oldest of these is the Edinburgh International Festival. The festival was founded in 1947, when Europe was recovering from World War II. Festival founders believed that some event was needed to draw the continent together and 'provide a platform for the flowering of the human spirit'.

In recent years, the festival has drawn as many as 400,000 people to Edinburgh, with acts by world-renowned music, opera, theatre, and dance performers, filling all the major venues in the city.

Edinburgh festival time can fill almost any artistic need . . . Edinburgh in August is an experience you are unlikely to forget!

— *The New York Times*

One

The confetti was a bit of a mystery. Two weeks after the wedding and the multicoloured flakes still kept appearing in every room of the flat. Sometimes they materialised in force under the new king-sized bed or piled up in small drifts behind the television in the sitting room; other times no more than a single fragment floated delicately on toaster thermals around the kitchen. At first, despite the need to vacuum every room on a daily basis, its presence had given Tess a warming sense of fulfilment, a constant reminder of everything that had happened on her Big Day. But now, as she pulled the polo-necked jersey from the top shelf of her wardrobe and a fresh flurry drifted down on to the polished floorboards of the bedroom, she felt it was all becoming a bit of an inconvenience and, like thawing snow, it had been around too long.

Tess had a sneaking suspicion that it was Allan who was to blame for it all. She had visions of him tiptoeing about the flat, sprinkling the tissue petals around like love dust so as to keep the spirit of their wedding day alive. But when she had broached the subject on the previous morning as he stood stark-naked shaving in front of the full-length bathroom mirror, he had rather disappointingly denied the whole idea. 'Nice thought, angel' – mouth to the left as he scraped away at the right cheek – 'but I'm afraid it's not been me' – chin pulled down for more scraping under nose – 'probably like sand after being on a beach,' – turns to look at newly wedded wife with perfectly formed shaving-foam goatee and gesticulates with razor in hand – 'you know, you find it between your toes and in your belly button and other places for days afterwards.'

That had been enough for Tess. The thought of 'other places' had cut any notion of romantic frivolity from her mind.

Seated on the edge of the bed, Tess pulled on her brown leather calf-length boots, wrestled the legs of her jeans over them, and then got up and walked over to open the wooden shutters on one of the room's tall sash-framed windows. Her spirits, which had been flying at Learjet height since the wedding, sank a little when she looked out on to another grey day in the Scottish capital. She could tell by the movement of the leafless trees just visible up by Heriot Row and by the way the pedestrians on the pavement below walked up Dundas Street clutching their coats closed at the neck, that the wind was coming from the north, sweeping cold and unguarded across the Firth of Forth. Spring is a season that's lost its reason, she thought to herself. The beginning of May and it could as well be February. An icy draught sought out a space at the side of the ancient window frame, surrounding her with a chill that made her shiver and clasp her hands under her armpits. It was about the one thing, being married, that she – regretted, having to leave her cosy little tenement block flat in West College Street and move here to Allan's great barn of a place, situated in the infinitely smarter New Town.

Tess picked up her mobile from the bedside table and thumbed a couple of buttons. She held it to her ear as she pulled on her woollen jacket and shouldered the strap of her laptop case. When Allan eventually answered, his greeting was unintelligible through a mouthful of food.

'It's me,' Tess said, picking up her keys from the table in the hallway.

She heard Allan swallow. 'I know. Your name came up. Sex Maniac.'

'It does not say that!'

'No, you're right. It says Mrs Goodwin.'

The name change was something else Tess was having difficulty getting used to. Back in her schooldays, her jotters had been covered with the test autographs of soon-to-be-famous Tess

Hartley, but now her pen found it impossible to flow from the *s* of Tess to the *G* of Goodwin, and her signature had taken on the appearance of that of an incompetent forger.

'That's nice,' she said with a smile, as she double-locked the door of the flat and began descending the stone steps, the clipping heels of her boots echoing up the chilly stairwell.

'So, where are you?'

'Sitting in a traffic jam on the M8, twenty miles from Glasgow.'

'What time did you leave this morning?'

'Six-thirty. I would have woken you but you were out for the count, so I just gazed hungrily at you and left. Are you still in bed?'

'No, I'm on my way out.'

'My word, that's a bit keen, isn't it? It's only just gone seven-thirty.'

'I know, but I've got to be up at the Hub early. Alasdair's calling in from Budapest at eight.'

'What's he doing there?'

'Sounding out some dance company he thinks might fill an empty slot in the programme.'

'What gives with Sarah then? I thought she liked hogging the morning phone calls with the great Sir Alasdair Dreyfuss.'

Tess smiled wryly as she pulled shut the heavy entrance door and walked the few steps down on to the pavement. Allan was right. Sarah Atkinson, the marketing director of the Edinburgh International Festival and her own immediate boss, liked to be the one who liaised with the director, especially when he was on one of his incessant scouting missions abroad.

'She's down in England, having a meeting with the Royal Shakespeare Company,' she replied, glancing down Dundas Street to see if there was a bus in sight. A double-decker, resplendently dull in the Edinburgh corporation colours of maroon and dirty-white, stood at the traffic lights. 'What time do you think you'll be home?'

'Sevenish.'

'Fancy something to eat out?'

'No, I fancy you.'

Tess felt a loved-up glow swell in her stomach. 'I know it. But that doesn't answer my question.'

'OK, we'll eat out. Hey, looks like the traffic's starting to move. Better get off the phone. See ya, angel.'

'OK, see you tonight.'

Tess slipped her mobile into the pocket of her jacket and boarded the bus, waiting for an elderly grey-faced gentleman dressed in a creased pinstriped suit and carrying a weary-looking leather briefcase to clear the stairs before she climbed to the upper deck and jolted into a seat, as the bus took off.

It hadn't been the best time to get married, what with Allan just getting a promotion and her working all hours at the International Festival office, but then again it had almost come down to a 'make or break' situation. If anyone were to ask her, she would say they'd been together for just over three years, but in truth that was a bit of a generalisation. Their relationship had always blown hot and cold, even to the extent that for a four-month period two years ago they had taken a complete break from each other. During that time, they slalomed into affairs and crashed out of them, coming back together to lick their wounds and begin to piece together the shaky confidence they had in each other. Those on-the-side flings were easy to forgive. The one Tess had the following year was not, yet even though it rocked their boat quite forcefully, it never succeeded in capsizing it. And that was the danger. It was Allan who said their relationship had become too comfortable, almost verging on the platonic, and that neither was doing the other any favours by continuing to live without any form of commitment. So he proposed to her, and Tess had agreed without even giving the question any thought. It seemed the most natural thing to do. It was just they'd never got round to doing anything about it.

In the same way that they'd never got round to organising a honeymoon. After the wedding, they'd both taken a couple of days off work to move her belongings into Allan's flat, but neither felt it the right time to head off on holiday. Maybe she would get on to the Internet this morning, if there was no urgent business to attend to once she'd spoken to the director, and see if she couldn't book a couple of weeks in September after the festival had finished. Right now, on this cold, raw day, she fancied somewhere sunny and warm, somewhere that sounded exotic, with white sandy beaches and palm trees and a blue sea that merged into the sky on the horizon. She smiled to herself and nodded decisively. Yes, somewhere like Barbados would just fit the bill nicely, thank you very much.

As the bus took the lights on Queen Street and edged its way slowly up the slope, Tess rubbed the sleeve of her jacket on the steamed-up window and gazed out at the sight of Edinburgh's citizens walking to work. Men and women dressed alike in formal, colourless clothes, adding to the general drabness of the day, but apt apparel for those who earned their daily crust in the city's many financial and legal institutions. It never ceased to amaze Tess that a city that seemed to wallow in a state of such stolid lugubriousness for most of the year should, for three weeks in August, suddenly behave as if its water supply had been spiked with amphetamine. But she knew only too well that this dichotomy had existed since the festival's inception in 1947, and even though it was now regarded as one of the foremost artistic and cultural gatherings in the world, it had only been in the past ten years that the opinion of the archetypal 'Edinburgh citizen' had really changed towards the event. Up until then, it had been viewed as a dreaded yearly inconvenience when taxis were impossible to find and restaurants were crowded out. Little was made of the cultural kudos the festival brought to the city, nor of the extra revenue generated for its businesses and householders by the thousands of visitors who came for those three late summer weeks every year. There was no doubt in the minds of everyone who worked in the International office that the favourable change of opinion was due, in no small part, to the present director, Sir Alasdair Dreyfuss, but he himself would be the first to deny it, being as reticent about promoting his own sizeable achievements as he was about using the 'handle' of his recently awarded knighthood.

Tess got off the bus and began to walk up Lawnmarket, the uppermost stretch of the Royal Mile. This was where she felt comfortable, the Old Town, with its small-windowed buildings of ancient, gnarled stone, its cobbled streets, its more youthful and exuberant inhabitants, its seedy but atmospheric public houses, its tacky tourist shops, selling everything from ghost tours to tartan ginger-wigged tammies, CDs of wailing Gaelic love songs, weaponry – the genuine article, of course – used by the Highland clans to fight the Jacobite cause in 1745; claymores so blunt that they would hardly give a clumsy sword dancer a bleeding toe, and studded-leather shields that bore not even the faintest scratch of a Redcoat bayonet. Every weekday morning, Tess made the journey from the New Town and it never ceased to give her a frisson of excitement to be back in her old stamping ground.

Crossing over the street, she entered the warm, aromatic interior of a Starbucks café, one of the few insurgent establishments in the street. As she took her place in the queue, two away from being served, the entrance door crashed shut behind her. Everyone in the chrome-strewn place looked up, clasping hands to rattling cups in saucers, deactivating jaws on half-eaten blueberry muffins to stare at the door, expecting the logo-ed glass pane to come crashing to the ground. When nothing happened, the stares were shifted to the young man with the frenzied mop of dark curly hair that spilled on to the shoulders of his far-too-large blue serge overcoat. He stood in front of the door breathing heavily, his hands held up as if surrendering, his eyes tightly closed and a pained expression on his face.

'Sorry . . . sorry . . . sorry.' He opened up one eye and surveyed his scornful audience. 'Sorry?'

Tess decided to help him out. 'That was some entrance, Lewis,' she said with a smile.

The young man took a couple of steps towards her. 'It was your fault, Tess,' he said quietly to her in a lilting Welsh accent.

'What d' you mean, *my* fault?'

'Well, I was just about to go into the Fringe office when I saw you get off the bus, so I've just had to run all the way up the High Street to catch you.'

Tess stared at him blankly for a few seconds, scanning through her memory files to work out if she'd forgotten an appointment or to make a telephone call. Lewis Jones was her direct contemporary in the marketing team of the Fringe, one of the seven independently organised festivals that were run under the conglomerate title of the Edinburgh Festival. Although their events were managed separately, each office still liaised closely on city issues and the general organisation of the Festival.

'What was so urgent?'

Lewis shrugged. 'Nothing, really. I just wanted to ask how married life was treating you. I haven't seen you since your big day.'

Maybe it *was* just the accent, but Tess was always aware of Lewis's disarming quality of being able to make people feel sorry for him. Right now, she felt like patting him on the head like a little boy and telling him not to get himself so worried – which was ridiculous, really. Not only did she know that Lewis was just shy of his thirtieth birthday – almost her twin, in fact – but also that he was a very shrewd operator, helping to co-ordinate in his laid-back-to-almost-horizontal way the logisitics for nearly two thousand performers during the three weeks of the Fringe.

'It's – very exciting,' Tess replied with a nod of affirmation. 'I strongly recommend it.'

Lewis sighed. 'No one on the horizon for me, I'm afraid.' He stepped in front of Tess when the girl behind the counter asked for the next order. 'Here, let me buy you a coffee and we can have a chat.'

'I can't, Lewis, sorry. I've got to be in the office in less than five minutes for a telephone call.' Tess turned to the girl behind the counter. 'A cappuccino to go, please.'

'Oh, well, never mind,' Lewis said sombrely. As soon as the girl had slapped the lid on the paper cup and put it on the counter, he picked it up and gave it to Tess. 'Here you are, this one's on me. You'd better get going up the road.'

Tess shot him a smile. 'Thanks, Lewis. See you around.'

If Lewis said anything in reply, she didn't hear it. She left the coffee house at speed, and with one hand clutching the cup and the other preventing the laptop case from thumping against her side, she ran as fast as her tottering boots would allow her up Lawnmarket, a Cinderella figure whose sole objective was to be at her desk before the bells of some nearby clock tower struck out its eighth peal.

The offices and headquarters of Edinburgh International Festival are housed in a converted church at the very top of the Royal Mile, the building having lost its ecclesiastical name along with its pews and pulpit and been 'rechristened' the Hub. Pushing her way through two sets of swing-glass doors, Tess hurried along the central passage, at one time the aisle of the church, with the Hub café behind a long glass partition to one side and the International Ticket Office on the other. She took the staircase two at a time, past the bright-red wall with its random shelves of sculptured figurines, and as she stopped momentarily on the upper landing to catch her breath, she heard the telephone ringing in her office. She ran in and reached across the desk for the receiver, simultaneously ridding herself of the coffee cup and allowing her laptop case to fall from her shoulder on to the ground with an ominous thump.

'International office, good morning.'

'Good morning, Tess. It's Alasdair.'

'Oh, morning, Alasdair.' Tess stretched out the telephone cable with her free hand and walked around the desk to her seat. 'I'm sorry, have you rung before?'

'No, I left it a little later just to give you the chance to get into the office.'

Tess couldn't tell from his tone whether he had said it with any seriousness, but nevertheless she felt her face pulse with nervous embarrassment. Her boss, Sarah Atkinson, was *never* late for her early morning telephone call with the director.

'So, how're things in Budapest?'

'All right. The dance company is good, but I don't think the choreography is up to scratch, so I'm not going to risk booking them for this year. I'll maybe see if I can't fix up some sort of collaboration with Hans Meyer for next year. He'll be coming to direct the Rombert at any rate.'

'Nothing you want me to do from this end, then?' Tess asked, tapping the point of a ballpoint pen expectantly on her desk pad.

'Not for this project,' the director replied, 'but listen, when I was flying out here, I noticed in the newspaper that Angélique Pascal is playing at the Barbican this Thursday. I know it's a bit early for publicity, but seeing she's going to be the International's star turn this year, try tracking her down and organising an interview, and then give Harry Wills a call at the *Sunday Times*. There's every probability you'll get stalled by Albert Dessuin, her manager, but give it a go.'

Tess jotted the names down on her pad, but it was only as a reminder. Both names, especially that of the young French violinist, were well known to her. 'Anything else?' she asked.

'Yes, I want you to ring up Jeff Banyon at the Scottish Chamber Orchestra and ask him if it's definitely Tchaikovsky they're going to be doing for the fireworks at the end of the festival. If not, then we'll have to change our theme to accommodate whatever they've chosen. Now, do you have anything else for me?'

Tess searched the top of her desk for any messages others might have left for the director. 'No, nothing at all.'

'All right. I'll be back in the office tomorrow late afternoon, if all goes well with Air Paperclip. When does Sarah get back?'

'This afternoon.'

'OK, let her know I'll speak to her first thing tomorrow morning. Bye, Tess.'

Tess replaced the receiver and whistled out a breath of relief. She really liked the director but had always felt quite in awe of him. He had an unsettling manner that could be taken as being ice cold if one did not understand the constant pressure he was under, and coming up to working at her third festival in the International office, she felt only now that he treated her as an integral part of the team. Yet the story could have been completely different if he'd ever discovered what had happened over the course of the previous two festivals.

Her affair with Peter Hansen had been clandestine, exciting, and fired by the creative energy that thrummed through the city at the time of the festival. Peter was one of Denmark's top artistic directors, brought in by Sir Alasdair Dreyfuss on a two-year contract to direct a number of theatrical productions, and it had been the director himself who had given Tess the job of chaperoning the man. In his mid-forties, Peter was famous, charismatic, and a practised seducer, and Tess, having just become involved in her first festival, had been flattered by his attentions, and soon accepted her energetic sessions in one of Edinburgh's five-star hotels as part of her duty. She and Allan had been going through one of their 'cool' periods, and even though they were still seeing each other quite regularly, there was never a question of him finding out about it. There was always the excuse of a reception or a dinner she had to attend, or a late-night tour of the city's nightclubs, entertaining the visiting classical performers. So, when the second year came round, both she and Peter took up where they had left off, and Tess knew at every moment of their affair that it was underhand and dangerous, not least because Peter Hansen just happened to be one of Sir Alasdair Dreyfuss's oldest friends, and that for the past five years their respective families had joined together for skiing holidays in Norway.

It had all come to an abrupt end a week before the end of the previous festival. She arrived at work one morning to find a note on her desk from Sarah Atkinson saying that Peter Hansen had rung to say he had no further need for her services and that he would be leaving for Copenhagen the following night, immediately after the final performance of the play he had been directing. Tess tried to contact him on his mobile phone, but he never answered. In time, she came to understand that her usefulness to Peter had run its course and that he had simply been using her as a form of diversion, just as he had probably done with a plethora of stupid, gullible young girls in cities where he had been working throughout the world.

Sir Alasdair Dreyfuss never found out about the affair. If he had done so, there was no doubt in her mind that she would have been thrown out of the International office without her feet touching the ground. But Allan had found out. It was her own fault, really, walking around in a gloomy daze and bursting into tears for no apparent reason. So when he eventually asked her what was wrong, she told him everything. It could have all ended there. That's what she was expecting, but instead dear, sweet Allan simply pulled his snivelling wreck of a girlfriend close to him, heaved out a long, painful breath and said, 'We're going to have to stop doing this to each other, Tess. We can't sustain a relationship when we're constantly ignoring the basic rules of trust and fidelity between us.' And just when she thought her own selfish stupidity had cost her the love of the one person for whom she had really cared, he said, 'Our only chance of survival is to get married. What d'you think?'

And she'd accepted without hesitation.

Tess jerked her head to break away from her thoughts, realising she had been sitting staring at the telephone ever since she had finished her call with the director. She leaned over and picked up her discarded case from the floor, unzipped it and placed her laptop on the desk. As it was booting up, she glanced at her watch and decided it was too early to start trying to trace the whereabouts of Angélique Pascal and her manager. Consequently, she thought it as well to wait until nine o'clock before making any of her telephone calls.

Which gave her all of forty-five minutes to do a Google

search on 'Barbados Holidays' and look for a September booking for her much-delayed honeymoon.

Two

Due to an inadequacy of space in the rented industrial unit on the outskirts of Cheltenham, the offices and storage facilities of the Exploding Sky Company had recently been moved to a block of outmoded farm buildings deep in the rolling country-side of the Cotswold Hills. Even though it was a transaction that had stretched the relationship with his bank manager to near breaking point, Roger Dent, sole proprietor of the company, was extremely thankful at that particular moment that he had under-taken the move, if only for the soothing vista of sheep quietly grazing with their lambs in the verdant pastures outside his window. He sat slumped in a high-backed swivel chair at his desk, open-mouthed with jet lag, hardly aware of the fact that Cathy, his wife and personal assistant, had succeeded in turning the once dark and smelly piggery into the company's new stately office during the two weeks that he had been away. White-painted windows now replaced the cobwebbed jute sacks that had once flapped in the open frames, hardboard floors were laid and carpeted, and the walls, now lined with plasterboard and resplendently fresh in Dulux 'Magnolia', were hung with photo-graphs that displayed some of Roger's most triumphant moments: the darkened silhouette of Blenheim Palace lit by a blinding shower of green and silver cascading from its roof; the huge shimmering palm tree of illumination that arced above the barge on the River Thames, catching in its brilliant rays the frontal elevation of the Houses of Parliament and the stolid, square tower of Big Ben; and the largest of them all, an aerial shot that showed a night sky emblazoned with incandescent spirals and trailing meteors that fell earthwards in flames of red and gold on to the battlements of Edinburgh Castle. These, and the countless other photographs still packed away in removal boxes, were testament to his skills as a master pyrotechnic.

Roger was brought out of his soporific state by a coffee mug being placed with a clatter on the desk in front of him and a kiss being planted on the side of his bearded face. He closed his mouth and turned to watch with heavy eyes as his wife came to lean her denim-ed bottom on the desk beside him, her arms folded across the front of a faded blue cotton shirt and a concerned smile sliding her mouth to one side.

'You look all in.'

Roger stretched his legs out under the desk and ran a hand over the top of his thinning hair. Even though he was yet to reach his mid-forties, he no longer had the wherewithal for the ponytail that had, at one time, trailed down his back, covering the ESC logo on the back of his navy-blue sweatshirt, a garment which he wore, along with a pair of heavy-duty cotton chinos, as his constant uniform.

'I am,' he replied, mid-yawn. 'There was a problem with the plane in Shanghai, so we were four hours late in boarding.'

'What time did you get back here?'

'Six-thirty this morning. I didn't bother coming to bed. Thought I'd just disturb you.'

'That was very considerate of you,' Cathy said with a smile. 'So, tell me, how did the trip go?'

'All in all, really good. We . . . had a couple of "red tape" problems, which I suppose is the norm for China, but we did manage to visit the factories in Beihai and Hengyang and they got pretty excited about the new material we've ordered from them. We spent two days on the test ground with this new lad from the research department in Hengyang and I have to say that some of the new multishot batteries he'd come up with were just mind-blowing.' Roger took a hefty slurp of black coffee. 'Talking of which, have you seen Phil this morning? I have to remind him to send an e-mail off to that lad this morning.'

'He's with Danny in the storeroom, getting the gear ready for the weekend.'

Roger eyed Cathy for a moment, then leaned across his desk and opened his diary. 'Oh, for heaven's sakes, I'd forgotten about Cardiff. Looks like we'll have to be back on the road tomorrow to get that one set up.'

Cathy pushed herself away from the desk. 'Well, I'm afraid the best news I'm saving for last. Jeff Banyon from the Scottish Chamber Orchestra called this morning to find out how you were getting on with the Tchaikovsky piece for the festival.'

'What did you tell him?'

'I told him that you and Phil were working on it and that everything was going well.'

Roger snorted out a laugh. 'That'll be right. We haven't even made a start to it.'

Cathy gave her husband's hair a ruffle. 'Don't worry. You always say that some of your best displays are the ones you've left to the last moment.'

As she moved over to the door of the office it opened with force, and a short, well-built man with blond hair and eager blue eyes walked in. He encircled Cathy's waist with powerful forearms, picked her up off the ground and twirled her around.

'Hi there, Cathy. Good to see you, babe,' he bellowed out in a thick Australian accent. He dropped her with little care back to her feet, moved over to the desk and gave Roger a solid slap on the shoulder. 'How're you feeling this morning, Rog?'

Roger did not reply, but turned and fixed his right-hand man with a caustic glare.

'Not very well, actually,' Cathy replied for her husband, 'which makes me slightly wonder why *you*'re so chirpy?'

Phil Kenyon planted his sizeable backside on top of the desk, covering Roger's diary in the process. 'Oh, I never get jet lag,' he said cockily. 'Comes from all those years of flying back and forth to Oz.'

'Bully for you,' Roger mumbled quietly, giving his diary a sharp tug to free it from captivity.

Phil leaned over, his annoyingly fresh face only a foot away

14

om Roger's scowling features. 'Not feeling our best today, are
e, Rog, mate?'

'Don't bait him, Phil,' Cathy said warningly. 'It's not the best
lea when he's in this kind of mood. In fact, I think I might
st leave you both so that I don't have to clean the blood off
e new carpet.'

'Oh, Rog wouldn't hurt me, would you, mate?'

The remark was met with a short disparaging laugh from
oger. 'I'd happily take you apart if we didn't have work to do.'

As Cathy closed the door behind her, Phil pushed himself
pright and jumped off the desk with a purposeful clap of his
ands. 'So what's on the cards today?'

'The Tchaikovsky piece for the Edinburgh Festival. We've got
 start programming it.'

Phil's smile changed to a joyless grimace. 'Oh, man, that's a
ll order.' He let out a heavy breath. 'Oh, well, we'd better
ive it a go, I suppose. Where d'you put the CD they sent
s?'

Roger's energy levels were sufficient only for a finger to be
ointed towards the row of filing cabinets against the wall. Phil
valked over to them, selected a drawer and pulled it open. He
etrieved the CD and returned to the desk, picking up a chair
 passing and thumping it down next to Roger. He placed the
isc in one of the CD players that were stacked to one side of
e desk and sat down.

'Right,' he said, pulling forward a thick block of lined paper.
Ready to make a start?'

Roger shook his head slowly. 'You know, Phil, I'm not really
oking forward to trying to get this one programmed. With all
ose quiet passages, I just don't see how it's going to come
ogether.'

Phil wrote, 'Tchaikovsky, Edinburgh' at the top of the page,
nd then dropped the pen on the desk and turned to his boss.
 always seem to get an appalling attack of déjà vu when you
ay that kind of thing. Listen, mate, you've been doing the
ireworks Concert in Edinburgh for over twenty years now, and

every year is more spectacular than the one before. I can't think of any reason why this one should be an exception to the rule.' He picked up the remote and pressed the 'play' button for the CD machine. 'So what d'you say we just chill out and get on with the job in hand?'

Roger laughed quietly. 'Were you born an optimist?'

'Na, mate, I was born in Wagga Wagga,' Phil replied, sticking his tongue in his cheek as the large floor speakers resounded with the opening bars of the classical piece.

Three

When the telephone rang, Lewis Jones made no immediate attempt to answer it. At this time of the year, it was almost certain to be some theatre company or comedy act leaving it to the last to book into the Fringe rather than anything to do with marketing. There were other people in the office whose jobs it was to handle such calls. However, when it continued on, he stopped reading through the gruesome forty-word description of Nick Cardean's forthcoming act, 'Four Weddings, Four Funerals and Four Acid Baths Somewhere-in-Between', got to his feet and looked over the partition that gave him a little privacy in the cluttered, open-plan space. There were eight others working in the Festival Fringe office at that time and each was engaged in a telephone call. So, with a resigned shrug, Lewis sat down again and picked up the receiver.

'Good morning, Fringe office.'

The man on the other end of the line spoke with a distinct North England twang, his words flowing out at a speed only matched in extreme by their inaudibility.

'All right, let's just go through one thing at a time,' Lewis interjected as the man avalanched him with information. 'What was the name of the performer again?'

The noise in the office was only a low hum of voices, but

nevertheless Lewis had to push a finger into his uncovered ear to be able to hear what the man was saying.

'So it's Rene Brownlow, is it? . . . No, I don't need to know what kind of act it . . . oh, it's comedy, is it? . . . Yes, I'm sure she's very funny – look, could you just hang on a mo' and I'll see if I can find her name on the database.'

Someone in the office had nicked Lewis's mouse mat, so he had to slew the mouse halfway across the slippery surface of his desk before he got the arrow on the icon at the top of his computer screen. He typed in the name, thumped on a key and the name appeared.

'Right, I've got Rene Brownlow, care of Andersons Westbourne Social Club, Hartlepool. That's the one, is it? . . . OK then . . . Well, it looks like you've paid the registration fee of twelve pounds, but nothing else.'

That set the man off like a train on a downhill stretch, his explanation gradually picking up speed until it was both unstoppable and incomprehensible. Lewis, however, managed to ascertain from it all that a venue had been booked in West Richmond Street (cheap, he thought to himself, but a comedian's graveyard down there), that money was coming from different sources and that it had all been very complicated to coordinate.

'I can understand all that,' Lewis cut in loudly, hoping that volume might scare the man silent, 'but in the monthly bulletins we sent out to you, it does say that to secure your place and get your name in the programme you have to pay three hundred quid before the end of April – and now it's two weeks into May.'

The man stuttered out some lightning-fast excuses, and then careered off sideways into a non sequitur about someone being 'very hard done by' and 'life dealing her a cruel blow'.

'Could you just hold it a moment?' Lewis asked, holding up a hand, a pointless and ineffectual action when trying to halt such a barrage of unseen verbosity. Hearing the man still speaking when he pressed the 'hold' button, Lewis got to his feet and once more peered over the partition. Everyone was still engaged in telephone calls, so he plumped on interrupting Gail at the next desk, waving a hand semaphore-like to try to attract her attention. She didn't see it.

'Gail, give us a help here, will you?' he whispered loudly to her.

Gail swung round in her chair to face Lewis. She asked her caller to hold the line before clamping her hand over the mouthpiece. 'What is it?'

'I've got some fellow from Hartlepool here who hasn't paid up the three hundred pounds yet.'

'Has he got a venue?' Gail asked.

'Seems so.'

'And has he got the money?'

'Apparently.'

'Well, just tell him to get it here by tomorrow latest, along with his act description. We won't be finalising the programme for another two weeks.'

Lewis gave Gail a solid thumbs-up, sat down at his desk and put the receiver to his ear. 'Hullo? Right, the story is this. If you get a cheque and an act description to us by tomorrow, then you'll be all right . . . yes, better to do "next day delivery" . . . Not at all, glad to be of help . . . no, I'm not Indian, I'm Welsh . . . that's all right, don't give it another thought . . . goodbye.'

Standing at the bar in Andersons Westbourne Social Club, known in all parts of Hartlepool as Andy's, Stan Morris replaced the receiver on the payphone and shovelled the remainder of the change off the dog-eared telephone directory into his cupped hand. He let it cascade with a jangle into his trouser pocket, and then turned to smile at the four men that eyed him expectantly.

'Well?' the smallest of them asked, his face wrinkled up to stop his bottle glasses from falling off the end of his snub nose. 'What did she say?'

'It was an 'e,' Stan replied importantly, clearing a path for himself through the eager band by holding the palms of his hands together like an old-fashioned diver. Everyone fell into step behind him as he headed back to the table in the corner of the sparsely furnished bar, where seven pints of beer in varying stages of consumption and a scattered set of dominoes awaited them. Wooden chairs were shifted back noisily on the linoleum floor as they resumed their seats. 'I thought 'e was Indian,' said Stan, taking a sip from his glass, then carefully wiping his mouth with a folded handkerchief he kept stored in the breast pocket of his tweed jacket, 'but 'e was Welsh.'

'Bugger 'is nationality,' exclaimed the little man with the glasses, taking a pinch of Golden Virginia tobacco from a greasy leather pouch and dexterously rolling himself a twig of a cigarette, 'what did 'e say about Rene?' .

Stan shot a haughty look at the man. 'I was merely telling ye that, Skittle, as a point of interest.' A universal groan went round the table. 'All right, the man said we were still in time as long as we got a cheque in the post tonight and sent it "next day delivery".'

A murmur of relief greeted the news.

'For a moment, I thought ye'd blown it,' said Derek Marsham, whose long face, sunken cheekbones and down-turned mouth gave the impression that he suffered constant and immeasurable unhappiness.

'I beg your pardon, Derek,' Stan retorted. 'What d'ye mean by that?'

'Well, ye prattle on so, ye do. It was a bloody wonder the man understood one word of what ye were saying to 'im.'

Stan puffed out his cheeks and pulled himself upright in his chair. 'I'll have ye know, Derek my friend, that at one time I was an accomplished after-dinner speaker. Sought after the length and breadth of Yorkshire, I was, and never before 'as the allegation been made that—'

'Come on, lads, this is getting us no place.' The voice abruptly stopped Stan's protest, and four faces turned to look at the man sporting the short denim jacket with the turned-up collar.

Even though Terry Crosland, in his mid-fifties, would have been younger than his companions by at least ten years, his long dark sideburns and Teddy-boy quiff seemed to put him in a distant and bygone era, while the others, who kept what was left of their hair barber-short and garbed themselves in cloth caps, mufflers and belted raincoats, were timelessly fashioned as their fathers and grandfathers would have been before them.

Stan Morris composed himself once more, but not before he had given Derek a sharp look of contempt. 'I quite agree with ye, Terry. Well spoken, that man.'

Terry rubbed his hands nervously on the legs of his jeans. 'What I think we should be discussing is . . . OK, so we've got the money together, but don't you think it's time we told Rene what we've been planning?' The suggestion brought about a rumble of agreement. 'Also, there's another three months before the festival, so 'ow's about we put the motion before the committee that we keep raising the money for 'er, because we can't send 'er off up to Edinburgh flat broke.'

Norman Brown cleared his throat and leaned forward to enter the circle of discussion for the first time. 'That's a good point,' he said, clutching a hand to his arm to stop the shake of developing Parkinson's. 'Our Maisie lives up Clavering way and 'er kids go to the same primary school as the Brownlow kids, and she says that the Brownlows took out a mortgage on one of those newbuilds just before Gary Brownlow lost 'is job with Daiwong Electrics, so they're just about skint . . .'

Norman tailed off, silenced by the hardened stare on Stan Morris's face. 'Thank ye, Norman,' he said, a condescending smile twitching his cheeks momentarily. 'I think we know that, otherwise we wouldn't be bothering to do all this for Rene.'

'Oh,' said Norman Brown quietly and shrank back out of the circle.

'I don't mind going up to see Rene and telling 'er what's been planned.' It was Terry who spoke, just after he had shot a wink at disheartened Norman to give his fragile confidence a bit of a boost. 'I 'ave to 'ead up toward Clavering any road this evening to do a paint job, so it won't be that much out me way.'

Stan Morris, who sensed that his commanding action in dealing with Norman's stupidity had brought proceedings back under his control, knocked a fist on the table. 'I think that's a very good idea. Much better to break the news to 'er in the comfort of 'er own home, rather than when she's all caught up pulling pints behind the bar 'ere. Everybody in agreement that Terry should take this on?'

The assembled company nodded their approval.

'Right, then,' Stan sang out, taking a ballpoint pen and a notebook from the inside pocket of his jacket. 'So what we 'ave to do now is come up with a forty-word description of Rene's act.'

Skittle squinted at Stan through his glasses, a quizzical expression on his face. ''Ow the 'ell can we do that when we don't know what she's going to be saying?'

'We have to use our imagination then, don't we, Skittle,' Stan replied in a schoolmasterly voice. He flicked a thumb over his shoulder. 'We've all heard 'er up there on that stage every Thursday night for the past six months, so we have a fair inkling of what 'er act's going to be about.' He creased open his notebook with the side of his hand. 'Right, then, I'll start the creative ball rolling. What about "'Ilarious comedienne from 'Artlepool"?'

'That's only four words,' droned sombre Derek Marsham.

Raising a long-suffering eyebrow, Stan threw the pen down on the table and crossed his arms. 'Ooh, I can tell this is going to be a long afternoon.'

Four

In the small sub-office of the *Sunday Times* in Edinburgh, Harry Wills opened the top drawer of his desk, took out a square of Nicorette chewing gum, unwrapped it with one hand and popped it in his mouth. At the same time, with the receiver jammed in against chin and shoulder, he continued to write his own form of shorthand on the spiralled notepad, sometimes interspersing the text with longhand words for which, in his thirty-odd years in journalism, he had never worked out abbreviations.

He clicked the top of the ballpoint pen and dropped it on the desk. 'Thank you, Monsieur Dessuin, for your time. I think that's all I need to ask. You said you were going to be at the Tower Hotel until tomorrow, is that right? . . . just in case there's anything else I need to know . . . good . . . well, thank you again . . . goodbye.'

Harry thumped the receiver down on its cradle in frustration and then briefly read through his spidery jottings before lobbing the notebook on to the desk and, with an angry groan, leaning his considerable bulk back in the old wooden armchair with force enough to make it creak violently in protest. There wasn't a story there at all. Not that it really surprised him that much. He had been trying to get a personal interview with Angélique Pascal for two years now, ever since she had become the 'great new discovery' after winning the coveted Prix du Concours Long-Tibaud at the Conservatoire in Paris, but never had he been able to get further than speaking to her manager and mentor, Albert Dessuin. He laughed quietly to himself and shook his head resignedly. Well, at least he knew he wasn't alone in his failure. It was a well-known fact amongst all his journalistic colleagues that Dessuin kept the young French violinist under such a tight rein that her existence could at best be described as reclusive.

Heaving himself out of the chair, Harry walked over to the window and gazed down on to the sun-striped lawns of Princes Street Gardens. This year, he thought to himself, right here in Edinburgh. With Pascal being located in the city for more than a week when she performed at the festival, there would never be a better chance to get that interview.

On the fifteenth floor of the Tower Hotel in London, Albert Dessuin also stood gazing out of the window, his picture-postcard view being no less spectacular than that of Harry Wills in the northern capital city. Small cutters and sightseeing barges plied the murky waters of the River Thames, appearing and disappearing under the majestic span of Tower Bridge. His mind, however, was not focused on the view. He stood with an elbow resting in one hand, the other playing with the collar of his cashmere polo-neck sweater. His thin lips were pursed and his eyes twitched rhythmically behind the gold-framed spectacles that were seated firmly on his long, thin nose. He was listening intently to the strains of the violin that drifted in through the closed door of the adjoining room, as it played through the first movement of Sibelius's Violin Concerto in D Minor. With every downbeat, he jerked his head, making the high cockscomb of jet-black hair pulse as if powered by an electrical current. Then, in an instant, he threw up his hands, simultaneously clicking his fingers, and strode over to the door and pulled it forcefully open.

'Angélique, what are you doing?'

The girl stopped playing instantly. She turned to look at him, her large brown eyes beneath the straight fringe of short dark hair eyeing him with uncertainty. She dropped the violin from her shoulder and began twisting the bow back and forth in her fingers.

'What do you mean?' she asked hesitantly.

'I can tell from through here in my room that you are not concentrating. You are missing so many beats.'

The girl's full mouth broadened into a wide smile. 'I know. I was looking out of the window. It is so beautiful out there with the sun glinting on the river. Have you seen all the boats?'

'Yes, I have,' replied Dessuin with little enthusiasm.

'Oh, Albert, I love London. It is such a wonderful place. I am going to come to live here one day.'

'Pfoo! Why would you want to live here?' Dessuin snapped. 'Paris is so much more superior. It has better shops, better restaurants, nicer people.' He moved across the room to the girl and dismissed the idea with a light backhanded brush to her shoulder. 'You are mad to even think about it.'

A sparkle of excitement glinted in her eyes. 'Maybe one has to do mad things at some time or other.'

'Of course, but not at *this* time. You are twenty-one years old and you are very fortunate that together we are being able to cut out an excellent career for you, and that is what you should be concentrating on right now' – he put a hand under her violin and guided it back under her chin – 'starting with you getting those downbeats right.'

Angélique lifted her bow to the strings and with a gentle dip to her head, closed her eyes and began to play. After the opening three bars, she stopped abruptly.

'I heard you talking on the telephone. Who was it?'

Dessuin shrugged his shoulders. 'Some *journaliste* from Scotland. Now keep playing.'

Angélique bit at the side of her mouth and tapped her bow on the strings of the violin. 'Why don't you allow me to talk to the press? I'm quite capable of doing so.'

Dessuin narrowed his eyes at the girl before fixing her with an insincere smile. He draped an arm around the shoulders of his protégée. 'Of course you are, but it is so much better for you to do what you are best at, and I will do likewise.' It may have been his imagination, but as he planted a protective kiss on the side of her head, he felt pressure on his hand as if she were drawing herself away from him.

'Your mother has been on the telephone,' she said quietly.

Dessuin dropped his arm from her shoulder. 'When was this?'

'About an hour ago.'

'Why did you not tell me?'

'Because you were away from your room at the time.'

Dessuin nodded slowly. 'And what did she say?'

Angélique played a merry trill on her violin. 'She thinks she is suffering from flu again,' she said lightly. 'She wants you to call her.'

Dessuin turned and strutted over to the door of his bedroom. He opened it, and then turned to glare angrily at Angélique. 'You know, my mother has been very good to you. You should

24

have more respect for her and not be so mean about her *fragilité*.' His rebuke was met with a blank stare from the young violinist. 'I think you are a very cold person sometimes, Angélique. I am going to call her now, and then I am going out to get some fresh air.'

'Oh, can I come too, Albert?' Angélique asked breathlessly. She hurriedly placed the violin and bow down on her bed and moved towards him. 'I know I should not have been so *flippante* about your mother. I am sorry. Please, when you speak to her, tell her I was asking after her.'

Dessuin huffily shrugged his shoulders. 'I suppose you could come, but are you sure you are ready for the concert tonight?'

'Albert, you know I can play Sibelius with one hand tied behind my back.'

'Five minutes ago, it sounded to me that you were.'

'You don't mean that.'

'Most certainly I do, and if you play it like that tonight, you will make yourself a laughing stock.'

Dessuin could tell from the look on Angélique's face that he had succeeded in casting doubt in her mind. He decided to push her a little further. 'And what about Mozart in two days' time? Your reputation would be shot down in flames if you screwed up in Vienna.'

The enthusiasm that Angélique had displayed visibly drained from her being. 'Maybe I should stay and do a bit more practice.'

He smiled at her. 'A good idea. Anyway, it's cold outside. We don't want *you* getting a chill like my mother, now, do we?'

Angélique stood watching as Dessuin closed the door behind him, then turned and picked up the violin from the bed. She closed her arms around it, holding it hard to her chest, feeling its shape press against her small firm breasts. It was her comforter, her friend these days, almost her only friend. Since leaving the Conservatoire two years ago, she had hardly seen any of her old acquaintances, and certainly she had not had the time to make any new ones. The routine had been constant. One hotel room after another, one concert hall after another. Of course, she understood what Albert was always telling her, that she had been blessed with a supreme gift of music and that it was her duty to share that gift with all the people of the world who did not possess it. But the pressure was becoming intense. She wanted a break from it all. She wanted to go out once more to the cinemas and to the bars in Paris with her friends from the Conservatoire, and she wanted to go home to Clermont Ferrand to visit her family and spend time with dear Madame Lafitte. Oh, how she missed that wonderful woman!

Without relinquishing her hold on the violin, Angélique sat down on the edge of the bed and blew out a long breath to steady the wave of nausea that flooded up from her stomach. She knew only too well, however, that the cause of this was not the onset of such an illness from which the dreaded Madame Dessuin constantly claimed she was suffering. This was worse, and had begun to take place more frequently over the past two months. It was brought on by the unthinkable realisation that she, Angélique Pascal, was beginning to feel bored of playing this wonderful instrument. How could she ever entertain such an idea when there were those who clamoured at the box offices of the great concert halls to hear her play? How could she tell such a thing to Albert Dessuin, the man who had nurtured her through her days at the Conservatoire de Paris and who had given up everything to become her manager and counsellor? And what would she ever be able to say to Madame Lafitte?

Angélique kicked off her shoes and lay down on the bed, pulling her legs up so that her ankles rested against the curve of her narrow-hipped bottom. As she nestled her head deep into the pillow, a tear slowly trickled down her cheek and was immediately absorbed by the white linen pillowcase.

'Hullo?' The voice on the telephone sounded weak and quavering.

'Hullo, Maman. It's Albert.'

'Oh, Albert, *mon cher*, why have you not called me before

now? Where have you been?' A pathetic cough followed.

'I am sorry, Maman. I did not know you *had* called until a moment ago.'

'Do you mean the girl never gave you the message?' Suddenly there seemed to be strength in the voice.

Dessuin rested an elbow on the dark-stained desk and rubbed the palm of his hand against his forehead. For eight years, Angélique had been living with him and his mother in their capacious apartment in the *quinzième* district of Paris, and still she could hardly bring herself to call her son's young protégée by name. 'I have been away from my room, Maman, and Angélique has been practising for the concert tonight. It was not her fault.'

'I am not feeling at all well, Albert.' The voice changed for the worse once more.

'So I understand. Have you called the doctor?'

'Pah! The doctor knows nothing. Anyway, he is too busy even to visit a sick old woman.'

'In that case, you must send Simone round to the *farmacie* for some paracetamol.'

'Albert, it is Tuesday. Simone only comes for two hours on a Tuesday. She has left already.' Another feeble cough sounded down the line. 'When are you coming home, Albert?'

'I cannot be back in Paris before Friday, Maman.'

'Ah, *mon Dieu,* Friday! I may very well be on my deathbed by then, if I have not gone before.'

'Maman, that is ridiculous,' Dessuin said irritably. 'You are as strong as an ox.'

'How would you know how I am feeling?' Again the strength in the voice returned. 'You have never considered how I am feeling. If that had been so, you would never have left your teaching job at the Conservatoire to fly around the world with that girl.'

'Maman, I have talked to you countless times about this.'

'You were never able to make the grade, were you, Albert? You are only doing this because you see in her the talent that you lacked. Don't forget that if it had not been for my contacts, you would never have got that job at the Conservatoire.'

'That is most unfair, Maman.'

'Pah! What age are you now? Thirty-seven years old? And you are going to be content to follow this girl around the world like a lapdog for the rest of your life?'

Dessuin did not reply, but leaned back in his chair and wound the telephone cord tightly around his fingers. He let out a short silent laugh. 'Isn't it strange how you always seem to sound so much better when you get angry?'

There was a moment's silence.

'Albert,' the suffering in the voice had returned, 'I am sorry to say such things to you. It must be the fever. I do feel quite delirious.'

'Well, I suggest you take yourself to bed with a cup of hot lemon and a shot of cognac, and if you are feeling no better by Friday, I will take you to see the doctor.'

'You are a good boy, Albert. I know that. *Mon seul fils, et je t'aime beaucoup.*'

'*Et je t'aime aussi, Maman.* I must go now. I have things to do. I will call you tonight.'

Dessuin replaced the receiver and sat for a moment focused on the letterheading of the Tower Hotel, stacked neatly with its matching envelopes in the leather stand at the back of the desk. He then leaned slowly forward and clenched his hair with both hands, squeezing tighter and tighter until the pain brought tears to his eyes. Why was it so much part of her very nature to belittle those who were closest to her? She had acted exactly the same with his father as well, so much so that the man had often been driven to vent all his pent-up emotions in an irrational rage that had left neither Albert nor his mother physically untouched. He had too vivid memories of his puny young arms braced against his bedroom door, jarring like shock absorbers against the power of his father's shoulder as he tried to gain entry, desperately reaching out a foot to hook round a chair so that he could jam it under the handle. And when his father would eventually calm down and Albert could hear him muttering to himself as he stolidly descended the stairs, Albert would then lay himself down carefully on his bed, fold his aching arms across his chest and feel the comforting coolness of the linen pillowcase against his throbbing, bruised face.

He knew it had never been his father's fault, but when, in his last year at school, he returned home one day to find an ambulance and two police cars outside the house and was then told by a gruff police inspector that Guillaume Dessuin had locked himself in the attic bedroom and had subsequently taken his own life with the revolver he kept as a souvenir from the last war, Albert's desolation was tempered by an overwhelming sense of relief. He had now escaped the violent reach of the unfortunate man.

Yet as the months went by thereafter and his mother's silent chagrin finally lifted from her sad, embittered being, Albert found himself becoming the new and unwitting target for her verbal abuse, now more vitriolic than ever before. And it soon came to him that Guillaume Dessuin, through his actions, had inflicted on his only son a wound more permanent than any received during those regular beatings. He had succeeded in doing something at which Albert himself was forever destined to fail, and that was to rid himself of the very cause of so much misery in his life.

Abruptly, Albert stood up and strode over to the minibar, the memory of his troubled youth and the matriarchal ball and chain he dragged through his adulthood being too prevalent in his mind. He took out two small bottles of whisky, poured their contents into a glass and drained it in two gulps, feeling his body give out an involuntary shiver at the immediate impact the alcohol had on both his throat and his brain. In that moment, he became aware that no sound was coming from the next-door room. He moved across to the adjoining door and opened it quietly.

Angélique was lying fast asleep on the bed, her stockinged feet curled up under her bottom and her violin clutched like a comforting teddy bear in her arms. It was a sight that made Albert smile despite his melancholy mood. He had watched that girl grow up, becoming more attached to her than she would ever know, and he knew only too well what that particular instrument meant to her. It was her childhood, her passion, her fairy-tale world to which she used to escape from the impecunious and uncultured lifestyle of her family in Clermont Ferrand. And, over the years he had witnessed it gently coaxing from her one of the most truly remarkable talents he had ever had the pleasure of hearing. Oh, how easy life would be, he thought to himself, if one needed only to take one's solace from a shapely piece of veneered wood with a few steel strings attached to it.

Dessuin soundlessly pulled the door closed and turned once more to raid the minibar of its anaesthetising contents.

Five

The shutters in the drawing room of the house in Clermont Ferrand were always kept closed during the summer months to protect the antique furniture from the sun, especially the lacquered top of the grand piano, which stood at an angle in the large bow window, squatting like a giant toad on its turned-out legs. It was covered with a white lace cloth upon which sat a weighty stack of music scores and the large blue Limoges terrine in which Madame Lafitte always kept an abundant supply of Nestlé's plain chocolate secreted under its patterned lid.

So efficient were the shutters that it was always impossible to see anything in that room, even at ten o'clock on a summer's morning when the sun was high enough to clear the trees that lined the rue Blatin and hit the front of the house full-on. But if one entered quietly when nobody else was about and took care not to bump into anything, it was actually possible to *smell* one's way around the room, which turned out to be so much more exciting than actually being able to see it. Starting on an anti-clockwise course, the fireplace came first with its acrid reek of cold, unswept chimney; next the long bookshelves, which gave off a heady whiff of leather; round past the grand piano, which was always sweet with beeswax; feel one's way to one side of Dr Lafitte's high-sided armchair with the rich aroma of hair oil on its linen head cloth; then along the smooth-fronted sideboard, which gave off first the obnoxious tang of spent pipe tobacco, followed by the fading bouquet of potpourri; and then, finally, journey's end came by the small Louis XV chair nestling beside the door, which ponged of Madame Lafitte's two elderly Pekineses.

It was during one of these unsighted sojourns, when the perpetrator had decided to widen the search for new discoveries behind the grand piano, that a foot came into contact with some form of solid object, causing it to sound off a muffled reverberation in protest. After a moment of thumping heartbeat, during which ears were sharply attuned to the possible approach of footsteps, small hands were used to explore the shape of the object. First curvaceous around its base, then into a narrow waist, then some smaller curves before its lines ran parallel to the top. Imagination could not help in any way to understand what the box contained, and that was not to be of any satisfaction to one so curious. Accordingly, ten little fingers sought to break the sacrosanct spell of darkness, gripping hard at the edge of one of the tall shutters and pulling it open to allow the narrowest sliver of light to fall upon the box and upon nothing else. The little girl in the shapeless cotton dress and dirty plimsolls, who now revealed herself for the first time to her inanimate acquaintances in the room, knelt down in front of the box and slowly undid the three spring catches on the lid, and then carefully, oh, so carefully, she opened it up.

She did not touch its contents. She just gazed at them, so mesmerised by what she saw that, after an unknown quantity of time, she felt no discomfort from kneeling on the hard parquet floor, nor was she aware of the commotion that had started outside the room.

'You try upstairs, Marie. I will look for her down here.'

A door on the opposite side of the hallway groaned open on unoiled hinges before being closed immediately with an echoing bang, and then the door to the drawing room was opened and a light turned on.

'Angélique? Are you in here?'

As she stood by the door, the woman, who, despite her advanced age, was tall and upright and elegantly turned out, her grey hair pinned in a circular plait to the back of her head, was puzzled by the crack of light that showed through the shutters. She walked over to the window and let out a cry of surprise when she came across the little girl huddled on her knees behind the piano.

'Oh, Angélique, what a fright you gave me,' she said, clutching a hand to her white-bloused heart. 'What are you doing in here, little one?'

The little girl looked up at the old lady, her face radiant with delight. 'What is this?' she asked, pointing at her discovery.

The lady was so warmed by the child's expression that any thought of reprimand quickly melted from her mind. 'That, Angélique, is a violin.'

'Is it very special?'

The old lady smiled. 'That one is, yes.' She held a finger up to the little girl. 'You wait right there. I must tell your mother I found you.' She walked over to the door and called out, 'Marie?' into the hallway.

'I have not yet found her, Madame Lafitte,' a panicked voice sounded out from some distant point on the upper landing.

'She is down here in the drawing room, Marie, so calm yourself.'

Madame Lafitte walked back to the bay window, placing her long, graceful hands on the back of a low armchair and pushing it on squeaky castors to where Angélique remained as instructed, her face no more than ten inches away from the instrument.

The old lady sat, tucking in her grey worsted skirt under her legs and shifting her knees demurely to one side. She reached down and lightly moved a thumb over the strings. The tone of the violin was muted by the thick green baize that lined its box.

'It was given to me by my father many years ago,' Madame Lafitte said, as if beginning the telling of a fairy tale. 'He was a very kind and generous man. I had not long started playing the violin when he came home with it one evening. "Lillian," he said to me, "if you want to be a really excellent violinist, you need the assistance of more than just a good teacher." So he gave me that case, and I, like you, opened it up and just stared at it in wonderment.' She reached down and pulled the violin case towards her. 'Of course, it is only a small one because I was very young at the time.'

'How old were you?' the little girl asked, briefly taking her eyes off the violin to look up at Madame's kindly wrinkled face.

Madame Lafitte laughed. 'Oh, now that is difficult. Not as young as you, at any rate. What are you now? Six? Seven?'

'Six and a half.'

'Well, I think I was probably about ten, and—'

Madame Lafitte was interrupted by the arrival of a heavy tread and the sound of an unhealthy wheezing in the room. In the doorway stood a large woman with a wild tangle of brown curls adorning the top of a very red and very round face. Her figure, which resembled that of an all-in wrestler, was encased in a sleeveless floral overall that looked large enough to double as a two-man tent and under which, judging from the expanse of bosom revealed, she wore little other than an overloaded, flesh-coloured brassiere, the straps of which were almost lost in the pudginess of her shoulders. Below the bivouac, her thick legs were sheathed in black calf-length stockings that ran amok with ladders, while her considerable weight was borne by a pair of battered, woollen bedroom slippers.

'Oh, Madame,' she gasped, as she rocked her way over to the piano. 'I am so sorry. I cannot understand what she was thinking of. She knows this room is *interdite*.' She placed her fists on her wide hips and frowned angrily down at her daughter. 'Angélique,' she boomed, her voice suddenly taking on the force and volume of a Marseillaise fishwife, 'you come out from behind that piano and apologise immediately to Madame.'

Seeing the fear on the little girl's face as she got to her feet and quickly backed away as far as the bay window would allow, Madame Lafitte held up a hand. 'It's all right, Marie,' she said in a calming voice, 'no harm has been done. It is good for little girls to be so inquisitive.'

'But not here in your house, Madame. That is unforgivable. She can be as inquisitive as she likes in her own home, but not here at my work.'

'And how much more work do you have to do this morning?' Madame Lafitte asked, trying to steer matters away from Angélique's trivial misdemeanor.

'I have yet to finish off the polishing in Dr Lafitte's study, Madame, and then if I might leave the dining room until tomorrow, I would be very grateful. I have to be home to make lunch for all my family.'

'What?' Madame Lafitte asked quizzically, knowing that the three Pascal sons and elder daughter laboured alongside their father in a furniture factory on the outskirts of the city. Marie Pascal had been working in the house for nearly eight years, and consequently Madame Lafitte knew that Angélique's birth had been a bizarre mistake, remembering well the woman's surprise and shock on discovering that she was pregnant fourteen years after her previous confinement. 'Why would they be home on a Wednesday? Do they not all have lunch in the canteen?'

Angélique's mother flicked back her head. 'Of course, that is usually the case, Madame, but today, they are all on strike.'

Madame Lafitte clicked her tongue. 'Oh, not another strike. How long is this one going to last?'

The housekeeper threw out her hands. '*Je ne sais pas*, Madame. I hope a very short time, otherwise there will be no food in the house for me to cook for them.'

'Well, Marie, you get yourself off home when you have finished the study, and while you are doing that, I shall keep Angélique here with me so that she does not feel the need to carry out any more of her explorations.'

'Oh, you need not trouble yourself. Angélique will come to sit quietly at the kitchen table and wait for me to finish my work. She has been—'

'Marie,' Madame Lafitte cut in sharply, 'I am very happy to have Angélique with me here. We are going to have a little talk about the violin.'

Marie frowned. 'The violin, Madame? Angélique would not know what such a thing is.'

'In that case, I would like to explain it to her.'

With a shake of her head and a low muttering to herself, Angélique's mother turned and headed towards the door, running a yellow duster she had taken from the front pocket of her overall along the full length of the sideboard before departing the room.

Madame Lafitte smiled conspiratorially at the little girl, who had waited for her mother to leave before sinking to her knees in front of the violin once more. Angélique watched with wide eyes as the violin was taken from its case and the bow unclipped from the lid. Madame Lafitte placed the violin under her chin and plucked at each of the strings, turning the small wooden pegs at the end of the fingerboard to tune the instrument.

'Oh, my word, it has been so long since I have played. My fingers are not so nimble nowadays and also the violin is quite small for me, so you must be ready to excuse a great many mistakes, Angélique.'

The little girl watched as the old lady straightened her back, held the bow lightly against the strings, and then began to play. Immediately the dark, soulless room was warmed by the sweetest sound that Angélique had ever heard. She stared open-mouthed at the hand that moved effortlessly over the strings, at the fingers that quivered to make every note resound more beautifully, and at Madame Lafitte's face, which suddenly seemed to have become so much younger than before. Oh, it's like magic, Angélique thought to herself; this is the most special thing I have ever discovered.

When Madame Lafitte eventually finished playing, she laid the violin and bow across her knees and smiled at Angélique. 'Well, that wasn't so bad, was it? Not so many mistakes after all.'

'Do you always have to pretend you're sleeping when you play?' Angélique asked.

Madame Lafitte laughed. 'No, my dear, I close my eyes to concentrate. One has to try to become part of the music, and if you are not looking at other things, like the piano there, or even at you, then you are not distracted.'

'If I closed my eyes, would I be able to play?'

'I don't know. Would you like to have a try?'

With a gasp of amazement, Angélique jumped to her feet. 'Am I allowed to?'

'Of course you are. The violin might still be *un peu grand* for you, but let's see if we can't play a note or two. Come here and stand beside me.'

When the violin was placed under the little girl's chin, her face was at such an angle that she had to peer sideways to look at the strings. Madame Lafitte bit at her lip pensively. 'Now, that does not look very comfortable.'

'Oh, it's very comfortable,' exclaimed the little girl, terrified the old lady would take the violin away from her.

'All right, then.' She put the bow in Angélique's free hand and raised the girl's arm so that the bow rested on the fourth string of the violin. 'We are only going to use this string, so that is the one the fingers of your other hand need to press, *tu comprends?*'

'*Oui.*'

'*Bon.* So let us start with that finger, which we call your fourth finger, and now gently move the bow across the string.'

Angélique did what she was told and the violin emitted an ear-piercing screech. The girl let out a shrill laugh. 'That sounds like the noise our cat makes when Papa stands on its tail by mistake!'

Madame Lafitte smiled. 'In that case, we must immediately stop the suffering of your poor cat! Come on, we shall try *encore une fois*.'

The note, this time, came out almost perfect.

'That was wonderful, Angélique. Well done, you. Now what I want—'

But Angélique had already begun to play again, this time with her eyes screwed tightly closed, and when she repeated the note, she mirrored the technique of the quivering finger that she had seen Madame Lafitte use. It resounded exactly as the old lady's had done. So Angélique pressed her third finger to the string and pulled the bow back across it, and again the lower note came out as pure as the last. And then she moved to the second finger, and after an initial screech, she readjusted her little wrist and the note once more came out perfect.

The old lady did not try to stop her, but watched the girl's tenacity with fascination. 'All right, now let's try the next string over. The same thing again.'

The bow and the fingers moved together to the next string, and following one false start, three perfect notes were sounded, the playing hand arched just as it should be to avoid coming into contact with the fourth string, and then, without prompting, Angélique moved back to that string and played the three original notes again.

'Do you want to try the second string now?'

Angélique did not reply, nor did she open her eyes, her fingers feeling instinctively for the next string. Madame Lafitte could tell from the expression on the girl's face that this was indeed an effort with fingers as short as hers. She managed almost immediately one clear note before the moment was broken by the sound of the drawing-room door being forcefully opened. Angélique's mother entered the room, pulling on an enormous raincoat.

'That's the study finished, Madame. Again, I am sorry about my daughter's behaviour and I can assure you that it will not happen a second time.'

Madame Lafitte did not give her a reply, but with a gentle smile took the violin from the little girl. She could tell, in that second, that a spell had been shattered, and she saw the longing in Angélique's eyes as the violin was replaced in its case.

'Marie, why is Angélique here today? Why is she not at school?'

'There was a holiday today, Madame. Oh, I cannot tell you how sorry I am that I brought her. In future, I will—'

'I would like you to bring her here at any time that you possibly can, schooldays or not.' She turned and looked at the housekeeper. 'Would you be able to do that?'

Angélique's mother was perplexed by the request.

'Madame? 'I'm not sure what you—'

'It's very simple to understand, Marie. Would somebody be able to bring Angélique to my house every day and then fetch her later?'

'May I ask why?'

'Because I want to teach her the violin.'

The housekeeper let out a short laugh. 'The violin? Ah, Madame, it is very kind of you, but you don't want to bother yourself trying to teach my daughter—'

'Marie, what I do in my own time is my affair. So, the question still stands. Can someone bring Angélique to my house every day and then collect her at a later time?'

Angélique's mother shrugged her huge shoulders. 'There are six of us in the house. I suppose someone can walk her round, but it would depend on the shifts that the others work.'

'It doesn't matter. Anytime. I am always here.'

'Very well, Madame.'

Madame Lafitte put her arms around Angélique, who had come to stand enthralled beside her. The old lady planted a kiss on the side of her short dark hair, before whispering in her ear, 'I think, Angélique, my dear, that one day you will become an exceptional violinist.'

And so it was that Madame Lafitte became the most important person in Angélique Pascal's young life. It was she who gave

Angélique her lessons until the ability of the ten-year-old outshone her own; it was she who arranged and paid for the teacher who continued to nurture her extraordinary talent, and together with whom Madame Lafitte put out a search for a full-size violin that had the same resonance and playing style as the one Angélique had been using, eventually tracking one down in a backstreet shop in Munich that held a scant but exceptional stock of stringed instruments, and subsequently purchasing it with little regard to its enormous price tag; it was Madame Lafitte who set up the interview and audition for the thirteen-year-old at Le Conservatoire National Supérieur de Musique et de Danse de Paris; and it was she who mollified the stupid prejudices of the Pascal family and made them understand that her attendance there would have no detrimental impact on their lowly finances, and that Angélique's future promised much more than working in a furniture factory in Clermont Ferrand.

It was Madame Lafitte also who accompanied Angélique to Paris for the first time, the girl holding tight to her hand as they rode below the streets of the city on the Métro before emerging at La Porte de Pantin station in front of the inspirational white structure of the Conservatoire. Then, having watched Angélique being taken off for her audition, carrying the new, but equally treasured violin, the old lady had sat alone in the echoing foyer, drinking a cup of coffee whilst keeping the fingers of her free hand tightly crossed, watching the music students struggle along the corridors with bulky instrument cases and the leotarded dance students who sat in the chairs around her, chatting to their friends as they effortlessly stretched their legs into positions that would be unachievable for mere mortals.

It was a full hour and a half before Angélique eventually returned to the foyer, accompanied this time not by the young public relations woman but by a tall bespectacled young man wearing a dark-green corduroy suit. When they reached the perimeter of the seating area, he put a hand on Angélique's shoulders and spoke to her. The girl smiled at Madame Lafitte and pointed a finger in her direction. Settling Angélique in a chair, the man bought her a bottle of orange juice from an illuminated dispenser next to the wall, gave it to her along with a reassuring smile and approached the old lady.

'Madame Lafitte?'

'*Oui, c'est moi,*' she replied, struggling to raise herself out of the awkwardly shaped chair.

'Oh, please, don't get up,' he said, reaching down to her an elegantly shaped hand that bore the hallmark of a musician. 'I am sorry that we have taken so long with Angélique. My name is Albert Dessuin and I am a teacher of the violin here at the Conservatoire.'

Madame Lafitte shook the hand and watched as the young man lowered himself into a chair on the opposite side of the table. She could not bear to wait for news of the audition.

'Monsiuer Dessuin, can I ask how Angélique got on?'

Dessuin leaned forward in the chair, resting his elbows on his knees and linking his hands together in front of his chin. 'Madame Lafitte, all I can say is thank you for bringing Angélique to the Conservatoire.'

The old lady felt her heart give a huge thump, and tears immediately sprang to her eyes. She opened up the blue leather handbag on her knees and extracted a white linen handkerchief. 'Oh, I am so pleased you said that. She has a wonderful talent, *n'est-pas?*'

'I certainly believe it, and that is why we felt the need to discuss at length her future here.' The young man dropped his hands from his chin. 'Madame, I have had a word with the *directeur* of the department and asked if he would allow me to take Angélique under my wing. I truly feel that I can make something wonderful out of this talent.'

The old lady shook her head slowly. 'I have always believed this,' she said quietly, almost to herself, 'from the first moment that I allowed her to lay hands upon that violin.'

'Oh, it is *your* violin. I wondered, because it is certainly a most beautiful instrument.'

'No, Monsieur Dessuin, I was talking about a small one given to me by my father many years ago. I shall always have that one in my house as a keepsake. The violin she is using now I bought for her.'

Dessuin smiled at the old lady. 'Then, what a wonderful gift you have made to her.' His face became serious. 'Now, Madame Lafitte, what I want to say about Angélique is that I feel that one so young, and one who has – how can I put this? – has not had a great deal of experience of the outside world, should not be put into the system of staying by herself in a students' residence.'

Madame Lafitte nodded. 'This has been one of my great worries, also.'

'Good, so I hope that the suggestion that I am going to make, which has been approved wholeheartedly by the *directeur,* will be acceptable to yourself as well. Madame, I live with my mother in a very large apartment here in the *quinzième* district, and we have customarily lodged some of the younger students from the Conservatoire. The girl who is with us at present is now of an age to move into the students' residence, which means that Angélique could take over her room. It would be a most beneficial arrangement for her because it would facilitate my supervision of both her music tuition and the educational studies that she will receive here at the Conservatoire.'

'Monsieur Dessuin, that would seem the most perfect idea, and would certainly take a weight off my mind. Of course, I will be the one to recompense you and Madame Dessuin for this.'

Dessuin held up a hand. 'Well, let us see what I can first arrange. For a girl from Angélique's background, I am sure that there are grants available to cover such costs.'

Madame Lafitte tilted her head to the side. 'Whatever you think, but if you cannot succeed in that, then I shall certainly meet all her costs. My husband and I were never fortunate enough to be blessed with children, Monsieur. Circumstances and *la guerre* put pay to that. Maybe it was then the plan of some greater being that I should wait until my eighties before being called upon to nurture a child as I now do Angélique. She need never worry about money, *comprenez-vouz?'*

'Of course, Madame. I can assure you that I will keep in close contact with you regarding all financial matters relating to Angélique.'

'I am very grateful, Monsieur Dessuin.' She tucked her handkerchief back in her handbag. 'So when are you thinking that she might start?'

'Next month, in September. Is that reasonable?'

Madame Lafitte nodded thoughtfully. 'I cannot give you a definite answer now, Monsieur Dessuin, because I must first talk to Angélique's parents. However, I am sure I will be able to persuade them by then.'

'Well, that is the start of the year at the Conservatoire, and I can tell you, Madame, that for once, I am very happy that it is starting so soon!'

Madame Lafitte glanced over to where Angélique sat, watching intently the comings and goings of the students around her. In her arms, she held the violin case as if protecting it.

Madame Lafitte smiled. 'Now, I think, would be a good time to give her the news.'

Every week for the next six years, Madame Lafitte received a letter from Angélique, telling her everything about the particular piece of music she was playing, about the friends she had made, and about the walks along the banks of the river Seine and the visits to museums and art galleries she had made with Albert Dessuin. In turn, Madame Lafitte would read these aloud to Angélique's mother, whom she knew had never received such a letter. Happiness seemed to radiate from these dispatches, so much so that it never occurred to Madame Lafitte that, not once, had Angélique mentioned her home life with Albert Dessuin and his mother. If she had but known about the tirades, the selfish hypochondria and the cold unfriendliness of the dreadful woman, the heavy clinking of bottle against glass that sounded from Dessuin's bedroom as Angélique passed by late at night to go to the bathroom, then Madame Lafitte would have taken the first train to Paris to make other arrangements. But Angélique never included a word of this in any of her letters, frightened that such a disclosure might end her time at the Conservatoire.

It was two days before her eighty-eighth birthday that Madame Lafitte received the news from Angélique that she had won the Prix du Concours Long-Tibaud. In another letter from Albert Dessuin, which arrived on the same day, he announced to Angélique's guardian that he had decided to give up his position at the Conservatoire and continue to teach Angélique and manage her affairs, as already she was being inundated with requests from concert halls around Europe to hear her play, and Dessuin felt that there was no way she could cope alone with such a pressure.

Madame Lafitte did not open, nor did she read, either of the letters herself. That was left to a young male nurse who sat on a chair close to the stroke victim's bedside in hospital. When he had finished, he looked closely at her face and nodded. Good news, he thought to himself, for both her and for the doctors. The smile was the first sign of understanding she had given since being brought there.

Six

The battered Transit van with the blown exhaust drove slowly through the confusion of streets, every one of them lined with identical stark-fronted, drab-harled houses, before coming to a halt at the entrance to a wide cul-de-sac. Terry Crosland rolled down the window and studied the street sign, just being able to make out the letters of Bolingbroke Close beneath a swirl of black graffiti. He swung the nose of the van around and reversed down the street to a point where he wouldn't interrupt the game of three-aside football that was in progress. As he opened the door, a deafening bang resounded around the tinny confines of the van and he saw the football dribble past him on the pavement. Thumping the door closed, he went over to the ball, pulled it towards him with his foot and deftly flicked it up into his hands.

A young boy came running down the street towards him. 'Sorry 'bout that, mister.'

'No 'arm done, lad,' Terry smiled at the boy and lobbed him the ball. 'Any idea which is the Brownlows' 'ouse?'

'Number seventeen, over there,' the boy replied, pointing to a house that seemed to have aged worse than others in the ten or so years of its life. 'That's Robbie Brownlow playing in goal for the opposition.'

Terry cast an eye towards the small figure that stood in front of the goal-chalked wall at the far end of the cul-de-sac. He was gazing up into the sky, seemingly more interested in the vapour trail of a plane flying overhead than he was in getting on with the game of football.

'Good, is he?' Terry asked.

'Nah,' the boy replied disparagingly. 'That's why we put 'im against the wall. We'd keep losing the ball if 'e was at this end.'

Terry watched the boy kick the ball back into play, and then walked across the road and entered the Brownlow property through a wrought-iron gate that a spare five minutes and a lick of black paint would have improved considerably. The pathway to the front door was blocked by a pile of large stones with weeds growing amongst them, a planned rockery never fulfilled, so Terry walked down the narrow passage with the high slatted fence that divided the twelve-foot gap to the adjacent house.

A quick glance at the back garden was more than enough evidence for Terry to realise that Gary Brownlow wasn't in the habit of frequenting the gardening department of the local DIY store. He went up to the back door and knocked twice, and then turned away to smooth back his greased hair and give his quiff a quick remodel. By the time the door opened, he was standing with his hands pushed into the pockets of his jeans, the collar of his denim jacket turned up.

The woman who stood at the door was short and dumpy, her streaked hair shaped in a pageboy cut. She was wearing black leggings with a pair of scuffed white trainers, her large hips and big bottom well hidden beneath the tails of a blue cotton man's shirt. Her face, however, was smooth-skinned, her cheeks healthily rosy, and the shape of her mouth and the slant in her eyes radiated humour.

'Well, if it isn't Elvis 'imself,' she said with a laugh, and then began to move her fat little body in the twist, whilst singing the refrain of "Return to Sender" in a deep, sexy voice. When she stopped she stretched her hand up the side of the door, pouting her unmade-up lips provocatively. 'If I'd known ye were coming round, I'd 'ave put on me see-through negligee.'

Terry smiled. 'I take it that Gary's not home, then.'

Crossing her arms beneath her huge bosom, Rene Brownlow raised her eyebrows. ' 'E's where 'e normally is. In the sitting room, watching telly. I doubt 'e'd notice if we had a *bonk* in front of 'im.' She dropped her hand from the side of the door. 'Nor would 'e probably mind, come to that.'

Terry cleared his throat uncomfortably. He liked Rene, but he was, in nature, a shy man and could never quite cope with her totally up-front frankness. But that was why she had the reputation of being probably the best comedienne on the Hartlepool circuit, and consequently the heroine of the members of Andy's Social Club, where she worked part-time behind the bar. Terry also knew from the general gossip in the club that her domestic relationship had been under a strain since her husband lost his job, but he certainly hadn't come round to get mixed up in all that. Rene sensed his unease and heaved out a sigh. 'So what can I do for ye, Terry me lad?'

'I need to 'ave a word.'

Rene leaned her back against the open door. 'In that case, ye'd better come in.'

Terry walked past her into a tight-spaced kitchen, still cluttered with dirty pans and dishes from the evening meal. Rene squeezed herself between Terry and the small kitchen table.

' 'Ere, let me clear ye some room,' she said, quickly stacking up some plates and moving them to the sink. ''Ave a seat there.' She pointed to a small plastic-covered stool. 'Like a cuppa?'

'Aye, that would be grand.'

Rene gave the water level in the electric kettle a cursory check by swishing it around. ''Ow d'ye take it?' she asked, flicking on the switch.

'Milk and two sugars, please.'

Rene let out a low growl. 'Ooh, I like a man with a sweet tooth.' She shot Terry a smile, but it went unreciprocated. She shook her head. 'I'm only joking, ye know, Terry. I can't 'elp it. It's the way God made me.'

Terry nodded. 'I know.'

Rene plopped a tea bag into a mug. 'And bloody 'ell, it's 'ard enough trying to keep joking round 'ere at this very moment in time.'

'Aye, probably,' Terry replied.

Rene pulled a stool away from the table with her foot and sat down. Instinctively, Terry shot a look at its thin wooden legs and wondered if it was going to be able to take the strain. He turned his eyes away before Rene had a chance to notice and, as a form of diversion, pulled a pepper pot across the table and began spinning it around in his fingers.

Rene leaned over and took it from him and pushed it to the far end of the table. 'Ye're worse than the kids, y'are. Always find something to fiddle with when they're going to tell me something . . . bad.'

Rene emphasised the last word and watched closely for Terry's reaction.

'No, it ain't bad, Rene. Far from it . . . I think.'

'In that case, let's be 'aving ye, then,' she said, getting up from the stool and pouring hot water into the mug.

Terry rubbed his hands on the legs of his jeans, as he always did to settle himself to talk. 'Well, it's like this, lass. The lads down at the club 'ave been 'aving a whip-round for ye.'

Rene frowned questioningly at him as she slowly stirred sugar into the tea. She placed the mug in front of him and resumed her seat. 'For what reason?'

'We've arranged for ye to go up to Edinburgh in August.'

'Edinburgh? Why on earth would I want to go up to Edinburgh? Are you and the lads trying to tell me the act's that bad, ye want to banish me to Scotland?'

'No. Listen, Rene, it's for the Edinburgh Festival – or for the Fringe, to be exact.'

'The Fringe?' Rene shook her head. 'I'm sorry, Terry, ye've lost me, lad. I don't understand what ye're saying 'ere.'

''Ave ye 'eard of the Fringe?'

'If we're talking about 'aircuts and the neat finishing on candlewick bedspreads, then I 'ave. If not, then ye'll 'ave to enlighten me.'

Terry scratched at the side of his face. This was not going as easily as he had hoped. 'The Fringe, Rene, is part of the Edinburgh Festival. It's the name for a whole load of different acts put on in different venues all round the city. There are all sorts of plays and reviews and things – and also comedy shows.'

'So what are ye saying?' Rene asked quietly.

'We think ye should go up there and put on a show.'

Rene let out a short laugh and stared incredulously at Terry. 'Ye're joking!'

'No, far from it.' He leaned forward on the table. 'Listen, Rene, ye're a bloody wonderful comedienne, but ye're never going to get anywhere just staying 'ere in 'Artlepool. The lads down at Andy's think ye could make it big, and the Fringe is known for being a really good launching pad for people like you.'

'People like me?' Rene exclaimed. 'You and the lads 'ave lost the plot, you 'ave, Terry.' She got up and began to slide dishes with a clatter into the sink. 'People like me don't do that kind of thing. We live in 'ouses with unemployed 'usbands. We go to the supermarket and 'ang around the shelves where all the stuff that's past its sell-by date is stacked. We take the kids on a Sunday to Ward-Jackson Park to feed the ducks with stale bread because

47

we can't afford to go to the cinema complex down at the Lanyard. We don't even entertain the idea of leaving 'Artlepool. I mean, a 'oliday for me would be spending a weekend with the "codheads" round on the 'Eadland!' She threw a washing-up cloth with force into the sink. 'We can't afford to have pipe dreams, Terry, about making it big and getting our names up in lights. It just don't work that way.'

'Who says it don't? What about people like Jim Davidson and Jimmy Tarbuck and the like?'

'Oh, yeah? They made it big "on the Fringe", did they?' she asked sarcastically.

'I'm not sure of *that*, exactly, but they both came from pretty 'umble rootings as well.'

'I know that, Terry, but they are them and I am me.' She sat down heavily on the stool. 'Ye know, I'm really touched you and the lads 'ave done all this for me, but go back and tell them to spend their money on something more worthwhile' – she laughed quietly – 'like getting something better than an 'ole in the ground for the ladies' toilet in the club, for a start!'

Terry shook his head. 'No, it's you going to Edinburgh or nowt.'

'Why's that?'

'Because we've paid the money and booked the venue.'

'Ye never 'ave!'

'So if you don't go, we'll all be out of pocket.'

'But why the 'ell did ye pay before telling me about it?'

Terry simply smiled at her, a knowing look on his face. Rene flicked back her head, understanding everything.

'You knew there wasn't a chance of me considering it otherwise, isn't that right?'

'Something like that,' Terry replied quietly.

Rene leaned her elbows on the table and rested her forehead in the palms of her hands. ''Ow long's it for? A couple of nights or summat?'

'Three weeks.'

Rene shot upright. 'Three weeks! Terry, I can't go up to Edinburgh for three weeks. For a kick-off, I couldn't afford it!'

'That's all been taken care of.'

'Oh, bloody 'ell, Terry! This has not been thought through at all! I mean, I couldn't just 'ead off and leave the kids to fend for themselves, could I?'

'What about Gary? 'E's not working.' Rene had her mouth open, ready to set off again with another stream of reasons-why-not, but was cut short by Terry's raised hand. 'Rene, don't find excuses for this one. We can work around it. You 'ave a real gift, lass, for making people laugh. Doesn't matter who they are or where they come from, ye could make anyone laugh. Why keep it for 'Artlepool when ye could make yerself some decent money elsewhere? It's only three weeks out of yer life, and if it doesn't work out, well then, ye 'aven't lost out on anything, 'ave ye?'

Rene did not reply, but sat biting at her bottom lip.

'But,' Terry continued, 'if you let this chance slip, ye could go regretting it for the rest of your life.'

The door leading from the kitchen into the front of the house opened and a tall skinny man, dressed in baggy jeans and a checked lumberjack's shirt, open to reveal a grubby white T-shirt, leaned his shoulder against the door pillar. 'What's going on in 'ere, then?' he asked, taking a long drag on his cigarette and exhaling the smoke through his hawk-like nose.

Rene smiled at the man. 'Ye know Terry, don't ye, Gary? Ye've met him at Andy's.'

The man nodded his head briefly in greeting. 'Terry.'

'Nice seeing ye, Gary.'

Gary walked over to the sink, ran water on to the stub of his cigarette and threw it into the bin. He turned around and leaned his bottom against the kitchen sink and folded his arms. 'So what gives 'ere? Voices were raised that much, I could 'ardly 'ear the telly.'

'Nowt, really,' Rene replied, narrowing her eyes at Terry in a bid to stop him from even starting on an explanation. Terry chose to ignore it. He had come this far and he needed an answer before he went off to do his paint job.

'What d'ye think of Rene as a comedienne, Gary?'

'She's damned good,' Gary replied with a flick of his head. 'Makes us all laugh, any road.'

Terry shot a look at Rene. 'Aye, that's what I was telling 'er.'

Gary snorted out a laugh. 'So that's what ye've come round to tell 'er, is it? That she's a funny person?'

'No, not exactly.'

'So, what's yer explanation for being 'ere, then?'

'Gary!' Rene reproached him tentatively, detecting the edge of hostility in his voice. She took in a deep breath. 'Right, then. I'll do the explaining. Some of the lads down at the club 'ave put money in a kitty to send me up to Edinburgh in August to do me act at something called the Fringe.'

'Oh, aye?' Gary said, taking a cigarette packet from the breast pocket of his shirt. 'And what 'ave ye said?'

Rene glanced at Terry. 'I've told 'im that I can't make a decision right now.'

Gary put a cigarette in his mouth and lit it. He took a deep drag. 'What would ye 'ave to do?'

'Just do me act.'

Gary shrugged. 'Why not, then? Ye could take the train up and get back next day.'

Rene looked at her husband. 'It would be for three weeks, Gary.'

'Three weeks? No way, then! Ye can't go off and abandon yer family for three weeks, especially not in August! That's when Robbie and Karen'll be getting ready to go back to school. Who's going to manage all that?' Gary took another long drag from his cigarette and shook his head. 'A nice thought, Terry, but it wouldn't work out at all.'

'Excuse me,' Rene exclaimed, her voice rising in volume, 'but is there any good reason why you shouldn't look after Robbie and Karen? After all, ye're not doing owt else at the moment.'

Gary leaned over, inches away from Rene's face, his eyes pierced with anger. 'It's not my bloody fault I don't 'ave a job. And anyway, what would 'appen if I got a job while ye were away? Who'd look after the kids then?'

'*I* don't know, Gary. I haven't given it that much thought yet!'

'Well, forgive if I'm wrong, lass, but it sounds as if ye've thought about it good and proper!'

Terry got slowly to his feet and pushed the stool under the table. 'Look, I'd better get off and leave you two alone to talk about it.' He eased his way between them, and then, with another pensive scratch to his cheek, he turned back and smiled at Rene's husband. 'Listen, Gary, I know it's 'ard for ye right now. I appreciate it all, mate. I got laid off at the shipyard back in '92, and it took me an age to get back on me feet after that blow. But you 'ave a wife with an amazing talent, and to 'ave that locked away here in 'Artlepool is a real waste. I mean, she could make a whole load of money doing what she does.'

'And are ye trying to tell me that I'm not capable of making the money then, is that it?' Gary replied irately, taking a step towards Terry.

Terry held up his hands defensively. 'No, I never meant that, mate.'

'I'm the one who's been bringing all the money into this family up until now, Terry, my friend. I wasn't to know that the bloody Koreans were going to pull the rug out from under our feet because of some sodding "global restructuring" plan.'

'I know, Gary,' Terry said quietly. 'I'm sorry, it was never meant to sound that way, 'onest, lad.' He gave Rene a sad smile. 'I'll let meself out.' He opened the door and closed it behind him, and as he stood on the step he blew out a long breath of both regret and relief. He walked around the side of the house, past the weed-ridden rubble and out through the paint-starved gate. The game of football had ceased in the road. No doubt a case of 'bad light, stop play', he thought to himself. He walked over to the van, jerked open the ill-fitting door and got in, cranking up the engine with a roar from the broken exhaust. He was just about to pull away from the kerb when again he was made to jump at the sound of something heavy hitting the side of his van. He glanced in his wing mirror only to find Rene standing beside him on the pavement. He rolled down the window.

'All right, lass?' he asked concernedly.

She nodded. 'Aye, I'm fine.'

He flicked his thumb over his shoulder. 'Sorry about that in there. I didn't—'

'I'll do it.'

'What's that, lass?'

'I'll do it. I'll go to Edinburgh for the whole bloody three weeks.'

'What about Gary?'

'For once in me life, Terry, I'm not even going to think about Gary. This is *my* chance, and I want to give it a go. Ye're right, it'll never come round again.'

'Ye can still think about it, if ye like.'

'I don't 'ave to. I've made up me mind this is exactly what I want to do.'

Terry gave her a wink. 'And, by God, you'll show 'em, lass.'

He rolled up the window and took off up the cul-de-sac, and as he drew out into the street he couldn't resist giving three long blasts on his feeble horn, even though he could hardly hear them above the noise from the broken exhaust.

Seven

Roger let out a long groan and pressed the 'pause' button on the remote with force. He leaned back in his chair and slapped both hands to his forehead. 'Dammit, we should have started on this before now. I just don't see how on earth we're going to make it work.'

Phil Kenyon drummed his pencil on the desk as he studied the two pages of roughly drawn diagrams, his supreme confidence at their being able to programme the piece beginning to wane. 'I reckon we're all right for the first fifty-nine seconds. The timings seem to be spot on.'

'Yes, but that section has the whole orchestra involved. Now we dive into these three quiet passages, followed by two crescendos before we get the volume back again. If we just sequence in a load of flares and fountains, the audience will either end up bored rigid or fall fast asleep by the time we reach that point in the music.'

Phil stuck the pencil behind his ear and pushed himself out of his seat. 'We'd better have more coffee,' he said, clamping together the two empty mugs on the desk with his fingers, 'otherwise we'll be in danger of doing the same.'

Roger glanced at his watch. It was only ten past five in the afternoon, but having only managed four hours' fitful sleep in the past thirty-six hours, all he really felt like doing was crawling into bed and flaking out for an eternity. He pressed the 'start' button on the remote and once again listened through the muted string section of the Tchaikovsky piece.

'OK,' he said, as Phil placed a cup of black coffee on the desk in front of him. 'Let's work first on the crescendos. We don't want them to overrun, so we'll use some of those short-timed items we're getting from Hengyang and then when the volume hits in again, we'll catch it with a battery of four-inch flash mines. How does that sound?'

Phil took the remote from Roger and scrolled back through the music. As he listened again to the piece, he thumped his fist on the desk, out of time with the music but knowing intuitively each moment of firing. He pressed the remote at the end of the section.

'Yeah, I reckon that would work. We'll have to back-time the mines by at least two bars, otherwise we'll lose synchronisation when the whole orchestra comes in again.'

'Shall we risk it?' Roger asked, feeling too tired to make a decision on it for himself.

'I don't see why not,' Phil replied, reaching over to the CD machine and switching it off, 'but my suggestion is that we don't make a decision right now and go sleep on it.'

Roger rubbed both hands at the side of his bearded face. 'That's about the best idea you've come up with all day.'

Eight

Rene Brownlow stood watching long after the van had pulled out of sight, its one-time presence in the cul-de-sac still marked by the lingering smell of exhaust fumes. Well, that's it, then, she thought to herself, ye've gone and done it, 'aven't ye? In the last fifteen minutes, ye've made a decision that's going to change the course of yer life. All right, let's be practical about it, everything could go belly-up and ye might well end up back here in 'Artlepool with yer tail between yer legs. But so bloody what! An opportunity 'as opened up to get away from this dreary little 'ouse in Clavering, to break into a new world outside of this cold, windy town teetering on the edge of Britain. Not that 'Artlepool is a bad place to live, but twenty-five years is a long time to be stuck in one place. Ye may have spent the first ten years of yer life twenty miles away on the North Yorkshire moors, but now ye're a real West Docker, through and through.

She turned and walked slowly back to the house, and as she reached the gate she stopped and looked back to the end of the street, her face thoughtful as something clicked in her mind. 'You'll show 'em, lass,' that's what Terry had said. And he'd said it once before, hadn't he? Rene kicked the gate shut with her foot and then walked along the narrow passage to the back of the house. Aye, it was quite fitting that it was Terry who should break the news. If it hadn't have been for him in the first place, this whole thing would never have come about.

Saturday night at Andersons Westbourne Social Club was always busy, but on that particular occasion, there was hardly room to move, due to the impending and much publicised visit of

Danielle Vine, a young singer who had recently been a finalist on the television show *Stars in your Eyes*, thanks to her superb – yet not quite superb enough to win – impersonation of Celine Dion. Consequently, Harold Prendergast, manager and licensee of the establishment, decided to come out front for a spell so that he could watch with eagle eyes as the money flowed in and out of the three cash tills that were spaced evenly along the shelf at the back of the long bar. He felt this was a necessary precaution, seeing that two weeks before, he'd had to sack one of his eight bar staff for having 'light fingers'. Not that he knew for certain it was that particular girl who was the culprit, but losing money in such a way ate into his profits, and he thought it necessary to show the rest of the staff that he would not tolerate such practice. OK, truth be told, he'd had to pay her off just to keep her mouth shut about what happened, or more to the point, what *hadn't* happened behind the closed doors of his office, but he'd always considered it a perk of the job, having a bit of fun with the girls, and he wasn't used to having his advances spurned in quite such a forceful manner.

He leaned against the bottle shelf at the back of the bar and crossed his arms as he eyed the new girl at work. This one wasn't so much of a looker as the last, her size certainly outweighed her beauty, but there was something definitely sexy about her. It was his theory that a girl could be as pretty as paint, but still exude as much sexual attraction as a cross-eyed donkey. Talking of which, he thought to himself, as he glanced over to the permanently reserved table next to the stage where his wife sat, chatting away primly with her set of friends from Thursday-night bingo. With a shake of his head, he turned away from the sight that, over the years, had come to offer him little attraction and found a space between the spirit-dispensing racks to look himself over in the mirror that backed the full length of the bar. He adjusted the striped bow tie, which drooped a fraction to the left, picked at a loose thread on his white double-breasted tuxedo jacket, and with forefinger and thumb smoothed his well-trimmed moustache from centre outwards. Out of the side of his eye he caught sight of the reflection of the new girl, wrestling to control the size of head on a pint of Guinness. He turned, shot a look over to where his wife was seated, before gliding over to the girl and putting his hand on top of hers on the tap.

'Come on, Rene, lass,' he said kindly, 'ye've been working 'ere two weeks now. Ye should really 'ave mastered the Guinness tap by now.'

Rene looked round and smiled. 'Sorry, Mr Prendergast. I think it's because Joe's just changed the barrel.'

'Never mind, we'll do this one together. Just pour the head off into the waste tray and we'll try it again.' He pushed up the tap and then eased it down, taking the opportunity to move his hand gently against Rene's. 'There, that's going wonderfully.' He took another brief glance towards the stage before leaning closer to Rene's ear. 'I think ye'll manage that now, won't ye?'

'I think so. Thanks for the help, Mr Prendergast,' Rene replied.

'That's what I'm here for,' he said soothingly, putting a hand on her shoulder and giving it a tight squeeze. He started to move away, then turned back and put a pensive finger to his lips. 'Actually, Rene, maybe ye could spare me a moment in me office after ye've finished that round of drinks. Just a few things I need to say.'

Rene looked anxiously at him. 'I can do them most times, Mr Prendergast. It was just the new—'

'No, no,' he cut in with a smile and a shake of his head. 'Nothing serious, lass. Just a couple of encouraging words.'

Five minutes later Harold was seated behind his desk watching the close-circuit television that relayed front-of-house proceedings to his office, when there was a knock on the door. Getting up from his mock-leather executive swivel chair, he ran a hand either side of his parted hair before moving over to the door and opening it.

'Come in, Rene.' He stood aside and ushered her in. 'Take a seat over there,' he said, indicating with outstretched hand the chair in front of his desk. Rene smoothed her black skirt over her large bottom and sat down. Harold scrutinised her actions, and then opened up the two doors of an ornate-fronted cabinet that hung on the wall next to a large black-and-white photograph of himself and Bernard Manning, the bear-like comedian, shaking hands with each other onstage.

'I think we could do with a little freshener,' he said, inspecting the bottles in the cupboard. 'What would yours be, Rene?'

'Nowt for me, thanks, Mr Prendergast. I've never been a great one for taking a drink.'

'An admirable quality,' he said, unscrewing the top from a bottle of Glendurnich malt whisky and pouring a large shot into a crystal tumbler, 'especially when ye work behind a bar. In my book, that's the kind of thing that can earn a girl like you pretty fast promotion.'

He took a sip from his glass before seating himself on the edge of the desk beside Rene. 'So, tell me, how are ye finding the work?'

Rene shrugged. 'Fine, I suppose.'

'Not too much of a strain?'

'No.' She snorted out a laugh. 'Not when the heaviest thing you have to lift is a pint of beer.'

Harold threw back his head in mirth. 'That's not what I meant, lass, but it's very funny.' His face became serious. 'No, what I really wanted to say to ye, Rene, is that if ever there comes a time when ye *do* feel stressed or ye find that things are beginning to get on top of ye, then ye must know that the door of my office is always open to ye.'

'That's very kind of ye, Mr Prendergast.'

'Not at all, Rene,' he said, putting his glass down on the desk and moving around behind her, 'because, ye see, I know all about tension, Rene. It just happens to be my speciality.' He placed his hands on Rene's shoulders and began to knead the back of her neck slowly and rhythmically with his thumbs. He leaned over close and whispered in her right ear. 'For I am a man, lass, who has been gifted with 'ealing 'ands.'

'Oh? That's summat, in't it?' Rene replied brightly, darting her eyes from side to side in an attempt to work out why he was doing all this. Surely Mr Prendergast wasn't trying to come on to her? No, that's a really stupid thing to think. He wouldn't pick on a dumpy girl like her, especially tonight of all nights, when the place was jam-packed with punters. And what's more, he knows there's a husband kicking about someplace, because she'd told him about Gary losing his job at the interview. No, Rene, you stupid twit, you're barking up the wrong tree here. Mr Prendergast is just trying to be kind.

Nevertheless, she wanted it to stop right there and then. She jumped to her feet and circled her arms, easing out her shoulders. 'Ooh, that was lovely, Mr Prendergast. Just set me up right for the rest of the night.' She turned to him and smiled, pointing to the door. 'I think I should be getting back now. Work to be done, and all that.'

'No, no, there's no hurry, lass,' he sang out, taking her by the arm and trying to guide her back to the chair. 'That's only the beginning. I've got to work on the full length of yer spine yet.'

Rene pulled her arm away from his grip. Keep smiling at him, she thought to herself. Don't make it look as if you're rebuffing him. 'No, let's make it another time, Mr Prendergast. We shouldn't really keep the punters waiting, should we?'

Rene saw the hand moving back towards her, but then a knock on the door made the manager retract it immediately and he moved swiftly round the back of his desk and sat down, his face masked in composure.

'Come in,' he called out.

Joe, the assistant manager, put his head round the corner of the door. He gave a brief smile to Rene before looking towards the manager. 'We've got a no-show, Harold.'

Harold sat bolt upright in his executive chair. 'What d'ye mean?'

'Danielle Vine's mother has just turned up and said her daughter's come down with tonsillitis.'

Harold slapped a hand to his forehead. 'Oh, bloody 'ell! That's all I need. Can't she do nowt at all?'

'I doubt it. Seemingly, her throat's all closed up and it's gone the colour of a ripe tomato.'

'Please, spare us the details. What about our reserve act, then?'

'Eddie's away in York doing a show tonight. He told you about it last week.'

Harold scratched the fingers of both hands hard at the back of his head. 'Right, then, ye'd better leave me, you two. I've got some bloody thinking to do to come up with an act in the next 'alf an 'our.'

With relief, Rene followed Joe out of the office and closed the door behind her. She took in a deep breath and let it out slowly to compose herself before walking along the passage and out into the bar. Most of the customers were sitting at tables, waiting expectantly for the act that Rene knew wasn't going to happen. The rest of the staff stood in a huddle at the other end of the bar, chatting amongst themselves.

'Be a lass, Rene, and give us a pint of ale.'

Rene turned to see Terry Crosland smiling over the bar at her. She hadn't been working in Andy's long enough to put a name to all the regulars, but she knew Terry because there had been a couple of quiet nights when he'd come in by himself and they'd both had a chinwag together. He always struck her as a bit of a loner, but there was something, she liked about his quiet and friendly manner.

'Coming up,' she replied quietly, still distracted by what had just happened in the office. Without saying a word, she drew the pint, put it on the bar, took his money and rang it up on the till. She placed his change in front of him and turned away.

'What's the matter with you tonight, lass? Cat got yer tongue?'

Rene smiled at the man. 'No. Sorry, Terry, I'm just feeling a bit . . . strange right now.'

Terry raised his eyebrows. 'Right. Well, that were a tenner I gave ye just then,' he said, knocking a finger on the bar next to his change, 'so ye owe me another fiver.'

'Oh, I'm sorry, lad.' She opened up the till and found the ten-pound note slid into the compartment that held the fivers. She moved it over, then took out Terry's additional change and shut the drawer. 'There y'are,' she said, placing the note on the bar. 'Sorry about that.'

'So what's wrong?'

Rene shook her head. 'Nowt, really.'

'Well, there must be summat up, because ye haven't come out with any of yer jokes yet.'

'I can't tell ye, Terry. Anyway, it's probably just my imagination, but the thing is I really do need this job, what with Gary being out of work an' all.'

Terry slowly nodded, his eyes narrowed as he began to understand the situation. 'Ye've just been in the office with 'Arold Prendergast, haven't ye?'

Rene stared at him. 'What d'ye mean?'

''E's tried to come on to ye, 'asn't he?'

Rene leaned forward on the bar, relieved that someone else had knowledge of her predicament. ''Ow d'ye know that?' she asked secretively. 'I mean, 'as 'e done it before?'

'Not that anyone would suspect, lass, but aye, 'e's done it before . . . countless times.'

'Who knows about it, then?'

'You, me, and the other girls who have had to leave because they told 'im to get lost!'

''Ow come you know?'

'Because I found out about it from the first girl that it 'appened to. Met 'er outside in tears just after she'd been given the sack. She was still 'olding the money in 'er 'and that 'e'd given her to keep 'er mouth shut.'

'And ye've done nowt about it?'

Terry shook his head. 'I know, it doesn't sound right, does it? The man's definitely got it coming to 'im, but the opportunity's never come up.'

Rene looked at him questioningly. 'I don't understand.'

Terry turned round, his eyes looking towards the table by the stage. 'You see that group of women over there?'

'Aye.'

'Third one from the left is 'Arold's wife.'

Rene stared with wide eyes in the direction of the stage. 'I don't believe it. D'you mean to say 'e'd try it on with . . . with 'is *wife* here?'

'That's the kind of man 'e is.'

Rene let out a long puff of breath. 'What a bloody *scumbag!*'

'Exactly,' said Terry, turning back to face her. 'So that's what I mean about the opportunity not coming up yet, but it soon will, Rene my girl, you mark my words.'

Rene did not say anything for a moment, but stood biting her lip and eyeing the stage, her eyes deep-set with hostility.

'I think, Terry, old fruit, that our opportunity has just presented itself.'

'Oh? Why d'ye think that?'

'There's a no-show tonight.'

'What?'

'Danielle What's-'er-face has got tonsillitis, and the reserve act's 'eaded off to York.'

'Oh, bugger me!' Terry exclaimed, looking open-mouthed at the hundreds of people in the packed club. He let out a high-pitched chuckle. 'Oh, my word, 'Arold's for the 'igh-jump!'

With that, the lights on the stage were brought up to full power and Harold Prendergast came out of the side wing, squinting blindly into the room. He was greeted by a thunderous hand clap and deafening wolf whistles, the audience expecting this to be the preamble to a wonderful night's entertainment of songs made famous by the French-Canadian diva. Harold approached the microphone too fast, making it screech with feedback. He took a step back and cleared his throat. 'Ladies and gentlemen, I'm afraid that I 'ave some quite bad news for ye.' This brought about an immediate and complete silence, which did nothing to help Harold's nerves. He now let out a couple of hacking coughs. 'I'm sorry to inform ye that our star performer, Danielle Vine, 'as been taken unexpectedly ill . . .' He got no further. The audience erupted with angry jeers and loud whistles, and a chorus of 'We want our money back!' soon took hold and boomed around the club. Harold held up his hands in an attempt to pacify them, but soon realised the battle was lost and reversed away sheepishly to the sanctuary of the side wing.

'Right, go up and introduce me, Terry,' Rene shouted above the noise.

Terry turned and stared at her. 'What?'

'Go up and introduce me,' she yelled louder.

'I 'eard you the first time. I can't go up there.'

'Terry, I know ye're a shy man, but this is our opportunity. All ye've got to say is something about the club being lucky enough to have some in-house entertainment tonight.'

'And what are *you* going to say?'

Rene burst out laughing. 'I don't know yet.'

Terry shook his head. 'Ye're mad, ye are.'

Rene nodded. 'Probably, but do it. Go on.'

Terry reluctantly left the bar and made his way slowly through the tables. Nobody noticed him until he jumped up on to the stage and walked over to the microphone. The noise abated to a questioning hum before there was silence.

'Ladies and gentlemen, we might not be able to 'ave what we came for tonight . . .' A voice yelled out: 'Too bloody right, we're not,' but others in the audience hushed the protester. Terry smiled and held up his hand in thanks. 'But I know this girl who is funnier than anyone *I've* ever seen up on this stage, and what's more, she works right 'ere in Andy's. So I ask ye now, ladies and gentlemen, to welcome 'er up 'ere by giving our own Rene Brownlow a big round of applause.'

There was a smatter of clapping and all eyes turned to watch Rene duck under the bar lid and make her way towards the stage. As she passed Terry, she reached out and gave his hand a squeeze. He leaned over and whispered 'Break a leg!' in her ear.

The first laugh came before Rene had even got on to the

stage. There being no steps at the front, Rene tried to get up by swinging one leg first and then the other before turning turned round and pulling two well-built lads out of their chairs to give her a heave-up. They carried out their task with such power that Rene's feet hardly made contact with the ground until she was centre stage and she had to grab hold of the back-drop curtain to stop her from falling flat on her face. She walked forward to the microphone. 'Thanks, lads,' she said, smiling down at the two men. 'I'll take your numbers later in case I ever want to get shot into space!' The remark brought some chuckles and she watched as the two guys had their backs slapped hard by those around them.

'Right. First I'd like to thank Elvis for that kind intro-duction.' More laughter as people turned to look at Terry, who reacted by running both hands over his quiffed hair. 'Not every girl who gets her act announced by the King himself.' That continued the laugh for a moment or two, sufficient time for Rene to work out what the hell she was going to say next. 'OK, my name's Rene Brownlow. I'm the short fat one who works over there.' She pointed towards the bar. 'Of course, anyone who's the same 'eight as me 'as probably never clapped eyes on me before. Either that, or ye've thought I was just a disembodied 'ead rolling backwards and forwards along the bar.'

That gave her another thirty seconds to get her train of thought going. Her eye was caught by a shadowy figure standing in the side wing. It was Harold Prendergast. She smiled to herself and moved forward to the microphone once more. 'Of course,' she said, moving her wide hips provocatively from side to side, 'I'm no Marilyn Monroe, but I'm extremely 'appy in me skin, and I'll 'ave ye know there are some who find me *most attractive*!' There was a loud cry of agreement that Rene didn't allow to end. 'OK, 'ands up, all you sexy gentlemen out there,' she yelled above the noise, 'who finds me outrageously attractive?'

It was working. She looked out on to a sea of hands, laughed and then turned towards the side wing. ''Ang on a moment!' she said, putting her hands on her hips and frowning theatrically. 'There just 'appens to be a man over 'ere who 'asn't put 'is 'and up.' She saw Harold begin to slide away, so she moved quickly over to the side wing and grabbed his arm. 'Oh, no, no, no, sunshine, you come right out 'ere.'

'What the *'ell* are ye playing at?' Harold Prendergast hissed angrily at her. 'Don't ye realise my *wife's* out there?'

Rene turned back to the audience. 'Oh, he says 'is *wife's* out 'ere. Where is she, 'Arold? Stop hiding yerself in there and come and point 'er out to us all.'

The laughter in the club was growing louder, but it was never as strong as the chorus of 'Come out, 'Ar-old!'

With a sneer of fury, Harold allowed Rene to drag him on to the stage and the audience applauded his arrival for at least half a minute. Rene held up her hand and there was immediate silence, and in that briefest of moments she knew she had the audience totally with her.

'So, go on, 'Arold, tell us all where yer good wife is sitting.'

Harold pointed down to the table in front of the stage and flashed an uneasy smile at his wife.

'That's no use, 'Arold,' Rene exclaimed, shaking her head from side to side in time with her words. 'I can see at least eight beautiful ladies sitting at that table.' She took hold of his arm and pulled him to the front of the stage. This time there was no resistance and he followed on after her like a lamb to slaughter. 'Which one is she, 'Arold?'

'That one,' Harold said quietly, pointing again to his wife.

Rene shielded her eyes against the glare of the lights as she made a show of appraising the manager's wife. 'Wow, 'Arold, you've got a real stunner there! Tell me, 'ow long 'ave you two been married?'

There was a look of intense concentration on Harold Prendergast's face as he carried out a quick bit of mental arithmetic. 'Twenty-four years,' he replied meekly.

Rene drilled a finger into her left ear. 'I'm sorry, 'Arold, my 'earing doesn't seem to be too good tonight. 'Ow long did you say?'

'Twenty-four years,' he repeated, only a fraction louder than the first time.

'Twenty-four years!' Rene exclaimed, jamming the microphone under her armpit as she joined in with the audience's applause. 'Well, that is what I call a wonderful achievement!' She moved close to Harold and leaned her head against his chest, anguish written all over her face. 'I can see now why ye never put yer 'and up. How could I *ever* compare with someone as beautiful as that?'

There was a cry from the back of the hall. 'Put yer bloody 'and up, ye tosser!'

Others began to join in the refrain and Rene saw with glee that even Mrs Prendergast's companions at the front table were calling out their disdain, their own hands shooting up into the air.

Very slowly, Harold Prendergast raised his hand, and Rene Brownlow began to smile serenely, as if she were Sleeping Beauty just aroused from her sleep by the handsome prince. She pulled Harold Prendergast's face down towards her and planted a lingering kiss on his cheek, and the club was filled with the hammering of feet and the beating of pint glasses on the tables.

Rene felt the manager's hand grip tightly to the back of her blouse and he leaned over towards her, as he continued to look out at the audience with a smile fixed on his face. Rene knew what was coming. As he made to speak, she leaned her hand against his right shoulder. He was so distracted with anger and humiliation that he did not realise that that was the hand in which she held the microphone.

'I want to see you in my office immediately afterwards, d'ye understand?'

He had meant it to be a whisper, but his words rang with instant betrayal around the club. There was no need for Rene to say anything, but she couldn't resist turning towards her audience with a knowing grin on her face and giving a slow continuous nod. To begin with, the audience burst out laughing, but then, as four hundred eyes focused on Mrs Prendergast to witness her reaction, the volume faded away to an uneasy silence. Even in the dim light of the auditorium it was possible to see her cheeks redden with embarrassment at the sudden and improper attention that her husband's remark had brought upon her. Glaring with hostility at his drooping form onstage, she got quickly to her feet, grabbed her jacket from the back of the chair, shouldered her handbag and, with her head bowed, started to make her way towards the exit. And as she ran the gauntlet, the only sound that emanated from the crowd was the uneasy clearing of throats and the creaking of chairs as her progress was followed across the hall.

By the time the door had closed behind her, Harold had disappeared from the stage, quickly making for the fire door in order to catch up with his wife and start to make immediate amends. Having captured her audience's attention once more with a quick-fire remark, Rene kept them engrossed for the next hour, never giving Harold Prendergast another thought nor mention. After the show, she went to his office as he had asked, even though she was not sure whether he would be there, and entered when a weak voice answered to her forceful knock. Ten minutes later she reappeared, clenching her fist in triumph as she closed the door behind her. She literally bounced back along the corridor and out behind the bar.

Business was going so well that the bar staff were having a hard time keeping up with the orders. For a while, Rene could do nothing to help out, as those who thronged the bar greeted her with loud cries of congratulations and thrust out hands for her to shake. Rene smiled and said her thanks while scanning the bar for Terry. She eventually caught sight of him over in the corner, leaning on the bar lid and watching her every move. She walked along to the end, ducked under the bar lid, and hardly had the chance to straighten up before she found herself enveloped in a tight hug in his arms.

'You were bloody fantastic, lass. That was absolutely spot-on.'

'D'ye think so?'

Terry pushed her away and eyed her suspiciously. 'Ye know fine well it was, don't ye?'

Rene smiled and nodded. 'Aye, I suppose I do, really.'

'I don't think ye've left 'Arold Prendergast much of an 'eart to try out his old tricks again, that's for sure.'

'No, I reckon 'e'll be well occupied trying to seduce one particular lady for the foreseeable future.'

'So, did ye go to his office to see him?'

'Aye, I did.'

'What 'appened?'

Rene shrugged her shoulders. 'We threw insults back and forth across his desk for five minutes, and then we negotiated.'

'Right,' said Terry, wanting to hear everything immediately. 'So what did ye come away with?'

Rene's face broke into an excited grin and she reached up and grabbed hold of the lapels of Terry's denim jacket. 'A bloody raise and an 'alf-'our comedy spot up on that stage every Thursday night!'

'Ye never 'ave!'

'I 'ave!'

Terry grabbed her by the shoulders and gave her a shake. 'That's just the best bloody news I've 'eard for a long time. Ye'll show 'em 'ow it's done, lass, ye'll damn well show 'em.'

Nine

Having shown the affluent-looking man into her pristine front sitting room, the small elderly woman politely excused herself from his company, closed the door and walked past the dark-varnished staircase to the kitchen. She filled the kettle from the tap, put it on to boil, then slid open one of the double-glazed doors that led out into the small garden at the rear of the house, allowing immediately the thundering noise of the traffic on the Kingston bypass to fill the room. With one hand on the door handle to steady herself, she stepped down on to the concrete-slabbed patio and walked out of the shadow of the house to the edge of the immaculately kept lawn, feeling the warmth of the mid-morning sun permeate through her woollen cardigan.

'Leonard,' she called out, 'are you there?'

There was no reply. She walked out on to the grass and made her way around the curved herbaceous flower bed where she found her husband kneeling on a black plastic sheet, carefully digging around the stubborn roots of a dandelion with a hand fork.

'Leonard?'

Leonard Hartson pushed himself upright and turned to look at her, shielding his eyes against the sun with an earthy glove. 'Hullo, Gracie. Coffee time, is it?'

'No, dear. It's Nick Springer. You remember, he called you two nights ago and said he was going to pop in today.'

'Oh, goodness gracious!' her husband exclaimed, getting laboriously to his feet. He took off his cap and pulled the back of his gloved hand across his glistening forehead, leaving behind a streak of dirt. 'I totally forgot he was coming. You should have reminded me, Gracie.'

'I did, dear, this morning at breakfast.'

'Oh, bother me, did you?' he said, pulling off his gardening gloves. 'How forgetful of me.' He cast an eye over his earth-smudged corduroys and ragged home-knit jersey. 'Do you think I should change my clothes before I see him? I do look rather scruffy.'

'I don't think he'll mind. He seems very nice.'

Leonard smiled at his wife. 'That sounds like Nick. He always was a charmer with the ladies.'

Putting a hand on her elbow, he guided her back towards the house, not relinquishing his hold until she had negotiated the step back in the kitchen. 'Where is he, then?'

'In the front room,' she replied, licking her thumb and rubbing away the streak of dirt from his forehead. She caringly ran her hand either side of his straggling grey hair to make him look slightly more presentable. 'You go through and see him, but take a raincoat or something from the coat stand in the hall and put it on the chair before you sit down. I've just had those loose covers dry-cleaned and I don't want you making them all dirty again. I'll bring through coffee and biscuits in a moment.'

Using the aluminium ledge of the sliding door to pull off the rubber gardening shoes, Leonard then pushed his feet into a pair of bedroom slippers that lay in wait for him and shuffled through to the hall, unhooking a sleeveless quilted jacket off the coat stand as he passed by. He opened the door of the sitting room and entered. Nick Springer turned from the mantelpiece where he had been studying the photographs spread along its length.

'Leonard!' he shouted out enthusiastically, approaching the elderly man with his hand outstretched. 'How wonderful to see you!'

Leonard winced a smile as he felt the grip send an arthritic jolt up his arm. 'Nice to see you too, Nick. What a real surprise.' He walked over to the sofa and spread out the jacket on the pale-blue loose cover. 'You'll have to forgive my appearance. I'm afraid it had completely slipped my mind that you were coming, hence the reason you find me in my gardening clothes.'

'I hope this hasn't inconvenienced you, then.'

'Not at all,' Leonard replied, waving a hand towards an armchair as an indication for Nick to take a seat before he lowered himself slowly on to the sofa. 'It's very rare that I see anyone from the old days in the film industry.'

Nick gave a sharp pull at the creases of his navy-blue suit trousers before sitting down in the armchair. 'It's been a long time. I was just working it out while I was driving down here, and I reckon it's all of twenty-eight years.'

'Really? That long?' Leonard shook his head slowly. 'Oh, well, time stops for no man, as they say.' He observed the younger man as he brushed a hand across his thick dark hair, noticing now that there were traces of grey showing above each ear. His recollection of Nick was that he had been one of his better camera assistants, a quick learner with a good sense of humour, an essential when one had to spend so much time in each other's company, both travelling and on location. However, he had always felt that Nick had an arrogant streak in him, and it seemed to show now more with age in the narrow set of his eyes, the determined jaw and the slide of his mouth when he talked. Whatever he had done with his life, Leonard could tell that he had accomplished it with some success. 'So, are you still behind the camera?' he asked.

Nick shook his head. 'No, I run my own production company now. I did operate camera for a time with Gerry Mansell. You'll remember him, of course?'

'Most certainly I do. We joined Pathé News together many moons ago. Gerry became a particularly gifted lighting cameraman and he and the director Doug Standing formed a most successful partnership. I remember on the film *The Man From Syracuse,* he shot a number of scenes with very little use of a key light. It was both a brave and brilliant concept and the effect was quite staggering.' Leonard chuckled. 'I tried it out myself once, but I'm afraid it all ended up a bit of a disaster.'

Nick smiled at him. 'The only reason I got the job with Gerry was that he knew I'd worked with you. He was equally complimentary about your work.'

'Really? Well, that makes a certain amount of pride course through these old veins of mine.'

The door handle of the sitting room rattled, but it did not open. Jumping up from the chair, Nick was there in two strides, opening the door with force and taking the tray from Grace Hartson's hands before she had even the chance to enter the room.

'Where would you like me to put it?' he asked, swinging the tray from side to side in a way that made Grace fear for the safety of her precious Royal Doulton coffee set. She scuttled around the back of the sofa and spread out Leonard's *Guardian* newspaper on the low stool in front of the electric fire. 'Here, I think, would suit you both,' she said, smiling nervously at the man. 'Thank you for your assistance.'

'Nick, you've met my wife, Grace, haven't you?' Leonard asked, making an effort to push himself to his feet, then deciding not to bother.

'Of course. I was reminding Mrs Hartson that we met many years ago, when I picked you up here once on the way down to Portsmouth for a shoot.'

Grace shot her husband a worried look. 'I'm afraid I had to tell Nick that you had so many assistants over the years, I couldn't quite remember—'

'No reason why you should, Mrs Hartson,' Nick interjected with a laugh. 'I was just saying to Leonard that it was all of twenty-eight years ago.'

'My word,' she said quietly, already making her way towards the door. 'Well, I'll leave you two to have your chat in peace.' She opened the door and closed it soundlessly behind her.

'Shall I do the honours?' Nick asked, squatting down on his haunches and picking up the coffee pot from the tray. 'How d'you like it?'

'Just milk, please.'

'What? No sugar, Leonard? I remember when we used to stop in transport cafés on our way around the country, you put so much sugar in your coffee that you could practically stand a spoon up in it.'

Leonard laughed. 'Goodness, you do have a good memory, don't you? I'm afraid I can't get away with that any more.' He patted his heart. 'Doctor's orders, you know.'

'Really?' Nick handed Leonard the cup of coffee and then sat back down in the armchair, precariously balancing his own cup on the arm.

Leonard pointed to it. 'You'd better not put that there. Just in case . . . you know.'

Nick grimaced. 'Sorry. Is it all right on the carpet, then?'

'Safer there, I think.'

Taking a sip from his cup before placing it and the saucer on the floor, Nick leaned back in the armchair. 'So, is that the reason you gave up work?'

'What?'

'The heart. Was that the reason?'

Leonard shook his head. 'Oh, no. That's only been a slight problem for the past five years.'

'So why did you give up? It really took everyone in the industry by surprise.'

'Now, I know you're overexaggerating on that account, Nick. I never did quite make *that* kind of a mark.'

Nick pushed himself forward in his chair. 'You always were a bit of a self-deprecating devil, Leonard. That is simply not true. I went up to Sammie's on Cricklewood Broadway to pick up some hire equipment about three months after you retired, and I was reliably informed that they'd received endless correspondence from the likes of David Watkin asking why you'd retired.'

'You're not being serious.'

'I certainly am. Come on, Leonard, you were at the top of your professional career and I know for a fact that you were only a stone's throw from being made a member of the British Society of Cinematographers. So, why did you choose that particular moment to give it all up?'

Leonard took a sip from his coffee cup, placed it back on the saucer and let out a long sigh. 'There were a number of reasons, Nick, but overall it was because I was becoming disillusioned with all the changes taking place within the industry at that time. The ACTT union had become far too powerful and was hindering a lot of new blood entering, and I really had no time for all the new video technology being introduced. I hated the lack of refinement in the way that one was supposed to just blast a set with lights. There was no delicacy any more in the technique of lighting, no artistry. Everything was just too immediate. I used to love those nail-biting twenty-four hours when one had to wait for the rushes to come back from the lab, and then see the results up on the screen in the viewing theatre. I really thought it to be the death knell of the industry as I had known it. I even believed that features would eventually end up being shot on video.'

'But they haven't.'

'No, that's true, but you have to remember I was working more and more in documentaries, using sixteen mill, and that was the part of the industry hit hardest by the surge in popularity of video. It was much cheaper, less of a risk, and, to my mind, it all seemed to be becoming so . . . amateurish.'

'The quality of video production has really improved in leaps and bounds, you know, especially now with the introduction of High Def Digital.'

Leonard laughed. 'I'm afraid you've lost me on that one, which really only goes to confirm my belief that if I'd stayed on I would have just become a bit of an old dinosaur.'

'So what did you do after you left? You could only have been in your mid-forties.'

Leonard let out a short laugh. 'It was a difficult one. I had no training to do anything else. I'd left school at the age of sixteen with no qualifications and went straight to work at Ealing Studios as a general dogsbody. I'm close on seventy-three now, so yes, you're right, I would have been in my mid-forties, and prospects for further employment at that age were not very bright. I did do a brief spell in financial services but found it appallingly dull, so I gave that up and became a taxi driver.'

Nick started with amazement. 'What? A London cabbie?'

'No, just a private hire company here in Kingston. Actually, I found it quite a relief. I'd spent so much time away from home and from Grace, I really enjoyed getting back to my own house every night . . . or in the morning, if I was working night shift.'

Nick picked up the cup and saucer from the floor, drained his coffee, then leaned forward and placed them on the tray. 'Do you have any regrets now?'

'What about?'

'Leaving the film industry.'

Leonard pulled at his earlobe thoughtfully. 'I would say that

73

I *did* have regrets, but they have faded with time. You have to understand, Nick, that film-making was in my soul, and I never quite came to terms with the fact that, in my mind, I had never accomplished what I would have considered to be my definitive film. There were just so many different facets of lighting that I wanted to try, being able to push the film stock to the limit, but the type of jobs I was getting didn't allow me to try them out. I'm an old man now, Nick, and I'm quite happy pottering around in my garden, but if you really want to know the truth, I did harbour a very deep frustration for a number of years after I'd given everything up.'

Nick nodded slowly. 'Do you still remember much about how you worked?'

Leonard smiled. 'You don't forget how to ride a bicycle, do you?' He knocked a finger at the side of his head. 'It's all still up here. I don't know what I'd be like at operating a camera now. My hands may be a bit shaky, but no doubt equipment will have improved and someone will have invented a tripod that's even superior to the great Miller fluid head. And I'm sure film stock will have changed for the better too. I would have thought a much finer grain to it.' He let out a quiet, nostalgic laugh. 'My word, you've got me harking back, haven't you?'

Nick had not sat back in the armchair, but rested his arms on his knees, his hands clutched together. 'Do you remember a job we did at the Royal Ballet?'

'Of course I do. We shot it all on 7242 Ektachrome with available light. All pretty grainy, but it turned out to be quite effective.' He pointed a finger at Nick in recollection. 'You operated on that job. First one I ever allowed you to do.'

Nick laughed. 'Now whose memory is working overtime! I don't even remember that.'

'You did a damned good job of it too. It was after that one I was convinced you were going to make the grade.' He let out a sigh. 'But you gave it up too and went into production, right?'

'Yes,' Nick's face became serious, 'and that's really the reason I've come down here to talk to you today.' He rubbed his hands together as he gathered his thoughts. 'Leonard, I'll get straight to the point. Would you ever consider coming out of retirement?'

Leonard observed the man for a moment, his eyes and forehead creased in question. 'Did I just hear you correctly?'

Nick laughed. 'Yes, you did.'

'To do what?'

'A job for me. I want you to film a Japanese dance company at the Edinburgh Festival in August.'

Leonard continued to stare at Nick, and then, with a slow, disbelieving shake of his head, he turned and fixed his eyes in silence on the electric fire.

'Look, Leonard, let me explain the situation,' Nick said, leaning so far forward with intent that his bottom was only just in contact with the edge of the armchair. 'I received a telephone call last week from an old friend of mine, Alasdair Dreyfuss. I used to play tennis with him on a regular basis at Queen's Club before he moved north to become director of the Edinburgh Festival. He told me one of the big Japanese conglomerates is sponsoring this traditional dance company at the festival this year, and consequently one of the broadcast companies from Tokyo has been in contact with me, asking if I could arrange the filming of the event. There are, however, certain stipulations, or a better word might be "complications" attached, in that the commissioner has given express instructions it should be shot on film rather than on video, so that, in his words, "the essence of the dance can be captured in its purest and most natural form".'

Nick was becoming uneasy at Leonard's total lack of response to his proposal, but he decided to continue with his explanation.

'Now to be quite honest, Leonard, my line of work is strictly corporate, and we have always centred our business on video production, but the moment that Alasdair told me about this particular project, my mind was taken back to that job we did with the Royal Ballet—'

'That was all of thirty years ago, Nick,' Leonard cut in quietly.

'I know it was, but you said yourself that the knowledge is still there.'

'Maybe so, but that doesn't mean I could suddenly take on a job like this. For heaven's sakes, I'm seventy-two years old, Nick!'

'So? There are plenty of DOPs still working at your age, and if I'm not very much mistaken, the great Freddie Young was still making films way into his nineties! I'd get you a full working crew, Leonard. You wouldn't have to lift a finger other than just light the set and shoot it.'

Leonard slowly shook his head. 'My word, Nick, what an extraordinary proposal.'

'Three weeks of shooting in August, Leonard. That's all it would be. I'm not asking you to head off for four months to shoot a feature. Three weeks and you just make your own time. The dance company knows it's to be part of the sponsorship agreement to have the show filmed and therefore the director of the company will go out of his way to help you.'

Leonard bit at the corner of his mouth. 'You said I would have to light the set. Surely the company would be performing in a theatre with fixed lighting.'

'I'm going to send a location scout up to Edinburgh to see if he can't find an unused warehouse with a three-phase supply, just in case you want to use heavy lighting. I would suggest that some you shoot under theatre light during the perform-ance to get the atmosphere and the rest you shoot in the ware-house.'

'How would that edit?' Leonard's eyebrows arched with worry. 'And what about film stock? For goodness' sakes, Nick, I'm so out of touch, I wouldn't have the first idea what to use!'

'We have three months before the festival, Leonard, and by the time it comes around, I'll make sure you know as much about the equipment and the film stock and the lighting as you did thirty years ago. It would be as if you'd never left the industry.'

Leonard rubbed at his forehead with splayed fingers, as if kneading away a headache. 'I really don't understand why you are suggesting all this to me, Nick.'

'Well, truth be told, I did have someone else lined up to do the job, but he asked if I could let him off the hook so he could go shoot a big-money documentary in Canada.' He clicked his fingers. 'And then you just happened to spring to mind, Leonard, because word still has it in the world of cinematography that no one has ever come close to being able to film the medium of dance as well as you.'

Leonard thought to rebuff the remark, but then felt such a sudden and long-lost feeling of pride and achievement well in his being that he realised he had no wish to suppress the compliment.

'This could turn out to be your definitive film, you know,' Nick said quietly, taking the retired cameraman's silence as need for further encouragement. 'Why not take the chance to achieve it?'

'I would have to speak to Grace about it,' Leonard replied eventually.

'Of course,' Nick said, shifting back in the armchair with relief, knowing now he had managed to sow the seed of acceptance. 'I'll give you a call in the next couple of days and you can let me know your answer. And if it's yes, then we'll start the ball rolling.' He pushed back the cuff-linked sleeve of his shirt and glanced at the Rolex watch on his wrist. 'I must be on my way. I have a lunch meeting in the West End at one.' He sprang to his feet and stood as Leonard raised himself stiffly from the sofa.

He moved slowly to the door, opened it and ushered Nick out into the hall.

'It was very good of you to remember me, Nick,' Leonard said, undoing the Yale lock on the front door. He held out a hand and when Nick grasped it with his own, Leonard wrapped his other hand over it and gave it an affectionate squeeze. 'I'll have an answer for you when you call.'

'I do hope you take the job, my friend. I feel I'd be repaying a great debt to humankind if I managed to persuade the great Leonard Hartson to get himself back behind the camera.'

Leonard followed the tall man out on to the gravelled path and stood watching as he opened and closed the gate and then slid himself into the dark-green Jaguar parked by the pavement. As the car sped away, he turned to find Grace leaning over a sad-looking azalea bush, plucking away some of its withered leaves.

'Hullo there, Gracie,' he said absently.

'This doesn't seem to be doing very well here, Leonard. I think we should move it to the back garden.' She straightened up and turned her gaze to the Jaguar as it turned out onto the main road and vanished out of sight. 'What a nice man that is.'

'Yes, he is,' Leonard replied quietly as he watched his wife.

'He has a very loud voice, though. Do you think that's requisite for being successful in business nowadays?' She turned to look at her husband and her face broke into a broad grin when she witnessed a sparkle in his eyes she knew had been absent for so many years.

'What?' he asked, perplexed by this sudden burst of humour.

Taking a step towards him, Grace put her hands on his shoulders and planted a long kiss on the side of his cheek. 'Are you going to do it, then?' she asked.

He pushed himself away from her, taking hold of both her hands and giving them a squeeze. 'I don't know. The idea of it all fills me with fear, but at the same time I am honoured he should have asked me. What do you think, Gracie?'

His wife was silent for a moment before replying. 'I could give many reasons why you should *not* do it, my dear,' she said. 'I would worry about you, about your health and about your physical ability to take on a project such as this. But this is not about me, Leonard. You have been given a challenge and an opportunity to counter all those lost years away from the industry that you so dearly loved.' She gave his hands a solid shake. 'So

78

I would suggest you go for it, give yourself this chance, and I am sure no one will be disappointed in what you achieve, least of all yourself.'

Ten

Fred Brownlow gave himself the once-over in the mirror that hung in the narrow hallway of the terraced council house in Wilson Street, Hartlepool. Taking hold of the lapels of his blazer, he gave them a sharp tug, adjusting the fit across his broad shoulders, before giving the sleeves a brisk smooth-down with his hands and turning slightly so that the shaded ceiling light shone on the gold-threaded emblem on his breast pocket. He stood to attention, admiring his turnout just as he had done three decades before when serving as a company sergeant major with the Durham Light Infantry.

'Is that you ready to go?'

He turned to see his wife come along the passage from the kitchen. She was wearing her 'indoors' attire, a floral housecoat with woolly bedroom slippers, and those sparkling eyes that had attracted his attention almost forty-two years ago were made brighter still by the blue frames of her spectacles.

'Aye, Agnes me luv,' he said, taking the white cap down from the hook on the hallstand and fitting it snugly on to his head. 'Ready for action.'

Agnes approached him and began to scrutinise the front of the white V-necked sweater he wore under his blazer. 'That stain came out nicely, didn't it? You make sure to use a paper napkin now when ye 'ave yer tea after the match. No more chocolate down yer front.'

Fred laughed. 'I'll be a good lad, Mother,' he said, giving her a kiss on the forehead. He took a bunch of keys from the stand and put them in the pocket of his light-grey slacks, and then scooped up the bag that contained his bowls from the floor. 'I'll not be late the night. I said I'd give Bert 'and at his allotment tomorrow.'

'Right. Well, play well and don't get all moody if ye get beaten.'

Fred flicked back his head at such a notion. 'As if I ever do,' he scoffed.

And as he left the house, Agnes gave a shake of her head. Although to anyone else her husband's answer may have sounded ambiguous, she knew from experience that one followed the other more often than he cared to admit.

Fred closed the latch on the iron gate, giving a proud glance at the tidiness of his cobbled front patio, and began to walk up Wilson Street. As he hit his stride, he caught sight of the man with the two children walking towards him, seemingly unaware of his presence. He quickly sidestepped off the pavement and crouched down in front of a parked car, but he had hardly time to complete his act of concealment before two high-pitched yells rang out and the slap-slapping of feet came running up the pavement towards him.

'We know ye're there, Grandpa!' he heard the voice of his grandson call out. 'We saw you 'iding!'

Fred stood up just as Robbie came to stand beside the car, a beaming smile on his face. 'Rats! I thought I'd managed to outsmart ye that time,' he said, giving the boy's hair a rough tousle. He turned just as Karen reached him and launched herself into his arms.

'Oh, my word!' he cried out, dropping his bowling bag with a clatter to the ground and catching her up and swinging her around in a full circle. 'Ye're almost getting too big for that kind of thing, lass. Nearly had your old grandpa off his feet.' He put her down and gave his son a welcoming nod as he approached. ''Ow ye're doin', Gary? All well?'

'Aye, good enough,' Gary replied sullenly, dropping his cigarette butt to the ground and grinding it out underfoot.

'Come to pay us a visit, 'ave ye?'

'That was the idea, but looks like ye're on the way out.'

'Aye, I've got a bowling match on. Semi-finals of the district league.' He cocked his head back towards the house. 'Yer mother's in, though. Go pay her a visit. She'd like to see the kids.'

'Ah'll do that.'

'No luck yet, then, with the job-'unting?'

Gary shook his head. 'Bugger all. There's nowt much doing.'

Fred gave his son's arm an encouraging squeeze. 'Ah, well, summat'll turn up, lad. Keep yer spirits up.' He picked up his bag. 'Best be off, then. Can't keep the boys waiting.'

'See and play well,' Gary replied, raising a hand in farewell as he turned to follow the children, who had already disappeared into the house.

The television in the front room was on at full volume when Gary shut the front door behind him. He glanced into the room in passing and saw Robbie and Karen squeezed together into one of the maroon velour armchairs, their eyes transfixed on the screen.

'What d'ye think ye're doing?' Gary asked heatedly as he entered the room. 'Ye're here to see yer nan.'

'She said we could,' Robbie replied, turning to him with a plaintive look on his face.

'Aye, I did that,' Agnes said as she came in carrying two glasses of orange juice. She placed them down on the lace mat she had arranged on the small occasional table next to the children's armchair. 'Fancy a cup of tea, luv?' she asked, giving her son's arm a loving rub.

'Aye, that would be grand.'

'We'll go through to the kitchen, then, and leave these two to their programme.'

Gary followed the small figure with her neat grey curls along the narrow passage to the kitchen. He pulled out a stool at the end of the Formica-topped table and sat down, instinctively putting his hand to the breast pocket of his shirt for a cigarette. He stopped, remembering that his mother had banned smoking in the house since the day her husband had stalwartly kicked the habit six months before.

'Rene working today?' Agnes asked, freshening up the brew in the china teapot with boiling water.

'Aye, she was asked to do the afternoon shift down at Andy's.' Gary drummed his fingers agitatedly on the table. He really could do with a cigarette. 'Probably just as well. She's not in the best mood with me.'

''Ow's that, luv?' Agnes asked concernedly as she poured out two mugs of tea.

Gary sighed. 'This lad from Andy's came round the other day, said that they'd been raising money to send Rene off to Scotland for this Edinburgh Festival thing, you know, to do her comedy turn, and she wants to do it – only I've sort of put a dampener on the whole idea.'

'Oh? Why's that, then?' Agnes asked, concentrating on carrying the brimming mugs over to the table.

'Because it was for three weeks, Mum, that's why! She can't go off for that length of time. Anyway, it's just when the kids will be getting ready to go back to school.'

Agnes sat down opposite her son. 'And that makes a difference, does it?'

'Of course it makes a difference!'

'Why?'

'Well, because . . .' Gary hesitated, his eyes flashing around the small orange-walled room. ''Ere, I thought you'd support my point of view on this one.'

'Oh, luv, I am supportive of you, and the lads at Andy's must be pretty supportive of Rene as well if they're willing to pool their 'ard-earned cash to send 'er all the way up to Scotland to do 'er comedy bit. They must think she's really good.'

'Oh, she is. There's no question about that,' Gary replied with enthusiasm. 'It's just that . . .' He paused and Agnes noticed his shoulders slump with dejection.

'Just what, luv?'

'I was 'oping I might 'ave found meself a job by then.'

Agnes reached across the table and patted her son's hand. 'And I'm sure ye will, Gary, but even when that happens, we can all still manage. I can do my bit with the kids and so can yer dad. It's a pleasure for us, ye know.' She gave a thoughtful shake of her head. 'She's a real brave one, is our Rene.'

''Ow d'ye mean?'

'Well, she's considering taking off from 'Artlepool, a place she's 'ardly left in her life, and spending three weeks away from 'er family in a place where she'll know absolutely nobody. That's not a decision to be made by the faint-hearted. She must really feel she can make a success of 'erself at this festival.'

Gary bit at his lip as he watched his mother smiling encouragingly at him. 'All right, I get yer point.'

'In that case, why not just get right behind 'er and give 'er the encouragement she needs? After all, ye never know what might come of all this.'

Gary nodded slowly. 'Ye reckon she should go then.'

'Absolutely, and if ye want to show how much ye love her, which I know ye do, then ye'll be waving her off up to Scotland with flags unfurled.'

At that moment, Karen sidled into the kitchen and came over to sit on her father's knee. 'Dad, I'm feeling hungry,' she said, looping an arm around his neck.

'Are ye, my luv?' Agnes said, pushing herself to her feet. 'In that case, what d'ye say to yer nan making us all a nice big plate of bangers and mash?'

Gary laughed and gave his daughter a tight squeeze. 'I think we'd all say that's a really good idea, Nan, wouldn't we, darlin'.'

Eleven

On a warm, cloudless morning at the beginning of August, Jeff Banyon strode along Princes Street at a brisk pace, feeling a bead of sweat break out from under the collar of his shirt and trickle slowly down his back. There was still one week to go before the Fringe started in earnest and two weeks before the

International, but already there was an increase of tourists on the street. He body-swerved a tall blonde probably Scandinavian couple, heavily laden with haversacks, who had suddenly stopped to consult a street map, then almost stumbled over a young Japanese photographer who was squatting down on his haunches trying to work out the best angle to capture the line of sail-like pennants that hung on every lamp post from the Scott Monument to the junction with Lothian Road, heralding the forthcoming festival.

When his mobile rang, Jeff had to juggle with his briefcase and jacket, which he carried forefinger through hanging loop and slung over his shoulder, to free up a hand to answer the call. As he walked, listening more than he was speaking, he looked down over Princes Street Gardens to where the railway track broadened out before entering Waverley Station to see if the eleven-o'clock train to London was yet in sight. He quickened his pace to a loping run as he turned down Waverley Bridge, seeing the slanted front of the dark-blue-and-red GNER engine appearing from the tunnel below the castle. It was a natural reaction, but then, on glancing at his watch, he realised he still had a good ten minutes before its scheduled departure, so he slowed once again to a fast walk, not wanting to be soaked with perspiration by the time he boarded the train.

As he made his way into the station he ended the call and slipped his mobile into the breast pocket of his jacket, letting out a sigh of relief. It was his fourth season working with the Scottish Chamber Orchestra and dealing with the organisation of the Fireworks Concert, yet time and experience did not seem to make it come any easier. Over the last three months he had managed to speak with Roger Dent, the owner of the Exploding Sky Company, on just four occasions, and it was only now that it had been confirmed to him they had finally succeeded in scoring the Tchaikovsky piece and had already begun to stockpile the required equipment and hardware needed for the show.

Dealing with Roger had always been one long run of high-octane stress. The man was a law unto himself, totally unorthodox in the way he conducted his business, but at the end of the day he never failed to come up with the goods, always producing a display that left the audience open-mouthed in awe, something his company had succeeded in doing for the past twenty-odd years. However, Jeff knew that Roger Dent would never be aware of the amount of bluffing and downright lying he himself had to solicit on the part of the pyrotechnic to appease the demands and enquiries of both the sponsors of the Fireworks Concert and Sir Alasdair Dreyfuss, the director of the International Festival.

He flashed his ticket to the stern-faced official at the barrier and made his way down the long platform towards the front of the train. Thank goodness he had known well in advance about today's meeting in Newcastle. It had resulted in his acquiring a first-class ticket off the Internet at a much-reduced rate. That gave him at least an hour and a half of comfort and tranquillity to gather his thoughts before meeting with Sir Raymond Garston, the man charged with conducting the Scottish Chamber Orchestra when it accompanied the Fireworks Display on the final Saturday night of the festival.

At the rear section of the train, Leonard Hartson eventually managed to squeeze his suitcase into a luggage rack, half a carriage away from where he had his reserved seat. He edged his way back along the central aisle, his path hindered by children who stood staring in blank fascination at other passengers, and old ladies who were hoping to rely on the goodwill of others to help them put their bags and coats up onto the overhead racks. Eventually, he found his seat and excused himself past his travelling companion, a man of stocky build and unshaven face wearing a woollen plaid shirt and jeans tucked into rigger boots. As Leonard squeezed past him he noted from the reservation ticket on the man's seat he had boarded the train at Aberdeen and already there were several empty cans of McEwans Export on the table in front of him. Leonard smiled briefly at the beery-breathed man before sitting down in his seat with a puff of relief and turning to look out of the window at a young family on the platform who were mouthing words of farewell to an elderly lady seated in the row in front of him.

Despite Gracie's encouragement, he had taken his time over his decision to agree to Nick Springer's request. In the cold light of day after the producer's visit, Leonard began to doubt his ability to take on the Edinburgh job and to question Nick's judgement in not using a cameraman who had both age and technical knowledge on his side. Nick, however, was not to be swayed and arranged for Leonard to study the work of a young freelance cameraman for a week, saying that Leonard could give him an answer after that period.

It turned out the cameraman knew well of Leonard's reputation and appeared more agitated and nervous at the prospect of working with the cinematographer than Leonard was of starting from scratch. Leonard had stood aside as the young man set his lights, watching in fascination as he positioned the small 1K redheads to illuminate an area that would have required at least two 5Ks as 'fillers' in his day. Leonard politely questioned the man about the speed of his film stock, doubting whether he had enough lights to shoot the scene without the need to 'bump it up' a stop or two during processing in the laboratory. The cameraman had told him there had been a huge improvement in both the quality and speed of Eastman Colour over the years, and then, knowing the reason for Leonard's question, he had cast a look at his lighting set and said with a smile that he thought he would probably get away with it. Leonard continued to study the young man's technique as fine adjustments were made, and as his own knowledge came flooding back, he found himself having to bite his tongue at times to stop himself from suggesting the use of a piece of diffuser scrim here or the partial closing of a 'barn door' there. But then later, when he had walked around amidst the nostalgic blaze of lights with his old leather-cased Weston light meter held out in front of him, Leonard was very glad that he had held back any form of criticism. The set was not lit for any great effect, but it was certainly perfectly balanced.

However, it wasn't until Leonard touched the redesigned body of the Arriflex 16SR3 camera that he suddenly felt back where he belonged. His hands moved instinctively around the grainy cast of the apparatus, accustoming himself to the new positioning of handles and buttons and focus lugs. With a steadying hand on the rear-mounted film magazine, he levelled the tripod head, unlocked the tilt and pan levers and with his eye pressed to the foam eyepiece on the adjustable viewfinder, he swung the camera through a smooth figure of eight, exactly the same movement he had practised so many years ago with the old two-wheeled mechanical Moy head on the studio floor at Ealing. The young cameraman watched his action closely, and then changed the static lens for a Canon 10:1 zoom, inviting him to try it out. Leonard pressed the button on the automatic zoom, marvelling at its smooth action and thinking that long gone were the days when a jerky movement on the manual lever would have resulted in a scene reshoot. With the zoom tight in, he focused on a book that lay on a table in the centre of the set, and then returning to wide angle, he once again went through the figure of eight, ending up close in on the book, perfectly focused. When he had finished, he locked off the tripod and stood back from the camera and smiled. Nothing had changed, and he knew from that moment on he still had the knowledge and the ability to accept Nick's commission.

And now, having carried out his recce in Edinburgh, and having seen the warehouse the location scout had found, Leonard knew exactly what he required. He had made out the list the night before in his hotel bedroom and faxed it to Nick's production manager. In two weeks' time, he would be back here in Edinburgh to meet up with his assistant cameraman and two electricians who would be bringing the equipment up from London, ready to start the job.

The train eased off slowly on its journey south, and Leonard watched as the young family waved frantic goodbyes to the woman in the train, moving quicker along the platform in an attempt to keep up with the carriage as it accelerated away. Then, just before they were out of sight, Leonard witnessed the effects of a sudden gust of wind blowing at the woman's cotton dress, making her push it down between her knees, her mouth oval with embarrassment.

Three miles to the north of Waverley Station, over the genteel crescents and ordered rows of the New Town, that same surge of wind blew hard through the weathered concrete five-storey blocks of council flats on Pilton Mains before losing its force somewhere out over the expanse of the Firth of Forth. It billowed out the lines of faded washing that hung on the small railed balconies, a flash of green breaking the grey starkness of the scene as a Hibernian football strip fluttered earthwards from a washing line on the top floor. It landed noiselessly beside a young boy with a shaven head and a silver stud in his ear who had been ambling across the bare swathe of litter-strewn grass. Darting his eyes around the buildings to make sure no one was looking, he quickly picked it up and bundled it into the folds of his zipped jacket, before walking on with practised nonchalance.

In Thomas Keene's bedroom, situated on the third floor at the end of one of the blocks, an empty Tesco baked beans tin, positioned on the extreme edge of the broken-backed chair by his bed, also fell victim to the gust that blew in through the uncurtained window. It clattered to the ground and rolled noisily across the bare floorboards, leaving in its wake a trail of ash and self-rolled cigarette butts, adding little to the detritus already covering every square inch of the room. The figure on the bed stirred under the crumpled, uncovered duvet and a leg shot out in a long juddering stretch, revealing a dirty green undersheet that was too short for the grubby, swirl-patterned mattress. After a moment of complete stillness, the duvet was thrown back and Thomas Keene, known to those few friends he had in the locality as T.K., greeted the brightness of the new day with a rub at his

tinging eyes, a long and successful sniff, and a string of expletives.

Swinging his legs over the side of the bed, T.K. sat for a
moment in his T-shirt and shorts, scratching his head and dragging fingers with difficulty through his thin tangle of greasy
brown hair. He stood up and pulled on a pair of jeans that had
lain in wait since he had removed them the night before, and
then, progressing a step further, he pushed his bare feet into a
pair of dirty trainers, their laces already tied, and kicked them
on as he walked over to the bedroom door. Pulling a hooded
sweatshirt off the bare screw in the wall that had at one time
supported a shelf, he opened the door and walked into the sitting
room, where his father slumped low in a battered armchair,
smoke curling from the cigarette he held cupped in his hand,
as he eyed vacantly the chatty banter of the presenters on the
television.

'Whit's there tae eat?' T.K. asked, pulling the sweatshirt on
over his head. He stood rubbing a hand down the soft, unshaven
stubble on his pockmarked cheek, his mouth hanging open as
if the weight of his flabby bottom lip were too much for his
narrow jaw to bear.

His father answered with a negative flick of his head.

'Could ye gie's some money, then?'

'Awa' tae hell,' his father replied, without taking his eyes off
the television. 'D'yae think ah'm daft or summat?'

'It's fi food.'

'Oh, aye?'

T.K. shook his head slowly at his father's mistrust. 'Ah'm clean,
you know. Ah havnae touched the stuff fi twa months. Gie's
some credit fi tha'.'

Putting the cigarette in his mouth, Thomas Keene senior
turned, a sneer on his face, and began to slow-handclap his son
in strong, aggressive beats, the action making the long ash fall
from the cigarette on to his mountainous belly. He scattered it
with a flick of a finger and turned back to the television. 'Try
getting yersel' a joab then, if yuv stopped fryin' yer brains.'

'Ah cannie.'

'How no?'

'There's naine aboot.'

'Well then, dae wha ye did last year. Awa' an' tak' photies of a' thae tourists aw aboot the toon.'

'Ah cannie,' T.K. replied morosely.

'How?'

'Ah've flogged the camera.'

His father turned and glared at him 'Fi a fix?'

'Na, fi cash!' T.K. replied angrily. 'Ah told ya before, ah'm clean!'

His father shook his head and leaned forward to stub out his cigarette in the overflowing ashtray on the table in front of the television. 'Mon then, get yersel' uptoon and see wha gives.'

'I've nae change fi the bus.'

His father let out a long sigh. 'God gae ye legs, lad. Awa' an' use 'em.'

T.K. shambled over to the door of the flat and opened it with force. He turned and gave his father a middle-finger salute before slamming the door behind him.

He always used the stairs, because the lift never worked, and if it did, there was more likelihood of being roughed up inside it. Nevertheless, he was now in the habit of sticking his head around every turn in the staircase as he descended, just in case there was a dealer hanging about or someone waiting for the chance to dish out a bit of GBH. He took the concrete steps two at a time, his hand sliding down the graffitied wall, trying to hold his breath for as long as possible so he didn't have to take in the mixed odour of disinfectant and urine that came at every turn. He burst out into the sunlight at the bottom, heaved in a gulp of fresh air and made his way across the estate to the cul-de-sac where the dustbins were kept, the entrance to the shortcut uptown.

As he turned into the cul-de-sac, he stopped and quickly pulled back against the wall. He edged his head around the corner of the building and eyed the two policemen who were walking around the dark-blue Ford Mondeo. One was talking in a low monotone while the other was writing details down in his notebook. The police car was drawn up alongside the stolen vehicle, its blue light flashing, but T.K. could hardly make it out in the glare of the sun.

He had no option now other than to go the long way round. If he was seen anywhere near a stolen car, he knew he'd be roped in for it. No doubt within the hour his father would be getting a visit from the two policemen, asking of his son's whereabouts last night. But this time it hadn't been him. He hadn't nicked a car for the past few months, ever since he had given up on the hard stuff. It had been hard graft trying to break both habits, but he owed it to his solicitor, Mr Anderson, for somehow getting him a two-month probationary order with compulsory rehab instead of the expected spell in borstal. 'I can't help you any more, Thomas,' Mr Anderson had said to him afterwards outside the juvenile court. 'One more offence like this and you'll have me looking a real fool and you'll be facing lock-up for at least two years.'

T.K. ran out to the front of the estate and turned eastwards on to the main road that headed towards Leith Docks. Not that he didn't miss it, though. The joy-riding, that is, not the drugs. He still took the 'script', the prescribed methadone, but he was determined not to go back on the hard stuff, not after suffering those interminable days of gut-wrench and vomit and shivering and hallucination.

But the joy-riding was a different matter. First time he'd done it was when he was fourteen years old. It was a Ford Fiesta, parked up for the night in Northumberland Street Lane. The boy he was with got into the car and hot-wired it within one hundred seconds, and with a heavy burn of rubber they'd headed off on an exhilaration trip that took them up on to Queen Street, down Leith Walk and then back along Ferry Road, eventually ending the evening triumphantly by abandoning the car with its front wheels on the top step of the war memorial in the centre of the gravel sweep at Fettes College. As they made their escape across the playing fields back towards Ferry Road, the boy had panted out proudly that on their journey they had come across ten sets of traffic lights showing red and he'd never stopped at one of them.

After that, T.K. had been hooked, and in the two years that followed he took off no fewer than fifty cars. He became an artist at his craft, being able to break into the most sophisticated German car, disabling its alarm, hot-wiring its supposedly fool-proof ignition system, all within the space of two and a half minutes. He did get caught once in his early years, and that's when he'd first met Mr Anderson, who managed to get him off on the grounds of his age and it being his first-time offence. T.K. hadn't asked for the seven cars he had stolen previously to be taken into account.

And then he had done the contract theft of the BMW for the man in Craigmillar and he suddenly found himself with two hundred pounds in his pocket. He didn't go looking for the drug dealer. Word just got around the estate that Thomas Keene junior had money and the man came knocking on the door of the flat. And after that, he never again had the concentration nor the ability to carry out his craft. He had tried on a number of occasions, but his brain lacked any degree of coordination and his hands shook so much that he would set the car alarm off before he had even the door unlocked. And so he had come to rely on petty theft to feed his habit, hanging around the bus stops and coffee shops uptown, watching out for an open handbag or a jacket or coat slung casually across the back of a chair.

Then three months ago, impulse had made him jump into the Vauxhall Vectra left outside the newsagent on West Granton Road with its engine running, the owner having rushed in to buy something like cigarettes or a newspaper. T.K. had been pretty loaded up at the time and only managed to drive it for a mile before sideswiping a parked car at speed. The impact slewed him across the road, and although somehow he managed to thread an unscathed path through the oncoming traffic, the car ended up with the driver's door caved in against a tree. His brain had been so completely rat-arsed that it never occurred to him to make his escape through the passenger door. He just waited patiently until the police came to free him. And it was following the resultant court case that T.K. decided to take Mr. Anderson's advice to heart.

After an hour and a half's walk, T.K. found himself heading with aching legs up Broughton Street towards the top of Leith Walk. He stopped for a rest, leaning his shoulder against a lamp post, and glanced across the street at a small coffee shop, its stone surround painted in pastel green with the words 'The Grainstore' written in looping purple italics above the door. Even at that distance, T.K. could still smell the rich aroma of ground coffee beans and warm bread drifting out through the open door, and his stomach began to ache with hunger, not having had anything since his paltry meal of a slice of pizza and half a can of baked beans the evening before. Pushing himself away from the lamp post, he shambled across the street and peered in through the plate-glass window at the coffee shop's busy interior. Customers were talking or reading newspapers, some seated at the small round tables, other perched on high stools, their coffee cups resting on the narrow wooden ledge by the window, while a long but orderly queue snaked along the full length of the display counter. He let out a resigned sigh and ambled into the establishment. Ignoring the queue, he approached the girl with the short blonde hair and black hairband who was operating the till at the far end of the counter.

'If you want something, you'll have to join the queue,' she said, not looking up at him as she counted out change in her hand.

'Nuh,' replied T.K. abruptly.

'I'm sorry?' the girl asked, now giving him a quizzical frown.

'Ah mean, ah'm no' aifter some' in' tae eat or drink. Ah'm aifter a joab.'

The girl let out a short laugh of disbelief. 'Oh, you are, are you?'

'Yeah, ah'll dae onythin'. Waash dishes, whativver ye waant.'

The girl's humour disintegrated from her face and she turned to catch the eye of a tall thin man wearing a red-striped butcher's apron, who was in the process of laying succulent strips of rare roast beef on to a baguette with disposable-gloved hands. She beckoned him over with a flick of her head.

'Can I help you?' the man asked, his brow creased questioningly as he took in T.K.'s dishevelled state.

'Ah've just said tae the girl here that ah'm needing a joab,' TK repeated.

'I'm afraid we're fully staffed,' the man said curtly, an uncertain smile flickering across his mouth. 'Now, if you want to buy something, please join the queue. Otherwise, I must ask you to leave.'

T.K. shrugged his shoulders. 'Aye, cheers onyway, mate.'

He turned and made his way over to the door. The queue had now grown to such a length that it stretched out on to the pavement, causing a bottleneck in the entrance with those who were trying to leave the coffee shop. As T.K. joined the throng, he was pushed hard against the back of a chair, and he shot an apologetic smile at its elderly occupant, who turned around enough for T.K. to spy the small American flag stuck into the lapel of her cotton jersey. And then he saw the open bag slung over the back of the chair and the silver glint of the camera inside. It was so close he could make it out quite clearly to be one of the new compact JVC digital video cameras. He scratched at an imaginary itch on the side of his leg, judging the camera would be no more than nine inches from his outstretched hand once he was upright. A feigned stumble would be all it would take.

During the next ten seconds, T.K.'s mind went into turmoil as images of right and wrong flashed in his brain. His father's words of 'Awa' an' tak' photies of the tourists' spun around his head, merging with Mr. Anderson's 'I can't help you any more, T.K.' He looked back at the counter and saw that both the girl and the man were too preoccupied in serving customers to bother looking in his direction. And then the crush of the bottle-neck started again, and T.K. felt a dunt on his shoulder from behind, powerful enough to make him nearly lose his balance, and he was pushed along with the crowd and out on to the street.

T.K. turned left down Broughton Street, walking swiftly until he had cleared the corner of the coffee shop, and then, tucking the camera into the front pocket of his sweatshirt, he pulled up the hood and took off as fast as his tired legs would carry him. Even though he heard no cries of alarm behind him, he was still convinced that some silent fleet-footed coffee drinker was giving chase, and there was no lessening in his pace as he raced around the corner into London Street. At that point, he felt he had to look back to see if there was need for him to jettison the camera and make a break for it. He did not see the lad walking towards him with the two paint cans in his hands, moving from side to side in an attempt to avoid a col-lision. As T.K. turned again with relief, he veered to the same side of the pavement as the paint carrier. Their shoulders came into heavy contact, sending the two cans clattering to the ground.

T.K. heard a yell of anger behind him, but he didn't turn round nor did he stop running until he came to Dundas Street, at which point he thought he would be safe enough from any pursuit.

Twelve

Jamie Stratton stood rubbing a hand at his throbbing shoulder and watched with annoyance as the hooded figure with the sagging jeans disappeared at speed around the corner.

'Effing junkie,' he said quietly and then walked across to the edge of the pavement and stepped down into the gutter where the two paint cans had come to rest. Both bore large dents but somehow they were still intact. He picked them up and held them out at arm's length, just to make sure there were no leaks, then, switching them to one hand, he took the bunch of keys from the pocket of his paint-spattered jeans, walked up the wide stone steps and opened the heavy black entrance door.

He had got into the habit of taking the stairs to his third-floor flat at a run, two at a time, as it helped to keep his leg muscles toned for rugby, both in and out of season. He let himself in, stooped down to pick up the mail and then walked into the large kitchen, depositing the keys, the paint cans and the pile of mail on the table. He moved across to the sink and removed a couple of dirty saucepans so that there was sufficient space to fill the kettle. He put it on its base, flicked the switch, and then, folding his arms, he leaned back against the Formica worktop and listened to the eerie, unnatural silence in the place.

He had bought the high-roomed Georgian flat at the beginning of his second year at Edinburgh University, his father being the instigator of the purchase. He had lent Jamie the deposit for the mortgage, saying that it would be a good investment and that he could pay off the monthly instalments by renting out the three other bedrooms to fellow students. Having bought the flat at a knock-down price because of its appalling condition, Jamie had cajoled four friends to help him to gut the place during the summer holidays with the promise of a party-to-end-all-parties on completion. They stripped the walls of several layers of ingrown wallpaper, filled the cracks and buffed them down to their original state. They teetered precariously on makeshift scaffolding to fit new roses for the lights and clean and paint the endless cornicing, then sanded acres of dark stain from the pine floorboards. They defied gravity when stretching from stepladders to replace the broken cords on the tall sash windows, and retched with disgust as they pulled rubber-gloved handfuls of human hair from the shower outlets and delved into the mechanics of the lavatory Saniflo to clear blocks caused by certain unsavoury items. Then, having painted the place from top to bottom, they sought out auction rooms within a radius of thirty miles of Edinburgh and spent hours chatting up traffic wardens to allow them to park the Land Rover and Ifor Williams livestock trailer, lent to them by Jamie's father, on the single yellow line outside the flat while they unloaded the furniture. And when they had finished their two-month slog, they had the party-to-end-all-parties. The problem was Jamie had then set the precedent by it and over the next three years the place had endlessly thumped with the sound of music and laughter, to such an extent that he was more than relieved at the end of his university career, two months before, to walk away with a 2:2 Honours degree.

And now it had all come to an end. His three flatmates had left, two to start jobs in Newcastle and Manchester and the other to travel the world, while he had been offered a September placement with a publishing company in London. He had discussed the future of the flat with his father, being reluctant to let it go, but his father had persuaded him it was time to move on and better to sell the place and roll his capital over into a small property in London. So, with heavy heart, Jamie had decided to heed his advice. The plan was made for the flat to go on the market in mid-September and that Jamie would ready it for sale over the summer months, eradicating all signs of the four years' worth of hell-raising (a job which the two cans of paint would finish off completely), and covering the intervening mortgage payments by renting out the three empty bedrooms during the three hectic weeks of the festival.

Jamie sighed nostalgically and turned to shake a heavy dollop of Nescafé into a mug before pouring in the now-boiling water from the kettle. He walked back to the table and sifted through the mail, lobbing the circulars and catalogues directly into the bin by the cooker. He kept in his hand the two letters that remained, one a heavy, buff-coloured A4 envelope from the *Edinburgh Fringe Review* and the other from the accommodation agency that was to be renting out his flat. He tore open the envelope from the newspaper and emptied its contents on to the table. It enclosed a Fringe programme, a heap of flyers on the forthcoming acts and the treasured yellow ticket that would allow him free passage into any of the shows. He read quickly through the accompanying letter, confirming they were pleased he would once again be joining their team of reviewers and setting out the conditions of use of the ticket and the deadlines for the submission of articles. The job generated little money, but it did mean that he could see as many of the Fringe shows as he wished as well as keeping his writing skills honed before joining the London firm in September.

Jamie spun the letter on to the table and set to opening the smaller envelope. He unfolded the crisp parchment paper and glanced through its short message.

'*Shit!*' he yelled out, whacking the letter ineffectually on the side of the table. He gritted his teeth and closed his eyes tight in exasperation before reading through the letter once more.

'What the *hell* do I do now?' he said with a shake of his head, as he refolded the letter and repeatedly creased its edges so hard that it would have become three separate pieces with no more than a flick of a finger. Tossing it on to the table, he ran his hands over his thick blond hair as he tried to work out what options were now open to him. With a further loud expletive, he strode out of the kitchen into the hallway, extracting a battered Moleskin notebook from his back pocket, and walked over to the dark mahogany sideboard upon which sat the telephone. He pulled the elastic band off the notebook, opened it at the back page, and then picked up the receiver and dialled a number.

'Good afternoon, R. and J.L. Mackintosh, Solicitors,' a female voice sang out in a refined Edinburgh accent.

'Yeah, can I speak to Gavin Mackintosh, please?'

'May I ask who's calling?'

'Jamie Stratton.'

'Just hold the line, please, and I'll see if he's in his office.'

The line went on to hold and Jamie drummed his fingers irascibly on the top of the sideboard.

'Hello, Jamie, Gavin here.' The solicitor spoke in a slow, deep, methodical voice, one that Jamie had always found strangely comforting, as if Gavin Mackintosh had the ability to sort out any problem, regardless of its complexity.

'Hi, Gavin.'

'How's that father of yours keeping? Still chasing sheep over the Lammermuirs, is he?'

'Nothing changes,' Jamie replied with a chuckle. His father and Gavin Mackintosh had been friends since their time together at Loretto School, and consequently Gavin had become his father's solicitor almost from the moment he joined the family firm, hotfoot from university. He and his father still played fierce rounds of golf against each other at Muirfield and the two families always came together for the international rugby matches at Murrayfield.

'So you've finished with university. Did you get what you wanted?'

'Yeah, a drinking degree.'

'A what?'

Jamie laughed. 'A 2:2. I was hoping to squeeze a 2:1, but what the hell, I've still managed to get a job with a publishing company in London, starting September.'

'Good for you. And what about the rugby? Are you going to keep that up?'

'Yeah, I'll try. I'll go and see if either Rosslyn Park or London Scottish have any need for a stand-off who moves like a dead turtle.'

'Don't think so little of yourself, lad. Scotland has dire need of a player with your skills.'

Jamie scoffed. 'I'm afraid that's wishful thinking, Gavin. There are about three or four lads from the Border clubs who'll get a trial before me.'

'I'm not so sure. You played for the under-21 team, so it should be a natural progression. Anyway, let's get ourselves down to business. How can I be of help?'

'I just wanted a bit of advice about the sale of the London Street flat.'

'Right. So just remind me, it was September, was it not, when we were going to be putting it on the market?'

'Yeah, but the thing is I had the flat rented out for the festival through an agency and they've just written to say the theatre company involved has cancelled. Trouble is I really need the money to cover my last mortgage payments, and the agency won't be able to get anyone else so close to the start.'

'Oh, what a blessed nuisance for you!'

'It's more than that. I'm not sure what to do now. Maybe we should think about bringing the date of the sale forward? I've practically finished doing the place up, and if I sold it off quick-like, then I'd get some money to pay off the mortgage.'

Jamie heard Gavin hum thoughtfully on the other end of the line.

'My first instinct, Jamie, would be that you wouldn't benefit much by doing that. We could certainly put it on the market now, but I would advise you against going for the quick sale. You might well find yourself undervaluing the property if you hurry it along, and anyway, conveyancing can be a long, drawn-out affair. Even if you sold it immediately, I wouldn't think you could expect payment for a good couple of months, which really doesn't help your predicament, does it?'

'Not really,' Jamie replied despondently. 'So what d'you suggest I do?'

'Take one step at a time would be my best advice. I know the festival is only a week away, but there are still quite a number of notices in shops and newsagents all over the place advertising rooms to let, so why don't you do the same? I can't believe there aren't people out there still desperately looking for somewhere to stay for the duration.'

'Yeah, that's not such a bad idea. Certainly worth a shot.'

'And while you're doing your rounds, drop a couple of flyers into the Fringe office. That might be a good bet as well.'

Jamie twisted his fingers around the telephone cord. 'But if nothing comes of all that, how the hell am I going to pay the mortgage?'

Gavin hadn't really given much thought to the fact that it was festival time again until that moment when he had spoken with Jamie. It always posed a bit of a quandary for him, because although every year he had great intentions of going out and enjoying some of the events, unfailingly his workload seemed to increase at that time and the whole three weeks came and went without him hardly noticing anything out of the ordinary had ever taken place. His wife, however, persevered regardless, booking tickets for concerts and operas, but she usually ended up having to take a friend or prising one of their two daughters away from their ever-increasing young families to accompany her. The previous year, one small window of opportunity had arisen and he had managed to counter the growing exasperation of his wife by attending a production of De Rojas's *Celestina,* but his mobile phone had vibrated in his breast pocket just before the end of the first act and he had had to leave, shrouded in a black cloud of unpopularity, to answer a call from the police station in Portobello and interview a young man who had been caught in the act of breaking and entering.

Pushing himself out his chair, Gavin walked over to the stack of brown cardboard folders on the long refectory table beside the door, selected one and returned to his desk. Maybe this year would be different, he thought to himself. There was one particular event he did especially want to attend, a welcoming reception for the young French violinist Angélique Pascal, in the Sheraton Grand Hotel. He had been more than surprised when he had come across the stiff-backed invitation sitting on the drawing-room mantelpiece at his house in Ravelston Road. Despite constant badgering from friends, he had always been pretty sceptical about how much additional fee income could be generated from sponsoring an event at the festival, and consequently he and his wife had never made it on to the 'preferred' list of guests. However, this time he was going to make every effort possible to attend the party, even though it might lead to a barrage of requests for financial support. It would be worth it just to get a glimpse of the extremely talented and extremely attractive young musician.

Opening the folder, Gavin pulled his chair in close to the desk and put on his spectacles, and began reading through the Last Will and Testament of Mrs Annie Dalgety, a long-time client of the firm who had just failed to reach her one hundredth birthday by a mere six weeks. It was destined to be a lengthy wrangle, as she had always been a crusty old soul, constantly falling out with her three sons in turn and changing her will to benefit the one who happened to be in favour at the time. It was further complicated by the fact that her lineage stretched to three generations below her, and there were no fewer than thirty descendants all looking for a share in the carve-up of her estate. This included a three-storey town house in Royal Crescent, one of the remaining few not to have been divided up into flats, and a substantial share portfolio built up over many years by her late, but in his time very shrewd, stockbroker husband.

Gavin had just begun to note down a few diplomatic observations on his pad, readying himself for the second, and no doubt confrontational, meeting scheduled for four o'clock that afternoon in the partners' room, when there was a loud knock on the door. He put down his pen, took off his spectacles and called out for the person to enter. John Anderson, one of the firm's junior partners, stuck his head round the door.

'Have you got a moment, Gavin?'

'Certainly, John.' He indicated the chair at the other side of his desk. 'Come in and have a seat.'

The lean, bespectacled solicitor moved in an ungainly lope across the room, placing the large pile of folders he had been carrying under his arm on the desk in front of him. He positioned himself in the chair as if about to answer Mastermind questions.

Gavin eyed the folders suspiciously. 'What have we got here, John?'

John Anderson clenched his teeth. 'Ah, I *thought* you might have forgotten,' he murmured.

Gavin leaned back in his chair, an expression fixed on his face that would indicate his lack of recall was about to cause him a considerable amount of physical pain.

'OK, let me have it.'

John rubbed his hands together apprehensively. 'I'm off on holiday for two weeks on Monday.'

'Och, jeezy-peeps!' Gavin exclaimed, hitting the palm of his hand hard against his forehead. 'Of course you are. It had completely slipped my mind.'

'I'm sorry. Maybe I should have reminded you earlier.'

Gavin waved a dismissive hand at him. 'No, it's my fault entirely. It's been in my diary for at least three months, and what's more, I should know by now. This is about the third year I've been covering for you on the Legal Aid cases, is it not?'

'Fourth, actually,' John replied with an apologetic smile.

Gavin let out a rueful laugh and shook his head. 'Funnily enough, I was just thinking about how I never seemed to find enough time to go to any of the festival events. Now I remember it's *you* I've got to blame for that.'

John leaned forward in his chair uneasily. 'Listen, Gavin, if you want, I'll see if I can get someone else to—'

'No, no, I was only joking,' Gavin interjected. 'Of course I'll handle them for you.' He pointed at the pile of folders on the desk. 'Are those your ongoing cases?'

'Yes, but I promise it's not as bad as it looks. Three of them are appeals that probably won't be called to court until I get back.'

'And the others?'

'Five pleas of guilty and two of not guilty. I'm due to be in the magistrates' court for the next couple of days and hope to clear up two of them, so I won't be leaving you with too much.'

'Depends what comes up when you're away, though, doesn't it?'

'Yes, I suppose it does,' John replied quietly.

Gavin slapped his hands down on the desk. 'Never mind. You

go away and enjoy yourself, John, and come back refreshed and raring to go. Where are you off to this year?'

John got to his feet and picked up the pile of folders. 'Majorca again,' he replied, his tone much lighter now that he had accomplished his mission. 'It suits the kids. They get to go to the night-club while Deborah and I can just crash out on the beach.'

'Sounds a good arrangement. You have a good time, then.'

'I will, and thanks for taking this on yet again, Gavin.' The solicitor made his way towards the door and opened it. 'I'll leave those cases I haven't cleared with your secretary on Friday after-noon, if that's OK with you?'

'That'll be fine, John. I'll read them up sometime over the weekend.'

As the door closed, Gavin screwed up his eyes and rubbed his fingers hard on top of his balding pate. Oh, well, he thought to himself, looks like another few weeks of uncultured bliss. No doubt you'll hear the boom of the fireworks from the house and realise it's all over for another year. One thing for certain, though, you'll be getting yourself to that reception in the Sheraton Grand come hell or high water, even if it does mean leaving some young whippersnapper in the clink overnight.

Slipping on his spectacles, he picked up his pen and resumed his quest to sort out the estate of the indomitable Mrs Dalgety.

Fourteen

Phil Kenyon carefully lowered the heavy silver fireproof case to the floor, his knees bent to avoid giving his suspect back a twinge. He straightened up, letting out a puff of effort, and turned to look over to the far end of the old grain shed as one of the large double doors was slid open. Roger Dent entered and heaved the metal door closed with an echoing clang. He walked towards his Australian colleague, pushing a folded piece of paper into the pocket of his chinos.

'Did you speak with Jeff Banyon, then?' Phil asked as his boss approached.

'Yup, all went well,' Roger replied, giving a thumbs-up. 'I think I came out with all the right things to appease him.' He sat down on the case that Phil had just been handling and crossed his arms. 'He's on his way down to Newcastle to meet up with the fellow who's going to be conducting the orchestra on the night.'

'Have we worked with him before?'

'No, so we'll just have to hope he doesn't go apeshit, knowing he's got the eyes of about a quarter of a million people glaring down on him. If he rushes his way through this one, our timings are certain to go all up the creek.'

Phil raised his eyebrows. 'And what about the score reader? Have they got that fixed up yet?'

'Yes, it's the same girl we had last year from the BBC Scottish Symphony Orchestra.'

Phil bit at his lip. 'Ah, Helen,' he said quietly.

Roger smiled knowingly. 'Of course, I'd forgotten you'd had a bit of a fling with her.'

'Could be a bit awkward,' Phil murmured.

Roger got to his feet and gave his sidekick a hard slap on the shoulder. 'I'm sure you'll cope with the situation quite manfully, Phil.' Taking the piece of paper from his pocket, he unfolded it and quickly scanned through the handwritten list. 'How're you doing with the trucks for Edinburgh? Have you booked them yet?'

'Yeah, they'll be here on the Friday night.'

Roger nodded. 'OK, so let's just stick to the same game plan as we had last year. We'll aim to get up there on the Sunday before the final night, and that'll give us the full week to get set up.' He folded the piece of paper and stuck it back in his pocket. 'I'll go up in the first truck with the workshop equipment, and then you and the crew can stop off in Birmingham en route and pick up all the hardware from the store there.'

'No worries. We've got four weeks in hand, so that's time aplenty for getting it all ready and putting the final touches to the programme.'

Roger fixed the stocky Australian with a humorous look of subterfuge. 'If you ever happen to pick up the telephone in the office and find yourself speaking to Jeff Banyon, please, whatever you do, don't tell him that.'

'Why? What did you say to him?' Phil asked with a conspiring twinkle in his eye.

Roger shrugged his shoulders. 'That the programme was complete and we had most of the gear stockpiled.'

Phil laughed. 'Oh, well, you've got to lie a little to live a little.'

'Exactly my sentiments, mate,' Roger replied as he turned and threaded his way through the equipment back towards the entrance doors, 'especially seeing we've got four more displays to get through before we head up to Edinburgh.'

Fifteen

''Ere, Robbie, quit doing that and come over and stand by me!'

Rene Brownlow's yell was barely audible above the cacophony of noise on Darlington Station, dominated at the precise moment of her reprimand by a crackling announcement on the tannoy system heralding the imminent arrival of the Intercity service to Edinburgh. Robbie pushed the luggage trolley at speed along the platform towards his mother, giving it a final spin to extract one more squeal of delight from his sister, who clutched hard to the handle, her feet splayed out across its bars.

'They're doing no 'arm,' Gary Brownlow said quietly.

'What d'ye mean? They could quite easily go right over the edge and under the train.'

Gary smiled at his wife. ''Ow're ye feeling? A bit nervous?'

Rene blew out a shivering breath. 'Only as much as I'd be

feeling if I was 'eading off to me own execution. Before now, an excursion to Darlington for me was about as rare as a mule with offspring, and 'ere am I going even further off the beaten track.'

Gary laughed and put his arm around his wife's shoulder and gave it a reassuring squeeze. 'You'll be fine, girl, I know it.'

Rene gazed up at her husband. 'Are ye sure ye're all right about me doing this, Gary? We don't seem to have spoken much about it recently, what with one thing and another, but I can't 'elp remembering yer first reaction when Terry—'

'Oh, forget that, lass,' Gary cut in with a wave of his hand. 'That was me just voicing me own frustration. I should've kept me big mouth shut. What I want you to do is get yerself up to Edinburgh and knock 'em all dead.'

Rene smiled fondly at her husband. 'It'll turn out all right for ye, Gary. I know it will. But listen, if something comes up while I'm away or ye find ye can't cope with the kids—'

'Don't worry yer 'ead about that,' Gary interjected again. 'Between me and me parents, we'll cope.'

'Aye, I reckon ye will.' Rene turned her head and looked past Gary. 'I feel like the bloody Queen,' she said out of the side of her mouth.

''Ow d'ye mean?'

She glanced sideways. 'My entourage.'

Gary glanced round at the five committee members of Andersons Westbourne Social Club, who stood smiling at them from a distance of twenty-five feet.

'D'ye think we could get a photo now, Rene, seeing that the train's approaching?' Stan Morris asked, taking Gary's look as an opportune moment to cut in on the couple's farewell.

Rene laughed. 'Aye, why not, Stan?' she called over to him.

As the committee chairman slipped the camera out of the leather case he had dangling from his neck, the other members rushed forward and gathered themselves around the Brownlow family. Putting arms around shoulders, they grinned inanely in the direction of the camera.

Stan squinted through the eyepiece. 'Right, all squeeze in a bit. That's better. Skittle, I can't see ye, so get in front beside the kids. No, Norman, not you! You stay where y'are! OK.' He took the camera away from his eye, just to give a final check that it was loaded with film. 'Right, one, two, three . . . oh, 'ang on a minute, the train's pulling in.' There was a universal groan from the assembled group. 'All right! All right!' Stan said shirtily, 'I'm an experienced photographer, I'll 'ave ye know, and it wouldn't do to 'ave the background go all blurry.'

'Well, stop yakking and get yer skates on, then,' said sombre Derek Marsham. 'We've only got the minibus booked until two o'clock.'

Derek's remark produced the laughs that were to be captured for posterity on film. The group broke up as the first of the carriage doors started opening.

'Ye're in the one down 'ere, Rene,' Terry Crosland said as he scooped up her suitcase and hurried off down the platform, the farewell committee following on his heel like ducklings. Rene ambled along, holding hard to Gary's hand. 'I'll call ye every night.'

Gary nodded. 'Aye, you do that.'

Reaching up, she pulled his head down towards her and gave him a long kiss on the lips. 'I'll miss ye, lad. I wish ye were coming too,' she whispered into his ear.

'Ye'll do fine on your own,' he said, putting his arms around her ample body and giving her bottom a tight squeeze.

Rene broke away and gave each of her children a kiss and a hug. 'Ye look after yer dad now, you two, and don't be giving 'im any bother.'

Robbie and Karen both replied with a nod before breaking away from their mother's loving hold, eager to head off once again on their trolley.

'Come on,' Gary said, grasping her arm. 'Let's get ye on board.'

Leaning out of the window as the train pulled out of the station, Rene watched the cluster of waving hands until they bend in the train hid them from sight. She pushed up the window and let out a long nervous breath. Well, that's it, lass, she thought to herself, ye're on your own now.

Thomas Keene junior had worked up quite a tidy little business for himself over the week. Having discovered how to take digital stills with the video camera, he had set himself up on the junction of Princes and Hanover streets and started waylaying tourists as they passed, offering to take their photograph with Edinburgh Castle as the backdrop. It was a success from the start. Once he had at least ten different customers on record, he would whip out the memory card, take it up to the Kwikflick shop halfway up Hanover Street, put it in for a half-hour service and have the prints back on Princes Street within the hour, catching the punters on their return. Of course, at the outset there had been a few problems to sort out. Having not one bean to his name, T.K. had had to persuade an elderly Dutch couple to pay him upfront and then get them to stand outside the shop for the time it took for the photographs to be printed. Then the woman in the shop started complaining about his ever-increasing appearances, so he ended up agreeing to pay her the full hourly rate. He was pretty sure the extra money was going straight into her pocket, but it didn't really bother him that much. At the end of the day, he always had enough money to get himself a double cheeseburger and large Coke from McDonald's on Princes Street and then catch a bus back home afterwards.

That day, however, had not been the best for trade. T.K. didn't really know the reason, but he thought maybe it was because the street theatre had already started up on the Royal Mile, seeing as the Fringe shows were due to begin the following day. He waited until the Kwikflick shop had closed, then pulled his meagre takings from his pocket. It was a toss-up between the meal and the bus. Seeing it was a warm, cloudless evening and he was in no great hurry to get home, he opted for food and headed along the street to get himself a burger.

The cardboard cup and polystyrene container were discarded

over the railings of a basement flat at the bottom of Dundas Street, just before T.K. started out on one of the many complicated short cuts he knew to get back home. He zigzagged through narrow cobbled alleys, climbed walls, squeezed his narrow frame through loose wooden fence panels and swung himself over arrow-tipped railings by grabbing the branches of overhanging trees. He jumped up on to the precipitous wall that ran above Glenogle Road and walked along its length until he came to the point where he knew a number of near imperceptible footholds existed. Lowering himself over the parapet, he eased his way down the wall, jumping the last six feet to the ground. He crossed the road and began to make his way past the many narrow cul-de-sacs that made up the rabbit warren of two-storey terraced houses known as the Stockbridge Colonies.

As he turned the corner to cut down the last street, he stopped and drew himself back against the end gable of the row of houses. He peered around the corner and watched the two boys who ambled slowly along the road towards him. One was positioned on the pavement, nonchalantly looking about him, studying the windows of the houses and occasionally casting a glance down to each end of the street, while the other walked parallel to him on the street, looking for the nod from his mate before glancing quickly in through the driver's-side windows of the row of parked cars.

T.K. drew back behind the wall and laughed to himself. He knew exactly what they were doing, but what he found so ridiculous was they were about to attempt a car theft in broad daylight. Six o'clock in the evening during the winter months maybe, but not at the height of summer. He put his head around the corner once more and noticed them spending time over one particular car. Good choice, lads, he thought to himself, an old Ford, easy to get into, easy to start and plenty of room to make a quick getaway.

It was at that moment T.K. remembered the video camera. He pulled it out of the front pocket of his sweatshirt and switched on the power. Right, he thought, let's see how fast you two can pull this off. Clicking the camera on to 'standby', he stuck the lens around the corner of the building, adjusting the viewing screen so that he could see what was going on. His timing was perfect. He started the camera running the moment the boy on the street ducked below the level of the roof. He straightened up, took one last cursory look around him, and then wrenched the door open and got in, leaning over to pull up the lock of the passenger door. The accomplice jumped into the car, and there followed a moment when T.K. could hardly stop the camera from shaking, as he watched a silent, yet obviously desperate shouting match develop while the driver struggled to hot-wire the car. Then suddenly the engine roared to life, and with a squeal of tyres the car shot out of the parking space and sped down the street towards him. Without stopping at the T-junction, the car veered right out on to the main road and headed away.

He kept the camera rolling until the car disappeared at the end of the street. Putting his hand over the screen to shield it from the glare of the evening sunlight, he read the length of the recorded scene on the time code. Four minutes twenty seconds. He laughed out loud. That is effin' lousy, lads, he thought to himself. If you go on like that, you may as well just *drive* yourself to the juvenile court.

Closing up the screen, T.K. stuck the camera back in his sweat-shirt pocket and swaggered off down the street in the proud knowledge that he, Thomas Keene junior, just coming up nine-teen years old and without a driving lesson to his name, was not only a veteran of the game, but also still one of the unbeaten artists at the job.

Sixteen

When Rene Brownlow arrived the following evening at the Corinthian Bar in West Richmond Street, half an hour early for her first show, the last thing she felt like doing was standing up on a stage and being funny for an hour. The first wave of apprehension and homesickness had engulfed her the moment she got off the train on to the crowded platform at Edinburgh, and thereafter events conspired to reduce her fragile confidence to rubble. Not wanting to waste her scanty finances on a taxi, she had dragged the heavy Samsonite suitcase, bought for her by Terry Crosland at a car-boot sale, to her digs in Morningside, not realising beforehand the two-mile distance nor the orienteering nature of her journey. The first part seemed to be interminably uphill from the station until she reached George IV Bridge, where there was eventual but momentary respite from the incline. Despite consulting the map that had been included in the package from the Fringe office, wrong turnings were frequent, and even though the streets were swarming with people, the majority of those from whom she breathlessly asked directions also turned out to be visitors to the city.

The woman who eventually responded to the third knock on the front door of the unspectacular little bungalow in Greendykes Terrace eyed suspiciously the plump figure with the bright-red face that sat wheezing on the suitcase at the bottom of the stone steps.

'You'll be Rene Brownlow, then,' she stated, folding her arms defensively across her fawn-jerseyed bosom.

Rene had simply nodded, not having the essential breath left in her body to answer her.

'Right, I'm Mrs Learmonth, your landlady. You'd better get yourself inside, and I'll show you to your room.' Ignoring Rene's load, the woman turned and walked back into the house.

As Rene used her last ounce of energy to carry the heavy suitcase double-handed up the steep staircase, Mrs Learmonth stood on the top landing watching her ascend and lambasted her with the endless rules of the house. Only one shower to be taken every day, and that between half past seven and eight o'clock in the morning; breakfast at nine o'clock on the dot; no visitors; no use of the house telephone, but she would give directions to the nearest call box; keep the noise down at all times; and the room should be vacated between the hours of eleven o'clock in the morning and three o'clock in the afternoon to allow for cleaning. When Rene cast a spirit-sapping eye around the small, sparsely furnished bedroom that had been built into the low sloping roof of the bungalow, she couldn't quite work out why the tight-mouthed Mrs Learmonth needed five hours to clean such a minute area. However, she was too exhausted to pass comment either on that or any of the other conditions, just wanting the woman to leave her alone so that she could rest her weary body on the low wooden-framed bed that looked more suited to the dimensions and weight of an undernourished pixie. Later on that evening, after she had picked at a near inedible meal of overcooked stew and boiled vegetables in Mrs Learmonth's dingy little dining room, with only the scraping of cutlery on willow-patterned plate to keep her company, Rene had stood in the littered telephone box three hundred yards from the house desperately trying to maintain her self-control when Gary's quiet, laid-back voice had sounded at the other end of the line.

At precisely eleven o'clock that day, Rene had left the house, eager to spend as little time there as possible, even though it meant facing the prospect of killing time in a strange city with little money. She sat for two hours on a bench at the top of the Meadows, watching the joggers and the people walking their dogs and the golfers practising their swings; she walked all the way back to the High Street to locate the Fringe office and then tagged on to a small gathering which had formed around a brightly dressed young man who was shaping a dog out of balloons for a young toddler in a pushchair while she washed a tasteless ham sandwich down with a can of Coke; and when the sky clouded over and a bitter wind picked up, she sought out the warmth of a crowded pub where she sat alone at a corner table, trying to eke out the last inch of her half pint of shandy for as long as possible whilst reviewing her act in her head.

But it was to no avail. All day long, she had only been able to think of what Gary and the kids would be doing, picturing their weathered little house with its untidy garden in Bolingbroke Close. She thought of Stan Morris and his cronies sitting round their usual table in Andy's, snapping down their dominoes and talking excitedly about what she, Rene, would be doing at that precise moment. She thought about what food she should be buying that week from the discount shelves in Morrison's supermarket, and then her imagination took her across Marina Way and down to the end of Jacksons Landing, where the seagulls glided lazily on the wind, the riggings clinked against the tall masts of the yachts and the water lapped lazily against their sleek bows. And then she wished above all other wishes that, right there and then, she could somehow transport herself away from this alien city back to the familiar, warm-hearted surroundings of her own Hartlepool.

Taking in a deep steadying breath, Rene pushed open the heavy glass door of her venue and entered. The Corinthian Bar was obviously a new establishment, equipped from top to bottom with all things chrome. The tables, chairs, handrails, footrests below the bar all sparkled, reflecting myriad small low-voltage lights that were suspended from wires cobwebbing the ceiling. To the right of where she stood there was a small ticket booth with racks of coloured leaflets on its counter, advertising the forthcoming shows; and to the left, a flight of stairs that led down to the toilets and, as indicated by a temporary sign, to the theatre. The whole wall at the back of the stairs was covered with posters, all larger versions of the front covers of the leaflets. Rene took one of her own from a rack on the counter and glanced through it as she walked along the wide ceramic-tiled passage to the bar.

Whilst every other eating and drinking establishment Rene had passed that day seemed to be filled to capacity, the Corinthian Bar had barely any business at all. There were only about ten people in the place, two couples eating at tables, while the rest sat on stools or stood leaning on the dark granite surface of the bar. As Rene approached it, a young barman with gelled spiky hair came over to her, greeting her with a flick of his head.

'Hi there, what can I get ye?'

'Oh, nothing, thanks,' Rene replied. 'I'm actually here to do a show.'

'Oh, right. Just hang on a minute then.' He scanned the floor before catching sight of a girl coming up the stairs. 'Hey, Andrea!' he called over to her. 'This is the woman who's doing the show tonight.'

Rene felt immediately downhearted by the boy's introduction. He didn't call her a 'comedienne', or even by her name. Just 'the woman'. She turned to watch Andrea approach, a sleek blonde who dressed to accentuate her elegant contours in a pair of black tight-fitting jeans and polo-neck jersey.

'Hi, you must be Rene,' she said, offering out a hand that gushed blood-red nails. She spoke in a twanging English voice with no softening trace of a regional accent.

'That's right,' Rene replied with a smile, conscious of the podginess of her own hand when clasped in Andrea's talon.

'Good. Well, look, I think the best thing is for me to take you straight downstairs and show you where everything is.' She turned on the stilettoed heels of her boots and Rene followed on behind her as she headed back along the passage and clipped her way down the stairs.

The grandly named 'theatre' turned out to be nothing more than the pub cellar, hastily converted by way of a black backdrop being strung across the width of its combed ceiling. About ten plastic tables with matching chairs, two apiece, were crammed into the small auditorium, some sloping at weird angles because of the uneven flagstoned floor. The place was dingy, damp and stank of stale beer, and Rene was only thankful that it was brightly lit by two spotlights positioned on stands against the back wall, their beams focused on the microphone that stood in the centre of the backdrop.

''Ow many people d'ye expect will be coming?' Rene asked flatly as she stood with her handbag hanging limply at her side and casting an eye over the paltry seating area.

Andrea crossed her arms over her neat little bosom. 'It

depends, really. We're a bit off the beaten track here, but if the word gets round there's a good show going on, then it can really fill up. Believe it or not, we've had as many as thirty people in here.'

The girl shot her such a bright, enthusiastic smile that Rene felt she had to muster up some sort of jovial response. 'Oh my, that's summat, in't it?' she said, with the thought going through her mind that any wild hope of her 'making it big' in Edinburgh had just suffered the worst form of spontaneously combusted.

'Of course,' Andrea continued, 'it also depends on how well you've been able to publicise the show yourself.'

Rene looked at the girl questioningly. ''Ow am I meant to do that?'

Andrea's smile faded away. 'Have you not been handing out leaflets?'

'What d'ye mean?'

'Leaflets, like the one you have there. You should have been handing them out all day up on the High Street.'

Rene glanced at the leaflet in her hand. 'I didn't know that.'

Andrea raised her eyebrows. 'How else do you expect anyone to come? That's where all the punters are during the day. You've got to go up there and attract them.'

'Oh,' Rene replied quietly.

'Otherwise you could find yourself well out of pocket when the show comes to an end.'

Rene swallowed hard, feeling her cheeks suddenly glow with apprehension. ''Ow's that, then?'

Andrea let out a sigh that gave off little sympathy. 'Don't you know about the conditions?'

'No, I don't,' Rene replied quite forcefully, becoming irked by the girl's attitude. 'I didn't arrange this 'ole thing. It was done for me.'

'All right,' Andrea countered defensively, holding up a hand to steady Rene's mood. 'I'll explain then. We rent out the theatre to you for a fixed sum over the three weeks. If you don't manage to cover that figure through box office takings, then you are liable for the shortfall.'

'And 'ow much does the theatre cost?'

'Seventeen hundred pounds.'

Rene stared at the girl with her mouth open. 'Bloody Aunt Ada,' she exclaimed, as the figure flashed in her mind like a neon warning light. 'That means . . .' She looked around the room, counting the seats, trying to calculate what chance she might have of bringing in that amount of money. Twenty times, say five quid a ticket, gives a hundred quid a night; times twenty-one nights equals . . . just over two thousand pounds! And that was with a bum on every seat! 'Oh, bloody Aunt Ada,' she said again, rubbing a hand at her forehead. 'That's damned near impossible! I don't suppose there's a chance I could do an afternoon performance as well?'

Andrea shook her head, her eyes almost managing to register kindly concern. ''Fraid not. The theatre is booked morning, noon and night.' Her look brightened in encouragement. 'But it does mean you'll have the whole day to hand out leaflets and woo your audience. And then, of course, you might get a brilliant review in one of the papers and find yourself playing to a packed house every night.'

'I s'pose,' Rene replied unhopefully.

The voice of the barman rang down the stairs. 'Andrea, there's a couple of people waitin' here tae buy tickets.'

Andrea glanced at her wristwatch and walked over to the door. 'On my way!' She turned back to Rene. 'If you could be ready to start in about ten minutes . . .' She nodded her head towards the backdrop. 'I'm afraid it's a bit cramped behind there, but you'll find a small table with a mirror if you want to get yourself made up or whatever.' She cast a look at Rene's handbag. 'I don't suppose you use your own props or anything.'

Rene shook her head. 'No. What ye see is what ye get.'

Andrea shrugged her shoulders as if signifying there was nothing further she could do to help Rene. 'All right. I hope it goes well, then. Billy will be down shortly to make sure the sound system is working properly.' And she swung round on her sharp-heeled boots and left the comedienne to her fate.

Rene's first show was played to a grand audience of five, and despite the glaring spotlights she could tell from the moment she took up her position at the microphone that at least three of them were foreigners. From their reaction to her first joke, which had never before failed to produce a roar of hilarity, it was also quite apparent that what ability they had to understand the English language did not stretch to the complexities of a North Yorkshire accent. During her performance Rene struggled to raise one good laugh, finding herself having to fill in the dreadful silence between jokes with feeble ad libs that fell on her own ears like an appalling speech impediment. As she watched two of her audience noisily scrape back their chairs and make their way towards the door halfway through her act, it took every ounce of concentration to keep talking and not to silently gawp at them as they departed. After forty-five long minutes, during every second of which she wished the greasy flagstone floor would open up and devour her hopelessly unfunny self, she called an end to her suffering fifteen minutes early. She waited behind the backdrop until her remaining audience quickly made their exit, and then came out and sat down at one of the tables in the deserted theatre. Covering her face with her hands, she relived every cringe-making moment of the show and wondered to herself how on earth she was going to be able to take another three weeks of similar disasters.

'How did it go?'

Rene dropped her hands to the table and turned to see Andrea's smiling face pop round the side of the door. Rene bit at her lip and slowly shook her head.

'Don't worry,' Andrea said as she flicked off the switch of one of the spotlights. 'First one's always the worst. Once you've got used to the intimacy of the theatre here, you'll find it much easier.'

'Maybe,' Rene replied solemnly, wondering how Andrea had the ability to distort her marketing jargon to such an extent as to describe this subterranean torture chamber as being 'intimate'. Picking up her handbag from the table, she got slowly to her feet and made her way towards the door.

'It's a bit of a pity, though,' Andrea said, turning off the other light and plunging the place into coal-mine darkness.

Rene stopped at the bottom of the stairs. 'What's a pity?' she asked.

'That you felt it didn't go too well tonight,' Andrea said brightly as she pulled the door to the theatre closed. She edged her way past Rene and began climbing the stairs. 'There was a reviewer from Radio Scotland in the audience.' She turned and gave Rene a thin smile. 'Never mind, he might not bother saying anything about it at all.'

Rene kept staring up the stairwell long after Andrea's tight little bottom had disappeared from view, and then, putting a steadying hand on the chrome banister rail, she lowered herself slowly on to the bottom step, clutched her handbag to her chest, and burst into tears.

Seventeen

Harry Wills sat at a small metal table in front of the Costa coffee stall in Edinburgh Airport, toying with a small cup of espresso, as he kept an eye on the two photographers who stood chatting together at the entrance through which the recent arrivals on the British Airways flight from London flooded into the baggage reclaim area. He saw them separate, their movements suddenly becoming more animated, and when a series of blinding flashes went off, Harry got to his feet, draining his coffee, and began to make his way towards them. The two photographers were now moving backwards away from the entrance, focusing their lenses on a tall bespectacled man in a navy-blue raincoat who accompanied a young dark-haired girl with a violin case in her hand. The man paid little attention to the photographers as he approached the cluster of uniformed drivers. He spoke to one, who immediately lowered the sign he had been holding up, and guided them with outstretched hand over to the luggage carousel that had just begun to move.

As the two photographers hurried away towards the terminal exit, their assignments successfully completed, Harry pushed his bulky figure through the mass of people gathering around the carousel and approached the man from behind.

'Monsieur Dessuin, Mademoiselle Pascal, welcome to Edinburgh.'

The man turned round, a questioning frown creasing his high angular forehead, and slowly put out a hand to the one that Harry offered in greeting. 'I'm sorry, I'm not sure if we have—'

'Harry Wills, the *Sunday Times Scotland*.'

'Ah, of course,' Albert Dessuin murmured, giving Harry's hand a single shake, his face registering no sign of pleasure at meeting the journalist.

'I thought I'd come along today just to introduce myself in person. We've spoken often enough with each other on the telephone.' Harry switched his attention to the young girl who stood watching the luggage go past on the carousel. 'However, I haven't had the pleasure of speaking to you before, mademoiselle.'

'Mr Wills,' Albert Dessuin cut in, 'we arrived early this morning in London after an all-night flight from New York, and after a long delay at Heathrow we have now made it here to Edinburgh. Tonight we have to attend a reception that will no doubt drain us of all our energies, and tomorrow Mademoiselle Pascal will have to have recovered sufficiently to start rehearsing for a concert the following evening in your Usher Hall. I would suggest, therefore, that this is the wrong time and the wrong place to try for an interview.'

'Of course, I understand that. I was just hoping to fix—'

'I seem to remember also, Mr Wills,' Dessuin continued, clicking his fingers at the driver and pointing to a large brown suitcase on the carousel, 'that it was only a few months ago that I gave over a great deal of time for an interview with you. I would not think, so soon afterwards, there would be much I could add to that.'

Harry Wills took in a deep breath before clearing his throat noisily in an attempt to cover for the anger he felt at the man's measured hostility. Then, on an impulse, he decided to go for broke. 'Monsieur Dessuin, what I really want to do is to write a story from Mademoiselle Pascal's point of view. I want to write about her influences, about her background, about her interests . . . and about being Angélique Pascal. She is becoming one of the most famous violinists in the world and everyone, including the young people, want to know about her.' Harry turned to Angélique, who, having just pointed out another suitcase to the driver, now stood watching the journalist with a look of silent intent. 'Mademoiselle Pascal, would there be any time over this next week when you would be willing to do an interview with me?'

'Mr Wills,' Albert Dessuin exclaimed irately as he grabbed the full luggage trolley from the driver, 'over the years you have continually tried my patience and now I will not take it any more.' He put a hand against Angélique's back. 'From now on, I will not consider one further interview with you, and please remember in future that it was your own dogged stupidity that led to this.'

Harry Wills stood watching as the driver hurriedly escorted his charges towards the terminal exit, Albert Dessuin guiding Angélique Pascal almost forcefully with a hand on her arm. Letting out a derisory grunt, Harry scratched hard at the back of his head and then ambled off to get his car.

As the Renault Espace came on to the Western Approach Road, Angélique broke the silence that had existed since leaving the airport twenty minutes before. 'Albert?' she said, as she stared out of the window at the traffic that sped past.

'*Oui?*' Dessuin replied, without looking up from his copy of *Le Monde*.

'I want to ask you something.'

'What?'

'Tonight at the reception, I want you to allow me a little space.'

Dessuin glanced across at her. 'What do you mean by that?'

'Just let me move around by myself.'

'Do I not always allow you to do that?'

Angélique let out a quiet laugh. 'No, Albert, you do not.' She turned and fixed him with a smile. 'I know you have my best interests at heart, but sometimes you can be quite . . . suffocating.'

Dessuin shrugged his shoulders. 'It may seem that way to you at times, but it is my job to protect you and I know that Madame Lafitte would—'

'Please, Albert,' Angélique interjected, 'don't bring Madame Lafitte into this. You are always using her name like . . . some kind of blackmail.'

Dessuin shook his head, and with a huffy expression on his face turned back to read his newspaper.

Angélique leaned across to him. 'So will you give me a bit of freedom tonight? I'm not going to run away from you.'

Dessuin lifted a hand dismissively. 'Do as you please, but no talking to *journalistes, tu comprends*?'

'*Oui, bien sûr.*'

In the office of the International Festival, Tess Goodwin ended her telephone call and once more ran through her checklist for the reception scheduled that night in the Sheraton Grand. The hotel's events manager had confirmed that the function room had been set up as Tess had requested, and all arrangements for the finger buffet and wine had been put in place. The public relations agency who were helping her out during the festival had already hung the two large photographic posters of the Italian baritone, Guiseppe Montarino, and the young French violinist, Angélique Pascal, in whose joint honours the reception was being held. Now all that was left for her to do was to make a few courtesy calls to those sponsors of International

123

events who had been remiss in replying to the invitation. As she stretched out a hand for the telephone, she saw the director's intercom light flash a split second before it began to ring. She picked up the receiver, noticing the outside call he kept on hold.

'Yes, Alasdair?'

'Are we all set for tonight, Tess?'

'Yes, everything's ready. I'm just about to call up some of those sponsors.'

'OK, but before you do that, I've got an old friend of yours on the line. He wants to have a word with you.'

'Who is it?' But the director had already put down his receiver and Tess addressed the question to the person who wished to speak to her.

'What do you mean, "who is it"?' a male voice replied with a laugh. 'Did your boss not tell you?'

Tess felt her face flush with panic, recognising immediately the smooth voice with its precise foreign accent. It was one she had hoped never to hear again.

'Is that you, Peter?'

'Of course it's me. I'm sure you did not really need to ask.'

'Why are you wanting to speak to me?'

'Why not? Alasdair is not the only one in the International office with whom I share some pretty wonderful memories.'

Tess closed her eyes tight, feeling the skin on her back tingle with nervous apprehension. 'Listen, Peter, I think—'

'So, how is everything going? I wondered if you would still be working in the office?'

'Why shouldn't I be?'

'No reason.' Tess heard Peter Hansen sigh. 'Listen, I thought it would be a good time to make amends for the way I behaved towards you at the end of the festival last year. It was just that things got a little bit difficult back in Copenhagen. I thought if we could meet up—'

'What do you mean? Where are you?'

'Here in Edinburgh. I came over for the festival . . . and to see you, of course.'

Tess gave a short cry of disbelief. '*What?* Are you being serious?'

'Never more so.'

Tess shook her head at the sheer gall of the man. 'Peter, I really am too busy to meet up. For a start, I've got a reception tonight, and anyway, the last thing I really want—'

'In that case, I could be round in your office in five minutes. It would be good to see Alasdair as well.'

'You will do no such thing,' Tess exclaimed, knowing only too well the director's intuitive nature would pick up on her uneasy vibes.

'Then where shall we meet?'

Tess pressed a hand to her forehead. 'I really do have a lot of work to do, Peter.'

'OK, then. Why not invite me to the reception tonight?'

'No!' She bit hard on her bottom lip, realising he was leaving her with little alternative other than to meet up with him there and then. 'Right, where are you?'

'About two hundred yards away. There is a church on the right-hand side of the High Street. I am standing on the steps.'

'Give me five minutes then, but I warn you, I haven't got long.'

'I'll be looking out for you — and, Tess?'

'What?'

'I'm longing to seeing you again.'

By the time Tess had made arrangements to cover for her short absence from the office fifteen minutes had elapsed before she reached the small paved square where the church was situated. Peter Hansen was instantly recognisable in the crowd. Tall, lean, with a shock of Viking-blond hair that curled against the collar of his dark-green jacket, he possessed an almost visible aura of self-admiration about himself. As soon as he caught sight of her, he lifted his hand in a brief wave, pushing himself away from the stone pillar against which he had been leaning at the entrance to the church. He descended the steps and threaded his way through the mêlée of pedestrians and street entertainers towards her, and as he approached he held out his arms, enveloping her in a hug and planting a kiss on the top of her head.

'Tess, it is so good to see you.' He pushed her away from him, resting his hands on her shoulders. 'My word, you look fantastic. Life is good for you, yes?'

Tess gave him a brief smile. 'Yes, it is. Never been better.'

He put an arm around her shoulders. 'Come on, let's go and get a cup of coffee.'

Tess pulled herself away from his hold. 'I said five minutes, Peter, and that's all I'm going to give you.'

'I think we can down a cup of coffee in that time,' he said, already starting to make his way across the High Street to a small café outside which a few metal tables and chairs took up half the width of the pavement. Tess stood her ground for a moment, and then, with a resigned shake of head, followed on after him.

Having ordered up a cappuccino for Tess and a herbal tea for himself, Peter leaned his elbows on the table and smiled affectionately at her, accentuating his annoyingly good looks, although Tess was pleased to see that a few age lines now creased his tanned face. When she met his gaze with an ice-cold stare, he reached across the table to place his hand on hers, but she avoided the contact by sitting back in her chair and folding her arms.

'I think you are still very angry with me,' he said with a quiet laugh.

'I was, but I really haven't dwelt on it too much.'

He nodded his head slowly. 'Listen, it was wrong of me to leave last year without talking to you. I had to get back to Copenhagen pretty urgently.'

'So your note said.'

'It was just that my wife . . . well . . . she had not been in very good spirits . . .'

'I hope she's better now.'

Peter paused for a moment, eyeing Tess, unsettled by her quick-fire remarks. 'Yes, thank you, she is. But what I really wanted to—'

'Why was it you never answered your phone?' Tess asked,

leaning forward on the table and glaring at him with intensity. 'I called enough times.'

Peter held out his hands apologetically. 'I had no alternative, believe me. My wife is very . . . untrusting of me . . .'

'With every reason, too,' Tess interjected sharply.

Peter twisted his mouth to the side. 'My word, you are being quite sharp today.'

'What are you doing back here, Peter?'

The question once more disarmed him momentarily. 'I have come for the festival, but more to see you. I cannot tell you how much I have missed you. I don't think a day has passed when I have not thought of you.'

Tess nodded. 'Right, so let me get this straight. You just want to take up where we left off.'

'Of course not. That would be asking a great deal of you, but maybe I thought we could meet for dinner and remember the good times . . . because they were good times, Tess. You know it as well as me.'

Tess choked back a laugh. 'To be quite honest, I hadn't given them another thought. And I'll tell you why, Peter. You see, I'm not free now, for you or anyone else, because I'm married.'

Peter shrugged. 'I know all that. Alasdair told me on the telephone. You married Allan, didn't you?'

'Yes, I did.'

'And if I remember right, you had been going out with him ever since we first became . . . involved.'

Tess bit at the side of her mouth. 'So?'

'So, if that is the case, nothing really has changed. A very innocent dinner, that is all I am asking. What difference would that make to your relationship with him?'

'Every difference.'

'But there's no reason for him ever to know. You could simply treat it as part of your routine entertainment at the festival.' He paused to take a sip of his tea. 'To make it legitimate, maybe I could speak with Alasdair.'

Tess swallowed hard. 'No, I don't want you to do that.'

Peter raised his eyebrows. 'Ah, yes, of course. We certainly don't want the director to find out about our little affair. That could make your life very difficult.'

'And yours too.'

'Not really. Alasdair knows the way I am, but maybe he would think it rather unprofessional of you.'

'Are you saying you would tell him?'

Peter laughed. 'Of course not. It's just that if I have to take more formal action to arrange a simple dinner date with you, well then, it might put you in a bit of a predicament, don't you think?'

Tess stared at him for a moment. 'That's as good as blackmail.'

Peter frowned. 'Oh, I hope nothing so serious as that, surely, but I think it does prove how much I want to see you again.'

Needing time to consider her options, Tess turned her head and fixed her eyes on a young female street performer who was juggling with three blazing torches whilst standing on the shoulders of two worried-looking young men she had obviously pulled out of the crowd. God, Tess thought, the girl's not the only one playing with fire here. She had been right in saying that Peter's proposal was as good as blackmail, but then again, she had brought it upon herself. There was really only one option open to her. Have dinner with the man and finish it for good, and then neither Allan nor Sir Alasdair Dreyfuss need ever be the wiser.

She turned back to Peter. 'All right, we'll have dinner.'

Peter's face registered victory. 'I'm so glad to hear it. When shall it be, then?'

Tess took her diary from her handbag and flipped through the pages. She shook her head. 'This week's out. It'll have to be either next Tuesday or Wednesday.'

Peter nodded. 'OK, I'll call you.'

'No, I'll do the calling.'

'You still have my number?'

'If you haven't changed it.'

Peter shot her a knowing wink. 'No, it's exactly the same.'

Tess glanced at her watch. 'Dammit, this is ridiculous. I'm so late.' She drained her coffee, pushed back her chair and stood up, slinging her bag on to her shoulder. Peter got to his feet at the same time. She made a move to walk back up the High Street before turning back to glare with hostility at her ex-lover. 'The dinner next week will be the last, Peter.'

'In that case, we will have to celebrate it in style.' He came round the table, hoping to bid her an affectionate farewell, but she had already gone.

As soon as Angélique Pascal entered the vast function room of the Sheraton Grand that evening, she was sure she would not be wanting to leave Albert Dessuin's side during the course of the event. As she descended the wide carpeted steps to the crowded floor, she felt three hundred pairs of enquiring eyes turn to look at her and reacted to it by putting out a hand to grasp her manager's arm for reassurance. She shyly returned the smiles that were beamed her way as Albert led her through the parting crowd to a small group gathered by the window. A thin, studious man with black-rimmed spectacles and wearing a dark-blue suit that looked decidedly crumpled detached himself from the group and came towards Albert and Angélique with his hand outstretched.

'Albert, I am sorry. I didn't see you enter. Welcome to Edinburgh.' He shook Albert's hand, and then turned to his charge. 'Angélique, what a pleasure it is to meet you at last. I'm Alasdair Dreyfuss, director of the International Festival.' He gave her a light kiss on the cheek and she turned her head, expecting the second, but the man was already walking back towards the group. 'Come on over and I'll introduce you to some of my colleagues, and then I'll organise some drinks for you. Right, this is our marketing director, Sarah Atkinson . . .'

Angélique listened to the introductions, but she did not catch any of them, as the man spoke English too fast, a trend that seemed to be set thereafter. Whenever a question was asked of her, she turned to Albert and he answered on her behalf, turning to smile at her every time as if to say, 'So who thought she could manage without me, then?' It made her determined to try to understand so that she could answer at least one question for herself, but the noise in the room was deafening, and no matter how hard she concentrated, she could not pick up the gist of one single conversation. After three quarters of an hour of listening to unintelligible words being spoken to her, she suddenly felt very tired, realising now Albert had been right in saying to the journalist at the airport that they would be drained of all energy by the time the reception was finished. She looked around the function room and noticed a small recess over by the huge floor-to-ceiling windows. Squeezing Albert's arm and gesturing with a finger for him to lean over, she whispered in his ear that she was going to look out of the window for a few minutes. He nodded his approval and she moved quickly over to the recess, her head down, in case someone else should take the opportunity of engaging her in yet another incomprehensible discourse.

The recess was luckily much deeper than she had imagined, a twenty-foot carpeted passage that ended at a wall on which a large gilt-framed mirror was hung. Finding herself completely hidden from those in the function room, Angélique crossed her arms and leaned against the window, looking down on to the bustling crowds and the slow-moving traffic in the street below. As she then turned her gaze to the huge dark-stoned castle sitting high above the city, she let out a long, lingering yawn.

'You must be exhausted,' a female voice said.

Angélique turned to see a girl approach her tentatively along the passage. She was carrying two glasses of champagne in her hands.

'I saw you didn't have anything to drink,' she said, handing Angélique a glass.

'Thank you,' she said, smiling at the girl. She had noticed her before at the back of the group when Albert had greeted the festival director, and it had occurred to Angélique at the time that they must have been about the youngest two people in the room. Although the girl was a few years older than herself, Angélique had immediately liked the way the she looked. Her close-cropped brown hair framed an honest, happy face, and she was dressed quite informally in comparison with the other women at the reception, in a light red wrap-around dress over a black polo-neck sweater and blue jeans.

'I'm sorry, we weren't introduced,' the girl said, offering a small light-skinned hand. 'I'm Tess Goodwin. I work in the International office.'

'I am pleased to meet you, Tess,' Angélique said, shaking her hand.

'You speak English very well. I'm afraid my French is almost non-existent. Languages were never my strong point at school.'

'Oh, my English is not so good, and I find it very difficult when there are many people in a room,' Angélique said, casting her eyes along the corridor from where the noise of the reception boomed. 'I cannot concentrate enough.' She took a sip from her glass and looked out of the window. 'Edinburgh is a very beautiful city, I think. Do you come from here?'

'No, I'm originally from Aberdeen, which is much further north, but I live and work here now.' Tess stepped closer to the window, her eyes searching above the roofs of the buildings to one side of the large square in front of the hotel. She pointed a finger. 'Do you see the church spire there?'

Angélique nodded.

Tess smiled at her. 'I was married there five months ago.'

'How wonderful for you!' Angélique exclaimed with genuine excitement. 'I think you must be a very happy person, then.'

Tess laughed. 'Yes, I suppose I am.'

'What is your husband's name?'

'Allan.'

'I like the name *Alain*,' Angélique remarked decisively, giving the name its French pronunciation. 'It is very strong, very . . . er . . . the French word is *sûr*.'

Tess grimaced embarrassedly. 'I can only guess at something like "dependable"?'

131

'Yes,' Angélique replied with a confirming nod of her head. 'That is exactly right. Does *Alain* work in Edinburgh, too?'

Tess studied the interest in Angélique's face. She was really beginning to warm to the open friendliness of this young celebrity whom she had only seen before on television, hiding her face from the cameras. 'Yes, here and in Glasgow. He's just recently been promoted in his company, so he's having to work very long hours.' She gazed out of the window, her mind caught up with the clandestine arrangement she had made with Peter Hansen only hours before. 'We don't see much of each other at the moment.'

Angélique screwed up her nose. 'That is very hard for you both, *n'est-ce pas*?'

Tess turned and smiled at the girl. 'Very. We didn't actually even have time to go on honeymoon for that very reason.'

'*Oh, ça c'est triste!* But you will go eventually, will you not?'

'Yes, once the festival is over and done with. We're going to Barbados for two weeks.'

'Ah, I believe it a very beautiful place. It is one place I have never been.'

'It must be one of the *only* places you've never been.'

Angélique gave a short, hollow laugh. 'You are right, but unfortunately, my life means I am never in one place long enough to enjoy it or to learn about it.'

'I can understand that. I'm sure constant jetting around the world isn't as glamorous as it sounds.' Tess put down her glass on the low windowsill and opened the zip on her small suede shoulder bag. 'Listen,' she said, taking out a business card and handing it to Angélique, 'maybe you'd like to come out one night with Allan and me? We would both love to show you around Edinburgh.'

Tess noticed sadness glaze over the violinist's eyes as she studied the card. 'That is very kind of you, Tess. I'm afraid I don't think I will have the time, but I am very happy you have asked me this.'

Tess shrugged her shoulders. 'Well, keep the card anyway. If you do find you have a spare moment, or even if you just want to have a chat, you can always contact me at any time on my mobile phone.'

Angélique's eyes never lifted from the card. 'Thank you very much, Tess. I would like to do that.'

'Excuse me, I hope I'm not breaking into a private conversation here.'

Both girls turned to look at the balding middle-aged man who stood peering around the corner of the recess at them. He was smartly dressed in a dark-grey pinstriped suit with a striped shirt and yellow silk tie, but his most striking feature was the kindly smile that he beamed in their direction.

'I just wanted to have the opportunity of saying to Mademoiselle Pascal how much I enjoyed her playing,' the man said as he came along the passage towards them.

Tess turned to Angélique. 'I'll leave you with your fan,' she said with a quiet laugh.

The young violinist came forward and gave Tess a kiss on both cheeks. 'I have enjoyed meeting you, Tess.'

'Me too,' Tess replied, making her way along the corridor past the man. He watched her until she had disappeared back into the reception.

'I'm sorry, I didn't mean to cut in like that,' the man said, seemingly quite flustered about having invaded Angélique's privacy, 'but I really did not want to leave tonight without saying to you in person how marvellous it is that you are here in Edinburgh. I have greatly admired your playing over the past few years.'

'Thank you very much,' Angélique replied, accepting the compliment with a small bow of her head. 'That is a nice thing to say.'

The man put out a hand to her. 'My name is Gavin Mackintosh, Mademoiselle Pascal, and I am most honoured to meet you.'

'And it is also an honour to meet you, too, Mr Mackintosh,' Angélique replied with a laugh as she took his hand.

'Please, you must call me Gavin.'

'And you must call me Angélique.'

'I would like that,' Gavin said, suddenly realising he was holding a hand that must be insured for millions. He quickly relinquished his grip. 'So, I'm right in saying this is your first time here in Edinburgh?'

'Yes, it is.'

'And how do you like it?'

Angélique turned to look out of the window. 'This is all I have seen of Edinburgh. It appears very beautiful from here.'

'So you've just arrived?'

'Yes. I was in New York last night.'

Gavin sighed. 'I don't know how you have the stamina. You must be extremely tired.'

Angélique shrugged her shoulders. 'I get accustomed to it.'

'And how long are you going to be here?'

'I think seven nights. I am rehearsing tomorrow and then I will be playing in concerts the following two evenings in the . . . how do you say? . . . Ush . . .'

'Usher Hall.' Gavin pointed to the large round ornate stone building on the opposite side of the road. 'That's it over there.'

'Ah,' Angélique said, moving her head slightly so she could see the building. 'Not far to walk, then.'

Gavin laughed. 'No, not far. And for the rest of the week?'

'I think there are also some late-night concerts when I am to be playing some of the Bach violin sonatas.'

'And then you head off again?'

Angélique gave him an uncomprehending look. 'I'm sorry?'

'And then you travel to another place.'

'Ah, yes. To Singapore.'

Gavin shook his head. 'I don't know how you do it.'

Angélique laughed. 'It is sometimes quite hard. Do you also live here in Edinburgh?'

'Yes, I do, and have done all my life. I went to school here, and then university, and now I work here.'

'What is your job?'

'I am a solicitor.'

'I'm afraid I don't know that word. What would it be in French?'

Gavin burst out laughing. 'Don't ask me! I have no idea. It's all to do with law, anyway.'

'Oh, I understand. And do you have a family?'

'I do. I have a wife, who is somewhere next door probably trying to find me, two daughters and four grandchildren.'

'Four grandchildren! That is wonderful. But you do not look old enough for that.'

Gavin slowly nodded. 'You know, that's probably the nicest thing anyone has ever said to me.'

'*Mais, c'est vrai!*'

'And that's even nicer.'

Angélique pushed herself away from the window. 'I think maybe I have been hiding in here too long,' she said, threading her hand through his arm. 'Please, will you take me to meet your wife, Gavin? I would very much like that.'

Gavin placed his hand on hers and gave it a light squeeze, totally captivated by the charm of the young violinist. 'Nothing would give me greater pleasure.'

They had taken no more than a couple of steps towards the function room when Albert Dessuin suddenly appeared and looked along the short corridor towards them. Gavin could see his eyes focus on the hand that was nestled under his arm. 'Angélique? What are you doing? Why have you been in here so long? There were so many people whom you should have met, but they have left already.' He spoke his French very fast as if to ensure that Gavin, if he had any knowledge of the language, could not understand what was being said.

'Albert, I have been speaking to Tess and Gavin, who are both new friends of mine,' Angélique replied in English, 'and I am now going to be introduced to Gavin's wife.'

Gavin felt Dessuin's glare of distrust almost burning into him. 'I am sorry, but there is no time,' he replied, this time in English. 'Our plans have changed. We are now having dinner with Sir

Alasdair Dreyfuss in a restaurant and already he has left. We are to follow immediately in a taxi.'

'Oh, Albert, can I not please first meet Gavin's wife?'

Gavin noticed her tone had suddenly changed to that of a little girl pleading for a favour.

Dessuin came over and took hold of her free arm. 'I am sorry, but we have wasted enough time.' He looked at Gavin, his mouth creasing into a smile that displayed not one ounce of friendship. 'I apologise, monsieur. It will have to wait until another time.'

'Of course,' Gavin replied, knowing full well the occasion would never present itself again. Unfolding her hand from his arm, he bent down and gave her a kiss on either cheek. 'It's been my pleasure, Angélique.'

The young violinist looked up at him with a smile. 'I hope I might meet your wife another time, Gavin.'

'Please, Angélique, we must go now,' Dessuin said sharply, hustling her away long the corridor.

Gavin watched them as they walked away, his mind filled with two conflicting emotions – how much he liked her, and how much he disliked him. He put his hands into the pockets of his suit jacket and began to walk slowly back to the function room. Just at that point, Angélique appeared again.

'Two tickets for the concert.' She turned away. '*Albert, j'arrive!*' She looked back at Gavin. 'I shall leave them at the concierge desk. Please come.' She blew him a kiss and disappeared.

As Angélique followed Albert Dessuin across the hotel foyer, she stopped momentarily to put down her handbag on the floor and shrug on her jacket. She watched Dessuin forcefully push the heavy glass door open, nearly knocking off balance a small elderly man who was about to enter. She let out a gasp at Albert's total lack of manners and ran towards the door just as the man entered, looking visibly shaken.

'I am so sorry,' she said, putting a hand on his arm. 'Are you all right?'

'Yes, thank you very much,' the man replied with a nod, but

Angélique could tell from his ashen face the incident had given him a tremendous shock. He smiled distractedly at her and hurried off towards the concierge desk.

Angélique pushed open the door and ran down the steps to where Albert was standing, hands on hips, on the pavement. 'Albert, why did you do that just then?' she said fiercely. 'You could have seriously injured that old man.'

'Oh, never mind about him. Look at this problem we have now!' he exclaimed, throwing up his hands in frustration. The taxi that had been waiting for them was completely hemmed in by two large white vans, one of which had the name 'CinElectrics' emblazoned on its side.

Dessuin stepped off the pavement in front of the taxi and hammered his fist on the window of one of the vans. The young driver, who was speaking on a mobile phone, slowly lowered the window.

'What's up, friend?' he asked.

'Could you please move your van? You are blocking in our taxi.'

'Hang on a minute,' the driver said, holding up his hand to stop Dessuin's protest. 'OK, so that's final, is it?' he said into the mobile. 'You definitely want us to head back to London tomorrow with all the gear . . . all right, if that's the order.' He jabbed angrily at the button on the phone to end the call. 'Bugger this for a larf.' He tossed the phone on to the dashboard and turned to Dessuin. 'Sorry about that, mate. We'll get out your way now.'

Eighteen

Having been watching the departure from the hotel of the famous violinist Angélique Pascal, the young female receptionist had also witnessed the incident at the entrance door. She made a move to go around the front desk to check on the well-being of the elderly man, but then stayed where she was when she realised he was fast approaching her.

'Are you all right, sir?' she asked concernedly, seeing his obvious agitation.

'Yes, I'm quite well, thank you,' the man replied, casting an eye around the hotel lobby. 'I wonder if you could tell me where I might find a telephone.'

'Certainly, sir, there's a payphone in the corner over there,' she replied, pointing to a glass door beside the lifts, 'or might I ask if you are staying in the hotel?'

'Yes, I am. Hartson, room 215.'

'Ah, Mr Hartson, a gentleman has been trying to contact you quite urgently.' She turned and took an envelope from one of the cubbyholes at the back of the desk. 'No message was left, but he asked that you ring this number as soon as you returned to the hotel. I was going to suggest you might like to use the telephone in the seating area over there and I'll just add it to your bill.'

'Yes, that would be the best idea,' Leonard Hartson replied absently as he moved away from the desk without acknowledging the girl's kindly aid. He made his way across the lobby to the seating area and pulled the chair away from the small telephone desk. Taking a spectacle case from the pocket of his tweed jacket, he placed it on the desk along with the envelope and sat down, and once he had fussed over both for a moment, he drew the telephone towards him and dialled the number.

'Good evening, Springtime Productions,' a female voice replied immediately.

'I would like to speak to Nick Springer, please.'

'Who's calling, please?'

'Leonard Hartson.'

'Oh, Mr Hartson, we've been trying to get in touch with you all day. Hold the line and I'll put you straight through to Nick.'

Leonard took off his spectacles, folded them in one hand and put them back in the case.

'Hullo, Leonard?' It was Nick's voice.

Leonard sat forward in his chair. 'Nick, there seems to be a great deal of confusion up here. Have you any idea what's going on?'

'I'm sorry, Leonard, I have tried to get in touch. It's a pity you don't have a mobile phone.'

'Well, I don't because I've never had need of one, so please tell me now what's happening.'

'This is all very difficult, Leonard. I know how much of a disappointment it's going to be to you.'

Leonard slumped back in the chair and pressed his thumb and forefinger into the corners of his eyes. 'So it's true, then. You are recalling all the equipment.'

'I'm afraid so.'

'For what reasons, Nick?'

'I had an e-mail today from the Japanese broadcast company that commissioned the film. It was pretty abrupt, to be quite honest, but the gist of it was that they're presently shedding jobs like crazy and a freeze has been put on all recently commissioned works, and, unfortunately, your job just happens to be one of them.'

'Oh, my word,' Leonard said, pressing a hand to his brow. 'Is there nothing we can do?'

'The dance company will obviously still be performing at the festival, but I'd never be able to find another broadcast company to take on the commission at such short notice. That's really why we've got to cut our losses now and get the equipment back to London as soon as possible.'

'Nothing more to be done, then,' Leonard murmured despondently.

'I'm afraid not. I really am sorry about this, Leonard. I know how much you were looking forward to doing this job.'

'Not your fault, Nick.'

'Listen, the boys are heading back tomorrow with the vans, but there's no reason for you to return straightaway. Why not stay up there for a day or two and go to some concerts or whatever, and I'll foot your hotel bill? That's the least I can do.'

'No. I think I'll just catch the train tomorrow morning and get back home.'

'All right. I quite understand.'

'It would have been a wonderful film to make, Nick, and I can't thank you enough for entrusting it to me.'

'Believe me, if there was anything I could do at this stage to continue with the project, then I would, but I really can't think of anything.'

'I know, and I appreciate that.'

'Keep in touch, and I promise I'll call in to see you next time I'm on my way down the A3.'

'You do that, Nick. Look after yourself.'

'And you do likewise, Leonard.'

The old cameraman reached forward and put down the telephone. He sat for a moment staring at the wall in front of him, and then, with a tired sigh, he pushed himself to his feet and made his way slowly back to the reception desk.

'All right, sir?' the young receptionist asked him with a smile. 'Did you manage to contact the gentleman?'

'Yes, thank you, I did. I'm afraid I'm going to be booking out of the hotel tomorrow.'

'Oh, I'm sorry to hear that, sir.' She looked down at her computer monitor and typed quickly on the keyboard. 'Your bill is going directly to Springtime Productions, so there'll be no need to settle up on anything in the morning.'

'Right, well, thank you for all your help, and I'm sorry if I appeared a bit distracted before.'

The girl laughed. 'It's a pretty crazy time for us all right now in Edinburgh, so there's absolutely no need to apologise. We all get caught up a little in the excitement of the occasion.'

'I suppose so,' Leonard replied resignedly. 'Well, I'm off to my room now, so I'll bid you good night.'

'Good night, sir, and I hope we have the pleasure of having you to stay with us again very soon.'

Leonard emptied out the pockets of his tweed jacket and placed everything on the dressing table alongside the key card to his bedroom. He shrugged off the jacket, slipped it on to a hanger and put it in the wardrobe, and as he made his way across to the bed, he loosened the knot on his woollen tie and undid the top button of his Viyella shirt. He sat down on the edge of the bed and eyed the telephone, wondering how on earth he was going to break the news to Gracie. He himself felt aged with disappointment, so he couldn't imagine how she, being the one who had encouraged him almost to the point of vehemence to take the job, would react to the news.

He reached out a hand for the telephone, held it hovering above the receiver for a moment as he gathered his thoughts, and then picked it up and dialled the number.

'Hullo?' Grace answered. Even in that one word, Leonard could sense an air of excited expectancy in her voice.

'Gracie, dear, it's Leonard,' he replied, trying to force light-heartedness into his own voice.

'Oh, I've been longing to hear from you, my love. How's everything going?'

'All right.'

'And has all the equipment arrived safely?'

'Yes, about an hour ago.'

'Oh, how exciting! So when do you think you will start shooting?'

Leonard did not answer, but closed his eyes tight and clenched his fist, banging it up and down repeatedly on his knee.

'Leonard?' Gracie asked quietly, her voice filled with concern. 'Is everything all right, dear?'

'We're not going to be shooting, Gracie,' Leonard replied, his voice suddenly weak with emotion. He cleared his throat to control it. 'I've just spoken to Nick. The job's fallen through.'

'What? But why?'

'The funding's been withdrawn, and he says there's no time to find it elsewhere.'

'Oh, Leonard, I can't believe this. Is there nothing that can be done? It all seems such a dreadful waste of time and effort.'

'I know. I had such wonderful ideas as well, about how I was

141

going to film it. With all this new equipment, I was going to take risks I'd never dared to try before. I really do believe, Gracie, that I could have done a wonderful job here.'

'Your definitive film,' Gracie replied in a voice heavy with chagrin.

'Yes, I think it might well have been.'

There was a silence before Grace spoke again. 'So what happens now?'

'We're all returning tomorrow. I should be back home some-time tomorrow evening.'

'And what will happen to us, Leonard?'

'Nothing will happen to us, my dear. We will just continue with our lives in gentle retirement, just as we have done for the past seven years.'

'With nothing to look forward to except our eventual demise.'

Leonard laughed. 'I don't think we need to be considering that *just* yet, Gracie.'

'Well, then why don't you and I take some risks? You were going to do it in the making of the film. Why don't we do it together?'

'How do you mean?'

'Leonard, we have no children nor grandchildren to bless with an inheritance. We just have each other, and time is running out for both of us.'

'What are you saying?'

'Have you any idea what the budget for this film was?'

'No. Nick never told me, and I would have no idea what the costs are nowadays.'

'More than three hundred thousand pounds?'

'I wouldn't have thought it would be *that* much. I remember reading about a low-cost feature being made recently for a quarter of a million pounds. This film was only to be a forty-minute documentary, so probably around a hundred thousand.'

'In that case, I think you and I should fund it ourselves.'

'*What?*'

'Leonard, my dear, when we thought about moving to a smaller house two years ago, the estate agent valued this one at two hundred and seventy thousand pounds. It must now be worth much nearer three hundred thousand. We don't have a mortgage, so why don't we just use it as collateral against a loan for the film? If, in the worst scenario, we don't make any money from it and we lose a hundred thousand pounds, well, then that's the time we move to a smaller house.'

Leonard held the receiver away from his ear for a moment, staring at it in disbelief at what Gracie had just suggested. He put the receiver back to his ear. 'Gracie, my dear, have you gone quite bonkers?'

'No, I have never been more serious in my life, neither have I ever come up with such a sound idea. Leonard, you know yourself that you have rued the very day you gave up work in the film industry, and you were heading into the twilight days of your life feeling dissatisfied and unfulfilled. Living with you over the past few months has been an exhilaration, a complete joy for me. I have seen you returned to me as the man I knew thirty years ago, and I love it, and I love you. If you came back now, everything would change, and with nothing to look forward to, I doubt much time would pass before one of us would just fade away. Leonard, we are only talking about a third of the capital value of the house, but in all honesty I would rather risk losing everything we own than to lose you, the way you are right now.'

Grace's impassioned monologue brought tears to Leonard's eyes and he dug into the pocket of his trousers for a handkerchief and gave them a wipe. 'Gracie, you truly are a remarkable woman, you know.'

'Shall we do it, then? Shall you and I take the risk?'

'We've always been so careful with our finances, Gracie. We've never done anything quite so foolhardy in all our lives.'

'Yes, but how rejuvenating for us both it would be.'

Leonard laughed. 'Well, in that case, why not? Let's just cast our fates to the wind.'

'Good, and no regrets, my dear, whatever the outcome. No regrets.'

Leonard pushed the handkerchief back in his pocket. 'I'll give Nick a call now.'

'You do that, and first thing tomorrow morning I'll go down to the bank and organise the loan.'

'No, don't do that just yet, Gracie. Let me first find out from Nick how much the film was going to cost and then I'll see if I can't work out a way of shaving a bit off the budget. I'll give you a call tomorrow night.'

'All right, my darling. You get a good night's sleep now and don't go mulling it over in your mind. We've made the decision, and you will be needing all your energies over the next few weeks for making the most wonderful film.'

'Goodnight, Gracie. I love you, my girl.'

'I know you do.'

Having sat there motionless for five minutes, taking in what he and Gracie had just agreed and trying to work out some of the more immediate logistics, Leonard got to his feet and sought out Nick Springer's mobile number. He stood, apprehensive, as he dialled it up.

'Hullo, Nick Springer.'

'Nick, it's Leonard Hartson.'

'Oh, hullo, Leonard. Just give me a moment while I pull the car over.' Leonard heard the rev of an engine and then quiet. 'Still there?'

'Yes, I am.'

'Are you all right?'

'Yes, fine. Nick, I wonder if you might be able to tell me what the approximate budget for the film was?'

'Why do you ask?'

'I just wanted to know.'

'Well, off the top of my head, I think it was about one hundred and fifty thousand pounds, perhaps a bit less.'

'Right. Nick, could you do something for me immediately?'

'Certainly, what?'

'Could you call up both the camera-hire company and CinElectrics and cancel the return of the equipment?'

'What are you saying, Leonard?'

'Gracie and I have decided we're going to fund the film ourselves.'

'*What?*'

'We're going to take out a loan against the value of our house and make the film ourselves. We've decided.'

'No, I can't allow you to do that. You mustn't.'

'Is there any reason why not?'

'Because . . . you and Grace can't put your security at risk like that, Leonard.'

'Yes, we can. Anyway, if you say the full budget is between a hundred and a hundred and fifty thousand pounds, then we would only have to take out a loan on about half the value of the house, and I have a few ideas already on how to reduce the costs still further.'

'By doing what?'

'By sending the electricians and the assistant cameraman back to London. I'll find someone local to give me a hand. I'll move out of this hotel, of course, and look for somewhere a little cheaper.'

'Leonard, are you really being serious about all this?'

'Never more so in my life.'

'Then I have to come in on the deal.'

'Nick, you don't need to—'

'No, I insist. I feel totally responsible for having brought you both to this decision and I simply cannot allow you to take on such a financial risk alone. I shall put up a figure of fifty thousands pounds and you, Grace and I will produce it as equal partners under the umbrella of Springtime Productions. I'll give you backup for whatever you need and arrange for all processing and post-production work to be done here in London.'

'Are you sure, Nick?'

'In your words, Leonard, never more so in my life. I'm just so delighted you're still going to be able to make the film. Dammit, if I wasn't so busy, I'd come up and assist you myself!'

Leonard laughed. 'Now, that would make it just like old times.'

'Yes, but I'm afraid an idea that's totally unviable. Are you sure

145

you're going to be able to find someone to help you? I haven't got one single contact in Edinburgh.'

'Don't worry. I have a couple of days in hand to get myself sorted. I'll put the word around at the theatre where the dance group are performing, and I've also met the man who owns the warehouse where we're doing the shooting. He appears to have his fingers in enough pies.'

'Well, don't go doing anything rash, Leonard.'

'In what way?'

'You won't try going it alone, will you? It really is not worth the cost cutting. You have to remember you're not as young as you were, and you have to consider your health.'

'Nick, I know my limitations.'

'I sincerely hope so. Have you been in touch with the dance company yet?'

'Yes, I'd just got back from their hotel when the equipment arrived. They have a young Scottish girl acting as an interpreter, and together we spoke with Mr Kayamoto, who is the director. A very nice and courteous man. He didn't mention any changes to the schedule, so I doubt he knew at that time. I'll give the girl a call now and arrange another meeting for tomorrow. I'm sure Mr Kayamoto will be willing to continue as planned.'

'One problem has just occurred to me, Leonard.'

'What might that be?'

'You have two van-loads of equipment up there. How are you going to manage to drive both? And what will you do with all the equipment overnight?'

Leonard pondered on this for a moment before replying. 'I think, Nick, having seen the warehouse, that I can afford to get rid of some of the equipment, so I'll just keep hold of one of the vans and get the boys to drive the other back to London with what I don't need. And you don't have to worry about security. I can lock the van and the equipment in the warehouse.'

'That's good, then, and listen, my contribution to this venture is accessible now, so if you're in need of any money short-term, you must just get in touch. Is that understood?'

'Thank you, Nick . . . for everything. I can't tell you how happy I am this is going to go ahead after all.'

'Not half as happy as I am now that we've managed to come up with this solution. My heart has felt like concrete ever since ending that last call with you. But now we're into exciting times, Leonard, exciting times!'

Leonard chuckled. 'Yes, we are, aren't we, if not a little precarious.'

Nineteen

The following morning, Leonard left the hotel after an early breakfast and took a taxi over to the lodgings where the rest of the crew were staying. He found them in a gruff mood, having had the night to mull over the fact that they had lost out on three weeks' work, but Leonard managed to mollify their anger by telling them that he would ask Nick to seek some form of compensation for them from the Japanese company. This news seemed to have a visible effect on their spirits, and by the time they set off back to London in the spare van, having helped Leonard to sort through the equipment at the warehouse, any ill feeling had dissipated and they left with hands waving from the windows and cries of well-wishes.

The day, however, did not continue in such a positive vein. Having booked himself out of the Sheraton Grand the previous evening, he spent the lunch hour and the early part of the afternoon on the telephone in the hotel lobby, with local newspapers and magazines scattered on the table in front of him, vainly trying to track down somewhere to stay. At three o'clock, he realised that it was all to no avail. With little alternative open to him, he approached the reception desk to ask if he might have his room back for one more night, only to be told that it had been taken almost the moment he had handed in his keys. In desperation, he explained his circumstances to the receptionist, who had little to suggest other than he should try going to the offices of the International to see if they could be of any assistance to him.

The taxi took Leonard the short distance up past the castle and dropped him off outside the old church at the top of the Lawnmarket. He entered the building towing his suitcase behind him, and made his way along the passageway to the ticket office. He approached a young man wearing a festival logo-ed sweatshirt, who sat in one of the booths.

'Can I help you, sir?' the young man asked with a cheery grin.

'Yes, I wonder if it would be possible to speak to someone in the International office?'

'Do you have an appointment?'

'No, I'm afraid I don't, but my name is Leonard Hartson, and I'm up here to film the Japanese dance company that's performing this year.'

'Ah, right.' He picked up the receiver on the telephone and pressed an intercom button. 'Hullo, Tess, there's a Mr Hartson here in the ticket office who's needing to speak to someone . . . no, he doesn't, but he's filming the Japanese dance company . . . All right I'll tell him.' The young man put down the receiver. 'Mr Hartson, Tess Goodwin will be down to see you in about five minutes. If you go across to the Hub café on the other side of the corridor Tess will meet you there.'

'Thank you very much,' Leonard said with an acknowledging smile and walked the few steps across the corridor and pushed open the glass entrance door of the coffee shop.

Ten minutes later, as he drained the last drops of his now-lukewarm coffee, the door of the café swung open and a young woman came in, dressed in a pair of jeans and a brightly coloured shirt and holding in her hand a spiral notepad. She scanned the tables before catching sight of Leonard, who had risen to his feet on her entrance.

She came over to his table. 'Mr Hartson?'

'Yes, that's right.'

'Tess Goodwin,' the young woman said, offering out a hand to Leonard. 'I work in the International marketing department.'

'Miss Goodwin . . .' Leonard began, shaking her hand.

'Tess, please.'

Leonard nodded. 'Tess, thank you for sparing time to meet me. I know you must be very busy right now.'

'Up to the eyeballs, actually.' She pulled out a chair for herself. 'But never mind, let's sit down and you can tell me how I can be of help.'

Leonard resumed his seat once she had slipped a mobile phone from her back pocket, put it on the table beside her notebook and made herself comfortable. She opened up the notebook to a fresh page and hovered her pencil expectantly above it.

Leonard took this as a sign that she did indeed have little time to spare for him, so he started his explanation immediately. 'Tess, this might not be part of your remit at all, but I'm afraid I didn't quite know who else I should ask. The fact is that, for reasons that I won't bore you with, I have to find other lodgings for the duration of the festival, and so far I've had absolutely no joy.'

'Where are you staying at the moment?'

'At the Sheraton Grand, but there have been unforeseen changes to the budget of the film, and I can't afford to stay there any longer.'

Tess bit at her lip thoughtfully. 'You're right. This is not usually my remit. We have an artiste liaison team which handles everything to do with the International performers, and they're usually booked into the more expensive hotels in Edinburgh.' She tapped the end of her pencil on the notepad. 'I can't promise you anything,' she said, picking up her mobile, 'but I'll try the Fringe office. They have many more performers than we do, so they might have something available.' She dialled a number and held the mobile to her ear. 'Hullo, can I speak to Lewis Jones, please? It's Tess Goodwin at International.' She smiled reassuringly at Leonard as she waited to be connected. 'Lewis, good afternoon, it's Tess . . . absolutely hectic . . . no, you're right, no time to enjoy married bliss at all. Listen, Lewis, I am with a Mr Hartson who is in

Edinburgh to film one of our events and he needs to change his accommodation arrangements . . . Yes, he's staying in the Sheraton Grand right now, but he's looking for somewhere a bit cheaper. You don't know of anything available, do you? . . . No, I understand that.' Tess looked across at Leonard. 'He says the whole of Edinburgh is chock-a-block.' She listened once more to the man on the line. 'Oh, right. Yes, I can hold.' She took the mobile away from her ear. 'He says someone came in a couple of weeks ago who had rooms to let, due to a cancellation. He's just trying to find the piece of paper now.' A voice sounded down her mobile and she listened once more. She raised her eyebrows hopefully at Leonard as she picked up her pencil and began writing. 'Jamie Stratton . . . OK . . . was that number seven London Street? . . . Right, and telephone number? . . . that's brilliant, thanks, Lewis . . . Yes, a drink would be good, if I can find the time . . . bye.' She punched the 'end' button on the mobile. 'Well, that sounds hopeful. Let's give this Mr. Stratton a call.'

'If you would prefer, I could—'

'No, let's see if he has anything available first,' she cut in, dialling the number written down on her notepad. She bit at a fingernail as she listened for the telephone to be answered. 'Hullo, Mr Stratton? . . . yes, this is Tess Goodwin at the International office. I believe you had some rooms to let . . . you still do . . . oh, that's wonderful . . . just the one, it's for a Mr Hartson . . . Right, and are you going to be in this morning? . . . Good, so Mr Hartson could come round anytime . . . Many thanks indeed . . . bye.'

'You're in luck,' she said with a smile as she ended the call and laid the mobile down on the table. She tore off the sheet from her notepad and handed it to Leonard. 'London Street is quite central, so you should be able to find it easily enough. You can make your move whenever you want.'

'I can't thank you enough, Tess,' Leonard said, folding the piece of paper and tucking it into the top pocket of his tweed jacket.

'I'm glad we managed to sort something out for you,' Tess said, rising from her chair and picking up her notepad and mobile.

'Now, if you'll excuse me, I must really dash.' Giving him a brief wave, she turned and hurried away towards the glass door.

Walking out on to the Lawnmarket, Leonard crossed over the cobbled street, feeling the late afternoon sun warming his back, and began walking down towards the High Street where the street theatre was in full swing. People thronged the closed-off thoroughfare and gathered around the acts in progress. There was first a jazz band, and then a juggling stilt walker, and further on an escapologist, naked to the waist, his face crossed in the blue and white of the Scottish saltire, who appeared to be hanging himself from a lamp post. His attention being captured by this alarming form of entertainment, Leonard never noticed the small dumpy woman who kept abreast with him on the other side of the street, trying to keep the large Samsonite suitcase that she dragged behind her from keeling over on the uneven paving slabs.

Rene Brownlow bumped the suitcase uncaringly up the two stone steps and pushed open the door to the Fringe office. She towed the suitcase into a corner where it wouldn't be in anyone's way and, puffing out a breath of exhaustion, she approached the long counter that was piled high with flyers and leaflets. A girl, dressed similarly to the appalling Andrea from the Corinthian Bar, left her computer screen behind the counter and approached her.

'Can I help you?'

'Yes. My name's Rene Brownlow. I've been doing a show in the Corinthian Bar, but I want to—' She didn't get any further, feeling the lump rise in her throat and the tears bubble in her eyes, just as they had done endlessly for the past twelve hours.

The girl smiled at her. 'Don't worry. I know exactly who you need to talk to.'

She went back to her desk and picked up the telephone. 'Lewis,' Rene heard her say, 'you have another tortured soul to deal with.'

The girl put down the receiver and came round from behind

the desk and put a hand on Rene's shoulder. 'Come on, I'm going to take you to see Lewis Jones. He'll sort everything out.'

These were about the first kindly words that had been spoken to Rene since she had arrived in Edinburgh a week and a half before, so by the time that she took her seat at the desk in front of the young man with the unruly mop of dark curly hair, she was snivelling uncontrollably. Lewis leaned forward on the desk, spinning a pencil about in his fingers, a huge grin spread across his stubbly face.

'Come on, things surely can't be going that badly, can they?' he said in a lilting Welsh voice. He took a handful of tissues from a large box of Kleenex at the side of the desk and passed them over.

Rene nodded as she peeled one off the pile and blew her nose with force. 'They couldn't go any worse,' she sobbed. 'I've 'ardly had anyone come to the show, and no one understands me 'umour and I'm never going to be able to cover the theatre cost. I just want to go 'ome now.'

Lewis leaned back in his chair, the grin still fixed on his face. 'Rene, would you believe you are the fifth person I've had in today, saying exactly the same thing?'

Rene wiped at her eyes, her sobs slowing down as his words sank in. 'Really?'

'Yes, really. You're not the only one in the boat, you know.'

'But I'll never be able to cover the—'

'Look, it's early days,' Lewis said, leaning forward on his desk once more. 'Quite a number of the performers get a bit despondent about this time. That's why I get a rash of visits about now. My advice to you is to stick it out, because you're sure to regret it if you don't.'

At that point a dark-haired girl put her head over the partition that separated Lewis's desk from the rest of the office. 'Lewis?'

Lewis watched Rene turn her head away to stop the girl from seeing she was crying. He looked up at the girl. 'Not now, Gail, I'm busy.'

'I know, but is that Rene Brownlow you've got with you?'

'Yes. Why?'

'I thought you might like to see this.' She handed him over a folded copy of a newspaper before disappearing once more behind the partition. Lewis scanned through the piece that Gail had highlighted in fluorescent yellow.

'There you are, you see,' he said, turning the newspaper round to face Rene. 'You are being a bit hasty, aren't you? That's in the *Scotsman*. Everybody reads that in Edinburgh.'

Rene picked up the paper and stared at the black-and-white photograph of herself. She glanced quickly through the words written underneath. 'Rene Brownlow . . . an original wit . . . splitting my sides at her characterisation of the members of Andersons Westbourne Social Club in her home town of Hartlepool . . . this act is definitely worth a visit.' Rene placed the newspaper back on the desk and let out a short laugh that was caught up in the last of her sobs.

'Not bad, eh?' Lewis said.

'No,' she replied quietly.

'I wish I could have produced reviews like that for the other four people who came to see me today.'

Rene smiled at him. 'I'd better get on with it then.'

'I think that would be the best idea. You wait until tonight. I bet you'll find the place packed.'

Rene lowered her head and pulled another handkerchief from the pile and once again began wiping at her eyes.

'What's up now?' Lewis asked in a baffled voice.

'I don't want to go on living where I am right now,' Rene said with a renewed sob. 'I'm in this 'orrible 'ouse with this dreadful woman, and I 'ave to be out every day at eleven o'clock and I just 'ave to walk the streets all day.'

Lewis puffed out his cheeks in disbelief. 'Oh, that's all a bit violent, isn't it? It sounds like that particular lady deserves to lose your custom.' He sucked in air through his teeth as he gave Rene's predicament some thought. 'Hang on a minute.' He began sifting through the piles of paper that littered his desk. 'Now where the hell did I put that address?' He shifted his attention to a wire tray, going through its contents. 'I only had it in my bloody hands about ten minutes ago.' He ducked out of sight for two seconds and came up brandishing a scrumpled piece of paper. 'Here it is. Under my foot, it was.' He put it on his desk and smoothed it out with a hand before picking up the telephone and dialling a number. 'Let's just keep our fingers crossed,' he said, shooting a wink at Rene.

'Hullo, is that Jamie Stratton? . . . Right, well, this is Lewis Jones at the Fringe office. I've just given your name to a colleague of mine . . . yes, that's right . . . ah, so do you have any more rooms available? . . . oh, you do. Well, in that case, I've got someone here who would like to take one of them . . . Yes, her name is Rene Brownlow . . . Yes, how do you know that? . . . ah, well, there you go then. I've just given it to her to read . . . Right, so she can come round any time, then? . . . Good, thank you, Jamie.'

Lewis smiled at Rene. 'There you are, you're famous already. Your new landlord has just read your review.' He quickly copied out the address on to a notepad, tore it off, then pushing himself out of his chair, he came round the side of his desk and handed it to Rene. 'You're going to be in London Street, which is just down the road a bit from the top of Leith Walk, so it's a good place to stay. He says you can go round anytime you want.'

Getting to her feet, Rene reached up and threw her arms around the lanky Welshman's neck. 'Lewis, you're a real star. Thanks for being in the right place at the right time.' She gave him a big kiss on the cheek. 'And sorry about all that blubbing.'

Lewis laughed. 'That's what I'm here for. That's why they call me Jones the Sponge.'

Twenty

Putting down the receiver, Jamie Stratton punched the air and let out a loud whoop of relief. Thank God things were looking up at last. One month had passed without any income coming into the flat, and his bank balance was just about at its limit. Now, in the space of twenty minutes, he had managed to rent out two of the rooms. He glanced at his watch, working out that he probably had enough time before anyone arrived to head round the corner and get a celebratory cup of coffee from The Grainstore. He scooped up his keys from the hall table and left the flat at speed, descending the three flights two at a time.

Jamie bought more cups of coffee per day at The Grainstore than was probably good for him, but he had an ulterior motive for his visits. It was his considered opinion that, underneath her red-striped apron, Martha had a body to die for, an uncommon asset for a girl who edged him in height by as much as three notches over his own 'approximate' six feet. Yet her attraction went much deeper than a mere clawing at his carnal senses. Humour constantly simmered in Martha's blue-green eyes, her face radiated so much health that make-up was a non-essential, and her complete zaniness was marked by the pointless black plastic hairband that permanently adorned her frenzy of short blonde hair. From the very first day she had started working in the coffee shop, Jamie had considered her his ultimate woman. The only slight problem was that, during their many brief encounters, he had found out she had six years on him and had been in a steady relationship for three of them. But inaccessibility only made the crush grow deeper.

The coffee shop was enjoying good custom that afternoon, but with the hometime rush yet to start, there was no queue at the counter. Martha caught his entry and immediately turned to one of her colleagues, slumping her shoulders and raising a long-suffering eyebrow. Jamie saw her every move, but undeterred by her lack of amorous reciprocation, he approached her with a broad grin.

'Hi, there, Martha.'

When she turned at his greeting, Martha gave him only the briefest of smiles. 'Well, James, what is it you're wanting this afternoon?'

'Black coffee to go, please.'

Martha turned to the espresso machine, and unclipping one of the coffee strainers, she banged it forcefully on the waste tray to rid it of the old coffee granules. 'So what's been going on today? Still home alone, are you?'

'Nup, not any more. I've managed to get two of the bedrooms rented out.'

Martha glanced over her shoulder and shot Jamie a more meaningful smile that succeeded in floating butterflies around his stomach. 'That'll please the bank manager then.'

'Too right.' He dug in the pocket of his trousers for some change. 'And what about you? Busy as ever?'

Martha placed the styrofoam cup on the counter and pushed on a lid. 'Working at full throttle,' she said, holding out her hand for the money. 'We didn't close up until midnight last night.'

Jamie handed her the exact change. 'No more cameras going missing then,' he said with a laugh.

Martha narrowed her eyes at him as she rang up the amount. 'That's a very bad joke.' She shut the drawer of the till with force. 'It's not good for business, having people come in here and nicking things.'

'No, I reckon not.' He picked up the cup from the counter. 'Well, I'd better head back in case one of my punters arrives. I'll see you later.'

'Nothing in life could be more certain,' Martha replied quietly through clenched teeth as she turned to serve another customer.

Seeing the taxi pull away from outside his flat, Jamie ran the last thirty yards along London Street and spun around the railings that led up to his front steps. An elderly man, smartly dressed in a tweed jacket and cavalry-twill trousers, was standing at the entrance door with a large suitcase by his side, pressing one of the bells on the brass-panelled intercom.

'Are you Mr Hartson?' Jamie asked.

The man turned with a start and appraised the young man standing in front of him in the calf-length shorts, white baggy T-shirt and flip-flop sandals. 'Yes?'

'Hi, I'm Jamie Stratton. Sorry I wasn't here. I was getting myself a cup of coffee.'

'No need to apologise,' Leonard Hartson replied with a shake of his head. 'I have only just this moment arrived.'

Jamie pulled a bunch of keys from the pocket of his shorts and unlocked the door. Holding it open with a foot, he reached out his un-coffee-ed hand and grabbed the handle of the man's suitcase.

'Oh, I can manage that,' Leonard said, making a move to take the suitcase from Jamie's grasp.

'It's no bother,' Jamie replied. 'I'm used to carrying heavy loads up these stairs. The flat's on the third floor, so I'm afraid you've got a bit of a climb.'

Leonard laughed. 'In that case, I am sincerely grateful that I have a fit young landlord.'

By the time the man had made the stairs, Jamie had opened the shutters on the large windows and given the bedroom a quick visual appraisal, letting out a loud expletive when he saw the well-breasted front cover of a copy of GQ peeping out from under the valance of one of the beds. Picking it up, he rolled it up into a tight scroll in his hand and went out into the hall just as Leonard Hartson entered the flat, puffing with the effort.

'Oh, my word, that is some climb,' Leonard said, resting his hand on the sideboard.

'Yeah, sorry about that. Better to take it in stages.' Jamie held out a hand to guide Leonard towards the bedroom. 'You're in here, Mr Hartson. It's on the quiet side of the building, so you won't hear the traffic. The bathroom is on the left just outside your bedroom door, which I hope you don't mind sharing with me. The kitchen is down the hall on the right, and there's a large sitting room at the other end with satellite television which you're welcome to use whenever you like.' He looked around the room, wondering if there was anything he had missed. 'Does this seem all right for you?'

Leonard nodded his approval. 'Perfect.' He glanced a smile at Jamie. 'Almost as well appointed as my room at the Sheraton

Grand.' He walked across to the window and looked out on to the small gardens that were enclosed by the surrounding buildings. 'Very pleasant indeed.' He turned back. 'And what about cost?'

'Well, erm . . .' Jamie had given this some thought. The agency was to be charging £40 per room per night, minus their commission, from the start of the festival, but he had to try to make up some of the shortfall. 'How about fifty pounds per night?'

Leonard nodded. 'Would you consider sixty pounds a night and allow me use of your telephone? Only for calls within the United Kingdom, of course.'

Jamie raised his eyebrows thoughtfully. 'Yeah, sounds good to me. We have a deal.'

'Good.'

Jamie leaned his back against the wall and folded his arms across his chest. 'So, are you going to be here for the whole of the festival?'

'Yes, I am.'

'To see the events?'

'No. I'm going to be working.'

Jamie furrowed his brow, wondering what type of work an elderly man, obviously well past retirement age, would be undertaking at the festival. 'And what is it you do?'

'I'm a lighting cameraman.'

'Is that right?' Jamie replied, suitably impressed. 'What a fascinating job. What type of films do you make?'

'Well, I've worked on every kind of film in my time, but right now, I'm up here to do a documentary.'

'So you've done features as well?'

'I have, yes.'

'Would I know any of them?'

'Not unless you're a fan of very old movies.' Leonard chortled. 'The last feature I worked on was made long before you were born.'

'In that case, I'll bet my father would know it. He's a complete movie buff.'

Leonard nodded slowly. 'Is that so? I wouldn't suppose your father has any contacts up here in the film industry?'

Jamie laughed. 'No way! Dad's a farmer. Why do you ask?'

'Because I'm looking for someone to assist me, and I'm not really very sure where to begin.' He scratched a finger down the side of his lined face. 'I don't suppose you know of anyone who might be looking for a job for the next three weeks? Experience isn't really very necessary. I just need someone who has a bit of muscle and a bit of common sense about them.'

Jamie shrugged his shoulders. 'I'm afraid not. All my university friends have either headed off to jobs or they're on summer vacation. I'll have a think about it, though.'

'That would be most kind,' Leonard replied.

Jamie pushed himself away from the wall when he heard the front-door buzzer sounding in the hall. He excused himself from Leonard and walked quickly along the hall and picked up the receiver.

'Hullo?'

'Is that . . . Jamie Stratton?'

Jamie winced at the distorted voice that rang in his ear, the woman obviously having her mouth pressed hard against the speaker of the entry phone.

'Yes.'

'This is Rene Brownlow. I'm standing outside your front door.'

'Right. When you hear the buzzer going, push the front door open. I'm on the third floor.'

'What? I can't get this wretched suitcase one inch further. My arms have stretched that much in length, ye'd think my dad was an ape!'

Jamie chuckled. 'All right, hang on there. I'll be down in a sec.'

He jammed the doormat in against the door to stop it from shutting and headed down the stairs at his customary speed. He opened the front entrance door and a woman with short straight hair, her small but ample frame swathed in a loose-folded coat that appeared to have been manufactured from a couple of multi-coloured rag rugs, jumped back with surprise.

159

'My, that was quick! You must 'ave wings on your feet!'

'I'm used to taking those stairs at speed,' Jamie said, picking up her suitcase. 'By the way, I read your review this morning. Pretty good.'

Rene stared open-mouthed at the ease with which he had lifted her enormous Samsonite burden. 'Ah, well, nice of you to say so,' she replied distantly.

Jamie cocked his ear, catching the sound of a telephone ringing up the stairwell. 'Dammit, that's my phone. I'd better see if I can get it, so just make your own way up.' He turned and began taking the stairs two at a time, as if he were carrying nothing heavier than a paper bag.

Rene remained on the front steps for a moment, watching the point where he had disappeared. 'That lad must be superhuman,' she said, shaking her head in disbelief before starting her ascent to the flat at a much more sedate pace.

Dropping the suitcase with a thump on the flagstone floor at the door, Jamie crossed the hall and made a dive for the telephone. 'Hullo?'

'Good afternoon, Jamie. It's Gavin Mackintosh here.'

Jamie caught his breath before replying. 'Hi, Gavin. Sorry about the delay. I was down at the bottom of the stairs when you rang.'

'Is my timing a bit inconvenient?'

'No, not at all.'

'Good. I was just ringing to see if you managed to find any tenants for the festival.'

'Well, funny you should say that,' Jamie replied, glancing around to see that Mr Hartson's bedroom door was closed and Rene Brownlow was yet to make it to the top of the stairs. 'Two have just arrived today.'

'Oh, excellent. So does that mean you'll be all right for your mortgage payments?'

'Yeah, I've worked out I should be OK until the end of September.'

'I take it, then, your tenants will be there for the whole of the festival.'

'Probably not both of them. One is doing a show on the Fringe, so she could well leave before the final week. The other guy's a cameraman who's making some sort of documentary at the festival, so I reckon he'll be around for the duration. Talking of which, Gavin, you don't have any contacts in the film industry up here, do you?'

'No, I'm afraid that's away out of my network, Jamie. Why do you ask?'

'Well, this cameraman is an old boy and he's in need of an assistant, so he asked me if I knew anyone up here. I think he's a bit desperate because he said he'd be happy to take someone with no experience.'

'Nothing springs to mind, Jamie, but I'll certainly keep my thinking cap on.'

'That'd be great. Cheers, Gavin.' Jamie waved a greeting to Rene as she entered the flat and sat down with a flump on her suitcase. 'By the way, did Dad get hold of you?'

'No. What would that have been about?'

'A possible game of golf at Muirfield tomorrow evening, I think.'

'Ah, in that case, I'll have to tell him I won't be able to make it. Jenny and I are going to a concert to hear Angélique Pascal play.'

'She's the French violinist, isn't she?'

'Exactly.'

'Yeah, there was a photograph of her on the front page of the newspaper this morning, arriving at Edinburgh Airport. She's pretty fit-looking.'

Gavin laughed. 'You're not wrong there. I had the pleasure of being in her company at a reception yesterday evening and she is an extremely captivating young lady.'

'Sounds as if you're a bit hooked there, Gavin. Maybe you should consider ditching Jenny tomorrow evening and going it alone.'

'Ah, Jamie, I think maybe this would be an apt time to finish this call before you come up with any other suggestions, and

I'm tempted to charge you for my time. We'll keep in touch, though.'

'Right you are. Thanks, Gavin.'

Jamie put down the receiver and turned to his new tenant, who still sat on the suitcase catching her breath. 'Sorry about that.'

Rene held up a hand. 'Not at all. I'm not used to all this exercise. Living in Edinburgh is like being at a bloody 'ealth farm.' She got slowly to her feet. 'I tell you, I'm going to be returning to 'Artlepool a mere shadow of my former self.'

Jamie smiled at her as he picked up the suitcase. 'Come on, I'll show to your room and you can recover in a bit more comfort.'

Twenty-One

The police panda car was sitting at traffic lights in Stockbridge when the report of suspicious behaviour came through on the radio from the control room. Being only four streets away from where the supposed incident was taking place, WPC Heather Lennox took the call while her male colleague switched on the blue light, gave a short wail on the siren and swerved out of the queue, swinging the car left across the red light.

As they approached the street, the driver killed the blue light and drove slowly around the corner, hoping for an element of surprise in their arrival. He flicked the headlights on to full beam, illuminating the two youths who turned with expressions of panic on their faces, immediately stepping away from the car into which they were only a moment away from gaining entry. As the panda car accelerated towards them, the two boys took to their heels like a couple of frightened gazelles, and as the car drew level with them their desperation pushed them to perform a near impossible feat, scrambling up and over a seven-foot wall before disappearing from sight.

The driver unclipped his seat belt and threw open the car door, making ready to give chase, but was stopped by WPC Lennox.

'Dinnae bother, Jim. We'll never catch 'em.' She turned around in her seat and stared out of the back window. 'Did ye see onything a bit odd back there when we turned intae the street?'

The policemàn shrugged.

'I'm sure there was some'dy standing in that end doorway watching everything that was going on wi' something like a pair of binoculars.' She swung round and unslotted the radio handset. 'Come on, I think it's worth checking it. Better get the car turned so we don't have to reverse out o' here.'

The police driver spun the steering wheel back and forth until he had managed to turn in the tight space between the rows of parked cars. He drove to the end of the street and stopped at the junction with the road.

'Which way?' he asked.

WPC Lennox craned forward in her seat and glanced up and down the street. She could make out a number of pedestrians walking beneath the orange glow of the street lights, mostly in couples. There seemed to be only one person walking alone.

'That could be him up there on the left. Wait for a couple of cars to come and slot in between them, then just drive past at normal speed so I can tak' a look at him.'

Sixty yards away, Thomas Keene junior was still chuckling to himself. It had been the third time he had videoed those two boys from his housing estate attempting to nick a car, but that one really had to take the Oscar. He had had the zoom set right in to record every detail of the theft and consequently had seen the expressions of horror on the boys' faces when they turned to look up the street. Sensing then that something was going on out of frame, T.K. had zoomed out, catching the police car approaching, and he had kept the camera switched on until the two lads had disappeared from sight over the wall. He could not have captured the scene better, so well in fact that he could not resist the temptation of reviewing the whole hilarious scene right then and there. Opening up the viewfinder, he rewound the tape and pressed 'playback', studying the screen as he walked, oblivious to the cars that passed him on the street.

'Well, speak o' the devil,' WPC Lennox breathed quietly, as the car passed the slow-moving figure on the pavement.

'D'ye know him?' her colleague asked.

'That, Jim, is one Thomas Keene junior, a young man from Pilton Mains who has mair stolen cars to his name than the Queen of England has jewels.'

'Ye'd think he'd notice us, then. What was he doing?'

'I don't know. He was holding something in his hand, but I couldn't work out what it was.' She gestured with her hand. 'Turn into the street on the left here and we'll just wait to ask the lad a few questions, shall we?'

T.K. was so distracted by his latest masterpiece that he missed the step down on to the street at the end of the pavement and landed awkwardly on his foot. Wincing with pain, he closed the viewfinder on the camera and bent down to rub at his throbbing ankle. It was at that point he became aware of the two shadows that darkened the area around him.

'Evening, Keene,' the policewoman said in an airy manner. 'Remember me, dae ye?'

Thomas slowly lifted his head and saw the two uniforms standing above him. Shit, he thought to himself, the bloody polis. His first fleeting thought was that at least he was innocent of all crime, but then his eyes glanced down at the stolen video camera that lay by his right foot. Hell, he couldn't get caught with it. He'd stayed out of trouble for so long, he wasn't going to get pulled in for something as petty as that.

'Could you stand up so that we can ask you a few questions, Keene?' the policewoman asked, taking a step towards him.

'Ma ankle's sare.'

'Just get to yer feet, sonny,' the policeman said sternly, backing up his colleague's request.

T.K. put his hand on the camera and manoeuvred his feet into a position that was as near as possible to that of a hundred-metre sprinter about to push off from his blocks. The policeman sensed the lad's intentions and reached down to grab his shoulder, but his hand closed on thin air. Thomas Keene junior had taken off like a scalded cat.

'Bring the car. I'll get him,' the policeman called out to his colleague as he ran off in pursuit of T.K. After fifty metres he wondered if he hadn't been a bit premature in the surety of his statement because the gap between him and the wee bastard was increasing with every second.

T.K. glanced quickly behind him. He was certainly putting welcome distance between himself and his pursuer, but the policeman was still in full view, which meant T.K. wasn't yet in a position to jettison the camera unseen. He had to get out of sight.

T.K.'s knowledge of every short cut to the north side of the New Town was infinite, and so he knew from the moment he turned into the small mews street that he had made a fundamentally suicidal mistake. The cobbled lane, which was lined with small, pleasantly symmetrical stone houses with brightly painted garage doors, came to an abrupt end at an eighteen-foot-high wall that was topped, for some ridiculous reason, with a spiral of razor wire. Left with no other alternative, T.K. kept running until he came to the wall. He turned, at bay against it, thankful that the street was only lit at its entrance. He looked frantically around. To one side were a couple of potted bay trees at either side of the front door of the last house. No time to start digging, he thought to himself. On the other side was a cluster of pristine rubber dustbins tucked away into the corner of the wall where the house owners would deem them least unsightly. He dragged one of them out, pulled off the top and pushed the camera down deep amongst the plastic bags. Then a spur-of-the-moment decision made him retrieve it. Losing the stolen apparatus was unfortunately a necessity, but he was damned if he was going to lose his precious videotape. He ejected the cassette and once more rammed the camera back into its hiding place, and then, squatting down behind the dustbin, he slid the cassette down the side of his battered trainer shoe. He leaned back against the wall, drew up his knees and took in a deep, calming lungful of air. It was all he had time for. He watched the beam from the powerful torch light up the profile of the dustbin, hitting him full in the face ten seconds later. He held up a hand to protect his eyes, hearing the policeman's rasping breath.

'All right, lad, are ye going to come quiet now or am ah going tae have tae use a bit o' persuasion?'

Gavin Mackintosh rose to his feet along with the rest of the audience in the Usher Hall to give tumultuous applause to the performance of Mozart's Violin Concerto No. 3 in G Major. With outstretched hand, the conductor directed the acclaim toward the young soloist, then swivelled on his plinth and gave her a short Germanic bow. Angélique Pascal, dressed in a black strapless cocktail dress that hugged her small but curvaceous figure, reciprocated by blowing him a kiss before continuing on in similar style to the packed auditorium encircling the stage.

Gavin continued to clap until his was the last to echo feebly around the vast domed concert hall, his eyes fixed on the departing orchestra. Jenny, his wife, already with her coat on and her handbag shouldered, touched his arm to draw his attention to those others in their row who were waiting to get past him. Gavin held a hand up in apology, slipped the evening's programme into the inside pocket of his jacket and followed his wife up the steep staircase to the exit.

Outside, a cool wind blew up Lothian Road, swerving with force around the curved walls of the Usher Hall. Fastening the centre button of his suit jacket, Gavin took hold of Jenny's arm and manoeuvred a path for them through the crowds, at the same time taking his mobile phone from his breast pocket and switching it back to 'general' ring. It was as well he had remembered to turn it on to 'silent' before the concert because he had felt it reverberate against his chest halfway through and it had taken a steely glare and a brisk shake of the head from his wife to curtail his immediate reaction to answer it. Pressing the playback number, he listened to the message as he walked.

'Damnation,' he muttered, slipping the mobile back into his pocket and guiding Jenny over to the side of the pavement.

'Don't say you have a call-out,' she said in a voice which expressed both disappointment and long-sufferance.

'I'm afraid so. One of John Anderson's Legal Aid cases. The lad's been taken into Gayfield Square Police Station.' He held up a hand to hail one of the few taxis on Lothian Road with their 'For Hire' lights still on. 'It shouldn't be too complicated, but I'll have to stop in at the office to see if I can unearth some files on the boy. You take this taxi home and I'll be back as soon as I can.' As the black cab pulled up alongside them, Gavin opened the door and gave his wife a kiss on the cheek. 'At least this year we managed to *get* to see the concert.'

Jenny smiled knowingly at him. 'Just as well, too. I think you might have been in a bit of a grump if you'd missed out on both Madamoiselle Pascal's musical *and* physical attributes this evening.'

Gavin laughed. 'My dear, it is nothing more than a boyish infatuation.' He closed the door, and with a quick wave of farewell as the taxi pulled away from the pavement, he headed off down towards Princes Street, glancing behind him from time to time in the hope of spying another vacant taxi.

Thomas Keene junior sat slumped on the hard wooden chair in the windowless interview room, chewing hard on a fingernail that was already bitten down to the quick. God, how he hated the stink of these places. They were always the same, the sour aroma of disinfectant doing little to cover the ingrown stench of fear. It always made his stomach knot up in agitation, and this time his unease was exacerbated by the fact that he was beginning to break out in a cold and clammy sweat, being a good hour overdue with the methadone.

He glanced at the pair of battered trainers that sat incriminatingly on the table. 'Ah, fa *fuck's* sake!' he yelled out, thumping his elbows on the desk and slapping repeatedly at his face. Why in the name of hell had he kept the tape? He should have known they would give him a thorough search. Now, if he ever got out this bloody mess, his life wouldn't be worth shit. There was enough evidence on that tape to put at least nine lads in front of the juvenile court, and it wouldn't take long before everyone on the Pilton Mains estate knew exactly who was responsible for supplying the evidence. He leaned back in the chair, clasping his hands behind his head. He'd asked to see his solicitor the moment that damned policewoman had held up the video cassette between finger and thumb, eyeing it as if she was bloody Sherlock Holmes. 'What do we have here, then, Keene?' she had asked. 'A miniature timing device that'll blow yer hand aff in twa seconds,' he had wanted to answer, but then felt it wouldn't have helped his case any. Where the hell had that damned Mr Anderson got to? The polis must have put the call through a good hour and a half ago.

The door of the interview room opened and WPC Lennox entered, barely able to cover the smirk on her face. 'Your solicitor is here, Keene.'

A large man in a dark-blue pinstriped suit walked in and thumped a buff-coloured file down on the table. T.K. stared at him in alarm.

'Where's Mr Anderson?' he asked, a note of panic in his voice.

'On holiday, I'm afraid, Thomas. I'm Mr Mackintosh. You're going to have to make do with me.'

T.K. let out a groan of hopelessness on hearing the gruff tones of his new solicitor. This is it, he thought. There's no way ye're goin' tae escape dae'n time now.

Gavin turned to the policewoman. 'Constable Lennox, would you be good enough to allow me two minutes with my client?'

The policewoman flicked her head uncertainly. 'We should really just get on wi' it, Mr Mackintosh, but I'll give ye a couple of minutes, as long as ye don't hold back on anything during the interview.'

Gavin nodded. 'You have my assurance.'

As the door closed, Gavin pulled out one of the chairs opposite T.K. and sat down. He took a pair of half-moon reading glasses from his pocket, put them on, and then, flicking the bands off the file, he spent a moment in silence scanning through the reports on the first few pages. Pushing the file to one side, he leaned forward on the desk and eyed the young man over his spectacles. 'Well, it doesn't look too good, does it, Thomas?'

'Ah didnae dae onything,' T.K. mumbled disgruntedly.

Gavin found it difficult to suppress a laugh. 'I wouldn't know about that. On that videotape, you seem to have supplied the police with enough evidence to cut car crime in Edinburgh by half overnight.'

'Ah, *shite*,' T.K. spat out, throwing back his head and closing his eyes tightly.

'What happened to the camera, Thomas?' Gavin asked.

'Ah dropped it in the chase.'

'You didn't dump it, did you?'

'How should I? It wis mine.'

'Why did you take the tape out then?'

T.K. managed to pause only fractionally before replying. ''Cos I'd just loaded it wi' a new one.'

'You know Constable Lennox's colleague went back to look for the camera. There was no trace of it.'

'Some thievin' gypsy must hae picked it up then. That cost us a packet, that did.'

'What model was it, Thomas?'

'A JVC digi'al compact.'

Gavin nodded. He had a half inkling to believe the boy. His experience was that those who stole cameras usually had no idea or interest in what model or make it was, only in what money they could raise from its sale.

'You seem to be bit uncomfortable, Thomas. Are you back on the hard stuff?'

'No, I'm clean. I'm just sweatin' 'cos ah'm due ma "script".'

'Could you tell me why you've been filming people stealing cars?'

T.K. eyed the solicitor distrustfully before shrugging a silent reply.

'It would help your cause if you gave me some sort of answer, Thomas. How did you know who was going off to steal cars?'

T.K. sighed and stared up at the bare fluorescent ceiling light. 'They meet uvvy night on the estate. They talk aboot how they nick the different cars, some o' them learn themselves, others learn fi' the boys they meet in detention centres in other cities. That's how it works.'

'It's like a club, then?'

'Aye, s'pose.'

'And you were in this club, then?'

'No!' T.K. replied with vehemence. 'If ye want proof o' that, tak' a look at the film. I never went near 'em.'

'Are you running some kind of racket, Thomas?'

'Whit?'

Gavin leaned over and leafed through the pages in the file. 'Car theft does seem to be your speciality—'

'It wis,' T.K. cut in.

'Well, your knowledge of how it's done is probably infinitely greater than the lads you've been filming, and even I know that anti-theft devices on modern cars are making it more and more difficult to break into them, so I'm wondering to myself if you're not running some kind of elaborate training scheme.'

T.K. scoffed out a laugh. 'Ye're talking crap, mister. Ah dinnae wanna steal cars onymair, d'ya unnerstand that, ah wanna film stuff. Whit else is there tae shoot when ye live in a shitehole like Pilton Mains?'

Gavin studied the gaunt, loose-lipped face of the young man. 'Is that the truth, Thomas?'

'Aye, it is,' T.K. replied quietly, avoiding eye contact with the solicitor as if embarassed by what Gavin had just drawn out of him. 'Ah'm tryin' ti go straight, eh, but the breaks dinnae come easy.'

Gavin nodded and reached over and drew the buff file towards him. He closed it, replaced the rubber bands with a twang and got to his feet.

'Where you aff tae?' T.K. asked, sitting bolt upright in the chair, a sudden look of desperation in his eyes.

'I think it's time we started the interview, don't you, Thomas?'

T.K. held his arms across his chest to stop the shakes that were developing due to his condition and to the thought of what was going to happen to him. 'Honest, Mr Mackintosh, I didnae dae onything. Ye've gotti believe me.'

Gavin winked. 'Just stay cool, Thomas, and answer the questions. I'm on your side, lad.'

Fifteen minutes past the hour of midnight, Gavin walked out of the police station into the cool night air and stood on the pavement listening to the breeze rustling the leaves on the trees that stood in the grassed centre of Gayfield Square. A moment later, he heard the door of the police station open and he sensed someone come to stand beside him. He turned to see T.K. stick his hands into the pockets of his baggy threadbare jeans and pull in a long breath of relief.

'Cheers fae that, Mr Mackintosh,' he said, nodding appreciatively. 'I'm no' sure what ye said in there aifter the interview, but . . . cheers onyway.'

'I did stick my neck on the block for you in there, Thomas, and judging from your notes, Mr Anderson has done likewise in the past. However, I was willing to take the risk because I think you probably are making an effort to keep out of trouble. Just don't disappoint me, Thomas.'

T.K. shook his head and glanced up and down the street. He knew he wasn't out of the shit yet. He now had to go back to Pilton Mains, and God only knew what kind of reception would be waiting for him there. No doubt the police would have been knocking on doors already, which meant it would be highly unlikely he'd get by the evening without getting knifed or having a broken bottle slice open some part of his body.

He turned to Gavin and shot him a sad smile. 'Mr Mackintosh, I dinnae like tae ask ye, but is there any chance you could gie's some cash tae get hame? Ah'm skint.'

Gavin sucked on his teeth. 'Where'd you keep your methadone, Thomas?'

T.K. frowned quizzically at the solicitor's unrelated question. 'In ma bedroom in the flat. How?'

'Well,' said Gavin with a slow, pensive nod. 'I'm going to suggest we take a taxi back to my house, pick up my car and you can then show me where you live. Once I've fetched the methadone from your bedroom, I'm going to bring you back uptown and take you to a hostel for the night. It's no five-star hotel, I'm afraid, but I reckon it'll be a whole lot safer than you returning to Pilton Mains right now.'

'Ye're no' kiddin me,' T.K. mumbled disconsolately.

Gavin flicked a forefinger at the boy, gesturing for T.K. to walk with him up the road towards Leith Walk. 'I don't do this for all my clients, you know, T.K., but in your case, I do happen to have an ulterior motive.' He fixed the lad with a stern glare. 'I have a real aversion to being called out to police stations at a time when I should be in my bed, and if I can do anything to avoid it, I will. So tomorrow morning, I shall come and pick you up at the hostel at nine-thirty sharp. Is that clear?'

T.K. nodded dolefully.

'Because then I'm going to try out an idea of mine which, if it comes to a favourable conclusion, might hopefully result in my never having to encounter you in a police station ever again.'

Twenty-Two

Albert Dessuin arrived just over three quarters of an hour late for the post-concert reception in the Sheraton Grand. His mobile had rung almost the moment he had walked out of the Usher Hall and he had sought out the quietest corner of Festival Square so that he could placate his mother as she reeled off her trials and tribulations for that particular day. He had listened and reasoned and accepted responsibility for gross negligence, and when eventually he had exhausted every form of appeasement, he had abruptly ended the call with a stab of his finger and made to hurl the mobile phone as far across the square as he could. Now, as he entered the function suite, he could sense the black cloud of frustration and irritation that resulted from such a call descend upon him.

He swept a glass of champagne from the waitress's tray at the entrance door, downed it in one gulp and took another before skirting the outside of the room, hoping to locate Angélique Pascal and spirit her away before being engaged in conversation. He did not get far. A small grey-haired lady with a friendly smile approached him almost immediately and began to twitter away to him in bad French about the various concerts she and her husband had attended so far during the festival. Smiling disinterestedly at the woman, Dessuin looked up over the top of her head and scanned the assembled crowd, eventually fixing his eyes on the cluster of men who gathered around the unused bar in the corner of the room. In the midst of them, Angélique and another girl sat up on the high counter, chatting and laughing, and Dessuin immediately recognised the girl as being Tess Goodwin, the marketing assistant from the International office with whom Angélique had struck up a friendship at the welcoming reception two nights before. He watched as Angélique turned to Tess and, with cupped hand, whispered something in her ear. The girl reacted by staring at the young violinist with a wide-eyed, open-mouthed look of sheer disbelief, before both dissolved into fits of laughter. The men dutifully followed suit, even though they could have had no idea as to what had been said.

Albert left the woman still talking, hearing her conversation trail off to a stunned silence as he moved into a position where he could see the two girls more clearly, noticing immediately that the short length of their skirts and the high angle at which they were sitting no doubt afforded a greater attraction to the men than anything that was being said. Taking another glass of champagne from the tray of a hovering waitress, Albert started to walk across the room towards the group, but was waylaid by a hand on his arm, and he was introduced to the main sponsor of that evening's concert, a small man with an almost tangible air of self-importance, dressed in a perfectly cut dinner jacket with a deep-red Thai silk waistcoat. He had at his side a woman with long straight blonde hair and an over-tanned face, who not only had to be twenty years his junior, but also towered over him by at least four inches. Albert smiled and pretended to listen to what was being said, but his eyes kept glancing across the room to Angélique, his mind boiling over with anger and jealousy.

Ever since the concert in Munich two weeks ago, he had begun to notice unwelcome changes in the way Angélique was behaving towards him, and he had come to realise that she was no longer the pliable little working-class girl from Clermont Ferrand who, from the moment she had appeared at the Conservatoire, had held hard to his coat-tails in everything that she did. This new, grown-up Angélique Pascal was beginning to show too much independence and self-reliance, often questioning his judgement on a matter or taking little heed of the advice he gave her concerning her playing style. What's more, she had begun to display an obvious aversion to those congratulatory embraces that had been commonplace between them since he had first started to teach her. And that was something he could not allow to continue. She had, after all, become his property, he had invested his life in her, and eventually he wished to possess every part of her, even though sixteen years separated them in age, because he knew it was the one way he could truly prove to his mother that he was of some worth and importance in the world, and not just an impotent lackey as she had so often described him. And how that would succeed in rankling her! It was therefore imperative to his own interests, and to his financial survival, that he should continue to keep Angélique reined in, under his control.

Nodding his appreciation to the sponsor and his wife, Albert took his leave of them and turned to watch Angélique at the very moment she placed her hand on the shoulder of one of the men, drew him towards her and kissed him on his forehead. She then threw back her head with a laugh and pushed him away, waving her hands as if dismissing him from her presence. This action did nothing to help Albert's already darkened mood. It was indicative of yet another unwelcome change in the character of Angélique Pascal as she demonstrated awareness of what both her status and her sexuality could do for her. She was learning the arts of flirtation and manipulation, qualities that were no different from the cunning deception employed by the whores in the Quartier Latin to attract their clientele each night. And if that was the way in which she wished to behave, then it was obvious to Albert that now was the time to forgo his kind, fatherly influence and educate her in ways other than simply playing the violin.

Wiping beads of perspiration from his forehead, Albert made his way purposefully towards the group.

'Albert?'

He turned to the person who greeted him with forceful words of dismissal ready to bubble like a hot geyser from his lips, only to gulp them back when he found a smiling Sir Alasdair Dreyfuss standing beside him.

'I'm sorry, I've been rather negligent of you this evening,' the director said, putting a hand on his arm. 'I'm afraid Signor Montarino seems to be under the impression this whole party is for his own considerable self alone and he has rather commandeered my attention up until this point.'

Albert took in a deep breath and smiled at the director. 'Please do not worry. I have also been engaged in numerous conversations.'

'And most of them would have been about the concert tonight, I am sure.' Alasdair Dreyfuss glanced in the direction of Angélique. 'Quite startling. She seems to be becoming more accomplished every time I hear her play. You really are to be congratulated, Albert.'

'Thank you,' Albert replied distractedly as he too turned to stare at his protégée.

Alasdair eyed Angélique Pascal's manager concernedly. 'Are you all right, Albert? You're looking a bit pale.'

Albert shook his head. 'No, it is only a bit of a headache, but I was thinking I might slip away to lie down in my room for a while.'

'Well, I'd be grateful if you might just spare me a moment before you go,' the director said, taking his arm and guiding him away from the young violinist's admiring group. 'I want to have a quick word with you about the late concerts Angélique will be performing. Let's head over to the recess by the window so we won't be disturbed.'

And as Sir Alasdair led him across the room, Albert heard Angélique's laughter sound out once more and he turned with paranoid fury burning in his eyes as the distance grew between them.

As Tess stood by the door of the function room, thanking the departing guests for their attendance, she heard her mobile phone ringing in her handbag. She left Sarah Atkinson to carry on the duty and walked down the carpeted steps and into the centre of the nearly deserted room, scrabbling in her bag for the phone. She glanced at the screen, took in a long steadying breath and pressed the 'receive' button.

'What are you doing?' she whispered angrily, cupping a hand around the mobile and casting a furtive glance over to where Alasdair Dreyfuss stood chatting to a group of late departers. 'I said I'd be the one to make contact.'

'I know,' Peter Hansen replied, 'but I wanted to let you know I've booked a table for a week today in La Hirondelle at eight-thirty. I thought that as it used to be our favourite restaurant, it would be a good place to renew our friendship.'

'It's not going to happen, Peter. The only reason I agreed to have dinner with you is because I love my husband and I love my job and I am certainly not going to lose either because of you. Is that understood?'

'Come on, Tess, there's no reason to be like that. Let's just take one step at a time. I have made it my plan not to leave Edinburgh without mending all our differences.' Tess heard one of his slow, seductive laughs, the very thing she had been idiotic enough to find so attractive at the outset of their relationship. 'And I thought maybe you might wear that blue dress I bought for you? You always looked very beautiful in it.'

'What? You think I'd keep that?' Tess laughed derisively. 'I chucked that ages ago.'

There was a brief silence. 'OK, no matter, then,' he said, the tone of disappointment in his voice satisfying Tess. 'I am sure you will look wonderful in whatever you wear.'

'I have to go, Peter. Our guests are leaving.'

'All right. A week today, then, eight-thirty at La Hirondelle. I shall be there waiting.'

Tess did not bother to say any word of farewell. She ended the call and slipped the phone into her handbag, and then, taking a moment to compose herself, she fixed a smile on her face and returned to stand next to Sarah Atkinson.

Twenty-Three

Still dressed in the black cocktail dress she had worn for the concert, Angélique Pascal lay huddled on the bed in her hotel bedroom, staring at the distorted image of her violin case on the cream Regency-style chair that sat against the wall. The side of her face felt wet and sticky, due to the tears of frustration and fatigue that had been shed on her pillow, but she had neither the energy nor the inclination to make any move.

She had never before had such a row with Albert Dessuin. She had played her heart out at that evening's concert, and had consequently felt unusually buoyant in spirit during the reception afterwards, dissipating the smog of exhaustion that had enveloped her over the past month. But it had only lasted until the moment she had returned, or had *been* returned, to her hotel bedroom by Albert, who had caused an embarrassing scene at the crowded reception by extricating her from the room like a naughty schoolchild who was being marched off to see the headmaster. All she had said was she wanted to go out that night for a couple of drinks with Tess and her husband, and that was when Dessuin had lost his temper. In the privacy of her room, he had set about berating her for the sloppiness of her performance and the way she had acted both on stage in the concert hall and at the reception. And then, displaying an almost disturbing irrationality, he had literally *ordered* her to start practising part of the Szymanowski Violin Concerto, a piece not scheduled to be performed until the concert in Singapore in ten days' time. It was at that point she had retaliated. She did not lose her temper, she did not scream, she just told him in a quiet, controlled voice that she'd had enough. When Edinburgh was finished, she wanted to take a complete break.

'What do you mean by that?' Dessuin had blurted out, his eyes narrowed in anger.

'Albert, you must understand that I cannot go on like this, playing night after night. It is becoming too . . . automatic, impersonal, for me, and it affects the way I feel about the music. You are probably right to criticise me, although tonight I made a great effort to play well, but it does not make me happy, Albert, to have to *make* that effort and not have it come naturally to me. I need a rest. I want time to go back to Paris to see some of my friends, and also to return to Clermont Ferrand to stay with Madame Lafitte. I know that she would help me get my perspective back and help me regain my enthusiasm for music.'

'*Pah*, that ancient old crow could give you *nothing* now.'

'Albert, you have no right to call Madame Lafitte such—'

'*Tais-toi et écoutes-moi.* You will not go back to Paris, nor to Clermont Ferrand. You will continue to play until I tell you to stop. It is as simple as that.'

'But there is absolutely no way—'

'Exactly, there is no way you can back out of your obligations at this stage. Can you not imagine what the press would say about you? It would spell the end of your playing career.'

'Could we not just say that I am sick?'

'But you are not sick, are you? And I am not going to be party to such subterfuge. No, the tour continues, and let that put an end to all this *merde*. Now, once you have changed out of that dress, which I have to tell you makes you look like a tart, please get on with your practising.'

Angélique let out a short, quiet laugh and shook her head slowly. 'Oh, Albert, sometimes you are so like your mother.'

'How *dare* you say such a thing!' Dessuin screamed at her, raising his hand as if to strike her backhanded across the face. Falling back on to the bed to avoid the blow, Angélique crawled away from him, pushing herself against the headboard, and stared at him with horrified astonishment. He dropped the threatening hand to his side, turned on his heel and stormed out of the room, slamming shut the door that connected their bedrooms. And then, in the ensuing silence, Angélique had keeled over on the bed, exhausted and frightened.

Sitting up, she glanced across at the radio alarm clock on her bedside table. It was a quarter past midnight. Two hours had passed since Dessuin had left the room. She shuffled her bottom over to the edge of the bed and pushed herself to her feet. Intending to have a shower, she slipped out of her dress as she walked across to the bathroom, her nakedness spared only by a black lace thong.

She turned with a start at the sound of the connecting door being thrown open, and her immediate reaction was to cover her breasts with her hands and push her legs together in an attempt to hide what the thong did little to cover.

'Albert, what the *hell* are you doing?' she said to Dessuin, who stood framed in the doorway, one hand against the doorpost to steady himself. In the other, he clutched a bottle of J&B whisky by the neck. 'I am naked, so please get out of here *now*.'

Dessuin gave a short, scornful laugh. 'Oh, look at you, Miss

179

Modesty,' he said in a slow, slurring voice, 'trying to cover your self up as if you have something to hide from me.'

Angélique turned to get into the bathroom, but drunk as he was, Dessuin still made it across the room, blocking her pat before she was able to seek refuge. She backed away into th centre of the room, shaking with uncertainty and fear.

'Come on, Angélique,' he laughed derisively. 'Why bother actin so cold with me? You would have no doubt loved to have give one of those young men who clustered around you tonight th chance to see you as I am now seeing you.'

Angélique squatted down on her haunches, cupping her hand to her face and covering her breasts as best she could with he elbows. 'Albert,' she sobbed quietly, 'please leave me alone.'

'Leave you alone?' he whined. 'Why should I leave you alone? He came and leaned over her, and she could smell the alcoho surrounding him like a poisonous cloud. 'I *own* you – and s you will never get rid of me.'

Angélique took her hands from her face and stared up at him her eyes now afire with disillusionment and hatred. 'My God you are a screwed-up *bastard,* Albert Dessuin. I am beginning t realise it now. You are nothing more than a worthless, drunke *cochon*!'

The force of the blow was so great that it knocked Angéliqu on to her side and rolled her across the floor. She lay with he head spinning, trying to orientate herself, trying to work ou how she could avoid the next blow. She began to pull hersel into a fetal position to protect herself when he grabbed her b the arm and yanked her to her feet. Angélique let out a cry o pain as he dug his fingernails into her arm, dragging her acros to the desk so that he could rid himself of the bottle of whisky Then, with both hands free, he picked her bodily off the groun and threw her spreadeagled on to the bed.

'Right, Mademoiselle Pascal, world-famous musician, if you choose to call me that name, I will show you exactly what *cochon* excels at!'

He clumsily unbuttoned his trousers and pushed them to th

oor, but as he pulled his legs up to step out of them, the cuffs ought on his shoes, and in his inebriated state he lost his balance ad fell heavily to the ground. Angélique, seeing her moment o escape, jumped off the bed and grabbed her dress from the oor. As she ran towards the door, a hand grasped at her ankle nd she fell forward on to the desk, splaying out her hands for upport and knocking over the whisky bottle in the process. It oppled from the desk and hit heavily against a metal wastepaper asket, shattering its neck and spraying whisky liberally over the all and on to the carpet. Putting his near-spent energy into ne final heave, Dessuin brought Angélique crashing to the round, but even in his drunken stupor, the ensuing scream cut arough to his inner senses and he immediately released his grip n her ankle.

Dessuin crawled over to the wall and leaned his back against , and with lolling head fixed his drunken gaze on Angélique. ll thoughts of protecting her modesty now long gone, Angélique t on the floor with her legs apart, staring at her hand and at ae blood that flowed down her arm from the wound.

'Oh, *mon Dieu*, what have you done? What have you *done*?' ae cried out, her desolate sobs shaking every part of her body. You have just ruined my *life*!'

'Oh, Angélique,' Dessuin said, his voice slurring heavier than efore. 'I'm so sorry, *ma chérie,* I did not mean . . .' He tried to nake a move towards her, but the violent struggle and the amount f alcohol that was now coursing through his body took its toll nd he toppled over unconscious.

Never taking her eyes off her hand, Angélique got slowly to er feet and stepped over Dessuin's prostrate form. She went ato the bathroom and turned on the cold tap, wincing with ain as she held her palm upturned under the gushing stream. he held her hand up to the light to see if there was any glass ill embedded in the wound. The gash was long and deep but, s far as she could tell, it was clean. Taking a white hand towel om the rack, she bound it tightly around her hand and then, or the first time, viewed her shivering, naked form in the large mirror above the sink. Oh, Angélique, what has just happened in there? Everything has changed, everything has gone in the past few minutes. What are you to do now? You cannot stay here, not with this man who has betrayed your trust and put an end to your wonderful dream. But maybe you provoked it. Maybe everyone would believe it was your fault. He would certainly do everything to manipulate the story for it to appear so.

You have no alternative but to leave now, leave everything behind you. But where do you go? Where do you seek refuge when you are completely alone, knowing nobody in a vast foreign city?

She peered round the door of the bathroom and looked down at Dessuin. He lay gently snoring with his mouth open, his glasses pressed awkwardly into the side of his face. She noticed two small patches of blood on the carpet beside the desk and decided there and then to cover her tracks, removing as much evidence as she could of the struggle.

Moving guardedly around Dessuin's prostrate form, Angélique wiped away the blood from the carpet and soaked up the whisky with the help of half a roll of lavatory paper before flushing it away. She then took the whisky bottle and its broken neck through to Dessuin's bedroom and put it in his wastepaper basket. Returning to her room, she picked up her dress from the floor and stepped into it. Taking a linen jacket from the wardrobe, she pulled it awkwardly around her shoulders and kicked her feet into a pair of flats. She glanced over at the small card that lay next to the telephone on the bedside table and then walked across the room and picked up the receiver. She started to dial the number on the card, but then halted and put down the receiver. It was impossible for her to call Tess. She was too involved, and if she were to see her in this state, then questions would be asked and the story would be on the front pages of every international newspaper within days. And that was something Angélique knew she could never allow to happen.

She moved over to the door, and then turned to take one last fleeting look at those things that were now useless to her – Albert Dessuin, her former tutor and manager, and the black violin case that sat on the cream Regency-style chair against the wall.

For a moment, Angélique eyed the room key that lay on the desk, but then decided she would not take it. She would never have any need to return here again. She closed the door behind her and hurried along the corridor. She pressed the button for the lift, and as she waited for it to make its journey from the ground floor, her face crumpled and tears streamed unguarded down her cheeks, in the full realisation of all that she was leaving behind and the terrifying uncertainty of what she would face in her future and much-changed life.

Twenty-Four

During the three hectic weeks of the Edinburgh Festival, the city itself rarely succumbs to rest. At every hour of the day and night, each street corner, each darkened lane on both sides of the bridges becomes a venue for some aspiring musician, actor, comedian or entertainer, attracting an ever-shifting audience from the vast crowds that throng the streets and creating an inescapable cacophony of sound that drowns out even the constant drone of traffic. In the small hours of the morning, an ambling pedestrian on Princes Street, which would be as crowded as on the last Saturday before Christmas, might find himself first striding out in proud military style to the stirring skirl of the bagpipes before gliding rhythmically past a string quartet playing a Strauss waltz; and then staggering away in laughter from the comedian whose act had been conducted from the confines of a council wheelie bin. He might then be reduced to tears of compassion by a couple of teenage actors, using a long fold-away table as their only prop, performing the death scene from *Romeo and*

Juliet with as much passion and fervour as one might ever witness in the velveted splendour of the Old Vic.

And intensifying this atmosphere of revelry and bonhomie are the blazing lights that shine out from every misty-windowed restaurant, crammed public house, queued-up café and buzzing street stall, each staying open until the hour when city licensing laws stipulate their closure or when the last of their customers see fit to adjourn to their smart hotels and homely boarding houses, sparse lodgings and shared bedrooms.

It was against such a backdrop that Jamie Stratton, having spent the whole evening reviewing a plethora of Fringe shows at the Pleasance, made his way back to the London Street flat. A distant bell rang out two o'clock as the sound of the never ending street theatre faded away behind him. As he walked briskly down Broughton Street, he heard the frenetic finale of an Irish jig band floating out through the open doors of his local pub and his initial thought was to cross the road to squeeze in one final pint before closing time. But then he noticed that the lights of The Grainstore coffee shop were still ablaze farther down the road, and knowing that Martha usually closed up at midnight at the latest, his curiosity as to why it should still be open dispelled the need for another drink.

The coffee shop appeared to be completely deserted, with all the chairs upturned on the tables and the floor swept and mopped. And there was no sign of Martha. Suspicion gripped at his stomach as he slowly pushed down on the door handle. It was locked. He retreated back on to the pavement, his mind racing. What if that junkie who stole the camera had returned? Maybe he had waited until Martha was alone and then come in and robbed the place and left her tied up at the back of the shop. Maybe Martha was in real need of his help.

He approached the door once more and beat his fist on the wooden frame. 'Martha, are you in there?' he yelled. 'Martha! Can you hear me? Are you all right?'

He pressed his face to the glass, squinting through The Grainstore logo, and then, with relief, he caught sight of Martha looking up over the counter from her seated position behind it. Getting to her feet, she placed a thick dog-eared paperback on top of the microwave oven behind her, and then, with a disconsolate frown on her face, came round the counter and approached the door. She unlocked it and opened it only a fraction.

'What do you want, Jamie?'

'God, you had me worried. I thought something had happened to you.'

'Why?'

'Because you're usually closed up by now and I saw all the lights on, and I thought, well . . .'

'You thought what?'

'That you'd been robbed or something.'

Martha laughed mockingly. 'Ah, and I suppose you were going to do your 'Sir Galahad' bit and rescue me.'

'Well, no, but I was just . . .' He scratched self-consciously at the back of his head. 'Why *are* you open so late, then?'

Taking a quick glance behind her, Martha opened the door and came out on to the doorstep. 'Listen, Jamie,' she said in a quiet voice. 'Do you really want to be a help to me?'

Jamie shrugged. 'Yeah, sure. What d'you want?'

Martha jabbed a thumb over her shoulder. 'There's a girl in there who won't leave. I can't get rid of her. Every time I think she's about to finish up, she orders another cup of coffee. And I'm knackered and I want to go home and get to bed.'

Jamie peered through the window of the coffee shop. 'I can't see her.'

'Of course you can't. She's sitting at the table behind the drinks cabinet.'

'Oh, right. Well, why don't you just tell her to leave?'

Martha raised her eyebrows. 'Because I think she's French, or something foreign anyway, and I don't know what to say to her.'

'So you want me to tell her to leave – in French.'

'Da-ra!' Martha sang out, flicking open her hands, as if Jamie had just answered the million-dollar question correctly.

Jamie bit at a fingernail as he tried to recall some suitable phrases from his sparse GSCE French vocabulary. 'Well, I suppose I could give it a go.'

'You do that,' Martha said, jumping off the doorstep and walking round behind her saviour. She put two hands on his back and pushed him forcefully into the coffee shop. 'I'll go to the loo and get my things while you get rid of her.'

As he approached the counter, Jamie saw for the first time the dark-haired girl who sat at a table in the far corner behind the drinks refrigerator. She seemed oblivious to his arrival, staring out of the window into the darkened alleyway that ran alongside the coffee shop and slowly spinning her empty coffee cup around in its saucer.

. Jamie walked across to the girl's table and leaned his hands on the back of the chair opposite her. '*Excusez-moi, mademoiselle? Êtes-vous française?*'

From the moment she turned to face him, Jamie knew there was something very wrong. Her eyes were swimming with tears and the only colour in her pallid features came from an ugly bruise that spread purple across her right cheekbone. She sat awkwardly, hunched forward, keeping one hand hidden in the folds of something bulky inside her linen jacket.

'*Tout est bien, n'est-ce pas?*' Jamie asked.

'*Oui,*' the girl replied unconvincingly.

There was something strangely familiar about her, but he could not work out what it was, his thought process being taken up with trying to recall a few more relevant French words. '*L'heure est très tarde, mademoiselle, et mon amie veut fermer le café.*'

The girl nodded slowly, smiling apologetically at him. 'Yes, of course. I am sorry to have stayed so long.' Her grasp of English far outmatched Jamie's stuttering attempt at her own native tongue. 'I will leave immediately.'

'Ah, I'm sorry, I didn't realise you spoke English. I'm sure Martha would have talked to you if she'd known.'

'Please don't worry,' the girl said, dismissing his remark with a light wave of her exposed hand. 'Anyway, I was very distracted myself.' As she pushed herself to her feet, Jamie noticed her

186

screwing up her eyes, as if she had just suffered a sharp stab of pain. 'Maybe you would be kind enough to give me some advice before I leave?'

'Of course.'

'Would you know if there is a hotel close to here where I might get a room?'

Jamie began to explain that there was little chance of her finding anywhere to stay, never mentioning the fact that he himself had a spare room in his flat, because, as he spoke, he studied the girl's face, digging deep into his memory, trying to think where he had seen her before. And then suddenly, out of nowhere, the image on the front page of the newspaper came to him and he clicked his fingers in recognition.

'For heaven's sakes,' he exclaimed. 'You're Angélique Pascal, aren't you?'

Jamie witnessed the girl's eyes widen in alarm the instant the question had been asked. She lowered her head as if to avoid further recognition and walked past him towards the door. 'I must leave now, but thank you for your kindness.'

'Hang on a minute,' Jamie said with such force that the young violinist froze in her tracks. He moved quickly to put himself between her and the door. 'Listen, it may be none of my business, but why are you looking for a hotel? You, of all people, must have somewhere to stay tonight. You're one of the star attractions at the festival this year, so you have to be booked into one of the big hotels.' Jamie paused, giving her time to answer, but she continued to stare down at the floor. He took a step towards her, dipping his head to try to see her face. 'Something's happened, hasn't it? What's gone wrong?'

Angélique Pascal took a step to the side to make for the door. 'I must . . .'

Jamie moved to block her path once more. 'I think you're in quite a bit of pain, aren't you? What have you done to your hand?'

The violinist shot a frightened look of entrapment at the young man who stood in her way, and then renewed tears welled in her eyes. 'I have cut it,' she sobbed. 'Very badly, I think.'

Jamie put an arm on her shoulder. 'Come on, you're not in any fit state to leave. Let's go and sit down again.' He guided her back to the table, and once she had resumed her seat, he pulled round a chair and sat down next to her. 'Right,' he said, with hand outstretched, 'let me have a look at it.'

Angélique undid her jacket and slowly pulled out her hand wrapped in the bloodstained towel.

At that point, the door of the restroom banged shut and Jamie turned to see Martha staring at him transfixed, her handbag held limply at her side. 'What are you doing?' she mouthed at him. 'Get rid of her.'

'Martha, just come here for a sec.'

Rolling her eyes heavenward, Martha walked quickly over to the table, desperate to get the coffee shop closed up as fast as possible, and then she saw the girl's bandaged hand. 'Oh, for God's sake,' she murmured, immediately turning away from the bloody sight.

'Right,' Jamie said gently to the violinist, 'just lean your elbow on the table. I'm going to remove the towel really slowly, OK?' He carefully unwrapped the towel and handed it to Martha, who took it as if she were handling a garment newly stripped from a leper. Jamie narrowed his eyes at her and shook his head, and Martha reciprocated with a mouthed expletive.

As Jamie slowly unclenched Angélique's hand with his fingers, blood immediately dripped from the wound on to the table, and the young violinist cried out in pain. 'Martha, get me some paper towels to wipe this up and also something really clean to cover it with.'

Sighing impatiently, Martha dropped her handbag on the ground and clumped off behind the counter. Meanwhile, Jamie studied the uneven gash that ran across the violinist's now-swollen palm. 'Ow, that looks quite deep. How on earth did you do it?'

'I fell over on to broken glass,' Angélique answered in a faltering voice.

'Where? On the street?'

'No, in my hotel bedroom . . .' Her voice trailed off almost to silence as she cast a worried glance between Jamie and Martha, who had returned to the table with a large kitchen roll and two clean white tea towels.

Jamie bit at his lip as he studied the violinist's face. 'Well, let's just take one thing at a time. First, we need to get this cleaned up and then stitched. You'll probably need a tetanus jab as well.'

'I'm sure it does not need all that,' Angélique said quickly, trying to draw her hand away from Jamie.

'Oh, yes, it does,' Jamie said, exerting enough pressure on her hand to stop her. 'I've seen hundreds of wounds like this, and they all needed stitches.'

'Are you a doctor?' Angélique snuffled.

Jamie let out a short laugh. 'No, I'm a rugby player.' He pointed a finger at the wound on her hand. 'There are cuts like this in every game.'

As Jamie began to rebind the wound with one of Martha's tea towels, Angélique studied the face of the well-built young man who was being so kind, noticing now the small scars of battle that were quite familiar to her. 'My brothers used to play rugby as well, for a club in Clermont Ferrand, but they are now both too old.'

'Jamie played rugby for Scotland, didn't you, Jamie?' Martha stated knowledgeably from a distance, 'or that's what I was led to believe.'

Jamie looked quizzically at Martha, never having realised before the acerbity in her tone. 'Only for the under-twenty-one team.'

'C'est vrai?' Angélique asked, obviously impressed. 'You are quite famous then?'

Jamie laughed. 'Not nearly as famous as you.' He rose to his feet. 'Right, Martha, we'd better get Angélique to A and E at the Royal Infirmary, and—'

'What do you mean, "we"?' Martha cut in.

Jamie turned fully in his chair, his back to Angélique. 'You've got a car, Martha, and I don't.'

'Listen,' Martha said in a whisper, 'I've got to get this place

opened up at half past eight tomorrow morning. Can't you tak
a taxi?'

'For God's sakes, just do us a favour and drop us off,' Jami
hissed at her. 'We'll get a taxi back once the girl's been treated

Martha stood looking at Jamie, taken aback by the vehemenc
of his reply. 'All right, then. You don't have to get on your hig
horse. You'll have to give me time to get her table cleared an
the till locked up.'

Jamie gave her a short, sharp nod. 'OK, then.'

As he watched Martha sweep away the coffee cup from i
front of Angélique, Jamie felt saddened by the shattered illusio
he had of Martha, thinking that the next time he set foot i
The Grainstore, it would be for coffee and nothing else.

'Listen, Angélique, I'm trying to work things out in my head
Who else knows you've cut your hand?'

Angélique shook her head. 'Nobody.'

'Right,' Jamie said, rubbing hard at his forehead with his finger
'this is how I see it. I know for a fact you were playing in
concert in the Usher Hall this evening, and I'm pretty sure you'v
got another one tomorrow. Trouble is I think it's quite obviou
to both of us you won't be able to play with your hand in tha
condition.' He paused, catching the look of unease in the violinist
expression. 'So, I suppose we should tell someone you're goin
to be out of action.' Angélique dipped her head once more a
the suggestion. 'What about that man who was in the photograp
with you?' Jamie continued. 'Is he your manager or something
Do you think we should let him know?'

'No! Don't do that!' Angélique cried out, jerking up her hea
to glare at him with fear burning in her eyes.

Jamie held up his hands to calm her. 'All right, all right, w
won't do that.' He let out a long sigh and shook his head
'Angélique, I haven't got a bloody clue what's gone on thi
evening, but if you're trying to hide away from someone c
something, the press will get wind of it the moment you don
turn up for your next concert, and I'm afraid they'll come lookin
for you. There's a spare bedroom in my flat which you're mor

than welcome to have for a night or two, but I can't hide you there for ever unless I know who or what I'm hiding you from.' He leaned forward on the table when Angélique Pascal made no reaction to his reasoning. 'So, what do you want me to do?'

The violinist did not answer for a moment or two, but sat staring at her bandaged hand. 'Listen, maybe,' she said eventually, looking up at him, 'for an hour or so?'

Jamie nodded. 'OK, I'd be happy to.' He glanced round as Martha came out from behind the counter and scooped up her bag. 'Let's leave it for now,' he said quietly, giving Martha a nod.

She walked over to the entrance door and pulled it open. 'Come on then,' she said resignedly. 'Let's get you to the hospital.'

Twenty-Five

Cathy Dent and Phil Kenyon were deep in conversation when they walked into the office of the Exploding Sky Company just as the clock that hung amongst the framed photographs on the far wall clicked on to nine o'clock. Both stopped talking when they realised that Roger was already there, sitting with his feet up on the desk, a mug of coffee in hand, and staring out of the rain-lashed window at the dark Cotswold landscape.

Taking it that the boss was in one of his morning moods, Phil pulled a long face at Cathy before walking over to Roger and giving him a hearty slap on the shoulder. 'How're things this morning, mate?' he asked jovially. 'Raring to go, are we?' He dumped the files he had been carrying on to the desk and then went through to the small kitchen that led off the room to make some coffee for himself and Cathy.

Cathy pulled out the chair next to Roger and sat, pushing the button on her computer to boot it up. She looked across at her husband, who was yet to acknowledge her entry. 'You all right, love?' she asked with a hint of concern.

He turned to her and smiled. 'Yeah, I'm fine.'

'I didn't hear you get up this morning.'

'I know that. I've been here since six o'clock.'

'What have you been doing?'

'Nothing much. Just thinking.'

'About what?'

Roger shrugged his shoulders. 'This and that.'

Phil came through from the kitchen carrying the two mugs of coffee. Handing one to Cathy, he pulled across a wheeled secretary's chair from the other desk and then reached across in front of Roger for the schedule diary before sitting down. He placed his mug on the edge of the desk and opened the diary at the paper clip, moving it across to mark the page for the seventeenth of August. 'Right, so it looks like we're getting gear ready for Edinburgh today.'

Sliding his feet off the desk, Roger leaned forward and put his own mug on the desk. 'We're doing a bit more than that, Phil.'

Phil frowned questioningly at Cathy, but she answered only with a shake of her head. 'And what's that supposed to mean?'

Roger picked up the pile of papers in front of him, evened them up with a hard tap on the desk and handed them to his colleague without looking at him. 'Tell me what you think of that.'

Phil glanced through them quickly. 'This is the firing plan for Edinburgh.'

Roger nodded.

'You've changed it.'

'Yeah, I have.'

'But you've gone and added stuff.'

'I know.'

Phil went back to the beginning of the firing plan and silently studied Roger's alterations in detail. When he eventually turned over the final page, he blew out a long breath of frustration. 'Mate, this is going to screw up all the timings.'

'No, it's not. All the new firings will be simultaneous with those already programmed.'

Phil tossed the papers on to the desk. 'But we're completely full up on the slave units, Rog. There's no room for this lot.'

'I'm going to increase the number of slaves from thirty-seven to forty. That should do it.'

'And complicate the whole thing to hell as well. Jeez, mate, this isn't going to be easy to set up.'

'I know. That's why I'm rescheduling our departure from here for the twenty-sixth of August. That'll give us a day extra.'

Phil flipped through the pages of the diary. 'That's only in nine days' time!'

'Yes, so we've got a bit of work to do, haven't we?'

'And how! What about the crew? Are they going to be able to make it?'

'Not sure yet. Cathy can send round an e-mail to tell them about the change in plan. If not, then we'll just start rigging without them.'

Cathy had sat silently watching her husband during the interchange between the two men. Getting up from her chair, she went to stand behind her husband, encircling his neck with her arms and giving him a kiss on top of his thinning pate. 'Is this what I think it is?' she asked.

'Yeah, love, this is it.'

Phil let out a short laugh and shook his head. 'OK, you two, what's cooking? I'm obviously being kept in the dark about something.'

Roger held hard to his wife's hands as he looked across at his colleague. 'My swansong, old friend. I've decided Edinburgh's going to be my last show.'

Phil stared at his boss, open-mouthed. 'You're joking, Rog.' He paused. 'Aren't you?'

'No, I'm not.' Roger unwrapped his wife's hands from around his neck and rose stiffly to his feet. 'I've been doing this for twenty-five years now and I'm just . . . dog-tired of it all. This is a young man's game, Phil. This constant shifting around the country, the intensity of the workload, it's all getting too much for me. I just feel the time's right to move on. I want to take it easy, spend some quality time with Cathy, and maybe do something completely different.'

'Like what?'

Roger chuckled as he stuck his hands deep into the pockets of his chinos. 'I've always fancied the idea of breeding pigs.'

Phil threw back his head in laughter. 'Mate, you cannot be serious! What the hell do you know about breeding pigs?'

'About as much as I did about putting on a firework display when I first started out.'

'He's actually very knowledgeable,' Cathy interjected. 'He's been reading up on it for the past year.'

Phil shook his head in disbelief. 'God, is that how long you've been planning all this?'

'Maybe a bit longer,' Roger replied. 'It was one of the reasons I bought this place out here in the country. The thirty acres that were included in the sale are all I'm going to need.'

Phil sucked on his teeth. 'My word, Rog, you don't half take the wind out of a bloke's sails.' Discarding the diary on to the desk, he pushed himself to his feet and scratched at the back of his head. 'So, that's it, then. The end of the Exploding Sky Company.'

'Doesn't have to be,' Roger replied, picking up a lengthy typewritten document from the desk and handing it to the tough little Australian.

'What's this?'

'A partnership agreement.'

'Saying what?' Phil asked, glancing at the front page.

'That I keep a vested interest in the Exploding Sky Company, but hand over forty-nine per cent of the company to my new partner. The business is doing well, so there's no reason why he shouldn't be able to pay for his shareholding over a ten-year period on a no-interest loan basis.'

Phil's eyes never left the page. 'My name's on this.'

'Of course it is,' Roger replied with a laugh. 'I wouldn't take anyone else on as a partner. You, Cathy and I have built up the Exploding Sky Company together, Phil, and if you're not going to take it on, then I'd rather close the whole damned shooting match.' He shrugged. 'But it'd be a pity, especially seeing we're at the top of our profession.'

Phil stood for a moment in silence, biting on his bottom lip as he ran briefly through the pages of the agreement. 'It's a bit of a no-win situation for you and Cathy, ain't it?'

'Not at all. We have a company that keeps going and we retain a controlling shareholding. We don't lose out at all.' He eyed his colleague. 'So what d'you think?'

Phil shrugged his shoulders. 'What d'ya think I think! I'll go for it, mate, without a whimper of doubt.'

Roger put out his hand and the Australian grabbed it and shook it forcefully.

'Only thing is,' Roger said, holding up a finger, 'part of the payment is this.' He pointed at the new firing plan for Edinburgh. 'I want to put together a display that's going to break new ground, one that's just going to knock 'em all dead, and I want you to make it work.'

Phil laughed. 'You wanna go out with a bang, mate.'

Roger slid an arm around Cathy's shoulders. 'Quite literally, old friend, quite literally.'

Twenty-Six

While Gavin Mackintosh retrieved a parking ticket from the machine on the corner of the street, Thomas Keene junior stood next to the solicitor's Volvo, tentatively surveying his surroundings, wondering if there might be some ominous reason behind Mr Mackintosh's choosing to park his car in the exact location where, just over two weeks ago, T.K. had bid a hasty retreat with the stolen video camera. There seemed no interest in his presence there – cars passed noisily along London Street's wide cobbled thoroughfare, and a few pedestrians strode unconcernedly to and fro on the pavements – but to T.K.'s distrustful eye, it was the normality of it all that posed the greatest threat.

Sticking the ticket on to the windscreen of the car, Gavin shut the door and glanced across at T.K., witnessing the obvious unease in the boy's manner, but taking it solely as an attack of nerves at the thought of the imminent meeting. Gavin walked over to him and gave him a light, reassuring slap on the back. 'Come on, then. Let's go meet the man.'

They crossed the street and climbed the three wide stone steps that led up to one of the many entrance doors in the row of smooth-stoned, tall-windowed Georgian buildings. Running his finger down the list of names on the polished brass panel, Gavin pressed one of the buttons and stood back, whistling gently to himself.

'This is the residence of Mr James Stratton,' a woman's voice crackled from the speaker, affecting a smart upper-class accent quite unconvincingly. 'How can I be of assistance?'

Gavin chuckled to himself and pressed the button. 'Is Jamie there, please?'

'I 'aven't seen him this morning,' the voice replied, now in a strong Yorkshire accent. ''E's probably still in his bed.'

'I see. Well, my name is Gavin Mackintosh and I'm Jamie's solicitor, and I do need to see him quite urgently, so I would be most grateful if you could let me in.'

'OK then, hang on a mo'.' There followed an amplified crash and a distant expletive at the other end of the line, and after a few seconds the voice said, 'Oops, sorry 'bout that. I dropped the receiver.' A long pause then ensued. 'I don't suppose you 'ave the faintest idea 'ow this wretched thing is supposed to work?'

'I think there's a button on top of the phone you have to press.'

Immediately there was a long buzzing sound and Gavin pushed open the heavy entrance door. With T.K. following at his heels, he made his way up the three flights of well-worn stone stairs to Jamie's flat, where a small plump woman with short streaked hair was waiting to greet them at the door.

'Good morning,' Gavin said, holding out a hand to the woman. 'You must be one of Jamie's new tenants. I'm Gavin Mackintosh.'

'Rene Brownlow,' the woman replied, taking his hand and giving it one strong brief shake. 'Pleased to meet ye.'

Gavin revealed his young companion, who was lurking behind him. 'And this young man is Thomas Keene junior.'

Rene nodded a short, querying greeting at the boy before stepping back into the flat. 'Well, you'd better both come in, then.' She shut the door with a bang when Gavin and T.K. had entered. 'As I said on that phone thing, I 'aven't seen Jamie this morning. D'you want me to knock on his bedroom door?'

'Not necessarily straightaway,' Gavin replied, tilting his head thoughtfully. 'You wouldn't happen to know Jamie's other tenant, would you?'

Rene shook her head. 'No, not really. We've passed once or twice in the corridor, but we haven't got as far as a formal introduction yet.'

Gavin sucked on his teeth. 'Well, not to worry. Would you have any idea if he's here or not?'

'Aye, I know that for a fact.' She pointed to a door at the end of the corridor. 'I saw 'im go into the sitting room about ten minutes ago.'

'Right,' Gavin replied with a slow nod as he eyed the door, 'but you can't help me with his name?'

'I'm afraid I 'aven't a clue.' There followed a brief moment before enlightenment shone on Rene's face. ''Ang on a mo' though. I'm pretty sure Jamie's written it down on the wall chart in the kitchen.' She walked past them into the first room on the left. 'Aye, 'ere it is,' her muffled voice called out from behind the door, 'Leonard 'Artson.' She reappeared back in the hall seconds later. 'Did ye get that? Leonard 'Artson's 'is name.'

Gavin smiled broadly at her. 'Thank you.' He pointed at the sitting-room door. 'What I'm going to do then is just pop in there to see Mr Hartson with Thomas, and hopefully by the time we finish, Jamie might have surfaced from his bedroom.'

Rene shrugged. 'Fine by me. Do you want a cup of coffee or summat to take in with ye? I've just put the kettle on.'

Gavin shook his head. 'That's very kind, but I think we'll give it a miss. Thomas and I have something pretty important we need to discuss with Mr Hartson.'

Rene stood and watched as Jamie's solicitor, shadowed by the strange young man, walked down the hall and knocked on the door of the sitting room. When it was answered, he pushed it open and peered around the side. 'Mr Hartson?' she heard him ask, 'I hope I'm not disturbing you. Might I come in for a moment?'

Half an hour later, seated at the kitchen table, Rene looked up from the aged copy of *Hello!* she had been leafing through to see Jamie enter the room dressed in nothing but a bath towel tucked in around his waist. Seemingly oblivious to Rene's presence, he made his way over to the sideboard as if working on automatic pilot and switched on the kettle. Rene smiled as she cradled her cup of tea in her hands. 'Ye shouldn't go walking round the place like that, Jamie, when ye've got impressionable ladies as your 'ouse guests.'

Turning with a start, Jamie folded his arms across his chest as if attempting to cover his semi-nakedness and peered at Rene through bleary eyes. 'Yeah, sorry about that. I had a bit of a late night. I'm not really with it yet.'

'Out on the booze, were ye?'

'I wish,' he replied, turning to take a mug from the cupboard above the sink. He spooned in a large heap of instant coffee and filled it to the brim with boiling water, and then, walking across to the table, he pulled out a chair and sat down with a sigh of exhaustion, as if the very action had drained the last remaining cell of energy from his being. 'I had to take someone to the hospital.'

Rene looked concerned. 'Nothing too serious, I 'ope.'

'Not really. Three stitches in a cut hand.' Jamie replied, leaning forward on the table and rubbing at the gritty tiredness in his eyes. 'But that turned out to be only half the story.'

'Tell me about it.'

Jamie smiled at her. 'Well, I would, but . . . it's all a bit secretive, really.'

Rene nodded understandingly. 'OK, but let me know if there's anything I can do to 'elp.'

'Yeah, I will. Thanks.' He glanced at his watch and pushed himself up from the table. 'Listen, I've just got to make a phone call.'

At that point, a door slamming shut at the far end of the corridor jogged Rene's memory. 'Damn, I almost forgot to tell ye. Yer solicitor called in about 'alf an 'our ago, along with some dozy-looking young lad. They're in the sitting room right now with that gentleman who's staying 'ere.'

Jamie frowned quizzically at Rene. 'Gavin Mackintosh?'

'Aye, that's yer man.'

'He's here in the flat?'

'That's right,' a voice said from behind him, and Jamie turned to see the solicitor's portly frame standing in the kitchen doorway.

Jamie gave his head a quick disbelieving shake. 'How weird is that? I was just about to call you. What on *earth* are you doing here?'

'Just a bit of worthwhile networking. I've managed to find someone to give your Mr Hartson a hand.'

'What?' Jamie asked, still baffled by Gavin's presence in the flat. 'Who?'

Gavin came into the kitchen and flumped himself down on the sagging sofa that was pushed hard against the wall next to the fridge. 'A young man called Thomas Keene. I doubt you'd know him, Jamie.' He let out a short laugh. 'Not quite in the university scene, this one.'

'And what did Mr Hartson think?'

'He reckons Thomas will suit his needs extremely well, and all I can say is I hope to hell he's right.' Gavin crossed his legs and stretched his hands along the back of the sofa. 'Mind you, I was pretty amazed just how well the lad managed the interview. I doubt he's ever undergone one like that before in his life.'

'So what's he been doing up until now?'

Gavin wagged a finger at Jamie. 'Ah, that's between myself,

Thomas and Mr Hartson for the time being. Let's just say we're in a probationary period.'

Rene laughed. 'I think I understand where ye're coming from. I've known a lot of lads like that in my time.' She got up from her chair. ''Ow's about I make ye a nice cup of tea or coffee now then, Mr Mackintosh?'

'I think a black coffee would go down a treat, Rene. Thank you.' Gavin turned to Jamie. 'So what were you going to call me about?'

Jamie scratched a hand at the back of his neck and glanced furtively in Rene's direction. 'Well, it's a bit . . . delicate.'

'Don't worry,' Rene said, having caught the look, 'I can take a hint. I'll make myself scarce.' She made up the mug of coffee and handed it to Gavin. 'I've got to come up with some more funnies for my show tonight, any road.'

Jamie leaned his bottom against the work surface and folded his arms. 'Yeah, how's it all going? Did the newspaper review help?'

'A bit. I'm playing to about half capacity now, but it's still a struggle.' She smiled at the two men. 'But that's my problem, in't it? I'll let you get on with yer own.'

As she closed the door behind her, Gavin looked questioningly at his young client. 'What problem are we about to discuss now, Jamie?'

Walking back to the table, Jamie pulled out a chair, spun it around to face Gavin and sat down. 'Well,' he started, and then, with a brief shake of his head, he leaned forward on his knees. 'Gavin, you are *not* going to believe who I've got sleeping in the free bedroom.'

'Tell me.'

'Are you ready for this?'

'I'm all ears, Jamie,' Gavin replied, taking a sip from his coffee cup.

'Angélique Pascal.'

Gavin almost choked on his coffee. He hurriedly set his mug down and took a handkerchief from his jacket pocket.

'I think you're having your leg pulled, lad,' Gavin laughed, wiping his mouth.

'It's no joke, Gavin.'

Gavin stared at Jamie open-mouthed. 'Are you really being *serious*, Jamie?'

'Yeah, course I am.'

'In that case . . .' Gavin shook his head, momentarily lost for words, '. . . what in the name of goodness is she doing here?' He cast a calculating eye over Jamie's state of undress. 'You haven't, erm, become . . . involved with—'

'No, of course not,' Jamie remonstrated. 'It's nothing like that. I met her in a café last night, and me and this other girl ended up taking her to hospital, and then afterwards . . .'

'You had to take her to *hospital*? Why?'

'She'd cut her hand quite badly.'

'Her hand?' Gavin's eyes suddenly clouded over with consummate concern and he shook his head slowly. 'Oh, no, Jamie, she can't have cut her hand. Not *her* hand.'

Jamie bit at his bottom lip. 'Yeah, I know what you mean. That's why *she* was so terrified to go to the hospital. She really thought she was going to be told she'd never be able to play the violin again. However, as it turned out, it wasn't nearly as bad as it looked. The doctor said no tendons had been touched and that the swelling in her fingers would soon go, so I reckon she won't be out of action for too long . . . probably won't do anything else at the festival this year, though.'

'*You* reckon, Jamie? I'd be more interested in hearing the doctor's considered opinion.'

Jamie paused for a moment, caught in the solicitor's steely glare. 'Actually, Gavin, we never mentioned to the doctor that Angélique was a violinist. In fact, I did something that's probably against the law. I gave her a false name when we registered her at the hospital.'

'You did *what*?'

'Listen, she insisted on it. I couldn't go against that. She said she didn't want anyone to know who she was, because she was frightened the press would find out about her injury, and . . . she didn't want her whereabouts to be known either.'

Gavin tried to unscramble the baffling rationale behind the violinist's presence in the flat.

'Jamie . . . Jamie,' he stuttered, holding up his hands as if trying to steady his thought process. 'I'm completely in the dark as to what is going on, so could you please just start at the beginning and tell me everything that happened last night?'

'OK, but it could take some time. I was up until five o'clock this morning listening to the whole saga.'

Gavin nodded. 'Right,' he said, pushing himself up from the sofa. 'I think I'd better cancel all my appointments for this morning.' He thumped at the pockets of his suit jacket. 'Hell, I must have left my mobile in the car. Can I use your telephone?'

Jamie pointed at the door. 'It's out there on the sideboard.'

When Gavin had left the kitchen, Jamie got up and went to make himself his customary second black coffee of the morning. As he poured water into the mug, he heard a single knock on the door and turned to see Leonard Hartson standing outside in the hall with a tall, straggly-haired youth peering over his shoulder.

'I thought I'd let you know I have found myself an assistant,' Leonard said, 'due to the kind endeavours of your solicitor. I just wanted to thank you for putting the word around so promptly.'

'Glad it all worked out, Mr Hartson,' Jamie replied, carrying his coffee over to the door and leaning a shoulder on the doorpost. 'Hope all goes well for you. Are you going to start filming today?'

'No, not yet. My immediate plan is to give young Thomas here a crash course on all the equipment.' The cameraman turned and smiled up at the youth. 'It'll be a steep learning curve, but I am counting on my new assistant to be a very fast learner.'

Jamie gave Thomas a friendly smile which went unreciprocated. Studying the gormless expression on the assistant's face, it struck him that Thomas looked anything *but* a fast learner. 'Well, best of luck then, to you both.'

As he watched the two move off towards the front door, Jamie was taken by the almost comical incongruity of this new partnership, the tall lanky figure of the new assistant, with his threadbare hooded sweatshirt and baggy jeans worn at half mast, towering menacingly over the diminutive but dapperly dressed figure of the elderly cameraman. And then, for the second time in so many hours, Jamie found himself searching his mind for some glimmer of identification, knowing that there was something vaguely familiar about the boy – especially, for some reason, from the back view.

'Right,' said Gavin Mackintosh, taking a diary and pen from his inside pocket as he pushed purposefully past Jamie into the kitchen. 'The rest of the morning is yours, Jamie my lad, so shut the door behind you and let's be having the whole story.'

An hour later Jamie welcomed the chance to rest his voice as Gavin, with brow furrowed, sat in silence leafing through the copious notes he had written in the back of his diary.

'And that's about it, is it?' the solicitor asked eventually, glaring seriously at Jamie over his spectacles. 'She told you nothing else?'

'Well, it's not word for word, but near enough.'

When Gavin once more resumed the examination of his notes, Jamie began drumming his fingers on the table. 'So what do you think we should do?' he prompted quietly, eager to know what was going through the solicitor's mind.

Lobbing the diary on to the table, Gavin took off his spectacles and twirled them back and forth in his fingers as he stared thoughtfully out of the window. 'A very good question, Jamie. A very good question.' He let out a long sigh. 'I don't think anything can be done until I've spoken with Angélique myself and ascertained exactly what course of action she wants to take.'

Jamie pushed himself to his feet. 'I'll go and wake her then.'

'That would be the best idea,' Gavin replied, 'and if you wouldn't mind, I think I should speak to her myself. There could be some quite complicated legal procedures involved in this whole affair, and consequently it should remain as confidential as possible.'

'OK,' Jamie replied, quite content in letting Gavin take on responsibility for Angélique. 'Do you want me to do anything?'

'Not immediately, but I'd suggest you head off and get yourself showered and dressed, because I could well be in need of your assistance after I've spoken to her.'

Five minutes later, Jamie ushered Angélique into the kitchen. Her eyes were drowsy and the oversized dressing gown she was wearing trailed behind her across the flagstoned floor like the train of a wedding dress.

'She's a bit out of it, I'm afraid,' Jamie said. 'The doctor gave her some pretty strong painkillers last night.'

As Jamie settled her on a chair, Gavin smiled kindly at the violinist to put her at her ease, but his eyes were registering deep anger at the sight of the purply-black bruise that spread down one side of her face and the white elastic bandage that was bound around the palm of her left hand. He waited for Jamie to leave the kitchen before he sat down opposite her.

'Angélique, I don't know if you remember me, but my name is Gavin Mackintosh. We met the other night at the reception at the Sheraton Grand.'

'*Bien sûr,*' she replied woozily. 'You are the lawman.'

'That's absolutely right.'

Angélique's attention drifted to her unfamiliar surroundings and she gazed foggily around the kitchen before fixing Gavin with a look of bewilderment. 'What are *you* doing here? You do not live in this place as well, do you?'

Gavin laughed. 'No, I don't.'

The drowsiness faded instantly from the violinist's face and she glared at him, wide-eyed with panic. 'Then who told you I was here?' she exclaimed, pushing herself clumsily to her feet. 'How did you find out?'

'It's all right, Angélique,' Gavin said in a slow, calming voice, holding up his hands to steady her anxiety. 'You are perfectly safe. Nobody knows you are here, except Jamie and myself.'

Gavin fixed himself with his most reassuring smile as she studied his face to try to detect any sign of deception, and then, very slowly, she sat back down on her chair.

'Let me explain,' Gavin said, leaning forward on the table and interlocking his fingers. 'It just happens by chance that I am Jamie's solicitor. I have been a friend of his father for many years, and consequently have always handled the family's legal affairs. Now Jamie, quite rightly, was going to call me to ask advice about your . . . predicament, but it just happened that I had to pay him a visit this morning for a completely different reason.'

The violinist took in a faltering breath. 'So now Jamie has told you the whole story,' she said quietly.

'Yes, he has.'

'He is a very kind person.'

Gavin nodded. 'You were extremely lucky to bump into him last night.'

'I know that,' Angélique breathed out almost indiscernibly. 'I had been to so many places before, but they were all filled with a lot of people and a lot of noise, and I just wanted to be alone. I saw the café was empty when I passed by, so I went in. I did not realise it was about to close. Martha was very kind also, because she kept it open for me and she drove us to the hospital.'

'But Martha wasn't present when you told your story to Jamie?'

'No, she had gone home, but when she dropped us off at the hospital, Jamie made her promise not to say a word about me to anyone. He was quite . . . *brusque* with her. I do not think he likes her very much.'

At that moment, Gavin had no interest in Jamie's likes and dislikes. His greatest concern was for this vulnerable young girl whose world, in the past twelve hours, had been turned upside down and whose trust in her manager, tutor and companion had been decimated. He let out a long, disheartened sigh. 'Angélique, I am so sorry this has happened to you.'

Angélique averted her eyes from the solicitor and began fiddling with the cord of the dressing gown.

'How does your hand feel today?'

She shrugged her shoulders. 'It is quite sore.'

'I'm sure it is.' Gavin stroked a finger thoughtfully across his mouth. 'Angélique, I know this is a difficult question to put to you, but I'm afraid that it has to be asked. What action do you wish to take against your manager, Mr Dessuin?'

She jerked her head up and looked at him questioningly. 'What do you mean?'

'Well, I know that he has been your tutor and manager for many years, but in my opinion I think his immediate actions would suggest that he could well pose a real threat to you in the future, and accordingly my advice would be that we seek a restraining order against him as soon as possible.'

'How would you do that?'

'You and I would have to go to the court here in Edinburgh to ask for what is called an interim interdict.'

'I would then be in the newspapers?'

'It's not usual for the press to be at the initial hearing, but of course I can't guarantee that, especially when the case involves someone who is as much in the public eye as yourself.'

'Then I cannot let it happen.'

Leaning back in his chair, Gavin folded his arms and puffed out his cheeks. 'Can I ask you why not, Angélique? My real concern is that he might well try to repeat his actions of last night.'

Angélique shook her head. 'You do not understand Albert Dessuin. He is very . . . how would you say . . . complex?'

'I'm sure he must be, judging from what he's done to you.'

'No, what I am meaning is that I understand him very well, even though he probably would never believe it. If something bad was to be written about him in the newspapers, I know he would do something very stupid.'

'In what way?'

Angélique paused momentarily. 'He would probably try to harm himself.'

'You mean he would attempt suicide?'

Angélique shrugged. 'It is very possible. It is in the family, after all, because I found out that his own father had killed himself. And, besides that, there are so many *irrationalités* in Albert's head. I know, because I have been subjected to every one of them during the years we have been together. So, even though he treated me so badly last night, I cannot do anything to hurt him. It would always then be my fault.'

Gavin scratched frustratedly at his forehead. 'But you must understand I cannot allow you to leave Edinburgh with him. It would then be *my* fault if something were to happen to *you*.'

The violinist shook her head. 'I will not be leaving Edinburgh with Albert. It is all finished between us. I decided that even before I left my hotel bedroom.'

'And what will you do? Tour the world by yourself?'

Angélique appeared uncertain. 'I suppose I will have to find another manager.'

'But what about Dessuin, Angélique? You are a famous person. It wouldn't be difficult for him to find out where you are at any time of the day or night. You said yourself he is a complex person, and your leaving him could well spark off considerable paranoia in his mind – and if that were to be the case, you would never be safe from him.'

Angélique looked up at the solicitor with sad eyes. 'I know this, but I can never be the reason for him doing harm to himself.'

Gavin leaned back heavily in the chair and folded his arms. 'So, what *are* we to do then?' he murmured. 'What *are* we to do?'

'I do not know,' Angélique mumbled in reply.

Gavin got up from the table and began to pace the floor. 'OK, I shall reluctantly leave that issue aside for now. What we have to do, as a matter of urgency, is somehow break the news that you won't be playing tonight, nor probably for the rest of the festival. Because of the present circumstances with Dessuin, we must do it in such a way that nobody need know what really happened, and we certainly should not reveal your whereabouts.' He waved his hands as he thought. 'We could just say you've cut your hand in an unfortunate accident and you've had to return home to France to recover.' He pondered this for a moment. 'Actually, that's not such a bad idea. It might even act as a red herring for Dessuin.'

'A herring? What is that?'

'A false trail. It'll certainly get him away from the hotel and, at best, out of the country. You do have your passport with you, don't you?'

'Yes, it is in my handbag.'

'Good. That means he could quite easily take the bait. The only problem is your clothes. Jamie said you left everything in the hotel bedroom.'

'And my violin as well.'

'And the key to your room?'

'I left it there too,' Angélique replied sheepishly.

Gavin shook his head. 'Not to worry. We'll just have to find a way of getting everything out of your room while Dessuin is not about.' He blew out an anxious breath. 'My word, the plot thickens by the minute, doesn't it?' he murmured.

'Gavin, will I really be returning to France?'

'Well, it's entirely up to you, Angélique, but I would suggest it would be better if, for now, you just stayed here in Edinburgh and kept a very low profile. It'll give you time to recover, and at the same time it'll give *me* the chance to monitor Dessuin while you're still under my watchful eye.'

'But where would I stay?'

'No better place than where you are right now. I don't think it would be very wise for you to come to my house under the present circumstances. I'm quite seriously bending the rules of my profession with all this subterfuge, so it's better if I'm seen to be taking more of an impartial stance. Anyway, nobody else is using that bedroom you slept in last night, and I know for a fact Jamie's going to be around until the end of

September. I don't think you'd find anyone better to look after you.'

'But he might not want me to stay. I could make his life quite difficult with so much secrecy.'

Gavin smiled at her. 'I'll have a word with him. I'm sure he'd be more than delighted.'

'I could pay him, of course.'

Gavin clicked the fingers of both hands simultaneously. 'Jumping Jupiter, there's a problem.' He sat back down on the chair, clenching his fists together on the table. 'Angélique, does Dessuin handle your finances?'

The violinist shook her head. 'No, everything is managed by the lawyers of Madame Lafitte in Clermont Ferrand. They give me an allowance each month and pay Albert his salary.'

Gavin puffed out a breath of relief. 'Well, that's one thing less to worry about, but we'll have to notify them in due course.' He pushed himself to his feet once more. 'So what about this story we've concocted for the press? Would you agree to it?'

'Yes, I think it would be a good idea.'

'Right,' Gavin said, walking over to the window and gazing down at the bustling activity in London Street. 'So, all that remains for me to do is to find a journalist with a bit of integrity.' He gave a short, cynical laugh. 'Now, that is a tall order.'

Angélique sat in silence for a moment, her brow creased in thought. 'I know of a man, a journalist, here in Edinburgh. He has been trying to interview me for many years, but Albert would not allow it. Maybe we could ask for his help?'

'Do you know his name?'

The violinist stared up at the ceiling. '*Qu'est-que c'est? Qu'est-que c'est?* He met us at the airport.' She held up her hand as a name flashed into her mind. 'Will, I think is his surname. No, Wills. He is called Harry Wills. He seems to be a nice man, although I know that he does not care much for Albert.'

Gavin nodded. 'Good, sounds like the perfect contact.' He bent over the table and wrote down the journalist's name in his diary. 'I don't know him personally, but I've read his articles in the *Sunday Times*. I'll see if I can arrange a meeting with him straightaway, because it's imperative that we get this story into the *Evening News* tonight. I'm also going to ask Mr Wills to liaise with the International office as well. They'll need to be told as soon as possible so that they can arrange for another soloist for the concert tonight.'

A sudden pinpoint of clarity shone in Angélique's eyes. 'Of course, he must speak with Tess Goodwin. Do you remember her?'

Gavin stared bemusedly at her for a moment. 'No, should I?'

'She was the person I was speaking to at the reception when you came to talk to me.'

Gavin nodded. 'Ah, yes.'

'She works at the International office and she has become a friend of mine. I was going to call her on the telephone last night, but I was frightened the true story would then be put in the newspapers.'

Gavin wrote down the second name in his diary. 'Yes, I think you were probably wise not to call her. We won't involve Tess right now.' He slipped both the diary and the pen into the inside pocket of his jacket. 'The only other person I am going to tell about this incident is my doctor, who is a good and trusted friend of mine. I'll get him to come round to see you and he'll be able to keep an eye on that very special hand of yours.' He smiled at the young violinist. 'Now, I want you to take yourself back to bed and rest well, and don't worry about a thing. We have it all under control now. If you want to contact me at any time, just speak to Jamie. In the meantime, I'll make sure he looks after you.'

As he turned to leave, Angélique got up from her chair and moved across the room towards him, putting a hand on his arm. 'Gavin?'

'Yes?'

'I was very lucky to meet you at the reception the other night. Thank you for being such a kind friend.'

Gavin grinned broadly at her. 'My dear,' he said, 'the circumstances are not what I would wish for, but it is indeed a pleasure to be of some assistance to you.'

Twenty-Seven

Albert Dessuin sat slumped forward on the chair in his bedroom, his throbbing head cradled in shaking hands, trying desperately to trawl through his befuddled thoughts for some recollection of what had taken place the previous night. Coming round from his alcoholic stupor, he had found himself on the floor of Angélique's bedroom, but his memory of the events that had led him to being there had been completely wiped out. Evidence only showed that Angélique's bed linen was rumpled, but not slept in, and the bottle of whisky he must have consumed was in two pieces in the wastepaper basket in his own room.

He tried to convince himself that nothing untoward had happened. He always drank in private – he had never allowed Angélique to see him in an inebriated state – so maybe he had come into her room last night just to check on her, and found she wasn't there. But if that was the case, where was she now? No, it was more likely he had only been lying there for an hour or two and that Angélique had risen early from her bed and had left the room before he had come in. But then that didn't add up either. She had not slept in her bed – unless she had made it up herself. And, why would she do that in a hotel?

He got to his feet and moved slowly across the room to the bathroom, clutching his arms around his shivering body. A cold shower was what he needed. It always helped to clear his head.

At the top of Lawnmarket in the Old Town, on the fourth floor of the Hub, Tess Goodwin sat at her desk in the International Festival office, listening, open-mouthed with disbelief, to the gravelly male voice at the other end of the telephone line. When she ended the call, neither a word of thanks nor salutation passed her lips. She was too shocked to speak.

Getting to her feet, she moved around the desk and hurried over to the door that led into Sir Alasdair Dreyfuss's office. His meeting with Sarah Atkinson and the morose director of the Estonian National Symphony Orchestra was scheduled to run for another half-hour, but this was something that definitely could not wait. She gave one cursory knock on the door and walked in without waiting for a reply.

Both Alasdair Dreyfuss and Sarah Atkinson looked up at her immediately, enquiry and annoyance in their eyes, while the Estonian turned his corpulent figure around in the armchair with a flatulent squeak of leather.

'I think you might have your time wrong, Tess,' Alasdair Dreyfuss said pointedly, pushing back the cuff of his shirt and consulting his wristwatch. 'I said we wouldn't be free until midday.'

'I'm sorry to interrupt, Alasdair, but something extremely important has come up, and I wonder if I might just have a couple of minutes with you and Sarah.'

'Can't it wait, Tess?' Sarah asked tersely, but she was stopped from enquiring further by a hand on her arm from the director, who could tell from the troubled expression on his marketing assistant's face that something was seriously amiss.

'Valdek, would you please excuse us for two minutes,' he said, getting to his feet. 'I do apologise for this.'

The man in the leather armchair gave his consent with a flick of his pawlike hand, and both Alasdair Dreyfuss and Sarah Atkinson followed Tess out of the room and into the open-plan office.

'Now, what's wrong, Tess?' the director asked, as he closed the door behind him.

'I've just had a journalist on the phone who says that Angélique Pascal had an accident last night. She's cut her hand pretty badly and she's heading back to France.'

'What?' her two superiors exclaimed in unison.

'He said the story's going to be on the front page of the _Evening News_ tonight, and that he was only telephoning the international office to give us warning so we could find another soloist to take over from Angélique Pascal at tonight's concert and rearrange our programme for the rest of the festival.'

'Is this genuine information, Tess?' Sarah Atkinson asked. 'Who was the journalist?'

'He didn't give his name, and I'm afraid I didn't recognise his voice.' Tess shook her head. 'I can't believe this has happened. I spent the whole evening at the reception with her last night. She was going to come out afterwards with Allan and me, but then her manager spirited her away.'

'Maybe it's some kind of hoax, then,' Sarah Atkinson said, glancing between Tess and the director.

Alasdair Dreyfuss stood staring intently at Tess, lost in thought as he chewed on the nail of a forefinger. 'We've got to take it as being true,' he said eventually. He turned to his marketing director. 'Sarah, you head back to my office and give my humblest apologies to our Estonian friend and finish off the meeting with him, and once you've done that, get hold of Julia Parfitt and put her on standby for tonight's performance.'

'What are you going to do, Alasdair?' Sarah Atkinson asked.

'First off, I'm calling the _Evening News_ to see if they're genuinely going to run with this story, and if so, then I want to get hold of Albert Dessuin and ask him what the hell is going on and why he hasn't let me know about this sooner.' He took off his spectacles and rubbed a hand across his face. 'Dammit, I thought everything was going too smoothly.'

Albert Dessuin stood in the middle of the hotel dining room and scanned the few tables that were still occupied for breakfast. Apprehension gripped at his stomach when he realised Angélique was not there, and he hurried out of the room and down the stairs to the reception area. There was a queue of people shuffling their suitcases forward as they waited to check out, but he bypassed them and went straight up to the desk.

'Excuse me,' he said ungraciously to the young female receptionist who was trying unsuccessfully to swipe a credit card.

'I'm sorry, sir,' she replied with a smile, 'but there is a queue I'm afraid you'll have to wait your turn.'

'I have not time to wait. You must tell me, have you seen Angélique Pascal this morning?'

The girl looked questioningly at him. 'Do you mean the violinist, sir?'

'Of course I mean the violinist. There is no one else of that name staying here, is there?'

Dessuin's tone made the receptionist's face colour. 'I'm sorry, sir, I've only just come on duty, and I certainly haven't seen her this morning.'

Dessuin snorted angrily. 'Well, then, who *was* on duty? I need to speak to them immediately.'

'I'll see if I can find out, sir.' She smiled apologetically at the couple with whom she was dealing and walked off to the door at the side of the desk. Before entering the room, she turned back to Dessuin. 'Can I ask who you are, sir?'

'I'm her manager, Albert Dessuin. Now go and find out if anyone knows where she is. This could be a very serious matter, you know.'

'Excuse me, Mr Dessuin,' a voice said from the far end of the reception desk.

Albert turned to the other receptionist, who stood with her hand cupped over the mouthpiece of a telephone. The expectant guests in the queue were now regarding him with increasing impatience.

'Yes?'

'There's a telephone call for you.'

'*Enfin!*' Dessuin exclaimed, striding along the desk and causing the man at the front of the queue to take a hurried step back to avoid being forcibly thrust out of the way. 'Thank you,' he said to the receptionist, jerking the receiver from her hand, and

214

meeting her surprised look with the thinnest crease of a courteous smile. He turned his back on his hostile audience. 'Angélique, where the hell are you?' he hissed into the receiver.

'Oh, so *you* obviously don't know what's happened, then, do you?' a man's voice replied.

'Who is this?' Dessuin demanded.

'It's Alasdair Dreyfuss, Albert.'

For a moment Dessuin stood speechless, his eyes screwed up tight with embarasssment. 'Ah, Alasdair – I apologise,' he stuttered out eventually. 'I have had rather a bad morning. I did not mean to be so abrupt with you.'

'What on earth is going on, Albert?'

'I'm sorry?'

He heard the director let out a sigh of impatience. 'Albert, I have just been on the telephone to the *Evening News* and they are about to run a front-page piece about Angélique Pascal.'

'No – no, that could not be right.'

'It's very right, I'm afraid, Albert. Seemingly Angélique had an accident last night. She cut her hand quite badly and is flying back to Paris as we speak, which of course means she'll be unable to fulfil her commitments here at the festival. How on earth did you not know about all this, Albert . . . Albert? . . . are you still there?'

The words of the director of the International Festival were enough to start clearing the fog of alcoholic amnesia from Dessuin's brain. He saw Angélique's naked form flash into his mind, the raised hand coming down with force on the side of her face. He slowly clenched and unclenched his fist, noticing a tightness in the skin on the back of his fingers which he had not noticed before. 'Oh, no,' he murmured, dropping the receiver limply to his side. 'Oh, no, what have I done?'

'Albert, for God's sake, are you still there?' Alasdair Dreyfuss's distant voice asked again.

Dessuin slowly brought the receiver back to his ear. 'Yes,' he replied weakly.

'This has put me in an extremely difficult position, you know,

Albert. It's one thing rearranging the late concerts for next week, but trying to find another soloist at the eleventh hour for the concert tonight . . . well, it really would have helped if you—'

As if in a trance, Dessuin reached across the desk and dropped the receiver back onto its cradle. He turned and walked across the reception area to one of the chairs that were grouped around a low glass-topped coffee table and sat down. Covering his face with his hands, he began to piece together all the missing scenes of what had taken place the previous night, and then tears of remorse and shame began to flow. 'Oh, Angélique,' he sobbed quietly to himself, 'I did not mean to hurt you. I never wished to hurt you. Please do not tell anyone I have done this terrible thing. *Please* do not tell.'

He felt a hand press lightly on his shoulder. 'Are you all right, sir?' a female voice asked.

Dessuin uncovered his face and looked up at the young receptionist who had left to find out about Angélique's whereabouts. 'I am fine, thank you,' he replied in a quavering voice.

'I'm afraid I can't get hold of any of the receptionists who were on duty last night.'

Dessuin shook his head. 'It does not matter now.' He reached for the girl's hand and held it tight. 'Would you do something else for me, please?'

'Of course, sir,' the girl replied in an uncertain voice as she eyed her clamped hand.

'Angélique cannot leave without me. I need to find her.'

'I know, sir,' she replied quietly. 'We're doing everything possible.'

'No, what I mean is, can you please find out for me what flights leave from Edinburgh to Paris today?'

There was relief in the girl's smile on seeing her chance to get away from the strange Frenchman. 'Yes, sir. I'll get on to the Internet straightaway.'

'Thank you very much,' Dessuin said, releasing her hand. 'I will go to my room now.' Pushing himself to his feet, he made his way across to the stairs and began to climb them, moving like an old man, every tread an effort as he dragged himself up on the broad wooden banister rail. Halfway up, his mobile rang and he eagerly glanced at the screen, hoping that it would be Angélique.

It was not. He continued to climb the stairs, allowing the mobile to ring in his hand, not answering until he reached the next floor. He pressed the 'receive' button as he walked along the thick-carpeted corridor towards the lift. '*Bonjour, Maman. Ça va?*'

The other four people in the lift would hardly have known he was engaged in a telephone call had it not been for the fact that he had his mobile held to his ear. He never spoke, but listened with an empty, forlorn expression on his face. When the lift eventually stopped at his floor, he walked out and waited for the doors to close.

'Listen to me, you spoiled old woman. When will you ever consider how I am feeling? You never do. Never, *never!*'

He punched the button to end the call and dropped the mobile into his pocket, and as he walked along the corridor to his room he felt the weight of hopelessness and despair bear down upon him, realising that he had now succeeded in alienating himself from the only two people who played any part in his sad, pathetic life. Just as his father had done.

Twenty-Eight

In the middle of the vast empty warehouse deep in the docklands of Leith, Thomas Keene junior sat uneasily on the silver camera box, a look of painful concentration on his face as he felt around in the black changing bag on his lap, attempting to load the dummy roll of film into the camera magazine for about the twentieth time in the past hour. He glanced at the wristwatch Leonard Hartson had left hanging on a light stand for him to time his progress, but it only served to remind him that it was nearly three o'clock in the afternoon and his stomach was aching with hunger.

He shut his eyes trying to envisage what his fingers were doing inside the bag as he threaded the film through the slot into the pick-up chamber of the magazine and doubled over the end so that it sat tight in the spool before clicking the spring catch closed. When he thought all was in place, he pulled his arms free from the constraints of the elasticated armsholes, just as the fire door at the far side of the warehouse opened and banged shut again, stretching a momentary beam of bright sunlight out across the floor. Pulling back the Velcro flap on the changing bag, T.K. watched Leonard Hartson pick his way over the electric cables, ducking to avoid the lights that they had already set up earlier that day.

'There you are,' the cameraman said, handing T.K. a brown paper bag and a can of Sprite. 'Two ham-and-cheese rolls.' He sat down opposite T.K. on a long lighting box. 'How did you get on this time?'

'I think ah've go' it,' T.K. replied, putting the black bag to one side and making to flick back the ring pull on the can.

'Don't do that yet,' Leonard said sharply.

T.K. glared at Leonard. 'How no?'

The cameraman pointed a meaningful finger at his assistant. 'Another golden rule, Thomas. Never handle food or drink while you're loading a film magazine. If one single foreign body gets into that changing bag, it could gum up the whole roll of film.'

'Ah've finished loadin' onyways.'

'No, you haven't. What did I tell you? Magazine out of the bag, check it's secure, tape it up and write on it the stock number and film roll. That's the order of things.'

T.K. let out a disgruntled sigh and, with great deliberation, put down his can and picked up the black bag.

'I'm sorry, Thomas,' Leonard chuckled. 'I told you it was going to be a steep learning curve.' He leaned across and gave the boy a solid pat on his knee. 'But don't worry, you're doing well.

You've had more thrown at you in one day than many assistants would have to learn in about a month.'

T.K. undid the zip on the changing bag and pulled out the magazine. As he placed it on his knee, the cover on the load reel fell off in his hand. 'Aw, *shite!*' He glanced apprehensively at Leonard. 'Ah mean, sorry.'

Leonard raised an admonishing eyebrow. 'Don't worry. It's only an end-roll, but remember, you must check the cover plate is fitted securely into its grooves before you lock it. If you'd just loaded that magazine with an unexposed roll, we would've had to throw it away.'

'Ah'm no' goin' tae get a-haud o' this,' T.K. murmured solemnly.

Leonard studied the boy's face for a moment, trying to judge the meaning of T.K.'s last sentence by the expression on his face. Eventually, he just shook his head. 'Thomas, if our partnership is to work successfully over the next couple of weeks, I think it's going to be of paramount importance that we understand what we're saying to each other. Now, please believe me, I'm not saying anything derogatory about the Scottish accent and it is probably my fault entirely that I have never taken the time to study the colloquial intricacies . . .' He stopped mid-sentence when he saw a broad grin stretch across T.K.'s face. 'What's the smile for?'

'Are ye saying that ye cannot understand what I am sayin'?' T.K. asked, mouthing out the words in laborious fashion.

Leonard nodded. 'That, I'm afraid, is exactly what I'm saying.'

'That's good, 'cos I wis goin' tae say the same thing tae you.'

They eyed each other for a moment before both burst out laughing, rocking back on their makeshift seats.

'Well,' Leonard said eventually, taking a handkerchief from the breast pocket of his jacket and wiping a trickling tear from his cheek. 'I think we might have just had a breakthrough there, Thomas.'

Still smiling, T.K. carefully pulled the film out of the magazine and placed everything back in the changing bag. 'You can call me T.K.,' he mumbled as he refastened the zip and pressed down the Velcro flap.

'What was that?' Leonard asked.

'T.K.' His cheeks flushed with embarrassment as he once more pushed his hands through the elasticated armholes. 'All my friends call me tha'.'

In that instant, Leonard realised there had been more than just a breakthrough in their language barrier. 'In that case, I would be delighted to call you T.K.'

'Ah think ah've got the hang o' this now.'

'All right,' Leonard said, reaching out to take his wristwatch from the light stand. 'I'll time you.'

Just under two minutes later, T.K. pulled his hands free of the changing bag, opened it up and held the loaded film magazine out to Leonard. First checking that the covers were secure, the cameraman then opened up both sides to make certain the threading of the film was correct.

'Perfect. Couldn't have done better myself,' he said, handing the magazine back to T.K. 'After you've had your lunch, you can have a go at loading the real McCoy.'

Whilst Thomas Keene junior had happily found gainful employment that day, the case was not the same for Rene Brownlow's husband, Gary, in Hartlepool. Having dropped Robbie and Karen off at their school in the morning, he had taken a bus downtown and spent the best part of the day sitting in the Employment Exchange staring vacantly at the plethora of posters that told of the consequences of being caught 'working on the fly' while drawing unemployment benefits. Then, when his long-awaited interview eventually did take place, he had to leave halfway through to get back to the school to pick up the kids again. His parents were busy that afternoon, his father at his mate's allotment, his mother doing the weekly shop at Morrison's, so he had no alternative other than to head back into town with the kids in tow.

When he entered Andersons Westbourne Social Club, his

immediate impression was that the spacious lounge bar was completely deserted. There was nobody up at the bar and the two women who stood behind it were idly chatting away before both turned at the sound of the swing doors banging shut. It was only when he heard the clink of dominoes from the table near the stage at the far end of the room that he surmised that some, if not all, of Rene's 'Fringe committee', were there.

He walked over to the bar and shot a wink at the elder of the two women. 'Hi, Mags. I 'ope ye don't mind me bringing the kids in. I just wanted to see Terry Crosland for a moment.'

'Aye, they'll be fine,' Mags replied. 'Mr Prendergast is away for the day, so ye've got nowt to worry about.' She glanced over Gary's shoulder and her glossy lipsticked mouth stretched into a broad grin. 'Was it just Terry ye wanted to see, or the whole bang shooting match?'

Gary turned round to find that the five domino players had left their table and had come to gather around him, their faces alight with enquiry.

''Ave ye 'eard 'ow Rene's doing?' Stan Morris, the self-appointed chairman of the committee, asked.

'All right,' Gary replied noncommittally, catching Terry's eye and greeting him with a brief nod.

' 'As she been on telly yet?' Skittle asked, squinting up at Gary through his bottle glasses.

'No, not yet.'

'Give 'er a chance!' Stan Morris said, glaring at Skittle. 'It takes time to build up fame.' He pushed his hands into the pockets of his tweed jacket. 'Now, I remember the time I appeared on the television—'

He was interrupted by sombre Derek Marsham's disparaging laugh. 'We all know about that one, don't we? All ye did was walk back and forth behind the reporter when 'e was doing that bit on the marina, just so ye could get yer ugly mug broadcast.'

Stan Morris's face puffed with indignation. 'I'll 'ave ye know that I was asked to be—'

'All right, let's give it a rest, lads,' Terry Crosland cut in, pushing past Stan and leaving him to swallow his explanation. He gave young Robbie's hair a firm ruffle. 'Ye're wanting a word with me, mate,' he said to Rene's husband.

'Aye, if ye can spare a couple of minutes.' Gary replied, glancing briefly at the other members of the committee, who pressed claustrophobically around them.

Terry turned to his fellow domino players and waved his raised hands towards their table, as if guiding back a reversing car. 'Go on, lads, just get on with the game. I'll be over once I'm through talking with Gary.'

'But what if it concerns Rene?' Stan blustered out. 'I am the chairman—'

'I know y'are, Stan,' Terry interjected in a quiet, diplomatic tone, 'and if any part of our discussion might have some relevance to those business matters over which you 'ave jurisdiction, then of course I will inform you of them accordingly.'

'Right,' Stan said, shrugging up his tweedy shoulders importantly. 'That's fair enough. Come on, lads, let's return to the table and allow Terry time to converse with Gary.'

'Sorry about that,' Terry said to Gary once he had seen the four members of the committee settle themselves back at the table. 'Stan likes to do things by the book.'

'Might be better if someone 'it 'im over the 'ead with one.'

Terry laughed. 'Aye, ye might be right.' He leaned an elbow on the bar. 'Fancy a pint or summat?'

'Just a Coke would do me, thanks.'

'And what about you lot?' Terry asked, looking down at Gary's children. 'Shall we make it four rounds of Coca-Cola?'

Robbie and Karen nodded in agreement to the idea.

Terry turned to the bar girl. 'Mags, make it four glasses of Coca-Cola and give the kids a set of those darts ye keep behind the bar. They can knock 'ell out of the dartboard for a moment while Gary and I have a chat.'

The two men carried their glasses over to the table in the furthest corner from where the game of dominoes had resumed and sat down.

'So, 'ow 'ave things been with you?' Terry asked. 'Any luck yet on the job front?'

Gary shook his head. 'Not yet.' He lit up a cigarette and then looked around the interior of Andy's, as if embarrassed to make eye contact with Terry. 'Listen, mate, I never said owt to you that day we put Rene on the train, but the first thing I want to do is to apologise for being bloody rude that time ye came round to see 'er. I 'ad no right.'

Terry waved his hand dismissively. 'No need to do that, lad. As I said then, I understand your situation.'

'Aye, maybe, but ye shouldn't 'ave been the one to cop the flak for my frustration.'

'Enough said,' replied Terry, taking a drink from his glass. 'So 'ave you 'eard from 'er?'

'Aye, I 'ave.'

''Ow's she getting on?'

'Not too good, I don't think.'

'Oh?' Terry leaned forward on the table, a look of concern on his thin face. 'What's gone wrong?'

'It's just not working for her. I spoke to 'er two nights ago and she said she's not getting the punters coming to 'er show and she's dead worried she's going to end up 'aving to foot the bill at the end of the run.'

'She don't 'ave to worry about that!' Terry exclaimed. 'That's all taken care of!'

'Aye, well, that's just one of 'er problems. She's living in some bloody awful out-of-the-way place and she 'as to be out of the 'ouse for most of the day.'

'Can't she find some place else to stay?'

'She was going to 'ead off this morning to see if she could find out about that, but I tell you, Terry, it took all me limited powers of persuasion to stop 'er from packing 'er bags and coming 'ome.'

'Oh, bloody 'ell,' Terry murmured, running a hand lightly over his Teddy-boy quiff. 'That doesn't sound too good, does it?'

'Not really.'

'Mind you, there's another week and an 'alf to go. If she can stick it out, things could change.'

Gary shrugged. 'Aye, they could, but it's my way of thinking what she could do with is a bit of encouragement from the 'ome crowd.'

'What are ye saying?'

'Well, it's the last thing I can afford to do, but I'm going to take the kids up to Edinburgh at the weekend to go see Rene's show. Give 'er a bit of moral support, sort of thing.' He stubbed out his cigarette in the ashtray. 'I was wondering if ye might like to come with us.'

Terry repeatedly sucked on his teeth as he contemplated Gary's suggestion. 'Mate, I don't think there's any way I can make it this weekend. I've got that much work on. I don't suppose you could leave it until the following one?'

Gary's laugh had a cynical edge to it. 'There's nowt pressing in my life right now, Terry. I could make it any weekend. The only thing about that is we'd be only there for Rene's last show, but I don't suppose it would matter too much.'

'You could all travel back to 'Artlepool together then.'

'Aye, that's true.' He pulled another cigarette from the packet and lit it. 'OK, let's make it next weekend.'

Terry flicked his head towards the group of domino players at the far end of the room. 'What about that lot? I don't think I'd make myself that popular if I 'eld back on telling them our plans.'

Gary took a long drag on his cigarette. 'Tell 'em then. I don't mind if they all come. They deserve it, really, 'aving raised all that money for Rene. Anyway, it'll help swell 'er audience, even if it is only for the last night.' He drained his glass of Coca-Cola and got to his feet. 'Well, I'd better take the kids back to do their 'omework.'

''Ow're you planning on getting up to Edinburgh?' Terry asked.

'I 'adn't really thought. Probably by train, though I sure as 'ell can't afford it.'

'In that case, I suppose we could take me van. Strictly illegal, but I'm quite 'appy to risk it.'

'D'ye reckon it would make it?'

Terry laughed. 'Aye, I reckon. I'll do a bit of tinkering with the engine beforehand and get a new exhaust stuck on. It's long overdue.'

'We'll be needing to fix somewhere to stay as well, won't we?'

'That's true,' Terry replied, rubbing thoughtfully at his chin. 'I'll 'ave a word with Stan Morris. 'E's always going on about is great contacts, so let's see what 'e can come up with.'

Gary nodded and stuck out a hand to Terry. 'I appreciate yer elp, mate.'

Terry stood up and shook it. 'Don't think anything of it.' He looked over to the far table where the four other members of he committee were now staring at them expectantly. 'Well, I'd better get over there and give me report.' He shot a wink at Gary. 'I doubt there's going to be much dominoes played for he rest of the afternoon.'

Twenty-Nine

In the space of one day, the world had suddenly become a brighter place for Thomas Keene junior. That evening, having first accompanied Leonard Hartson back to his lodgings in a taxi, he now made his way across town to the hostel, walking with a purposeful spring in his step and his shoulders held high, a young man displaying an element of pride in himself.

And he had every reason to feel that way. Not only had he now found himself a job, he had also received considerable praise from his new boss in the way he had picked up so much technical information during the course of the day. 'I called it a steep learning curve,' the old cameraman had said to him in the taxi, 'but, so far, you seem to have diminished it to nothing more than a gentle incline.'

As he walked, T.K. went over in his head all the skills that he had learned that day. The loading of the magazine and how to slot it on to the back of the camera, the threading of the film in the camera gate, leaving the correct-sized loop above and below, the raising and lowering of the tripod legs and the levelling of the 'head', and the assembly of the lights on their stands. When he turned into the street where the hostel was situated, he was so preoccupied with his thoughts that he never clocked on to the two boys who were leaning against the railings on the opposite side of the street. As soon as they saw him, they began to make their move. They crossed over to meet him at a diagonal keeping their faces turned away to avoid recognition.

T.K. only became aware of their presence behind him when he had begun to climb the stone steps leading up to the door of the hostel. He felt a hand grabbing his arm, another on his shoulder and he was spun round and slammed against the railings with such force that he let out a scream of pain as the iron-work jarred against his spine. One of the boys took hold of the neck of his sweatshirt and twisted it in his hand, and T.K. found himself choking for breath as it tightened like a noose.

'Whit the fuck hae *you* been dain', ye bloody toe rag?' the boy said, his face contorted with hatred.

'Jeez, Lenny, let go,' T.K. gasped out in a high-pitched voice, his face beginning to turn puce. 'Ah cannae breathe.'

'Tha's the whole idea, ye wee bastard. Ma younger brither wis takin' aff by the polis this mornin', and guess wha the cause o' that wis?'

''Onest, Lenny, it wisnae—'

The other boy stepped forward and backhanded T.K. hard across the cheek. 'Dinnae ye try tae fuckin' well deny it, mon. A'body kens it wis you. The word's a-roond the estate, a' aboot you takin' videos o' the lads nickin' the cars.'

T.K.'s eyes filled with tears of terror and his legs gave way underneath him. He began to slide slowly down the railings to the ground. 'It wis a mistake, Rab. Ye gotta believe me.'

Lenny eased off the pressure on T.K.'s neck. He didn't want

226

him to black out just yet. 'An fuckin' mistake!' He let go T.K.'s sweatshirt and aimed a violent kick at his side. T.K. let out another cry of agony.

A man dressed in a dark suit and carrying a leather briefcase slowed down as he passed by, a look of concern on his face. Rab turned and flicked a thumb at him. 'Git on yer way, mister. This is private business.' The man shot a glance at T.K., then back at his shaven-headed assailants. The sight of the ragged tattoo on the neck of the youth who glared at him quickly dissipated any thought of further intervention on his part and the man continued on his way up the street with quickened step.

Lenny squatted down on his haunches, his face only a few inches away from T.K.'s. 'So ye thocht ye could hide awa' frae us, did ye? Jist yer luck, then, that auld Peesy McGill from ma block decided tae get guttered last night and ended up in yer fuckin' dosshoose. It wis him wha' saw ye and him wha' telt me.' He gave T.K. a knowing wink. 'As Rab said, Thomas Keene, the word's oot. A'body's efter ye. Ye're bloody done fer, pal.'

The door of the hostel was suddenly flung open and a huge man appeared on the doorstep. He was wearing a vast pair of jogging pants and a dirty white T-shirt that strained hard to cover his enormous belly, yet the size of his arms seemed to be in complete proportion with the rest of his body. 'Whit the hell's goin' on here?'

'It's naine of yer business, fatty,' Rab said, pointing a hostile finger at the man.

The man stepped down from the threshold and seized the lapel of Rab's denim jacket with one hand, lifting him almost clear of the ground. 'A'thing that happens on these steps is ma business, ye wee tosser,' he said through clenched teeth, glancing momentarily at T.K.'s sprawled form on the step, 'especially if it's tae dae wi' wan of ma lads.' He jerked the youth closer to him. 'And whit's mair, ah dinnae like bein' called "fatty", so if ah wis you, ah'd git the hell oot o' here afore I call the polis, is that understood?'

He let go his grip on the lad, giving him a violent push that made him stumble down the steps. Lenny stood up and backed away to join his colleague on the pavement. He balled his fist and flicked out a thumb, affecting the action of a switchblade 'Ye'll be gettin' it comin' tae ye, Thomas Keene. You canna hide awa' fae us.' He cleared his throat noisily and then spat at T.K. with such force that the gob passed more than a foot above the head of its intended target.

'Get awa' wi' ye!' the caretaker yelled out with an angry wave of his hand. He stood watching after the two boys as they ambled off down the street, every so often casting a glance behind them, and then, letting out a long sigh, he looked down at T.K., who lay on the steps rubbing at his aching ribs. 'Ye dinnae half pick yer friends, dae ye, lad,' he said with a shake of the head. Leaning over with effort, he put a hand under T.K.'s armpit and pulled him to his feet. 'Ye'd better get yersel' inside and ah'll hae a look-see whit damage they've done tae ye.'

'Ah'm fine,' T.K. replied dolefully. He took in a long deep lungful of air. 'Ah'll jist stay here fer a minnit and catch ma breath.'

The caretaker gave a brief nod of his head. 'A'right. Come in when ye're ready,' he said as he turned and walked back into the house.

T.K. waited until the man's huge frame had disappeared from sight, and then, casting a quick glance up the street to make sure the two boys had gone, he descended the steps and headed away in the opposite direction, clutching a hand to his side.

Even though T.K. was only one amongst the thousands of people who crammed the centre of Edinburgh that night, he kept walking until well after midnight, never being too sure that somewhere, a hundred yards back on the crowded pavements, the two boys weren't following him. Eventually, he took the risk of ducking down a dimly lit alleyway off the bustle and noise of Rose Street, where he squatted uncomfortably behind a large industrial refuse bin for a good half an hour, waiting to see if his fears were to be justified. There did come a moment when he was set ready to make a dash for freedom, hearing two male

oices talk quietly to each other only twenty feet away from
im, but then he heard a splattering noise on the cobbles and
ealised that it was just a couple of revellers finding an unseen
orner to relieve themselves. After they had gone, he left it for
ve minutes before quitting his hiding place. Rubbing at his
ching legs, he began to make his way back along the narrow
reet, walking unexpectedly into the warming blast of air coming
om a heating duct set into the side of one of the buildings
hat fronted on to Princes Street. He stood in its comforting
olds for a moment, feeling its warmth penetrate his chilled body
nd relieve the aching in his side, and his eyelids began to give
vay to fatigue. He realised then that he would be unlikely to
nd a more comfortable place to pass the night than right there
n that spot. Returning to the refuse bin, he pulled out a couple
f cardboard packing cases and carried them back to a recessed
loorway where he could still feel the warmth from the duct.
aying one on the ground, he pulled up the hood of his sweat-
hirt and drew the strings tight around his face. He sat down
n his hard, unforgiving bed, propped his back against the wall
nd covered himself with the other piece of cardboard, punching
t with the side of his hand to mould it around his legs and
ody. He then leaned his head back and, with a deep sigh of
lespair, focused on the clear, cool starlit sky. Please, he thought
o himself, if there's onybody up there, please gi' us a break.
Dinnae let it end like this . . . please.

His head lolled heavily to one side and he fell into a deep,
ear-comatose sleep, blanking from his mind all the frustration
nd anger he felt at the innumerable injustices the world had
eaped upon him.

Thirty

Albert Dessuin stood in the queue at the British Airways desk
t Edinburgh Airport, his face lowered as he looked over the

top of his dark glasses to see if there was any sign of movemen
up ahead. Gone was the bravado and impatience he had displaye
the previous morning when he had pushed his way to the fron
of the queue at the hotel. Now, he was prepared to stand an
wait, not wishing to draw attention to himself.

Since being informed of Angélique's injury and her unscheduled return to France, Albert had hidden himself away in hi
bedroom in the Sheraton Grand, not daring to leave, even
though the receptionist had given him details of at least three
direct flights that would have taken him to Paris that day. He
had sat in the armchair staring trance-like out of the window,
not wishing to watch the television in case it featured some
damning news item about himself and not even glancing toward
the small refrigerated minibar that was built into the corner
of the wardrobe. When he had eventually left the room early
that morning to check out, he had even averted his eyes from
the complimentary newspaper lying on the ground outside his
door. He just couldn't bring himself to learn whether Angélique
had spoken to anyone about what had happened two nights
before.

As the queue inched forward, he bent over and pushed the
two suitcases along the ground, making sure the violin case
remained hidden between them. He could hardly bear to look
at it. It was only when he had returned to Angélique's bedroom
in the hotel after speaking with Alasdair Dreyfuss the previous
day that he had realised how serious a situation had arisen.
Under those appalling circumstances of the preceding night, he
could well understand why she had run off without taking any
of her clothes, but to abandon her most treasured possession,
the violin, was beyond comprehension. Oh, Angélique, he
thought to himself, I cannot believe I allowed myself to do such
a thing to you. Please let me find you so that I can try to make
amends.

He did not mean to look round. It was just that he was so
filled with guilt and self-loathing at that particular moment
that even looking at the violin case brought the now clear

memory of what had happened on that fateful night back to mind. He found himself staring directly at a man dressed in jeans and a multi-pouched body warmer, a large camera slung round his neck, who leaned against a pillar in the centre of the departure lounge, idly scanning the long queues that formed at the various check-in desks. The man glanced briefly in his direction, looked away, and then did a double take. He pushed himself away from the pillar and made his way quickly over to Albert.

'It is Mr Dessuin, isn't it?' the man asked, adjusting the dials on his camera and taking the cap off the lens.

Albert did not reply, pretending that the photographer had mistaken him for someone else. The camera flashed and Albert reacted instinctively, holding up his hand to shield his face. It was all the verification the photographer needed.

'Mr Dessuin, why are you travelling alone?' the man asked. 'Where is Angélique Pascal?'

The other people who stood in line at the British Airways desk had now begun to take interest in what was going on, turning to look at the tall man wearing the sunglasses and the belted mackintosh with the collar turned up, to whom the questions were being directed. Leaving his bags on the floor, Albert walked quickly away from the queue, and then turned to confront the photographer, who had followed, hot on his heels.

'I have no comment to make about anything,' Albert hissed at the man. 'I'm sure your newspapers have said it all.'

'It's all a bit airy-fairy, though, Mr Dessuin. All that's been reported is that Angélique Pascal had an accident and was returning to France.'

Dessuin bit at the side of his mouth as he contemplated what the photographer was telling him. Maybe Angélique had not disclosed the true facts after all. If so, for what reason? Maybe, despite all he had done, she was still displaying a sense of loyalty, protecting his reputation. If that was the case, there was hope of reconciliation after all. He decided to go along with that assumption, making a mental effort not to display the sense of elation he was feeling to the photographer. 'And that is all tha[t] happened. Mademoiselle Pascal has returned to Paris, and I ar[e] about to catch a plane to join her, so if you will now pleas[e] excuse me . . .'

The photographer put a hand on his arm as Albert prepare[d] to return to his place in the queue. 'That's all very well, but [I] can tell you Angélique Pascal has definitely not returned t[o] Paris.'

Albert stared at the man. 'What do you mean?'

'Mr Dessuin, over the past twenty-four hours my colleagu[e] and I have been doing shifts here at the airport waiting to ge[t] a photograph of her, and there hasn't been one person who eve[r] vaguely resembles her booking in for a flight to Paris, or anywher[e] in France for that matter.'

Albert shook his head. 'You are mistaken.'

'No, I'm not. I've even had an acquaintance of mine chec[k] the passenger lists. Angélique Pascal has not left from this airport[.]'

Albert looked around at the queue. Those who were behin[d] him were now moving forward, skirting around his luggage o[n] the floor. 'She has obviously then been directed to a flight fron[m] another airport.'

The photographer let out a short, disbelieving laugh. 'M[r] Dessuin, this is big news, you know. The festival's top performe[r] has an accident preventing her from fulfilling her engagements and heads off home to Paris. The word's got round to ever[y] freelance news photographer in Scotland. We've had all majo[r] airports and train stations covered for the past day, and there'[s] not been even a glimpse of her. Now, having seen you here b[y] yourself, it just confirms to me my own journalistic instinct o[n] the matter.'

'Which is?'

'That Angélique Pascal is still in Edinburgh. The whole stor[y] about her returning to France is a sham, for some reason o[r] other. Have you any idea why that might be, Mr Dessuin?'

Albert stood looking at the man, speechless, working throug[h] the logic of his reasoning. If the photographer was indeed correct[,] then where was Angélique? She knew no one in Edinburgh except those she had met at the receptions, and certainly Alasdair Dreyfuss was under the impression that she had returned to France. Of course, there was that girl, Tess Goodwin. Angélique seemed to have become friends with her, but how was he to find out? It could be that Angélique had confided in the girl, in which case he didn't want to question her, otherwise she might declare to the press the true events of that night.

He realised now, though, that he had to remain in Edinburgh to find Angélique, but first he had to think of a way of throwing this photographer off the scent. He could not allow press speculation to continue on her whereabouts. If she was still in Edinburgh, he needed the time and space to find her.

Albert smiled at the man and shook his head. 'The story is not a sham. I know that for certain.'

'How, may I ask?' the photographer asked, his eyebrows arched in uncertainty.

'Because I planned for Mademoiselle Pascal to leave before me, and I spoke with both her *and* my mother on the telephone last night. They are together in my house in Paris.' He cocked his head at the man. 'So, it would seem you have not been so efficient after all. Mademoiselle Pascal must have eluded you.' He gave a short bow of his head. 'So if you will now excuse me, I should like to continue with my plans to return to Paris and allow you to get on with some more lucrative work than standing around this airport all day.'

He left the man and walked back to the queue. Those who had been standing behind him had now shuffled forward past his luggage, but he was not concerned. It gave him time to see if the photographer had fallen for his ruse. He watched him out of the corner of his eye, studying his body language as he talked on his mobile phone. When the man had finished, he never turned to look in Albert's direction, but walked quickly over to the revolving doors and left the terminal.

Letting out a sigh of relief, Albert flicked back the cuff of his shirt and glanced at his watch. He would give the photographer five minutes' grace, and then he himself would take a taxi back to the city.

Thirty-One

In the London Street flat, Jamie Stratton sat cross-legged on a large threadbare Turkish carpet that covered only a fraction of the floor space of the cavernous sitting room, scratching perplexedly at his thick mop of blond hair as he stared at the backgammon board on the low cluttered coffee table.

'You've done it again, haven't you,' he said, eyeing his opponent with suspicion. 'You can't tell *me* you haven't played this game before.'

Leaning her elbows on the table, Angélique cupped her face in her hands and grinned at him. 'Not very often.'

'Hah! I knew it!' Jamie exclaimed, pointing an accusing finger at her. 'You're nothing more than a damned hustler.'

Angélique laughed. 'Of course,' she said, getting to her feet and immediately flopping back into the drape-covered sofa. 'There is no other way to be in life.'

Jamie pushed himself away from the table and leaned his back against an armchair. 'OK, so you'd better tell me about your other hidden talents, just so as I don't get duped again,' he said, smiling at her.

Angélique pulled the large towelling dressing gown tight around her neck and tucked up her feet on the sofa. 'Well, I could tell you all the names of the French rugby fullbacks all the way back to Serge Blanco.'

'You're joking.'

'I am not. My brothers thought it was a very necessary thing for their little sister to know. Shall I tell you the names?'

'No, spare the details, I'll believe you,' Jamie laughed, holding up his hands as if to defend himself from what was to come.

Angélique challenged his cowardly rebuff by wrinkling her

234

nose disdainfully at him. 'You are just frightened that I might know more about rugby than you.'

'Probably,' he replied, watching her closely as she ruffled her short dark hair, still wet from the shower, with the fingers of her unbandaged hand. It was funny, he thought to himself, how he had always been magnetically drawn to tall, shapely blonde girls with sparkling blue eyes in the past. Martha in the coffee shop was certainly a case in point. But now, having spent two days in the isolated company of Angélique Pascal, he realised that this preference had been narrowing the field quite unnecessarily. He studied the brown eyes that mischievously stared back at him, the downy softness of the sallow-skinned cheeks that were creased with humour, and the small dark-lipped mouth that challenged him with its smile. Everything about her – her diminutive size, her boyish figure – was a complete antithesis to those qualities that had fulfilled his youthful fantasies, but now he was beginning to see this young French violinist as one of the most mysteriously attractive and outrageously captivating members of the opposite sex he had ever clapped eyes on.

'Anything else?' he asked.

Angélique rocked her head from side to side in consideration. 'I suppose I am quite good at playing the violin as well.'

Jamie smiled. 'Maybe you should take it up professionally then.'

'I suppose it's a consideration,' she replied quietly, the smile on her face fading away and Jamie realised immediately his joke had been crass and badly timed, a stark reminder of her present situation.

'Sorry, that was a stupid thing to say.'

Angélique shook her head. 'No, I understand you did not mean it that way. I can only imagine everything would be much worse if I hadn't met you and Gavin.'

'Yeah, well,' Jamie replied, dismissing the remark with a wave of his hand, although his true feeling was that their meeting was one of the more fortuitous things that had happened to him. 'So, how's the hand feeling today?'

Angélique flexed the fingers of her bandaged hand. 'It seems to be better. I do not have so much pain now.'

'In that case, I've got something for you,' he said, clambering to his feet. He walked over to the fireplace and began tipping out the contents of each of the chipped china bowls that lined the dark polished granite mantelpiece. 'Where the hell is it? I know it's in one of these.' He eventually found what he was looking for in the last bowl. 'Here you are.' He turned and lobbed something small and black to Angélique. She caught it by instinct and then turned the object around in her fingers, studying it with a baffled expression on her face.

'I think this is a ball for playing squash,' she said.

'Yeah, it is.'

Angélique laughed. 'So, are you now challenging me to a game of catch or something?'

'No, but it's not such a bad idea. I might have a slight advantage over you with two good hands.' He pushed the backgammon board to one side and sat down on the table in front of Angélique. He took the ball from her hand and began squeezing it repeatedly in his fist. 'Last year, this enormous rugby prop forward from one of the Borders teams decided it would be fun to grind his studs into my hand during a game. By the time I'd been helped off the field of play, my fingers had lost all feeling and had swollen to the size of sausages. I used this squash ball to get them working again, and I was back on the rugby pitch within two weeks.' He put the ball back in her bandaged hand and gently folded her fingers over it. 'How does that feel?'

Angélique's mouth screwed to one side, as if she was trying hard to suppress a laugh. 'Very nice. Quite sensual, actually.'

Jamie smiled at her in surprise. 'Just keep squeezing it. You'll find it does help.' He got to his feet and pushed his hands into the back pockets of his jeans. 'Listen, I've got to get on with writing some of these reviews. I'm a day behind and I have a deadline for this afternoon, so I hope you don't mind if I leave you to fend for yourself for an hour or two.'

Angélique swung her legs off the sofa. 'Jamie, have you heard et from Gavin?' she asked concernedly.

'No, I haven't.'

'So we don't know what Albert is doing.'

'I'm afraid not.'

Angélique nodded. 'It's just that I would really like to have ny violin. I have never been parted from it for so long, and I eel . . . lost without it.'

Jamie scratched thoughtfully at his head. 'I don't think we hould do anything until Gavin gets in touch, but tell you what; f I don't hear from him by midday, I'll give him a call.' He valked over to the door and opened it. 'In the meantime,' he aid, turning back to her, '*work the ball!*'

An hour later the telephone began to ring shrilly in the hall, naking Jamie type faster than his fingers would allow as he tried o commit to his computer's memory what he knew was the perfect description of the Fringe comedy show before it faded rom his mind. He swore under his breath when he looked up nd saw nothing but a plethora of misspelled words on the creen. Pushing himself out of the chair with a frustrated yell, e ran through to the hall and made a dive for the telephone.

'Hullo?'

'Jamie, it's Gavin here. How's everything today?'

'Oh, good enough,' Jamie replied absently, picking up a biro o scribble down the sentence on the back of an unopened enve-ope. When the biro refused to write, he threw it with force against the wall. '*Bugger!*'

'Obviously not a good time,' Gavin laughed.

'Sorry, I was just trying to write something down before I forgot it.'

'Do you want me to call back?'

'No, don't worry. I'll probably remember it.'

'How's Angélique this morning?'

'Doing OK.'

'And the hand?'

'On the mend, I reckon. She's not in so much pain now.'

'A good sign, then. Listen, Jamie, I think our little plan about getting her luggage back from the hotel might have backfired.'

'In what way?'

'Dessuin didn't leave the Sheraton Grand yesterday, so that's why I never called you about collecting Angélique's belongings. Now it would appear that he's gone and checked out of the hotel at about eight o'clock this morning and taken a taxi to the airport. I can only deduce from that that he's following her back to Paris.'

'He hasn't taken Angélique's stuff with him, has he?'

'That I can't tell you. My source of information couldn't confirm it one way or the other, but I'm afraid it's highly likely.'

'So, what happens now? Angélique was just saying she was desperate to get her violin back.'

'Well, let's not write off everything at this point in time. Dessuin will have been pretty distracted before leaving, so there's the slimmest chance he might have left something behind. I would suggest you just go round to the Sheraton Grand and see what's what.'

'OK, but what do I do if he *has* taken everything?'

Jamie heard Gavin sigh resignedly at the other end of the line. 'Then we'll just have to consider what our next step is going to be, but let's just rule out one thing at a time, shall we?'

'All right. I'll call you when I get back.'

'You do that. Thanks, Jamie.'

Jamie replaced the receiver and turned to go back to his bedroom but stopped when he saw Angélique leaning against the door of the sitting room, silently watching him.

'How long have you been standing there?' he asked.

'Long enough,' she replied.

Jamie nodded. 'Right, well, you probably gathered I'm going to try to pick up your things this morning.'

'If they are still there.'

'Yeah, that's right,' he replied, moving off towards his bedroom door. 'I'll go as soon as I've finished off writing that review.'

'Jamie?'

She had not moved away from the door, but was following him with her dark-brown eyes.

'What?'

'Do you want me to leave?' she asked quietly.

'No. Why do you ask?'

'Because I am causing you a lot of problems. It would be easier for you if I was not here.'

Jamie shrugged. 'Yeah, that's true.' He grinned at her. 'But life would be a helluva lot more boring.'

'Do you mean that?'

'Course I do. Anyway, you can't go.'

'I know that Gavin says I should not—'

'It's got nothing to do with Gavin. You're not leaving here until I've beaten you at backgammon.'

The haunting shadow of worry evaporated from Angélique's face as she contemplated this challenge, eventually answering it with a shrug of her shoulders. 'I cannot be here for ever, you know.'

Jamie narrowed his eyes and jabbed a finger in her direction. 'Tonight, Mademoiselle Pascal, you are history.'

'Ça m'étonnerait!' Angélique exclaimed, pulling back her arm and throwing something at him with force. Jamie ducked to one side as the squash ball thudded against the wall behind him. She rushed forward and bent down to retrieve it, and as she straightened up she stood on her toes and planted a kiss on his cheek. 'You were supposed to catch it,' she said, her face so close to his that Jamie felt her breath brush past his ear. He had time to see one small, squint-toothed imperfection in her teasing smile before she turned and walked assuredly back towards the sitting room. 'That, I'm afraid, is another game I have won.'

Leonard Hartson adjusted the knob on the back of the 1K Redhead to balance the contrast of light hitting the chalk-white face of one of the Japanese dancers and the reflective gold thread that was intricately woven through the silk of her deep-red kimono. He walked forward to the dancer and scanned her with his light meter before returning to the row of canvas chairs T.K. had set up beside the camera, two of which were occupied by the dance company director, Mr Kayamoto, and Claire, his young interpreter.

'Right,' Leonard said, slipping the light meter into the pocket of his jacket. 'I think we're about ready to shoot.' He smiled reassuringly at Kayamoto as Claire translated his words. 'And I would suggest that after we've finished this particular scene, the company breaks for lunch. That'll give me time to reset the lights for some close-ups.' He glanced towards the unlit area of the warehouse behind the camera. 'Right, T.K., if you could start the music and then mark the scene.' He stepped up on to the camera box he had positioned behind the tripod legs to give him extra height, set the aperture on the lens, checked his focus through the eyepiece and waited for the music to start. Nothing happened. He turned and looked across to where the darkened shape of his assistant leaned forward in front of the rack of amplifying equipment. 'T.K., when you're ready.'

Again, nothing happened. Leonard heard a scrape of chairs as both the director and his interpreter turned to see why the music hadn't started. He stepped stiffly off the camera box and walked away from the dazzling pool of light. In the few seconds that it took him to reach his assistant, Leonard's eyes became accustomed to the obscurity of the warehouse and he could tell immediately that T.K. had not heard a word he had said. He placed a hand on the shoulder of the boy's slumped form and gave it a gentle shake. 'Are you all right, lad?'

T.K. jumped to his feet too quickly, lost his balance and fell hard against one of the large loudspeakers. It toppled over with a low resonant thump.

'Sorry about tha',' T.K. said, heaving up the speaker and gingerly returning it to its position. He dipped his head, not wishing to make eye contact with the old cameraman. 'Sorry, Leonard. Ah think ah drapped aff.'

Leonard stared hard at the boy. Because T.K. had not turned

up that morning until well after the dance company had arrived, Leonard had decided to hold back from saying anything to him about his general state of appearance and his sloppy, wordless demeanour during the morning's shoot, but he certainly would have to address it during the lunch break. T.K. was wearing the same clothes he had worn the day before, his hair was greasy and dishevelled, and his whole being emanated a sour smell of body odour and unkemptness.

'Yes, well,' Leonard said curtly, 'if you're ready now, maybe you would be good enough to turn on the music and then come and mark the scene.'

It took three takes before Leonard managed to put the shot in the can. He noticed that one of the dancers had looked straight at the camera during the first, a jerky camera pan put pay to the second, but the third worked beautifully. Having congratulated the director and the company on a good morning's work, accompanied by many a reciprocated bow, he watched as the little ensemble in their bright, out-of-place clothes filed through the fire door at the side of the warehouse and closed it behind them.

'Shall ah turn the lights aff?' T.K. asked, his voice tentative as it echoed around the vast empty space.

Leonard took off his spectacles and let them drop to his chest on the neck cord. He rubbed a hand at his eyes, unaccustomed as they were now to working under the glare of the lights, and then pressed it to the slight pain he felt at the left side of his ribcage. Maybe it had been a foolhardy idea of his to take on the making of the film in this way. Of course, both he and Gracie knew he had to take this one-off, God-given opportunity to show the world that Leonard Hartson, the once famous director of photography, had not lost his touch. But maybe it was all happening twenty years too late, and trying to do it now was really biting off more than he could chew. If he had a full working crew as was originally planned, things would be different, but to have only this young lad who knew little about what he was doing and who could hardly keep his eyes open was going to test both his patience and his fading stamina to the full.

He turned and made his way back to the studio floor. 'What was that, T.K.?'

'Ah didna know if ye wanted me tae turn aff the lights.'

Leonard let out a despondent sigh. 'Yes, you can do that.' He walked over to the camera and unlocked the tripod legs, allowing them to sink down, and spun the lens round to face him.

T.K. switched off the last light and came to stand beside him. 'If ye're goin' tae check the gate, ah've already dunnit,' he said quietly. 'It's clean.'

Leonard smiled at the young lad. He was trying his best. 'Well done. I had forgotten to do it.'

T.K. hunched his shoulders and stuck his hands deep into the pockets of his sagging jeans. 'Ah'm sorry ah dozed aff, Leonard. Ah'll no dae it again.'

Leonard shook his head. 'Listen, I do understand you're being thrown in at the deep end here, but before we go any further, there are a few things we've got to get straight.'

'It wis jist that . . .'

'I know,' Leonard said, holding up his hand to curtail T.K.'s further excuses. 'Just hear me out, if you would. When one is making a film, T.K., it is extremely important that you are seen to be totally professional in everything you do, because that is what impresses the client. Now, this not only makes itself apparent in the way you work around the set, but also in the way you present yourself. I know you'll probably think my dress sense is a bit old-fashioned, and I wouldn't dream of asking you to wear a jacket and tie like myself, but tomorrow I want you not only to turn up for work on time, but also having smartened up your appearance quite considerably.' Leonard paused, seeing the lad dip his head in embarrassment at the reprimand. 'Now, I don't want you to get disheartened. You had one slip-up today – that was all. Other than that, I thought you worked pretty well.' He put a hand on the boy's shoulder. 'Appearances are crucial, T.K., so when you finish up this afternoon, I want you to go home, get yourself cleaned up, look out some clean clothes and then have an early night. Is that understood?'

The young man nodded dolefully in reply.

'Right, enough said,' Leonard said, turning to check the footage left in the film magazine. 'Let's get ourselves set up for the next scene. I want to do some close-ups on the faces, so if you could move the camera forward to the edge of the dance area . . .'

'Leonard?'

Leonard turned back to the boy. 'Yes?'

T.K. stood with his head still lowered. 'Ah don' like tae ask ye this, because ah know ah havna earned it yet, but could ye lend us some money so as ah can turn up fer work tomorrow?'

Leonard looked questioningly at him. 'Would this be for a bus fare, T.K.?'

T.K. shook his head. 'So's ah can get ma claithes washed.'

'Do you not have a washing machine at home?'

'Aye, it's just that . . .' T.K. scratched the back of his greasy head. 'Ah'm no' livin' at haim at the minnit.'

'Oh, right, I understand. And there's no washing machine in the place you're staying now, is that it?'

T.K. moved over to the camera, swung it round and locked off the tripod head. 'Ah'm no' stayin' onyplace,' he said quietly. He picked up the apparatus and began pushing the tripod spider towards the dance area with his foot.

'T.K., would you just leave the camera for a moment?'

The boy settled the tripod back into the grooves on the spider and turned slowly to face the cameraman.

'What do you mean, you're not staying anyplace? Where did you spend last night?'

T.K. shrugged his shoulders and began pushing one of the snaking electrical cables into a loop with the toe of one of his dirty white trainers.

'Where did you spend last night?'

'Jist aff Rose Street,' he mumbled.

'What do you mean, just off Rose Street?'

'Doon the back o' Marks and Spencer's. There's a hot-air duct comin' oot the back o' the building, so it's good an' warm, but people kept walking past so ah didna get much sleep.'

Leonard let out a long sigh, understanding now exactly what the boy was saying to him. 'You're sleeping rough, aren't you, lad?'

T.K. nodded.

'How long have you been doing this?'

'Jist the once. Mr Mackintosh had paid fer me to stay in a hostel fer a week, just so's I could get started wi' you.' He paused, his head lowered as he scratched at his downy stubble. 'But ah didna want tae go back there.'

Leonard sat down heavily on one of the lighting boxes. 'And why would that be?'

''Cos there's folk wha are efter me. They know ah wis staying there.'

'And what's the reason for these "folk" being after you?'

'Jist because.'

Leonard nodded, realising the boy did not wish to elaborate on the circumstances. 'So, in a nutshell, you have nowhere to stay and you have no clothes other than those you're standing up in, is that right?'

'Aye, ah suppose,' T.K. muttered.

Leonard leaned forward on his knees and covered his face with his hands. 'Oh dear, oh dear, oh dear,' he stated rhythmically. This was certainly the last thing he needed. The making of this film was going to take up enough of his time and energy without having the additional hassle of sorting out both the accommodation and security problems of this young waif-and-stray. He felt the lid of the lighting box sink slightly as T.K. came to sit beside him.

'Ah'm sorry, Leonard. I wis hopin' you widna find oot.'

The old cameraman reached across and patted the boy's knee. 'That's all right. I'm glad I did sooner rather than later.'

'Ah could always sleep here, if ye'd allow me tae. Naebody wid find me here, and ah could look efter a' the equipment.'

'No, that would not work. You'd be no better off.' He looked across at his assistant, studying the sad, hopeless expression on his face. 'T.K., do you really want to work with me?'

The boy jerked round his head, a look of alarm on his face. 'Aye, ah do, Leonard. Ah promise ah won't be late again, and ah'll get masel' sorted oot, honest ah will.'

'I can't have you sleeping rough.'

'Ah willna dae it,' he replied, his voice rising in agitation at the thought of losing his one big chance.

'No, what I mean is that I can't *allow* you to sleep rough. If you work for me, then you are part of my crew, and it is my responsibility to find you lodgings.' Leonard rubbed his wrinkled hands on the knees of his cavalry-twill trousers. 'Trouble is I can't really afford to pay for your accommodation, and what's more, I doubt I'd find anywhere for you stay right now . . .' He paused a moment before murmuring, '. . . which leaves only one option.' T.K. got to his feet and took a couple of paces towards the lighting stage. He stood with his back to Leonard, his shoulders slumped dejectedly and his hands thrust into the pockets of his jeans.

'Ye're goin' tae say ah canna work fer ye, aren't ye?' he sniffed.

'No, I am not. I'm certainly not going to find anyone else to assist me at such short notice, and anyway, I offered you a job and I'll stick by that, so you have no worries on that account.'

T.K. turned to the cameraman. 'So, whit did ye mean aboot the wan option?'

Leonard clambered wearily to his feet. 'Well, it's certainly not the most ideal arrangement and I'll have to clear it with my landlord, but there are two beds in my room, and—'

'Whit are ye sayin'? That ah can come and stay wi' you?' T.K. stared at Leonard, wondering if he had misunderstood what the old cameraman was saying, but desperate to grab at any opportunity.

'I don't think there's much alternative, is there?'

T.K. eagerly approached Leonard, realising now all was not lost. 'If ah did that, I widna be a nuisance tae ye, ah promise, and ah dinna snore or a'thing, and onyways, it's a good idea 'cos we can talk aboot whit we're goin' tae dae the next day, so ah can get ready fer it in ma heid . . .'

Leonard smiled and held up a hand to halt T.K.'s exuberant outburst. 'All right, let's take one thing at a time, lad. After we've finished shooting this afternoon, I would suggest we go uptown and get you kitted out with a few things, including a pair of jeans with a decent belt. I don't want you to continue exposing half your backside to our assembled company every time you bend down to unplug a light.'

As if trying to make amends already, T.K. pulled up his own drooping trousers and ran a hand around the waistband to tuck in his grimy T-shirt. They immediately slipped to their original position when he launched himself at the cameraman and grabbed hold of his hand. The shake it received was so enthusiastic that Leonard had grave worries a serious shoulder dislocation was imminent. 'Cheers, Leonard. I willna let ye doon, ah promise.'

The result of T.K.'s energetic arm action was to immerse Leonard in a suffocating waft of body odour. He pulled his hand free from the boy's grip and took a few paces back to escape the unsavoury cloud. 'And the first thing you do when we get back to the flat is have a long hot shower, is that under-stood?'

T.K. grinned broadly at him. 'Aye, ah will.' He turned and hefted the tripod and camera up on to his shoulder and kicked the spider across the floor. 'Tell us how far ye want this in now.'

Shrugging on a corduroy bomber jacket, Jamie descended the stairs of the flat and flung open the front door. Without lessening his speed, he ran out on to the broad stone steps, managing to swerve in time to avoid a thumping collision with the small solid figure that swung around with alarm at his sudden appearance, crumpling an open street map of Edinburgh against her ample chest.

'Is there ever a time when ye slow up?' Rene Brownlow asked

Jamie's momentum took him clear off the three remaining steps to the pavement.

'Yeah, waking up in the mornings is a pretty slow affair, as you've witnessed,' Jamie laughed.

Rene pulled a long face and glanced about her. 'More's a pity there's no one about to 'ear you say that,' she said, stretching out the map in front of her with a flick of her wrists.

'Where are you off to?'

'I thought I'd try to find a quicker route uptown than the one I've been taking the last couple of days.'

'Come with me, if you like. I'm heading up there now.'

'At what speed?' Rene asked, folding up the map and slipping it into her large shoulder bag.

'I'll let you set the pace,' Jamie replied with a smile.

'That'll do me,' Rene said, descending the steps and pushing her hands into the pockets of her rag-rug coat. They headed off side by side along the street. 'So, did ye manage to get it all sorted out with your nice lawyer chap yesterday?'

'We're getting there.'

'Don't think I'm prying, like, but has it got something to do with that nice French violinist who's staying in yer flat?'

Jamie's step faltered as he fixed her with an open-mouthed look of amazement. 'How come you know about *her*?'

'Well, ye could 'ardly stave off our eventual meeting, Jamie. Her flat is large, but it's not exactly Buckingham Palace.' She lifted her bag up on to her shoulder. 'Any road, to answer yer question, we bumped into each other this morning on the way to the bathroom.'

'What did she say?'

'Well, I can't remember her exact words, but it was something like "Please, you must use ze basroom first."'

Jamie was too eager to hear what had passed between them to react to her light-hearted quip. 'And that was it?'

'No. I asked what she'd done to 'er 'and and she told me she'd put it on glass and 'ow sad she was because she wasn't going to be able to play the violin for a bit.' Rene slowed her pace as they started up the incline of Dublin Street. 'And then when I got back to my bedroom I was leafing through some of the festival brochures and suddenly there she was, staring out of the pages at me. Angélique Pascal, world-famous violinist. I tell ye, ye could 'ave knocked me down with a feather. It's not every day ye get to talk with someone like that, let alone share a bathroom!'

Jamie kept walking without passing comment. It had never occurred to him that Angélique might talk to one of his tenants. He had only foreseen problems coming from without the sanctuary of the flat. Not that it was the fault of either Angélique or Rene. They were just making normal conversation with each other, and like as not, Rene would still have found the photograph of Angélique in the brochure. But it did add up to a huge complication. If Rene was to keep her ears and eyes open, she was bound to find out sooner or later that Angélique's presence in Edinburgh was contrary to everyone else's belief. She seemed to be a decent, down-to-earth sort of person. Maybe his best option was just to confide in her.

'Oh, thanks for that,' Rene gasped, taking Jamie's reason for stopping at the corner of Heriot Row as a chance for her to catch her breath.

'Listen, Rene, if I tell you something about Angélique, will you honestly swear to me you won't mention it to anyone else, most of all the press?'

'My, this all smacks of intrigue, don't it?'

'Do you promise?'

'Jamie, I don't 'ave an 'otline to *News at Ten,* you know, and I don't reckon the press will be queuing up to ask Rene Brownlow, small-time comedienne from 'Artlepool, for her weighty views on world affairs.'

'If they discover you're living in the same flat as Angélique Pascal, they'll find what you have to say pretty important, I can tell you.'

Rene nodded. 'Right,' she said, realising now that her young landlord was seriously concerned about something to do with the violinist's welfare. 'In that case, of course I promise. Ye've en me bloody saviour up here in Edinburgh, Jamie Stratton. he last thing I'd want to do is get ye into trouble.'

So, as they continued on their way up to the lights on Queen reet, Jamie told Rene about his chance meeting with Angélique the coffee shop. By the time they turned into George Street id he had told her of the assault the violinist had suffered at e hands of her manager, Rene was so captivated by the story e forgot all about her lack of fitness and made sure she kept ice with Jamie, even breaking into an awkward trot at times avoid missing one word of what he was telling her. When e one-o'clock gun thundered out from the battlements of dinburgh Castle and the pigeons, sitting high on the flat stone illustrades of the buildings, rose momentarily in panic, Rene tened on, seemingly immune to the sudden, ear-pounding sturbance. They stepped off the pavement in unison to avoid e disorderly but boisterously good-natured queues that mean- ered along the street, readying themselves with plastic beer asses in hand to squeeze into unlikely basement venues for the irly afternoon Fringe performances. And then, on reaching harlotte Square, where crowds mingled on the grass outside e white marquees of the Book Festival, dappled with shadow nder their sun-glistened umbrella of trees, Rene let out a loud xpletive describing her thoughts on Albert Dessuin and stepped it into the street without looking. Had it not been for Jamie's straining arm, she no doubt would have ended her days beneath e wheels of one of the vehicles in the ever-constant stream of affic, with the vulgar word frozen on her lips.

'So, this is where they were staying, is it?' Rene wheezed when ey eventually came to a halt, looking across Festival Square at e glass-fronted rectangle of the Sheraton Grand.

'Yeah, it is,' Jamie replied distractedly as he cast an eye around e packed area.

'Do ye think 'e's still somewhere abouts?'

'No, I'm pretty sure he's headed back to Paris.'

'So what're ye going to do?'

Jamie exhaled a deep breath. 'Just go in, I suppose.'

'D'ye want me to come in with ye?'

'No, don't worry. You should go off and do what you've got to do.'

'Oh, I've got nowt pressing. Anyway, ye've got me 'ooked now, lad. I want to 'ang around and see the outcome.'

Jamie smiled at Rene, secretly pleased she was there with him as an accomplice, her quirky banter calming the nervousness he felt at carrying out the task in hand. 'All right. Maybe you could stay here then, just in case I am followed out of the hotel.'

'D'ye think that's likely?'

'Anything's possible.'

Rene shot him a wink. 'OK, then, consider it done. I'll 'ave a seat over there at the café and keep me eyes peeled.'

As Jamie hurried across to the steps and entered through the swing doors of the hotel, Rene walked across to the café, put her bag on an empty table and flumped down into one of the metal chairs facing the hotel entrance so that she had an unhindered view of all that was going on in Festival Square. She was taking this whole 'private eye' business pretty seriously.

And had she not been so attentive while waiting for her cup of cappuccino to arrive, she would never have noticed the woman with the wild mass of red hair and the huge pink scarf wrapped around her neck get up from the table beside her, nor the brown leather purse that lay dropped beneath her chair.

'Excuse me!' Rene called out, pushing herself to her feet. She leaned over awkwardly and picked up the purse. The woman had not heard her, continuing on in the same direction as Jamie had taken five minutes before. Rene bustled off across the square after her. 'Excuse me!' she called out again, this time much louder.

The woman turned and looked back at her, a querying frown on her freckled, moon-shaped face.

'Ye dropped yer purse,' Rene said as she approached her. 'It was under yer seat.'

The woman's mouth dropped open in horror. 'Oh my God!' she said, taking the purse from Rene's outstretched hand. 'I can't believe I'd do that. My whole life's in this purse. How can I ever thank ye?'

Rene smiled at her. The woman spoke with an accent not dissimilar to her own, and although Rene could tell she didn't hail from Yorkshire or County Durham, just the very tone of her voice was like a homecoming, a comfort to hear.

'Think nowt of it,' Rene replied with a shrug of her shoulders. 'Lucky I saw it.'

'Well, let me at least buy you a coffee.' The woman flicked a thumb behind her towards the Sheraton Grand. 'I'm going into that 'otel there.'

Rene shook her head. 'Thanks, but ah can't. Ah'm waiting for someone. Any road, ah've just ordered a cappuccino back there at the café.'

'Right, well, in that case, what can ah say other than thanks.' Rene stuck her hands deep into the pockets of her huge coat. 'It was a pleasure.'

A quizzical frown came over the woman's face once more. ''Ave we met before?'

'Ah don't think so.'

'It's just that you look quite familiar.'

'Maybe you've seen my double in *Vogue* or summat like that.' The woman laughed. 'Aye, maybe that's it.'

'Ah'm always being mistaken.'

'Ah'm sure y'are.'

Rene turned to see the waiter put her cup of cappuccino on the table. He lit the patio warmer that stood next to it, and then glanced around for his customer. She caught his eye and raised a hand. 'Ah'd better get back, then,' she said, pointing a finger.

'Aye, ye'd better. And thanks again for the purse. That was a real lifesaver.'

Giving her a brief wave of farewell, Rene turned and walked back to her table.

She was savouring every sip of her frothy cappuccino, floating with an overabundance of flaked chocolate, when she saw Jamie appear back through the swing doors of the hotel and cast a searching look around the square. When he caught sight of Rene, he beckoned for her to come quickly. She stood up, her eyes darting back and forth between him and the inviting cup of coffee. 'Oh, damnation!' she said under her breath, rummaging in her handbag for her purse. She showered some coins on to the table, slung her handbag on to her shoulder and hurried over to the steps.

'What's up?' she asked.

'Bloody Dessuin's standing in the queue right now at the reception. He was meant to have gone back to Paris.'

''Ow d'ye know it's 'im?'

'Because I've seen his picture in a newspaper. Anyway, he's also got her blue suitcase and the violin with him.'

'But I thought yer lawyer had said he'd booked out.'

'I know. That's what's puzzling me. He must have come back, which means . . .'

Rene saw the gaunt look of realisation on Jamie's face. 'Means what?'

'Somehow he's worked out Angélique is still here in Edinburgh.'

Rene blew out a long breath. 'Aye, that *would* seem the logical answer. So what should we do?'

'Only one thing for it. I've got to get her suitcase and violin now. There's never going to be another opportunity.'

'But 'ow?'

'I'm not sure yet,' Jamie replied, turning back towards the swing doors. 'Come on, you'd better come with me. If the worse comes to the worst, you'll have to set up some kind of diversion.'

Rene pushed through the swing doors in pursuit of Jamie and scurried along the carpeted corridor to catch up with him. ''Ow do I do that?'

'I have no idea,' Jamie said as he descended the wide black-banistered staircase leading down to the reception area. 'Hopefully it won't be necessary, but you'll just have to use your imagination, if need be.'

'We're not going to break the law, are we?'

But Rene got no answer to her question. She stood trans-fixed on the final landing of the stairs, watching Jamie as he made his way over to the reception where a tall thin man with a belted mackintosh was in heated debate with the young recep-tionist, his hands gesticulating in annoyance as he tried to put his point across to her.

Rene slowly descended the remaining few steps in a knee-knocking trance of panic, her eyes never leaving Jamie as he nonchalantly reached down to pick up the blue suitcase and the violin that stood in the row of luggage behind the man. This is not going to work, she thought to herself.

'Oh, I've suddenly come over all faint,' she said shrilly to no one in particular, theatrically grabbing hold of the large square banister knob and weaving her body in a circular motion, not unlike a spinning top that was coming to the end of its centrifugal momentum. The true fact was that the tension of the whole situation was making her feel particularly light-headed, which helped to reassure her of the realistic nature of her performance. Unfortunately, though, she delivered her line with such clarity and volume that she not only attracted the attention of all those who were present in the hotel lobby but also the very person whom Jamie was so far doing a very good job of evading. There was a brief moment when he glanced over to her with an agonised look on his face before he made a fast and furtive dart for the back entrance of the hotel, clutching Angélique's suit-case and violin. Through her oscillating vision, Rene watched as the Frenchman's unsympathetic glare turned from her, the lady in distress, to Jamie, the boy in quick retreat, his expression changing in an instant from annoyance to open-mouthed horror.

'Hey, you, come back with those!' he yelled out at the top of his voice as he took off after Jamie, who had by this time disap-peared out into the street. Rene glanced down at the floor, measuring her distance, and with a final, desperate prayer that the Sheraton Grand had not scrimped on its furnishing budget and that the carpet was indeed a plush, top-of-the-range

Axminster with a deep spongy underlay, she fell poleaxed to the ground, on the very spot where Dessuin was about to plant his neat black, highly polished shoe. Like a racehorse that had an obstacle the size of a Grand National fence suddenly dropped in front of it, Dessuin could do nothing to avoid the prostrate form. His foot caught the side of Rene's body with such force she momentarily opened her eyes wide, muffling a cry of pain, as Dessuin's charcoal-worsted legs flew over her in a horizontal arc. As she heard the thump of his body coming to rest next to hers, she hurriedly closed her eyes and feigned serene uncon-sciousness, hoping that her face was giving off the colour of insipid magnolia rather than the much more likely raging red of a well-stoked brazier. She sensed people gathering around her, some giving helpful commands like 'Stand back and give her air,' and then, rather alarmingly, hands started to undo the top buttons of her shirt. If ye go to the next one down, she thought to herself, I'm going to slap yer bloody 'and away, regardless. And then she heard a female voice, further away from those surrounding her, say something that certainly had the effect of draining any excess colour from her face.

'I'll call the police immediately, sir.'

'No, don't do that,' came the immediate reply. 'I do not want to involve the police.'.

'But, sir, you've just had some luggage stole—'

'I said I do not want you to call the police.' Rene heard Dessuin let out a short unconvincing laugh. 'It is all a bit of a misunderstanding. I know who has taken the cases. I will get them back from him.'

There was a pause, during which someone raised Rene's head off the floor and slipped a soft cushion underneath it.

'Well, if you're sure, sir.'

'Quite sure. I will deal with it all once I am in my room.' Rene heard the man's soft tread skirt round the foot of her supine body. 'Does anyone know who this woman might be?' he asked.

Oh, no, Rene thought to herself, this is it. I've been found out. This must 'ave been 'ow it felt for a member of the Resis-

nce to be picked up by the Gestapo. I wonder 'ow I'll 'old
) under interrogation. Oh, please, God, all I ask is that I can
t to go to the loo first.

'Aye, she's a friend of mine,' a female voice replied, very close
Rene's head. 'We were about to have tea together when she
id she was feeling faint and headed off to the ladies' toilet.'

There was a pause before the Frenchman's voice replied, 'Very
ell,' and then Rene heard him walk away. She flickered one
e, trying desperately to see who it was that had come to her
scue. Through the diffusion of her eyelid, she could make out
e wild tangle of curly red hair and the huge pink scarf.

'That's about five minutes now,' the woman's voice whispered
) her. 'I reckon that's sufficient time to be in your so-called
int. Just flutter your eyelids a bit like you're seducing Brad Pitt
id then let out a bit of a moan.'

Rene smiled, her eyes still tightly shut. 'I'm 'oping those were
ur 'ands that were getting dangerously close to my cleavage.'

'No such luck, pet. That was Brad Pitt.'

Rene fought hard to suppress a giggle, but it spluttered out
:vertheless.

'I said moan, you daft cow, not laugh!'

Rene did as was requested, and with a dazzling flicker of
'elids looked up into the round freckled face of the woman
hose purse she had returned. There was such an expression of
larity in her greeny-grey eyes that Rene had a strong urge to
irst out laughing there and then. Not that it would probably
ive mattered. She realised the woman was now the only person
ho was paying any attention to her.

'Ye're Lancashire, aren't ye?' Rene said, seeing no reason now
) speak in hushed tones. 'I've just worked it out.'

'Aye, and you're Yorkshire ... or were at one time.' The woman
rinkled up her squat little nose. 'I remembered where I recog-
ised you from. Ye're Rene Brownlow, aren't ye? I've seen yer
iow.'

Rene raised her eyebrows in astonishment. 'Well, fancy that.
ame at last.'

'You should write that fainting bit into your repertoire,' the woman said, giving Rene's arm a light shove with her hand. 'It was one of the funniest things I've seen in years.'

'I thought it was quite convincing,' Rene replied, feigning pique.

'Well, if you're ever thinking about getting a bit part in *ER*, you'd have to improve on that performance.'

Rene grinned at the woman. 'Thanks for stepping in just then. I thought my cover was blown.'

The woman shrugged. 'One good turn deserves another. Anyway, us comediennes had better stick together, isn't that right?'

'Oh my word, is that what ye do too?'

'Aye, every day, every night.' The woman stuck out her hand. 'Matti Fullbright.'

Rene took the hand and shook it. ''Ullo, Matti Fullbright. Listen, while ye've got an 'old of me 'and, d'ye think you could 'eave me back up on to me pins?'

'Aye, sure, but you'd better make it look as if you're still a bit unsteady, just for authenticity's sake, OK?'

Rene accomplished the upward movement and held hard to Matti's hand as she weaved her body round once more.

'Right, you can stop that now,' Matti said, glancing around her. 'No one's taking a blind bit of notice. Listen, how d'ye fancy a nice cup of tea?'

Rene flicked her head to the side. 'I'd really like that, lass, but I think I'd better get back to me flat. I've got to make sure of a few things.'

'Like if your young friend made it back there with the suit-case and violin?'

Rene smiled. 'My, what intuition you 'ave, Matti Fullbright.'

'Can I ask what the hell all that was about?'

Rene bent down and picked up her handbag. 'I can't tell you right now, but believe me, we were both doing someone a good turn.'

'Aye, I'm sure you were,' Matti replied. 'I didn't like the look of that man from the moment he came into the hotel. He gave me the once-over as he walked past, and from the expression on his face ye'd think he'd just stepped in a bloody great dog's mess. Took every ounce of my female gentility not to give him the finger.' She took hold of Rene's arm. 'Come on, let's get out of here. We'll go out the front, so it don't look as if we're following in the path of the suitcase snatcher.' As they began to climb the stairs, Matti stopped and turned round. 'Who'd give a damn anyway?' she said, surveying the people who criss-crossed the reception area. She shook her crazy mop of red hair. 'Typical, in't it? Ten minutes ago you were the centre of attention, and now not one person's paying you the blindest bit of notice.'

Rene shrugged. 'That's an entertainer's life for you.'

They turned and made their way up the staircase, both unaware that the person with the dark-rimmed spectacles and the belted mackintosh, who had been sitting out of sight on the other side of the staircase, had paid a great deal of notice to everything that had passed between them during the previous five minutes.

Halfway across Festival Square, Rene stopped and looked back at the imposing frontage of the hotel. 'So what were *you* doing in that place? A bit posh for the likes of us, in't it?'

'I had a meeting with my agent.'

Rene looked suitably impressed. 'Really? My word, you must be at the top of the game.'

Matti stuck her hand into her blue canvas tote bag, pulled out a leaflet and handed it to Rene. 'Come and see the show sometime. I'll make sure it's a freebie, all right?'

Rene glanced at the leaflet. ''Eaven's sakes, you're on at the Smirnoff Underbelly!' she said in astonishment. 'That's one of the top venues, in't it?'

Matti shrugged her shoulders. 'Well, I've been lucky. I was there last year and they asked me to come back.'

'You must be damned good, then.'

Matti reached out and squeezed Rene's arm. 'Come and see for yourself.'

'I will,' she replied, pushing the leaflet into her handbag, 'and thanks again, lass, for yer help back there.'

'And likewise, thanks for my purse. See you around, I hope.'

And as Matti Fullbright strode off across the square, Rene let out a long, satisfied breath as she watched her go, realising that her lonely existence in Edinburgh had taken a change for the better over the past hour or two. Jamie had *needed* her confidentiality and help that morning, and she liked nothing better than to feel *needed,* to take over, step into the fray, just like when that singer never turned up at Andersons Westbourne Social Club and she took to the stage for the first time. And then in meeting Matti Fullbright, with her peculiar zany looks and wild sense of humour, Rene realised that, for the first time ever, she had come across a person who was *just like her.*

She smiled to herself as she saw Matti disappear out of sight. 'Aye, see you around,' she murmured.

Thirty-Two

Albert Dessuin flicked back the net curtain of his newly designated bedroom, situated now on the fourth floor of the hotel but still with the same wide panoramic view over Festival Square. Even through the diffusion of the curtain, it had been easy enough to single out the bumbling little figure with the loose-fitting multicoloured coat that threaded its way through the crowds and then turned down Lothian Road towards Princes Street. Letting go of the curtain, he took off his mackintosh and threw it on to a chair. He was not unduly worried by the way things had turned out. In fact, they could not have turned out much better.

This was contrary to the blisteringly angry mood he had been in when he had arrived back at the hotel an hour earlier. Whilst returning from the airport in the taxi, he had had time to mull over all the facts leading up to Angélique's disappearance, and it had slowly begun to dawn on him that, from the start, she had been playing him along in a cruel and calculated game of deception, making him feel wretched and guilty for

mething that had never been his fault in the first place. She
d orchestrated the whole affair, displaying her naked body in
ont of him like that, knowing that he had already admonished
r for her sluttish behaviour. His reaction of fury was totally
atural, one that came from a deep sense of protection for his
otégée, but she had twisted his motives, using them as the
ry reason for which to walk away from him, from everything
at he, Albert Dessuin, had bestowed upon her. And this story
out her having cut her hand and returning to France was just
other way in which she was trying to manipulate him, to put
m off the scent and literally to blackmail him into keeping
vay from her by not disclosing the full story, which they both
new to be nothing more than a harmless row between them.
Vell, she had made a grave mistake. She certainly would not
t rid of him that easily.

There was no chance of him ever being able to recognise the
oung man who took the suitcase and the violin, save for the
ct that he had blond hair and was stockily built. He was undoubt-
lly one of those who had clustered around Angélique with
eir tongues hanging out at the post-concert reception, their
es fixed on the glories that lay beneath her short dress as she
t on the bar, shamelessly crossing and uncrossing her legs. But
en his instincts had been right about that red-haired girl. He
d seen her the moment he had walked into the reception area
n his return from the airport. She had been sitting on one of
e sofas lining the walls of the hotel lobby, talking across a low
offee table to a dark-haired woman dressed in a sombre pencil-
kirted suit worn over a cream cashmere polo-neck sweater.
eauty and the Beast, he had thought to himself. He did not
ke red-haired girls. He had always thought them the unattrac-
ve product of recessive genes, and this one in particular had
ot one redeeming feature to speak of, with her wide-set eyes,
er moon face and a nose which made her look as if she had
alked at speed into a plate-glass window. And her dress sense
d been almost offensive to the eye. Why would anyone choose
 wear a pink scarf with hair that colour?

He knew she had never before laid eyes on the fat little woman who had foiled his pursuit of the young man. That's why he had decided to hang around, out of sight but within earshot, after the mêlée had died down. He hadn't been able to decipher everything they had said to each other in their brogueish accents, but he had understood enough and had heard every derogatory word she had had to say about him.

He walked over to the bed and picked up the thick copy of the Fringe show guide that he'd found on the display stand next to the reception desk. He opened it up at the index and ran a manicured fingernail down the first column, and then the second. He found what he was looking for halfway down. He memorised the venue reference number and leafed through the guide until he came to the correct page. 'Hilarious Comedienne from Hartlepool' was the strapline above the photograph of the woman whose face he had first seen as she lay flat out on the carpeted floor of the hotel lobby. *Mon Dieu,* she must be bad, he thought to himself, if she can come up with no better advertisement for her act than that!

Creasing the guide open at the page, he spun it on to the desk and walked over to the minibar and took out a miniature of Scotch and a bottle of mineral water. It was really too early to start drinking, but what the hell! His plans had changed now. There was no reason for him to go off immediately in search of Angélique Pascal. He would take his time, let the heat die down. After all, the show was on every night in the Corinthian Bar.

Pouring himself a drink, he let out a short quiet laugh and raised his glass. 'Here's to you, Rene Brownlow. I'm sure in time you will prove very useful to me.'

Thirty-Three

Desperate to get away from the vicinity of the hotel as quickly as possible, Jamie had bundled himself and Angélique's luggage to a passing taxi and slumped down into the seat beneath the level of the rear window, expecting to hear at any moment the ominous sound of a police siren threading its way through the traffic towards them. He was actually quite amazed he had got as far. Because of Rene's extraordinary outburst in the hotel, he knew that Dessuin had caught sight of him before he had even left the place. Under normal circumstances, he was sure he would have outpaced the man quite easily, but burdened with the suitcase and violin, he thought he would have had the Frenchman breathing down his neck before he'd even reached the street. Maybe Rene had managed to set up some kind of diversion, but he couldn't imagine how. There had only been a moment for her to react.

By the time the taxi dropped him outside his flat, Jamie was beginning to have serious concerns about the comedienne's welfare, realising now that it had been both unwise and unfair to have involved her to such an extent. It would have been pretty obvious to anyone with half a brain in the hotel foyer that her coming over all faint at the very moment when he was making a run for it with the suitcases was more than coincidental, and he was convinced she would now be closeted in some back office of the hotel being interviewed not only by the police, but by a very interested Albert Dessuin as well. And if that was the case, then not only would she be forced to identify Jamie as the 'mastermind' behind the bag snatch, but also Angélique's whereabouts as well.

Having paid off the taxi, he let himself in through the entrance door and ran up the stairs, his heart in his mouth as he tried to work out his next move. Maybe he should ring Gavin straightaway and tell him what had happened. At least then, if the police did come to arrest him, Gavin would have had time to prepare some sort of defence for him and get him out on bail. He wasn't too sure what police procedure would be. Or maybe he should hang fire for twenty minutes or so, just in case Rene came back by herself.

He entered the flat and hurried over to the telephone. He

couldn't risk waiting for Rene. He picked up the receiver and began to dial the number of Gavin's law firm, but just before he hit the fourth digit he stopped, his finger poised in mid-air, and stood listening to the low reverberation of voices coming from the sitting room. He slowly replaced the receiver as he heard Angélique speaking a long, drawn-out sentence before it was answered by the lower and much more resonant tones of a male voice. Jamie exhaled with relief, realising it could only be his solicitor, and he walked quickly along the hall passage to the door of the sitting room and threw it open.

'Gavin, thank goodness you're—'

Angélique and a heavily built middle-aged man in a gabardine raincoat were sitting on one of the sofas, their mouths frozen in mid-conversation as both looked round in surprise at his sudden entry, the man's ballpoint pen still hovering above a spiral notepad.

'What's going on?' Jamie demanded, his eyes ablaze with both concern and distrust for the man. 'Who are you?'

Angélique quickly uncurled her feet from underneath her and stood up. 'It's all right, Jamie. This is Harry Wills. He is a journalist who is an acquaintance of mine. It was he—'

Jamie shook his head, never taking his eyes off the man. 'I told you not to let anyone into the flat. What the hell's the point of me trying to hide you away if you allow any Tom, Dick or Harry into the place?'

He knew as soon as he had said it, it was the wrong metaphor to use. Angélique frowned at him and unwittingly capitalised on it. 'Who is Tom and Dick?'

'This is not a joke, Angélique.'

Harry Wills flipped over his notebook and stood up. 'I'm sorry, this is my fault. You're absolutely right. I should never have come round without giving you both some warning.'

'How did you find out she was here, anyway?' Jamie asked abruptly.

'If you will just listen to me for a moment, Jamie, I shall tell you,' Angélique said, her voice rising in frustration at his hostile attitude. 'It was Harry who wrote the story about me having cut my hand and leaving the country. I suggested his name to Gavin, and they both met to work out what should be written in the newspapers. Harry knows what has happened, Jamie. He is helping us, along with Gavin.'

The explanation did little to lighten the thunderous expression on Jamie's face as he glanced from one to the other. 'Well, that's just great. Maybe it would have been an idea to let *me* know about all this as well.'

Angélique bit at her bottom lip in an effort to stop smiling at his moody reaction. She walked over to him and gave the sleeve of his corduroy jacket a tug. 'I am very sorry. It was very bad of me not to tell you, and I promise I will not overlook such a thing again.'

'I'm being quite serious, actually,' Jamie mumbled.

Angélique pulled a long face, stood to attention and gave him a brisk salute. 'I quite agree, and I am now taking it very seriously, don't you think?'

Jamie smiled reluctantly. 'Oh, get lost,' he said, waving a hand in the general direction of the hall. 'Your suitcase and violin are out there.'

'*Oh, ce n'est pas vrai!*' Angélique exclaimed. She jumped forward and gave him a quick peck on the cheek before rushing out into the hall.

Jamie turned to the journalist when she had left the room. 'Sorry about the misunderstanding.'

Harry Wills waved his notebook dismissively. 'No bother. Anyway, you were quite right to question my presence here. You're obviously doing a good job of looking after her.'

Jamie shrugged off the compliment. 'Were you doing an interview?' he asked, nodding towards the notebook.

'Not about immediate events, I can assure you, and anyway, nothing will get printed until this whole situation has rectified itself.'

'Well, we've a long way to go before that happens,' Jamie murmured ruefully.

'What makes you say that?'

Jamie pushed his hands into the pockets of his jacket and took a backward step to glance along the hall, just in time to see Angélique beam him a broad smile as she disappeared into her bedroom with the suitcase and violin. He closed the door of the sitting room with a shove of his foot and turned to the journalist. 'Listen, Dessuin's figured out that the story about Angélique returning to France is untrue. He knows she's still in Edinburgh, and by now he could very well know she's here in this flat.'

Harry Wills's expression showed immediate concern. 'Why do you think that?'

'Because I've just seen him booking himself back into the Sheraton Grand. What's more, he saw me, or at least the back of me, when I took Angélique's cases.'

'You took the cases from in front of his eyes?' the journalist asked incredulously.

'No, they were actually sitting behind him. I reckon I would have got away with it, only . . . well, let's just say he turned round at the wrong time.'

'But he didn't follow you?'

'No, for definite.'

'Then what gives you reason to believe he might find his way round here?'

Jamie told him briefly of Rene's involvement in the suitcase snatch and his uncertainty as to what had happened to her. When he had finished, Harry Wills stood in silence, slapping his notebook rhythmically against the side of his raincoat.

'Well,' he said eventually, 'this poses a bit of a problem for us all, doesn't it?'

Jamie felt almost angry at this ridiculous understatement of facts. 'Of course it poses a problem – especially for me! I could well get arrested for what I've just done.'

Harry waved a hand at him. 'I don't think you need worry about anything like that happening. If the worst comes to the worst, then we'll tell the true story. Remember the only reason we're in this situation is because Angélique wanted to protect

Dessuin's name. My instinct tells me the man will do his utmost to avoid involving the police, just for that very reason.'

Jamie stood for a moment considering the journalist's logic before breathing out a sigh of relief. 'Yeah, that would make sense, wouldn't it?' He clicked his fingers as a thought came into his head. 'But wait, we're forgetting about Rene. If Dessuin knows she was helping me, then he'll surely find out from her where I'm living, or even if he *doesn't* question her, he could still just follow her around here.'

'Would there be any reason for Dessuin to think she *might* have been helping you?'

Jamie blew out a derisive laugh. 'God, yes! She would have been as well having a notice hanging round her neck saying, *Hey, look at me! I am the thief's number-one accomplice*"!'

While Harry looked thoughtful over this new predicament, Jamie heard Angélique in her bedroom play a cautious scale on her violin. Although the notes were clear and resonant, the speed at which she played them seemed falteringly pedestrian. Nevertheless, Jamie knew it was a major achievement and a boost to the violinist's shattered confidence, and if he hadn't been so concerned with the seriousness of the situation, he might well have felt like letting out a whoop of triumph there and then.

'Is there anyplace you and Angélique could lie low for a couple of days?' the journalist asked.

'Here in Edinburgh, d'you mean?'

'No, preferably away from the city.'

Jamie looked dubious. 'I'm not sure. I'm meant to be writing fringe reviews, but I suppose I could get out of that. What about my tenants, though?'

'Hopefully, it would only be for a few days. I'm sure they could fend for themselves during that time.' He paused, seeing Jamie still vacillate over making a decision. 'I'd strongly recommend the idea.'

Jamie shrugged his shoulders. 'In that case, I suppose we could go to my parents' place in East Lothian.'

'That will be good,' Harry said, nodding his approval of the idea, 'and then while you're away, I'll stick myself outside your flat and keep an eye out for Dessuin turning up here.'

'Really? Would you mind doing that?'

Harry laughed. 'I was an investigative journalist for a good number of years, Jamie, so I'm quite used to spending many a lonely hour sitting in my car outside people's houses.'

Jamie stared at the man for a moment. 'Can I ask you a question?'

'Shoot,' Harry replied.

'Why are you willing to give us so much help? Surely, with the festival on, you've got a hundred better things to be doing with your time?'

Harry sat his sizeable bottom down on the arm of a sofa. 'Quite simply because I have absolutely no time for Albert Dessuin. He happens to be one of the most discourteous human beings I've ever had the displeasure of meeting.'

'You *know* him?'

'Let's just say there have been numerous occasions over the past few years when I've been party to the more unpleasant side of his nature. Ever since Angélique Pascal left the Conservatoire in Paris, I have been trying my damnedest to get a personal interview with her and Dessuin has always been there to thwart my attempts.' He clicked the top on his ballpoint pen. 'Does that answer your question?'

'Yes, I suppose it does,' Jamie replied with a smile.

'OK, so what I suggest is that if there's been neither sight nor sound of the man over the next few days, then I'll give the all-clear for you both to return to the flat. Do you have a number I could contact you on?'

Jamie reeled off the number of his mobile and the journalist wrote it down before slipping his pad into his coat pocket and getting to his feet. 'Right, you and Angélique should get yourselves ready to go as soon as possible.'

'Which brings us to another problem,' Jamie said tentatively. 'I don't have wheels.'

Harry pushed back the folds of his raincoat and delved into

a trouser pocket. 'In that case,' he said, taking out his own mobile phone, 'I think it's time we involved Gavin Mackintosh.'

The sound of the front door slamming shut had both men looking questioningly at each other. Jamie walked over to the sitting-room door, opened it a fraction and squinted down the hall. 'Oh, hell! It could be too late!' he exclaimed quietly, glancing round at Harry. 'It's Rene.' He opened the door fully to see the comedienne stagger exhaustedly along the passage towards him.

'Glad to see ye made it back,' she said, taking off her coat as she walked past him into the sitting room and dumping it, along with her handbag, on to a chair. She gave a quick nod of greeting to Harry Wills before flopping herself down on to a sofa and kicking off her shoes. 'I am absolutely dead beat,' she puffed out, awkwardly pulling a stockinged foot up across her knee and giving it a rub. 'That's far too much excitement for one day.' She glanced up at Jamie and Harry, who had now come to stand side by side in front of the fireplace, observing her closely, trying to work out from her demeanour whether they had an imminent problem to face. 'So, aren't you going to introduce me to yer friend, Jamie?'

'Oh, yeah, sorry; this is Harry Wills.'

'Nice to meet ye, 'Arry,' Rene said, holding out the hand with which she had been rubbing at her foot. She then thought better of it and just waved it at him. 'Let's just forgo that formality.'

'Rene, what happened?' Jamie asked, eager to ply her for information. 'Why didn't Dessuin come after me?'

'Because I set up a diversion, just like ye asked me.'

'How?'

'I pretended to faint right in 'is path.'

Jamie pulled his hands across his head in desperation. 'Oh, God. What did he do?'

'He gave me a kick in the ribs, and then flew through the air and fell with a thump to the floor.'

'OK, but what happened then? Were the police called? Were you questioned at all?'

Rene closed her eyes tight as if in deep concentration. 'I think the answer to that is, nothing, no, no,' she replied before resuming her foot massage. 'It was all a bit odd, really. I was lying on the floor with me eyes closed, pretending to be out for the count when some girl – I think it was probably the receptionist – asked if she should call the police, and the Frenchman went all sort of panicky and said he didn't want them involved. He said he knew who ye were and 'e'd sort it all out later.'

Jamie frowned apprehensively at the journalist, who answered it immediately with a dismissive shake of his head.

'That's exactly what I thought he'd do,' Harry said, 'and he was just bluffing when he said he knew you, so don't worry about it.'

Jamie turned his attention back to Rene. 'But he must have known you were helping me. Weren't you asked any questions at all?'

'No. Mind you, I've little doubt I would 'ave been, if it 'adn't been for this girl coming to my rescue.'

'How?' both Jamie and Harry asked in unison.

'Well, when I was still flat out on the floor, the Frenchman asked, in a sort of general way, whether anybody knew me, and this girl said she did and that I was a friend of 'ers, and we were going to have a cup of tea together when I'd come over all faint.'

'And Dessuin believed her?' Harry asked.

'I'm certain of it. 'E just stormed away after that, probably went straight up to 'is room.'

Harry and Jamie glanced at each other, relief written on their faces.

'So, there's absolutely no chance Dessuin could have followed you back here?' Jamie asked.

'Why would 'e want to do that? The girl made it pretty clear I was just an innocent bystander. Anyway, I had to stop off in a pub on the way back to go to the loo, and when I came out I certainly didn't see anyone lurking about.' She let go of her foot and stood up. 'Now, unless you've got some more furtive action planned, I think I might just get back to my normal pace of life.'

Jamie approached the comedienne and planted a kiss on her

ot round cheek. 'Thanks, Rene, for being a real star. I could
ave ended up in deep shit if it hadn't been for you.'

Rene smiled at him. 'Glad to be of assistance,' she said, moving
ff towards the door. 'Just don't expect me to do it every day,
ight? Otherwise I'll 'ave to be charging ye the full union rates
or a thief's assistant.'

When she had left the room, Jamie turned round to the jour-
alist. 'Looks like we're in the clear, then,' he remarked hope-
illy.

'We might be,' Harry replied with a reserved flick of the head.

'You don't think so?'

'Let's just say Dessuin is no fool. He's now back in Edinburgh
n a mission, and as yet he has no leads. He doesn't want to
nvolve the police and he certainly won't want to involve the
nternational office, so I reckon he'll be looking to grasp on to
ny small oddity or coincidence. Maybe Rene and her friend
lid manage to convince everyone in the hotel with their act,
ut it just could be that Dessuin saw it all as being a bit suspect.'

'So what are you saying? That he could be standing outside
he flat right now?'

'No, I'm pretty sure Rene was right in saying she wasn't
ollowed here. However, we don't want to give Dessuin any
pportunity to be doing clever things behind our backs, so I
hink we should still continue with the plan for you and Angélique
o leave Edinburgh. If he doesn't show up here over the next
wo days, I reckon then, and only then, we can probably say
ve're in the clear.' He thumbed a couple of buttons on his mobile
hone. 'OK, so let's see now if we can't get hold of Gavin
Mackintosh.'

Thirty-Four

Leonard Hartson had a smile on his face as he climbed the
teps to the entrance of the London Street flat. It had been

there ever since T.K. had appeared out of the small barber's shop next to The Jeans Warehouse on Princes Street, where, on his own insistence, he had had his greasy mane reduced to a very presentable and very clean fuzz of hair. It had had the immediate effect of not only transforming his features, but some of his more unsavoury characteristics as well as if, in its cutting, T.K. had rid his body of some virulent, energy-sapping, brain-numbing amoeba. His vacant eyes now looked alert, his pallid cheeks flushed with colour (although Leonard knew that that was initially due to T.K.'s embarrassment at his new look), and there was even a determined rigidity to his loose-lipped mouth. But the most extraordinary by-product of the barber's clippers had been to unlock the floodgates on a verbosity Leonard would never before have thought to exist in the lad's slow-witted head.

With the shopping bags bearing his new purchases gathered round his feet in the taxi, T.K. had questioned Leonard incessantly on all aspects of film-making, hardly waiting for a reply before he was on to the next query. Even now, while Leonard extracted the keys of the door from his jacket pocket, T.K. stood beside him eager to find out how long it had taken Leonard to be considered proficient enough to operate a camera. While the cameraman paused in his action of putting the key in the lock, casting his mind back over countless years in an attempt to come up with an accurate answer, the entrance door flew open and his young landlord appeared, shouldering a rucksack. His presence had the immediate effect of cutting off T.K.'s verbal assault, which Leonard greeted with a clandestine sigh of relief, likening it to that first brief moment of silence after a plug has been pulled on a blaring radio.

'I'm glad I've caught you, Mr Hartson,' Jamie said, as he came down on to the steps, his eyes momentarily glancing with astonishment at T.K.'s incongruous new hairstyle. 'I have to head off for a couple of days, so just use the flat as your own. I've left my mobile number on the hall table if you need to contact me for any reason.'

Leonard was about to speak when Gavin Mackintosh, the solicitor who had introduced him to T.K., appeared at the entrance door carrying a canvas zip-up overnight bag and a violin case. 'Ah, Mr Hartson, I do hope everything's going well for you both,' he said, before catching sight of T.K. and almost doing a double take. 'My word, Thomas! You've changed into a dapper-looking fellow. Well done, you!' He gave T.K. a pat on the arm before hurrying off down the steps. He was closely followed by a young girl who had appeared through the door wearing a short jacket with the collar turned up and a large pair of sunglasses that obscured her features. Gavin opened the back passenger door of a Volvo estate car and waited for the girl to get in before walking around to the back to put her luggage in the boot.

While this furtive operation was in progress, Leonard noticed Jamie casting searching glances up and down the street. 'Right,' he said, making a move to join them once the man was seated behind the driving wheel. 'I'll see you when I get back.'

'Could I just have a moment of your time?' Leonard asked quickly, realising there seemed to be a degree of urgency in their departure.

Jamie paused on the bottom step. 'Sure,' he replied, turning.

'I had hoped to get the chance to explain this in more detail, but I do see you're pressed for time, so I'll be as brief as possible. It's just that T.K. here has unfortunately found himself to be temporarily without lodgings, and I wondered, therefore, if you might have any objections to him making use of the other bed in my room.'

Jamie bit on his bottom lip to stop himself from laughing at such an absurd idea. He immediately had this mental vision of them both tucked up in the two beds gazing into the darkness whilst they indulged themselves in a bit of Deep Meaningful Conversation.

'Yeah, that's fine by me.'

'Of course, it goes without saying that I shall pay a bit more for the rent of the room.'

'Oh, don't bother about that,' Jamie replied, dismissing the suggestion with a shake of his head.

'No, I insist. What would you say to eighty pounds per night for the both of us?'

'Seventy-five,' Jamie said in reply as he made his way to the pavement and opened the front passenger door of the Volvo. He dumped his rucksack into the footwell and glanced back at the two roommates. 'That's my final offer.'

Leonard smiled at him. 'That's very kind. Thank you.'

'Ring me if you have any problems,' Jamie called out as he got into the car, which began to move out into the street before he had even time to shut the door.

Leonard turned and raised an eyebrow at his crop-haired assistant. 'Well, looks like we're in business then.'

While T.K. went off to have his much needed shower, Leonard made use of the telephone in the hall to speak with Nick Springer in London, telling him of the progress he had made during the initial day's shooting and giving him the name of the courier service that would be delivering the exposed film stock to his office the following morning. Although Nick sounded pleased to hear from him, Leonard could sense from the producer's lack of reciprocative chat that he had caught him at a busy time, so he kept the call short. He then rang Grace and gave her a more in-depth account of what had passed that day, including news of the unavoidable, but somewhat irregular, sleeping arrangement he now had with his young assistant, T.K. He did not, however, mention to his wife the facts that led to this happening, knowing that it would only perturb her to hear he had taken a young vagrant off the streets, simply giving the reason that T.K. lived too far away for him to travel to work every day. Neither did he mention to her the doubts he had harboured earlier in the day about taking on both such a physical and financial burden at his advanced stage in life, and he certainly was not going tell her about the pain that had begun to nag intermittently at the left side of his chest. Nevertheless, as if by telepathy, while he now pressed a hand to the troublesome area, Grace told him that he was not to overdo it and asked him if he was remembering to take his pills. 'Of course I am, my dear,' he replied. 'Don't worry about me, I'm quite capable of looking after myself.'

When he replaced the receiver after the call, Leonard turned to find a young man standing in front of him whom he hardly recognised. His own expression must have been enough to convey this because T.K.'s face immediately broke into a broad grin.

'What d'ya think, then?' he said, his arms outstretched as he gave himself the once-over.

Leonard nodded approvingly as he appraised the new-look T.K., with his clean white T-shirt, stiff new Levi's tightened at the waist by a wide belt with a Harley Davidson buckle, and the virginal-white pair of Adidas trainers. Slung over his shoulder, a finger through its hanging loop, was the new Timberland jacket at which T.K. had gawped longingly in the shop while Leonard was paying the bill for two identical pairs of jeans, six white T-shirts, a four-pack of boxer shorts and a six-pack of white socks, one cotton sweatshirt, one belt, and a pair of Adidas trainers. 'And I think we'd better take that jacket as well,' Leonard had said quietly to the shop assistant.

'Well?' T.K. asked again.

'I think you look very . . . clean.'

'Is that a'?' T.K. exclaimed.

Leonard laughed. 'No, I really am very impressed, T.K.'

T.K. smirked bashfully. 'Cheers, Leonard.'

'And I think it's only right that we should celebrate your new and much improved appearance by searching out a suitable eating establishment that can provide us with some well-earned sustenance.'

'Eh?' T.K. remarked, reverting too easily to his imbecilic look, his mouth curled up at one side.

'How would a very large beef steak and a glass of beer suit you?'

'Oh, aye, tha' sounds great,' T.K. replied enthusiastically, his face brightening with comprehension. He swung the new jacket off his shoulder and shrugged it on.

A door opening at the far end of the hall made them both turn, and their fellow tenant appeared, her attention caught up with trying to find something in her large handbag. Rene looked up and saw them.

'My word!' she said, her eyes fixed on T.K. as she came along the passage. 'What 'appened to you? Did ye fall in front of a street cleaner or summat?'

Leonard held out a hand as she approached them. 'We've met in passing, but not yet introduced ourselves. My name's Leonard Hartson.'

Rene shook his hand. 'Nice to meet you, Leonard. Rene Brownlow.'

'Are you just on your way out?'

'Aye, I am.'

'In that case, you wouldn't care to join us for something to eat? T.K. and I were just going out to celebrate a very successful day's work.'

Rene sucked her teeth disappointedly. 'Oh, what a grand thought, but I can't, luv. I've got to do a show in 'alf an 'our. Maybe another time.'

Leonard opened the front door and stood aside to allow her to leave the flat first. 'Well, consider it a firm invitation then.'

'I'll tell you what, though,' Rene said as she walked past him. 'Seeing as Jamie's gone and left the lot of us 'ome alone, what about me cooking us all a meal tomorrow night? Wouldn't be until after me show, but if about nine o'clock would suit?'

Leonard glanced at T.K., who answered with a shrug of non-commitment. 'Well, I think that would suit us both very well,' Leonard replied with a nod. 'We shall look forward to it.'

'Right,' the comedienne said as she began to descend the
stairs. 'In that case, see you tomorrow night at La Maison de
Scene.'

Thirty-Five

During the journey out to East Lothian, what little conversation there was in the car was between the two men in the front,
though Jamie would occasionally glance round and ask
Angélique if she was all right, sensing she might be feeling somewhat excluded from proceedings. She was not, however, in a
great mind to talk. At first, when the car was travelling slowly
through the sprawling, colourless suburbs of Edinburgh, her mood
had been rock-bottom, the road seemingly taking her further
and further away from her previous life, and there was a moment
when she wanted to end all this craziness and tell Gavin to turn
the car around and take her back to the Sheraton Grand, regardless of the consequences. But then, as the fast dual carriageway
left behind the city, her spirits improved as the endless rows of
houses and industrial estates gave way to open countryside, and
it dawned on her that this was almost the first time since leaving
the Conservatoire she had not been viewing a country from
thirty-three thousand feet up in the air. Her troubled thoughts
and heart-aching doubts subsided as she looked out of the
window, shielding her eyes against the glare of the early evening
sun that shone gold on the ripe rolling wheat fields and glinted
off the bulky bodies of the combine harvesters that cut their
laser-straight paths through the crops. And when the car turned
off at Haddington and breasted the hill above the village of East
Linton, Angélique could not help but let out a quiet breath of
wonderment as she looked out across the wide panoramic view
of the rugged Lammermuir Hills shouldering in the velvet-green
coastline as it bent its way southward, leaving nothing but the
endless expanse of the North Sea before it.

Gavin swung the car to the right, curtailing Angélique's enjoyment of the vista, and took a narrow high-banked road tha wound its way up towards the hills. They drove through a sma village boasting both a pub and a post office but hardly of a siz to merit the thirty-mile-an-hour speed limit, and then turne left down a smooth dirt-track road with overgrown verges, pas a number of long, low livestock sheds with slatted sides and tid concrete aprons. A hundred metres on, they entered through stone-pillared gateway leading on to a gravelled drive bordere by well-tended lawns that were shadowed long by the sprawlin limbs of two ancient cypress trees. For a moment they hid from sight the tall white house with steep slated roof and craw-steppe gable ends that stood proudly defensive of a broad circular swee

As Gavin brought the Volvo to a scrunching halt in front o the house, a couple of black-and-white sheepdogs appeared from nowhere, made a beeline for the car and started biting ineffec tually at the front tyres with bared snarling teeth. Jamie imme diately opened the door and gave them a yell as he got out, bu it did little to stop their attempted mauling of the car. It wa only when a voice like thunder rang out around the grounds so loud it echoed off the side of the house, that the dogs cease their endeavours and slunk off to lie side by side on the lawn their eyes fixed on the quad bike that came at a breakneck spee up the drive. Angélique got out and stood gazing at her nev surroundings as the bike swung round at the back of the Volvo spurting up gravel that landed dangerously short of the car' gleaming paintwork.

'Hey, quit that, Stratton!' Gavin shouted angrily as he jumpe out and stomped round the back of the car to inspect it. 'I there's so much of a scratch, I'll have you foot the bill for complete respray.'

Angélique smiled at the grinning man who sat astride th mud-spattered quad. He was dressed in a heavy cotton lumberjack shirt and waterproof trousers pulled over wellington boots a battered baseball cap jammed back to front on his head. He put a dirt-ingrained hand up to his ear and delicately dislodge

earphone. The thumping beat that emanated from it was so
[lou]d that Angélique could hear it quite clearly from where she
[wa]s standing. 'I'm sorry,' the man said, looking at Gavin with a
[a]mused expression on his tanned weather-beaten face. 'I didn't
[qu]ite catch that. Did you say anything of interest just then,
[M]ackintosh?'

'God, he's such a lad,' Angélique heard Jamie mutter as he
[ca]me to stand beside her. He raised a long-suffering eyebrow at
[he]r. 'Come on, I'll introduce you to my father.'

They walked over to where the two men were already engaged
[in] a friendly but sparring banter.

'Dad, this is Angélique Pascal.'

The man swung a leg over the handlebars of the bike. 'Good
[to] meet you, Angélique,' he said, taking her by surprise by flip-
[pin]g off his cap and landing a bristly kiss on both her cheeks.
[I] understand you're a bit of a violinist.'

'A bit of a violinist!' Gavin exclaimed. 'God, you really are an
[un]educated heathen, Stratton.'

'Not at all,' Rory laughed, encircling his son's shoulders with
[a] pair of wiry arms and giving him a welcoming hug. 'Just
[be]cause our tastes in music differ somewhat.' Moving over to
[th]e car he opened up the boot, and took out Angélique's bag
[an]d her violin case. 'Come on, then,' he said, heading off towards
[th]e house, 'I reckon it must be time for a drink.'

'Count me out, Rory,' Gavin said, closing the boot. 'I have to
[be] getting back to Edinburgh.'

[Ja]mie's father turned, a disappointed frown on his face. 'Not
[ev]en a quick one?'

'Can't do, I'm afraid. I have a mountain of work to get through
[at] the office before I call it a day.'

'Oh, how deadly boring of you.'

Gavin smiled at his old school friend. 'Maybe another time,
[bu]t give my love to Prue and tell her I'm sorry to have missed
[he]r. I'll call you about golf, as well.' He waved to Angélique as
[h]e followed Rory towards the house before turning back to
[Ja]mie. 'How have you left things with Harry Wills?'

'He's going to call me in a couple of days' time if all's well.'

'And you can make your own way back?'

Jamie nodded. 'I'm sure I can persuade Dad to give us a lift.'

'Right, well, give me a call if you need anything.'

'Will do, and cheers, Gavin, for bringing us out here.'

'My pleasure,' the solicitor said as he got into the car. 'Let's hope this whole business has resolved itself by the time you get back.'

'Yeah, let's hope,' Jamie replied, giving him a wave of farewell as he turned towards the house.

The large, ornately furnished sitting room was warmed by the dusty rays of the setting sun streaming in through the three west-facing windows. When Jamie entered he found his father standing in jeans and stockinged feet in front of the unlit fire, a large glass of whisky in his hand.

'Where's Angélique?' Jamie asked.

'Your mother's showing her to her bedroom.' Rory took a healthy swallow of whisky and cocked his head to the side. 'Nice-looking girl, that.'

'Yes, she is,' Jamie replied indifferently, walking over to the drinks table and removing the ring pull from a can of beer.

'*Very* nice-looking, in fact,' Rory continued, a smile on his face as he eyed his son.

Jamie shook his head. 'Leave it out, Dad.'

Rory laughed. 'Just a bit of a leg-pull.' He sat down heavily in one of the pale-blue loose-covered armchairs. 'Oh, by the way, I bumped into Gordon McLaren in Dunbar today and told him you were coming out for a couple of days. He said there's a pre-season warm-up game tomorrow evening at the club if you wanted to play.'

Jamie shrugged. 'I suppose I could. I'm not that fit, though.'

'Do you some good, then, wouldn't it? Give him a call, anyway, and in the meantime you can start your fitness training early tomorrow morning by going up on to the hill and looking round the sheep for me. I've got some lambs going through the ring at Kelso, so I won't be able to do it.'

'Thanks for that, Dad,' Jamie replied morosely.

'Well, seeing you're home, you may as well do some work! Anyway, it's not that much of a slog. You'll be able to get the Land Rover as far as the gate above the high burn and then walk from there. You should take Angélique with you, as well. I'm sure she'd appreciate a taste of the Scottish wilderness.'

The door of the sitting room opened and Angélique entered with a small blonde woman dressed in a long denim skirt and white cotton shirt. Her face lit up when she saw Jamie and she came over to him, her arms outstretched. 'Darling, how are you?' she said, giving him a kiss on either cheek that left traces of her pale-pink lipstick.

'I'm good, Mum,' Jamie replied with a smile, 'except Dad's giving me grief as usual.'

Jamie's mother looked over at her husband, her expression turning to one of horror. 'Rory!' She hurried over to where he was sitting and delivered a resounding thwack to one of his knees. 'I'll give *you* grief, you dreadful man. Get out of that chair!' Rory leaped to his feet as if suddenly finding himself sitting on hot coals, and Jamie's mother dusted off the vacated seat with her hand. 'How many times do I have to tell you *not* to sit on these new loose covers in your filthy jeans?'

Rory twisted himself round to inspect his backside. 'They are not filthy. They were clean on this morning. Anyway, I've been wearing overtrousers all day.'

'That's as may be,' Jamie's mother said, puffing up the flattened cushions, 'but you still stink like an old tup.'

Rory pulled a schoolboy face at Angélique that made her smile unwittingly. 'I hope you've been treated a bit better by my wife.'

'Prue could not have been kinder to me,' Angélique replied.

'Just you wait. After two days in this house you'll be bossed around like the rest of us.'

'Oh, you do talk such rubbish!' Prue scoffed, taking hold of his arm. 'Come on, you old moaner. You can give me a hand to get supper ready.'

'See what I mean,' Rory said over his shoulder as his wife led him to the door. 'Boss, boss, boss.'

'They are very lovely people, your parents,' Angélique said t
Jamie when they were alone in the room.

'Yeah, they're good. I wonder sometimes how she puts u
with him, though. He's incorrigible.'

'They are very happy, I think. A good mixture.'

'Probably. Talking of mixtures, what can I get you to drink?

'Just a Coke, if you have one.'

While Jamie searched the drinks tray, Angélique walked aroun
the room, running her fingers lightly over the furniture. 'I lov
your house, Jamie. It is filled with so many old things.'

Jamie clinked ice into a tall glass and poured in the content
of the can. 'Well, everything's been here for quite a long time
I think about four or five generations of Strattons have live
with this furniture.'

'It reminds me very much of Madame Lafitte's house i
Clermont Ferrand.'

'Who's she?'

Angélique traced a finger around the central diamond-shape
pane of glass in a tall veneered display cabinet. 'She is the lad
who started me playing the violin. She is very old now, but sh
is the kindest, most wonderful person I know.' She turned an
smiled at Jamie. 'You would like her very much.'

'Is she a relation of yours?' Jamie asked, handing her the glas
of Coke.

'No, but I suppose she is as close to me as any of my family
It was Madame Lafitte who paid for me to go to the Conservatoir
in Paris.'

'Really? A bit of a fairy godmother, then. How did you com
to meet her?'

Angélique walked over to the sofa and sat down. 'My mothe
worked for her in the house.'

'What did she do, your mother?'

'She was Madame Lafitte's cleaner.'

Jamie was so taken aback by this revelation, he could not hel
but stare aghast at Angélique. 'Oh, I see.'

Angélique smiled at him. 'Your look is very disapproving

Jamie. Is it because you now learn I am from a very humble background?'

Jamie shook his head. 'Don't be silly. Of course not. Anyway, look at you now, a world-famous concert violinist. That's an incredible achievement for someone . . .'

'Whose mother was a cleaner?' Angélique suggested, a teasing glint in her eyes.

'That was *not* what I was going to say,' Jamie replied, raising his eyebrows. 'Tell me more about Madame Lafitte. Have you seen her recently?'

The light expression on Angélique's face seemed to change immediately to one of deep sadness. 'No, I have not. My schedule has never allowed me the time. She suffered a stroke just before I finished at the Conservatoire and she is now confined to a wheelchair in her house. It is my greatest regret that she has never been able to come to one of my concerts.'

'Are you still in touch with her?'

'Oh, yes, every week I either write to her or speak with her on the telephone. She talks very slowly because of the stroke, but her brain is as sharp as ever, even though she is in her ninetieth year.'

'She sounds a pretty remarkable person.'

Angélique smiled at Jamie. 'That is exactly what she is, and that is why I long to see her again.' She paused, rubbing a finger against the strapping on her hand. 'It was one of the reasons why Albert Dessuin got so angry on that night.'

Jamie nodded understandingly. 'You wanted to go back to France to see her.'

'I did not think it was so much to ask.' She lowered her face to hide the tear that ran down her cheek. 'I just have this very bad feeling that I will not be seeing her again.'

Jamie walked over and sat down on the low kilim-covered stool in front of her. 'Hey, don't think that,' he said, giving her knee a couple of gentle but reassuring thumps with his fist. 'Of course you'll see her again. Sounds to me as if she's strong as an ox.'

Looking up at him, Angélique wiped her cheek with the cuff

of her shirt and forced a smile on to her face. 'Why is it, Jamie, that you always manage to say the things I most want to hear?'

'Well, maybe because . . .' His forehead creased in thought '. . . no, sorry, I've no idea.'

Angélique snuffled out a laugh. 'I think it is because inside that tough exterior of a rugby player you are covering up the heart of a *romantique*.'

'Oh yeah?' Jamie said with a quizzically distasteful look. 'That sounds just like me.'

'Hah, you are not prepared to admit it, are you? I think you are very fortunate to have such a perfect balance in you. For me, playing a violin is not just a physical process. I cannot rely on my hands alone. I must use every bit of my soul to understand the emotions that a composer has written into a piece and sometimes I must make my violin take me to a . . . a different level of maturity and understanding to achieve the balance between the emotional and the physical. And when I do achieve it, it is the most beautiful feeling. It is like . . . how do you say it? . . . an "out-of-body" experience?'

Jamie scratched at the back of his head. 'Yeah, I can understand that, but I don't think you can compare it with playing rugby. If I walked out on to a pitch and was confronted by fifteen socking great lads who knew I had "the heart of a romantic", I'd be subjected to an "out-of-body" experience within the first five minutes of the game!'

Angélique shook her head. 'Now I am beginning to see a great similarity between you and your father. You are as incorrigible as he.'

'Maybe,' Jamie laughed. 'By the way, talking about your violin, I heard you playing it this morning.' He pointed to her strapped hand. 'How's it getting on?'

'It is feeling much better. Look' – she leaned back on the sofa and delved into the pocket of her jeans – 'I still have the squash ball.' She began squeezing it in her hand. 'I used it all the way out here in the car.'

'That's good, but you should be trying to increase the pressure

bit more.' He wrapped his hand around hers and gently closed
s fist until he could feel the ball flatten against the palm of
:r hand. 'Is that OK?'

'I don't feel any pain,' Angélique replied.

He opened up her hand and inspected each of her fingers.
Bruising's almost gone and so has the swelling.' He scowled seri-
usly at her. 'It is my considered opinion, mademoiselle, that you
ill very shortly be resuming your career as a concert violinist.'

Angélique grinned at him. 'It would never have been possible,
onsieur, without your wonderfully inventive cure. How can I
er repay you?'

'Don't worry, I shall be sending you an enormous bill which
ould keep me in squash balls for forty years.'

'In that case, I had better start to play my violin as soon as
ossible.'

Their faces had been edging closer together during this inter-
hange, so when the door of the sitting room burst open they
rang apart and began to act with unnatural nonchalance.

'Oh, sorry,' Jamie's father said, glancing from one to the other.
Hope I wasn't interrupting anything important.'

'No,' Jamie replied, leaning back on his hands on the stool,
id fixing his father with a challenging stare, daring him to say
nything about what he had just witnessed. Rory answered the
ook with an understanding raising of his eyebrows, a thinly
isguised smirk and an almost imperceptible wink at his son.

'Well, in that case,' he said with a brief, subservient bow of
is head, 'if you would care to follow me, I shall show you to
e kitchen where your evening meal awaits you.'

Thirty-Six

.K. lay in bed with a contented grin on his face, staring up at
he fixed shaft of orange light that shone through the gap in the
urtains and cast its funnelled shape on to the bedroom ceiling.

All was quiet except for Leonard's fast, shallow breathing in the bed next to his. He could not believe a room could be so quiet. Back in Pilton Mains, there was always constant movement and the banging of doors outside in the stark, echoing corridor, or raised voices coming through the paper-thin wall that divided his room from the next apartment, or the whine of a police car somewhere on the estate. He moved his feet back and forth over the smooth, clean undersheet, feeling the weighty warmth of the duvet moulding itself around his body. He slowly pressed three fingers, one after the other, into the soft, springy mattress, counting out under his breath as he went. Three days. What was that in hours? He imagined the multiplication sum in his head. Three times four is twelve, carry one; three times two is six, plus one is seven. Seventy-two hours. In seventy-two hours, everything in his life had changed. Out of nowhere, out of a hopeless situation when all that faced him was a lengthy spell in the slammer he had, by some extraordinary turn of fate, got the break he so longed for. And here he was now, not huddled beneath a torn cardboard packing case at the back of a city centre department store, but experiencing, in this warm, quiet room, a level of comfort he had never before dreamed could have existed. And across from him was the decent old bloke who had given him that break, who treated him . . . like he was worth something.

'Leonard, are ye awake?' he whispered.

He heard the cameraman catch his breath before letting out a long, sleepy groan. 'Did you say something, T.K.?'

'Aye, ah asked if ye wis awake.'

Leonard turned laboriously over in his bed. 'Well, I am now. What is it?'

'I wis just thinkin' aboot whit we did today.'

'Yes?'

'Will we get the chance tae see the stuff we shot?'

'Not until it's finished. Once it's gone through the film labora- tory, it'll go straight to the cutting room in London.'

'That's the master copy and the black-and-white cutting copy, is it no'?'

'Good for you,' Leonard said sleepily. 'You were obviously listening.'

T.K. grinned smugly to himself and linked his hands behind his head on the pillow. 'Dae ye no' get worried that nothing's goin' tae come out on the film? I mean, it's no' like video, is it, when ye can see whit ye've shot the moment ye've dunnit.'

'No matter how long one is in the business, T.K., one constantly worries. Sleeping is enough of a problem without . . .'

T.K. listened for Leonard to finish the sentence. 'Without what?'

Leonard let out a long breath. 'Never mind.'

T.K. looked over at the darkened shape of the old cameraman. 'Leonard?'

'Yes, T.K.,' Leonard replied with drowsy impatience.

'Are ye all right?'

'Sorry?'

'It's just that ah saw ye kept hauding on to yer side a' day. Have ye got a pain there or somethin'?'

'Just old age, T.K. Just old age.'

'Aye, but ye're fit, Leonard, aren't ye? Ye're as fit as onyone wha's twenty years younger than ye. Ye're fitter than ma dad and he's only fifty-twa, but that's no' surprisin' 'cos he does bugger all except sit in his chair watching TV and he gets through aboot fifty fags a day.'

'Good night, T.K.'

T.K. stretched out his legs and once more smiled contentedly to himself. 'Good night, Leonard. See you in the morning.'

Leonard flickered his eyes open and glanced at the luminous hands of his alarm clock. 'I do believe, young man, that we've just had that pleasure.'

Thirty-Seven

The quad bike ascended the hill at speed, kicking up loose stones as it went and brushing before it the tall fescue grass that grew in the centre of the deep-rutted track. Unused to rising from her bed at such an early hour, Angélique stifled a yawn as she sat astride the small pillion seat behind Jamie, her arms tightly encircling his waist. The sun ribbed the high-clouded sky in pinky red, promising warmth for the day, but as it had yet to appear above the top of the hill, she shielded her face from the freshening wind by pressing her cheek against Jamie's back. The high-revving engine of the quad cut out any possibility of conversation, but Angélique was happy to watch the view down onto the low ground unfold before her and feel the comforting warmth of Jamie's body radiate into hers through his sleeveless fleece body warmer.

They came out into the sun at the head of a long deep gully that frothed with clear fast water tumbling down the hillside. Jamie left the track and drove alongside a wire fence that followed the contours of the top of the hill, dipping and rising until it fell away from sight over the horizon. When they came to a wide metal gate swung between new pine strainer posts, Jamie turned the quad to face out over the view and cut the engine. In the resultant silence Angélique could hear the sound of sheep bleating beyond the fence and the throaty cackle of a pheasant somewhere down in the bracken that lined the bottom of the gully.

'What d'you think of that?' Jamie said, sweeping his gaze around the view.

Keeping her arms around his waist, Angélique rested her chin against his shoulder. She took in a deep inhalation of air, the sweet smell of the damp vegetation on the moor mingling with the faint aroma of shaving cream on the side of Jamie's face. Without moving, she focused her eyes on the mass of blond hair, pushed back behind his ear and curling down to his shirt collar, and she wanted, there and then, to reach up and push it to one side so that she could press her mouth against his warm downy neck. 'That is one of the most beautiful sights I have ever seen,' she replied eventually to his question, without averting her gaze.

'That's the North Berwick Law over there,' Jamie said, pointing to a conical-shaped rock that jutted up along the coastline.

'What would that be?'

Jamie looked over his shoulder and smiled at her. 'Do you really want to know?'

'Of course.'

'OK, it's a carboniferous volcanic plug, composed of phonolytic trachyte and formed over three hundred and thirty-five million years ago.'

'How very fascinating.'

Jamie laughed. 'Not at all. It's about the only thing I remember from my geography lessons at school. Local interest and all that.'

'There are some extinct volcanoes where I come from, too. Les Monts Dôme, les Monts Dores, and les Monts de Cantal.'

Jamie shot a quizzical frown at her. 'Where on earth are they?'

'In the Massif Central. Your geography is obviously not so good if you did not know Clermont Ferrand lies in the heart of one of the most beautiful mountain ranges in Europe.'

'Right,' Jamie said with a nod. 'In that case, the good old North Berwick Law is a just a bit of a bump to you.'

'But it is a very nice bump, as far as bumps go.'

'Well, thank you for saying so. And I guess this view will be pretty unspectacular to you as well.'

'I think it is . . . different.'

Jamie sighed. 'I'm beginning to wonder why the hell I bothered bringing you up here in the first place.'

Angélique laughed and tightened her grip around his stomach. 'I would not have missed it for all the world.'

Jamie gave her hands a light slap. 'Come on, let's go check these sheep out.' Swinging a leg over the handlebars, he took a beaten-up duffle bag from the wooden box strapped to the front pannier rack on the quad.

'What do you have in that?' Angélique asked as she clambered off the bike.

'Well, besides the usual veterinary stuff, there's a Thermos flask filled to the brim with undrinkable coffee and a couple of tepid bacon rolls.'

'Ah, breakfast on the moor. That is a wonderful idea.'

'Actually, it was the old man's. I think he's taken a bit of a shine to you ever since he found out it was you who was playing the violin on the one classical CD that he owns.'

'He is then surely a man of impeccable taste,' Angélique remarked airily.

'On that account, I think you should leave off judgement until you've tried his coffee,' Jamie replied doubtfully.

Three quarters of an hour later they sat in the warmth of the morning sun with their backs against a large smooth-sided boulder, looking out over a small loch that was surrounded by grazing sheep and on to which wild duck noisily landed and took off as frequently as planes at Heathrow Airport. Pouring out two cups of coffee from the Thermos, Jamie handed one to Angélique and waited for her to take her first mouthful.

'What's your verdict, then?'

'It's' – she swilled the liquid round in her mouth and then licked her lips – 'quite disgusting, actually.'

'There you are, I told you it would be,' he laughed, taking the bacon rolls from their foil wrappers and passing one over to her. 'Not really Parisian café quality, is it?'

Angélique smiled at him. 'No, it is not,' she answered quietly.

Jamie took a bite of his roll. 'You miss Paris, don't you?'

'Yes, I do. I miss it very much.'

'Will you head back there after all this is over?'

She took a small piece from the side of her roll and began rolling it between her thumb and forefinger. 'I don't think so. I have commitments to fulfil.'

'Where?'

'All over the world.'

'D'you reckon you'll be able to do them by yourself?'

Angélique sighed. 'For now, I don't think I have any other choice.'

'What about getting a new manager?'

She threw away the rolled ball of dough and turned her head away from him. 'I actually don't know how to start to find one . . . one that I will be able to trust.'

'Yeah, under the circumstances I can understand that,' Jamie said, taking a mouthful of coffee. 'Dessuin's really succeeded in messing up your life, hasn't he?'

Angélique turned and looked at him with glistening eyes. 'I have been with Albert Dessuin since I was thirteen years old. I suppose I revered him for all that time. It is very difficult when someone like that shatters all your illusions.'

Jamie could only nod his head in reply. He knew he didn't have the experience or understanding of life to come out with anything that wasn't going to sound crass or light-hearted, but he did wish he could have the pleasure of meeting Dessuin alone down some secluded alleyway one dark night.

He felt a hand settle on his knee. 'And what about you, Jamie?' Angélique asked, a brave smile on her face. 'Are you going to stay in Edinburgh?'

'No, I'm heading down to London in September to start a job.'

'That will be good fun for you. I would very much like to live in London.' She paused, toying once more with her now-cold bacon roll. 'Maybe we could meet up if I have a concert there?'

'Of course. I'd like that.'

'I would too.' She threw away what was left in her cup and handed him the bacon roll. 'You have this. I'm not very hungry.' She lay down, resting her head on his lap and tucking herself up into a ball. 'I hope you don't mind.'

'What? Eating your fingered bacon roll?'

She hit him playfully on the leg. 'You know what I mean.'

A flight of ducks whistled over their heads and Jamie munched on the roll as he watched them coast down on to the loch, breaking the dark water in parallel wakes.

'You know, last night was the best fun I have had for a very long time,' Angélique said. 'Being with you and your parents, I sensed what it would be like to be part of a close and contented family, and I have not experienced that very much. When I was a little girl in Clermont Ferrand, there was always something wrong in my house. Either my father was in a very bad mood because he had drunk too much, or he and my brothers were arguing over some industrial problem at the factory; and then, of course, my mother was *always* complaining about how she did not have enough money to feed everyone. So that's why last night shall become a very special memory for me.' She paused before letting out a long, sad sigh. '*En fait*, I really don't want it to end.'

Jamie looked down at the side of her face, seeing one curved eyelash flick open and shut and her short dark hair lying wind-blown against her cheek. 'What don't you want to end?' he asked, putting the last of the roll into his mouth.

She turned her body and looked up at him. 'Any of it. Being up here alone with you. Being so far away from all the travelling from one country to another.' She smiled wistfully at him. 'When one does not know any other way of life, it is easy to accept. But now, with all this happening, I don't know if I will ever be able to return to the normal things again. I feel . . . very lost, Jamie.'

Jamie took hold of her bandaged hand and rubbed a finger against the strapping. 'Listen, you'll do OK,' he said, smiling down at her. 'You've got a lot of healing to do, not just this hand here but . . . well, in yourself as well. When all that's happened, you'll be crying out to get yourself back in there and you'll find yourself playing your violin better than ever before.'

'Why would you think that?'

'Because you'll be a free spirit, because your life will no longer be ruled by that creep Dessuin, and I know you have the courage and the talent to go it alone.'

Pulling her hand free from Jamie's grip, Angélique reached up and pressed a finger to his chin. 'There goes that heart of yours saying all the right things again.' She pushed herself upright and shuffled her bottom over so that she sat between his legs. Leaning back against his chest, she pulled his arms around her. 'I think that I will have to tell all your rugby-playing friends about it this afternoon.'

Jamie pushed his fingers deep into her side, making her let out a short scream and squirm her body to the side. 'If you do that, it'll be the end of our friendship.'

'I don't think so,' Angélique said, rubbing her hand against the soft blond hairs on his muscled arm as she looked out across the sunlit moor.

'For Chrissakes, lads, what the hell are you doing?' the coach of the Dunbar First XV yelled as he stood at half-time in the middle of the crouched semicircle of sweating bodies, everyone of them heaving with effort. 'This lot's a division below us and you're letting them walk all over you!' He slapped a hand frustratedly against his forehead and let out a long breath to steady his anger. 'Right, Billy,' he said, addressing a giant of a man whose muddy face was covered with congealed blood from a gash above his left eye. 'Their game plan seems to be based on kicking for touch, so I want you to contest every line-out. Get up in the air, spoil their tactics. If you have to, use an arm to keep the other jumper down, but keep it subtle, like. I don't want you sin-binned.' He pointed at a player who leaned forward, his hands on his knees, revealing a neck that was as thick as a bullock's. 'Callum, you're letting that tight-head prop control the scrum. You've got to get on top of him, otherwise there's no way we can get good ball to the three-quarters, is that clear?' The player raised his shaved head and nodded. 'And you, Jamie,' the coach continued, staring fixedly at his stand-off half, who was tipping the contents of a water bottle down his throat, 'I know you're used to playing in dizzier ranks than this motley crew, but their backs are lying flat, so I want you to break the gainline by running every ball, is that understood?' Jamie nodded, wiping a dirt-streaked arm across his mouth. 'Right, just go out there, you lot, and start working as a team. I want this deficit turned round in the first fifteen minutes of the second half, otherwise you won't have a hope in hell against the team next week.'

As the coach stomped off the field, the semicircle broke up and the players dejectedly sloped off to their positions to wait the few minutes until the referee restarted the game.

'There's someone over there trying to attract your attention, Jamie,' the inside centre said as he stretched a leg up behind him to keep his muscles from seizing up.

Jamie turned and looked over to the touchline where Angélique was waving at him. He lifted a hand to acknowledge her, but it only made her beckon more frantically.

'You'd better go,' the inside centre said with a teasing smile. 'I don't think she can wait until after the game.'

Jamie raised a finger at him as he ran over to the touchline. 'Yeah? What is it?' he asked Angélique.

'You are playing very well,' she said, a broad grin on her face.

Jamie pulled a hand across his head and rubbed at the back of his neck. 'We're losing, Angélique.'

'I know, but *you* are playing very well.' She gazed over to where the opposing team were thumping one another on the back in congratulations of a job well done so far. 'How fast is your left wing?' she asked.

Jamie turned and looked across at the player on the far side of the pitch. 'Andy? He's fast. Beats me by about two seconds over a hundred metres.' He turned back to her. 'Why do you ask?'

'Their three-quarter line is lying very flat.'

Jamie eyed her with amusement. 'That's what the coach has just said.'

'Well, I was just thinking that if Michalak was playing in your position and he had a very fast player like Dominici on his left wing and he saw a gap behind the three-quarter line of the opposition, he would put the ball there for Dominici to chase.'

Jamie smiled at her. 'You do know about this game, don't you?'

'I have told you that before.'

'Well, I'm afraid your idea doesn't match our coach's. He wants us to run every ball.'

Angélique shrugged. 'In that case, you will lose the match.'

Jamie crossed his arms. 'I'm glad you're so confident. Anything else you want to say?'

'No, but if you do not try it, I shall embarrass you,' she said with a wicked smile.

Jamie pulled his mouth guard from the pocket of his shorts. 'Just watch your step, Mademoiselle Pascal,' he said before placing it in his mouth and running back to his position just as the referee readied himself to blow his whistle to start the second half.

Five minutes later, after Jamie had started a number of abortive three-quarter-line movements, a scrum was called right in front of Angélique. She found herself standing next to the coach, who had been patrolling the touchline yelling out ineffectual orders at his players.

'Go on, lads, you've got one against the head! Hold it there now, hold it there.'

Angélique glanced over to the opposition's three-quarters and saw that their fullback had joined in the line as it edged forward to cover their opposing backs. 'Try it now, Jamie,' she yelled out at the top of her voice.

As the scrum half waited for the ball to be released from between the number 8's feet, the coach turned to Angélique, a querying look on his face. 'Try what, love?'

The scrum half picked up the ball from the base of the scrum and spun it at speed out to Jamie.

'Now move it down the line!' the coach yelled. 'Oh, no! What the effing hell are you doing?' He clapped both hands to his head as he watched Jamie kick a lobbing cross-field ball over the heads of the gawping opposition. The coach spun round and buried his face in his hands, not wishing to see the outcome of such an insane tactic.

Jamie's left wing was indeed a flyer. Timing his run to perfection, he scooped up the awkward-bouncing ball in one hand and tucked it under his arm, swerving his heels to avoid the last desperate attempt at a tap tackle by his opposing wing. Once he realised he had a clear path to the try line, he changed his running angle towards the centre of the posts and touched the ball down unchallenged between them. The cheers that erupted from the small crowd of home spectators made the coach turn slowly to watch what was going on.

Angélique jumped up and down, clapping her hands. 'It worked perfectly!' she said excitedly to him.

The coach stared at her open-mouthed for a moment before turning with a shake of his head and walking off in subdued silence down the touchline.

At the end of the game Jamie ran across the pitch to Angélique, pulling a sweatshirt over his head. 'Well, that was quite a turn-around, wasn't it?' he laughed. 'I owe you one. That tactic of yours really screwed them.'

'I told you it would work,' Angélique replied smugly. She took hold of the neck of his sweatshirt and pulled his head down towards her and gave him a kiss on the cheek. 'You played well. In fact, it is a pity you were not born a Frenchman.'

'That'd be no use. I have a phobia about snails,' Jamie said, giving her a wink before he turned and looked over to where his team was standing, watching them both. 'The lads want to have a drink with you in the clubhouse.'

Angélique shook her head. 'No, you go by yourself. I will wait for you in the car.'

'Come on, why not?'

'Because I do not know them . . . and they might know me.'

Jamie took hold of her arm and gave it a squeeze. 'Listen, *I* know them all and I can guarantee there's not one of them who would say a thing. Anyway, the person they're more concerned with meeting is the great rugby tactician who's just won them the game, not a world-famous violinist.'

Angélique looked over towards Jamie's teammates. 'Are you sure it's all right?'

'Yeah, of course it is. You're more likely to be offered a contract to sign rather than be asked for your autograph.'

'All right, then,' she replied and began to walk beside Jamie across the pitch. 'I hope you all take a shower first, though. I don't want to be drinking with a lot of sweaty men.'

Jamie laughed. 'Well, better get used to it, then,' he said, putting a filthy rugby-sleeved arm around her shoulders and pulling her tight in against him.

Thirty-Eight

Albert Dessuin threw a pound coin into the cardboard box of the young juggler who shared his stance in the doorway of Marks & Spencer on Princes Street, and without acknowledging the boy's gratitude he turned and looked into the brightly lit store, wondering if he shouldn't go in to try to find the woman. He had every reason to do so, because the place was packed with shoppers and there was a good possibility she could slip out of a back entrance, but nevertheless he decided to wait. It had been four days since he had first encountered her sprawled on the floor of the reception area in the Sheraton Grand, and so far that evening, he had done a good enough job of keeping himself out of sight, even in that dank little cellar where he had suffered a gruelling hour listening to her appallingly incomprehensible show. Because of that alone, he wasn't going to risk ruining his chances at this stage.

He moved away from the doorway, pulling up the collar of his mackintosh and thrusting his hands into the pockets. The wind was getting up and there was rain in the air. He looked up towards the castle where the vast bank of spotlights, lighting the Esplanade for the evening performance of the Military Tattoo, spilled upwards on to the dark threatening clouds rolling in from the west of the city. The audience would be getting wet tonight, he thought to himself. Later on, the streets leading down from the castle would be thronged with people wearing the free refuse-sack rainwear the organisers handed out, looking like an army of pink-shrouded ghouls sent forth from the ancient ramparts to ransack the town. He could not understand why they never went better prepared for an open-air show in the first place.

He saw her coming out of the store and standing in the doorway, her arms weighed down by two bulging plastic bags. It was the coat he recognised, that extraordinary multicoloured dog rug of a creation, a fitting garment, he thought, for someone as unattractive as she. He quickly turned towards the castle once more, watching her out of the side of his eye. She looked one way and then the other, maybe judging her moment when to step out into the crowded street or perhaps vacillating as to which way she should go. She moved off away from him, west-bound on Princes Street, lumbering along with her shoulders hunched and her coat-tail trailing along the grubby pavement.

It was easier than he could ever have imagined. She gave no indication that she might have suspected she was being followed, no furtive backward glance, no quick escaping dash into a dark-ened side street. It was child's play. As she laboured her way up the gentle slope of Hanover Street he decided to make it more interesting for himself and hurried his pace so that he was no more than twenty feet behind her, close enough to hear her gasping breath, stopping when she stopped and starting again when she continued her plodding ascent. He laughed quietly as he closed the gap further. It would be fun to go up and touch her on the shoulder, just to see her reaction when she turned round.

And then, as she reached the junction with George Street, the handle on one of her overloaded shopping bags gave way and the contents fell with a clatter on to the pavement. He stood frozen as he watched a tin can roll down the street towards him and veer off into the gutter, and then she turned to face him, bending down to retrieve her goods. At this point, he quickly moved over to the side of the pavement and pretended to study the window display of a fast-print photographic shop.

'Oh, bugger, bugger, bugger!' said Rene as she watched the tin of oxtail soup roll off down the road and disappear over the edge of the pavement. 'That's all I need.' She put the shopping bags on the ground and bent down to try to fashion a makeshift loop out of the broken handle. 'I hope this bloody well holds,' she mumbled irately to herself as she picked up the dirt-spattered packets and returned them to the bag. She straightened up, gingerly testing the strength of the new handle. 'Right, should get me 'ome. Now where on earth did that oxtail soup get to?'

She had taken no more than two steps down the street when her attention was suddenly caught by the figure of a man, not more than twenty feet away from her, studying intently the display in the window of a small photographic shop. It was the coat she recognised, a Maigret-style mackintosh with a double fold across the shoulders and a belt that was done up so tight that it puckered the material around his waist. And then she saw the high cockscomb of hair and knew instantly who it was.

'Oh, bloody 'ell!' she murmured to herself, and without even bothering to attempt to retrieve the lost can of soup, she took off across the street, dodging the traffic, and with her head bowed low as if trying to evade sniper fire, she scurried away along George Street as fast as her tired legs would carry her.

Albert Dessuin looked down at the bottom left-hand corner of the shop window as a way of being able to snatch a glance up the street, and then spun round fully when he realised the woman had gone. After a quick appraisal of Hanover Street, he ran up to the junction with George Street, and in his haste collided with a jovial group of beer-carrying young men.

'Oh-oh, watch it, mate!' one of them exclaimed as he steadied his plastic pint mug at arm's length. 'That's expensive stuff, you know.'

'I am sorry,' Albert replied curtly, holding up his hands in apology. He waited until the group had moved off before continuing his search for the woman. The full length of the street, however, was heaving with jostling pedestrians competing for space on pavements narrowed by queues awaiting entry into show venues. There was no sign of her. Albert smiled to himself. Maybe she had seen him, maybe not, but it did not matter. There was always another night, and he had the time to wait.

Rene peered tentatively round the side of the shop doorway and looked along the length of George Street. A momentary gap opened up in the mass of people and she caught sight of the mackintoshed figure of the Frenchman standing at the junction, leaning his head one way and then the other as he searched the street.

'Oh, 'eck, it is me 'e's after,' Rene murmured to herself as she hurried off down the street once more, weaving her way in and out of the crowds to keep herself hidden. 'You've got to get yourself off the street, lass.'

She passed by a long queue formed outside a wide glass-doored entrance. She veered off towards the brightly lit haven only to feel a hand grasp at her shoulder.

'Hang on, love, you need a pass or a ticket to get in here.'

Rene looked up into the faces of two black-shirted, shaven-haired bouncers, both wearing earpieces with curly leads that disappeared down their collars.

'What kind of pass do I need?' Rene asked in desperation. She transferred her shopping bags to one hand and delved into the folds of her coat, pulling out the Fringe pass she had suspended around her neck. 'Is this any use?'

'That's all we need,' one of the bouncers said, pushing open the door for her. 'You'll find the bar at the end of the hall.'

Rene didn't quite know how the man knew she was gagging for a stiff drink but she wasn't going to hang around to question him. She bustled her way across the pillared, stone-floored hall and entered the double doors at the far end.

The bar was crammed with people, every inch of seating space taken up – on sofas, chairs, even on the tables. She pushed her way towards the bar and set her shopping bags down on the floor, blowing out a long breath of nervous exhaustion.

'Rene!'

Her immediate reaction on hearing the voice was to make ready to get down on all fours and crawl round the side of the bar to hide, but then it dawned on her that the caller's tone was distinctly female. She stood up on the footrest and scanned the room, seeing no one that she knew, and she was just coming to the conclusion there must have been someone else called Rene in the place when she spotted the bobbing mass of red hair threading its way towards her. A few seconds later, Matti Fullbright appeared at her side, a broad grin on her large freckled face.

'Hi, there, girl. How're you doing?'

'Matti Fullbright, am I pleased to see you!' Rene exclaimed, rolling her eyes in relief.

'You look all in. Let me get you a drink.'

'Aye, I'm needing one bad, luv,' Rene said, leaning heavy-elbowed on the bar. 'Bacardi and Coke would go down a treat.'

With a click of her fingers, Matti attracted the attention of the barman and ordered up two drinks. 'So what's been going on?'

'Ye won't believe who I've just seen out there in the street.'

'Not the bloody Frenchman!'

'Aye, right first time. The bloody Frenchman.'

'What was he doing?'

'I don't know, but I think 'e might 'ave been following me.'

The barman put the two drinks down on the bar and Matti handed Rene her Bacardi and Coke.

'I doubt there's any way he could have been doing that. It's just a coincidence, that's all.'

'Some bloody coincidence!' Rene exclaimed, taking a hefty slug from her glass. 'Edinburgh's a damned big place to go bumping into someone like that.'

'It happens all the time during the festival. I'm forever meeting people I know on the street.'

'Oh, well, I suppose ye could be right,' Rene said with a flick of her head. 'After all, 'ere's you and me meeting up again. That's pretty extraordinary, in't it?'

Matti screwed up the side of her mouth as she scrutinised the naivety of Rene's remark. 'That's not so out of ordinary, you know.'

'What d'ye mean?'

'Haven't you been here before?'

Rene gazed around the bar. 'No, never. Why should I?'

'Because this is the Assembly Rooms. All the Fringe acts congregate here at the end of the day.'

'Really? D'you mean all these people . . . ?'

'Yeah, they're either Fringe performers or guests.'

Rene shook her head in disbelief. 'Would you credit that? I'd no idea this place existed.'

'In that case, you didn't read all that bumf you were given.'

'Obviously not.'

Matti laughed. 'So, how did the act go this evening?'

'Same as ever. Three foreigners who couldn't understand one word I was saying and a drunk who slept all the way through.'

Matti sucked her teeth despondently. 'I know what you mean. It's not been a brilliant time for me, neither. I think I might have overstayed my welcome here.'

'Ye're not being serious, are ye?'

'Too right I am. I reckon I'll have to do a major overhaul of my act quite soon, but I'm not sure how.'

Rene's face broke into a smile. 'Maybe you should try doing it in the nude.'

Matti almost choked on her mouthful of gin and tonic. 'For God's sake, I'm trying to woo my audience, Rene, not have them run screaming for the exits!'

The laughter that ensued between the two women was so loud it made those that stood around them stop mid-conversation and turn to stare. Matti blew out a deep breath to control herself. 'Oh, my word, it does you good, don't it?'

'Tell that to the audience,' Rene replied with a giggle.

'Aye, maybe we should.' Matti took a drink from her glass and then turned to Rene, her eyes narrowed in thought. 'Listen, what're you doing tomorrow afternoon?'

Rene shrugged. 'Nowt at all.'

'Right, d'ye know the Royal Scottish Academy on Princes Street?'

'No, but I s'pose I could find it.'

'Good. Meet me there at, say, one-thirty.'

'Why?'

'I want you to come to see my new show.'

'What? Ye've worked something out already?'

'I think I might have just done that very thing, Rene, my girl,' Matti replied, swallowing the last of her drink and slamming her glass down on the bar. 'Come on, let's set up another round.'

Rene shook her head. 'I can't, thanks, lass,' she said, bending down to pick up her shopping bags. 'I've got be off. I've sort of taken on the evening cooking duties for these two lads in the flat.'

'Right,' Matti said disappointedly. 'Oh, well, I'll just have to drink alone.'

'Sorry.'

Matti shot her a conciliatory smile. 'See you tomorrow, then, and watch out for skulking Frenchmen.'

Rene raised her eyebrows. 'Oh 'eck, I'd almost forgotten about 'im.'

'Oh, don't let him get your knickers in a twist. If he's still around, I suggest you just run straight up to him and throw your arms around his neck and give him an enormous tongue sandwich. That should make him hightail it back to his lair in the Sheraton-bloody-Grand!'

'Right, that's it,' Rene said, her mouth drooping in disgust. 'I'm leaving before you make me physically sick.'

Thirty-Nine

Why this evening of all evenings, Tess Goodwin thought to herself as she leaned over in her seat to get an unrestricted view through the windscreen of the bus, hoping to see what had caused it to remain stationary for the past ten minutes. There was no traffic coming down Hanover Street, so she knew there had to be some sort of blockage up ahead. She glanced at her wristwatch. It was half past seven. She was going to be so late and the last thing she wanted to do was to arrive at the restaurant in a flustered state. Tonight she had to be in the mood to play it ultra-cool, bordering on iceberg-cold.

Getting to her feet, she slung the strap of her laptop case on to her shoulder and walked down the aisle to stand by the driver. 'Are we going to be moving soon?' she asked, peering up the street.

'Nae idea,' the driver replied, masticating heavily on a piece of gum. 'Looks like an accident. Ah've just seen a police car head down past the roundabout on George Street.' He turned to her. 'How far are ye goin'?'

'Dundas Street.'

'D'yae want tae walk then? Ye'd be better tae.'

'Yes, I think you're right.'

The doors opened with a swish and Tess jumped down on to the pavement and began half walking, half running up the incline.

This had to be the most imperfect climax for what had already proved to be a gruelling week. The dinner date with Peter Hansen had been permanently at the forefront of her mind. She was distracted at work, forgetting to attend at least three meetings and to organise press calls that would normally have been second nature to her, and then, because Peter had gone against his word and had kept calling her constantly, she had become near paranoid about her mobile phone ringing. She considered turning it off altogether, only she knew it was her constant lifeline during the festival.

But the worst had always been when her day's work was over and she had gone home to Allan. She tried to act as naturally as she could with him, but everything that she said or did seemed so false, so deceiving, that eventually she resolved to plead utter exhaustion and keep all conversation between them to a minimum, hoping that he would not question the sudden change n her mood and character. So every night she would lie beside him in bed, her eyes fixed on the television but taking nothing in, while he would give up on his nightly attempts to make love to her and fall asleep, resigned to his sudden celibacy, with his head leaning heavily against her shoulder. She dreaded the coming of the day when she would have to meet Peter Hansen at the restaurant, yet she also longed for it so that she could put an end to this appalling charade and get her life with Allan back to normal.

Just before arriving at the flat, she took her mobile from her bag, thumbed the keys and put it to her ear. Her call was answered immediately. 'Yes, it's Tess,' she said in a voice that was distinctly cryogenic. 'I'm going to be late . . . I don't know, maybe half an hour, depends on the traffic . . . can't do that, I'm on my way home now. I want to have a shower first . . . no, Peter, you read nothing into that. You really could not be more wrong.'

Angrily, she put the mobile back into her handbag as she shouldered open the entrance door. She ascended the stairs quickly, praying she still had time to get changed and away from the place before Allan came back from the office. Tonight, she thought to herself, when this whole thing is over and done with, I'll make it up to him.

Her heart sank as soon as she walked into the flat, dropping her case on the chair in the hall. She could hear the blare of the television coming from the bedroom. She took off her coat as she walked along the passage and entered the room. Allan was lying propped up on the bed drinking a mug of tea, still in his suit trousers but with stockinged feet and his tie loosened. An open newspaper lay beside him. His eyes momentarily left the television screen and she saw immediately the deep sadness in his eyes.

'Allan?' she asked quietly, feeling her heart give a jolt of apprehension. 'What's happened?'

He smiled at her. 'Nothing.' He zapped the television with the remote. 'Just been watching the end of some stupid romantic film. Got to me a bit.' He dropped the remote on the bed beside him. 'I came home early 'cos I thought we could go out to dinner.'

Tess bit at her bottom lip. 'I can't, Allan. I've got to attend another reception tonight. I've just come home to change.' Feeling her face colour, she turned away from him and walked back over to the door. 'I'm just going to have a quick shower.'

She returned five minutes later wrapped in a towel, her skin tingling from the scalding she had given herself in the hope it would purge away her guilt. Allan was still sitting on the bed, still looking at her. She smiled at him as she walked over to the open wardrobe and took out a dark-red silk cocktail dress on a hanger.

'We need to talk,' Allan said.

Tess glanced round at him. 'What about?'

Allan shrugged. 'Anything you want. We haven't communicated for about a week, or maybe you haven't noticed.'

Tess placed the dress on a chair and walked across to the bed and sat down next to him. 'I know and I'm sorry. It's just—'

'Work,' Allan interjected morosely.

She put a hand on his arm. 'After tonight, things will be different, Allan, I promise. We could go out for dinner tomorrow night?'

Allan shrugged and picked up the newspaper. 'Have you any idea what happened to Angélique Pascal?' he asked, the change of subject seeming to Tess a ruse to avoid giving her an answer, yet she was glad of it. She shot a glance at the radio alarm on the bedside table. It was almost eight o'clock. Peter Hansen would no doubt be sitting in the bar at the restaurant waiting for her.

'No,' she said, getting to her feet and walking over to a chest of drawers and taking out a pair of pants and a bra, 'other than she's returned to France.'

Allan let out a hollow laugh. 'You're really a strange one, Tess. A week ago you were beside yourself with worry about her, and now you're acting as if you couldn't give a damn.'

Dropping the towel to the ground, Tess slipped on her pants

and her bra, and then stood for a moment staring at her reflection in the mirror that sat on top of the chest. He was right, of course. She hadn't given Angélique another thought ever since she'd left. She was too preoccupied with her own damned problems. 'I *am* concerned about her,' she said, picking up the dress from the chair and slipping it off the hanger. 'It's just that—'

'*How* concerned are you?' he cut in.

'What do you mean?'

'Well, it's been over a week since she left Edinburgh,' Allan replied, giving the newspaper a thump with the back of his hand, 'and we've heard nothing more about her. Wouldn't *you* think, as someone who deals with the press all the time, that a story about a world-class violinist who has had to cancel a whole load of concerts because she'd cut her hand badly would be pretty big news? I mean, there's been no follow-up story, no progress report, not even a photograph. Don't you think that's a bit weird?'

Tess rubbed her fingers against her brow. Again, he was absolutely right. Even though she'd had her nose buried in the newspapers for the past week looking out for reviews and articles on artistes, it had never occurred to her there had never been a mention of Angélique.

'Maybe she's asked for some privacy during her convalescence,' she offered hopefully. 'She is quite a private person, after all.'

'Come on, you know as well as I do the paparazzi don't give a damn about the privacy of *any* celebrity. It's all just money to them. And don't you think it's quite odd she hasn't been in touch with you? You became pretty chummy with her and she did have your mobile number.' He closed the newspaper, spun it on to the floor and then folded his arms. 'I think you should try to find out more about her, because to tell you the truth, *I'm* concerned even if no one else appears to be.'

Tess gazed at him for a moment. 'You're right. She should have been in touch.'

'I know.'

She glanced once more at the time on the radio alarm. This was an issue she was not going to be able to avoid. Peter Hansen was just going to have to wait for a bit longer. Pulling on her dress, she walked over to the door and left the room. She returned a few moments later with her mobile phone and address book. She sat down on the bed next to Allan, turned quickly through the pages and then began dialling a number.

'Who are you calling?' Allan asked.

'A reporter called Harry Wills,' Tess replied, putting the phone to her ear. 'I tell you, this is really breaking a cardinal rule. I never ask information from the press.'

Allan swung his legs over the side of the bed and got to his feet. 'D'you want a cup of tea?'

'Hullo, is that Harry Wills?' Tess asked, shaking her head at Allan's offer.

Five minutes later, Allan returned to the bedroom, a brimming mug of tea in his hand, to find Tess staring thoughtfully out of the window, her mobile held limply in her hand. 'How did you get on?' he asked, putting the mug down on the bedside table.

'He's coming round here now.'

'Why? What did he say?'

'Well, to begin with, he seemed quite adamant that Angélique had gone back to Paris, but then when I told him she was a good friend of mine and that I couldn't understand why I hadn't heard from her, his whole attitude changed.'

'In what way?'

'He just started asking me a whole load of questions about how I'd met her and when was the last time I'd seen her, and then when I told him I worked in the International office, he just immediately said he thought it would be best if he came round to see me.' She laid the mobile and the address book down on the bedside table. 'Funny thing is, I think I now recognise his voice. I'm pretty sure it was him who called the International office to break the news about Angélique's accident.'

'Sounds as if I was right, then,' Allan said, sitting down on the edge of the bed and rubbing his face with his hands. 'My word, there seems to be a hell of a lot of cloak-and-dagger stuff going on at the festival this year.'

He said the remark in such a strained voice that Tess shot him a worried glance out of the corner of her eye. She decided silence to be the only fitting reply.

Forty minutes later, Tess closed the door of the flat behind Harry Wills and walked back along the corridor and into the bedroom. Allan was pulling on his suit jacket, studying the piece of paper the reporter had ripped out of his notebook.

'Where are you going?' she asked.

'Out to East Lothian. Someone's got to go see Angélique.'

Tess bit at her lip. This was decision time, but already, in her heart, she knew where she had to go. 'I'm coming too.'

'Don't bother,' he said, studying her face intently. 'You'd better go to your reception.'

She glanced at her wristwatch. A quarter to nine. It was all too late now anyway. She didn't know what Peter Hansen's next step would be, but she was prepared to face the consequences. She picked up her handbag from the chest of drawers. 'No, I want to come.' She walked towards the door. 'I'll just make a quick phone call to Sarah Atkinson to say I won't make the reception.'

It was not a good time to be attempting to cross over to the other side of Edinburgh. The streets were clogged both with traffic and with pedestrians, and for the greater part of the journey through the city Allan drove in silence, only breaking it to mutter some oath under his breath as the traffic lights incessantly changed to red as he approached them. Tess didn't care. Her mind was completely set on the confrontation that was now inevitable between herself and Sir Alasdair Dreyfuss. She kept imagining the scene of her being called to his office, trying to work out what she would say when he questioned her about her affair with his friend, Peter Hansen, knowing that whatever she said in reply would make little difference. Her future as an employee of the International Festival would be considered untenable.

When she had spoken to Peter Hansen on the telephone before leaving the flat, he had been surprisingly understanding of her reasons for not being able to turn up at the restaurant. 'How disappointing,' he had said. 'In that case, we should make it another night.' And she had replied, 'Maybe.' Now she thought to herself how much easier, how much more self-preserving it would have been to have answered, 'Yes, of course we can,' but then she glanced across at Allan, shaking his head in frustration as he edged the car forward another few feet, and she knew she had made the right decision not to continue with this stupid, foolish, damaging game any longer. Her job was expendable, but not her husband. This was the man she loved, and this was the man she did not want to lose.

She didn't want to think about it any longer. She switched her mind to Angélique and wondered if she should ring her at the house in East Lothian to warn her they were on their way out to see her. She took her mobile from her handbag and picked up the slip of paper next to the gear stick on which Harry Wills had written the address and the mobile number of Angélique's friend, Jamie Stratton. She read his name again, trying to work out why it seemed so familiar, and then her mind registered on the meeting she had had in the Hub café with the elderly cameraman who had been desperate to find somewhere to stay in the city. Distractedly she put her mobile and the piece of paper back beside the gear stick and leaned her head against the window, thinking to herself how extraordinary it was that she'd already spoken to this man.

The next thing she knew she was jolting herself awake, blinking her eyes to accustom them to the glare of the oncoming headlights. The car was now travelling at speed along a dual arriageway. To her left she could see the illuminated block of he power station at Tranent. She reached across and squeezed Allan's hand. 'Sorry about that. I dropped off.'

'You must be exhausted,' he said.

'I am quite.'

'Too many late nights, burning the candle at both ends.'

Tess frowned. There was almost a frenetic edge to his voice. Not really.'

'Are you sleeping with him again then?'

Tess felt her face go on fire. 'What?'

'Peter bloody Hansen. You just can't stop yourself, can you?'

Tess swallowed hard. 'I don't know—'

'Of course you know what I'm bloody talking about. I saw him this evening. He was round at our flat knocking on the door when I got back from work. He recognised me and scutled off like the rat that he is.'

Tess shook her head. 'Allan, I—'

'Don't even start to tell me you didn't know he was here. Who was it you called just before you left the flat? Sure as hell wasn't Sarah Atkinson, was it?' He picked up her mobile phone from beside the gear stick and punched at the buttons. 'Look,' he said, holding the screen inches from her face. 'Lo and behold, if that isn't the name of Peter Hansen. Now, are you going to tell me that's just coincidence?'

Tess closed her eyes tight. 'Stop the car.'

'Why? Do you want to get out here and walk all the way back to his loving arms? Is that what the hell you want?'

'Please, just stop the car.'

Allan swerved into a lay-by at speed and slammed his foot on the brake and turned off the engine. The silence was absolute. Tess heard him let out a deep, quivering groan and turned to see him slump forward on the steering wheel, his head in his hands.

'I really didn't know he was going to turn up, Allan. He just did and the arrogant bastard expected everything to be exactly as it was before.'

Allan raised his head and looked at her.

'And was it?'

'No, of course it wasn't. Why would it ever be? I'm married to you now. I don't want anyone else in the my life, least of al him.'

'But you were going to go out with him tonight, weren' you?'

Tess paused, realising at that moment how badly she had handled this whole situation. She should never have kept it from him. 'Yes, I was. I was going to have dinner with him.'

'Jesus!' Allan muttered angrily, thumping his hand against the steering wheel.

'Let me finish – please! I agreed to have dinner with him only because he, in so many words, threatened to tell Alasdair Dreyfuss about our' – the word momentarily stuck in Tess's throat – 'relationship. I didn't want to lose my job and I certainly didn' want to lose you. I was going to have dinner with him and, I really mean this, Allan, that was going to be the end of it. I hate the man and I hate myself for getting involved with him in the first place, because I nearly lost you as a result. I decided not to tell you about him being here, because . . . well, I thought I could handle it myself.'

'Why? Did it never occur to you that this all involves me as well? If you screw up your life, you screw up mine as well.'

Tess looked down into her lap, feeling tears of stupidity and hopelessness begin to well up in her eyes. 'I know, and I'm really sorry. I should have told you.' She opened the glove box in front of her and took out a box of tissues. She pulled out a wodge and wiped her eyes. 'I have hated this week more than any in my whole life. I've felt I've been betraying you every moment of it, and to do that to someone you really love is just the most painful thing to bear.'

There was a long silence before Allan broke it. 'I don't know what to say, Tess. Maybe it's slipped your mind, but after we'd sorted everything out last year, I thought we'd made an agreement we would never hold back secrets from each other. Hell, that was the fundamental reason we got married! And now you've just blown the whole thing out the window, as if all those endless talks we had on trust and reconciliation were just trite and totally expendable. And yes, that's exactly how you always end up making *me* feel – totally and utterly expendable.'

Tess reached across and laid a hand on his arm. 'Please, you must never, ever think that. I know I've made a hash of things but you have to remember that nothing happened, Allan, and nothing similar will ever happen again in the future, because you are the only person I want in my life.'

With a shake of his head, Allan turned the key in the ignition, pumping his foot on the accelerator and making the engine roar angrily to life. 'We'd better go find Angélique.'

'Can't we call a truce first?' Tess asked quietly

Allan considered her question for a moment before turning to her. 'OK, but for your friend's sake only, because, Tess, you think back on what you've just said about nothing similar happening again. You used almost exactly the same words last year.'

'I know what is going to occur next,' Angélique said as she and Jamie lay on the sofa in the sitting room, the only source of the light coming from the television.

'OK, go on then, let's hear it.'

'The man with the beard who was on the bus with her has followed her home and has got into the house.'

'How?'

'I don't know. Through an open window, maybe?'

'Wrong.'

Angélique lifted her head from his chest and turned to look at him. 'Why do you think that?'

'Could be intuition.' He smiled at her. 'Or could be because I've seen the film before.'

'Oh, you are such a cheat!' she exclaimed, reaching for a

cushion. The imminent blow never struck its target, as her arm stopped mid-arc when the door of the drawing room opened and the lights were turned on. Both she and Jamie turned to see Rory Stratton standing there in his dressing gown.

'Hi, Dad,' Jamie said. 'I thought you'd turned in.'

'Yes, well, I was on my way upstairs when I heard a car arriving. You've got visitors.'

The news brought them both immediately to their feet. Jamie stared in bewilderment at the young couple that entered the room, having never set eyes on either of them before. Both were dressed as if they had been to a party, the man in a suit, the girl in a dark-red cocktail dress with her face made up. Jamie spun round when he heard Angélique let out a gasp of astonishment.

'Tess!'

She ran across the room and flung her arms around the girl's neck.

'Hullo, Angélique, how are you?' the girl said, giving her a kiss on both cheeks. 'We've only just found out what happened to you. We came straight out to see you.'

Angélique pushed herself away. 'I cannot believe this. How did you know I was here?'

'Yeah, good question,' Jamie said, still looking suspiciously at the couple.

'Well then, find out over a drink, Jamie,' his father retorted, still standing by the door as he shot a steely glare of disapproval at his son's lack of welcome. 'I'm off to my bed, so I'll bid everyone good night.' He was about to leave the room when he glanced back at Jamie. 'If you want to talk into the small hours, Allan and Tess can stay the night if they want. The double bed's usually made up in the top spare room.'

Jamie nodded. 'Thanks.'

As Rory shut the door behind him, the two girls walked across to the sofa and sat down, already engrossed in a deep private conversation. Still nonplussed as to what was going on, Jamie forced a smile on his face as he approached the man, his hand outstretched. 'Hi, we haven't met. Jamie Stratton.'

The man shook his hand. 'Allan Goodwin.' He pointed over to the girl sitting next to Angélique. 'That's Tess – my wife.'

'Right . . . so, what can I get you to drink?'

'A beer would do me fine.'

'And for Tess?'

Allan shrugged. 'Just something soft. She's driving home.'

'Where exactly *is* home?' Jamie asked as he walked over to the drinks tray, not yet willing to extend his father's offer of a bed until he had found out more about the couple.

'Edinburgh,' Allan replied, following him across the room. 'In fact, Tess says she knows you.'

'Really?' Jamie shot a quizzical glance at the girl seated next to Angélique. 'I can't say that I ever remember—'

'She spoke to you on the telephone.'

'Concerning what?'

'Renting a room to a Mr Hartson? She said he was a cameraman.'

Jamie stared hard at the man. 'I seem to remember that call came from the International Festival office.'

'It would have done. Tess works there.'

'Oh, I see,' Jamie replied, glancing apprehensively at the girl. 'But it couldn't have been Mr Hartson who told you we were here. He had no idea where we were going.'

'No, that information came from a reporter called Harry Wills.'

'*Harry Wills?*' Jamie exclaimed incredulously, just stopping short of overflowing a glass of Coke over the floor. 'Excuse me for asking this, but why did he think it necessary to tell her?'

'Because Tess hadn't heard one word from Angélique since she left for France. She called Harry because she knew he'd had contact with Angélique in the past.'

'And Harry . . . told you everything?'

'Yes, he thought it would be safe enough now. He said he'd stopped his vigil outside your flat about three night ago.'

'Yes, I know that, but I didn't expect him to start telling people we were here.'

'Don't worry, neither Tess nor I will be breathing one word on her whereabouts to anyone.' Allan studied the look of distrust on Jamie's face as the young man carried the glass of Coke across the room and handed it to Tess. 'I think, quite honestly,' Allan continued quietly when Jamie had returned to pour him his beer, 'that, until this whole situation with Angélique is well and truly over, the more allies you two have in your camp, the better. Tess has become a good friend of Angélique, and she would never do anything to jeopardise either her safety or her privacy.'

Jamie handed Allan his beer, and then looked over to where Angélique and Tess were chatting, seemingly oblivious to his and Allan's presence in the room. He gave a shrug. 'I had no idea Angélique knew anyone else in Edinburgh. I wonder why she's never mentioned Tess to me before.'

Allan shot a withering look at Tess and shook his head. 'I'm afraid that's the female mind for you,' he said, raising his glass of beer in salute. 'They have a bloody awful habit of keeping secrets from us men.'

Even though Jamie had no way of knowing the poignancy of Allan's remark, it was sufficiently male-bonding to break the unease Jamie had felt since the young couple's unexpected arrival at the house. He too raised his glass to the man. 'Listen, sorry about being a bit . . . well, unfriendly towards you. I was completely thrown into this whole game and I suppose it's just made me quite . . . protective towards her.'

'Yes, I can see that,' Allan replied, glancing briefly at Angélique before turning back to Jamie with a grin on his face, 'and I think I can probably understand the reasons why.'

Jamie felt his face colour instinctively at Allan's quip. 'So, how about it?' he asked, deciding to change tack to avoid further discussion on the subject. 'Do you want to stay the night? As my father said, the bed's made up.'

'That's very kind, but we wouldn't want to impose ourselves on you.'

'No imposition at all,' Jamie replied, looking over at the two girls on the sofa. 'I doubt we're going to stop those two talking for a while.'

'Looks that way, doesn't it?'

'So you'll stay?'

Allan shrugged his shoulders. 'All right, why not?'

'Good,' Jamie replied, walking over to the drinks tray. 'In that case, we have no excuse now not to hit the hard stuff.'

Forty

Hang on, lass, stop kicking around,' Rory Stratton muttered, squeezing his legs tighter around the body of the upended ewe to stop her from trying to make a break for freedom. He heaved her round in the pen so that he could cast light on the infected foot from the reddened glow of the early morning sun. 'Right, let's see if we can't get you back into shape.' He took a penknife from the back pocket of his jeans and began paring away the side of the hoof, wrinkling his nose at the foul smell of the foot rot. 'My word, that's not a good one, is it? I should have spotted you before.'

He turned round to pick up the aerosol can of antibiotic from the ground and started when he saw the figure standing behind him. Holding hard to the ewe's feet, he stood upright, stretching out his aching back and looked across at the young man whom he had welcomed to the house the previous evening.

'You're up bright and early,' Rory said, giving the aerosol a shake as he appraised the man's attire. 'Not the ideal clothes to wear for a visit to a sheep pen.'

Allan glanced down at his dark-blue suit and the expensive black loafers, already spattered with mud, and then smiled at the man. 'Yeah, you're right, but I just felt like getting out of the house and having a walk.' He leaned on the wooden railing, clasping his hands together. 'Do you always talk to them like that?'

Rory laughed. 'A bit mad, eh?' He bent down and gave the ewe's foot a spray. 'My wife sometimes accuses me of speaking more to my sheep than I do to her. She calls them the other women in my life.'

Allan pushed his hands into the pockets of his trousers. 'At least your wife only has to compete with a load of woolly animals,' he said, turning round to look back at the house.

Rory glanced briefly at the young man, detecting an obvious tone of melancholy in his voice. He eased the ewe forward on to her front feet and let her go and watched as she ran to the far side of the pen, turning to eye him distrustfully. He walked over to the railing and put the aerosol can in the bag that hung on one of the strainer posts. 'That sounds as if you've experienced a similar problem.'

Allan let out a long sigh. 'Sort of.'

Rory took a towelling rag from the pocket of his padded waistcoat and wiped his hands. 'Have you been married long?'

Allan turned and stared questioningly at him. 'Why do you ask?'

Rory leaned an elbow on the railing. 'Well, it's probably none of my business, but I just saw that shiny new ring on your finger and wondered why someone would prefer trudging around a muddy farmyard at this time in the morning, rather than be tucked up in bed with a beautiful young wife.'

Allan bit at the corner of his bottom lip as he studied the weather-beaten face of the farmer, wondering whether he should rise to this line of questioning. 'Sometimes things just don't appear how they seem, if you get my meaning.'

Rory laughed. 'I know exactly what you mean! I'm afraid, my friend, that's just one of the anomalies of marriage. You'd think after twenty-seven years of being wedded to my wife, there'd be an almost Zen-like plane of understanding between us and we'd go out of our way to avoid the pitfalls which we know put us at loggerheads – but no, we both still get attracted to them like moths to a light bulb. What you've got to consider, though, is how boring it all would be without those little annoyances and niggling differences.' He flashed a wicked smile at the young man before pushing himself away from the railing and walking across the pen to release the ewe into the adjacent paddock. 'I think it's much more healthy to have a bit of fire in a marriage rather than let it smoulder aimlessly along. That can lead to problems.'

'And what about trust?' Allan asked.

'That's fundamental to any relationship.'

'So there should be no secrets, nothing hidden?'

'That depends on their context, whether they're being deployed for deception or protection. One represents total breakdown in communication, the other pure love.' Rory took the bag from the strainer post, slung it over his shoulder and climbed over the railings. He smiled at the young man. 'Look, don't think marriage is always going to be a bed of roses, but it's infinitely better than sitting on a dung heap by yourself for the rest of your life.'

Allan smiled at the farmer. 'That's a good quote. I might use it sometime.'

'Well, remember where you heard it first. It's a Stratton original.' He nodded his head in the direction of the house. 'I think you might have company.'

Allan turned to see Tess coming towards them, her arms crossed as she walked along the road from the house. He glanced back at Rory. 'We'll be heading back to Edinburgh quite soon, so if we don't see you, many thanks for letting us stay the night, and, erm . . . for the advice as well.'

'My pleasure,' Rory said, shooting him a wink. 'Have a good journey back.' He made his way across the concrete apron to the lambing shed and hung up the bag on a nail inside the door, and then walked over to the grain store to turn on the drying plant for the day. Ten minutes later he was back in the lambing shed, climbing astride the quad bike. He fired up the engine and drove it outside. A hundred yards away, he spotted the young couple still standing in the middle of the road talking with each other, and then he witnessed the man putting his arms around his wife's waist, drawing her into him and kissing her long on the mouth. Rory grinned with satisfaction at the sight, gave a brief self-congratulatory nod of his head and then set off at speed up the dirt-track road towards the hill, trailed closely by his two fleet-footed sheepdogs.

Forty-One

Sir Alasdair Dreyfuss placed the cup of coffee on his desk and sat down, leaning forward on his elbows and rubbing at the fatigue that was smarting in his eyes. For the past ten days, the earliest he had been to his bed was two o'clock in the morning, and it was really beginning to tell on him. He pulled forward his diary and glanced through the appointments he had listed for the day. The telephone began to ring and he muttered angrily under his breath, wondering why, at nine-fifteen in the morning, it had yet to be switched off night service.

'Oh, where the hell is everyone?' he exclaimed, grabbing the receiver on its sixth ring. 'Hullo, International Festival.'

'Alasdair?' a woman's voice asked.

'Yes,' the director answered, a quizzical frown on his face. 'Who is this?'

'It's Birgitte Hansen.'

'Birgitte!' Alasdair exclaimed, leaning back in his chair, relaxing immediately in the knowledge it was to be a social call. 'What a lovely surprise. How are you?'

'I am good.'

'And the family?'

'All busy doing different things. Kirsten is working close to us here in a restaurant in Charlottenlund, making some money before she goes back to university, and Henning starts his new school next week, so there is a lot to do, as you can imagine. I don't seem to have stopped all summer, so I am very much looking forward to our holiday with you and Paula and the kids in Lillehammer next April.'

Alasdair laughed. 'That goes for me too. We're bang in the middle of the festival here and it's chaos in the office. So, tell me, how's Peter getting on?'

His question was met with a long silence, and for a moment, he thought the line had gone dead. 'I'm sorry,' Birgitte said eventually. 'What did you say?'

'I wondered how Peter was?'

'But you should know how Peter is. He is with you in Edinburgh, is he not?'

Alasdair sat forward in his chair. 'Peter? I don't think so, Birgitte.'

'Of course he is. He is directing some plays for you.' Alasdair began to note a rising level of desperation in her voice. 'I am sending him something in the post today as a surprise, but I do not know the address of his hotel and I don't want to contact him on his mobile phone, so I wondered if you might be able to tell me.'

Alasdair rubbed at his brow. 'Birgitte, I'm sorry, but if he's here in Edinburgh, I'm afraid it's for a different reason other than the festival, because I haven't seen him and he certainly isn't directing anything for me.'

He heard her mutter something forcefully in Danish, and deciphered the word God as part of the phrase.

'Birgitte, are you all right?' he asked concernedly.

There was a long sigh. 'Yes, I'm all right,' she replied in a resigned, almost sad voice. 'Tell me, Alasdair, do you know of a girl called Tess?'

'Well, I suppose you'll be referring to Tess Goodwin. She works in the office here.'

'Ah, she still works there, does she? I found out she was quite a friend of Peter's.'

'I suppose she was. She looked after him a couple of years ago, when he first came here to direct.'

319

'And she did a very good job of that, not just for one year, but for two.'

Alasdair frowned. 'I'm not sure quite what you mean by that, Birgitte.'

He heard her letting out a deep breath. 'Peter had an affair with this girl. It went on for the two years he was in Edinburgh and I found out about it just before the end of the festival last year.'

Alasdair stared with shock at the door of his office. 'Are you sure about all this?'

'Of course I am. I heard it from Peter himself. He is like a little boy, Alasdair, he cannot keep secrets. He has to tell me everything to . . . what is that word? . . . to . . . to exonerate himself.'

Alasdair ran a hand across his head. 'Birgitte, I had no idea. I'm so sorry.'

'Oh, it is not new. It has happened before. He goes off to work abroad and I never know what he is going to tell me when he gets home.'

'Why on earth do you stand for it?'

'Because of Kirsten and Henning and because – this may sound stupid to you – but because he is so honest about his indiscretions.' She sighed again. 'However, it looks like his affair with this Tess has continued, so maybe this time I have to make a decision.'

'Birgitte, to be quite honest, I really don't think you're right on this one. Tess got married earlier this year and I know she's head over heels in love with her husband. I can't see her jeopardising that relationship.'

'Do you know how long she went out with her husband before they got married?'

'Yes, quite some time. I think about three—' Alasdair stopped abruptly when he realised what he was saying. He pressed a hand to his forehead and closed his eyes. 'Oh, Birgitte, I really don't know what to say.'

'It's all right. It is my problem, not anybody else's. I shall speak with him and find out the truth.' She laughed quietly. 'He will no doubt tell me. Goodbye, Alasdair.'

He returned the farewell and thumped the receiver back on its cradle, and then sat drumming his fingers slowly on the desk, lost in his thoughts. The telephone began to ring again, this time it was an internal extension that flashed. He answered it.

'Hullo?'

'Good morning, Alasdair.' It was Sarah Atkinson. 'I've got Peter Hansen holding for you on line one. Do you want to speak to him?'

'Well, speak of the devil. Yes, I most certainly do. Sarah, is Tess coming in this morning?'

'She's just arrived. She had phoned in to say she was going to be a bit late.'

'Would you send her into my office as soon as I've finished with this call?'

'Will do.'

As soon as she had hung up, Alasdair heard the smooth voice of Peter Hansen greeting him with his usual self-confident charm.

'Peter,' Alasdair cut in vehemently, 'I've just spoken to Birgitte, and if I were you, you stupid bastard, I'd zip up your trousers and get back to her as fast as you bloody well can.'

He slammed down the receiver and jumped to his feet, and thrusting his hands into his trouser pockets, he turned and looked out of the window, trying to steady his anger and gather his thoughts before Tess came in. He had no more than a moment because there was an immediate knock on the door.

'Come in!'

He turned as Tess walked in and he could tell from the apprehensive expression on her face that Sarah had obviously warned her some kind of confrontation was imminent.

'Take a seat, Tess,' he said, gesturing towards the wooden armchair at the other side of the desk. He watched as she sat down, nervously smoothing her skirt over her knees. 'Are you all right?'

'Yes, fine. I just had a few glasses of wine over the top last night, but,' – she blew out a long breath – 'I'm ready now for what the world has to throw at me.'

'Right.' He cleared his throat. 'Tess, there's no real easy way to ask this question, but did you . . . or maybe I should say, have you been having an affair with the creative director Peter Hansen?'

She nodded slowly. 'You've obviously spoken to him.'

'Very briefly, but as it happens, it was his wife who's just broken the news to me.'

Tess closed her eyes tight and lowered her head. 'I had no idea she knew.'

'So it's been going on for three years.'

She jolted up her head. 'No, it all finished last year. I had no idea he was going to turn up again. He rang you out of the blue, don't you remember, about a week and a half ago, and you put him through to me?'

'He was here in Edinburgh at that time?'

'Yes, and he quite literally forced me into meeting with him.'

'How did he do that?'

'By implying that he would tell you about our affair if I first didn't see him, and then later, go out for dinner with him.'

Alasdair pressed a finger to his brow. 'For heaven's sakes, that's as good as blackmail.'

'I know,' Tess replied quietly.

'But, Tess, you didn't, er, succumb to him this time?'

Despite the seriousness of her predicament, Tess could not help but smile at his formality. 'No, of course I didn't. I'm married now, Alasdair, I'm extremely happy and I certainly wouldn't put all that at risk for a man like Peter Hansen.'

The director nodded. 'I'm glad.'

'I agreed to have dinner with him last night, but that's all. I've no doubt he viewed it as the necessary stepping stone in order to rekindle the affair, but it was going to be my opportunity to tell him to get the hell out of my life.'

'And did you say that to him?'

'No. For one reason or another, I didn't turn up.'

Alasdair nodded slowly, beginning to piece together Peter Hansen's resultant actions in his mind. 'So that's obviously why he called me this morning. To let the cat out of the bag.'

'I'm sure of it.' Tess leaned forward, resting a hand on the desk. 'I don't even know how to start apologising to you, Alasdair. I know he's a great friend of yours and I can't imagine what his wife is thinking right now . . .'

'Well, she's thinking it was all still going on.'

'I promise you, that's not true. It all ended pretty acrimoniously last year, but nevertheless, I do still feel so guilty for allowing it all to happen and letting you down so badly.'

Alasdair gave a dismissive wave of his hand. 'Tess, you've no reason to feel that way. *I'm* the one that's guilty.'

She stared at him, perplexed. 'I'm sorry?'

'I didn't admit knowledge of it to his wife, but I've known for years that Peter is a philanderer. He's had girls in every country he's worked in. I should *never* have put you in charge of him for that first year. I realise now it was as good as sending a lamb to slaughter. So, you see, it's me that owes *you* the apology.'

Tess remained silent for a moment. She could never imagine he would have reacted in such a way. 'Thank you,' she said quietly. 'I can't tell you how good that makes me feel.'

Alasdair smiled at her. 'And how bloody awful it makes me feel.'

Tess sat back in the chair and rubbed nervously at the palm of her hand. 'And . . . what about my job? Do you want me to continue?'

The director stared incredulously at her. 'Of course I do. Did you think you were in danger of losing it?'

'To be quite honest, yes.'

He shook his head slowly. 'How dreadful – not, I may add, because you thought you'd lose your job, but I realise now how little you understand my ways.' He stopped prowling around behind the desk and sat down, linking his hands in front of him. 'You have become a very important part of the team here, Tess.

I would go so far as to say you're invaluable, and I think, quite honestly, you could not have handled this appalling situation with Peter Hansen any better.'

'Yes, I could.'

'Why do you say that?'

She paused for a moment. 'I told Allan last year about the affair and that was the main reason we spurred on the marriage, but I never told him about Peter Hansen returning again and he found out.'

'Oh, my word, no,' Alasdair replied quietly. 'Has it caused great difficulties?'

'There was a moment when I thought I'd blown it completely, but we eventually managed to reason it out. If there's any upside to this whole stupid situation, it has to be that it's made me appreciate even more what a special person Allan is and just how much I love him.'

'Well, what a lucky girl you are to have hooked him.'

Tess grinned. 'Yes, I know.'

Alasdair shook his head. 'Well, I can only reiterate how sorry I am that this all took place, Tess, and if you feel you can, I really hope we might be able to treat this whole episode as water under the bridge.'

'I'd be happy to.'

'And if Mr Hansen ever so much as utters one word to you again, will you let me know?'

'Without a moment's hesitation.'

'Good.' The director thumped a hand down on his diary and smiled at her. 'In that case, maybe the time has come for us both to get on with some work.'

Forty-Two

Following hard on the heels of Matti Fullbright, Rene entered the Smirnoff Underbelly at the top door beneath a narrow bular archway from which a sign of an upside-down cow with gravity-defying teats was suspended, and descended the stone steps into a claustrophobically small, but brightly painted reception area.

'Is this it?' Rene asked as she looked around, wondering why so much hype surrounded this Hobbit-sized venue.

'Just you wait,' Matti replied, beckoning her on. 'Don't make judgement until you've seen the whole place.'

She led the way down a circular stone staircase, hardly wide enough for two undernourished people to pass without contact, each step worn into a curve by centuries of use. Spotlights played on the thick dark walls, plastered from top to bottom with posters advertising the acts that were being staged. At the bottom of the flight it opened out into a small but crowded space, off which led two doors hung with signs reading 'Quiet, please. Show in progress,' each attended by a girl wearing a red T-shirt emblazoned with the inverted-cow logo.

'Come on, keep up,' Matti said as she led on down another identical flight of stairs.

'I don't know if I'm enjoying this very much,' Rene said, putting her hands against the cold dank walls to steady her descent. 'It's like we're going into the bowels of the earth.'

'Aye, it does feel a bit like that,' Matti replied as she momentarily disappeared from sight.

'What is this place?'

'Old bank vaults,' Matti's disembodied voice echoed up the stairwell. 'They're supposed to be haunted.'

'Oh, bloody 'ell,' Rene mumbled, hurrying her step to catch up with her tour guide.

They continued to descend more winding stairs, each one ending on a floor packed with show-goers, standing outside venues or crammed into bars with low-vaulted ceilings that rang with laughter and conversation.

'How big is this place?' Rene asked as she squeezed past a portly American woman who had picked an inopportune place to stop and study her programme.

'Ten venues, three bars and a nightclub,' Matti replied. 'I think they continuously stage about one hundred and thirty shows a day.'

They eventually ran out of staircases, coming out into a large bar that was again filled to bursting point.

'This is the famous Beer Belly,' Matti said as she pushed her way through to the blue-fronted bar. 'I'll get us some drinks up and meet you outside in the yard.' She pointed a finger towards an entrance at the far end of the room.

Rene threaded her way through the crowd and walked out the lower entrance door into a narrow cobbled alleyway, its fifty-metre length strung with a dazzle of lighted bulbs. Small open-doored rooms and arched alcoves lined the street, each set up as a temporary coffee stall or fast-food kitchen, their wares being consumed at wooden tables that sat against the walls of the ancient stone buildings. Rene stopped in front of a huge board that showed the full programme of events, smiling at the clever puns that gave names to each of the venues – Belly Button, Belly Dancer, Delhi Belly. She scanned the list of acts, eventually finding Matti's name under a column headed Belly Laugh.

'Here y'are,' Matti said as she arrived beside Rene and handed her an enormous glass brimming with spitting bubbles.

'What is it?' Rene asked, holding it away from her and studying its swirling contents.

'A very large Bacardi and Coke.'

''Eavens, lass, I'm not used to drinking in the middle of the day.'

'You're going to need it,' she said, grabbing Rene by the arm. 'Come on, I'm running late.'

The musty-smelling changing room was as small and sparsely furnished as a nun's cell, yet it was a hundred times more salubrious than the conditions Rene had to endure at the Corinthian Bar. 'Take off your coat and sling it on a chair,' Matti said as she hurried to get herself ready, 'and then go out on stage and have a squint through the curtains. I need to know if there's anyone out there.'

Shrugging off her coat, Rene walked out of the room, around the side wing and out on to the stage. She tiptoed over to the curtain and pulled it aside a fraction, catching her breath when she saw that the auditorium was jam-packed. She dropped the curtain and scuttled back to the changing room.

'It doesn't look as if there's a spare seat in the place!' she said to Matti, who was leaning over in front of the mirror on the makeshift dressing table, trying to fix a red rose in her hair with a kirby grip.

'Fantastic!' she exclaimed, picking up the plastic bag she had brought with her. 'Just what I wanted.' She extracted a white rose and another kirby grip from the bag and handed it to Rene. 'Stick that in your hair, girl.'

'What for?'

'Don't ask, just do it.'

Moving over to the mirror, Rene arranged the rose above her right ear and secured it with the grip. She stood back, swinging from side to side as she admired herself. 'Look at that – a touch of Carmen, don't ye think?'

'You look perfect,' Matti said, pulling Rene by the arm out towards the stage as the announcer began his rambling introduction.

'I'd better go try find a seat out there,' Rene said, trying to wrest her arm free from Matti's grip.

'Leave it to the last minute, would you? I'm feeling dead nervous about my act today.'

'. . . so, ladies and gentlemen,' the announcer's voice crescendoed through the sound system, 'will you please welcome that red-haired lady from Lancashire, MATTI-I-I-I FULLBRIGHT!'

As the curtains drew back and the audience burst out into applause and loud whistles, Rene tried once more to free herself from Matti's vicelike hand.

'I'd better get off now,' she said.

Matti turned round to face her, a broad grin on her freckly face. 'Too late. We're on.'

She gave Rene an almighty heave that nearly took her off

her feet. The next thing she knew she was standing in the middle of the stage in front of the largest audience she had faced since being in Edinburgh.

'Good evening, everybody, good evening!' Matti yelled out, waving her hands in the air in acknowledgement of the thundering applause. 'OK, calm down, calm down.'

She turned to Rene and eyed her in a strangely hostile way as the noise abated. 'I decided tonight to bring along a friend with me. Well, not really a friend, actually. How could she be?' She nodded knowingly. 'She's from Yorkshire.' She turned and walked towards Rene, giving her a wink as she approached. 'Ladies and gentlemen,' she said, putting her arm around Rene's shoulders, 'this is Rene Brownlow, one of the funniest women I know, but unfortunately' – she reached down and patted Rene's stomach – 'coming from Hartlepool, she's too fond of her fish suppers.'

As the audience burst out laughing, Rene looked up at Matti, aghast that she could have said such a thing, but then her fellow comedienne smiled and leaned over and whispered in her ear, 'Come on, defend your rose.'

And then Rene understood. The red rose of Lancashire, the white rose of Yorkshire. Matti was setting up a double act. No rehearsals, no scripts. She wanted a duel of head-to-head ad-libbing, one bouncing off the other. The audience was suddenly deathly silent, waiting for the riposte, waiting for the next scheduled line to be spoken. But there was none. She slowly unwound Matti's arm from around her shoulders and stood her distance from her, appraising her from head to foot. 'You're a fine one to talk, ye red-'aired tramp. Bad breeding, that's what it is' – she held out her hands to the audience – 'but what can ye expect, coming from Lancashire.' And with that, the partisan spirit of the audience was unleashed with whoops of support and cries of umbrage.

It was the perfect ice-breaker, but neither Matti nor Rene could keep up the animosity during the performance. There was too strong a rapport between them, too much good umour, and they settled into an off-the-cuff routine that had both the audience and themselves in fits of laughter. They kept it going without one faltering moment for a full hour, and at the end of the show the audience would not allow them to leave the stage, clapping and banging their feet for a full ten minutes before the curtain finally fell on the two bowing performers.

'Read that!' Matti exclaimed, striding across the bar in the Assembly Rooms and throwing a copy of the *Evening News* at Rene.

'What is it?' she asked, leaning forward on the sofa and putting her drink down on the table.

'I'm not telling you,' Matti said, her face aflame with excitement. 'Just read it and see.'

Rene watched Matti move off with a spring in her step towards the bar before spreading the folded paper on her knee. She scanned the newsprint, trying to find what she was meant to be looking for, and then her own name bounced out at her. She moved quickly to the start of the small review article, entitled 'War of the Roses'.

This had to be written today, it read. *It couldn't wait. At two o'clock this afternoon, the Belly Laugh venue truly lived up to its name when two comediennes took to the stage for a raucous side-splitting, hour-long ad-lib session.*

Wacky-haired Lancastrian Matti Fullbrook, a favourite with audiences at the Underbelly for the past three years, teamed up with feisty little Yorkshire lass Rene Brownlow (currently appearing at the Corinthian Bar in West Richmond Street) to produce one of the most pulsating double acts seen so far on the Fringe this year. And rumour has it that it's not going to be a one-off either, so go beg, steal or kill your best friend for a ticket. It's just a pity they hadn't pooled their considerable talents before now, because there's no doubt they would have been up there with the front-runners contesting the Perrier Comedy Award for this year.

'Did you find it?' Matti asked, placing two wineglasses on the table in front of Rene before applying all her strength to prising the cork out of a bottle of Cava.

Rene could not reply. She read through the article again, taking in every word, every accolade, every nuance of what the reviewer was implying.

'What have we done?' she asked eventually, her eyes registering total incomprehension.

'We've cracked it, Rene, that's what we've done.'

'But what's all this about the show continuing? We never said that.'

Matti grinned as she overflowed the glasses with frothing liquid. 'I did.'

Rene dropped the newspaper on the sofa and stared at Matti in disbelief. 'Why?'

'Why not? We're electric, Rene. We've taken the punters by storm. I've never had a reaction to any of my shows like that. Have you?'

Rene looked at Matti open-mouthed. 'Are ye saying that . . . we should team up, like?'

'Of course I am! We've got it made, girl!' The grin slid from her face, taking Rene's blank expression as one of rejection to the idea. 'What's the matter? Don't you want to?'

Rene slowly shook her head. 'Matti, ye're successful. Ye've been working the Fringe for years. For God's sakes, ye've even got an agent! It's a really wonderful thought, lass, but ye don't want to be saddled with me.'

'What d'you mean, saddled with you? Rene, it's vice versa! I told you I had to change my act. I need you. Obviously though, the question is do you need me?'

'But . . . what about my own show in the Corinthian? What do I do about that?'

'Ditch it! You said yourself you weren't getting the punters
in. If we team up, we'll go fifty-fifty on everything. That'll cover
all your costs and more, I know it will.'

Rene bit hard at her bottom lip to stop herself from bursting
into tears. It didn't work. She got up from the sofa, walked
round the table and put her arms around Matti's neck. 'Thanks,
lass, thanks so much.'

Matti chuckled. 'Do I take that as a yes, then?' she asked,
pushing Rene away from her.

Rene snuffled out a laugh. 'Aye, why not? Let's go for it.'

'Oh, that is great, girl!' Matti said, punching her fists in the
air. 'You and I are just going to take this whole damned world
apart!' She picked up the two glasses from the table and handed
one to Rene. 'Here's to us, my love, here's to the War of the
bloody Roses!'

Forty-Three

On the Thursday, two days before the last acts of the Festival
Fringe were to be staged and nine days before the final curtain
was brought down on the International Festival, four white trucks,
each emblazoned with the Exploding Sky Company logo, drove
slowly across the castle esplanade through a chevron of tourists.
They lined up, one behind the other, waiting while the first
truck was guided through the low tunnel leading into the inner
sanctum of Edinburgh Castle, its roof having barely six inches
clearance at either side of the ancient stone archway. Once it
was parked in the inner courtyard, drawn up in front of the
portcullis gate, Roger Dent jumped down from the cab and
stretched his arms above his head, ridding himself of the stiff-
ness in his body after the ten-hour drive. He walked over to the
battlements and looked out across the all-too-familiar view of
the New Town while the other trucks came through the tunnel
and drew in close to his own. As the drivers disembarked, Roger

pushed himself up on to the wall and sat watching as they made their way over to him.

Every one of his crew had at least two years' experience of doing this particular job with him, each choosing to spend his two-week summer holiday helping him to put the show together. They were really a crazy bunch of misfits – Dave Panton, a weapons expert for the Ministry of Defence; Graham Slattery, a computer programmer with IBM; and Annie Beardsley, an air traffic controller at Gatwick Airport – but they seemed to gel as a team with both humour and ease, their work of setting up the display a far cry from the stress and worries of their everyday employment.

And it was just as well he had an experienced team with him this year. The programme he and Phil Kenyon had eventually devised for the climax of the Edinburgh Festival was to be the most complex and work-intensive display his company had ever dared to stage, the intricately timed detonation of over five tonnes of fireworks in thirty minutes. It was to be his swansong, his final flourish, but yet, even now, the thought of the logistics involved was enough to make his stomach knot tight in trepidation.

'Right, before we adjourn to the pub,' Roger began, a remark that received an immediate cry of approval from his attentive audience, 'I'm afraid there's a good bit of work to be done. We'll start by unloading all the workshop equipment and get it set up under the stairs in the master gunner's office. There's no need to change a plan that works, so lay it out exactly as we've done in previous years – all electrical gear at the far end of the store, radios near the sockets for recharging, and the firing plan and safety regs on the wall above the table. If we get all that done this afternoon, we'll start loading the small-calibre shells first thing tomorrow morning.' He pushed himself off the wall. 'OK, make a move.'

As the crew headed back to their respective vans, Phil Kenyon appeared from a small doorway at one end of the narrow terrace and made his way across to Roger.

'All looks good,' the stocky little Australian remarked, handing Roger a clipboard with pad attached. 'No new safety measures, so we can just go ahead as planned.'

'When are the riggers due to arrive?'

'First thing Saturday morning. I reckon the briefing will take most of the day, so we won't start getting the multicore cabling laid out until Sunday morning.'

'And when are you due to meet up with the score reader?'

Phil shot him a wink. 'The beautiful Helen, d'ya mean?'

Roger narrowed his eyes at his colleague. 'Just watch it, Phil, don't cause a fallout, this of all years.'

'No worries, mate, I'll keep it under wraps. She's coming across from Glasgow tomorrow afternoon, so we'll make a start then on the timing plan.'

'It could take quite a while. A lot of those new cues will be completely alien to her.'

'We'll make it, as long as we don't have too many unscheduled interruptions.'

As Phil said this, a young woman dressed in a dark business suit came through the castle tunnel and strutted meaningfully towards them, a gash of a smile on her lipsticked mouth.

'Oh-oh, I spoke too soon,' Phil said, turning his back on the woman. 'You deal with her and I'll go help the others.'

As Phil headed off to the vans, Roger crossed his arms and leaned back against the wall, watching as Pauline McCann, the PR coordinator for the Scottish Bank, the main sponsor of the Fireworks Display, approached him. 'Hi there, Pauline, how're things with you?' He gave her a welcoming peck on the cheek.

'Working away, Roger,' the woman replied jovially. 'No rest for the wicked, and all that.'

'I'm surprised to see you. I thought you were planning on leaving the SB to set up your own agency.'

'You're right, it was a thought,' she said, digging a hand into her large shoulder bag and extracting a Moleskin notebook, 'but then the company made me an offer I couldn't refuse.'

She undid the elastic band on her book. 'Right, let's get down to business. First off, I have a few messages for you. Jeff Banyon wants to meet with you at the Scottish Chamber Orchestra office tomorrow evening, so he asked if you give him a call. And Sir Raymond Garston, the conductor, will be here on Tuesday morning and would like to meet up around lunchtime at the Balmoral Hotel.' She turned a page. 'Now the International office has scheduled the press call this year for Monday morning at ten o'clock. I know this is a bit earlier than usual, but the weather forecast for Tuesday and Wednesday is a bit iffy, so I thought it would be a safer bet for the photo opportunity. Does that sound all right for you?'

Roger shrugged. 'As long as you keep it as brief as possible.'

Pauline smiled at him. 'I'll do my best.' She closed the notebook and put it back in her bag. 'Now, I'll need to send out a blanket e-mail to all the papers, so is there anything you can tell me about what you've got planned for this year?'

Roger let out a quiet laugh. 'It's going to be the largest and the most complicated display I've ever staged.'

'Really? That's quite a statement.'

'I'm throwing every bit of caution to the wind this year.'

'Any reason for that?'

Roger nodded slowly. 'It's to be my last show.'

'*What?*' Pauline exclaimed, her eyes wide in disbelief. 'But you can't . . . you've been doing it for . . .'

'This is the twenty-third year,' Roger offered.

'So . . . does this mean it's the last year the Exploding Sky Company will be doing the Fireworks Display?'

'I hope not. Phil Kenyon is taking on the business, so I suppose it'll be up to him and the Scottish Bank as the sponsors. In fact, you'd be doing me a favour in letting them know before the story hits the press.'

'You don't mind me using it as a hook, then?'

'Not at all. You can entitle it "Going out with a bang!"'

Pauline laughed. 'That's not such a bad idea, actually.

Maybe you should think about starting a second career as a journalist.'

Roger rubbed a hand against his beard. 'Listen, by the time his show is over, I reckon the only establishment that will invite me into its folds is a secure lunatic asylum.' And he turned with a wave and headed off towards the vans to help the crew, eager to finish off the day's work as quickly as possible so he could get to the pub for the first of many pints of beer that evening.

About the same time as the clientele of the Queen's Head in Grassmarket was swelled by the ranks of the Exploding Sky Company, a mud-spattered, long-wheel-based Land Rover was pulling up outside the flat in London Street. Killing the engine, Rory Stratton clambered out and walked around to open up the back door. Jamie was already waiting there on the pavement with Angélique, ready to pull out the luggage.

'Thanks for the lift, Dad,' Jamie said, hoisting the straps of the two bags on to his shoulder and taking the violin case in his hand. 'Do you want to come up for a drink?'

Rory shook his head. 'No, I'll head home. I half promised your mother to take her out for a meal in the village pub this evening.'

'You should do that. It'll give her a break. I don't think she realised she was going to have to put up with us for a whole week.'

Rory put a hand on his son's shoulder. 'It was a great time. We both loved it.' He walked over to Angélique and gave her a kiss on either cheek. 'And what a bonus meeting you, my beautiful French girl. See and keep in touch with Jamie's old fogies now, won't you?'

'Of course I will,' Angélique replied, reaching up and putting her arms around Rory's neck and giving him a long hug. 'Thank you so much for having me to stay, Rory. It has been the most wonderful time.' She pushed herself away from him. 'I will send

335

you some more CDs that I think you will like. Maybe you can play them along with the Rolling Stones?'

Rory smiled. 'I'll make a point of it.' He turned back to Jamie. 'I hope you don't have any more problems with . . . you know who,' he said quietly.

'I doubt it very much. Harry Wills was outside the flat for three days. Never saw a thing.'

'Good.' Rory put his arms around his son's shoulders and gave him a squeeze. 'Look after yourself, boy, and keep in touch.'

'Will do, Dad, and thanks again for everything.'

They waited on the doorstep until the Land Rover had pulled away from the kerb before Jamie put the key in the door and they both entered into the building.

No more than twenty seconds after the door had closed behind them, a dishevelled figure hurried across the street and up the steps and pressed his hands against the door, as if willing it to open. Albert Dessuin turned away, his fingers splayed against his throbbing head, and slowly slid his back down the door to sit on the cold stone step, feeling the damp seep through the fabric of his raincoat. He cared little for that, or for the general grubbiness of his appearance, because now, at last, he had found Angélique Pascal.

Five days had passed since he had followed the fat little comedienne back to this address. It had been luck that he had made the decision to wait for her in the bar at the Corinthian, rather than in the theatre, because for some reason she had not performed that night, only turning up long enough to have a word with the blonde girl at the box office before she had left again. Five days. How his whole life had changed in that time. At first, he thought the refusal of his credit card at the restaurant in Randolph Place had been a mistake, a mere fault of the electronic banking system, but then when he had tried it in four different automatic machines without success, he knew something was definitely amiss. Returning to his hotel, he had phoned his bank in Paris and was informed that his monthly cheque had not been paid in and would he therefore write a tter immediately, authorising them to transfer money from is deposit account to cover the weekly standing order made ɔ his mother's account. Because of the embarrassment and ıconvenience this had caused him, anger blinded any consid- ation of the outcome of the next telephone call and he had ıstantly rung the lawyers of Madame Lafitte in Clermont errand, demanding to know why his salary had not been aid. Even before he had finished haranguing the female recep- ɔnist he was transferred to a Monsieur Chambert, who intro- uced himself in a quiet but frosty voice as the recently ɔpointed secretary of the trust set up by Madame Lafitte for ngélique Pascal. Albert could do nothing but listen in mute orror as the man recounted to him in a controlled, precise ıanner every detail of what took place between himself and ngélique on the night of the sixteenth of August in heraton Grand, and, as a result of which, it was considered y the trustees that he, Albert Dessuin, was an entirely unsuit- ɔle chaperone for Angélique Pascal and that his contract of mployment was to be terminated with immediate effect and ıat no consideration should be given to financial compensa- on. At that point, Albert Dessuin could hear the change in ıe lawyer's voice as he spat out his closing line with such ehemence and hostility that Albert was left shaking as the eceiver buzzed in his ear. 'And if you ever chance to go near Iademoiselle Pascal again, I will make sure every police force ı the world has knowledge of what you have done and I can uarantee there will be no safe haven for you. Goodbye, Iessuin.'

He had booked himself out of the hotel immediately after ıe telephone call, realising that he could no longer continue ɔ afford to stay there and wanting desperately to distance imself from the place. Monsieur Chambert had confirmed to ım for the first time that Angélique had been divulging the ue facts of what had happened that night, and consequently thers would no doubt know about it here in Edinburgh. rom that moment on he could sense a thousand pairs of judging eyes upon him, watching his every move with distrust and loathing.

He had eventually ended up staying in a grubby, stale-aired room above a pub in Tollcross. It was being used as a storeroom, but the barman, who had taken pity on the drunk foreigner who sat alone with his suitcase in the corner of the bar, had cleared out the boxes and the empty beer crates and had then gone back to his own flat, returning with blankets and sheets to put on the metal-framed bed with the sagging mattress. There were no washing facilities on the upper floor, so Albert had to make use of the rank-smelling gents' lavatory downstairs, only being able to do that during the time when the pub alarm was switched off. Consequently, he had spent many a lonely hour in those sordid surroundings, his self-esteem shattered and his mind becoming increasingly embroiled with hatred and revenge, having too much time to think about the hopelessness of his situation and about those whom he knew to be responsible for it all happening.

He put a hand into the folds of his mackintosh and pulled out a half bottle of whisky from the inside pocket. He held it up in front of him, studying the inch of amber liquid still remaining in the bottle. This now was his only true solace, a mind-numbing refuge from all his crazy, distorted thoughts. Unscrewing the cap, he tilted it to his mouth and drained the bottle in two gulps. He placed it on the step beside him, carefully resting the cap upside down on the top, a small token of order in his disordered world. He got to his feet and steadied himself on the cast-iron handrail as he descended the steps. After five days, the waiting was over. He had found Angélique Pascal. A few more hours, even a few more days would make no difference. Eventually he would be able to confront her and ask her why, after all those years he had sacrificed for her, she had chosen to ruin him completely.

The delicious aroma of roast chicken was floating around the hallway when Jamie and Angélique entered the flat. Dumping the bags on the ground, Jamie followed the herb-laden smell to source, pushing open the door of the kitchen. Rene Brownlow, Leonard Hartson and his young assistant, T.K., were seated at the table, all in the throes of eating, a glass of red wine in front of each. The conversation halted when he and Angélique walked in, and his three tenants turned to look their way.

'Well, if it's not our absentee landlord,' Rene said with a smile.

'Yeah, sorry about that,' Jamie replied, scratching embarrassedly at his head. 'We sort of stayed a bit longer than was expected.' He eyed the plates piled with food on the table. 'You seemed to have been coping all right, though.'

'Aye, well, someone had to play mother for these poor starving lads.' She laid down her knife and fork and pushed herself to her feet. ''Ow about some for yourselves?'

Jamie held up a hand. 'No, don't worry. I can make something up for Angélique and myself.'

'Don't be stupid. There's masses left over.' Grabbing a cloth from the sideboard, Rene opened the door of the oven and took out an enormous roast chicken, one side of it still untouched. 'Come on, join the party.'

'Are you sure?' Jamie asked.

'Of course you must,' Leonard Hartson cut in, getting to his feet and pulling an unoccupied chair away from the table. 'Move yourself round the table, T.K., and allow the young lady a bit of space beside you.'

'Hullo, we have not met,' Angélique said, reaching across the table to shake hands with the two men, young and old. 'My name Angélique Pascal.'

'Ah, my word, what a pleasure!' Leonard said, bowing his head as he took her hand. 'I have long been an admirer of your wonderful playing.' He introduced both himself and T.K. to Angélique.

Rene placed two steaming plates brimming with chicken, vegetables and potatoes on the table. 'Right, grab yourselves a knife and fork and get stuck in.' She took two wineglasses from the cupboard above the worktop and put them next to the plates.

'And I'm sure Leonard wouldn't mind if you had some of 'is wine

'I'm afraid it's only a very humble Bordeaux,' Leonard said smiling apologetically at Angélique as he leaned across to pou her a glass. 'I'm sure you will notice that as soon as you try it

Sitting down next to T.K., Angélique took a sip from he glass. 'It is delicious. You are obviously quite knowledgeable abou wines, Leonard.'

'Leonard knows a lot aboot everythin', don't ye, Leonard T.K. stated with pride.

Leonard laughed. 'Flattery will get you everywhere, T.K.'

As Jamie took his seat, he looked across the table at th cameraman. Although he appeared to be in good spirits, the ol man seemed to have aged visibly since Jamie had last seen hin His eyes were twinkling with enthusiasm, but they were set dee into a face that was lined with either worry or pain, its colou drained to an unhealthy chalky-white.

'So, how's it going with the filming?' Jamie asked.

'We're doing reasonably well,' Leonard replied. 'A little b behind in our schedule, but hopefully we'll be able to complet everything in the next nine days.'

'The stuff we've shot so far s'been great, isn't that righ Leonard?' T.K. said, looking eagerly at the cameraman.

'I think it would be safer to say that the reports from Londo have been quite encouraging.' He shot a clandestine wink a Jamie. 'My assistant is not only an invaluable asset to me whil shooting, but also a constant boost to my morale.'

Jamie swallowed a mouthful of food. 'Well, I'm glad all's bee going so well while we've been away.'

'Aye, an' for Rene, too,' T.K. said.

Jamie turned to the comedienne. 'Really?'

'Go on, Rene, tell 'em whit's happened tae you's,' T.K. prompted

Rene's face flushed to a colour similar to that of the win she was drinking. 'I've . . . erm . . . started a new show.'

'What?' Jamie asked perplexedly. 'Where?'

'In the Underbelly.'

Jamie stared at her. 'You're kidding!'

'What is an Underbelly?' Angélique asked.

'Only probably the best Fringe venue in the whole of Edinburgh.' He turned his attention back to Rene. 'How did you manage that?'

'I teamed up with another girl who was doing a show there. We're now on as a double act.'

'Who is she?'

'A lass from Lancashire, Matti Fullbright.'

Jamie's jaw dropped. 'Matti Fullbright! Rene, she's fantastic! I reviewed her show last year when she was short-listed for the Perrier Comedy Award.'

It was Rene's turn to gawp. 'Ye're kidding me! She never told me that!'

'Well, all I can say is that you've got yourself teamed up with one of the funniest women I've ever seen. Is this to be a permanent partnership?'

Rene shrugged. 'I reckon it could be. We've been playing to packed audiences every day. They've even shifted our act on to twice daily.'

'How did they organise that?'

'They found someone who was quite 'appy to move to my old venue at the Corinthian.'

Jamie nodded slowly. 'You've got it made, Rene. That's great news. What do the folks back home in Hartlepool think about it all?'

Rene grimaced. 'I 'aven't actually told them.'

'Why not?'

'Because there's a lot to discuss before I make a decision one way or t'other,' she replied, and not wanting to enlarge on the problems her new partnership would doubtlessly cause in her already troubled domestic life, she left it with a smile and turned to Angélique. 'So, 'ow's your 'and getting on, luv?'

Angélique held up her injured hand, showing no sign of a strapping, only a small pink scar across the palm. 'It is back to normal, I think.'

'Oh, that looks brilliant,' Rene said, taking the violinist's hand in hers and scrutinising the healed wound. 'You'll be back to playing the violin in the blink of an eye.'

'She already is,' Jamie said. 'In fact, Angélique reckons she's ready to play in public again, so we're just hoping the International office can arrange for her to do one of the late concerts next week, just before the close of the festival.'

'Oh, I'm glad to 'ear that, lass,' Rene said, giving Angélique's hand a pat. 'Ye're doing exactly the right thing, jumping back on that 'orse straight after ye've fallen off it.'

Jamie thumped his hands down on the table. 'Right, I think all occupants of number seven London Street have got quite a bit to celebrate, so how's about we adjourn to the local pub and have a drink?'

There was no voiced approval to the idea but all jumped to their feet and started to clear away the plates. All, that is, except Leonard. 'If you don't mind,' he said quietly, 'I think I might just give it a miss on this occasion.'

T.K. clattered the plate he was carrying down on the sideboard and stared at the elderly cameraman. 'Whit's up, Leonard?' he asked concernedly.

Leonard held up a hand. 'Nothing at all, T.K. I'm just a little tired. Nothing a good night's rest won't cure.'

Jamie glanced worriedly at Rene. 'We don't need to go out.'

'Of course you must!' Leonard replied heatedly as he got slowly to his feet. 'I'm perfectly capable of looking after myself.'

'Ah'll gie ye a hand tae the bedroom,' T.K. said, putting a supporting hand under Leonard's elbow.

'Really, T.K., there's no need.'

'Aye, there is,' T.K. replied resolutely. 'Ye're goin tae yer bed.'

Leonard smiled at the rest of the party. 'Quite an assistant, is he not?'

'Do you think he's all right?' Jamie asked, pulling on his jacket as he came down the steps to join Rene and Angélique on the pavement.

'I'm not that sure,' Rene replied as they began walking up ondon Street side by side. 'To be quite 'onest, I think 'e's bitten ff more than 'e can chew. 'E told me this is the first film job e's done for about twenty years.'

'Never!' Jamie exclaimed.

'Aye, and what's more, 'e was meant to have a whole load of eople 'elping 'im, and now it's just 'im and the young lad.'

'Maybe we should ask that nice doctor who treated my hand o come round to see him,' Angélique suggested.

'Good idea,' Jamie replied. 'We'll see how the old boy's getting n in the morning and make a decision then.' They turned the orner and began walking up Broughton Street. 'Come on, let's ake a short cut,' he said, turning down a narrow cobbled street t only by a few dim lamps fixed high on the dark walls of the urrounding buildings. It was deserted save for a large ginger cat hat jumped clear of an open dustbin and disappeared down ome steps as they passed.

'Ooh, I'm glad I'm in the presence of a tough young man,' 'ene said, wrapping her coat around her. 'I wouldn't fancy walking own 'ere by myself.'

'Do you think T.K. will know where we are?' Angélique sked.

'I don't know if he'll come, but anyway I told him the name f the pub before we left. He should find it.' There was the ound of footsteps running quickly up the street behind them. amie turned. 'Speak of the dev—'

The force of the blow to his shoulder was so great that it nade him spin round through three hundred and sixty degrees. Ie put out his hands to try to grab hold of something that vould keep him on his feet, but he knew immediately it was lost cause. The side of his head hit hard against the cold stone f the building and his knees gave way, his eyes swimming in nd out of focus as he slowly sank down the wall to the ground. lutching his head in his hands, he heard Angélique scream nd Rene shout, their voices sounding to him as if both were tanding in an echo chamber. The words 'Let go of 'er!' resonated through his brain, followed by a hollow slap like a fish being thrown down on to a wooden chopping board. A heavy weight fell across his legs and through blurred vision he saw Rene lying in front of him, whimpering and clutching at the side of her face. 'Albert, stop this! Please, stop this!' he heard Angélique cry out.

The name rammed into Jamie's brain, causing an adrenalin rush that cleared his head and brought feeling back to his legs. Pulling himself free of Rene's weight, he levered his body up the wall and staggered towards Dessuin, who had Angélique gripped firmly by the wrists. He was yelling at her in French, his eyes demonic with hatred and rage. It was only then Jamie realised that, in all the physical encounters he had experienced on the rugby pitch, he had never been rendered quite so hopelessly weak. Dessuin turned to see him approach and let go of Angélique.

'You filthy bastard!' he spat out, as he came towards Jamie. 'You think you can turn her against me?' He grabbed hold of Jamie's hair with force and yanked his head down, at the same time bringing his knee up into the pit of Jamie's stomach. Jamie keeled over, fighting for breath, but still Dessuin was not finished with him. He pulled his head up by the hair and slammed Jamie against the building, clutching him by the lapel of his jacket. Jamie saw the fist being drawn back and knew now that he was without the energy either to duck or to parry the blow. His only act of resilience was to keep his eyes open while the finishing blow was administered.

But it never came. He suddenly saw Dessuin spin round in front of him and the Frenchman's head rock backwards. He turned slowly back to face Jamie, clutching at his nose as blood spurted out between his fingers, and Jamie watched as he sank down to his knees on the cobbled street. Gulping in air, Jamie now focused on the figure that stood before him.

'Jeez,' T.K. groaned as he rubbed hard at his forehead. 'Ah never got the hang o' the head butt.'

Jamie shook his head. 'You did bloody well, mate. I owe you

ne.' He looked past T.K. to see Angélique enveloped in the bearlike folds of Harry Wills's arms. 'God, the cavalry arrived in the nick of time, didn't it?'

Jamie stumbled round Dessuin's hunched form and squatted down beside the little comedienne's supine body. 'Rene,' he said gently, taking hold of her hand, 'are you all right?'

Rene opened one eye. 'Aye, I'm fine. I just decided to play dead until that bloody French madman had gone.'

Jamie smiled at her. 'Well, you're safe enough now,' he said, pulling her to her feet and giving her a hug. 'Sorry about that. Wasn't much good.'

Rene glanced down at Dessuin with a sneer of disgust. 'You didn't get much of a chance, lad.' She leaned over Dessuin's hunched form. 'The little sewer rat played dirty, didn't ye?'

Jamie felt an arm slip around his waist and he turned to find Angélique looking up at him, her face puffy and stained with tears. 'Are you badly hurt?' she sobbed.

'No, I'm fine. Just aching a bit,' he replied, putting an arm round her shoulders and giving her a squeeze. 'Don't worry. It's all over and done with now.'

'I'm sorry about all this, Jamie,' Harry Wills said, coming to stand beside Dessuin and looking down at him with pure dislike. 'I never saw sight nor sound of him while I was outside your flat. I really had no idea he knew where you lived.'

Jamie shook his head. 'No matter. Where did you spring from, anyway?'

'I dropped in at the flat just after you'd left to go to the pub. I was coming round with T.K. to join you for a drink.'

'Just as well,' Jamie replied, clutching a hand to his aching stomach. He nodded towards Dessuin. 'So what are we going to do with him?'

Harry Wills bent down and heaved Dessuin to his feet. He put a hand into his pocket and pulled out his mobile phone. 'I think this game we've been playing has run its course. It's time to call in the police.'

As he began punching in a number, Angélique glanced at

345

Albert. He still clutched at his nose, covering his face with his hands, but she saw new tears well up in his eyes.

'Please wait, Harry. Don't do it just yet.' Walking over to Dessuin, she reached up and took a hand away from his face and held it in hers. 'Albert, you must understand it's all over. Please, will you go home now? I promise you not one other person will ever know about what happened between us. You are such a talented man and you must use that talent to help others as you have helped me. And Albert, you must find someone else to look after your mother because she will continue to make your life a misery and you do not deserve that. So, please, Albert, go back to Paris and find yourself some happiness there.'

Dessuin lowered his face and his body suddenly heaved with sobs. 'I'm so sorry, Angélique,' he cried. 'I'm so sorry.'

Putting a hand on either side of his face, Angélique lifted it up and planted a gentle kiss on his cheek. 'Will you go?'

Dessuin bit hard at his bottom lip to control himself. 'I would do anything for you.'

'I know you would.' She pressed his face between her hands. 'You are not a bad man, Albert. You must take courage and start on a new life without me.'

Harry Wills slipped the mobile back into his pocket. 'I'll take him back.'

'What d'you mean?' Jamie asked. 'To Paris?'

Harry nodded. 'I feel responsible for tonight, so it's the least I can do. Anyway, I'm not quite so forgiving as Angélique, and I'll not rest easy until I've seen this chap out of the country. I'll have him stay with me tonight so as I can keep an eye on him and then we'll get the first flight out tomorrow.' He gripped Dessuin firmly by the arm. 'Come on, let's make a move.'

'Harry?'

The reporter turned round to Jamie. 'Yes?'

'Could you give me a call tomorrow before you leave? There's something I want to discuss with you.'

Harry nodded. 'Sure.' He shot them a smile. 'I'd get to bed, you lot. I think you've all had enough excitement for one night.'

Having watched Harry guide Albert Dessuin down the street and round the corner, Jamie leaned over, resting his hands on his knees, and took in a couple of deep breaths. 'Angélique, would you head back to the flat with Rene?'

'Why? What are you going to do?' she asked.

'Just recover for a moment. T.K. and I will be along soon.'

Angélique took the comedienne by the arm and they walked off slowly down the street.

'Hell, I didn't want to let on,' he said to T.K. once they were out of earshot, 'but that bloody man's really managed to hurt me.'

'D'ye need a hand?' T.K. asked.

'No, just give me a minute.' He looked up at T.K. 'Can I ask you something?'

'Whit?'

'Have we met before . . . I mean, before you came round to the flat with Gavin Mackintosh?'

T.K. grinned at him. 'Aye, we coulda done.'

'Where?'

'I think it wis you I bumped intae roond the corner there. Ye were carrying somethin' in yer hand and ye drapped it.'

Jamie nodded slowly as the mental picture of the paint cans rolling off the side of the pavement came to mind. 'Of course. That was it. You went haring up London Street.'

T.K. laughed. 'Aye, I thocht someone wis efter me.'

Jamie scrutinised him. 'It wouldn't have had anything to do with a stolen video camera from the coffee shop, would it?'

T.K. scratched at the back of his head. 'Aye, well, sort of.'

Jamie had a sudden fit of coughing and he gripped the side of his ribcage in agony.

'Whit's the matter?' T.K. asked. 'Are ye all right?'

Jamie lifted his head. 'Yeah, don't worry. I'm just laughing and it bloody hurts.'

'Whit's so funny?'

'Nothing, really,' he said, pushing himself upright and giving T.K. a thump on the shoulder, 'only that both you and I have damned good reasons not to set foot inside that coffee shop ever again.' He began to walk slowly down the street. 'I could kill for a pint of beer. What about you?'

T.K. smiled to himself and then hurried to catch up with Jamie. 'Aye, why not?'

Jamie felt the relieving effects of the two power-plus painkillers, swallowed with the aid of a large malt whisky, drift over his body like healing hands as he lay in the darkness of his room. He was only a moment away from deep, restful unconsciousness when it happened, so he could not tell whether it was an incipient dream of unrequited desire rather than sublime reality. It started with a beam of light falling across his face for a brief second before darkness enveloped him once more. A sliver of cold air hit him as the duvet was lifted away and he felt the mattress sink to the pressure of another person and the form of a female body melt its contours into the arch of his back. He lay there without moving, sensing every part of her on him, the push of her breasts and the squeeze of her stomach against his spine. He smiled to himself in total contentment and then turned to face the truth.

'Hi,' Angélique whispered.

'Hi,' he replied, leaning up on an elbow and reaching out a hand to the silk-soft skin of her face.

'Did you know it was me?'

Jamie grinned into the darkness. 'Well, as much as I like her, I was hoping it wasn't Rene.'

Angélique muffled a laugh into the duvet. 'How is your head feeling?'

'Throbbing.'

'And your body?'

'Aching.'

348

'Shall I make you feel better?'

'How do you plan to do that?'

He sensed Angélique raise her head from the pillow and then felt the pressure of her lips against his mouth. 'I don't think you really need to ask,' she breathed out.

Forty-Four

Gavin Mackintosh sat in the Hub café toying with his empty coffee cup as he watched the group of Japanese tourists at the next table sifting through the pile of festival leaflets they had laid out before them and discussing with incomprehensible excitement their viewing plan for the day.

'Gavin?'

He turned to find the young woman whom he had first seen talking with Angélique at the welcoming reception at the Sheraton Grand. He stood and offered a hand. 'Tess, how good to meet you at last.' He pulled out a chair for her at the table and sat down next to her. 'I just felt I should come to see you in person to say how grateful I am for all your help during the last week. The confidence and support you have shown towards Angélique has been invaluable to us all.' Gavin stopped talking when a waiter came and hovered beside him. 'What can I get you?'

'A cappuccino, please.'

Gavin ordered two cappuccinos and then leaned forward on the table. 'No doubt you've been in touch with Angélique?'

Tess nodded. 'I had a long chat with her this morning. It seems all your fears over Dessuin were well justified.'

'They were, and I think we were very lucky it didn't all turn out a great deal worse than it actually did.'

'How's Jamie? I hear Dessuin gave him quite a beating.'

Gavin smiled at her. 'He's a tough lad. He'll make a speedy recovery.'

'And Angélique?'

'Despite what happened, she seems a very different person this morning. I think a whole weight has lifted off her shoulders with the departure of Dessuin.'

Tess raised her eyebrows. 'I can well believe that, and I—' She stopped when the waiter approached their table and placed the two cups of cappuccino in front of them. She waited for him to leave before continuing. 'I'm just so glad it's all over for her.'

Gavin took a sip from his cup. 'She's ready to play again, you know.'

'Yes, she told me. I'm going to see Alasdair Dreyfuss this afternoon and break the news to him. It's going to be tricky to arrange it all, but there's no doubt he's going to be over the moon.'

'What will you say to him?'

'Just that Angélique's hand has healed much faster than was expected, and she's decided to return here from France so that she can at least fulfil a small part of her commitment.'

Gavin nodded. 'Yes, I think you're right to keep it quite simple.'

Tess blew out a breath. 'I have to. One way and another, I've been keeping too many secrets back from Alasdair this year. Anyway, once we've rescheduled one of the concerts, I'll get Sarah Atkinson, my boss, to arrange rehearsals for her. And then we can publicise it.'

Gavin drained his cup of coffee. 'I'm sure it will be a sell-out within hours of you doing that.' He glanced at his watch. 'Now, I really must fly,' he said, pushing back his chair and getting to his feet. 'I have a meeting in fifteen minutes.' He took out a five-pound note from his wallet and placed it on the table. 'It's been good meeting you properly, Tess.'

They stood and shook hands. 'And you too, Gavin. I know how much you've done for Angélique.'

'For me, it's been nothing but a pleasure.' He held on to her hand, laying his other one across it. 'Actually, Tess, there is one

her thing. Would you be able to reserve two tickets for me
r this concert before the word gets out?'

Tess laughed. 'Consider it done,' she said, 'and seeing you've
id for the coffee, I think we can put them on the house.'

Forty-Five

mie and T.K. stood up from the kitchen table as the tweed-
ited doctor walked into the room, unhooking his stethoscope
om around his neck and slipping it into the leather case he
as carrying.

'How is he?' Jamie asked.

The doctor gazed seriously at them both over the top of his
ectacles. 'Rest, and plenty of it. That's all he needs.' He put his
ag down on the table. 'I really am of the opinion that it was
retty unwise of Mr Hartson to take on this film job of his,
pecially in light of the fact that he's not been used to doing
ch work for the past twenty years or so.'

'Whit's the matter wi' him?' T.K. asked, a worried frown on
is face.

'Mr Hartson, I'm afraid, has quite a serious heart problem.
e has been taking all the correct medication, which has worked
ell in controlling his condition up until now, but the extra
hysical effort and the undoubted mental strain of making this
lm has certainly exacerbated it.'

'Are ye saying he's gotta stop makin' the film?' T.K. exclaimed
disbelief.

'I don't think whatever I have to suggest will stop him from
oing that. The making of this particular film obviously means
great deal to him, but nevertheless, my advice would be that
e should take a couple of days off, just so he can recharge his
atteries a bit.' He pulled back a tweedy sleeve and glanced at
is watch. 'Now, I must be getting off,' he said, picking up his
ag. 'I was given rather short shrift by my receptionist this morning

for taking on a house call.' He studied Jamie's face. 'You look as if you've been in the wars, lad. That's a nasty-looking bruise on your cheek.'

Jamie smiled at the old man. 'I'm fine, honestly.'

'Right, well, in that case, all I'd advise you to do is to take a couple of arnica pills.'

'I'll get some. Thanks.'

While Jamie showed the doctor out of the flat, T.K. walked along the hall and gently pushed open the door to his and Leonard's bedroom. The old cameraman was sitting fully dressed on the edge of his bed, leaning over with effort to tie up his shoelaces.

'Whit are ye daen', Leonard?' T.K. asked as he entered the room.

Leonard looked up. 'Oh, hullo, T.K.'

'Ah said whit are ye daen'?'

'Getting ready to go out, of course.'

'But, Leonard, the doctor said—'

The cameraman cut him short with a dismissive wave of his hand. 'Oh, the doctor says! I know exactly what I can do and what I can't. I've had this condition for the best part of five years, T.K., and I know exactly what my limitations are.' He pushed himself to his feet. 'Anyway, we simply cannot afford the time for me to be languishing in my bed,' he said as he approached his assistant, giving him a light pat on the arm, 'so let's get on with the work.'

As the cameraman opened the door of the bedroom, T.K. did not move, but stood with a worried expression on his face. 'Leonard?'

'Yes?'

'This is no' a good idea.'

Leonard turned and smiled reassuringly at the boy. 'I really am all right, T.K. Anyway, I decided myself last night that, due to present circumstances, I should try to take things a little easier, and for that reason, my plan for today is that you should take over the role of camera operator.'

For a moment, T.K. stared open-mouthed at Leonard, not quite believing what he had just heard. 'D'ye mean that?'

'Well, I've thrown you in at the deep end all the way through this shoot, so I don't see why we should stop now. It'll mean I can concentrate on the lighting.'

'In that case, what are we waiting for?' T.K. said excitedly as he bounded towards the door.

As his young assistant left the room and headed off down the corridor, Leonard shook his head. 'I think it was for you, my boy,' he laughed, closing the door behind him.

The lights shimmered and flared on the garishly bright silk kimonos of the Japanese performers as they dipped and turned and rolled with liquid precision through the ancient ritual of their dance. The shadows cast out by their bodies crossed over and merged together on the stage, arms and hands weaving like the high branches of a tree caught in the wind. The dancers, however, were not Leonard's focus of attention. He sat in the canvas-backed chair watching every move that T.K. made with the camera as he followed the action exactly as he had been directed. From what he witnessed, there was no doubt in Leonard's mind that the boy had the knack, using the top of his right arm to operate the panning handle of the tripod so that he could release his right hand to operate the automatic zoom. At every moment that Leonard thought the camera should pan or tilt, T.K. would carry it out, moving smoothly through the syncopated motions of the six dancers.

Oh, to be able to get the chance to live my life again, Leonard thought to himself as he slipped a hand inside his jacket to press against the pain that was once more building in his side. Why did I ever conceive the idea of giving up this kind of work? It was always my passion, my calling in life. Why did I allow myself to be cast out into the wilderness for all those years, to turn my back on so many potential opportunities to make films such as this? Yes, it had come about eventually, but only through a quirk of fate, and maybe, in the end, it was all going to be too late.

He took a neatly folded handkerchief from the top pocket of his jacket and dabbed at his watering eyes as he turned his attention to the lighting stage. He smiled sadly to himself as he glanced from one light to the other, following their perfectly balanced beams down on to the dancers on the stage. Maybe Nick Springer was right. Maybe now he should start admitting to himself that he was, indeed, still one of the best directors of photography in the business.

'Shall ah stop rolling, Leonard?' T.K. asked, taking his eye away from the viewfinder of the camera.

'Are you quite happy with it?'

'Ah think so.'

'Good lad. In that case, cut it.'

Forty-Six

The battered white van was sitting so low on its tired suspension, due to the weighty human load it was carrying, that Terry Crosland could hear the new exhaust he had had fitted before leaving Hartlepool scrape the ground at every bump as he drove up into Edinburgh via London Road. The journey had taken a good hour longer than he had envisaged, due to the heavy volume of weekend traffic on the A1 and the half-hourly pit stops requested by the committee members of Andersons Westbourne Social Club, who proved incapable of synchronising their interminable needs to relieve themselves. Much against Terry's expectations, it was the two youngest members of the rear-seated party, Robbie and Karen Brownlow, who had endured the six hours of bum-numbing discomfort the best, hardly opening their mouths as they sat on the makeshift seats, passing the time by listening to music on their MP3 players.

'Where do we go from 'ere?' Terry asked as he approached he roundabout on Leith Walk.

Gary Brownlow studied the Edinburgh Streetfinder they had ought at a filling station near Berwick-upon-Tweed. 'Left and hen straight on at the next roundabout.'

Terry did as he was instructed and was immediately confronted y a long line of stationary traffic. He glanced at his wristwatch. We're cutting it fine, you know,' he murmured to Gary.

A head appeared between their seats. 'I told you we'd 'ave een better staying on the City Bypass and coming in on the)alkeith Road,' Stan Morris said.

Gary turned and looked aggravatedly at the man's ruddy face. Oh, aye, and 'ave ye got some built-in bloody radar that tells e traffic was running smoothly there or summat?'

'I'll 'ave ye know that when I served in the Royal Signals—'

Terry pressed his foot down on the accelerator, seeing an pening on the inside lane. The sudden forward motion made tan disappear into the back and a gonglike sound resonated ound the van as he hit his head on the roof before being eturned to his seat with a forceful thump.

.''Ave a care, Terry!' his voice moaned from the rear of the ehicle.

Terry caught Gary's eye and gave him a wink and both men it on their bottom lips to stop themselves from laughing out oud.

'How far now?' Terry asked as he turned the van left at the raffic lights on to North Bridge.

Gary turned the map round and counted off the roads with is finger. 'West Richmond Street is about fifth on the left.'

'Bloody marvellous!' He glanced round at the seven other occupants of the van. 'Panic over. I reckon we'll make it by a good ten minutes.'

tan Morris walked quickly to the front of the party as they urried down the pavement towards the Corinthian Bar, eager that he should resume his role as spokesman once more. He pushed open the heavy glass door, letting it swing back on Terry's face, and approached the tall blonde girl in the black T-shirt who stood behind the ticket-office desk.

'Good evening, lass,' he said importantly, leaning an elbow on the desk. 'Would ye be so kind as to supply us with eight tickets for tonight's performance, please?'

Without even a welcoming smile, the girl began to rip off the tickets out of a book.

'And I don't suppose,' Stan continued, giving her the benefit of his most persuasive smile, 'that ye might see fit to give a reduction for juniors?'

The girl glared at him, a deep frown on her face. 'Juniors? What age are they?'

Stan turned and pointed at Gary's children in turn. 'That there is Robbie and he's ten and his sister, Karen is . . . how old are ye, lass?'

'Eight,' Karen breathed out, embarrassed.

Stan turned back to the girl, who was staring concernedly at the two children. 'There y'are. Ten and eight.'

The girl cleared her throat. 'Are you sure you want to take them to this show?'

Stan laughed. 'Of course we do, lass! It's their mother who's performing. They especially want to see her!'

The girl looked even more bemused, her mouth dropping open as she glanced back and forth between Stan and the children. Eventually, she shook her head. 'Well, if you insist,' she said, continuing to tear the tickets out of the book, 'and seeing it's the last night of the show, I'll let them in for free.'

Stan turned and smiled smugly at the group, feeling justly proud of his negotiating skills.

'There you are,' the girl said, handing him the tickets. 'Just go down the stairs behind you and the theatre's on the right.'

There were only seven other people in the dark little basement theatre, all occupying tables that were grouped around the small curtain-shrouded stage. Stan Morris stood with his hands his hips, contemplating which of the remaining tables would fer the best view, but the rest of the party pushed past him d proceeded to group themselves around the three nearest the ck of the theatre.

Stan let out a resigned sigh as he went over to join them. 'I ouldn't have chosen these meself. I think . . .'

'Aye, and we're getting tired of what you think,' replied sombre erek Marsham, who had sat himself next to the diminutive ittle. 'The place is no bigger than a public convenience, any ad, so what the 'ell does it matter where we sit?'

'Aye, just take that chair there,' added Skittle, as he polished s thick-lensed spectacles on a grubby handkerchief, readying mself for the show.

'Well, I 'ave to say—'

'Just sit down!' the five voices of the senior party commanded m.

As Stan moodily rested his cavalry-twilled bottom on the hard ooden seat, the lights dimmed and a voice boomed out from e loudspeakers set up in opposite corners of the confined space. adies and gentlemen, welcome to tonight's performance of the ruit Sundaes. We all know that an apple a day keeps the doctor vay, but on this occasion, a word of warning: DON'T EAT THE RUIT!'

'What's all this about?' Gary whispered to Terry, a look of comprehension lining his face.

'No idea, lad. Maybe she's changed her act.'

Loud music now blared from the speakers and the curtains rew back to reveal a pair of identical female twins, quite bviously past their prime, standing centre-stage, the lumpy ontours of their bodies swathed in voluminous aquamarine lk dressing gowns. Their arms were outstretched, and in each and they bore a small wicker basket laden with a variety of uit – tangerines and bananas and plums and grapes. As the arty from Hartlepool cast querying glances at one another, camp little dwarf of a man, dressed in a minute tuxedo, anced on to the stage, and with a muselike flourish took

357

the baskets from the women. And then, stretching their deep-red-lipsticked mouths into wide teasing smiles, they undid the ties on their dressing gowns and simultaneously allowed them to drop to the ground.

'What the *'ell* . . . ?' Gary exclaimed, desperately trying to put his hands in front of his children's eyes.

'You've got me,' Terry replied, a look of revulsion on his face. 'What's she going to do with that banan— oh, God, no!'

'I'm getting the kids out of 'ere,' Gary said, grabbing the hand of both his children and heaving them to their feet, causing a chair to crash backwards to the floor.

As he hurried them off towards the door, with Terry in close pursuit, the committee members of Andersons Westbourne Social Club rose slowly to their feet and began shuffling their way between the tables, never diverting their eyes from the act. All that is, except Skittle, who had not witnessed his associates move away from him. He got up from his chair and walked a couple of paces towards the front of the theatre, holding up a hand to cut out the blinding light that shone out from the stage, and squinting through his spectacles. 'Is that you, Rene? My, you've lost a lot of weight, lass.'

A hand reached out and grabbed the sleeve of his raincoat, giving him a heave that nearly took him off his feet.

'What the bloody 'ell's going on down there?' Gary angrily asked the girl behind the ticket desk.

'I'm sorry?'

'That act. That wasn't what we came to see.'

'I'm sorry, sir,' she said, displaying little interest in his complaint as she continued to tidy up the desk. 'That's the spirit of the Fringe, I'm afraid. Anything goes.'

Gary felt the rest of the committee pressing up behind him, eager to hear her explanation. 'But what 'appened to Rene Brownlow?' he asked. 'She was meant to be on 'ere.'

The girl slapped her hand to her mouth. 'But the gentleman didn't say,' she exclaimed, looking directly at Stan Morris, whose face coloured red when he felt the accusing eyes of the party upon him. 'Rene Brownlow isn't on here any more. She moved venues.'

'Where's she on, then?' Gary demanded.

'At the Underbelly.' She bent down and rummaged behind her desk, coming up with a bulky programme. 'Hang on a minute,' she said, flicking through it. 'She swapped venues with the Fruit Sundaes, so I should be able to find it.' She drew a red-nailed finger down a page. 'Here we are. She's on at the Belly Laugh, and there's a show at eight o'clock.'

Terry looked at his watch. They had twenty minutes before it began.

'I don't know if you'll get in, though,' the girl continued. 'Her new show's been a sell-out for the last week.'

'Is that right?' Gary asked with astonishment.

For the first time, the girl's face creased into a smile. 'She's been the talk of the town.'

Gary looked down at his children and gave them a proud wink. 'D'ye 'ear that, kids? Yer mam's the talk of the town.'

'Come on, lads, we'd better get going,' Terry said, pulling open the entrance door and ushering the party out into the street.

'Hang on a minute!' the girl cried out after them, pulling open the cash drawer and quickly counting out some money. She handed Terry a wad of notes. 'I think you deserve a refund. I'm sorry about the mix-up. If the gentleman had just said . . .'

'Don't worry,' Terry said, giving her friendly flick of the head. He held up the money in his hand. 'And thanks for this, love. Much appreciated.'

He went out of the door and then immediately opened it again. 'No idea where this place is, do you?' he asked the girl.

'Turn right out of this road, head back into town for about four hundred metres and then take a left on Chambers Street. Go to the end and turn right and you'll find the Underbelly about a hundred metres on the left.' She glanced up at the clock on the wall behind her. 'Have you got transport?'

'Aye, I 'ave.'

'Then I'd suggest you drive it, if you want to get there in time.'

Terry gave her the thumbs-up and ran out into the street.

The numbed silence in the van as they drove back towards town was broken by the quiet voice of timid Norman Brown, who had hardly opened his mouth since they departed from Hartlepool. 'They were very entertaining, those girls.'

Every head, including Terry's, turned to look at the mouse of a man.

'I think we'll draw a veil over that memory, thank you, Norman,' Stan Morris said prudishly.

'I reckon two large paper sacks would be more fitting,' Gary murmured in the front of the van, without lifting his eyes from the map.

A damned sheepdog, that's what we need 'ere, Terry thought to himself as he stood outside the ticket office in the cobbled courtyard of the Underbelly. Gary Brownlow and his two kids were the only members of the party in sight, standing at a fast-food stall where they were consuming hot dogs and Coke. Stan Morris and Derek Marsham had inevitably headed off to find a gents', and he had no idea where Norman Brown and Skittle had got to. Probably trampled underfoot in the crowd that was trying to get down the spiral staircase. With a shake of his head he turned and walked into the ticket office, digging into the pockets of his jeans for the wad of money.

'Can you give me eight tickets for Rene Brownlow's show?' he asked the red-T-shirted boy behind the counter.

'I'm sorry. That show's a sell-out. Has been for the past week.'

'Oh, 'ell, no!' Terry exclaimed, running an exasperated hand over his quiff of hair. 'Are ye saying there's no chance at all of seeing it?'

'I'm afraid not.'

'But it's 'er last show.'

'I realise that, sir.'

'But we've come all the way up from 'Artlepool to see 'er. We've got 'er 'usband and kids with us an' all!'

The boy did not reply for a moment. 'Hang on a minute,' he said, getting to his feet and grabbing the arm of a woman who was hurrying past him. They talked together in low voices before the woman nodded and then approached Terry.

'We can let you all in, but I'm afraid you'll just have to stand at the back of the auditorium.'

'Aye, that'll do us fine,' Terry said as he began to count out the money.

'Don't worry about that, sir,' the woman said with a smile. 'Seeing you're all from Rene's home town, I think we can let you in for free.'

'Thanks, lass,' Terry replied, pocketing the money. 'That's really good of ye.'

'You'd better hurry, though. It's just about to start.'

Terry ran back out into the courtyard where he found, to his relief, that the committee members had reunited and Gary and the kids had finished satisfying their appetites.

''Ave ye got the tickets?' Gary asked.

'None available,' Terry replied as he hurriedly led the way to the entrance of the Belly Laugh venue. 'The show's been a sell-out, so we're standing at the back.'

Arriving at the door, Terry gave it a push, but felt a pressure holding it closed.

'Come on, Terry,' Stan Morris called out impatiently from the back of the group. 'What are ye waiting for?'

''Old yer 'orses.'

The door was opened by a girl who pressed a finger to her lips. 'Are you the party from Hartlepool?' she whispered.

Terry nodded.

'Right, follow me, but be very quiet. The show's started.'

The auditorium was already echoing with laughter as the girl led them along the back aisle, the committee members of Andersons Westbourne Social Club jostling and bumping into one another in the dark, their eyes fixed on the stage. Rene stood close to one of the side wings with a white rose fixed behind her left ear, while on the opposite side a woman with a ruddy freckled complexion was passing comment on the red rose she wore in her wild entànglement of carrot-coloured hair.

Karen Brownlow tugged on her father's jacket sleeve and Gary bent down so that she could whisper something in his ear. Gary nodded and straightened up and leaned close to Terry. 'Kids can't see. Can you stick Karen on yer shoulders and I'll take Robbie?'

Terry gave the young Brownlow boy a hand to clamber on to his dad's shoulders before hefting up Karen on to his own. 'Who's the other woman with Rene?' he said to Gary.

'No idea. I've never seen 'er before in me life.'

'They seem to work well together.'

'Aye, they do.'

As they spoke, Rene walked across the stage and put a hand on the redhead's arm, cutting her off in mid-sentence. Rene turned, narrowing her eyes in the glare of stage lights, and looked up into the obscurity of the auditorium, directly to where Gary and Terry and the rest of the Hartlepool crew were standing.

'I've got great 'earing, you know,' she called out. 'Matti and me are dying for a rest, so seeing as you lot at the back seem to be in a talkative mood, we'd much appreciate it if you came down 'ere and did the show for us, so's we can get off to our beds.'

The audience tittered, and to a man turned round and looked towards the back of the auditorium, an action that made the committee members of Andersons Westbourne Social Club cast embarrassed glances from one to the other.

'Oh, shurrup, girl, and just get on with it,' Gary called out at the top of his voice.

Rene's mouth fell open in amazement and she walked to the front of the stage, shielding her eyes with her hand as she sought out the location of the heckler. 'Gary?' she said in a querying voice.

Terry took over the shout. 'Aye, get on with the show, lass. You just show 'em 'ow it's meant to be done.'

On hearing those all-too-familiar words, Rene started to laugh. 'You 'n all, Terry?'

The red-haired girl put her hands on her hips and scowled impatiently at her partner. 'Here, Yorkie, are you just going to gawp at the audience all night, or shall we continue? They've all paid good money, you know.'

'Oh, keep yer 'air on,' Rene replied as she returned to stand beside her fellow comedienne. She put a hand to her chin as she pensively scrutinised the untidy mass of red curls that tumbled around Matti's moonlike face. 'On second thought . . .'

And with that they slipped back into their routine, the initial slanging match between them turning, as it had done over the past eighteen shows, into a hilarious and warm-hearted ad-lib session that had both performers and audience alike falling over one another in laughter. An hour and a half later, after Rene and Matti had taken at least three more curtain calls than at any of their previous performances, the lights in the auditorium brightened and the audience rose from their seats in a hum of excitement and good humour.

'That was bloody marvellous!' Terry said, lifting Karen from his shoulders and putting her down on the floor. 'What d'ye think of yer mam, lass?'

'Can we go and see 'er now?' was all that Karen had to say in reply.

Terry rubbed a hand gently on her head. 'Aye, I'm sure we can.'

The girl who had shown them in led the Hartlepool party round the back of the stage to the small dressing room where Rene and Matti sat, slumped and exhausted, on a couple of wooden chairs.

'Oh, my Go-o-o-od!' Rene cried out, jumping to her feet when Robbie and Karen rushed towards her. She put her arms around them both and held them tight against her, raining kisses on their heads. 'Oh, 'ow I've missed you lot.'

'My word, Rene, you've got a real fan club here, haven't you?' Matti remarked as she surveyed the six faces peering round th doorway at differing heights.

Rene raised her eyes from her children's heads and glance towards the door. 'Oh, for goodness' sakes, you're all 'ere,' sh laughed, letting go of her children and hurrying over to the door giving each of the committee members a kiss on the cheek. 'Hov wonderful ye've all come. Whose bright idea was this?'

'Gary's,' Terry replied. ''E thought you needed some mora support, but obviously 'e got the wrong end of the stick.'

Rene grinned at her husband. 'Oh, you beauty, come 'ere she said, grabbing hold of his hand and dragging him round th side wing and out on to the stage. She reached up and pullec his face down to hers and gave him a long, smacking kiss or the lips. 'Ye're a great man, Gary Brownlow, so y'are.'

'Not 'alf as great as you. That was a bloody fantastic show.'

'D'ye really think so?'

Gary clenched his fist. 'Just the best, lass, just the best.'

Rene gave him another long kiss before letting go his fac and taking hold of his hand once more. 'So tell me, 'ow's i been?'

'No problems. We managed fine, but we 'aven't 'alf missec ye.'

Rene squeezed his hand. 'And I've missed you lot so much as well. Dare I ask 'ow the job 'unting's going?'

Gary smiled and gave her a wink. 'Don't let's talk about that Tonight's your night,' he said, leading her back to the edge o the stage, 'so let's get celebrating.'

As they squeezed back into the changing room, Matti poppec the cork on the second of the two bottles of Cava she and Rene had bought to celebrate their last night. 'You're the only twc without,' she said, pouring the frothing liquid into two pape cups and handing them to Gary and Rene.

'Gary, this is Matti,' Rene said, grinning at the redhead. 'She' my new partner.'

Gary leaned towards her and gave her a kiss on the cheek

Please to meet you, lass. I was just saying to Rene you two were just tops tonight.'

Matti raised her eyebrows in appreciation of the compliment, and without taking her eyes off Gary, she gave Rene a nudge on the arm. 'Oh, I like him, girl. Has he got a brother?'

'If I could 'ave yer attention for a moment, please,' Stan Morris called out above the laughter that ensued, 'I would like ye all to raise yer glasses and drink a toast to the future success of these two girls, and I am pleased that it was due to my efforts – and of course, the other committee members of Andersons Westbourne Social Club – that talent such as Rene's has had a chance to be aired at a time when—'

'Oh, do shut up, Stan,' Terry cut in with a laugh, holding his paper mug in the air. ''Ere's to ye both. Ye really showed them out there tonight.'

'I couldn't agree more,' a softly spoken American voice interjected. Everyone turned, their cups halfway to their mouths, as they stared at the smartly dressed woman with coiffeured hair and glistening diamond studs in her ears who stood leaning against the doorpost. 'I apologise. I didn't mean to interrupt.'

'Not at all. Come in and join us,' Rene said, picking up a spare cup of sparkling wine from the dressing table and carrying it over to her. The woman took the cup and held out her hand to Rene.

'It's Rene, isn't it?'

Rene nodded as she shook her hand.

'My name's Mary Steinhouse. I've been in the audience for the last three nights, and I just wanted to say how much I've enjoyed your show. You and Matti have one of the most refreshingly original acts I've seen for a long time.'

'Thanks for that,' Rene replied, glancing round at Matti and shooting her a wink.

'And I'm sorry that I had to come round here and cut in on your celebrations,' the woman continued, 'only I'm heading back to the States first thing tomorrow morning, and I really wanted to see you both before leaving.'

'Oh aye?' Rene said, a questioning frown on her face.

'You see, my husband and I sponsor a large cultural festival held annually in Boston, and it just happens that it goes back-to-back with the one here in Edinburgh. I come over each year and seek out the best acts on the Fringe and invite them over to the States to take part in our festival, and I was very much hoping you and Matti might consider coming.'

Rene's jaw dropped. 'Are ye being serious?' She turned to Matti, seeing her face register similar disbelief. 'When would this be?'

'The week after next. I'm returning here for the Saturday-night Fireworks Concert, which I adore, and then those acts I have chosen to take part in our festival will fly back with me on the Sunday.' She paused, tilting her head to the side. 'That is why, I'm afraid, I need an answer as soon as possible.'

Gary cleared his throat self-consciously. 'I can't speak for Matti, but as far as Rene is concerned, she can do it.'

Rene looked at her husband, her heart missing a beat and emotion pricking her eyes at the support he was continuing to show for her. 'Gary?' she said quietly.

'What about it, Matti?' Gary said, pressing her for an answer.

'Oh, God, yes!' Matti exclaimed, coming over to Rene and throwing her arms around her. 'Yes, yes, yes!'

'I'm so glad,' Mary said with a clap of her hands. 'So, if we could meet up next Saturday afternoon at the Balmoral Hotel in Princes Street. I have half a dozen rooms booked, so you are invited to stay with me there. We'll have an early evening reception, during which I will brief all those who are coming as to what will be happening during the following week, and then afterwards we can all go out to watch the fireworks together. How does that sound?'

Rene uncoupled Matti's arms from around her neck and drew a hand across her damp cheeks. 'I can't go.'

Her remark caused a rumble of concern to sweep around the room.

'You can't?' Mary queried.

'No . . . not without my family, that is. I've been away from them for three weeks and I need to spend some time with them.'

Gary came forward and put a hand on his wife's shoulder. 'Come on, Rene, we'll be—'

'No, Gary,' she cut in, shrugging his hand away. 'I've made up me mind.' She smiled apologetically at the American woman. 'I can only go if me family comes too.'

Mary glanced at the strange little group in the room. 'What, all of them?' she asked in a surprised voice.

Rene spluttered out a laugh. 'No, just me husband and the kids.'

Mary shrugged resignedly. 'All right, I don't see why not. I'm sure we can find somewhere for you all to stay.'

Rene grinned at her. 'In that case, ye're on. America, 'ere we come.'

'Wonderful,' Mary said, pushing herself away from the door-post. 'Until next Saturday, then, and enjoy your celebrations. You really deserve it, both of you.'

After she had left there was a momentary silence in the room before Matti let out a whoop of joy, and grabbing hold of the first person she could lay her hands on, who just happened to be sombre Derek Marsham, she began dancing around the room with him. Rene put her arms around her husband's waist and pulled herself against him, leaning her head against his chest. 'I think you'd better pinch me 'ard,' she said quietly.

'What?'

'Is this really all 'appening?'

Gary gave his wife a kiss on the top of the head. 'Aye, I think it is, lass.'

Having almost danced Derek Marsham off his feet, Matti sat him down on one of the two chairs to catch his breath. 'So, what d'you suppose we should do now?' she asked, turning to Rene. 'We can't stay up here for a whole week.'

'If I might be allowed to make a suggestion,' Stan Morris said quietly, already anticipating the usual cry of disapproval. When none came and everyone turned to hear what he had to say, he was, for a moment, too surprised to continue. 'Right, well, I was thinking about all this before that lady turned up, and what I'm going to suggest is that I ring up Harold Prendergast at Andy's and say to 'im that we are very lucky to have available for us one of the star turns of the Festival Fringe – that, of course, being Rene and Matti – and that they would be willing to come to our social club for a five-night run before taking their act over to the United States of America. Understandably, the performance fees would be greater than 'e would ever have considered previously, but I'm sure that a quick call to the newsroom of the *'Artlepool Mail* would 'ave everyone in the borough clamouring at the door for tickets.'

This was greeted with a complete hush as all those in the room contemplated his suggestion. 'Well, it was only a thought,' Stan mumbled dejectedly.

'Aye, and a damned good one at that,' Terry said, giving him a congratulatory thump on the shoulder. 'You always were the right man for the job, weren't ye, Stan. Spokesman extraordinaire.' He turned to the assembled company. 'Now before there 'appens to be any more interruptions, ladies and gentlemen, let's get back to unfinished business.' He raised his glass. ''Ere's to you two girls. Ye're both on the way to the top, ye are.'

Forty-Seven

The rain eventually came to Edinburgh on the Wednesday evening, more than eight hours later than had been predicted by the weather forecasters. However, it was as if the darkened clouds that had been rolling across the city since the early morning had held hard to their load until then, because the torrential downpour that ensued had every street awash with water, every gutter flowing like a river in spate. Yet the energy and enthusiasm of the festival continued unabated, the post-Fringe straggle of street performers in the High Street pressing on regardless with their shows, sheltering in the lea of buildings or the high-columned entrances to churches, while the tourists and punters and office workers still filled the streets under a seething mass of umbrellas, walking to their next point of interest, or to yet another venue, or to the peaceful sanctuary of their homes.

High on the castle battlements, where the wind caught the rain and threw it in violent blasts against the pitted, uneven walls, just as it had done over the past nine hundred years, Roger Dent held hard to the hood of his waterproof jacket as he raced across the courtyard to the steps leading down to the store, jumping over lines of multicore cabling already connected up to the forty-odd slave units that would power the explosions on the night. Hurrying down the steps, he threw open the door and entered into the fuggy interior of the small vaulted room.

'Bloody hell!' he exclaimed, shaking the water from his arms. 'That is just filthy out there.'

His crew looked up from the various maintenance jobs they were doing and laughed at his appearance.

'Jeez, mate, you look like a drowned rat,' Phil Kenyon said, getting up from the table and taking a pair of earphones off his head. 'How's about a cup of coffee?'

'Not just yet,' he replied, hanging his sodden jacket on the back of a chair. 'I'd rather find out what stage we're all at. How did you get on with Helen?'

'Really good. The score's written up with all the cues and the back-timings. We met up with good old Sir Raymond today and went through the whole piece with him, and he seems happy enough with it all.'

'Did you tell him to watch the speed when he's conducting?'

'Yeah, he listened to the recording we used to set up the programme, and he reckons he'll be able to stick quite close to that.'

Roger let out a nervous sigh. 'Well, as long as he doesn't tense up on the night and rockets through the whole thing. We just don't have the leeway for it to underrun.'

'I wouldn't worry too much about that. The old boy seems pretty laid-back about everything.'

Roger nodded and turned his attention to the small bespectacled figure of Graham Slattery, the computer programmer from IBM. 'Gray, what's the story with the bell wire?'

'Annie and I have got about six hundred metres of the stuff laid out. The tunnel, the gardens and the ground under the gun are all wired, which just leaves the rock face to be done.'

Roger stared at the man, a look of thunder on his face, his eyes burning with anger. 'What the *hell* do you mean, the rock face has to be done? The riggers were supposed to have that completed today.'

Graham's face coloured when the rest of the crew turned to look at him. 'It started to rain, Rog. They said it was too dangerous.'

'Jesus, that's what I pay them for, to risk their sodding necks. What happens if it rains tomorrow? Are they expecting to sit around drinking tea all bloody day?'

Graham cleared his throat, summing up courage to continue. 'They don't like the idea of doing the rock face, Rog. It's never been done before, and they just reckon it's not on.'

'I couldn't give a damn what they think. This is my final show and it's bloody well going to be done.'

'Don't get yourself all stressed up, mate,' Phil cut in, realising Graham was in need of some moral support. 'We'll get it done tomorrow.'

'We don't have time tomorrow, Phil,' Roger exclaimed, grabbing a web harness and karabiner off a hook on the wall. 'We're behind schedule as it is. If this isn't done tonight, there's no hope of us being ready on time.'

'Hell, Rog, you're not thinking of doing it now?'

Roger bent down and picked up a coil of thick climbing rope off the floor. 'Too right I am.'

'But it's bloody near dark! You'll kill yourself.'

Roger threw him the rope. 'Not as long as you're holding on to the other end of this.' Taking his jacket down from the all, he pulled it on and picked up a large drum of bell wire om the corner of the store. 'Right, are you coming?'

Phil glanced at the concerned faces of the crew and shook s head slowly as he picked up his jacket. 'You're mad as a bull ith ticks, mate.'

Roger beamed a smile around the room. 'Of course I am. hat's why I'm in this business.'

Fifteen metres below the parapet of the castle, Roger flattened mself against the rock face as the wind tore the jacket hood ff his head, the incessant rain soaking his hair even before he ad managed to search out his next handhold on the slippery urface of the rock. He was getting into a routine now. Handhold rst, then foothold, then uncoil the bell wire from the drum spended from his waist. It was all right as long as he didn't ok down. Whatever happened, he didn't want to look down. Ie was working so fast he felt the rope above him go slack and e realised Phil wasn't keeping up with him.

'Phil?' he yelled out as loud as he could.

'You all right, mate?' he heard Phil's faint voice shout out om above.

'Keep the rope taut.'

'Sorry, will do.'

Roger felt the rope once more reassuringly take his weight.

'How many of you have got hold of it?' he called up.

'All of us,' came the reply.

Roger smiled to himself as he put out his hand and felt for ie next cleft in the rock. Only a few metres more and then e could start making his way back up to the safety of the errace. Not before time, either. His hands were beginning to ramp up and the muscles in his arms were exhausted. He ushed his fingers deep into a crevice and swung his leg out, ut as he did so his hand went numb and he lost his grip. He et out a cry as he dropped away and spun around in open air efore the rope jerked taut, pulling the harness deep into his roin. His back slammed painfully against the solid wall and he wung, unsupported and spreadeagled against the rock face, looking down the sixty-metre drop to Princes Street Garden below.

'Shit!' he murmured as he gulped in air.

'Rog?' Phil's worried voice yelled out from above. 'What happened? You all right, mate?'

Roger took in a deep steadying breath. 'Yeah, I'm fine. I lo my grip.' He let out a laugh of relief. 'I think my balls have sho up into my throat, though.'

Phil laughed. 'Well, you're not sounding like a choirboy, s your manhood's obviously still intact.'

'Thanks for that,' Roger replied, not bothering if his colleagu heard him or not. He closed his eyes and laid his head bac against the rock. 'Phil?' he called back.

'Yeah?'

'Is the rope safe?'

'As houses. We've wound it round one of the bollards.'

'I need a couple of minutes to recover.'

'No worries. Take your time.'

Roger relaxed his body and stretched his arms out to the sid to relieve his knotted muscles as he looked out across the glisten ing lights of Princes Street and over the roofs of the New Towr and it suddenly dawned on him that, as he hung there, high an isolated above the streets of Edinburgh, he felt strangely like th statue of Christ the Redeemer on the pinnacle of Corcovad above the city of Rio de Janeiro, enfolding its inhabitants in th benevolent protection of his arms. And in that moment he fel neither sacrilegious nor irreverent to think such a thing, and h wondered to himself if fate had not brought him to this. Because for twenty-three years, this had been his city, and those diminu tive forms far below him crowding on to buses and driving thei cars and walking the streets were his followers, each year throngin, to watch the spectacle that he himself conjured up for then from his exalted position high up on the castle walls. He felt sense of well-being and peace come over him and a sudde overwhelming burst of love for those people radiated throug the cold and fatigue in his body. 'Bless you all,' he murmure

himself, 'and thank you for those years, and when that final
rburst lights up the sky, may your paths run true and your
es be filled with peace from then on.'

He broke away from his solitary meditation, feeling a hand
ong the rock face to find a new hold and heaving himself
und so that he was once more facing the wall, and as he began
climb slowly back up towards the parapet, he let out an
nbarassed laugh. That really was a bit of a weird thing to go
d say, he thought to himself. And anyway, what difference
uld the idiotic pseudo-religious rantings of an ageing old
ppie make to anyone's life?

'Phil?' he called out.

'Yeah, mate,' came the distant reply.

'Take the strain again, will you? I'm on my way back up.'

Forty-Eight

eonard Hartson stood on top of the small stepladder adjusting
e spotlight so that it fell on to the face of the solitary female
ncer he had called to the location that afternoon. There were
ly a couple of small insert shots to do, so he had decided not
involve either the director of the dance company or his young
male interpreter. After three weeks of arduous and energy-
pping work, there were two things now prevalent in Leonard's
ind: first, that what he had just completed was indeed his
asterpiece; and second, that it had come at a drastic cost to
s own health.

He glanced across to the other side of the lighting stage, where
K. was shifting the camera to its new position, levelling the
ipod head with an experienced hand. When he was sure the
d wasn't watching him, he climbed slowly down the ladder,
utching hard at the lighting stand for support, and then dragged
s feet back to the canvas chair, grimacing with pain, and sat
own heavily upon it. As T.K. left the camera and came towards

him, Leonard forced an excited smile on to his face, taking a deep breath before speaking, hoping to make his voice sound as normal as possible.

'We've just about done it, T.K.,' he said.

His assistant smiled at him. 'Aye, looks like you and I are going tae get tae see the fireworks this evening, efter a'.'

'You could well be right,' Leonard replied, clandestinely slipping a hand inside his tweed jacket as he felt the tightness in his ribcage building. 'Are you ready to shoot?'

T.K. picked up the clapperboard from beside Leonard's chair and scribbled a new scene number on it with a piece of chalk. He handed it to Leonard. 'Could ye mark it, then?'

The clapperboard felt a dead weight in his hand and he let it fall on to his lap. 'Let's not bother with that,' he said with a shake of his head. 'It's only an insert, so just roll the camera when you're ready.'

Leonard watched as T.K. walked out on to the stage and held Leonard's own trusty Weston light meter up to the face of the young dancer to check the skin-tone exposure. He returned to the camera, set the aperture on the lens and then unlocked the pan and tilt levers on the tripod. He checked his focus at the long end of the zoom lens before locking off the tripod once more. 'Right, Leonard,' he called out.

'In your own time, my boy, in your own time.'

T.K. turned on the camera and watched the flickering image of the girl's motionless face through the viewfinder. He pressed the zoom, bringing out the frame to head and shoulders, and let the camera run for a further fifteen seconds. 'I've got it, Leonard,' he called out. 'D'ye want me tae cut?'

The camera ran on as T.K. waited for a reply, never taking his eye away from the viewfinder. 'Leonard? Shall ah cut it?' he said again.

The sound of the clapperboard clattering to the ground made T.K. slip a hand over the eyepiece and glance round at the old cameraman, and he knew the moment he laid eyes on him that something was dreadfully wrong. Leonard lay slumped to one

de of his chair, his head lolling awkwardly against his shoulder
id his right arm dangling down towards the ground.

'Leonard!' T.K. cried out, quickly turning off the camera
id running across to his mentor. He gently pulled Leonard
pright and placed a hand either side of the cameraman's ashen
neeks. There seemed to be no sign of life in him. T.K. heard
gasp and glanced round to find the young Japanese dancer
anding beside him, her tiny hands clasped to her mouth. He
ood back, clapping his hands to his head. 'Jesus, whit d'we
ae? Whit d'we have 'tae dae?' he yelled out in a panicked
oice.

The young girl held out her hands in a hopeless gesture, not
eing able to understand one word that was being said to her.
.K. pushed roughly past her and grabbed his jacket from where
lay on one of the lighting boxes. He rummaged in the pocket
or the mobile phone he had made Leonard buy so that they
ould be in constant touch with Springtime Productions in
ondon, and with shaking hands pressed in the number for the
mergency services.

'I need an ambulance doon at Leith Docks right now,' he
elled urgently into the phone. 'Where d'ye think it is? It's in
dinburgh . . . address? There isna one!' He scratched impatiently
the back of his head. 'In that case, jist get the ambulance doon
e Commercial Street and ah'll stand and wait fer it.' He glanced
ver at Leonard. 'Ah don' know. Ah think it could be his hert.'
Ie stood listening for a moment longer before ending the call
nd then walked slowly back to Leonard's side. He reached over
nd pressed his fingers against the cameraman's neck, feeling for
pulse as he had been instructed. There seemed only the faintest
gn of life.

'Leonard, ah'm jist goin' tae get the ambulance,' he said quietly,
ears beginning to blur his eyes as he covered the old man with
e jacket that had been bought for him, tucking it in carefully
round his still body. 'Ye'll be all right, Leonard, I know ye will.
ist, sit nice and easy, mon, an' ah'll be back wi' lads who can
elp ye. Jist haud on, Leonard. Please, jist haud on.'

He turned to the young dancer to ask her to look afte Leonard, but then realised it was a hopeless cause. 'I'm sorry, bu ye have to stay here,' he said to her, pressing his hands dow towards the ground, his speech slow and distinct in the hop she would be able to understand him. 'Just stay here.'

He ran across the warehouse floor and opened the fire doo and stood there a moment, bathed in a watery beam of sunligh

'I'm no' going far, Leonard,' he called back to the unconsciou figure in the chair. 'I promise ah'll be back with ye in no time

Forty-Nine

When Tess Goodwin entered through one of the back door of the Usher Hall, the high curving passage was alread resounding to a cacophony of instruments warming up for th concert. She slipped off her coat as she followed the passag round, stopping outside a large dark-panelled door on which small brass slide bore the name of Angélique Pascal. She stoo listening for a moment, hearing the strains of a single violir going through a fast and complicated scale, before she knocked The sound ceased immediately and a voice called out for he to enter.

Angélique was standing in the centre of the room, dressed in the same figure-hugging black dress she had worn for th opening-night concert, her violin and bow held loosely in he hands. Her face lit up when she saw Tess and she hurried ove to give her a kiss on either cheek.

'How are you feeling?' Tess asked, placing her coat on a chair

Angélique blew out a long breath. 'Rather nervous, actually It has been quite a long time since I have done this.'

Tess folded her arms. 'I still feel bad about you having to perform at this final concert, but there was such a response to the announcement of your return we felt we couldn't jus schedule one of the "lates" for you.'

Angélique shook her head. 'You must not worry. I have a feeling it will go very well. I have always loved the Brahms concerto, so all I have to do now is to play it properly.' She laid her violin and bow down carefully on the chaise longue that sat against the wall. 'How is Allan today?'

Tess laughed. 'Not feeling too good. He was called in early to the office this morning for some reason, so he decided to walk it, just to clear his head.'

'That was good fun last night,' Angélique said with a grin. 'I have not danced like that for so long.' She picked up a lipstick from the dressing table and applied it lightly to her mouth in the mirror. 'By the way, have you seen Jamie this evening?'

'Yes, I saw him in the foyer – oh, and he asked me to give you a message. He's going to be sitting in the third row back in the central block and he wants you to look out for him when you get up on the stage.'

Angélique turned to Tess with a quizzical frown on her face. 'For what reason?'

'I can't tell you. It's a surprise.'

'Ah, so you know what it is?'

Tess laughed. 'I said I can't tell you.'

Angélique approached her friend, her eyes wide with intent and her fists clenched. 'Tess, I am going to make you tell me, or I promise I will . . . play all the wrong notes and you will get the sack from your job for being the one who arranged this concert.'

'Well, that's just tough luck,' Tess said with a hardened glare, 'because you're not going to get anything out of me.'

At that moment there was a knock on the door. Angélique called out for the person to enter and an elderly woman put her head round the door.

'Mademoiselle Pascal, the orchestra is ready.'

'Thank you,' Angélique replied, turning to pick up her violin from the chaise longue. She walked towards the door and stopped by Tess, taking in a deep steadying breath. 'Well, this is it, then.'

Tess put an arm around her shoulders and gave her a hug. 'Believe me, you're going to have a wonderful time. Just enjoy every moment of it.'

As Angélique walked out on to the stage the orchestra rose to its feet along with every member of the audience, and the huge domed building rang with the sound of spontaneous applause. Angélique walked over to the conductor, and, as had been her custom at every concert at which she had played, she beckoned for him to lower his head towards her so that she could plant a kiss on both his cheeks. The applause increased in volume, the audience charmed by the gesture, as she moved to her position on the stage. She bowed first to the side galleries and then to the front, at the same time scanning the nearest rows for Jamie. She caught sight of him and gave him a broad smile, and then noticed that Harry Wills, the reporter, was beside him. She watched as Harry turned to his left and her eyes followed, and there, sitting next to him in a wheelchair in the aisle, was a tall, upright, old lady with white hair, her hands clasped together in her lap, her pale-blue eyes transfixed on where Angélique stood on the stage.

'Oh, *mon Dieu! Mon Dieu!*' Angélique murmured, clasping a hand to her mouth. She moved back towards the conductor's plinth, never taking her eyes off the old lady, until she bumped into the brass rail that surrounded it. 'Please,' she said, turning to the conductor, 'can we wait for a moment? I have to see someone. It is very important.'

The conductor beamed her a smile and reached down to take the violin and bow from her. 'Of course, my dear. You take your time. I had a warning this might happen.'

As Angélique quickly walked over to the side of the stage and descended the steps, the audience went so quiet that her footsteps echoed around the concert hall. She approached the old lady, her hands cupped over her face as tears streamed down her cheeks. '*Oh, je ne le crois pas!*' She got down on her knees and gently took hold of the limp wrinkled hands. 'Madame Lafitte, you are here! You are truly here!' She kissed the hands and held

378

em against her hot wet cheeks, looking up into the woman's
nd smiling face.

'I . . . have . . . been brought . . . to hear you play,' Madame
afitte said in a weak faltering voice.

'But who brought you?' Angélique asked breathlessly.

Madame Lafitte turned her head slowly to look at the man
ated beside her. 'Mr . . . Wills here.'

'Oh, that is so wonderful!' Angélique got to her feet and flung
er arms around Harry's neck. 'Thank you, Harry, thank you so
uch.'

'Not my idea, I'm afraid,' he replied, his face pumping with
nbarrassment. 'Jamie thought that seeing I was going to Paris,
might do a bit of a detour via Clermont Ferrand on the way
ome.'

For a moment Angélique stared open-mouthed at Jamie before
e pushed past Harry's legs and sat herself down heavily in
mie's lap. She took his face in her hands and pressed her lips
gainst his for so long that by the time she broke away from the
nbrace he was left gasping for air. The audience loved it,
ngélique's spontaneous action breaking through their customary
aid demeanour, and reacted with wolf whistles and loud yells
f approval. One man, high up in the gallery and still dressed
n the suit he had worn to his law firm that day, even stood up
o applause, his claps resounding around the auditorium, before
e was pulled back to his seat by the red-faced lady sitting next
o him.

Leaving Jamie with a whispered message in his ear, Angélique
ot up and edged past Harry, and stood once more beside Madame
afitte, looking down into her tired smiling eyes. 'I shall play for
ou now,' she said, brushing the back of her hand gently against
e old lady's cheek.

'I . . . have waited . . . too long . . . for this moment,' she
eplied.

Angélique bent down and kissed her lightly on the forehead.
And you will wait no longer.'

And as she walked back on to the stage the conductor raised

379

his hands in the air to bring the orchestra once more to its fee
to greet the second entrance of the young French maestra.

Every day since Angélique Pascal had left the Conservatoir
in Paris, Lillian Lafitte had listened to her young protégée play
her music filling the large sitting room of the house in the ru
Blatin in Clermont Ferrand. But never before had she heard he
play as she did this evening. There was a powerful intensity,
newly discovered emotion present in her delivery, every not
striking at her own inner being, making her feel that her passing
years had been scrolled back in time, and she had the image o
herself as a young girl once more, walking amidst a carpet o
spring flowers in a mountain meadow high in the Massif Central
clutching hard to the hand of her companion, the dashing D
Jean-Pierre Laffite. And then, breaking from her reverie, sh
realised what it was that made Angélique play in such a way
The girl had found love. It was the missing part of the jigsaw
completing her full understanding of the music she was playing
a part that could never be taught, but could only be foun
through the explosion of longing, and then belonging, in th
heart. She turned her head slowly and looked along the row to
the powerfully built young man with the blond hair who sa
next to her chaperone. He was watching Angélique with a fascin
ation, a boundlessness that would make it seem that he was th
only person sitting in this vast concert hall. Lillian smiled to
herself. She doubted very much he was listening to one note
she was playing. How wonderful it is, she thought to herself
that in this modern day, when there seemed such reticence in
the young to commit to love, the feeling between these two
should be so entirely mutual.

She looked down into her lap and slowly interlocked the
quivering fingers that Angélique herself had separated. Age ha
struck your body, Lillian, but your mind is still as sharp as a
razor, so now use it, for Angélique's sake, while you still have
the time.

She raised her head to watch the small delicate fingers dance
across the strings of the violin, exactly as they had done so

many years before in the sitting room in her house in Clermont Ferrand.

So, the young man is moving to London . . .

Fifty

Roger Dent pulled back the sleeve of the new jacket that his wife, Cathy, had had made up for him for the final show, a blousy black windcheater with the ESC logo embroidered on the back in gold thread and studded with sparkling diamante buttons. His watch read ten to nine. Ten minutes more and the display would begin. There was nothing more he could do now. Every connection, every cable, every slave unit and every shell rack had been checked a hundred times. Preparation was complete, and it now just remained for Phil to call the show.

He walked quickly across the courtyard to the firing position under the one-o'clock gun. Annie Beardsley gave the thumbs-up when she saw him and slipped her earphones on to her head. Returning the gesture, Roger ran off to do a last check with Dave Panton and Graham Slattery, who were manning the other two firing positions in the tunnel and in the gardens. Five minutes later he entered the small glass-fronted box where Phil Kenyon and Helen, his score reader, sat next to each other, looking down on to the huge white-shrouded stage set up in Princes Street Gardens where members of the Scottish Chamber Orchestra were readying themselves for the concert.

'Are we ready to go, Phil?'

The Australian leaned back in his chair and turned to him with a broad grin on his face. 'Yeah, mate, we're just about to hit it.'

Roger simply nodded in reply, letting out a long nervous breath.

Phil laughed. 'Jeez, Rog, don't get so uptight. It's going to be fine.' He pulled out the chair next to his. 'Come and sit down and enjoy your finest hour.'

Roger shook his head. 'Not this time.'

Phil looked at him quizzically. 'What d'you mean? You always sit here.'

Roger flicked a thumb towards the door. 'I'm going to be out there. I want to stand on the castle walls and watch the people in Princes Street. I want to watch those hundred thousand faces look up and marvel at what we've created for them.' He shot his colleague a knowing wink. 'Because that's what it's all about, Phil. Sheer, unadulterated entertainment.'

Phil grunted sardonically and shook his head. 'Go on, get outta here. I think you've finally flipped.'

A loud roar went up from the crowds below and Phil turned to look down on to the stage. 'That's our conductor on,' he said, taking the earphones from around his neck and putting them on his head, 'so let's get ready to roll.'

Four hundred miles to the south, in a tall office block overlooking Victoria Station in London, Nick Springer sat with his feet up on his desk, flicking through the remote control as he reran the video that had been delivered to his office late that afternoon. Stretching his arms above his head, he let out a long contented yawn before pulling back the cuff of his Turnbull and Asser shirt and looking at his watch. It was nearly bang on nine o'clock. Definitely time to call it a day.

He swung his feet off the desk and got up and took his jacket from the back of the chair. Pulling it on, he walked across to the television and switched it off and made his way over to the door. As he opened it, the telephone on his desk began to ring. He stared at it for a moment, thinking about just letting it go on to the answerphone, but then returned to pick it up.

'Nick Springer . . . oh, hi, T.K., how're things going? I've just been watching the footage you sent down yesterday. It really is quite fantastic. Leonard and you have done a hell of a job . . .

I'm sorry, T.K., I was talking over you. What did you just say?'

As he listened the colour drained from his face and he sat down heavily on the side of his desk.

'When did this happen?' he asked in a quavering voice, pressing his hand to his forehead. 'Oh, my God! And where is he now?'

He wound the telephone cord so tight around his fingers that he could feel their tips go numb. 'And were you with him?'

He felt his eyes prick with tears of emotion as the boy talked on. 'Oh, T.K., I know exactly what you mean. If it's any comfort, I think he saw you a bit like a grandson as well . . . yes, I know, lad . . . no, don't you worry yourself about that. I'll drive straight down to Kingston and break the news to her.' He took in a deep sad breath. 'So where are you now? Are you still in the hospital? . . . Why on earth have you gone back to the warehouse? . . . Have you really? . . . Well, you're a great lad, T.K., Leonard would be really proud of you. I'll see if I can fly up tomorrow with Grace and I'll arrange for someone to pick up all the equipment. You say the remainder of the exposed stock is in the camera case? . . . Right, and will the place be locked?' He turned and picked up a pen from his desk and began scribbling on a pad of paper. 'Under the brick below the rubbish skip outside the door. OK, I've got that, T.K., and you have the mobile if I need to get in touch with you . . . T.K.? . . . T.K., I'm sorry I didn't understand what you just said. Your voice sounds a bit slurred . . . T.K., are you there, lad?'

Nick hung up the telephone and put his hands to his face, pressing his fingers hard against his eyes. 'Oh my God, what I have done?' he murmured to himself. 'What the hell have I done?' He pulled his hands down the sides of his face. 'And how on earth am I ever going to tell Grace?'

T.K. sat in pitch darkness in the centre of the empty warehouse, the packed camera and lighting cases clustered about him. He pushed the mobile phone into the pocket of his jacket and bent down and picked up the half-empty bottle of vodka from the cold concrete floor. He took an enormous swig, coughing involuntarily as the neat alcohol ran down the back of his throat, burning his gullet. He got to his feet and began to stagger unsteadily towards the door. He stopped and then turned to walk back to pick up something that lay on top of the camera case. He cradled Leonard's Weston light meter in the palm of his hand, and for a few brief seconds, brought it up to his nose to inhale the smell of its old time-worn leather case before putting it into the pocket of his jacket alongside the mobile phone. He walked aimlessly across the warehouse floor for the last time and opened the door, seeing the dark night sky above the buildings opposite light up in blues and greens. The fireworks had started.

He turned the key in the heavy padlock and then placed it under the brick next to the rubbish skip. He straightened up and took another swig from the vodka bottle and then realised that the street, usually empty save for the film company van, was now lined with cars. He nodded his head in comprehension. The fireworks. People would have had to park this far away and walk uptown.

He began to make his way along the street, and then stopped, casting an admiring eye over the brand-new BMW parked there, its dark gleaming body reflecting the light of yet another firework that hit the night sky. He stood weaving back and forth as he eyed its plush cream-tan interior and leather-covered steering wheel. He let out a drunken laugh and walked back to the rubbish skip, and ten seconds later returned to the car with a heavy metal rod he had found buried in it. T.K., the master car thief, he thought to himself. That's all that's left for ye now. No broken windaes to attract attention, 'cos you know exactly how tae handle this joab.

Walking round to the front of the BMW, he raised the metal rod and brought it crashing down against the front bumper, caving it in. The effect was immediate. The airbags ballooned out from the steering wheel and the dashboard in front of the passenger seat, the locks clicked and the doors sprang open. Approaching the driver's door, T.K. placed the metal bar against the side of the car and took a last long swig from the vodka bottle before shattering it against the wall of the warehouse. He pulled open the door, and leaning in, slashed at the airbags with the broken glass. The interior was showered with white powder, settling itself on every square inch of the car's leather upholstery. T.K. clambered into the driver's seat, not caring about the powder now covering his clothes, and threw the broken bottle out on to the pavement. He reached for the metal rod and wedged it between the spokes of the steering wheel, and using every bit of his strength, he yanked it downwards until the steering lock gave way. He freed the rod, jammed it into the plastic covering below the steering wheel and removed it with a simple turn of his wrist, exposing the multi-coloured wiring. He dropped the iron rod into the gutter and rubbed his hands hard on the legs of his jeans. Right, T.K., he thought to himself, this is where the fun starts. If ye can get past the immobiliser on this beast withoot haein' tae use a laptop computer tae break the code, then ye truly are a bloody master at yer craft.

Lillian Lafitte sat in her wheelchair at one side of the crowded lobby of the Caledonian Hotel, listening to the thunderous booms of the fireworks exploding and the appreciative roar of the crowd outside in Princes Street. She lifted her hand with immense effort and brought it down on top of Angélique's.

'Now . . . you must . . . go . . . to watch . . . them,' she said, smiling at the girl.

Angélique glanced across to Jamie, who sat, cross-legged and relaxed, in an armchair next to the old lady. 'We do not need to see them, do we?'

Jamie shook his head. 'No, I've seen them often enough before.'

'I would prefer to stay here and talk to you,' Angélique said, rubbing her hand gently against Madame Lafitte's arm.

'No . . . I insist,' the old lady continued, 'but first . . . I tell you something.' She looked sternly at Angélique. 'You are twenty-one . . . years old now and you can handle . . . your own affairs. I am therefore . . . instructing my lawyers . . . to buy you a house . . . in London. It will be . . . a good place . . . for you . . . to base yourself.'

Angélique clasped her hands to her mouth in amazement. 'Oh, Madame Lafitte, that is . . . that is what I've always wanted!' She jumped to her feet and made to put her arms around the old lady's neck, but again Madame Lafitte raised her hand a fraction to stop her.

'And I have also . . . spoken to someone . . . who I hope will become your . . . new manager . . . and you will travel together . . . to your concerts.'

'Who is this person?' Angélique asked.

'I cannot say yet . . . because the . . . answer will be given . . . tomorrow.' She let out a tired sigh. 'Now . . . I cannot talk more . . . so please . . . go!'

Madame Lafitte visibly slumped in her wheelchair at the sheer effort of speaking. Angélique leaned over her and gave her a kiss on either cheek. 'I love you so much, Madame,' she said quietly to her. 'You have been so good to me.'

The old lady raised her eyebrows. 'Go . . . Angélique.'

Taking this as the definite cue to leave, Jamie got to his feet and took hold of Angélique's hand and began to pull her towards the entrance door of the hotel. 'Come on, those were our marching orders.'

'You will still be here when it is finished,' Angélique called back as Jamie hurriedly dragged her away.

Lillian Lafitte smiled her reply and watched as they entwined their arms around each other and left the hotel, talking excitedly together.

Five hundred metres along Princes Street from the Caledonian Hotel, high above the mass of spectators, Gavin and Jenny

Mackintosh stood on the balcony of the New Club, gazing up at the streams of light that showered down upon the castle. He waited with anticipation, slipping a hand around her waist, as the orchestra in the gardens below built up to a crescendo, and then, at the precise moment when the kettle drums pounded and the cymbals crashed, the whole of the rock face below the castle exploded into colour, cascading downwards, never losing its blazing flare until it hit the ground sixty metres below.

'Oh, my word,' Gavin murmured in astonishment. 'I don't think I've ever seen that done before.'

Jenny turned and smiled at him. 'When was the last time you ever saw the fireworks display?'

Gavin laughed and gave her a squeeze. 'True, very true.'

'Well, you certainly got yourself involved this year, didn't you?' she said, leaning her head against his shoulder.

'Yes, I can quite honestly say that, for myself, it's been a very satisfactory three weeks' – he let out a relieved sigh – 'but I am extremely glad it's all over.'

Jenny looked up at him, her eyebrows raised questioningly. 'No misgivings, then? You won't go pining after your young girl too much?'

Gavin leaned over and gave her a kiss on the top of the head. 'My dear, there's only one young girl in my life and she's standing right next to me.'

Across the roofs of Waverley Station, in a building adjacent to the North Bridge, Harry Wills sat in his office, oblivious to the noise and celebration that was taking place outside his window, as he typed away on the keyboard of his computer. He watched the final word of the article come up on his screen and then thumped the full-stop button with a flourish. Blowing out a satisfied breath, he scrolled back to the beginning of the document and began to read it through. It was headed 'The Inquisitive Little Girl Who Became a Worldwide Star' and opened with the line *'Once, long ago, in the darkened drawing room of a house in Clermont Ferrand . . .'*

It had been Madame Lafitte's suggestion that they should wait until they were on the plane before he started to ask her questions about Angélique, so as soon as they were airborne and climbing high above the jutting peaks of the Massif Central, Harry had taken his tape recorder from his briefcase and switched it on. Due to Madame Lafitte's faltering speech and her constant need to rest, the story was not finished being told until they finally touched down in Edinburgh. But during the course of the two-hour flight he gleaned from the old lady every bit of information he had been seeking over the past three years.

He saved the document and then selected the 'send e-mail' icon at the top of his computer screen, and as the flash of a firework lit the dingy interior of his office he pressed the button on his mouse, sending the article off for inclusion in the next day's edition of the *Sunday Times*.

Tess Goodwin climbed the final staircase of the tall Georgian block in Dundas Street and blew out a long breath, the result of both exhaustion and trepidation, before putting the key in the front door of her flat and opening it.

'Allan?' she called out when she saw the lights in the hall were on.

'Yup,' she heard his voice reply.

'Where are you?' she asked, taking off her coat and lazily dropping it on the chair along with her laptop case.

'In the sitting room.'

She made her way along the stone-flagged passage and pushed open the door. Allan was standing to the side of one of the large windows, looking out at an angle.

'I thought you might have gone to the fireworks,' she said, walking over to him and slipping herself under his arm.

'No, I didn't feel like facing the crush in Princes Street,' he replied. 'I thought I'd just watch the high ones go off from here.' He gave her a kiss on the top of the head. 'What about you? Why aren't you there?'

Tess shook her head. 'I had to meet up with Lewis Jones from the Fringe office for our customary end-of-festival drink, and then I just felt like getting back here.'

'You'll be quite relieved it's all over.'

'Yes, I am.' She smiled up at her husband. 'I'm glad everything's over, and I'm just longing for our honeymoon.'

He looked at her thoughtfully. 'Yeah, roll on the honeymoon,' he replied with little enthusiasm.

'What's the matter?' Tess queried, pulling herself away from his arm. 'You don't sound too keen all of a sudden.'

Sticking his hands in the pockets of his trousers, Allan looked down at the ground and began dragging the leather sole of a shoe back and forth across the stripped-pine floor. 'Tess, listen, you know I had to be in the office early this morning.'

'Yes,' Tess replied, her face frowned with worry.

He looked up at her. 'Well, I've been offered a new job in London.'

Tess stared at him, stunned. 'I don't believe this.'

'It's a hell of an opportunity, Tess,' Allan continued immediately, wanting to get out the explanation he had been conjuring up for her all day. 'The salary is twice what I'm getting up here, so it means we can sell this flat and buy a bigger house, which will be great when we come to have kids – which, OK, won't be for a bit, because this job at the outset involves a fair amount of overseas travel, and, well . . .' He ground slowly to a halt and studied her closely for her reaction. 'What d'you think?'

With a laugh, Tess reached up and kissed him on the cheek. 'I think it's a wonderful idea, and I'm very proud of you.'

'Really? You mean, you'd be happy to move down to London?'

'Yes, I think it's exactly what we both need, a new beginning to our lives. We can just leave all the old baggage back here in Edinburgh and start all over again.'

Allan shook his head in disbelief. 'Wow, that's weird! Those were exactly my thoughts too. It's almost as if you'd been considering it as well.'

'Oh, I have.'

'For any particular reason?'

'A very good one. I've been offered a job too – in London.'

Allan stared at her, aghast. 'You're kidding me.'

Tess laughed. 'No, I'm not.'

'What is the job?'

'Working for Angélique Pascal as her new manager and chaperone.'

'You never are!'

'I am.' She let out a relieved breath and shook her head. 'And to think I've been trying to work out how to break the news to you.' She reached up and brushed a kiss on to his lips. 'So now we both seem to have got our lives in order, why don't you fetch that bottle of champagne out of the fridge and we'll go celebrate this all in style?'

Allan laughed and looked at his watch. 'Let's give it ten minutes.'

'Why ten minutes?' she asked, looking amazed at his reaction to her blatant call for seduction.

'You obviously haven't been reading your *Scotsman*.'

'Yes, I have, actually. What have I missed?'

'Only that it's the last show this fireworks chap is going to be doing.' He positioned Tess in front of him, put his arms around her waist and gazed out the window. 'He's decided to hang up his Catherine wheels, so the finale's expected to be pretty awesome.'

Tess disappointedly folded her arms and in protest at his untimely rebuff looked down at the ground, where her eye was caught by something that had been dislodged from between the floorboards by Allan's foot. Bending down, she picked it up and held it in the palm of her hand. 'Hey, d'you think we should take this to Barbados with us?'

Allan held her hand up to his face and studied the one tiny pink shred of confetti lying in the centre of her palm. 'Yeah, why not?' he laughed, giving her a kiss on the ear that made goose bumps rise on her arms. 'I love you, Mrs Goodwin.'

'Woooooo,' said WPC Heather Lennox as she leaned her head out of the window of the unmarked Vauxhall police car to watch a trailing meteor arc its way down from the sky.

'Whit wis that?' her young male colleague asked through a mouthful of egg roll.

'I jist said "woooo" at that firework,' she replied, still craning her neck out of the window.

'Ah, right.' He swallowed the remainder of his roll and wiped his hands on the legs of his trousers. 'Here, d'ya think we should get on the move?'

Heather brought her head inside the car. 'Why? Have we had a call-out?'

'No, but we're meant tae be driving aroond, no' just sitting here at the side o' the road.'

'Och, dinnae bother yersel',' Heather replied, knowing that his keenness came from his recent qualification as a police driver. 'Just relax and watch the show.' She looked up as yet another firework hit the sky. 'Onyway, there has tae be some compensation for being seconded tae traffic division for the night,' she murmured.

With a sigh, the police constable slumped back in his seat and crossed his arms and turned to look at the queue of traffic forming at the red lights at the top of Leith Walk. He followed each car down, glancing at the number plates, and then turned to the dark-coloured BMW next to him. 'Nice car, that,' he mumbled.

'Whit're ye saying now?' Heather asked.

'Nothin',' he replied morosely. He glanced across at the driver of the BMW. 'Here, d'ya fancy nicking a driver wha's no' wearing a seat belt *and* using a mobile phone on the move?'

Heather turned to him, a scowl on her face. 'Whit is it with you tonight?'

The police constable jabbed a finger in the direction of the BMW. 'Look for yerself. That lad there, a' dressed in white. No seat belt, mobile phone.'

Heather leaned forward to look past him. 'Jeez, Willie,' she said, pulling the radio handset out of its holder. 'That lad's no' dressed in white. He's got powder a' over his face and hands. We've got oorselves a ghost runner.'

'Eh?'

Heather strained her eyes as she peered through the window of the BMW just as it was taking off. 'Oh, for heaven's sakes, I know exactly who that is. Get after that car, Willie, and don't let him know ye're following him.'

As the Vauxhall powered away from the kerb, Heather called in to the control room to report their involvement in the pursuit of a stolen car.

'OK, can ye tell me now?' the police constable asked, as Heather replaced the handset in its holder. 'Whit's a ghost runner?'

'It's someone wha's broken intae a car by activating the airbags. The doors automatically spring open when that happens. Trouble is ye canna get behind the wheel unless ye burst the bags and they're filled wi' white powder, so that's why that lad's covered wi' the stuff.'

The police constable powered the car into the central lane of Queen Street to overtake a slow-moving vehicle, desperate to keep the BMW only two cars in front of him. 'But he's drivin' wan o' thae new BMWs. How the hell did he get past the immobiliser?'

Heather shook her head. 'If anyone's going tae dae it, he is.' She slammed her fist against the dashboard, just as another burst of fireworks flooded the night sky. 'Dammit, I thocht he wis going straight. His solicitor rang me up the ither day to tell me a' aboot him working wi' some film company.' She clicked her fingers as the police constable took the orange lights on the junction with Hanover Street at speed. She took her mobile phone from her pocket and started to press buttons.

'Whit are ye dain'?' the police constable asked.

'I'll hae his number here in "received calls". Aye, here it is, and it's a mobile number tae.' She punched the button and held the phone to her ear. 'Hullo, Mr Mackintosh. This is WPC Lennox here from Gayfield Police Station. Mr Mackintosh, I'm presently in pursuit of a stolen vehicle being driven by one Thomas Keene junior. Do you know whit . . . ?' She stopped speaking when the solicitor cut into her question, and for the next minute she listened intently to every word he said, every now and again grimacing at what she was hearing. Eventually, she took the phone from her ear and pressed the 'end' button, letting out a long sigh. 'All right, you can tak' it easy now, Willie. We know where he's goin'.'

'Whit d'ya mean?' the police constable asked, making no apparent effort to lessen his speed.

'The lad must have been on the phone to his solicitor at those traffic lights back there. Mr Mackintosh has arranged to meet him at his house in Ravelston Road in half an hour. He's on his way back from Princes Street right now.'

The police constable shook his head. 'Whit the hell's going on?'

Heather turned to him. 'It seems the old cameraman Keene wis working fer died this efternoon in the Royal, and the lad's real cut up about it. Mr Mackintosh reckons he's in a pretty fragile mood, no' helped by the fact that he's been drinking to drown his sorrows.'

'He's drunk!' the police constable exclaimed as he swung the Vauxhall into Randolph Crescent. 'Had we no' better tak' him, then?'

Heather glanced at the clock on the dashboard. It was twenty-six minutes past nine. 'No, just let's leave him be. He's no' driving dangerously. We'll have him in aboot five minutes.'

The police constable turned through the traffic lights into Queensferry Street and saw the BMW accelerate to take the next set of lights on orange. He gunned the engine of the Vauxhall to keep up and, on total instinct, reached down to his right and flicked on the switches for the siren and the row of blue lights set into the grille of the car.

'For Chrissakes, Willie, whit the *hell* are ye daen'!' Heather screamed at him.

'He's getting' awa'!' he yelled back.

'But we know where he's goin', ye daft bastard! Turn the bloody things aff!'

The noise of the siren broke through the hopeless mist of T.K.'s drunken misery. He glanced in the rear-view mirror with tear-filled eyes, seeing the blurry outline of the blue lights veering round a car that had pulled over to the side of the road. 'Oh, *shit*!' he yelled out, pressing his foot down on the accelerator, feeling the power of the car press his back into the soft leather upholstery.

'Oh, no, that's it. He's bloody well seen us now,' Heather moaned as she suddenly saw the gap between the two cars increase significantly.

The police constable pressed his foot down to the floor and the tuned engine of the Vauxhall roared. 'Dinnae worry, I'll keep up wi' him.'

'Hold on! It's against regulations tae give chase now.'

'I'm no' gi'in' chase! I'm jist keepin' him in front o' me.'

As T.K. drove fast along Queensferry Road, he glanced up into the mirror and saw that the police car was gaining on him. There were no blue lights now, only headlights fast approaching. This was all a completely new experience to him. He had stolen cars, but he had never been chased before, and a sudden terror gripped at his stomach, panic boiling up its sour taste into his mouth. Seventy yards in front of him, he saw the lights at the top of Orchard Brae change to orange and he pushed the accelerator to the floor, glancing down at the speedometer to see the needle move smoothly, effortlessly, through the hundred-miles-per-hour mark. He closed his eyes and braced his body for impact as he approached the red lights and then opened them as he heard the screech of a crossing vehicle being left far behind. He looked in the mirror. The headlights that were following him disappeared for a second, then reappeared from the wrong side of the road and continued the chase.

T.K. wasn't the only one who was frightened. Heather glanced across at the police constable and saw the determined set to his jaw, the steely intent burning in his eyes, his resolve being to capture at any cost. Red-mist syndrome, they called it in the police force. She had witnessed the results of it before. Three young lads, none of them more than fourteen years old, their decimated bodies being cut from the crushed mass of metal that once was a car, hounded to their deaths by an overzealous police driver. That had been the main reason for her requesting a transfer away from traffic division a year before.

She reached across and thumped the police driver on the arm. 'If ye dinnae pull over right this minute, Constable, I'm goin' tae put ye on report.'

But the driver was in no mood to reply to her, nor was he for stopping. He saw the BMW rock over on to its springs as it took a hard left at the roundabout on Queensferry Terrace, and ten seconds later he was actioning the same maneouvre.

'The little bastard's skidded,' the driver said in a controlled voice, his mouth showing a hostile smile. 'We're right up on him now.'

'Oh, God, this is a' wrong,' Heather said with a shake of her head, knowing now that she was unable to control events. 'This is goin' tae end in disaster.'

As the BMW slid broadside across the road, T.K. spun the wheel as fast as he could to the right to correct the skid, glancing over to his left through the rear passenger-seat window to see the police car turn the corner at the roundabout. He pressed his foot down to the floor once more, and with a squeal of rubber took off, looking in the mirror to see the full beams of the police car no more than twenty yards behind him. The powerful BMW almost left the road as it hit the crest of the hill and he accelerated down Belford Road towards the sharp left-hand bend at the bottom.

'Oh, no. Please, God, no,' Heather murmured as she saw the

BMW go straight across the corner and head down a narrow lane. 'Stop the car, Willie. For Chrissakes, stop the bloody car!' she screamed, as she watched the BMW career down the lane with no sign of its brake lights coming on.

'Whit the hell's up wi' you?' the police constable exclaimed, bringing the car to a juddering halt.

'He's jist gone down a cul-de-sac,' Heather cried out, her eyes wide with horror, 'and he's no' got any airbags or seat belt!' She shut her eyes tight and covered her ears with her hands, anticipating the appalling sound of the impact.

The muffled explosion was so powerful that the police car shook, and for a second, it seemed to suck the air from inside it. Heather opened her eyes, immediately having to shield them with a hand against the blinding glare of light blazing in the sky, so powerful that it was as if night had turned to day. The craggy outline of the houses and buildings in Edinburgh stood out, solid and erect, unperturbed by the constant shower of colour that appeared to be raining down upon their roofs. Open-mouthed with shock and amazement, she turned and looked towards the narrow lane down which the BMW had disappeared, and in the brief seconds of flickering darkness between the starbursts that lit up the street, she saw that all was quiet, all was safe.

'Oh, thank God! Thank God!' she cried out with relief as she undid her seat belt and threw open the door of the car. She got out and began to run as fast as her stocky little legs would take her down the road.

T.K. never lessened the power of the car as he drove at break-neck speed down the lane, his hands clutching hard at the wheel as he steered it through the narrow gap between the parked vehicles on either side of him. He had no knowledge of this part of the city and he had no idea where this was going to take him. A resounding bang made him jerk his body away towards the gear shift and he glanced at the dangling wing mirror, taking his eyes momentarily away from the direction in which he was travelling. And then suddenly, a dazzling flash of light fell upon the street, making him turn to see, in its glaring brilliance, the wall that was looming up in front of him at the end of the lane. He let out a scream of panic, bracing his arms against the steering wheel as he transferred his foot to the brake pedal and slammed it to the floor. The car screeched angrily at the sudden transference of command, its sophisticated anti-lock brake system keeping it to a straight path through the parked vehicles, and it came to a tyre-burning halt no more that three feet away from the end of the cul-de-sac.

T.K. sat shaking as he stared wide-eyed at the solid stone wall in front of him, catching his breath in great gulps of fear and relief, wondering what kind of extraordinary phenomenon had just occurred to save his life. And then it dawned on him that it could only be that someone didn't want this to happen, someone who really cared for him was watching over him, and he bent forward, resting his head on the steering wheel, and began to cry once more. Another blaze of light shone out and he looked up, knowing now that it was a sign from Leonard, calling out to him. He opened the door and staggered out and leaned on the car roof, tears streaming down his face, as he stared up at the gigantic starburst that exploded high in the night sky, stretching its flaming tentacles up towards heaven and, as only he knew, carrying with it the spirit of the man he had come to admire and to love.

He raised up a hand. 'See ya, Leonard,' he murmured. 'See ya, mon.'

He turned and began to walk away from the car, his body now shaking both with grief and adrenalin, and then he saw the figure, wearing a luminous yellow vest, run down the lane towards him. The woman police constable slowed to a walk the moment she caught sight of him. T.K. focused his bleary vision on the uniform and, in that moment, he was hit by the forgotten reality of his situation. He looked around desperately, trying to find some way to escape.

'It's a' right, Thomas,' Heather called out. 'It's me, Constable Lennox. I know aboot Mr Hartson, Thomas, I know aboot everything that's happened.' She held out her arms to the side, only to show she had no means of restraint about her person. 'Come on here, lad, ye'll be a' right.'

She saw him start to run towards her, and as he got nearer she saw the wild, seething anger in his eyes and she took a couple of steps back, bracing herself to stop him from pushing her off her feet in his attempt to make a getaway. She opened her mouth to yell out for support from her colleague, but her breath was forced from her body when T.K. flung himself into her arms, clutching tight to her as he sobbed inconsolably on her shoulder.

She stood there until she could no longer support the full, sad weight of his body against hers. 'Come on, Thomas,' she said quietly, giving him a pat on the back. 'Let's get you away from here.'

And linking a steadying arm through his, Heather Lennox began walking him back up the lane.

Two miles away, in one of the west-facing bedrooms in the Balmoral Hotel, Gary and Rene Brownlow lay in bed in the darkness, propped up against soft down pillows and gazing out of the open window at the fireworks display as they sipped their glasses of champagne.

'I bet the kids are enjoying all this,' Rene said as she cuddled herself in against her husband's naked body.

'Aye, I bet they are,' Gary replied, too mesmerised by what was going on outside even to look at his wife. 'It was good of Matti to take them.'

Rene sniggered as she traced a finger down the centre of her husband's chest. 'What do kids of that age think when their parents say they're going to bed at nine o'clock in the evening?'

'No idea,' Gary replied, taking a drink from his glass. He turned to her briefly. 'Ye 'aven't told them, 'ave ye?'

'Told them what?' Rene said with a smile.

'About, you know, the birds-and-bees stuff.'

'No, don't worry. I 'aven't said a thing.'

'Good,' Gary said with a nod and continued to look out of the window.

Rene let out a contented sigh. 'America tomorrow.'

'Aye.'

'Are ye looking forward to it?'

'Bloody 'ell!' Gary exclaimed as a blinding incandescence of light filled the room like an atomic explosion. He threw back the duvet and ran over to stand at the window.

'Gary!' Rene screamed in hilarity. 'Get away from there! Ye're stark-bollock naked!'

'Don't be stupid! No one's remotely interested in seeing me tadger,' he said as a second explosion lit up the outline of his lean body. 'They're all looking up at the castle, any road.'

A sudden roar rose up from the crowd in the street and Gary pressed his hands against the windowpane to see if he could work out what had caused it. He looked back towards the castle and immediately saw the reason for the cry.

'My God, Rene!' He turned and beckoned urgently to his wife. 'Come over 'ere quick, lass. You've got to see this.'

'I can see more than enough from 'ere,' Rene replied, leaning on an elbow as she studied with satisfaction her husband's neat rounded buttocks.

'No, come quick! Now!'

Clambering out of bed, Rene grabbed a towel off a chair and wrapped it around her as she walked towards the window.

'Look up there on the battlements of the castle,' he said, putting an arm around her shoulders and guiding her line of sight with an outstretched hand.

Rene followed his direction, and beneath the giant palm-tree spread of shimmering light she saw the tiny figure standing high up on the castle wall like the cross of St Andrew, his legs apart and his arms raised towards the sky as if commanding the multicoloured tempest taking place in the firmament above to cease.

'What d'ye suppose 'e's doing?' Rene asked.

'No idea. It's a powerful sight though.'

'It's a bit creepy, in't it?'

Gary shook his head. 'No, I think it's quite . . . well, biblical, like.'

Rene crossed her arms and looked disappointedly at her husband. ''Ere, I thought we were meant to be doing something during all this?'

Gary glanced round at her and gave his chin a thoughtful rub. 'Aye, ye're right, we were.' He flicked a thumb towards the window. 'D'ye want me to go and ask them to do it over?'

'No, don't bother,' she laughed, her attention suddenly caught by the largest starburst of all, exploding high above the city, illuminating the thousands of people who lined the length of Princes Street and showering its trailing beams down upon them. She put her hands up to her towel and let it fall to the ground. 'But the show's not over yet, you know.'

Gary smiled at her, his eyes twinkling. 'No, it's not, is it!'

And, together, they ran across the room and dived on to the bed.

Epilogue

It was mid-November the following year, when another festival had come and gone, and already the ticket hall at Waverley Station was being decked out for Christmas. A large tinsel-covered tree brightened up the starkness of the seating area while paper streamers were jauntily looped along the full length of the glass-fronted ticket desk. Gavin Mackintosh took off his leather gloves and undid the buttons of his overcoat as he approached one of the two clerks manning the desk, the place being considerably warmer than outside, where a freezing mist hung over the city, settling its thick rimey blanket on the sparsely populated platforms of the station. He purchased a return ticket to London King's Cross, only because it was better value than buying a single, but there was no doubt in his mind that the return leg would never be used. Slipping his credit card back into his wallet, he took out two twenty-pound notes before returning it to the inside pocket of his suit jacket. He turned to the young man who stood behind him carrying a large rucksack on his back, the straps cutting deep into the brown Timberland jacket he wore, along with a woolly hat pulled down over his ears to cover his shaven head.

'There you are, Thomas,' he said, handing the ticket to T.K. before glancing up at the departures monitor on the wall. 'Your train is the ten-thirty from platform one, but it looks to be running about five minutes late.' He looked at the lad. 'Once you're on it, you don't have to think about changing or anything like that. If you have any worries, just ask someone. Do you know what you're doing when you get to London?'

'Aye,' T.K. replied, putting his hand in the pocket of his jacket and pulling out a well-thumbed letter and handing it to Gavin. 'Mr Springer's written it a' doon there.'

Gavin opened the letter and read quickly through it, the offer of a job at Springtime Productions, the plans made for T.K. at Christmas, and the directions he was to give the taxi driver on his arrival in London. Gavin refolded the letter and handed it back to him.

'I see you're going down to Kingston for Christmas.'

T.K. nodded. 'Aye, ah'm spending it wi' Grace.'

'Well, that'll be good for you both. No doubt you'll be looking forward to seeing this great award Leonard's film received at this year's Film Festival.'

'Ah've seen it, 'cos Grace sent me a photo of it. She'd written on the back, "This is yours as well".'

Gavin smiled. 'Nothing could be truer, T.K. Leonard couldn't have made that film without you.' He reached out for T.K.'s hand and pressed the two twenty-pound notes into his palm. 'This is just to wish you on your way.'

T.K. glanced down at his hand, opening it a fraction to see what was there. 'Cheers, Mr Mackintosh,' he said, without lifting his head.

'Best of luck with your future, Thomas,' Gavin said, giving the lad a pat on the shoulder. 'You've served your time, so now you can just put all that behind you.' He laughed briefly. 'And for goodness' sakes, don't go driving any cars unless they belong to you, is that understood?'

T.K. looked up with an embarrassed smirk on his face and glanced across at the woman police constable who stood next to them.

Gavin consulted his wristwatch. 'Well, I must be getting back to the office,' he said, holding a hand out to T.K. 'Keep in touch now.'

'Aye, ah will,' T.K. replied, shaking his hand.

When their goodbyes were finished, Heather Lennox to gave T.K. a brief hug. 'Cheerio, Thomas. Look after yersel'.'

'Aye, and thanks for pickin' us up this mornin'.'

Heather smiled, raising a stern finger to him. 'Well, you mak' sure that's the last time *you* ever get tae ride in a police car again, right?'

She gave a short wave of farewell and turned and walked with Gavin towards the doors of the ticket office, leaving T.K. with a broad grin on his face.

'Well, Constable Lennox,' Gavin said as he stood on the pavement doing up his overcoat, 'it looks like things have turned out all right for that young man.'

Heather rubbed her hands together to stave off the morning chill. 'Aye. He's the lucky one.'

'Very true,' Gavin replied, 'and consequently I doubt very much this will be the last time you and *I* will be meeting up.'

He left her with a smile and crossed over the taxi sweep and, setting a brisk pace, began making his way back up the ramp towards Princes Street.